MW00891931

The Rage of the Woodlands

Book One of the Realm Weaver Trilogy

B.B. Aspen

The Rage of the Woodlands

Book One of the Realm Weaver Trilogy

Copyright © 2023 by B.B. Aspen

All rights reserved.

ISBN: 9798850519162

Edited by: Danielle Kalland & Kacie Baumgartner

Cover Art by: My Shire Sister

For permission requests, contact BBAspenBooks@gmail.com

B.B. Aspen's Instagram @B.B.Aspen_Author

To all the women this world calls too wild, too headstrong, too *much*.

Rage on.

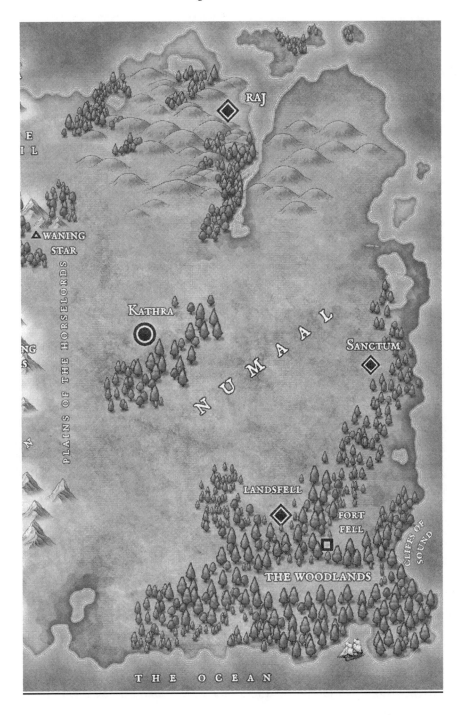

Chapter One

The blood drenching my face and forearms took what seemed days to dry. Time passed differently in the depths of the duke's dungeons. Surely, I had been there for well over two turns of the moon since Ferngrove was burnt down, my family along with it. My crying had long stopped for I doubted I had the ability to produce tears nor strength to stir a sob from my lungs after all the torment my body had met. The only peace on my open wounds were the soft, foreign vespers of a prisoner further down the dungeon corridor, someone kept below in the stench and shadows. A male, with no name or origins or known crime, but he had a voice that saturated the hallows of the prison like sun warmed honey dripping over warm toast.

It had been weeks without water, I was human—a red blood, I should have been dead.

That was what Duke Stegin Monte, the Southland's lord was expecting, although I don't know why he wanted me dead. He was to be the province's protector and held accountable for keeping us safe. Only those who pose a threat should be imprisoned, right?

The sole reason my heart still beat was because of the blood Anna forced me to drink.

My eyes burned with the mere memory of the duke stabbing his barbed spear into my shoulder. I had never known pain like that, it was far worse than a fractured wrist or the sting of poison oak. The rusted metallic spikes caught on my muscles, tearing my tendons as he twisted the point and withdrew it. I stifled my scream and gag by falling onto Anna's lap. I bit the cotton fabric of her tunic and felt the plunge of his iron headed spear push into the center of her chest. Her breathing gurgled, I shook with disbelief. The centuries of her long life had come to a violent conclusion, far away from her home in the land of the Gods.

She fell against the rock wall and I against her, pain replaced with panic. Duke Stegin's slicked backed blonde hair gleamed with potent jasmine oil as he darted up the stairwell. The light of his torch faded. The heat of my hatred followed him out.

"Ivy? Ivy?" she cooed for me and yanked on the short chain that held us tethered. I collapsed on her, my wrists throbbing under the iron cuffs.

I didn't bother to move her cherry red locks away from the gaping wound in her chest, they matted there. I pressed my palms over the streams of blood gushing out and pushed my forehead onto hers willing whatever Ilanthian magic she had to activate. And quickly. Our fragmented breathing mingled. Had I known these moments were our last together, I would have done less wishing and more tasting the last of her precious life. "I'm here Anna. I'm not going anywhere."

"Yes, you are. You will get out of here and do what I could not...prevent a war between nations."

"We will. We will unite the world together. Uproot the seeds of unfounded hatred and cut the stem of confusion."

"Seems unfair, that for all my lifetimes of living I had not felt alive until I had met you. Thank you Ivy, for proving me right," her lips darkened to a dangerous shade of blue. "There is good in this world worth saving, Maruc needs to come to that realization before it's too late."

Her skin cooled beneath my touch, I pulled her cloak over her hair and face, bringing her closer.

"I don't know how to do that," I confessed, biting back tremors.

"My brother chose you to stand face to face with the last God and tell him our tale. Demand he give you an audience at the Opal Lake. Tell him the Vulborg are here. Unite the realms of Kinlyra to stop the war of creation."

I was shaking now. "What are you on about! We will tell the king and Emperor our tale and find peace. We!" I reiterated fiercely.

"I love you, Ivy. I need you to drink my blood."

I shook my head. "You said you weren't that *kind* of immortal. I don't want it."

"It's too late to explain," Anna pinched my nose leaving me gasping through my mouth.

"I don't want this! This doesn't feel like love!"

The light in her eyes had almost dimmed, a stray tear formed and trailed down her high cheekbones. "This way I will always be with you. Fear not the path beneath your feet for the courage of your heart can overcome even the most impossible of tasks. My brother will not forsake you." What she meant at that time went unregistered. Anna had bitten her own wrist and sucked the last of her life force out. She descended on me, her cheeks swollen in holding the precious liquid. Then, pressing her lips onto mine, she demanded I drink and wouldn't release my breath until I had all but drained her. There was no fighting her, not because she was stronger, but because there was no use in arguing with a corpse.

Our last kiss was one of death, unlike our first which was as playful as new life blooming in spring. I wanted to vomit. I wanted to scream. I wanted answers. Damn it, did I want answers as much as I wanted to bring her back to life! I hadn't had her in my life nearly as long as I needed her, there was so much about the world I had yet to learn beyond the Southlands.

The songs that followed in the long nights ahead were nothing shy of a generous act to ensure I didn't lose my damn mind nor choke on the hatred coursing through me. Whoever had been dropping eaves kindly sang burial hymns and didn't press with unwanted questions. My tongue was heavy, I couldn't sing along when he arrived at the one familiar chorus I knew, but I did hum along and quietly asked Oyokos, God of Death and Justice, to permit my parents and Anna, onto his sandy shores of eternal joy. When bitterness twisted in my gut, I demanded that all those responsible for the deaths of innocents be tortured at the crossroads of life and death for thousands of years before being sent to Oyokos' flogging pole for an eternity.

A muffled laugh and sigh came from the dungeons.

There was a distinct coppery smell that struck the back of my palate with each inhalation. It was horrid, and yet that was where I had to concentrate my attention for if I had remembered the decaying body I was chained to, another wave of grief, sadness or hopelessness threatened to take me beyond the veil. Those were useless emotions. But, anger. Rage. Fury. Those brought heat to my chest and sparked the wild storm of revenge in my heart.

My teeth gritted, nearing the point of shattering and as the sweet melodies beyond my barred cell continued, I attempted one last look at her, at Anna.

In that moment, I swore to take the life of the man who had robbed me, and so many others, of happiness and love merely because we were born in different lands. "From this moment until Anna's immortal life is avenged by Duke Stegin's death, I will seek justice by summoning death for those who have stolen the lives of innocents and conspired with those who wield the swords and words that command evil. I will break down the doors of the White Tower and deconstruct the royal palace one brick at a time until I have answers. Until the innocent have answers. Until this madness is stopped and my heart stops, I will do my best to honor the second chance at life forced upon me." I laughed a little. An insane, tired laugh. "Unless, I kill myself first. Then I ask you to burn my corpse so I don't become claimed by my enemy." I chuckled darkly.

The singing stopped.

My pulse pounded in my ear drums at the sudden onslaught of eerie silence. Silence only paused for a breath. The prisoner cleared the hurt and weariness from his throat. He spoke unnervingly steady, "To whose oath of retribution did I bear witness?"

I tried to form words. A few choking noises escaped my cracked lips, nothing coherent. I bit on the soft tissue of my mouth to help instigate moisture. I tried again, sounding horrid compared to his honey tongue. "A woman whose allegiance is solely unto herself. Who fears nothing for death himself is but an old acquaintance. My name spoken to a stranger while chained in the dim to..." my swallow was painfully dry and my chest tightened. "What's it to you?"

"You have piqued my interest. Your oath held more passion and honesty than those who've spoken wedding vows. I trust you will accomplish *what you set out to do, but you cannot do it from inside a prison cell nor without an ally in this vastly dangerous world. I want to help because our intentions appear to be aligned."*

"Even if you are Ilanthian, you are still a captive."

"I am not an Ilanthian nor am I a captive, I allowed myself to be captured and just as I planned to sit in this cell, I have a plan to get out. Help is coming. Help, should you give me your full name, will also be extended to you."

Unlikely. *"Why did you want to be captured?"*

"My motives are my own. Name?"

"If they are your own, how can I concur if our intentions are aligned? What do you have to gain?"

"You have a lot of questions. Name?"

"I'm not inclined to give my name away should it end up in the wrong hands. Those in these lands who have encountered silver bloods are hunted and their memories turned into ghosts. You've been listening, you know we are... were... more than acquaintances."

"You loved her. There is no shame in that. Just as there is no shame in accepting help on a damn near impossible duty you've assigned to yourself to stop a war between nations and realms, between deities and mortals." His voice grew raspy. There was anger in his tone. Hunger too. He had been down here for months and not fed just as I. *"If you fail in this task or fail to recruit thousands of like-minded beings into an army, millions will die. There will be no Ilanthia, no Numaal, no dreamer realm or rest for the dead. Accept my aid, for I do not give it often, nor ever as freely as I am trying to give it to you."*

"Why do I sense frustration in your tone? I am not inclined to respond to such a manner."

He groaned. I heard the thunk of his skull fall back and hit the iron bars. *"I am trying to do the right thing, stop making it difficult. So, fucking stubborn."*

"Fucking resilient too."

"Anna called you Ivy."

"She did." My voice shuddered at the use of past tense. Glancing around the dingy corner of blood, rusted metal and death it appeared I would need some aid, at least in managing to escape. Then I could run back to Keenan—should he still be waiting by our safe spot, should he be alive.

Yes, I had to take advantage of this opportunity for Anna had given me a second chance at life and I could not waste it. Even if I did not want her blood. It was mine. "My parents called me Wisteria. Wisteria Woodlander."

"Wisteria," he said my name as if he would a prayer in the temple of Morial, the Goddess of beauty, bounty and sensuality. It purred off his lips. Anna had said that Morial's temple of white slabs of stone was always her favorite to visit in Akelis. He said it again in the same reverent manner. "Wisteria Woodlander, I, Zander Veil Halfmoon di Lucent, extend to you my oath of protection and aid. I will hold your health and needs above my own from this moment until my last." The rest of his vow was spoken in a dead language. When his words stopped, a thread of violet and one of gold connected to the center of my left and right palms and disappeared just as suddenly. I blinked, not sure if my eyes had deceived me.

"I have more questions, Zander Veil Halfmoon di Lucent."

This time there was a hint of humor in his exasperated sigh. "They will have to wait. Our prison break is currently underway. Any moment now."

As he spoke to himself, two soft bodies tumbled down the steps, and the dim light of the open door made the man with long white hair appear to have a halo. His eyes rapidly assessed my dire situation and his lips pressed together when seeing exactly what lay on the other end of my chain. "Fen?" Zander piped up from where he was locked away in the dungeons with relief saturating his tone. Fen dashed to the depths of the cells. Before a cycle of breath passed two dark figures resembling men hovered outside my cell. Zander stood a full head taller. Was he part giant? Anna never mentioned anything about gargants residing in our world. "She comes with us," my self-designated protector stated. Fen cocked his head towards his comrade, the unseen eye contact between them telling a story of its own. It unsettled my nerves.

"I felt our thread fray off. It anchored," he whispered while crouching onto his knees, the metal grew white hot in his grip as the bars melted away. He continued talking over his shoulder at Zander. "Can we kill those idiots yet or are you sticking with your original plan of patience?" Fen tried prying at my face, I lowered my hood and kept it there. He slowed his movements, as Anna and Keenan had done when we first met years ago, to not frighten me with their faster speed of doing things. Predicting his next request, I lifted my wrist ahead of me and he promptly melted the binds.

He froze, his breath baited while watching me.

"Thanks," I hushed, using the remaining bars to pull myself upright. I stacked my knees over my feet and straightened my neck above my spine. I thought I had done a good job of standing and not making a fool of myself, until my wildly pounding heart switched rhythms leaving me breathless and too close to collapse. Zander threw my thinning, lean arms around his neck and repositioned my legs around his surprisingly muscular waist. Definitely a giant. My face was buried in his dense hair and grey cloak; we were two shadows merging. I kept my eyes shut ignoring the searing pain of blood flow to my numb extremities and the queasy sensation from tilting my world sideways.

"Burn her. I don't want them to have her," I uttered. The man with the moonlit halo and heat power complied. Anna's body burned ash white and into dust before I blinked. It was so fast, there was no scent of burnt flesh or smoke to suffocate me.

Fen sounded distant. "You've got a lot of explaining to do." My heart pounded against the slow, steady beating that was inside the broad chest of that man I hung to.

"Later," the word grumbled softly from his lips just above the curve of my left ear. His exhale so close did nothing to settle my nerves or stop the heat rampantly swimming in my veins. I thought the flushed feeling would consume me until I caught a draft of lilac. Anna could always be found lounging in lilac fields when we hadn't herbs to gather, swords to draw or trouble to find. Anna's blood stirred in me, only calming when I said her name. The man next to me gave a somber sigh.

Fen shifted a slow gaze to the tangle of bone dust, fabric, blood and metal, saying nothing as he tapped Zander's shoulders. Mist, fog and steam crept in from the floorboards above, shouts of confusion and disarray were heard. The hollers of the guards and anointed priestesses continued, each time with more worry saturating their tone. After prayers failed, the room above went quiet as it was abandoned. "I'll let you hold me as tight as you need should you find yourself scared," Zander said lightly after wrapping us both in dark layers of fabric. I tried pushing back to find him pinning me against his hip with the mere width of his left hand.

I spotted a leather hilt of a dagger on Fen's waist line. I plucked it from its sheath and threatened the tip just below Zander's belt clasp. "I'll let you keep your loins and life should you not go back on your word." My body shook as Zander succumbed to a fit of giggles. Fen, who stiffened as I made my threat, made a jolt to retrieve his dagger. I spun it around my knuckles, holding it delicately by the red blade to safely offer him his weapon back by its detailed hilt.

In an untrusting motion, he swiped it back.

Now, calm. Zander educated, "My oath is breakable by death alone, Wisteria. Either yours or mine, but your death cannot be done by my hands or the decree of the Gods will see I join you on the other side of the living." There was little choice I had, but to believe him. "But, it does grant me comfort knowing you are skilled with a blade."

Fen growled, "And thieving."

I curled my lip at the man to Zander's side. "I took it with the full intention of giving it back to you and directly under your gaze. You're just bitter because you were too slow to realize that a pathetic mortal like me could pull that off."

He pivoted to Zander. "She talks too much."

"I won't hesitate to castrate should I feel it's necessary."

"I will give you no reason to castrate me, Wisteria. As I said, my interest in you grows exponentially each time you open your mouth. Bleeding me out by my manhood *would kill me and therefore end my entertainment. That doesn't make much sense now does it?" We would see about that. "Besides, Fen would be sad. We can't have that now can we, Wisteria?"*

"Shit. The Weaver mocks me. You both talk too much," Fen walked ahead of us, his wrist giving directions with slight movements. Zander took note and shifted his body against the northern wall. I retracted my face and opened my eyes using what light was offered in the fog and lantern lit passageway. There were no noticeable features, for his hood dropped to his bearded chin and he kept our cloak secure around us. I couldn't even see the color of his hair that cushioned my head. My vision blurred, it was troublesome to keep my eyes alert, not with fatigue fighting me for every effort made.

His weight began moving, his pace faster this time as we rounded the corner. Momentum rocked me on his side, as we hustled up the stairs our grips on each other tightened simultaneously.

It was an annoying sound, his laugh. Very childlike. Nothing akin to the beauty of his vocal cords honoring the death of my friend. "Don't say anything." I could practically hear the sarcastic commentary dipping off his snicker. I gripped him tighter as the two of them maneuvered around the duke's mansion and once I felt the cool kiss of fresh air burst onto my face, my grip eased as a dark mist blanketed me. I fell asleep in his arms.

I shot up in bed and wrenched onto the floorboards. Must it always feel tangible despite two years passing?

Fauna wasn't here to see my past come to haunt me; for once I was happy she was entertaining on the lower levels for she had witnessed this familiar scene too many times since I came to the brothel. Moving the drab woolen curtains aside, I peered down onto the dimly lit night of Horn's End, a makeshift town of a mere few hundred humans east of

Landsfell, compiled of underhills, seadrifters, ironsides, windriders, coalminers and woodlanders. There weren't many of us simple living peoples left in the Southlands to become much more than a tattered town of refugees. No one here had a method of obtaining information from beyond the nearest homestead that would help increase our defenses against the growing hordes of wraiths. Horn's End was a melting pot of poverty, disparity, rumors and fading will. The only thing that held us together was the fact we were not dead. We were the victims of wraith attacks who've no favor with the land holders or guards, definitely not the knights, to call them into the Wastelands to ask for their swords of service.

In the last decade, the untiring wraiths led us to burn down parts of our homeland. They stripped the soil and exploited the port, everyone who lingered or stood to fight, has died or been turned into one of them, a restless monster. A ravenous fleshless *thing* who I've yet to find an adequate name for, for nothing can capture its horridness. Wraith was the best term, shy of evil, fitting enough. Shivers danced down my spine as I hastily pulled the fabric shut over the glass. I grabbed my satchel from the nail protruding above the shelf.

It was dawn, time for work.

The brothel's madam, Madam Tidal, a former seadrifter and merchant, escorted me out the back so I didn't disturb her clientele. She gave me room and board several nights a week and in return I left her staff herbal tinctures to avoid pregnancy and stimulate desire. She was gracious and sent me off to the sickbays after slipping two apples in my scratchy woolen satchel. Kindness wasn't dead, not in Horn's End. Knowing the details of what each has suffered allowed us to extend a fair amount of grace towards each other in these darkening times of ambiguity.

"Oy, Ivy. Surprised I made it another night?" Brock piped up from his cot. His dark brow wiggled.

"Not at all. I am an expert in my craft. However; I believe I told you to go easy on the poppy milk. You will not be the last idiot to get slashed by the wraiths. I'd hate it if someone more deserving or nearer to death than you were to be brought in and need relief." I took the half empty vile of medicine away from him and locked it in my cupboard. Supplies were growing thin. "Stocks need to be replenished before the end of autumn, which is a day away. I'll need to treat your leg, or what's left of it, before I go." I mocked and pulled a laugh from him.

He snorted, "So, morbid." Brock shimmied over on the cot to make room for me to sit next to him. Carefully, I moved the stump of his leg onto my lap. His leg had been bitten and broken beyond repair, amputating it above the knee ensured he would not risk infection or worse, turn into one of them. The undead.

"Did you want to see it? It's healing marvelously, no infection in sight."

His eyes drifted towards the far wall. "Maybe by the time the sutures come out, I'll stop imagining I can run to my mistress and the sharp pain in my absent foot will cease to be."

I brought him a fresh basin of water and one of the apples Tidal gave to me. "It is called phantom pain, it's not an uncommon occurrence in those who have lost limbs. Better limbs than life," I offered.

"Maybe time will bring us in agreement. For now, I'm not sure I made the right decision. I'm more of a burden than I can bear." I swapped out the compress on his forehead for a fresh cooler one. "Rodrick says the captain's men were to be placing traps near the east route, maybe, they will prove useful this time around. Duke's celebration of winter solstice is around the corner, he probably wants the roads clear. He doesn't have a clue we're alive, does he?" Brock wasn't talking to me anymore; he was processing things over internally. "Doesn't matter, does it? Our existence doesn't change much of anything to the fancy folk."

My exact thoughts had mirrored his hundreds of times. Each time I arrived at a more and more unpleasant conclusion. There was only one fix for this. My hands itched towards where Stegin had stabbed me. There was no evidence of that fatal wound, however; the scars of my clumsy, reckless childhood still stained my flesh, as did the green and black ink markings of an advanced class woodlander. A master.

My spine was covered in delicate drawings of foliage, an ivy vine and a lilac to be precise.

Before I set out of the front gate, I returned the vial of opium within Brock's reach and left him with a soft squeeze on his shoulder. He gave

14

me a sarcastic goodbye asking that I not get myself killed, I suggested he do the same.

The soft wood of the fence groaned as I shoved the pickets with my palm. Travel fast by daylight to avoid wraiths, hide at night to avoid wraiths. Seemed as good a plan as any.

I fastened the bronze clasps of my cloak around my neck and shoulders and secured Orion to his spot on my waistline and a shorter blade on the upper of my thigh. Aside from the weaponry, my thighs were bare. I was in brothel attire of a strappy dress and long slits on either side of my hips, I enjoyed the numbness that prickled on my skin. The farewell kiss of autumn. My goat leather, ankle high boots crunched in the fallen orange leaves and as the wind blew, maple leaves landed in the tussles of my brown hair which hung to my waist. My deep hood fell over my face and blocked my vision, it mattered not. I knew these woods despite the remains of them being nothing but feeble pillars of ash and burnt brush. These were once lush and lively forests, just as its dwellers had been. The echoes of Cobar's laughter and my parents calling me home lingered loudly. I pinched the burning bridge of my nose. Would grief ever ease or was the phrase 'time heals all wounds' a crock of shit? The walk to more fruitful grounds would be a half day's trek if respite was evaded, a walk that would be mostly in solitude for Keenan was still in an abandoned cave seven miles north, by Maplewine Creek.

A smile crept onto my face. Oh, the fond memories I've had in that cold water creek. Anna and I had followed it to the Cliffs of Sound several times a summer and in my adolescent years where I gathered courage to dive in without even knowing how to swim. She would still believe my swimming skills to be abhorrent should she be alive to see them today.

The wind scattered my hair and I shook it out freely, welcoming the change in season and a few flurries of snow. Planting my feet in the soil I peered up at the barely awakened sky, my arms fell limply at my sides. The red of the maple tree further scattered my thoughts and I was lost into my memories.

Chapter Two

I was twelve when I met Anna, her presence and bright red hair was the promise of something new that drew me out of my parent's apothecary and onto the dock that spring day. I knew every resident in Ferngrove, for we were woodlanders who survived off the land in which we cultivated as a community, we survived with solidarity. And travelers, albeit very few wandered through our forested coastline, shifted the energy of our commune. It made many uncomfortable, especially my father for he was one of four who knew how to wield a sword with any degree of accuracy and was charged with keeping our village safe from threat or imposing violence. Although, in hindsight, he swung it around like a boy with a pitchfork, yet I will always think of him skilled with my youthful eyes. I heard him grumble my name as the wooden door frame prattled close behind me. I pretended not to hear.

I bustled past the livestock trade, Conrad was herding the last of the sheep into Maribeth's wagon, her wrinkled eyes meticulously inspecting the stock. The gambling merchants didn't raise a brow as I darted around their card tables, holding my breath as to not inhale their particular scent of stale sea voyages. For the scent that drenched their ragged finery often robbed me of my appetite or sent what food I had in my stomach to churn.

The hollow sound of my bare feet pattering the planks of the dock stopped when I paused toe to toe with a porcelain skinned redhead whose hair had become unbound during her travels. She looked about twenty. "Hello, I'm Wisteria! Where are you from?" I exhaled excitedly to find there were three more to deboard the white aspen ship lapping in the muddy waters. My jaw dropped when I found a young child among the caravan, a man who held the same demeanor as my father and a pregnant woman round enough to be delivering before the vines climbed.

"Call me Anna, those with me are my cousins." She smiled, flashing a dimple. Her hazel eyes moved beyond me and onto the suspicious adults collecting by the shoreline. "We come with kind intentions, void of deception and trickery from the far shores Ilanthia. Empress Athromancia, Goddess of wisdom, sent us to the southern lands of Numaal in search of peaceful times and a mutually prosperous future. One without war. Her departed brother of righteousness blessed our travels, Orion guided our efforts here and we hope that they are well received. We are all kin of Kinlyra, afterall."

Despite the loud silence of anger and disbelief behind me, my curiosity prompted me to move. I took her by the hand. "You're warm," I stated bluntly, the woman with a swollen womb covered her mouth as she gave a hearty chuckle that shook her. "For some reason I imagined silver bloods to be colder. I've never met one of you before. I bet you have loads of stories and are older than Marybeth," I thought out loud. My own blood, mortal blood, heated and rose to my cheeks. Her eyes narrowed slightly in the sweetest of ways that made the freckles on her cheeks rise as if she was stifling a booming laugh. Which later, yes, I discovered her laugh was obnoxious, loud and arose during the most inappropriate times.

"Alister, what are your thoughts? Do we deny the will of the living Goddess and the departed Temperance?" Conrad hollered to my father whose steps were heard behind me. Anna met his gaze beyond me as he continued to speak. "With war so close and the untiring so near, the duke and duchess forbade foreign blood on these lands; even mixed bloods must be reported and documented on the yearly census. We are mere herbalists and gardeners, we cannot afford the wrath of the duke, nor to be reported to the prince." The wind blew to fill the gap of hesitation.

My father's tone was deep. "If we were to deny you accommodations within our village, how would that redirect your Empress's plan? Does the Emperor Maruc condone your travel? If the last of the Eleven are fighting, we may have entered a far darker age than I had thought."

Anna held my hand, her thumb ran slowly over my knuckles and I dissected her bright attire with my green eyes. "We agreed to come to this soil from our own free will, this wasn't a simple order from the Empress that bound us to this fate just as it is not a mere coincidence in us meeting you fine folk. We've much to learn from each other; however, should you see us as an impossibility, we will walk north or perhaps east in search of kind hearts who also despise bloodshed. I heard from messengers on the sea that there is a watch tower and guards able to provide safety, perhaps they will see we wish no discord and deem us worthy of their sword's protection. No repercussions should find you or your home. As I said, we are not malicious, we've come here to learn."

I let a snort escape. "There are no guards that protect us from the night and the evils that live there. Here, we fend for ourselves," I mumbled under my breath. "It's a hassle for them to roam this way without taking a risk of injury from the rough landscape or the restless. They leave us be, not bothering to educate us in the formal ways as in the capital or provide proper defense." Since most woodlanders, windriders and seadrifters were not literate in written words, we didn't have to memorize the historical text as those in the cities and temples were. "My mother taught me all the names of The Eleven though! She's brilliant." I had always thought fondly of my mother, Lily. She was compassionate, smart, funny and a stickler for clean hands.

"Wisteria!" My father barked, forcing my chin to lower onto my chest with instantaneous guilt. His gentle hand on my shoulder did not match his tone. He spoke over me, "Should we provide provisions and you all agree to secrecy, how long is your intended stay?" My father's interrogation continued as he dipped his chin with courtesy.

"Until Ilanthians know Numaalians aren't selfishly insane with their crafting and Numaalians understand we are not rigid beings hellbent on domination. There is, in fact, little difference that separates us in our hearts, how we experience the world and what we desire. I can start by saying unless you are a God or Goddess, of which only two of the eleven remain, Ilanthians are not all immortal. As a collective we do live hundreds of lifetimes but with our growing population of mixed races on the range, we are seeing mortal lifespans as well. We accommodated everyone within our borders. Numaal just doesn't hear about it, since we took our blood out of Resig Torval's reach."

My father had a reply and Anna a rebuttal, but their words were lost to my fragmented memory. He said something along the lines of their rebel groups, sabotage and King Resig hellbent on war. I wish I paid attention to her reply, I was too busy counting her freckles to listen to the grand rationale of why Maruc and Athromancia removed pure and blended bloods away from us. Something I wish I knew now as an adult.

A farmhand spoke up, "She is with child and has come with children surely no more able bodied to handle this world than a four year old." I cocked my head and peered down at a chestnut haired boy who looked about as old as Elousie had said. I furrowed my brow in an attempt to guess his age. Silver bloods might not always be immortal but they were close descendants were the first peoples formed of the magical clay which gave them their extended life spans and set them apart from homely people like me. The human race was created secondly, almost like an afterthought. Anna assured me that was depraved thinking, that we were all equals to the Eleven because she has met them before.

"Thirteen," he cleared his throat. "I'm thirteen ma'am. My name is Cobar." We'd walked nearly the same amount of time on this earth and yet I've grown in height and softened in feminine features while he retained his youthful childlike years.

Elousie piped up again, "Still no better. You shouldn't be living on your own out here so far from your kingdom's reach and I'll be damned by the Eleven if I let you trek north. Duke Hammish and Koy are as aloof about the restless as Stegin. I don't have much to offer you little lad, but with my husband and mother passed beyond the veil, I have rooms for you and your immediate family. My son, Pine, went off to marry an underhill and will only come back to visit in the long days." Her weathered eyes shifted to the mother. "I'm somewhat of a midwife as well and would trust no one else to deliver your child in these here woodlands."

There was a grace to her swiftness, it was also the first time I had seen such delicate intentional movement in a human form so naturally I gaped at the pregnant women, Moriah, who darted and knelt at Elousie's feet. I was captivated. The lean man introduced himself as Keenan, the spouse, then withdrew his sword and placed it above his head. Then, he set the sword down on the dirt before Elousie's torn tweed shoes. During their private exchange of gratitude, welcoming and warning I took the time to lead Anna off the dock, her hand still in mine, and my father who followed closely with his metal sword clanging against his carving knife on his belt loop.

My father bent forward to kiss my mother's dark chocolate hairline and with a sigh he stated, "Lily, only a fool would make decisions without consulting the one who runs our homestead and family. I am no fool, the decision is yours. I will abide by your words as I have vowed sixteen years ago." He winked as my mother swatted the nape of his neck. They were nauseatingly affectionate.

"We've never turned away people in need, Alister, we know what happened to the lost and lonely in these parts. Go, fetch a down pillow and straw cot for our new guest," my mother commanded with kindness.

Anna leaned forward and muttered into my ear, "Your father is a wise man." We snickered and scurried behind my parents as we tread along the pine needle strewn path deeper into the familiar woods. Once behind our shared chambers, I wasted no time in bombarding her with questions and she promptly dispelled rumors as she changed out of her gauzy teal blues and into a woolen beige tunic and trousers. It was a shame to see such a lovely fabric be burned alongside the ship that carried them here. We destroyed the evidence of their origins over several weeks of cookouts, medicinal brewing and dehydrating herbs. The village wasted no time in teaching them the ways of gathering, sowing and honoring the natural order of nature; they needed to be woven seamlessly into our community so no scout would flag a guard. The ink of our trade didn't stain their skin, so each day I would draw it onto Anna's back with a plant-based henna while listen to her stories.

Over the following years many things happened, none of them short of magical or profound. Anna taught me to read and write. I taught her how to expedite healing with salves and tinctures, although Anna hadn't a need for such things, she still enforced how invaluable it was and thrived in our craft. She practiced herbalism devoutly, and in the same reverent manner I practiced Ilanthian combat with the beautiful blade I found tucked away under the hull of their boat. The same one that magically found its way under my pillow every night. The blade she had called Orion, named after the God of righteous intentions and firm resolute.

Ilanthian combat was complex, it held a fast tempo, as a two step dance would. I learned evasion and hand to hand combat for a year before Anna and Keenan thought it safe for me to pick up sword, dagger and archery. Keenan had trained me in several styles, he was part of the last Goddess's Bloodsworn Legion after all. I excelled in Ilanthian swordplay, but enjoyed the extemporaneity style of the Montuse, the extinct peoples of the Ice Jungles who lived in Ilanthian's northern hills some three thousand and odd years ago. Montuse fighting was a series of artful aerobics that allowed the civilization to dodge and weave through the treacherous landscape. Keenan would often get lost in describing the beauty of the northern region, how the vines of the rubber trees were covered in floral frost and their fire pits steamed because they were made of ice blocks. He'd had his future read by the region's visionary during the White Tower's exploration. The visionary could read the future from the steam and smoke.

To this day he hasn't told anyone what that visionary said. "Not even my Goddess knows," he replied when I asked, keeping his only secret behind that prideful smirk.

Keenan sat with my dad on the patio sipping their tea on lazy afternoons watching Anna and I fight until exhaustion, then he would laugh and bring out the ointments he had been working on and coat me with them. All while explaining where I had gone wrong in my footwork and that I was too aggressive in my stance or risky about my back flips. I rolled my eyes. It was the same conversation each time, "Less enthusiasm, more patience. Strike when the weakness presents itself, not when you feel the most confident."

To which I replied, "I'm always confident with Orion in my grasp." Anna was glowing. I swore she held a silver light under her skin.

"You are the first apprentice I have agreed to train in a long time, do not taint my reputation or tarnish my name with your haughtiness. Your footwork, agility, and blade control will speak for themselves. Do it again. Jump higher this time, try not to land in the mud or your mother will have my neck," Keenan added, hollering above the wind for I was already running, sword drawn down to the creek. His training methods had gotten more grueling in the months before the knights attack. My mother was discomforted when I came home after being gone from dawn to dusk, panting and shaking with fatigue. She almost reamed Keenan's neck once it became a routine practice that spanned weeks on end. With my father's help, I convinced her otherwise. I loved combat as much as I loved the plant medicine. The sheer physical difficulty of his training was Gods awful and humiliating, but the moment I drew blood on Keenan's cheek during a fight where he was truly invested—I deduced it had been worth it. Judging by his smile, he had thought so too.

During a literacy lesson, Cobar came knocking on our door. "Sissy! Sissy! Come quick," he called for me, his chosen sister. We, one dozen women of both red and silver blood, welcomed baby girl Rory into our blended world, that was the first time I've seen a grown man cry. Keenan wept joyfully for two days straight, reminding us all the tears were a natural way of expression. Anna gave a special blessing over Rory which involved a special jar of dirt, soil from the lands of the Gods, to be rubbed over the newborn. She smeared excess onto my forehead and planted a kiss on my brow.

We ran barefoot, often naked, into the deep of winter to dig warm bathing holes into the soil. In the spring, we'd track Numaalian guards to the borders of our wide woods using the dusting of frost that held the damage of their metal heel boots. They carried more sacks of heavy cumbersome materials for their traps than they did swords and arrows. Summer, we spent sweating beneath the hot southern sun, exchanging strikes until the muscles on my back burned with lean strength, so much so Anna had to massage the knots out at night and put her heated comfrey compress skills to the test. One evening, I sat at the edge of the bed with her hands kneading the tension out. I moaned, "You are very good at evading conversations regarding the magic of your blood line, also your age, but you should know that *this*," I pointed to her hands moving over my spine with castor oil. I sank into her skilled touch. "is nothing shy of magical."

Her touch stopped. Slowed. And wrapped around my bare shoulders. She nestled her cheek next to mine before burying her nose into my neck, I eased into her touch. "Ivy?" A nickname she had given me somewhere around my fifteenth or sixteenth year having seen me climb the rope vines up the second story trestle as well as a wild ivy would have.

"Anna." I stated my tone void of the question hers held. I pulled my face away from her enough to turn and view her complex hazel eyes which I realized had caught me like a bee stuck in the sweet syrup of its own hive. Her red hair tumbled over her shoulders save the strand that was draped across her oval blemish free face. I brushed it aside, not bothering to hide the consent and longing in my gaze.

After ensuring our bedroom door was bolted, she brought her mouth on top of mine. Her lips were soft, mine were full. She had experience, I had wild curiosity. I had questions, she had answers. Together, we were a spark of contagious liveliness, one that everyone saw, but no one spoke of. Except my mother. She had simply pulled Anna aside one morning after finding us sharing a mattress the prior night and calmly threatened her not to break my spirit to the point that not even a woodlander's knowledge or Moriah's physician skills could mend it. Anna agreed so long as after the conflict she could take our entire family to the land of the Gods to see a different kind of magnificence and the three seats of origin for the Emperor, Empress and Temperance. War, wisdom and righteousness. And observe the new process to refill the seats since Orion's departure. My mother agreed. We would try to find a ship for hire before the wraiths got worse.

"Do you miss your home?" I asked one night after we had stolen two bottles of spiced rum from a drunken merchant's tote bag. Her arms draped lazily across my shoulders.

"Yes. I'm old enough to miss what it was and what it should be. Cities of white stone where heat comes without flames and running water without coals. Lands of plenty, rivers of freshwater and fish, baths of sweet waters and golden shores. Green mountains and lush soils beyond the ice ranges and the lands of the horse lords. Temples of the Goddesses full of wisdom and fervor. Temples to the Gods dedicated to honesty and action. Now, earth and spirit realms are tearing at the seams. We are not without flaw, but once, centuries ago when the mountain ranges were born, it was as close to utopia as I could ever imagine it would be."

My eyes widened. "Centuries! Just how old are you?"

"Ancient to your measurements," she said after a swig of rum. "I am truthful about everything you've wanted to know thus far, let me keep some secrets for I fear you wouldn't want an old hag sharing your bed."

I rolled my eyes. "I don't care who you were, or what you are. To me you will always be just Anna."

Her head fell heavy on my arm, her soft curls rolled over me. "I've never felt more alive than I have in the past six years," she said with an undertone of sadness. "I wish it hadn't taken me this long to have left my homeland. The world you could have grown up in would have been vastly different."

"Anna, you are all but one person. Do not put the fate of the world on your shoulders," I reminded hoping to ease her regrets which were buried into a deep line on her cheek.

"You'd do well to remember that one person, deemed however small, can change the course of many." She sounded older when she dispensed wisdom. "All it takes it one choice. One spark."

I cracked a grin. "I'm not disagreeing with you, old lady. I'm telling you that you need to share your burden. I'm right here and willing to go the distance. Forget your yesterdays, we are here now and have a future ahead of us." Anna didn't speak for many moments. I finished the bottle and laid my back down on the grass when my cheeks warmed. Anna's silent tears fell onto my tunic as she lay there, perhaps revisiting the regrets of her centuries or envisioning a future side by side with me fighting the untiring and undead. Building families, traveling across all the provinces and arriving on the soil in Ilanthia with mixed bloods happily following us. I never asked that night what stories spun in her head, but come morning, when we saw the smoke rise behind us in billows as large as storm clouds, we knew our future of peace was in danger.

Ferngrove became the Wastelands.

Every living being within the grove was either killed or taken captive by the knights, save Keenan who had been out bartering with the ironsides for materials to strengthen our fences and collecting flowers as Anna had commanded him. Keenan had gone back and burned who he could find, but judging by the mass increase in numbers of things that haunted the night, Ferngrove forest wasn't the first to fall in the south province. If the corpses weren't burnt when the wraiths came, they rose into soulless, fleshless nightwalkers. Other areas had already succumbed.

That brought us to the present. Where the balance of life and death were tittering on the tip of a blade.

I skipped over the dried ditch of Maplevine Creek. Pausing, I honed in on the sounds around me. The rustle of leaves, the scurry of mice and a faint calling of a snowy owl. Keenan rounded the corner with a weak smile pulling the corners of his mouth up to meet his saddened eyes. He barely had his arms open before I launched myself into them. He smelt of cedar and tobacco. I nuzzled further into his chest, neither of us stopped our tearful reunion. I hadn't seen him in forty-seven days. Aside from my time spent in the dungeon, that was the longest span I had been away from him since he sailed into my life. "I must admit, I'm thrilled to see you and your presence warms my cold heart. However, coming here –"

I cut his fatherly concerns off. "I missed you too." I planted a kiss on his cheek and sauntered into an abandoned tunnel that he had set up with the basic comforts. It was far too dingy and stale to house a soul for too long without insanity seeping into the bones. I fondly touched the teapot and matching set of cups he had salvaged from Elousie's homestead. Keenan covered our tracks and followed me in. Per usual, he was handsome and dressed in brown leather and donned markings on his face serving as camouflage. "Horn's End is out of antiseptics and analgesics. Disease has taken any plant growth closer to our encampment. I cannot do my job well without adequate resources, you know how precise our art is."

He crossed his arms over his chest and raised a stern brow. "Then you should have gone two miles the opposite direction and not risk exposing your involvement with the likes of me. I doubt you've come to spar yourself into exhaustion." His lip fell. "Unless...you found a way in."

A wily beam flashed across my features. "A vulnerability in our enemies' disposition has presented itself. I'm done being patient." He sat on a stump of rotten wood he made into a stool, leaning forward onto his knees. "Guards are setting traps less than three leagues away from Horn's End. I'll meet them on their journey back to Cultee's fort and training grounds. From there it is a short two days on caravan to the duke's estate for the winter celebration, the captain is Stegin's second spear, he'll be invited for a long stent in his home or city at the least. It's the perfect distraction and it's not until several full turns of the moon so we have time for you to go and ready a ship for safe passage." He placed his knuckle on his low lip.

"While I set up transportation, what will you be doing, darling Ivy?" He knew the answer before the inquiry left his mouth. His teeth gritted, "You cannot expect me to sit here while you place yourself in grave danger to save... If I lose you, I truly have lost all my family. As painful as it is for me to admit, Anna has filled your head with crazy ideas, ideas that should have died when she did. And yet, I find you more self-assured, more determined and more eager despite perpetual hardships attempting to callus your heart."

I shook his nonsense away. "Had she not entered my life, my resolve wouldn't have been much different."

"Probably not. You both make outlandish decisions and try to outrun the consequences. Her choices caught up to her, I will not lose you too Ivy."

I touched his arm. "So, let's stand and face the consequences of loving you all. We are going to get them back. They are my family too. I'm doing this. You can help or hide, Keenan." He did all he could to hold the floodgates back. After my father had died, he had done all he could to fill the role without overstepping. I couldn't have loved the man more.

"I'm tired of hiding." He rose into a crouched position and walked beyond me to shuffle in his trunk. "If you are going in there, Orion can't be at your hip." His fingers wiggled, summoning my sword. My chest burned, as if I was losing a dear friend. My longest friend.

"First Anna, now him?" My hand pulled at my neckline trying to steady my heart.

"I shall keep it safe and you will reunite with it after this reckless endeavor."

I trusted his words.

No one else could have pried that blade from my side. "And you need a less obvious place to hold your dagger." He held up a petite sewing kit and thin leather strap from his overcoat. "Your strength does not lie in your quick wits or ability to fight a room of wraiths by yourself, it rests in being underestimated by the world, Ivy. Use it to your advantage as long as you are able. Anna gave you a second chance, do not squander it."

Chapter Three

Keenan and I traveled lightly on foot. I carried no more than what I arrived at his cave with, the addition being a satchel of water. He tracked the dozen horses that the guards were riding, estimating we had gained footage because we were dumb enough to travel at night under the faintest of starlight. Now, we were a half day's travel behind and when midnight descended, we were able to examine one of their traps up close. Six torches of light surrounded it, attracting humans and wraiths alike.

A red, rusted iron barrel that matched my height stood in the open, right off the most accessible trail to Horn's End. Keenan barred me from dashing ahead of him. It *was* a trap after all, he reminded firmly, his gaze locking me into place making me feel childish. He tiptoed ahead of me, I felt for the thin Ilanthian silver dagger sewn in just under the swells of my breast, above my exposed navel, protecting his flank as he strode forward. He peered inside. Retracted. Then repeated the gesture, his puzzled face rearranged into one of disbelief that stole the breath from my lungs. "What?" I whispered hoarsely.

His two fingers beckoned me towards him. With his hands on either side of my waist he lifted me up. Speechlessness found me as a stuttering sound fumbled from my lips. In the barrel were the fresh remains of body parts. Organs, hides and arms. Human and beast. Wraiths were mostly blind. The purpose of the fire was to heat the bloody barrel to lure them in. "It's not a trap. It's bait!"

Keenan stifled my words of rage by pulling me into a heavy hug to where my vulgar shouts were muted by his leather glove. "If our assumptions are correct, we have every right to be angry. We also cannot linger. They are coming for us."

"There is no other way to perceive this. My own country is feeding its people to the wraiths, luring them to their next meal." *Why?* My head throbbed with questions.

My flesh ached, Anna's blood had felt my wave of emotional intensity.

"We have to put out the fires, I'll run back and warn the people of Horn's End of the potential attacks. You..." He cupped my face in his gloved hands. "...You, run ahead and play naive with those guards. Don't do anything brash."

"No promises," I warned. His rapid kisses covered my forehead. "Next time you see me it will be a few days after the winter solstice on the orca moon by the apothecary's docks, you'll have a boat and I'll have your family. Swear to me that you'll be there."

"I swear," he whispered. We then yanked the torches off the pyres and kicked dirt on them to kill the flames. The heat vanished with it. "Don't be late." Keenan set my feet off in the direction of the nearest clearing as he dove fearlessly into the charred Wastelands which had slowly begun to come alive with the sound of strangled calls from the undead. My bones chilled as I willed my feet in the direction of the guards' last camp.

The wind carried more grotesque sounds; I hadn't the ability to distinguish whether they were bones or branches snapping. My feet ran faster. Even when I hit the gravel road I didn't stop, I continued east towards the gentle slope of earth and the steady smoke rising from the guard's night camp, my cloak whipped around me heedlessly.

Finally, a golden sliver of the sun cracked over the horizon casting a yellow, warming glow onto the four men and their mounts resting by the white coals. The one who was awake nursing his injured shoulder, stared right through me, as if I was a ghost. Spinning on my heel I turned to see what caught his attention. Smoke, lots of it, blotted out the entire northern sky.

Swearing internally, I scrutinized the trail of smoke southwest from where I had sprinted from. For now, Horn's End was not in flames. The guard that stood watch spoke, I faced him. "That overachieving bastard," he grumbled bitterly as if choking on poison. His tongue ran along the ends of his teeth as he sneered at the billows of smoke. Readjusting the red seal of Numaal pinned proudly to his collar, his brown eyes scouted me. "Looks like I'll get to share in the captain's praises." He kicked the cot next to him and three men stirred. "Fellas, look what the wraiths dragged in." As he shamelessly devoured my flesh with his stare, I tugged my cloak around me.

He rose to his feet. "How did you survive the night?" Stepping on the coals and ash of the dying pit he closed the distance between us. His tunic and scarf were cut, as was the open skin beneath his deltoid. It was a deep enough gash to require sutures.

The young guard popped up. "Drift is back! Look, Gimly!" His energetic joy was palpable.

"So he is," Gimly hissed, peering behind me where several sets of hoofs cantered closer. His fingers were firm, painfully so, as they pinched my elbow pulling me into his side. The seconds passed. Gimly's chest huffed and heaved under his attire. The banter of men and the stomping of the mounts approached. The guards who rested in the camp sprung up and offered celebratory shouts and greetings to the group gathering behind me.

Witnessing firsthand the betrayal of my country's guards on its own people left me in a very un-celebratory mood. I further dipped my chin; my hair fell in front of me, covering the disdain and hurt threatening to contort my face as I thought of Horn's End and the unknown fate of Keenan.

"Lured them right to the center of us! Drift got the mad idea to slick the dead leaves with oil and we burnt well over two hundred of those fuckers down. Not even dust remains!"

Another shouted, "Most brilliant thing I've ever seen. None of our lot got hurt."

There was a deep, youthful laugh that was modestly short. Someone dismounted behind me, their stride was long and their footwork light. Gimly sneered, he looked as though he got punched in the gut. His grip tightened when the shadow of a man hovered over us. Stiffening my spine, I braced myself for another pair of rough hands to befall my body.

The injured man holding me spoke. "She came to us as dawn opened, before you and your tribe of pubescent idiots arrived. We were just about to find out how she survived the night." He gave a yank on my arm. "What's your answer woman?"

I wiggled my well-worn boots, peeking the faded leather toes out from the brothel gown. "I ran."

"Obviously," he whispered harshly.

"I was out gathering resources on the edge of the Wasteland when I saw you set up the traps. Then I heard them coming, so I ran."

"Gathering? The only means to keep alive this far south would be on the coast, casting nets for fish and eels."

I retrieved a flake of willow bark from my satchel. He eyed it and let it be. "Healing is my primary trade. Chew that to ease the sting of your injury. If you take me to Landsfell, I'll happily examine and treat your shoulder along the way."

The guards behind me hopped down from their mounts. The one that spoke next looked the youngest for he had the roundest face. "Can't promise to take you all the way to the city, but we can give you passage to Fort Fell. Ain't that right, Gimly?" His audacity and gentleness earned him a hard smack across the face, there was blood on his cheek bone from where the ring of Gimly split it. I turned my eyes down, afraid they would see the ire behind them instead of meekness.

"You may search my satchel if you have doubts about my words and origins." I kept my tone pleasantly offended. "Guards of Numaal, I ran to you seeking refuge and the protection of your swords. There is no longer life here to sustain my own. I ask for your aid in taking me to the heart of the province, even as far as Fort Fell, so I may experience something more than death and hunger, even though I have become acquainted with them both enough times to call them my friends, despite them robbing my family from me."

"Your story is not special." Gimly's hot breathe wafted over me. "All the misery in the Southlands has grown the duke's legion of guards into quite a formidable size. Why half the men here have fled their trade to pick up arms, or risk being turned into a nightwalker. You are speaking to former crafters and myself, a lord of sorts." His fingers left my elbow to clamp my chin between his thumb and forefinger. I held my breath as he forced my face upward to lock our eyes. His complexion was pale. The surface of it scarred with acne. "You dress as a whore, which means you've not been in solitude. Hopefully, your good friend death has taken your clients swiftly before Drift burnt their corpses." I swallowed and squeezed the bit of bark in my fist.

Moisture left my mouth. "At least he is competent. I'd rather their bodies burn and souls passed on, then have to face them gaunt and fleshless in the war against humanity." Gimly wasn't expecting that response. His narrowed eyes told me as much.

"Tend to my scuff. If it is satisfactory, we will bring you to Fort Fell and use you there," he stated, pulling his tunic above his head. His *scuff* reddened angrily with the movement and friction of scratchy wool.

"No, she is one of us, a people of this nation, our blood." My mind stirred at Drift's words. My nightmare threatened to surface as his voice carried on. "We will bring her to Fort Fell and beyond if we can because it is our duty to guard her and her dreams as if she were our cousin, mother, sister and daughter. She represents the women in our lives who've not survived such a night of senseless terror. She will ride with us, *safely*, regardless of her abilities to mend the flesh." Drift's voice boomed behind me, the agreement of a dozen men around us echoed.

"Thank you, brothers," I said with an unexpected, half smile. "I mend the flesh as well as I can hide from wraiths, which is fantastically well if you were wondering." Some laughed politely. "If any of you have ailments, don't hesitate to seek me out." I offered calmly to those who have been setting bait traps along frequented paths. The same trap that lured Keenan and I in hours ago, the one that called the monsters close to Horn's End. I thought of the rickety village, Rodrick leading his men as he once led his fellow knights of Numaal, Brock in the infirmary, Fauna and Madam Tidal tending to the brothel. My swallow was uncomfortably dry.

Emotional discomfort flitted through me, refusing to ground itself.

"Do you have a name?" His voice subdued the turbulence rising in my chest.

"I do." I turned to him, words immediately stopped forming in my mind. The man called Drift hardly fit into the guard's red tunic, the poor seams around his wide shoulders and biceps were sewn many times, yet thinned and weakened to the point of holes forming. Once I adjusted to the sheer size of him, my gaze moved upwards. A third of his head was shaven, leaving the rest of his long hair pulled back in a messy, undone knot that at one point may have resembled a braid. Three braids. It was mostly black. A patch of white streaked his mane which drew my attention to his mismatched eyes. The right iris was a subtle blue, the left cloudy white. The opaque milkiness of his eyes was the color of blindness. I stared dumbly.

"Name?" He gave a white straight smile that dazzled me out of a trance.

Bitter, I muttered, "Ivy."

His bright grin spread to his eyes as he put a slight bend in his knees. Audible to everyone he commented, "Resilient indeed." Erect once more he addressed the small crowd. "Tend to your mounts and needs, we saddle up in a quarter hour and ride straight through. Right, Gimly? Wasn't that your strategy for the excursion?" The strain of authority on the hillside that morning could have been sliced with a dull butter knife. New to the caravan, burning bridges and being seen as a threat was something I could not afford to do. Either way the horses were saddled and fed over hushed conversations.

My grip on the willow bark eased, I extended it to the boy with a cut on his high right cheek, which swelled mildly. "It will take the sting away." He gave a goofy crooked smile and plucked it gingerly from my palm. "Soften it with your back teeth before rolling it under your tongue."

"Thanks, I'm Asher."

The faint hue of strawberry glinted from his bangs. "It's been some time since I've met a coalminer. I forgot how warm your hearts are." I kept walking pretending I didn't see his freckles disappear under a blush. Gimly sat on a horizontal aspen log, his belongings crumpled into a ball next to him. I approached his injured side. "Have you fresh water or rum?" I asked, rummaging through my bag for lavender oil and calendula salve.

"Rum is in the saddle pocket of the brown mare," his eyes pointed the way to a tethered chocolate horse with a silver plated mouthpiece. I fetched it and brought it back. He swiped it from me and took a swig. Placing it back in my grasp after he had his fill.

"Rum first, then the oils, stitches and salve. Feel free to bite your collar." He grunted. I wanted nothing more than to dump the alcohol on the wound and aggressively peel away the flaking dead tissue with a knife. I placed a docile look on my face and seated myself next to him slowly moving away greasy strands of his brown hair off his neck.

"On with it."

I liberally poured the rum over the gash the span of my hand from thumb to pinky tip. He made an unpleasant grunting sound as I used a package of clean cloth to wipe away the dirt. At least the lavender smelt better than the ripe scent of a filthy man, I thought, smearing several drops of the oil onto the edges of the wound. I wet the end of the spool and placed it through the eye of the needle. Many colorful swear words later, his deltoid resembled the repaired edges of Drift's tunic. I set clean gauze on top of the sutures and wrapped it with the scraps of his cot.

I had made good timing, the troop was packed and the mounts prepped when I had risen. "Get in my saddle." Gimly demanded, tossing a cape over his left side. "I doubt you can read, write or ride and I'm not opposed to a whore in my arms, rocking with me." My blood dropped to my toes. I didn't trust my mouth.

So, I said nothing. I couldn't get my body to move. For if it did, I would punch him.

Drift walked in leading a dusty colored horse that seemed too small for his statue. "Safety is a priority for our new lady comrade. Can we agree?"

"Ay, our captain would want the bitch alive." What little moisture I had left in my mouth vanished. My lips stuck together.

"You can't raise your dominant arm let alone wield a sword," he said in a whispered tone.

"I'll be dead before you take credit for her." The curl of Gimly's upper lip showed his crossed teeth.

"Cultee will know that you spotted Ivy before I on this particular morning. I'll claim the fires, but she rides with me and Rosie." Ice coated the last of his statements distracting me from my violent thoughts of slitting Gimly's jugular and bleeding him. Drift tapped my shoulder, "Would this arrangement be satisfactory with you, miss Ivy?"

Tying my satchel closed I merely nodded my head in agreement. A calloused hand was extended when my gaze settled. "What's this?" I asked Drift, noticing one of his white strands of hair had gotten free and blew across his face.

"Offering my assistance, unless you know how to saddle up already, in which case I apologize deeply." I scrutinized his square cut soldier's nails and mixed complexion that held a hue of dark golden and dirt from the days of travel. I didn't accept his hand for help.

Never had I ridden a horse. Never had I had the opportunity to, but Anna had spoken of them plenty enough. I often could feel the wind on my cheeks when she spoke of riding horseback through her homeland with her siblings. I identified the stirrups, saddle, bit, reins and horn. "Okay, place your left foot here. You'll have to swing your right leg up over the crescent," he directed, watching my eyes frantically move over the animal that weighed a dozen times more than I. "I may readjust you at the end because the stirrups are adjusted to my legs which, well... you're small." I hid my eye roll and placed the arch of my foot onto the metal bridge of the stirrups.

For the briefest moment, his hands found my hips as he floated me onto the saddle. Seconds later, he mounted behind me and I felt the entirety of his front body against my spine. "You can guide the reins after we've set out. Rosie is gentle," he stated coolly, bringing his right arm down in front of me to clutch the leather straps. I inhaled faint scents of cinnamon and sky from his sleeve when I reached for the saddle's horn between my thighs.

He must have glanced down taking notice of my exposed legs for he promptly readjusted my cloak to cover them and even whispered the suggestion I tighten my chest straps. Gimly led us east, charging into the rising sun, we brought up the rear. Drift kept his eyes on each member of his crew. The trot rapidly changed into a gallop. I was grateful for the recommendation to strap my chest down, however, I would have appreciated a fair warning of how intimately our bodies collided and moved together in the saddle. He never commented, I supposed he had ridden with others in this rough manner. An hour into our journey I found my legs and bum aching with newly formed bruises and my skin felt like ice. I desperately wanted to use peppermint oils and soak in a hot spring. "You'll get used to it," he finally broke the silence between us.

I couldn't ask him outright *what* he was, that seemed too crass for a first conversation. I led with, "Where are you from?"

"Much further east, by the Plains of the Horselords that guards the passage across the Thalren Mountains. My mother was one of the shield maidens who rode a white spotted mustang, and when I came into the world under the waxing moon looking as handsome as I do, she laughed at my markings for I had resembled the horse in which she loved dearly."

"Handsome? Perhaps that blind eye of yours screwed with your perception of reality far more than you care to believe." The two nearest riders chuckled and slowed to drop more eaves.

"Ouch, the little miss has offended me." He placed his left hand over his heart.

"Your mother, do you miss her and your homeland?"

He reared his horse up the twisted path. I promptly handed him back the reins in which he allowed me to hold for the briefest of minutes. I would not be held responsible for leading us off a cliff. "My mother died when I was not yet a young man. As for my land, it has changed much over the years, but I'll always remember it for what it was. Which was magnificent and vast."

"I'm sorry to hear that," I said, watching the way he wrapped the reins easily around his forefinger. "Are the undead rampant in the valley?"

"No. Not the undead." His tone turned cold. "I followed rumors of the wraiths and investigated the wreckage of cities and towns, all of which led me here to the Southlands. Although, I suspect the other provinces are dealing with the same plague." He paused and rested his chin atop my head. "That's how I got my name. You know, Drift? I *drifted* down from the northeast countryside and landed here among these fellows who said my name was too difficult to pronounce." His humorous tone became somber. "It's worse here than anywhere else, and yet, Landsfell hardly hears a whisper of the happenings under their noses. Seeing the state of the south, I couldn't leave so I started fighting them and one evening the duke spotted me, took me in and gave me over to Captain Cultee to train up a bit. So, here I am, killing evils that should never have been given life and training to be a good guard of Numaal." He clicked his lips and urged the mount to follow the others up the rocks.

He strived to be in the duke's good graces? Does he know what a wretched man he was? My empty stomach churned, I heard my breathing shake. Drift was going to evolve into a beast who shared the same values as his master. My sworn enemy.

"Aren't you going to ask me what my given name is?" He probed.

Drift was my ride to the encampment, and from there it was a less perilous track to Stegin's manor and flourishing estate. Where I would find a way into his locked chambers and out after the orca moon. "It matters not," I managed to reply.

He sighed. "So be it. We will go about this the hard way."

I'm embarrassed to admit I let a few whimpers of discomfort escape when we met a rocky incline that left me no choice but to rely on his arms around me to keep me from falling. I was so intent on not slipping off the horse's back I'd forgotten he was following orders from the man who killed Anna.

At our first rest, Drift had to balance me when my rubbery legs met the soggy mud of a creek bed. Before I realized I was tripping, his hand grabbed mine. The center of my left palm tingled, it felt as if lightning had struck it. Grimacing, I pulled away and found a young sapling to lean on. Drift's eyes stayed on me. I ignored him.

"Food, Ivy?" Asher offered, approaching from my right. I passed on his presentation of dried jerky. I wasn't sure what type of meat it was. It didn't matter. I passed. He blinked his innocent eyes. "You are a woodlander!"

I couldn't help but giggle. "How many other crafters do you know who can live off of a dead forest and heal ailments?" Had it really been so long since they interacted with us?

Drift snatched a large fistful of jerky from Asher's hand and devoured it in a few bites. He then dove into his own stash of food. More dehydrated meat. A slab of cheese. I wasn't surprised, and yet, I felt myself shaking my head appalled and disbelieving of his food consumption. "My Gods, just carry the carcass of a cow in your saddle bag next time."

"Can't," Drift said with his mouth full. His words muffled as he masticated. "Wouldn't leave room for pretty ladies to ride with me. Even ones who give me the silent treatment, I thought we were done conversing?"

"After watching you eat, I don't think any sane person, woman or man, would want to ride with you fearing you may consume them mistaking them for an undercooked steak. I'll ask Asher if he would care for the company." I attempted to distance myself from Drift's attention. Asher and company snorted and vocalized their agreement with my assessment of the carnivore who carried on chomping on the salted pork.

Drift swallowed and followed it with a deep swig from his pouch. "He has been riding for four months, I've seen him slip off his mount when sleep beckons or a shiny pebble distracts his brain. He just finished growing and his arms can't hold you, the reins and the hilt of his sword. Not yet," he called over his shoulder to the coalminer who peered hopefully into our conversation. "Asher will be a fierce companion, in time." Again, his ears reddened. "There is always Gimly," he whispered and wiggled his brows to his flank. I bit my cheek to prevent my lips from forming a thin line of aggravation. *Don't do anything brash.* Keenan had said.

The tree Drift leaned on moaned under his weight. He watched me unperturbed and I openly scrutinized him back, not bothering to hide my annoyance. His white eye combed over me slowly, not in a creepy way that made me want to shed my skin, but in a way of knowing. And that smirk of his held a hint of secrets.

The nearby trickling of the creek calmed the sarcasm eager to fire back to the guard, a traitor to humanity and he didn't even know it. Perhaps he did, that made it worse.

The trickle beckoned my ears, where there was moisture and weak currents there was also life. I hiked up my cloak and scant fabric of my dress over my knees and jumped across the creek bed landing on a flat limestone. Happily, I walked away from the crowd to comfortable solitude. A hollowed tree trunk typically was very promising for a meal. I crouched close to the ground. Pulling away the forest debris, my finger tip brushed against a soft, fuzzy texture. Carefully, I pried the moss off the porous rock and washed the dirt out of the shallow roots. I pinched the vibrant greenery between my fingers and inhaled the fresh scent of soil and water. It didn't taste of dirt nor was the texture grainy. It was quite delightful. I ate one handful and saved the other for a later time. Not knowing if the next stop would provide any sustenance, I ate sparingly. Nothing akin to that savage who'd eat my arm if it was a bit more meaty and better seasoned. Years of training made me toned and likely tough meat.

"It's time," a holler sounded upstream. I twisted my back and stretched my legs, my hips were tight from straddling the horse and it wasn't even mid-morning. Skirt in hand, I hopped across the stream narrowly avoiding a swampy portion of mud and strode back to Drift's mount. Ignoring him altogether, I placed my right foot in the stirrup and hoisted myself up the rest of the way. It wasn't pretty, or graceful, but I did it without assistance or having to ask for help. Keenan never said anything about stifling my prideful nature, which bordered on arrogance when my kindness wasn't deserving.

Drift landed behind me wasting not a moment to cover my bare legs and reposition the scraps of tattered fabric that constituted my attire. For in all my determination, I had left some bits, important bits, exposed. I pulled my hood over my face as Gimly called the men and their mounts into order, it was a quick stop and even quicker departure. My thighs shook, it was as if we had no respite at all.

"I've earned my fair share of cold shoulders, but I must admit *this* is a record. You've become voiceless in my presence after the briefest exchanges of words, I reckon you are angry with me. Although, I can't fathom why. I'm considerate, charming and devastatingly handsome," he muttered to himself.

"I'm not angry," I whispered.

In an exhale he said, "You're lying."

"Am not."

"Are too. And I wager ten gold coins and two hundred pastels that I know why."

I lowered my voice to only where he could hear me. "Doubtful." I immediately regretted retorting to his banter. I locked my gaze ahead and ignored the arm that loosely wrapped around me to hold the reins. I denied them when he offered them to me. Intentionally, I stiffened my back and tried my damnedest not to lean into the warm, wide chest behind me.

"My striking good looks have you tongue-tied. Not unnatural given I'm the most unique masterpiece you've ever seen." Thank the Goddesses that I didn't finish the moss, his narcissistic monologue was nauseating. "Save your words. We both know you'd be lying again if you told me that you didn't find me remotely attractive."

My tongue started to bleed from biting it.

When the road leveled out and the slopes and rocky breaks were behind us, I acknowledged Drift by way of wiggling the reins from his hand which made the leather straps appear as a petite string in comparison to his large grip. He surrendered without a fight and shifted his weight backwards to flex his limbs. This relieved me of his right arm wrapped around my side. Noon came and went. Visible on the horizon some leagues ahead were patches of greening fields scattered among the torched, black earth. The second respite was shorter than the first, for the dark navy line of night in the sky approached. The troop pressed hard, my hips left the saddle with our new cadence and my feet, far above the reach of the footholds, lost their grip on the mount's side. My legs were too wobbly to clutch any tighter and I started to fall. "You won't be asking for my aid, will you?" I shook my head fiercely as panic rose.

"Never."

"Stubborn indeed," his words were curt, his actions fast. Drift wrapped his left arm around the lowest portion of my pelvis and pulled my backside directing into his hips, anchoring me to him and firmly into the saddle. It felt intimate and animalistic.

Now grounded, he placed his right hand over mine and indirectly showed me how to tighten the slack and steady the gallop. His chest leaned into my back and together we lowered our torsos parallel to the ground, the wind no longer sent my small frame sliding off the mount. It soared over us.

As we strode late into the evening, conversations among the men grew sparse, only when the lights of the training camp and the surrounding town homes came into a dim view, did life rekindle within the boys. Stable hands emerged from the barn and one by one led the horses into their stall to be tended to. I stroked the warm neck of our mare and thanked her before it was recommended that I dismount. "Can you walk?" Gimly asked, pushing his way through the cluster of red and leather plated guards. I tested my balance. I was wobbly, but I could make due. I nodded.

"Good, yer coming with me." He turned his back, his black cape swooshing. He snapped for me to follow on his heels. Begrudgingly, I did. And I did it with the painful smile of a gracious survivor. I felt eyes on me as I wove out past Rosie and out of the stable and up the street of small pubs, inns and essential goods shops. Fort Fell was easy enough to spot, grey drabby bricks layered up to three stories high and archers tending their post on all fronts of the massive building. Two men uncrossed their spears and we walked in through the front doors. Crimson red and slate greys greeted me, it was harsh on the eyes. "Let the captain know, I've returned with success and a treat. We will be waiting in his office," Gimly announced to the room of scribes and several servant women in beige garb. I waved to the staff, they softened their faces and smiled back.

As we carried on down the southern hall and up two flights of stairs, I felt my knees protest. Gimly wasn't thrilled to alter his pace. He stood in the open doorway of a heavy oak entrance, his foot tapping. My eyes couldn't believe that so many books were to be found in one place, Anna and Moriah had read to me from scripts they rewrote from memory. Nothing I read was ever leather bound or ink pressed. My feet carried me to the library cabinet where I inhaled the scents of knowledge.

"These pages hold stories. Some of tragedy, some of love and some of the creation of our world." A new voice entered the small office, I turned to receive the proprietor of the military establishment.

"Captain Cultee, a pleasure. I'm Ivy." I lowered my head and did not raise it until he permitted me to do so.

"Rise," he stated dryly. "You've woken me up to present me with a lady? She can earn her keep in the kitchen with the rest of the rural workers who need a way to earn coin and comforts." I focused on my breathing. Inhale. Exhale.

Gimly tossed his cloak over the nearest chaise and presented to his superior with a cleaned and bandaged upper arm. "Not, just any girl, sir. A woodlander." The spark in their gaze turned Cultee's disappointed frown into a thin line. "The king will certainly turn his attention if he knows you've a woodlander in your grip. All the rest are rumored to have fled to the Southern Isles or succumbed to the bite. Our troops will be able to hold our ground better against the scum of the west if she can concoct us the right potions." *West? Not the scum on our own land?*

I almost laughed. Instead, a docile voice left my lips as I stated to the ground at his feet. "That is not how my craft works, it is about finding a body's equilibrium using nature to help dismiss disease. What you speak of is magic, no mortal wields the power of the Eternals."

Cultee examined his guard's wound. "Impressive stitch work," he addressed me. I looked up to meet his aging gaze. My angry heart pumped blood which burned and it pulsed through my body. I knotted my hands behind my back, preventing them from forming fists and slamming my knuckles into the side of his heavily bearded chin. I immobilized my face. "Anyone can learn to sow the flesh, for times are desperate and injuries unavoidable. Have you confirmed the claims she makes or were you swayed by her tender touch and full breasts?" Gimly watched us nervously. I choked on the sudden crude remarks watching Gimly shake his head.

Cultee turned to me, his scabbard swinging at the hip of his silk red tunic. "She has all the traditional piercings of a practiced earth crafter." That was true, each ear held several metal loops and some hanging vials, one of poison and another of an antidote. My lip, nose, tongue and most intimate parts had a rod through them. "What class of woodlander are you, Ivy?"

"Master."

His brow rose. "A master? This must be confirmed, I'd hate for the Fort to discover you a deceiver and have to watch you reap the repercussions of your foolishness." There was both an order and threat in his statement. His hand lay splayed open directly in front of my nose, demanding the cloak off my back. I unclasped the two brass chains and draped the green woolen fabric over his fingers. It was suddenly drafty. He twirled his finger and again, I complied. I spun to him to present my back.

I yelped, startled with Gimly's knife that appeared to cut away the fabric. Disbelieving that short scream of fright came from me I covered my mouth with my hands as my elbows held the remaining scraps intact preserving what little modesty was left. Gimly took liberating upon himself to overstep boundaries. My spine felt as immovable and frigid as steel when a set of fingertips caressed the low of my back along the intricate sprays of lilac and ropes of ivy.

"Hey, cap, we're back!" Drift spoke with his mouth full, we all heard him rounding the corner to the office. Hell, I'm sure the whole compound did. "Burnt a few hundred of them, definitely exceeded the assignment, wouldn't you say?" He stopped mid chew and choked down the rest of his turkey leg catching sight of me in the hands of his superior and fellow guard. His eyes grew as big as mine. "What the—?" There was a clatter as he dropped his clay plate and fork on the desk hurrying to shut the door. Confusion skewed his features when he moved into my line of sight. It was an intentional move. *What did he want?* I kept my arms secured across my chest and eyelids diverted down at his muddy boots treading on the floor. My body flushed under the intensity of the stares. It was a long humiliating minute.

"Drift, wipe that disapproving scowl off your brow and get your horselord ass over here to learn a thing or two about the Southlands," Cultee muttered across the span of the room. Drift slowly picked up his heavy boots. Surprisingly, his heels didn't make much noise as he walked. His chewing, however, was a different story.

An obnoxious, bothersome one.

Gimly gathered up my mass of hair and tugged it to the side. My neck strained to remain upright under the pressure of the firm clasp that snatched the nape of my neck, it felt like a tight collar of a hound. Swallowing was difficult. "There are seven levels to each craft. She has all the markings of a master," the captain educated and with the pronunciation of each word his minion drifted his finger down my spine, connecting the seven ink circles I earned, stopping only when the rope holding up my skirt cut off his trail. "She's a master woodlander. There never were many of them due to the complex nature of their skillset and their coven-like existence. I reckon she is one of the last if her family has passed on. She is young for a master, which means she probably is the girl all the Crescent Isles merchants chatted about. The holy healer? Prodigy child?" My face warmed, sadness and anger filled me at the lonely notion of being the last woodlander. "All things that live and grow are her domain. Ailments cured, farm soil made rich, animals rescued, bones set into place. A rarity, but irreplaceable when it comes to the battles to be fought and land to be lived on." My head was pulled backward until it met the chest of Gimly. His hot breath blew my hair as he continued to speak and wander his gaze down my neckline.

Gimly's mouth met my ear. "Pity what happened to the rest of the crafters in the province, either wraiths or ashes by now. The prince regrets not intervening sooner, had the Maruc himself not so openly announced his loathing of mortals, then perhaps his time could have been spent more wisely and we could have saved more." Inhale. Exhale. "The last God declared humans a grievous mistake. He is set on bringing down Numaal, starting with the undead feasting on the helpless. Ending with dethroning our beloved royals."

"What?" I exclaimed. Were so many things hidden from me in the woodlands?

Cultee allowed Gimly to banter under his watchful eye. "Disgusting, to turn their backs on their own creations. Either way, they are set on seeing Numaal's demise."

My chest felt empty. Abandoned, as if Anna didn't prepare me enough for the real world and this-this was only a small fort town of several hundred. Not a provincial city like Landsfell and certainly not Kathra, my country's capital. There was distress in my voice, "What of the Empress, the last Goddess, Athromancia? Surely, the embodiment of wisdom would counteract the insolent temper of the God of War?" I offered as Drift stiffly crossed his arms over his pectorals and his chin locked sharply as Gimly walked behind me.

"Rumors from Kathra reveal Athromancia sent her own army to the mountains. She is more eager than Maroc. Communication has gone awry between the nations. Don't concern yourself with political affairs, I'll summarize Numaal's history soon enough since you're unschooled in most matters outside of anatomy and dirt." Gimly stated behind me while Drift paced the office. I dared not raise my eyes to find his mismatched gaze full of unreadable emotions.

My own emotions were spiraling downward in a vortex of confusion. None of what he said was what I was taught, from my parents or the Ilanthian family.

The grip on my neck eased, my legs crumpled when I was released. My knees ached when they hit the wooden floor, I could practically feel the contusions forming. To ensure my dagger was still safe, I curled into myself, using my waist long hair to cover my discrete searching. Keenan's dagger was intact. "We've plans for you. The Gods have brought you to us to save what is left of our fellow mortals. To fight immortal supremacy. Fear not, I'll be by your side." I begged myself not to vomit, more from his promise to be near me rather than the impending war on humans.

My hands sweat with anger. "Have you an infirmary for me to manage?"

"We've a bar on second street that takes care of most woes and a whorehouse for the rest of our urges." He picked at his fingernails.

Captain Cultee shook his head at the guard. "There is an empty stock room by the smithy that will be plenty large enough for your botanicals. I expect you to create one there." I narrowed my eyes.

Drift threw my cloak over the tattoo with sloppy haste. "No need to keep her shivering if we've seen what we've needed to."

Captain gave an exasperated sigh. "Gimly don't be dumb enough to place your hands on a master crafter again, pursuing her will have consequences that we cannot fix." Gimly swore out of annoyance as his counterpart gave a smug look. "Drift, seeing as you remain a bleeding heart despite our best efforts to toughen you up, I'll leave you responsible for seeing Ivy to the female chambers. I'd like her to reside inside the fortified walls, woodlanders have a reputation of escaping. Sly little creatures they are."

Confusion must have crossed my face, "I've never heard that before, when my parents worked on the coast the sea merchants just called us content and reliable. Sometimes dirty for running around barefoot, never escape artists," I added, dumbly lost in memory.

Cultee sighed a gentle sigh, "Matters not, Ivy."

"It'd be my honor, cap," Drift said, watching his commander stride across the room.

"The lady's man will escort you to the stockroom tomorrow morn before he hands me an official report of this week's body count. Try not to linger with the kitchen maids or paddy clappers, ey?"

Gimly snorted then hissed across the office, "Drift frequents the whore house, yet, I'm the one that receives the warning to stay away from her? Unfair." He locked eyes with the captain. "Father wouldn't be happy."

Drift gave no emotion or reaction to the previous commentary directed at him. But he did take a jab before the red tunics shut the double oak doors. "See you after the first meal, captain. Oh and Gimly, next time at least *pretend* you got injured in combat, a bit embarrassing that you cut yourself on the lure trap you set. Good thing Ivy found you or that infection would have taken your arm. G'night!" The door frame shuddered and its lock rattled after Gimly slammed it on Drift's face. "We're competing for the same position you see." I felt the hunger in his words and pulled away from the extended hand steadily waiting to help me up. I looked at it and back down at my missing garments. "I need to get the captain's approval as his best sword for the duke to take me in his company to be trained as a knight in Kathra. Cap holds a gruff exterior, but sometimes he cracks and sentiments flood through. He's not all mad and salted with sadness."

He rubbed his neck. In one scoop he had me on my feet and a moment later he asked permission to tie the back of my dress. "It's a walk to the west wing and down some stairs. You will be passing the ranked guard's rooms across from the casual dining hall and you will be decent for that." There was no fighting against his tone.

I nodded. He proceeded and began to fumble with the clasps and straps. A full two minutes passed while he concentrated, I sensed his growing frustration. "What the bloody heavens is the point of these damn strappy *things*?"

"An allurement, they serve no real purpose."

"A waste of my time is what they are," he growled.

I dared, "Then leave them be."

"Sixty men sleep in the fort, and some hundred odd more in the bunks and inns. They are not all saints, this is not up for debate."

I was suddenly grateful my parents didn't have an older boy before me. The idea of a big brother sounded cumbersome. "Is that where you sleep, with the ranked guards?"

"Interested in coming to my chambers?" A flirt indeed.

"No. I need to ensure that when I sneak out, I am avid to avoid your window when I reenter."

He managed to connect the proper strings and plopped my cloak back onto my shoulders. "*When* you sneak out?"

"You heard your master, us woodlanders are notoriously sneaky little creatures," I mocked and collected my satchel off the floor.

Drift was walking towards his unfinished meal on the desk. "I figured that when I saw the dagger hidden under your breasts. Marvelous job bringing that in here by the way, *very* distracting technique." I didn't know what to say, my hand reflexed to grab the blade. "Aren't you pretending you don't know how to use one of those?" His dark brow wiggled.

I walked over to where he stood and watched the light from the chandelier over us cast odd shadows onto the floor. "For a blind man, you're very observant."

"I've never said I was blind." Damn me for thinking the next smile he let slip was gorgeous. There was even a charming dimple on the left side. That strand of his white hair fell in front of our dueling gazes. "Come, let's get you settled in."

"You are not going to report me for my dagger?" He opened the door with his spare hand, looking back at me with wide eyes standing there like a deer caught in the night.

"No, so long as you don't tell anyone that I am breaking you into the kitchen afterhours. What does a woodlander eat anyways?" He asked beckoning me to his side with his fork laced in his grip.

"Plants, oats, grains, fruits. Nuts and cheese- when there is someone to prepare it," I replied, suddenly starving. I pulled out the other handful of moss I had saved from this morning and took a bite. There was a stunned look on his mismatched face as he watched me devour the plant growth. "Did you want the last bite?" I offered, knowing he would reject me.

In shaking his head, he said, "Maybe another time. It looks like you need all the dirt and seeds you can get. No wonder you're so bloody petite, you eat like a rodent."

"I'm not small, you just so happen to be too big," I retorted bitterly as he led me down the stairs and across the main foyer where off duty patrols gathered. The drinking and card games stopped as we strode in. Drift cleared his throat to say something, but I was perfectly capable of introducing myself. I inhaled to state my name when my left hand stung and a strong pain of hesitancy flooded my mind.

Drift's voice boomed over mine, laced with humor and a lethal undercurrent. "This is Ivy, the new woodlander in the fort. Do try not to get yourselves killed or maimed until she has adequate supplies, alright fellows?"

They rose their beer mugs and goblets up as a manner of addressing the guard's statement. The respect in their eyes was evident, well, in most of their eyes. Some sneered. Drift gave a farewell wave and ushered me along in a maze of turns I mentally memorized.

We stopped at the most wonderfully scented room in the fort. The kitchen was absent except for a rounder woman, a decade older than my mother would have been. "Set this aside for you dear," she whispered to Drift as if there were others around to hear her secret. "Ah! Who do we have here?"

"Ivy, ma'am." I was happy to find my voice that had disappeared moments ago had returned.

Drift embraced the lady in a hug, she disappeared beneath his embrace. "Raina, you are a lifesaver." He kissed her head of grey hair. "Hopefully, you can help me just a wee bit more tonight?" He posed the last statement like a question.

I cut him off as he continued to speak for me. Stepping in I declared, "I'm a woodlander, this beast doesn't understand what I eat. If you've bread or lentils available, I'd be ceaselessly grateful ma'am. I'll work in your service to earn my meal if you are satisfied with such an arrangement."

The corner of her eyes turned up, soft winkles deepened when she spoke. "Glazed turnips and parsley wheat crisps sit well with you?"

My saliva glands activated. "Very well, ma'am. How may I service you?" I hopped on my feet and let my satchel fall onto the table where some of its contents tipped over. Raina hustled to the brick warmer and opened up a crock pot of sugary root vegetables and container of pressed crackers.

"Just grab a spoon darling," she called over her shoulder as she set the pot down on the table. "Second drawer on the left." Following her instructions, I obtained my utensil and on my return I slowed to observe all the drying herbs the cooks used for flavoring. Dill, fennel, basil, rosemary, licorice, mint, parsley, cilantro, cinnamon-all the common durable herbs. In the glass jars above some less common seasons, hordash root, sawle leaves and lapala greens. I sauntered back to where

Drift had made himself comfortable on the bench and rummaged through the vials and purses that had fallen out of my satchel.

"You may find me in your kitchen whether or not you need my help," I confessed with growing excitement as she headed two portions of food into a bowl and slid it in front of me. Drift was opening a paper bag of nettles. I grunted in a spark of annoyance. "Keep digging, there are pin quills coated with venom. I pray your clumsy hands get jabbed to teach you a lesson on respecting another's privacy." Raina eyed us with amusement, the guard swiftly took his fingers out of the bag and crossed them across his chest after inspecting them for punctures.

I shoveled food into my mouth, conscious that I didn't want to resemble the slob next to me. I chewed each bite thoroughly. "To your satisfaction?" Unable to stop eating, I gestured vigorously. The two of them carried on about the state of the king's wavering health, while I lost myself to the sweet glaze of the crunchy steamed roots. Once the spoon scraped the bottom of the bowl, I carried it to the sink, rinsed it and set it aside.

My eyes grew as heavy as my stomach. My feet moved slowly as Drift and I were directed out of the kitchen. Raina touched my wrist. "I accept your offer, Ivy. There is a great need for your skills among the females of Fort Fell." She was careful to avoid Drift's gaze. In understanding, I tipped my head.

"I was asked to conjure up an apothecary from an empty closet, that will absorb much of my time and of what little supplies I have on me." I grimaced at the painstaking task. "I have two available doses with me now. How many more should I be expecting to produce this month?

"Fifty, to be safe," she added, pressing my back down the hall alongside Drift who was stretching his long arms over his head. The man had nearly dismantled the faint light above with the careless swing of his arm. Was this clutz a man allowed to swing a sword?

Unsure I heard her right, I whispered with a hint of disbelief. "Pardon, five zero. Fifty?"

"Yes."

I bit my lip and handed her the last two tea bags of monthly tea. "I've taken mine already." I ensured. I had never missed a dose, the last thing

I needed, or wanted, was a child in my womb. Raina clasped her fingers around the bags and subsequently my hand. The touch was warm. It's been so long, over eight seasons, since I've interacted with a maternal touch. I retracted and stepped into stride with Drift. Two of my steps matched one of his. I practically sprinted at his side.

We halted outside a stone passageway lit with more fire and flickering electricity. Across the cold room was a mirror image of a passageway. Both hallways looked cold and uninviting. I swallowed hard pulling myself out of the memory of my iron and stone cell in the dark dungeon. "Will there be a window?" I whispered to hide the residual fear. I could not, I would not, be trapped again. A cold sweat broke on my forehead.

"Winter arrived this morning. Windows are typically deemed unfavorable for the weather wafts through the beams, you don't want that."

My jaw locked as if trying to cage my aggressive sentiments behind my teeth. "I don't intend on staying that long. Also, don't tell me what I want."

There was no verbal response. His feet led us a few steps into the women's quarters before he stopped at the door. An invisible boundary. "The empty rooms will have the door open and you are to choose one of them, I expect there to be several. You ought to find a gown and wash cloth on a side table. Somewhere in these chambers is a common room with a small lounge and a firepit to warm the pipes. There is a bathing room with a shower pour and a porcelain tub. Don't expect either to be warm," he warned, keeping his gaze set on me. I felt his attention studying my face and hands, which I kept laxed. "Just after first light I'll collect you here."

"Sure, after I watch the sun rise *from my window*, I can manage that."

His pale frosted eye fixated on me as I strode down the hallway. I went back and shut the door on his statue that took up the entire frame. "Good night to you too." His laugh was muffled behind the wood. The common room was empty, the fireplace a dying pile of coal and shavings of wood, offering little light and even less heat. A girl, some years older than me sleepily passed me leaving the privy too lost in the land of slumber to acknowledge me. I examined a half dozen stone rooms whose doors were ajar, only two had an opening large enough to fit my shoulders and hips through. I choose the one furthest away from the central area. The dress that sat folded on the end of the small cot was a lifeless color of beige and brown and the cut of fabric was not practical for... *anything*. It was too long to run, too drapey to measure plants with precision. I threw it on the floor just before I threw my body on the cot. The draft from under the fabric was cold but the pull of sleep was stronger.

Chapter Four

It was only a few hours after midnight when I woke up with my stomach twisting. Anna's blood was still hot on my lips, the coppery taste still thick in my mouth. Onlookers peered into my chamber, horrified by my screams. I waved them onward. My first stop upon awakening was the baths, I wished Drift had been lying when he said the waters were cold. I could hardly breathe when I ran the trickling stream over my head, lasting only a minute under the water. I was certain there was still soap in my hair when I left. Using mint leaves, I brushed my teeth and placed rose oil on my face. My previous garments were hardly clean enough to don so I took to scrubbing them in the remnants of the shower waters and hung them to dry on the single stool next to my cot.

In the common room, I stood thin and shivering in a billowing dress, while my hair dried. This wouldn't do. Returning to my room, I began to tear at the long sleeves, shortening them until my arms were exposed and nothing would be a burden. The excess material I wrapped around my waist, cinching it to wear my feet wouldn't catch. The sun rose as I made my way down the hallway to the central fort.

Drift wasn't there when I opened the door so I took to exploring the parameters of the main hall. There were no pictures, seldom a splash of color. Red curtains were hung on the banisters of the higher level and three guards patrolled in rotation, I watched them until I dizzied. Then I felt him. His hawkeyed watch and the chill of his shadow. "You're late," I stated, not bothering to turn around and greet him.

"Intentionally so. I gave you the courtesy of resting a few minutes longer." I hummed, doubting that very much. "You don't believe me?" He asked.

"Not in the slightest." I moved in his direction, avidly ignoring his brushed locks of hair that rivaled my mind in length and lush. Then I moved ahead of him, he caught up in little time as would be expected.

"Did you sleep well or were you too cold?"

Why couldn't he stop talking? "Take me to my destination and leave me."

"Are you always so obstinate?" He inquired too chipper for the early morn.

To which I retorted. "Are you always so loquacious?"

"No, actually. My preference is in the unspoken word which makes it difficult for me to form connections with people here due to the frequent misinterpretations of my actions versus the silent intentions." I let a moment of his precious silence pass hoping he could read all my unsaid agitation. "You don't believe me? I am starting to feel offended," he covered his heart. "I see we won't be making progress today. I'll try tomorrow."

"Please, don't," I prayed.

He smirked at the passing ladies filing out of Raina's kitchen. They giggled and batted their lashes, he turned to admire their hips swaying as they strode away from him. Taking advantage of his distraction I scrutinized his choice of weaponry. A sword hung on his left hip, its length an entire hand span longer than the traditional guard's sword and his black and gold belt buckle an obscured figure of a horse. With his tunic so tight there was no room to hide any smaller blades or pins and left each firm dip of his abdomen in plain sight. I pulled my attention back to the high ceiling of the foyer before he could accuse me of admiring him. The two spear holders uncrossed their pikes and permitted us outside where the onslaught of morning frost sent my skin into a frenzy. If only my cloak wasn't damp and left behind. My skin pricked.

"The smithy is between Crocker Street and the training fields, under the same pergola. You'll be sheltered on two of your four parameters and the smelting fires should keep you from becoming an ice statue. Peak sun is quite pleasant should you find yourself wandering out of your designated area craving a stroll to the civic." I made no gesture that I heard him for I was too occupied surveying the ground for signs of growth and vegetation. There was little life beneath the trampled surface. The paths were either too frequented or made of gravel. It was a brief expedition from the fort to the smithy, perhaps a quarter hour at my pace. The small street came to life with the rising sun. Two bakers began to gather their ingredients and cart it back to their stores while the barber shop on the corner pushed aside its curtains and propped the door open for customers to wander in off the dirt path.

The stockroom was no more than a closet. Even with its small capacity it would take me days if not weeks to fill the six shelves with the supplies needed to tend to the troops, the town's people and the women of Fort Fell. "What's the most common injury the guards endure?" I asked.

"Infection from deep wounds and bleeding out from a fatal strike. A fair share of injured egos, but not a single healer in all the lands can fix a man's shortcomings," I blew the dust off the shelves. I had my work cut out.

"Now, *that* I believe. You men are such delicate things," I commented, turning to watch the sun rise slightly high in the grey and smokey sky. "Best you run off to your master to tell him how you burnt down one of the last plots of inhabitable land left in the south province."

"It's becoming increasingly difficult to leave you unenlightened. But since your ire is palpable and company is not too far off, there is no choice but to let things remain as they are." Relief settled as the silhouette of him was absorbed by the massive block structure of Fort Fell. The training field was slow to arouse. Three men came into the pergola to grab chest armor while I was tidying the filthy cabinet and the stone floor. We all shared a friendly wave then directed our focus to our tasks.

Clank! Behind me the kiln's metal door swung open, the lock made more abrupt noises as it fell onto the hard work surface. There was no dagger for me to grab at my thigh, and yet, my fingers searched relentlessly for it. The man igniting the fire had on a soot covered hood and raised his hands into the air, in a gesture of innocence. His hands were scarred, calloused and blistering. "You're alright. I can see you mean no harm." His tired hands went back to work lifting firestarters from his cart and tossing them into the kiln which roared merrily as it was fed.

Twice, he winced at the large flames licking the outside of the clay oven, shielding his face with his rough hands. "Do you have insulated gloves for your work?" I asked the paddy clapper, wondering why he wouldn't take such obvious precautions in his line of work. He carried on as if I had said nothing. When I went to introduce myself-he shut the mouth of the kiln and scurried off with his wagon.

"Don't take it personally. He is a mute," Gimly added nonchalantly from the other side of the hut. "He is one of the best coalminers we've had, mostly because he keeps to himself and does what he is told. Odd fellow, but is vital to maintain livable conditions here as you'll find out this season." His injured arm had a stunted range of motion. He kept it tucked to his side while aimlessly swinging the sword with his other arm.

I forced a pleasant look and went about making a mental list of necessities for basic remedies. His voice intruded on my thoughts. "When shall I expect you to remove the thread in my skin?" Gimly crept over to the wooden fence that separated our halves of workspace from the clamor of shields and swords.

Assuming he kept the site clean and hadn't extended it overhead, I estimated, "Five days. I'll reassess it sooner if you find pain, swelling or drainage. I'm hoping to be granted some time in the kitchen this evening to prepare tea bags for mild cases of discomfort. But, I'll need to return to the Wastelands soon if I am to be of much aid here. There is no foliage." I moved my vision from him to the barrenness beyond.

"Least we know you are capable of running. Best to get an early start, you don't want to transform into a shadow of a soul and be forgotten like the rest of your family."

This *prick*! "You are quite right. I appreciate your concern." I collected the broom from the corner and thoughtlessly swept to deescalate the growing rage that fluctuated in my chest. Gimly walked back to his men and started barking orders, I found my way to the stables where I hid behind a stall and began punching a bale of hay. I had worked up a sweat by the time I felt moderately calm.

I can't do this! I thought, throwing myself into the haystack letting itchy straws tumble over me. I swore out loud. How was I supposed to get from this shit hole into the duke's mansion?

Keenan had been right to be worried. My brash self was moments away from making an appearance and I hadn't been here more than a half day. Shutting my eyes, I hummed one of the many memorable tunes that had been sung over the weeks of my imprisonment. Temporarily, my dread froze.

On my way to the kitchen, I stopped by Drift's mount who had carried us away from the traps and fires so bravely. "Hello, Rosie. Unfortunately, I wasn't in a mood to converse with your rider or I would have introduced myself sooner." She tentatively nuzzled her soft cheek on the side of my open hand before backing away. "I'm not a rider or skilled shieldmaiden, but I do understand reciprocating kindness." From my satchel I pulled out a pine cone covered with old spring sweet sap. The cone was devoured and my fingers free from the sticky substance within seconds of gifting it. "Glad you liked it." I wiped the horse spit on my bland attire, when I got to the kitchen, I scrubbed my extremities in the sink, hyper aware of the woman waiting to greet me.

"Good morning, is Raina nearby?"

The woman readjusted her garments, the drab color did nothing to distract the gauntness from her cheek bones. And yet, she was stunning. "She manages the late meals and after hours. I work the morning shifts and handle the prep work. I'm her granddaughter Sage." I shook her extended hand.

With a name like that...I couldn't stop myself from asking, "Are you a woodlander?"

"No, I get that often out here. My parents raised me in Landsfell, but grandmother says they dreamt about simple crafting and a quiet life." My eyes fell from her thinning face to her abdomen which her arms unconsciously guarded. "I've missed two cycles," she announced. "Let's keep this between us women for I work behind curtain six in the brothel."

I made a motion that sealed my lips tight. "I am here to ask about placing an order for some herbs the next time we refill the kitchen stock. Kitchen work is aligned with medicinal practice. So much healing comes from what we eat and ingest."

"I'll be sure to fetch you when the cart and scribes come to take inventory, won't be for another fortnight."

"You look unwell, Sage." I leaned across the center counter. "Are you not eating because of the nausea, fear of the rounding shape or poor finances?"

"I never wanted this babe. It came to be from a nonconsensual and violent encounter, I fear that when it's born I will loathe it. That I will think of nothing aside from the scum that forced this into my life." Her features saddened further as if she was hearing herself say the hard truths out loud for the first time. The tears welling in her eyes triggered mine to glaze over. "Yet, now that I can feel my womb grow heavy and expand, all I can imagine is the innocent life in me who never asked to be born, to be hated or to be alive in the dark times to come." We were now both openly sniffling back our tears. "I can't do it. End an innocent life. They do not have to be the sins of their parents. So, in answer to the question posed, uncertainty and frequent nausea prevent me from consuming proper meals."

Before I recognized my own actions, I had pulled Sage into a hug. She cried for a long while on my shoulder. Coming into a seated position I checked her pulse rate on her wrist and looked for any sign of swelling on her feet and damaged blood vessels on her legs. "I'll concoct you some ginger and lemon balm tea to help with the queasy stomach, it's alright to take the blend four times a day without consequences. You should be able to keep down a bland meal within a half hour of consuming it." I wiped my tears away as I took to boiling water on the stove top and mincing up the ginger roots on the top shelf.

"What's Landsfell like?" I asked Sage as she moved to my side mimicking how I peeled and sliced the roots. Behind us three more kitchen staff entered along with the clamor of dishes and gossip.

"Busy, gaudy, political. A horrendous place to anyone born of lesser stature, where a purebred horse would cost more than a human life. Where priestesses and landholders host formal events that turn the night sky into a dreamworld of glimmering distractions while they make political moves that thousands suffer for. Everything is a show, an audience is everywhere. It is not a kind place. I reckon the half million that live there ought to be barking mad to stay, but most love the games and the ritual of it all, even if it means never once living life on their own terms."

"And that's why you left. To live?"

Nodding, she scooped the ginger into the mason jar and brought down the large satchel of lemon balm leaves. I felt myself smile inhaling its scent that reminded me of strawberries growing in my mother's field and Cobar smashing them vigorously with his hands to make jam. He always enjoyed making a mess of things. Food, mud, paint, he thrived in being a tiny wrecking ball. I'd never loved a little disaster so much in my life. "These leaves are dry enough to crumple into the jar. One third ginger, two thirds lemon balm." Placing the knives down we rolled the brittle plant until the small pieces flitted down into the jar. "That should do it. Bring me a seep and cup. I'll then leave you ladies to your domain and make a hasty exit so as to not take up space."

"You're not a burden here. You'll be hard pressed to find someone who'd agree to such a statement," Sage replied, placing her full strainer into the hot water. "I promise I'll try and eat something if you take a loaf of bread with you. The ones that grow stale are given to the pigs," behind me a young girl who hadn't hit puberty yet handed me a wicker basket with two loaves of bread and apple cores.

"I've been alone, at least isolated, for so long, I wasn't sure what to expect when meeting others or if anyone would dare to welcome a lone woodlander, certainly not in the company of guards. I'm pleasantly surprised," I admitted, accepting the basket from the child who introduced herself as Lorelei. Sage allowed me to take the kitchen's supply of hops and stoneweed, two of the ingredients in the month tea, mosslace I would have to go back into the woods to hunt for. I was also given a variety of cooking oils which would come in handy for salves and poultices in the near future. The afternoon was spent hauling items back and forth from the kitchen to my pantry, stopping only when my stomach demanded to be filled. I'd eaten an entire loaf of sourdough bread by the time I collapsed onto my cot where a bath towel and another impractical servant's dress awaited me.

I was confident Drift would remain true to his words of *making progress with me tomorrow*—whatever that entailed. Finding my cloak and brothel attire from Horn's End were dry and relatively clean, I donned them with my boots and stuffed the brown clothes under my flat pillow. Sure, the brothel attire was less appropriate given the change in season, but that was what the woolen cloak was for. Besides, the smithy's kiln and the baker's ovens both radiated enough heat to keep me comfortable, I assured myself. I opted to leave from the window as an extra precaution to avoid Drift. It was a five foot drop, easily done. I hopped up off the dirt and tugged my hood over my face. The grass and ground beneath my feet were stiff and frosted. They made a satisfying crunch under my steps.

In the stable, I handed the last portion of the apple core to the horse who recognized me in my continuous efforts to befriend her. Efforts well spent seeing as I would need to ride out soon. The paddy clapper spotted me behind the stall and hid behind the nearest beam. He was a lean figure, yet still narrow enough to vanish behind a post. The manner in which Gimly spoke of him made it sound as if he was a workhorse, vital to the establishment, but in the way he carried himself it was obvious he wasn't showered with the appropriate appreciation. "Excuse me?" I called out into the early morning, my breath clouded and consolidated as I spoke. I rounded the corner of the back stables where the reins and saddles hung on the wall.

His grey and ash over coat hid his features. "Hello." My voice filled the air. I stepped cautiously in his direction, afraid he would bolt with any sudden movement like a doe being hunted. I wasn't expecting a verbal reply, but he gave me nothing. I bit my lower lip when I arrived at my decision. I just wanted to tend to the blisters on his palms. I laid the wicker basket with the last loaf of bread to rest at his feet and backed away. Knowing warmth awaited me in the stockroom, I ran with an extra skip over the white tipped grass.

A man in black leathers and a rubbery apron adjusted his goggles. The blacksmith set down his hammer and prongs watching me weave around his work station.

"Wisteria? Wisteria Woodlander?" He exalted.

"*Ivy* Woodlander," I educated the stranger.

He moved the circular goggles off his face, revealing the man beneath. His high cheek bones he inherited from his mother, Elousie. "Hello, again."

"Pine Underhill," I dropped the hood of my cloak. My satchel fell to the floor.

He opened his arms. "Now, I'm Pine Ironside. The wraiths stole my underhill family. The only means for me to be of use to those fighting them is to forge their swords." He looked me up and down as if not believing a spirit from his past had come to visit. "My mother would have had a field day lacing flowers in that hair of yours. My mother..." he trailed, words failing him.

"The woodlanders scattered and burned. I made sure our dead stayed that way, for watching them die twice may break my soul more than seeing their corpses the first time. I'm sorry, Pine." His arms found their way around my back and his wet nose buried into my shoulder.

I let him find comfort. Gods, his sobbing unsteadied my feet. I held him back as a means of resisting the push of falling over. "Your mother is at peace. As is mine. That was the day Wisteria died, please, just call me Ivy."

His shattered heart was thudding. "I'll miss her. Never a dull moment with Wisteria. She was as wild and lively as the violet she was named after."

I pulled back to see his face flush with loss. "You left us years ago to become an underhill. I'm not the ten-year-old child you knew." It was because of his absence that his mother offered her empty home to Moriah, Keenan, Cobar and short months later, Rory.

"Oh, I know that. I have a confession of sorts," His bushy brow rose. Releasing me, he set me on my feet and I watched his face twist with humor and guilt.

Captain Cultee arrived in the training field with his two favorite guards in tow, who stood examining the blades and armored plates displayed on the wall. Throngs of soldiers dragged their sleepy feet in two straight lines filing out of the fort and another from the inns. "It will have to wait." Conscious of his arm partially encircling me, we both tried to create distance between us, he shifted weight back to his molding table before we were spotted.

"Agreed," he whispered, moving his goggles back over his brown eyes. Wiggling my fingers as a farewell, I darted out the back, moving so fast the brisk wind hurt my cheeks and tip of my nose.

I looked up at the archer pacing on the first tier of the brick wall. The trail of men had ceased. "Excuse me, guard?" He dropped his chin down to me.

"Ey, miss."

"Are there seamstresses in the area willing to trade or barter? Or perhaps, old linens that are too torn to be reformed?"

"Coin is the preferred method of payment in these parts. If it is clothing you are seeking, the staff have a surplus of work gowns that would be of no cost to you." Coins. I'd never had a need for them, nor quite understood how items were delegated a price.

I pulled my cloak tighter across my forearms. "What about leather pants and tunics?"

He paused for a long moment. He stiffened back to his rigid gaze on the horizon. When I was sure he wasn't going to give an answer, I began to retract my steps. "The new recruits are fitted upon arrival. There are slender farmhands among them that would be about your statue. Search outside the laundering tubs. East wing. Ground floor."

He continued his patrol, ignoring my wide smile and words of gratitude that dispersed in a hazy cloud. The two guards uncrossed their spears for me, giving one another a cross look, they hadn't remembered seeing me exit the compound early on. Inside, I retraced my steps from two days prior. When I passed the informal dining room, I was rather surprised only to find one man drunk and asleep on the bench.

The work chambers of the fort were relatively quiet for the time of day, and of course, the authorities of Fort Fell were in the training field with about a hundred men forming lines of defense. The barking voices of Cultee and Drift sounded over the clashing of helmets on shield walls.

The stairwell upwards platformed into the hallway where the captain's office was, were it not for the three scribes moving between the parchment room and the tactic table, I may have followed my curiosity and ventured into all of the private chambers collecting all the books and information that tickled my fancy. When I came to yet another stairwell, I took the passage downwards following the plumbing pipes which, coming from the captain's privy, were warmed. The sporadic lightbulbs hanging on the weak copper wires provided just enough visualization for me not to stumble on a missed step. I knew I was getting close when the sound of rhythmically splashing water and echoing voices carried.

The washtub was warm and sudsy, the three women and two men around the parameters of the pool had perfected their motions and handed each article of clothes down the line with expertise. I eyed the hanging red guard tunics and a pile of folded black pants. "May I?" I asked the women clipping damp garments to a line.

"Anything ought to be warmer than that." Judgment hardened her tone. "If you can't find a suitable shirt, help yourself to the scraps." She pointed to an empty rum barrel full of cotton and wool, the shapes and sizes too odd or frayed to be of much use. "We use them to wrap our torches and start our fires until spring." My mind rapidly began to find the innumerous things I could do with the torn shreds of cloth.

"How many scraps may I take?"

She gave a disgruntled sound as I continued to disturb her work. "I don't care. Get your trousers and be on." I disappeared behind the hanging rack to undress and don the tiniest waisted pants I could find. They fit decently; it was a glorious sensation. None of the red tunics were made for a woman with breasts, which was fine, red never looked flattering on me. The green ones on the end, however, were only two sizes too big and if I left the top button undone, it allowed more breathability for my chest. I took three.

With my brothel dress and dagger crammed into my satchel, I was left to scoop up the scraps with my arms. The load I carried was so immense that I barely saw over the top. The scribes helped me in finding my way down the steps. I gave a weak smile and assured them I could find my way back to the sleep quarters.

That was where I spent the entirety of the next three days. Raina sent some of the younger kitchen aids to check on me and to bring me warm water, oatmeal and fruits. Lorelei stayed late one evening helping me cut the fabric into square sections with the bread knife she borrowed. "These will be made into tea bags," I explained, flexing my stiff and achy fingers. "They will keep better individually than a jar and already have the dosing set."

Lorelei grinned and held up the long reel of cotton I had cut into strips. "And this?" She danced around the room spinning it as any girl would have a ribbon to dance with on the first of spring.

"To wrap weeping wounds and hold bones in place." She stopped dancing and winced.

"Gruesome," she whispered.

"Very much so." She lingered and took her time in rolling up the wheel of cotton. "Do you want to talk about what's on your mind?" I hushed, taking the material from her. She shook her head. "No? That's fine. I'll see you back to the kitchen. There is a knife in need of returning."

"You have one." She pointed to the sliver of metal resting beside me. That dagger has gutted its fair share of wraiths and severed limbs of many more.

"I do. It's for uprooting moss, slicing bark and removing spores from infant fungi. Nothing more," I gave a half truth.

She stood and I followed. The kitchen's lighting was harsh on my eyes after spending time in the dim lighting of my temporary room. "Do you expect anyone here to believe that?"

"Yes. I do." The staff greeted us as they spotted us from the corners of their eyes. Raina was pulling a roasted duck, no, *two* roasted ducks out of the oven and handing the oversized platters to Drift who looked even more ridiculous than usual due to the orange floral mitts he wore. The staff dodged the sizzling platter and parted for the goofily grinning guard to exit the kitchen.

"You survived two years in the *Wastelands*. You can't tell me you've never fought the restless," Lorelei persisted as I pulled her from the course of Drift's giant boots.

"I know how to hide from sight and senses. Nothing more." Drift stopped at the frame of the door. Knowing he was invested in our chatter I said, "I hid among the twigs and flourishing leaves until the fires came and I had to resort to other means. Those massive fires that swallowed up the living and undead alike. I wonder whose brilliant idea that was?"

Lorelei looked up at him, while I openly grimaced at the dead carcass of two birds splayed out next to me. "If you are trying to cast the blame on me, you should know that I wasn't a guard at the time the Wastelands came about. Maybe if you stopped avoiding me, you'd have your answers. Gimly has been looking for you. Apparently, since he can't lift his sword, he's been ordered to read you Numaal's history and bylaws and all the shit that puts me to sleep. I'm not one for rules and regulations."

"Fantastic," I said dryly. "Enjoy your dead birds." I dipped under the tray into the hallway where I noticed there was extra liveliness in the foyer. Barrels of ale were rolled in and the men erupted.

"A gift from our Faceless Prince, son of King Resig Torval!" Cultee stood on the table with a frothy mug raised. He drew all the attention within ear shot to himself. "May the departed Gods bless the king with health and our prince with wisdom. May our battle cries of freedom be heard and our swords feared. May Oyokos greet us with an embrace, an ale and a woman should we die fighting for our country. May Maruc know we red bloods are not a mistake, but perfect, for it is we who see death and understand what it means to fully live." Drift came up behind me. The toast ended and the men all downed their beer in a swift swig.

Cultee stumbled upon me as he watched Drift usher in the main course. He raised his mug to me. Unsure of what to do with the unearned respect from a man I had distaste for, I tucked my hair behind my ear and lowered my eyes.

"Will you be joining us?" Drift called ahead of me.

"Absolutely not. I find your food and company *unpalatable*," I stated.

"Really?" He chew his full lip, tasting himself. "I am certain I am everybody's flavor. Stay a while and I'm sure you'll crave my company too. It's inevitable."

Hack. I made an audible gagging sound. "Since you are fond of unspoken words, this is for you." I raised my middle finger at him and the nearest table snorted. I'm fairly certain beverage shot out of one of their noses.

Drift laughed and collected a mug that looked petite in his hand. Gods did he grate my nerves. I found my way back to my cot after a cold shower. The fiddles and banjos blared late into the morning, I grinned into the sleepless night.

Tomorrow would be a great day.

Chapter Five

Today was the day I'd ride solo in the saddle.

Rosie had become familiar with my bribery. Once the stall gate opened, she walked forwards and shoved her nuzzle into my empty satchel. I giggled nervously and placed the bit piece in her mouth and fastened the reins under her strong neck. She willingly strode alongside me after I fed her the other half of my breakfast. The knot I tied on the rail was sloppy, making me grateful Rosie didn't fight me or try to roam off when I tossed the blanket and saddle over her back. I was breathless from lifting it over my head and was astonished my arms didn't crumple. I shortened Drift's foot straps significantly and stepped back to examine my work.

To the untrained eye Rosie looked ready to ride out. Being an untrained eye, I clutched my two empty potato sacks and led the mare out the stable gates.

I was ready to greet winter in my black pants and layers of two tunics under the cloak. My hair was braided and my boot straps secured. Rosie and I walked around the large barn to where Fort Fell was blind to our shenanigans.

The drab paddy clapper sat alert next to his cart, as if he had been anticipating my arrival. I pressed on. He jumped to his feet and grabbed the slack reins trying to reverse our progress.

Hell. No.

I dug my heels into the dirt and clicked my tongue for my mount to stop. "I'll only be gone a day and I can fend for myself," I hissed, holding up my sacks to be filled with whatever shrubbery I scrounge up. "I'm carrying out my assigned task, which is to help people. Do you think Cultee would be fond of you blockading me?" He straightened his spine, his humble appearance shattered at his display of assurance. With his hands now on his hips, it was clear that his figure wasn't emaciated nor his spine curved from his craft which demanded him to stoop into vents, pits and pyres. He was slightly taller than average I guessed and solid.

"I know what I'm doing." I prayed that I sounded confident. He cocked his head to the side and pointed to the dangling belts underneath Rosie I had in fact forgotten. I crouched down and firmly set the saddle in place. He inspected the footholds and flipped them around. He pointed at my mistakes in mockery, which in fairness were rather grievous. "Sooner or later, I would have figured it out." I led on. He moved in front of us.

I pivoted to the right, he followed. To the left, the same thing. My lips pursed in a flair of annoyance. I rubbed the crease in my brow and decided just to go for it. Make my break away.

Placing my right leg into the stirrup I swung my left over and shimmed my hips in the saddle. The coalminer seethed, ripping his hood down for our eyes to duel. They lit up like golden ambers. I challenged him, "You're not going to stop me."

He grabbed the horn on the saddle and pulled himself upright on top of Rosie. In the confusion, I didn't sense him taking the reins from my hand. His torso twisted to look back at me while he grabbed my right hand and wrapped it around his stomach, which was dense muscle. He gestured for my left to hold him as well. I did. "I need to find a creek or still water source. Probably southwest away from all the soot polluting the water system." His feet tapped mine out of the stirrups. He pointed to his lips. I clicked my tongue at the same time he reared her forward. "Come on, Rosie."

It was as if we were running away from the rising sun and into the blanket of darkness that was the outskirts of the Wastelands. The sun rose behind us but the heat wasn't on my shoulders or back, it was within my arms. Perhaps it was my mind imagining that coalminers had a natural warmth to them. I knew better, it was mostly because I'd never held a man in such a way before. I had never been the one pulling myself tight to a man's spine so we moved as one in the saddle.

Also, my pride felt squashed, damn well knowing I would have gotten lost a quarter hour into the trip. The heat feigned me—it was the blush of embarrassment, that's what it was.

He slowed our pace just after the full circle of sun was hanging in the sky, dispersing the grey clouds and melting the frost. "Do you have a name?" I asked dumbly. Of course, he had a name. I should have just shut up and let the urge to know things pass. But I didn't. I never could. One of my many traits that kept my father nervous and on his toes.

I placed my forehead between his shoulder blades and inhaled the scent of cedar and pine. Surprisingly, I felt him nod affirmingly. He tapped my right knee and pointed to the nearby pond and the slight trickle of water flowing into it from a creek. Without warning he dropped off the mount and led Rosie and I to the edge of an infant woods. It was not a dense forest by any means, but it wasn't dead yet either. Greenery was spared.

Once on the ground, I took off my cape and boots. Tiptoeing around as delicately as I could, cautious of every plant beneath my bare feet. Using a scrap of fabric, I tied my dagger to the meat of my upper thigh. He laid against the base of a skinny sapling and disappeared behind his hood. The crossing of his arms and ankles—a dismissive gesture. He brooded bitterly, so I let him.

I walked my way up stream to where the fresher moving waters oxygenated the root systems. I liberally grabbed fistfuls of dandelion, yarrow and feverfew. Luckily, I was fortunate enough to stumble across a bush of tarberries which I carefully isolated in a pocket. The first tweed sack I had filled within the hour. Up a little way more existed a water vein that veered off from the mainstream. It was warm. My heart fluttered with excitement.

I hadn't been in a hot spring since Anna's escapades drew us both out to the far side of Ferngrove. My skin ached in missing her touch and easy company, nothing akin to the cold shoulder of a mute. With a hundred yards separating me and my chaperone, I hastily stripped my layers and peeled my pants off. Steam blurred my vision, so I opted to shut my eyes. It was glorious. Not Fort Fell or Horn's End could manage heated waters, it was the first time in two years I felt my body relax.

The longer I stayed, the less I wanted to leave. Without much effort, I convinced myself to remain in the bubbling pool. I floated atop the slow currents and pulled my hair out of its tight braid. Freedom was all I could feel, all I wanted to feel, and leaving my private place of serenity to go back to the fort broke my spirit.

The fort was one step closer to Landsfell, I reminded myself daring to open my eyes.

They shot open, I choked on the water. His yellow hued eyes stared at me, more in frustration than fascination.

There was little sense to cover myself at this point and screaming indecencies at a man who wouldn't give me an answer seemed inappropriate. I settled for a softer approach to balance his sharpness, "Is there danger, must I leave now?"

He rubbed his brow as if trying to smooth out his sentiments. Eventually, he shook his head no and plopped to the ground facing away from me. "Thank you," I whispered to his back. I lounged in the pool until I pruned.

Using my cloak as a towel I dried myself off in the peak sun, I let the sun and air kiss all the intimate parts of me holding on to the last of this feeling. I tapped the coalminer's shoulder when I was decent, offering him a polite smile from behind my heavy curtain of damp hair. He rose and followed me close, yet not uncomfortably so, to the stagnant waters of the pond. Rosie stood across the water grazing merrily, her tail flicking away gnats and flies. She seemed at peace. I took the dagger off my leg and held the blade in my teeth to free up my arms. Slowly, I lowered my belly to the water's edge and peered at the growth of vegetation in the shallow rocky pool. My travel partner joined me on his belly, propping his chin up with the heel of his hand. His short shaggy hair shone a blond and white and with streaks of black ash as to be expected.

He watched me pull a miniscule vial from my breast pocket and uncork it. He gestured at its size. "Igmu snail secretions are potent. I don't need much," I educated softly. I took the fine edge of the blade and scraped it across the limestone behind the track of the bright green shelled snail. I found another one and repeated the motion. On the tip of the dagger rested a thick, near translucent droplet, enough to melt the flesh off a body in an hour. I scraped it into the vial and forcefully pressed it shut. He examined it with curious eyes. I scrubbed the knife well and moved on to collecting the rest of the ingredients needed for the women and anything of value I could carry in my bags. "Can you write?" I finally blurted out as he tied the bags closed and secured them to the hind quarters of Rosie. He left my side to fetch a stick and in the dirt he wrote. *Can you read?*

"Obviously or I wouldn't have asked," I said as his right cheek rose into a smirk of approval.

Nick, he spelt and kicked the dust and dirt over his evidence. For some dumb reason I had a flutter of success and happiness befall me, as if knowing his name gave me a foothold in this new place.

"How about Nikki?" I asked. Nick's regret was immediate. If his vocal cords functioned, I'm sure he would be spewing very vibrant language at me. He morphed back into his short, sharp tempered self and impatiently waited for me to seat myself behind him. "I have a lot of questions," I admitted, clumsily positioning myself behind him. I grabbed the sleeves of Nick's tunic to prevent me from slipping. "Can we stay and write in secret before going back?" He shook his head. "Well, can I ask you yes or no questions?" Again, the answer was no. "Fine, Nikki, have it your way."

He reared the horse, jostling me in the process. When the encampment came into view, I stiffened. Outside the stables stood a male and female barn hands looking cross. Her voice was shrill as we approached, "You had me believing we've a thief among us! Who'd be foolish enough to steal from Cultee's prime horses?" Nick dismounted onto his feet and dodged the barrage of discipline. "The new girl, perhaps aloof enough. But, the mute as an accomplice?" Nick didn't escape fast enough before she turned on him. "Best you hurry, dining hall has already had one cold meal today." Under the evening sky his shadow scurried into Fort Fell.

"Will he be reprimanded?" I asked unsure if I wanted to hear the answers.

"You've thought about your consequences too late in the day I'm afraid. Get down and let me see what in your pouches had you deciding such idiotic things!" I obeyed. While she raided my sacks, my stomach went turbulent thinking of Nick. "Weeds. Just a bunch of weeds. Hopefully, you can make something useful from them aside from a salad." I opened my mouth to reply. She intruded, "Get gone." I complied. I dragged the two large sacks to the pantry by the smithy and seeing the training field was empty, I hastily chased after Nick.

The kitchen was bustling and thankfully the ovens and stovetops had been lit. I searched for Nick. "Excuse me, Raina? Where is the paddy clapper?" Flour powdered her nose and collar.

"Afraid he just left. Been summoned to warm the tavern and pastry shoppe," she announced. "Are you alright, Ivy?" Raina's worried eyes found mine.

My mind was swimming, drowning in memories of my encounters with the fort's master. There were two interactions with him and neither were pleasant or kind. And for a mute who couldn't speak and defend himself? I shuddered. "Captain Cultee doesn't resort to any punishment for the residents of Fort Fell, does he?"

Raina put down her dough. Her tone dropped an octave. "Depends on the severity of the incident. Care to give me an example?"

"I took a horse from the stable this morning, with good intentions—I got supplies for the infirmary—the paddy clapper tried to stop me from leaving. And since he couldn't, he came with me." A sharp pain broke my chain of thought, I had bitten my lip too hard. "I don't want anything bad to happen to him."

There was a pause. She pondered a reply. "Cultee has a temper, but the mute has friendships that will offer protection and it doesn't appear well to the residents among these parts for the captain to harm a scrawny mute who the fort relies on, does it? Besides, we tolerated lukewarm lentils and salted rinds just fine. The people here were too hungover to care and most of us here have gotten on well enough long before he arrived two years ago. No harm, no foul I say," Raina pinched the high of my cheek and placed a full bowl of rice into my hands.

The effort it took to reciprocate a smile was immense, so I let my face fall.

"Lay low. Head down, work done. All storms pass, even the ones we create in our minds that never come to."

"You're probably right," I succumbed, pushing aside the uneasiness in my gut.

Waving a spoon, she pointed to the rice. "Eat. You will not waste away in my kitchen." When I came back for seconds, she applauded me.

The storm that blew and billowed in my head, didn't cease.

Grabbing my pipe and a pinch of hemp, I went to the common room and lit my smoke with the dim fire pit. The scent of a recreational high drafted down the hall and into the common room walked two more women who lay beside me beckoning a puff.

"This fragrance clung to my grandfather's clothes. He would mix tobacco in sometimes to fool mother that he wasn't high. No one bought into it," the blonde laxed onto her elbows. There was no time to inquire about her name or history, for she slumbered off. The girl next to her laughed and asked to share in the smoke circle. I obliged. Her name was Ronan from the Cliffs of Sound, an underhill, who was celebrating her twenty-ninth birthday this month, the eighth away from her family. She reckoned they were still out there in the extensive cave system they had.

"A very beautiful hope to have," I confessed, my head nodding off. I didn't tell her of the swarms of wraiths that claimed the cliffs, the seaside, the forest or the flat fields. Who was I to ruin the peaceful look on her face and the lively dreams that floated in her head? *Sleep.* The voice insisted.

I can't. I replied dizzily.

Why is that, Wisteria? They soothed.

The dreams.

They won't come tonight. I'll stand guard if you let me.

Curling up next to the warmth, I loosened the pipe from my grip. *You can't promise me that.*

I can promise that I won't be getting sleep if your guilt doesn't quiet down. Nick is safe.

Whatever trance the plant put me in, my awake mind broke free. Talking to myself was a new level of crazy, even for me.

Needless to say, the dreams never came because sleep never came.

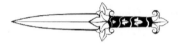

'Head down, work done.' That would be my mantra. I decided to follow the routine of the other women who served in the fort and lived locally, which meant an early meal together. I even wore the blasted beige gown. Drift was one foot out the door when he spotted me in the common meal hall. Swearing, I shielded my face from his clean shaven one, turning to my berries and tapioca.

"Morning ladies," he coyly addressed the entire table. "Ravishing as always." I shoveled food into the hole in my face to avoid replying to him. Ronan and the rest were all ogling his smile which he bestowed upon them. Just how many people did he have under his spell? It's no wonder that he believed himself to be everybody's flavor, the pheromones in the room were suffocating. My appetite vanished when he said my name. "Ivy," he directed. "Gimly is planning to collect you for a midday meal. I recommend bringing a pillow as a means of preparing yourself for his tedious saga of the Eternals and the formation of our continent." A funny feeling of sarcasm tickled up my left arm. I closed my fingertips over my palm.

"*His* tedious saga? I sense you aren't in agreement. That doesn't surprise me," I relayed, still refusing to look up from my food.

His presence hovered. The ladies looked from him to me and back again. The bench shook. I peeked over to find him straddling the log on stilts making himself comfy next to me. "I'll wait for you to finish up breakfast and accompany you to the stockroom. Captain informed the lot of us that you managed to 'borrow' a horse, *my* horse to be exact, from the stables yesterday. If the coalminer wasn't there who knows what ditch you'd find yourself in by now."

I held my breath to steady my emotions. "I'll consider myself lucky," I tried politely dismissing him. He stuck around like sap tangled in your hair after having washed it and combed it through. I felt his energy, it was persistently trying to call my attention but it succeeded only in overwhelming me. It was Captain Cultee who should consider himself lucky his town and soldiers have proper aid.

He lingered while I finished my food. Drift's energy wasn't going anywhere so I entertained it. "You should also consider yourself fortunate."

"Do enlighten me," he cooed, leaning into my personal bubble. Intrigue panged through me. The women at the table were practically drooling hearing his seductively low tone, but his eyes remained fixed on me.

I narrowed my green eyes and pouted my lips. I curled my finger towards Drift in a hither motion. He fulfilled my request and leaned his towering body closer to me, the static feeling up my arm pulsed as I pushed his hair aside. In his ear, I whispered for him alone to hear, "Because I haven't poisoned you. Not yet anyways."

The pink tip of his tongue flicked across his sharp canine grin. There was dark mischievousness in the manner in which he brought his mouth to hover by the shell of my ear. "I have no issue dying at the hands of a clever and beautiful flower, but I must wonder. Have I committed a crime deserving of such a wicked fate?"

My heart sped up. "If you don't stop stalking me, I'll happily introduce you to Oyokos."

The dimple in his cheek appeared. "Is there harm in me befriending you?"

I glanced around the table at all of the others he had befriended and gave an uncharming snort. "I've no interest in the companionship of you or any man," I stated, setting aside my empty bowl. I was on my feet before he registered that I was taking leave and heading to the door. "When you're done befriending these lovely ladies, feel free to get your lazy ass up and see your word through. Or don't. I prefer the latter," I said over my shoulder, my hair cascading down my back. Internally, I hoped he stayed behind toying his way through the kitchen and cleaning staff. By the time cold air hit my skin, he was in stride with me.

His blue rimmed eye tracked me instead of the horizon. "Alright, what gives?" I asked him midway to our destination, the nearest body was a pen of pigs many yards away. Humor trailed down my fingertips all while he kept his lips pressed thin. "I don't find any of this amusing."

"In hindsight, I expect your statement to change."

I hiked my pillowy dress up and bunched it at my core to prevent it from dragging on the wet grass. "Hindsight? What earth shattering information do you have for me?"

He bit back a wide smile. Nick and Pine readied the smithy's fire, I gave each a wave. Pine dipped his head in my direction. Nick disappeared behind the kiln. I stopped our trek far enough away to maintain privacy and faced Drift, gesturing I was impatiently waiting for his explanation. "I'm confident you'll figure it out. But, telling you outright deprives me from admiring that delightful inquisitive look that causes you to sink your teeth into that luscious lower lip of yours." I felt myself fluster, hoping it was the anger not the flattery that spun me off course. "To obtain the answers you so desperately seek, you simply have to speak my name. Ready for your hint?"

"Fine, have it your way. Release a clue and be on your way." I'd say anything to remove him from my presence.

"Very well, *Wisteria Woodlander*." My chest constricted. Had he overheard Pine say my birth name or had he known this entire week? I grappled for coherent words but he had since left towards the training field, flagging down several guards from the street to hustle over. They punched each other as a greeting and raced to the weapon shed. I stared blankly at Drift trying to place his face and failing. Even after he and his men evaporated from my line of sight, I stood vacantly until Pine called.

"Woodlander?" His voice carried on the wind. He beckoned me twice before I could engage my body to move. "You feeling alright?" He asked quietly after I walked under our roofing.

"Yes, just feeling the effects of foregoing sleep. Nothing an afternoon coffee can't fix," I reassured Pine whose concern was evident behind his goggles. He watched me haul down the two heavy bags of foliage. I knelt on the floor to sort them.

"That haul is plenty to have kept Ferngrove busy for days, are you planning on dehydrating and bottling all this by yourself?"

I glanced around us. "Do you know of another woodlander in a two hundred mile radius who's capable enough to portion off monthly tea or press the buds into oils?"

"I'm offended that I have not crossed your mind."

I shrugged and pointed to the hammer in his right hand. "Underhill and ironside, you are busy. Surely, the captain would be irritated if I prevented you from finishing your work just so you could help me hang calendula and feverfew upside down."

Pine paused. "I'm contracted to work until three in the afternoon. After that my schedule is free, I'll help you find canning jars and twine to hang the bulkier things from the rafts. There is a glass blower on the far end of Crocker. He is a hoarder, he won't mind if you stop by."

"Wonderful, because I can't reach that high." I pointed to the rafters. We both went to work, he with his shaping hammer and I with plucking sharp bristles from stems. I ran into the fort twice to withdraw a measuring spoon and spices from the kitchen and another time to bring out the cuts of square cloth Lorelei and I had made.

Midday, Gimly wandered in. His freshly oiled black boots left footprints over the fabric I laid out. "If you want me to use clean supplies to tend to your wound, I suggest removing your foot from my efforts."

He hummed. "Well, you can't remove the stitches from down there. Up, Ivy." He clicked his tongue at me as if I was a mutt or mount. I hurriedly placed rocks on the piles of leaves and flowers that were at risk of blowing astray in my absence, the finer, delicate blossoms I set back on the shelves and closed the doors.

I stood up and dusted the dirt and splinters from the hem of my dress. Taking only what I would need to dress his shoulder, I tucked strands of my hair back into a sloppy braid and settled myself with my hands interlaced at my navel. "I prefer the outfit you arrived in. This *homely* look doesn't suit your curves."

I hated to admit it, but I agreed. My Horn's End brothel attire, however lacking, was more practical. "I am ready."

We walked behind a cart hauling hay, stacked so high that with each breeze I held my breath when the tower waivered. In the captain's office a fire had been lit, the consolidated coal and nearby cart evidenced that Nick had recently been there. Gimly pulled a book off the credenza, one with blue bindings and sizably thick in length. "Are you familiar with The Eleven?"

"I am."

"What have you been told?"

I cleared my throat. "The Eternals created countless worlds before our own. The Gods and Goddesses collectively painted everything into existence from a thought which sparked light, clay and matter from darkness. Nine have since left to go back into Ether to continue dispersing life elsewhere and leave us to our own means. Two remain, Maruc and Athromancia. A third of their trio. Orion, the Temperance, left us, putting the White Tower's reign unbalanced between the final two powers."

He stripped his shirt and seated himself in the red velvet recliner, his feet on the oak table not showing any amount of respect for his captain's possessions. He skimmed through the pages of the book while I examined my work on his healing deltoid. "Maruc and Athromancia were left on the throne as a duo four hundred years ago. When a new trilogy is chosen, the world will have been remade. That divine day will mark the end of the Eternals and beginning of a creation ruling themselves with autonomy. Do you know how the Great Divide came to be?" After posing his question he gifted me a small set of pliers and a razor to initiate the removal of the threads. I didn't offer to premedicate him.

Not knowing about the divide, I shook my head.

"The Great Divide was the splitting of the two nations of Kinlyra over three thousand years ago by the sudden formation of the Thalren Mountains. The wise, long lasting folks of Ilanthia and the lively, hardworking humans of Numaal are physically divided by the mountain peaks that pierce the sky. The peaks cast mirages that lead wanderers astray and reveal demons who are restless beneath the crust of earth and the skies above. The Thalren range is a mostly impenetrable barrier for both silver and red blood wanting to cross on foot. The Gods forbade magic into our lands which brought on disease and strife.

"What they loathed most was the blending of our bloods. Some time ago, near Kathra and the plains of the wild cashmere horses were many who had the best of both worlds, a life of simple living and time to enjoy it, living over a hundred years or more in the newer generations. The Ilanthians found out and were disgusted about diluting their centuries long lifespan." Anna and Keenan spoke of an entirely different world, of blended bloods and varying lifespans. "King Resig first started to show signs of illness twenty years ago and fought to keep blended bloods *on* our land to show unity and kindly request their aid for his illness. The Emperor recalled every being with a trace of silver blood back to his White Tower in Akelis or the mountain cities scattered within the Thalren. Those who refused being displaced were instructed to stay and infiltrate, to dissemble Resig's family line. For that reason, the prince remains nameless and faceless in hopes to obtain methods on healing his father and restoring Numaal without being struck down by assassins."

"What ailments does Resig suffer from?"

"Suppose it was his liver once. Now, he fights age."

"Where did the wraiths come from?" I asked.

"Ah," he shook his head. "How else would one draw a king's attention away from enemy lines? Do wraiths seem a normal occurrence to you or are they rather *magical*?"

I was half way done pulling the stich out when I stopped to answer. "Neither, they are *unnatural*."

He countered, "You are familiar with nature. Could nature, as you know it, create such a thing or does the epidemic of a monstrous death derive from a source greater than a crafter and mortal, an Eternal perhaps?" My face fell. I knew the answer to that.

"What are King Resig and his son planning to do to service us in our efforts to rid them? We may not be a city of millions, but collectively we crafters are thousands and are the backbone of Numaal. We deserve peace. If he doesn't fight for us now against the nightwalkers, we will all perish and he will have no country left to fight for."

Gimly examined his closed wound. "Strategically speaking, would you rather use your forces to pin down the tail or cut the head off the snake?"

I wasn't prepared to answer that question, killing an Eternal had never crossed my mind. "Is that even possible?" I muttered, keeping my disbelieving gaze on his shoulder..

"The prince says it is. The details are reserved by the priestesses of Sanctum and Queen Ishma Torval in Kathra. The guards of the provinces and the knights of the capital are in demand, a resource that needs to be used wisely."

Sickness stirred in the low of my gut. "There has to be consequences for *ending* the life... of an Eternal. Of a creator."

"Who would reprimand us, Ivy? Nine have already exited this realm and the rules of the Eternals forbade them from reentering a world once they decided to depart it. They will be moving on shortly to create yet another entire world, a new sun, and sky full of stars for their next creations." That was true, Anna had mentioned something along those lines during one of our nightly stargazing adventures. "We are insignificant to them. If they won't assist and protect their own creations -us- during such an uneasy time, what purpose do they truly serve? Two Eternals remain and they are already preparing for their final departure from Kinlyra. Consider it a favor. A mercy."

"You're killing Athromancia too?"

His body jerked with laughter. "Not me, no. I anticipate someone else to take on that responsibility. I'm not in the high society circle, not yet." I opened the jar of coconut oil and brushed it on the two ridges of skin that were mending together nicely. The muscle beneath was no longer visible. Words failed me. He watched my work closely. "Does it sadden you to kill a God or does a God allowing thousands, soon to be millions, be swallowed by soulless spawn hurt your heart more?"

"Both, if I am honest with myself." I placed a swatch of cotton over the scar and wrapped it gently. "Your body will allow for some lifting now, nothing overhead, to be safe."

Gimly maneuvered back into his shirt and tested his range of motion. "By a stroke of dumb luck, your life may be spared from this madness because Cultee is a devotee of divine timing and happenstance. He's a love for the God Taite, because he found balance. He frequently recites prayers to the Eleven." He handed me the blue leathered book and opened it to the back centerfold. The gasp that escaped was authentic. I hadn't seen such a beautifully detailed painting *ever*, for my standards for art were limited to sketches with pollen and red rock mud. The Eleven were brightly depicted with all shades of skin tones and physical features only a visionary could think up. They adorned the parameters of the page and in the center lay a faded map of our continent. "We are here." Gimly pointed to an unlabeled portion of the map on the bottom right, a section so irrelevant to the maker that it failed to be named. He trailed his finger several centimeters northwest. "Landsfell," he read. Straight northeast was a larger spot. "Sanctum. The eastern city of priestesses and holy men, known for her spindles of might that jut into the sky and at night reflect the stars. Raj in the north, surrounded by dunes and oases. " Under the feet of Oyokos was a mountain range separating the landmass into two that ran from the northernmost border to the southern.

"The Great Divide?" I asked.

"Also, referred to as the Thalren Mountains, known for her perilous peaks of ice, storms and mirages of afterlife. Kathra lies here," he nudged my finger to the largest splat of ink on the page which lay between Thalren and the center of our country. "Kathra is the pearl of Numaal hosting private libraries, the royal palace, fine feats of electricity and the most fortified wall this world has ever known." Wicked curiosity flickered across his face. "I reckon even wraiths couldn't penetrate it if they came at it one hundred thousand strong and certainly no Ilanthian army with their fancy footwork could tear it down."

I pursed my lips into a thin line. Who decided who was worth saving and who got to be sheltered behind such tremendous walls? "How long did the walls take to construct?"

"Countless human lifetimes. I'm sure countless bones and bodies have been cemented in the barrier," he stood behind me. His breathing ruffled the paper outstretched in my hands. No longer could I inspect the map nor be dazzled by the illustrations of the Eleven, for my body protested Gimly's being in close proximity.

I pretended to be overcome by the chills and pardoned myself to stand near the fireplace. "Stunning picture, is it not?"

"Indeed, it is. Thank you for sharing." I ran my thumb over the feminine beauty of Morial and the astute gaze of Orion. There was an enchanting draw to the violet hued wings of Oyokos, a foreign exquisiteness in their strangeness. Dradion and Drommal, the twin God and Goddess who carved the earth like a pile of clay were pictured setting the elements loose over their landscape and conjoined by their hands which poured lava and rivers. Taite, a risk taker and fortune finder, gambled lives joyously and held his scale of fates in one hand and a bottle of wine in the other. Athromancia with her hair as bright as untamed flames pressed one hand to her heart and the other to the spot between her eyebrows. Misotaka, the Goddess of foresight was submersed in florescent colors that shimmered. "Who's the artist?"

"Aditi himself," he stated, prowling across the span of the office. "The Resig gave it to Cultee's father years before we were born. Well, that is the fanciful story that has been told to me." My fingertips tingled. If it was actually painted by the God of arts and music, I fear my clumsy touch would soil such a pristine parchment. "Why are there no dots and letters around Ilanthia?" I asked. "If this was made by Aditi surely he would know his own land."

Gimly retrieved the book and folded the paper with reverence. "We all have our theories on why the west remains barren of labels."

I couldn't resist. "What do you think?"

"I believe the ink vanished when it left the land of the Gods. Afterall, would you want your enemies armed with the knowledge of your land's resources and primary cities?" I shook my head and allowed my eyes to drift towards the shimmering fire. Bits of white ash blew out the chimney and twirled around the office.

"It's been an informative afternoon." I stated, tying up the strings of my satchel. "I'm not sure what to make of it all."

He demanded my gaze to hold his while he closed the distance between us. My skin crawled. His hand reached towards my waist and before I knew it–I spun out of his grasp with the quick shuffle Anna taught me in combat lessons. "Those are some moves. You'd make a fine dancer."

I softly puckered my lips and raised my brows. Diminishing my inner power, I spoke confused. "What?" He pointed to my feet. "I survived with only my plant knowledge and reflexes to rely on and I'm not fond of unwelcomed touches. Hasn't your captain spoken to you on such matters?"

Dismissing my latter statement, he carried on, "Those are quick reflexes. What else had survival forced you to do? You've arrived as a whore."

I pulled into myself and hid my small, but strong frame beneath the hanging fabric. My hands itching for my faithful sword. They found no hilt on my hip. "I figured out how to shoot a bow and arrow, not well, mind you. I took it off Conrad, our herder who supplied us with yogurts, cheeses and warm milk for oats. He was dead, nearly all his limbs were bitten off, I didn't think he would mind." I welcomed the memory of him and the glossy eyes of innocence it summoned for not all of my story was a lie, I watched many die before a sac was placed over my head and I was beaten unconscious. "I hid in the trees. Did you know wraiths seldom look up?"

"This world has been unkind to you, but blessed you with the fortunate incidence of finding me. I know some powerful people, it's in your best interest to please me and perhaps I'll take you into the luxurious lap of Landsfell." He tapered off his aggression, yet still approached me. My childhood was nothing shy of wonderful and joyful, not one unkind memory until the dungeons of the duke. And it wasn't a surprise that I stumbled into Gimly, for I tracked him and actively sought him out, the prick he was.

My neck heated and I opened my mouth to quietly suck in cool air. Nothing brash, I willed myself while tracing a jagged childhood scar along my forearm.

At the door there was a scraping and fumbled knocking. The guard crossed his brows and strode across the room in several short steps to open the double doors. Nick tumbled in and held a wrench in his bleeding hand with the other pointed to the fractured wheel of his cart. Gleefully, I took Nick by the wrist, mindful of the wrench in his grip. "Speaking of fortunate incidences, how timely is the hour in which the coalminer arrives. I have all the supplies with me to dress his hands and you, Gimly, are now able to make use of your left arm to fix his cart."

The guard's ears turned a raging shade of purple as I held out Nick's wrench to him. He wordlessly swiped it from my grasp, shoving me aside as he left the room to inspect the wheel. I ushered Nick in who refused to be seated in the captain's velvet chair, I joined him on the floor. As I cleaned, slathered and wrapped his palms, and several of his fingers, he made no eye contact nor any effort to connect with me. "You should really wear gloves." This earned me a mirthful headshake. This was the only solo time I would likely get with Nick, I had no idea how to vocalize an apology when he was the one who chose to ride with me.

Instead, my eyes combed over him ensuring there was no sign of a cane strike or bruise of a fist. He held no welts, limp or nursing of a joint. I saved my breath, he wouldn't reply in any manner, to my questioning of his well being.

I just lightly held his hand in the silent moments given to us while the guard tinkered with the cart. Nick didn't retract.

"Heat rat, your paddy wagon is mobile. It needs proper welding if it's to last." Gimly wiped soot and grime on his tunic, unaware he smeared black across the bridge of his crooked nose. His grin flashed his fowl teeth. "Girl, I'm off to the showers, however, the invitation to join me is always extended. If you're smart you'll seek me out."

"My refusal stands as does your captain's warning." I buried a blanch.

Gimly slid the book onto the top shelf where it was lost among the other protruding spines. Eighth from the right, I mentally tagged its location. I rose from the crouched position on the floor. "I'll see myself out," I had barely choked out the words before I was halfway down the hall.

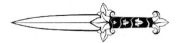

I ate my lunch late and alone.

I doubt anyone could squeeze in with me because I hid myself under an old cubie for perishables. Something about the tight, small space felt safe. Or something about the outer world felt threatening and unsure. Either way, I relished my solitude.

By the time I made it outside, Pine had already started hanging the weeds and beheading the buds. "You're a natural," I called from the pergola loud enough for him to hear me over the roar of Cultee disciplining the newer signups merely a few yards away. "Elousie would have scolded you for breaking the roots, but I shall defend your efforts as satisfactory. Who'd have thought the hands used for smashing iron were also able to scrap pollen off hundreds of frail petals without severing their shape?" He smiled and hopped down from the wooden stool.

"I found twine to cinch up the seep bags," he tossed casually. "Mr. Crest said we could stop by his glass shop any day to see if anything there suits your taste." He jumped back up on the step and hung another inverted bundle of dandelion stems and leaves.

Half of Raina's request would be fulfilled before week's end. "Pine, you didn't have to go through all this trouble."

"I know I didn't." He tied the knot off on the beam. "I wanted to test myself. Sure enough, the craft came rushing back to my hands and Alister's voice echoed in my ear telling me not to bruise anything. It feels good. Connecting with flora again," he admitted, the longing in his statement held a heavy tone of sadness that deafened even the ringing of steel beyond us.

He had accomplished what would have taken me a full day to conquer. There was a lightness to him as if he had been revived or perhaps memories and sentiments had been unlocked as he practiced his family's lineage. "Wonderful to hear because I need your aid tomorrow evening if you can be spared." His cheeks rose.

"I'll happily oblige."

Pine worked on separating the plants and bulking them together while I began to balance the mosslace, hops and stoneweed. We worked in unison for several hours. It wasn't until we lost our light and the sound of men fighting stopped did Cultee knock on the side panel. "I should have figured out you were born a woodlander, Pine. A man of many trades," he acknowledged. "Let's turn in. The farmers have witnessed the restless moving closer to the fort at night." That was all the motivation I needed. My hands were quick to seal and shut the stock doors. Pine closed the kiln which had been opened earlier for its radiating warmth. It groaned as the metal lock slid into place. Cold found me. I tucked my hands under my elbows. "Were you two acquaintances before the plague?" I looked up at the captain and forced my jaw to still.

"Yes," I said. "I knew his mother better than him. Pine left to pursue an underhill when I was nine or ten, he didn't visit much after that," I educated.

Pine scoffed and spoke factually, "You were eleven when I left. To marry my wife–I had to impress her father, who promptly put me to work digging inside the Cliffs of Sound for six consecutive seasons! My hands were a bloody mess when Plessa put the damn ring on my finger." He showed us the band snug around his ring finger. Even after her death, he wore it. The three of us started out into the moonlit night, the watchful guards lit the path ahead of our feet. "When Plessa and I were expecting our first child we rode out to Ferngrove to tell everyone the good news. We never made it." Pine fidgeted. "That was my first encounter with the wraiths. Ravenous rotting cadavers who had chased us back to the caves. The next month there were more, the gully became impassable and I am not the man to risk the life of my wife and unborn son."

"Elousie never held it against you. Her insightfulness always extended grace to those she loved. She knew shadows moved; she hid it well from me in my younger years. They all did." I was surprised how sour my voice sounded. It wasn't until Anna arrived with answers did my curiosity grow boundless, my sword eager and my feet antsy. A straggling group of guards in commoner clothes met us on the slope to Fort Fell, they moved close to stay within the glow of the lights.

Captain Cultee spoke next, "You were a sensible husband. I commend you." I don't know why, but his words surprised me. The praise sounded genuine, yet wasn't this the man who sent others to organize traps and to employ the duke's bidding? "Ivy, are you married with children of your own?"

"Definitely, no," I said. Pine laughed.

Even after Captain Cultee dismissed himself and the trainees scattered into the dining hall, he continued to laugh. "You laugh because you know I'd rather be dead than bound to a witless fool and trapped by duty."

"I laugh because I know you court women, not men."

My heart beat in my throat. "I won't deny my preference, if you tell me how you've come to know such *personal* information without seeing me in a decade. Unless, you've been filling my head with deception from the moment you realized I was from Ferngrove." Panicking, I combed over his facial features looking for malice or lies. Finding none still didn't settle my rising fear. It made it worse knowing there were people in the south province who knew things about me, maybe even about the llanthians we've befriended.

Nausea gripped my throat.

"It hurts me to see you gaze at me with such mistrust. You know I'd never bring harm to you, not after what you've done for my mother and our people, right?" There was authentic pain in his body posture as he humbly opened his hands to me. "After we finish tomorrow, come get a drink with me and I'll tell you whatever you want to know. It's not going to be a drawn-out story, if anything, it's fucking embarrassing on my behalf." He rubbed his neck which was red and splotchy. Across the room, the hallway was consumed by Drift's black cloaked presence.

"*How* can you possibly know*?*" I muttered, filled with both a threat and bemusement.

"Tomorrow, alright?" Pine insisted. He turned his feet to back out of the fort's hall, definitely trying to escape his awkwardness. "Do you still enjoy spiced rum?"

I repeated myself. Worry showed in my face. It was probably splotchy patches of red from the rising panic. He could not know. No one could know. "How can you possibly know? Were Misotaka's descendants among you?" He was slow, I blocked the hall that led to a sleeping wing. My tone came out more aggressive than I intended it to. He uncrossed his arms as a means of surrendering.

Behind him a darkness loomed. Pine was trapped between my pestering and Drift's impenetrable body of steel.

Drift rocked casually on his heels, he pursed his lips as he spoke, "Everything alright here?"

Pine's eyes pleaded with mine, he was intimidated into reserve. I moved my hand and foot off the side of the stone wall and looked to Drift whose eyes simmered like dying stars in the abyss of blackness. "Yes, we were just confirming our plans at the tavern tomorrow night. Pine was just telling me the first two rounds are on his coin. Isn't that right?"

"It is," Pine nodded. "We've much of our past to catch up, a conversation doesn't involve a third party prying." Pine managed to find his voice and even address Drift who straightened his shoulders, growing another five or six inches taller. "Kindly, let me pass." The guard side stepped, making a gap wide enough for Pine to pass through. A narrow space that intentionally made Pine uncomfortable as he squeezed by to avoid Drift's form. "See you in the morning, *Ivy*." I stuck my tongue out at him as he disappeared into the crowd settling to eat. The piercing in the center of my tongue and the bar in the tip clinked against my teeth.

Above me a hushed whisper spoke. "Unexpectedly, I'm insulted. Call me selfish, but I wanted to be the only one here who knows your given name, Wisteria. I thought we shared something special." I groaned and placed my hands on my hips, puffing out my chest to match whatever distinct presence he was trying to have.

"Apparently, this fort is nothing more than remnants of my past. Some I recollect, some I don't. Probably, for the better." I narrowed my eyes at his tense posture.

"No hard feelings in forgetting me, we will be better off after you remember how important I am in your life." He gave a forced grin. "I'm going to have a difficult time forgetting about that tiny glimmering gemstone in your mouth. I've never seen a bar horizontally piercing the tip of a tongue. Is there one in the middle too?" Something about him seemed off, almost as if he wanted to shed his skin but opted not to.

"I'm immune to your flirting," I disclosed. "Why are you here?"

He gestured to the passageway. "You were frightened. Or a better word would be 'apprehensive'. So, I came to offer assistance."

"Said who?" I stepped closer to him until the toes of our boots nearly touched. His scruffy jawline flexed, I noted hints of patchy white among the black hairs in his chin. "I'm not one of your damsels that need saving nor do I derive joy from being in your company. I deliberately isolated myself with Pine. And in case it failed to escape your notice, I'm not fond of you."

It was clear he wasn't listening. He pointed one of his index fingers at the center of my chest, "Something about that last conversation unnerved you."

How? I needed to shout. Just as I had asked of Pine who knew too much. Drift wouldn't give me answers either. "Good night," I said.

"That's it?" He countered.

"Shall I linger for you to drop a clue for this game you are imagining I'm engaged in with you? No? Very well, good night." Drift rubbed his face. "You look haggard."

He tried to keep his features tightened. "I look handsome."

"You're delusional."

"I'm delightful."

"Your personality is trying."

"My personality is charming; I am merely tired."

I took a long inhale. "Sleep is proven to help combat fatigue and deliriousness," I lectured. "Your inflated perception of self is a warning sign of mental instability. Do us both a favor and go to bed."

Drift hinged at his hips and made sure there was no method to evade him. He did appear exhausted, but there was a spark of vibrancy in the manner he said, "You've not rested well for years. I told you several nights ago, I would stand guard and shield you against your nightmares, yet, you once again ignored my sound advice." I swallowed. Everything about that moment felt like an enigma. The cool air from his mouth held a hint of clove and his damp hair that fell from the knot atop his head smelled of winter air and cooling oils. If it wasn't for his scent, I may have believed myself to have faded away. He further pulled me down to earth. "No, you are not crazy."

I sure felt crazy.

My hands pressed firmly against my chest at the low of my throat trying to pin down my heart which beat faster than a hummingbird in captivity. Drift readjusted the loose collar of his untucked shirt, this was the most disheveled I'd seen him. Not knowing what reply this warranted, I ran my tongue over my bottom lip. *Tell me.* I sounded firm, for I would not be found begging.

He was resolute when he shook his head. "Say my name."

I racked my brain and grieved silently when I arrived at the conclusion that I was practically a recluse growing up because my crafting commune had to keep the Ilanthians safe. I hardly stepped foot into this world.

I didn't know him.

My gaze fell from his wavy wet hair to his flexed forearm to his sculpted waist then to our feet on the floor. I shuffled mine and stared at the scuffed leather as they took me down the hall and collapsed onto the dingy cot in the dark corner of Fort Fell. I didn't bother to kick off my boots as I lay blankly staring at the low stone ceiling contemplating lighting a pipe of hemp to allow myself to relax enough to converse with myself or *Drift* this late in the night ... both sounded absolutely insane.

And as Drift said, I was not crazy.

Chapter Six

The first glass of rum went down easily, Pine gaped at me as I knocked on the bar table twice more to signal another round. The pub was crammed, save for the dance floor by the banjo and mandolin, no lad in here was drunk or brave enough to take the center. The barmaids held a cadence to their steps as they wove in and out of the tables delivering stews and ales. In the corner, Gimly wrapped his arms around the first pretty face he saw and pulled her onto his knee, "I'll be needing you for luck," he told her and pushed several shiny coins into the middle of the circular table. The girl was far too young to be dragged onto any man's lap, let alone one as vile as Gimly's. I could not watch the scene unfold for I fear if his hands ventured up her thigh any higher, I would cut them off.

The pub was a sturdy establishment, it had to be for the number of men stomping about recklessly would have broken the foundation had it been weak. The room hummed with a hundred different conversations and the strings of the instruments plucked uplifting tunes. I unbuttoned the top buttons of my green tunic and cuffed up my sleeves for the air was surprisingly warm. A glass of amber liquid was set next to my elbow, I gave the bartender a grin of gratitude as Pine took to leaving eight copper coins in his hands. "Upstairs is a bit quieter if you prefer less chaos."

"Chaos is fine," I assured.

He pointed to two backless stools in the back that had opened up. "Let's free up the counter for Joshua's customers." There was a grumble of thanks near the bottles as we maneuvered across the floor. "Alright, I warned you that it wasn't much of a story, it's more of a confession." Pine, who was in his third decade, became flushed with adolescent guilt.

"On with it," I coaxed, shifting my hips onto the round wooden surface.

"In the springtime, the underhills emerge from the coziness of our dwellings to greet the rising sun and longer days. One particular spring morning, the sound of shouts, giggles and *frolicking* awoke us. A group of us went out to see who had trespassed so boldly and directly on the green sweetgrass lay a girl I knew from my childhood, beholding a woman with such fervor and passion that honestly, it was beautiful to witness. So much so, that even when my Plessa came out with a babe at her breast, we paused to observe the love at work. And it was undeniably love between the two of you."

I swirled my drink. I could practically taste Anna as he spoke of us. "Your big secret is that you saw me fucking a woman?"

"This wasn't just a one time occurrence, mind you. Eventually, we grew to anticipate you and the redhead disturbing our peace in the spring and in the summer, and well—just how many times were you planning on jumping stark naked off the Cliffs of Sound without knowing how to swim?" His eyes were fixed in disbelief.

"I would have figured it out," I stated with assurance, hoping to deflect his stern questioning. Stern and ridiculous questioning. "What's done is done, no need to reprimand me."

He took a swig of his ale. And another. "Had it not been for your friend, the tide would have swept your scrawny ass across the ocean and down into the crevasse of the deep."

"I'm not scrawny!" I hollered at him.

"You were before they started teaching you how to swing a sword. And arrows. And dagger. And that spinning straight stick with curved blades. I'm sure that thing has a name too," he whispered to me. Now, it was I who looked at him in disbelief. "I am also an ironside," he reminded. "The quarries were my home as well and I know they trained you there often. I know damn well you can slaughter a third of this fort in one night before anyone notices *and* outlast any of these hopeful knight wannabes in one on one combat."

"They?" I bit down my bile. "You said *they* taught me... who do you think *they* were?"

"The red head and the man." Keenan. He had seen Keenan. Worry bubbled up inside me like champagne soon to blow its cork.

Putting the glass to my lips I discreetly said back, "Let this be our secret."

"The sex, swimming or swords?"

The rum heated my throat and warmed my core even more than uncertainty already had. "Mostly the swords and appearance of those who trained me."

"I don't even know their names and I haven't seen their faces in years, doubt I'd provide any significant details and I doubt anyone will ask." His brown eyes combed me over stumbling upon a realization. "Ah, okay. If others knew about them living in Ferngrove, they would expect me to also be familiar with the inhabitants of my home, in which I'm not. In that case, I will swear to you now that they never existed nor did any of my previous mentions occur." Drink in hand, I wrapped him in my arms. He hugged back and patted my shoulder. "Should I be worried for you wild Wisteria? Is there an agenda?"

He released me. "The Wastelands are soon to be the Deadlands. Our agenda, as a nation, should all be the same, Pine." He held up his finger to pause my tangent.

Pine downed the rest of his sixteen ounces and wiped the froth off his mustache. "Nope, I changed my mind, I don't want to be an accomplice." He retracted with a shake of his head. "For what you've done for my family, you will always have compliance and silence, that I can promise."

I grinned feeling my thoughts float on the rum. "How did you know about the spiced rum?" I wiggled my now empty glass at eye level.

"The hillsides were scattered with bottles, tobacco, smoke pipes and articles of clothing after you two ran amuck. And there is only one person in Ferngrove who had copious amounts of spiced rum and that was my mother. She had bought barrels of them off my father years before when he would dock from his seadrifting and stay the winter season with us." His eyes focused on the wall over my shoulder as he spoke of his past. "I suppose the docks are down?"

"Yes. It's been long months since merchants had stepped foot on south province territory," I said. This caused Pine to furrow his bushy brows.

"Odd. Considering that Resig prides himself on sea trade and the goods gathered are typical of the exports of the Crescent Lands, which are another week of sea travel south of the Southern Isles."

"I don't follow, sorry," I said, not entirely proud of my naivety showing through.

"No need to worry yourself." He looked at my toes. They were tapping. "Do you reckon the duo playing the banjo can whip up some field stomp?"

"Field stomp? That awful song my father and Conrad used to play late into the nights?"

He nodded eagerly, "The same one that drove your mother absolutely crazy, but she danced to it nonetheless. Yes, that one." His mug was down and he was up running to the musicians. When I tried to disappear behind a crowd Pine caught me by the hand and drew me into the center of the room. "One dance?" He asked.

"Fine," I grumbled seeing as I was already drawn onto the floor. "I'm an expensive date, you owe me one more drink for spinning in your arms and if you step on my feet, you owe me two." His beaming smile was agreement enough.

We lined up side by side and the moment the plucking started, our feet synced up in a fast heel, toe step. He spun me to face him so our kicks met in the air. The claps around us organized themselves to keep the upbeat tempo, but with my unclasped hair swaying around like a thick curtain I failed to view our audience. When the exhilarating few minutes were over, Pine and I were nothing but a heap of sweat and carefree exhaustion. Our next drinks at the bar were free of cost, Joshua gestured for Pine to put his coin purse away. The chatter in the pub intensified immensely after our jig was completed, several couples were debating whether or not to jump in for the next song having seen how easy it was to lose your cares in a matter of moments. And a few drinks.

When Gimly's voice boomed next, it wasn't a shout of celebration from his gambling. It was a roar that sealed the mouths of the entire room. "Silence!" The sirens outside screamed. The pitch hummed louder and at a frequency that made my eardrums ache.

"Guards to your post! Civilians into the fort! No exceptions!" Drift rose from a lounge chair tucked under a swinging window; I hadn't known he had been in the establishment that evening. But, I was glad he had been there. His calm and confident demeanor settled the jitters of the room and shortly after he barked directions people filed out both doors. Pine held my hand so I didn't lose him in the jostling crowd. When we made it outside, Captain Cultee was already atop his mount. The silhouette of him was an inspiring sight for he had his sword drawn in one hand and led another mount, Rosie. Drift flung himself into the empty saddle and quickly exchanged words with his captain. The more seasoned guards of Numaal sprinted out of the fort with torches and were seen running towards the encampments to gear up.

Those darting into Fort Fell were the shop owners, launderers, innkeepers and women and children. Pine tugged me in the direction of the fortified walls topped with dozens of archers, but my focus was on the blood curdling screams sounding from the east and the low rolling fog that nature had cursed us with. Visibility was low and the air was wet enough to freeze the bones. "Fucking hell," I swore a little too loudly, Cultee turned his head backwards.

Captain spoke. "Into the fort, Lady Ivy," his body language more rigid than his tone.

Drift cut in. Rosie shifted her weight anxiously. "*Lady*? Did you hear her vocabulary?"

"I did. My sister's mouth was worse, I'm accustomed to it." Cultee gritted his teeth watching his men line up with shields and blades just outside the encampment. "Into the fort. No exceptions." In the same moment I felt Pine's arms around me, hoisting me off the ground, I saw Drift slip him an affirmative nod. Did they assume they knew what was best for me? They both knew I was reasonable with a weapon and yet I was sent back with the untaught civilians to cower away and wonder what the outcome of the night was?

Pine dragged me up the hill, no matter how much I squirmed and thrust my head back, he held on. The small militia of sixty, split into two groups, one headed east and the other south. The siren on the watch tower fell silent after the doors behind us were locked and a long iron bar set into place. Hundreds of us were smashed into the main foyer and the casual dining hall. The mass of people filled the stairwells and second story hallways, where they sat in quiet, some prayed and some cried. Pine hauled me ungracefully to the nearest window. Only after he locked the clasp did he release me back onto my feet.

"It had to be done. I know you are mad, but you can thank me later," Pine stated.

I pressed my nose to the glass trying to catch a glimpse of the action. "I'm livid. Fuming. Irate," I corrected between collecting breaths. I should be out there, at least as one of the archers, I thought. Gimly already knows I've some skills with a bow, I've told him that myself and being the little snitch he was certainly captain would have been made aware by now and it would come as no surprise to find me perched upon the stables and armed upon their arrival. An arm snaked around my shoulders.

"I should have forged a lock and key to chain you in place had I known keeping you alive would be so taxing." I failed to see the humor in Pine's words. I felt myself go limp in his clutch as the memories of rusted iron bars, the coppery taste of blood and vision of my murdered lover chained to me fell over my eyes. Despite me surrendering to him, he didn't remove his arm. Some hours past midnight, a more subtle sound echoed outside, a brass bell chimed and continued to do so until the captain arrived with his men.

Those around me rose from the prayer pose on their knees and exhaled easier when the guards atop the balcony called down. "They've returned! Smoke rises from the south and the fog disperses, a sign of success," the guards' obvious relief transmitted to the town who grew eager to exit and took to lifting the bar across the front gates and stepping outside.

A dim sunrise greeted them.

I took advantage of the eventful movement and dropped low out of Pine's grasp. "Thanks for the dance," I commented and darted against the grain. I nestled in my corner room running my thumb along the silver blade of my dagger sipping cold tea to refresh my mind after a night of drinking and being locked down. I was as useful last night as a sitting duck in the dunes of the north. I slammed my head against the wall, wincing at the bruises forming on the base of my skull. Through my window, I heard the townspeople moving about, vocalizing their terror lingering from the night and their good fortune to be under the protection of Fort Fell. I didn't share their sentiments, I was busy dwelling on what remained of Horn's End and how Asher fared riding alongside his superiors, facing a mutilated form of deathlessness.

Mostly, I was enraged at the fact I had done nothing last night.

The fort town quieted midmorning when the rain came and lulled everyone to sleep with its sporadic pattering. It was days like these where Anna and Moriah would bring us all together for sharing stories and if parchment was available, I'd read and write stories of my own. In the afternoon, I braved the hallways of the fort, staff had nearly finished cleaning the waste and litter left behind and many of the guards sat nursing their mental and emotional wounds in silence around a pint in the common hall.

"Oy, woodlander!" The friendly archer shouted above by the chandelier. I looked up and spun around dizzily until I spotted him. I waved. "Off to the tactical room with haste, Captain's sent for you some time ago."

"Where is this *tactical room*?" I raised.

He pointed out the door nearest his post. "Out by the training field."

I backtracked to fetch my cloak and stopped by the men gathered on the dining table. "Pardon?" I approached the one with the most somber attitude. "Were there injuries or losses last evening?"

"Aye, two more dead. One farmer, one scout. That makes a total of seven and we ain't even seen the shortest days of winter yet." This man had given up the fight long before last night.

"I can't fix dead." I stated bluntly, bringing his eyes to meet mine, his finger circling his frothy mug. I let him sit with his defeated spiraling thoughts just as I had done all night and the remainder of the morning.

No spears stood standing guard at the gate, the mud beneath the toes of my boots squished and left small imprints next to the larger hoof prints and steps of men. I dropped the shroud of my hood when I stepped under the shelter of the smithy. There was no warmth or light pervading the space. "Lady Ivy? Come this way." A door clicked opened, a soft glimmer of electrical lamps shown across the hall. I crouched under the wooden fence and tip-toed over the scattered helmets and chest armor, I spotted the captain who waved me onward.

The tactical room was small, or perhaps the fact Drift consumed one entire side of the square table, made the furniture seem as if it was made for a doll's house. "I appreciate you stepping out of the fort, given the events of last night. Would you have stolen another horse to follow us into battle, woodlander?"

Cultee circled around me to close the door. I noted the black blood on his trousers, the same sticky guts clung to Drift's chest and spattered across his neck. "I don't steal, I borrow." I gritted my teeth and refused to meet Drift's twinkling eyes.

"Do you know why you're here?" He leaned on the table in which a map with landscapes had been carved from wood. The entire south province was represented and little black and red ponds were scattered around the hills.

I interlaced my fingers and rested them on my flat stomach. "I've been informed two have passed on. Are there other injuries I need to address?"

"None severe enough." He beckoned me towards the chair beside him where a sack of fresh apples, sandals and basket of tools were tossed. There may be a hope for the inhabitants of Horn's End after all. "These items were found by a scout a league off the old west road. Where exactly have you been hiding these late years?"

"In the heart of the Wastelands."

"Who did you say you were living with?"

I pursed my lips. "I hadn't said I was with anyone. If you are prying for information, I would like my honesty to be reciprocated with yours for I too have questions to pose."

Gimly spat on the floor. "Insubordination to your superior is punishable by whatever means seen appropriate." Cultee held his finger up in a blatant warning to his second, who made a noise like an infected rat.

"I imagine you do." The captain seated himself next to the discovered goods, he brought his elbows to his knees and, with a resounding sigh, flourished his hands. "Alright, ask away and in good faith, I expect you to do the same. One for one. Fair enough, Lady Ivy?"

What question shall I raise first? Gods, I had hundreds! My eyes ran along the simple decoration of the room, wooden framed with splotches of red. Numaal chose red to represent our nation for it was the color of our human blood. Blood that had been shed nearly every day for the last four years. It was a travesty. Anna's blood flowed in me and I shot out the words so fast that coated my mouth with venom. "Is the duke too preoccupied with his festivity preparations to send reinforcements or has he already surrendered Fort Fell to the restless as he had the rest of his lands?"

Gimly rose and in one swipe of his arm the map of the table was wiped clean and pieces tinkered as they crashed on the floor. Lethality crowded his features as he flipped the table onto its side and stepped towards me. "I don't like what you are implying about *our* duke for you are no more than a filthy girl mourning the loss of your woodlands unable to see the greater scheme." His comrade and captain let him prowl off the chains towards me, hyper aware of the tension in his movements.

I hated feeling little. So, I opened my big mouth. "Then, by all means, guide my stray thoughts with evidence of the truth. I'd love to know if Stegin was in the Wastelands as of late with noble knights sent from the prince to fight the decay of his lands." Gimly pressed his face next to mine and pulled his arm back to strike. The wall behind me splintered as his hand smashed through it. "Ah, he must not have wanted to summon the crowds or disturb the peace of the area with his mighty influence."

"Hold your tongue! The both of you!" Captain Cultee seethed through clenched teeth. He yanked the back of Gimly's collar and forced himself between us, his cautioning gaze fell onto me before turning to Gimly. "Compose yourself, guard of Numaal! Your actions and words represent our superiors and nation so if you can't formulate an apology to the lady or learn to restrain your temper, I'm going to ask you to leave and reconvene with me this evening."

Gimly stormed out. I exhaled.

Cultee turned to me equally enraged. "You should not prompt your own demise."

"You should not keep a rabid dog on a long leash," I let slip. The captain halted his steps. I lowered my head so he couldn't see how hard I was biting my lip. "Sorry, sir. I am lacking sleep and am entirely to blame for the incident. I will leave."

"Not necessary. Gimly is Stegin Monte's bastard son and rather sensitive when it comes to defending his lineage and making a name for himself. And to answer your previous question, the commencement of the winter solstice is the south province's most celebrated gala, just as the north celebrates spring, the east autumn and the west summer. His focus is undoubtedly on the lavish mascarade and accommodating the lords and ladies of the capital; he isn't aware of the extent of damage being done by the spawn of darkness. He will not entertain a whisper of a conversation about it. He placed a lot of faith in me, his son and the horselord—failure is not an option, he will hear nothing of the hordes of wraiths moving to the center of his lands. My letters have gone unanswered."

"Has he fought a wraith or seen one?" I asked, starting to feel more at ease with the threat removed.

"A good inquiry, one I'll respond to after I receive an answer from you."

Drift picked up the whole table as if it was weightless and set it straight. He pulled out two chairs and gestured to them. Captain seated himself. Drift pointed to the second seat. "That's for you. I broke that last one I tried to sit in and am now forbidden from rocking chairs."

I seated myself and said to no one in particular, "Thank you."

"Were you alone in the Wastelands?" Captain repeated as I settled myself.

"Some of the time. There are others, rural villagers. Survivors."

"Stegin has seen and fought wraiths before. Albeit, few and none recently." I nodded, preparing myself for his next questions. "How many of you are in the Wastelands?"

"Not many. Over the last eighteen months we've built up a spiked hedge and repaired homes from the fires, what started out as a small haven I stumbled upon one dark night morphed into a village. Horn's End is half the size of Fort Fell in terms of population, a little over two hundred and fifty."

Captain sunk into his chair. "That's a substantial amount. I assume that means there are those among you who can fight."

"Lives are frequently stolen; we are relatively defenseless." I gave him a grim smile. "Why the curiosity about Horn's End?"

The captain of the fort glanced at the sack of goods his men had found. "There are more signs of life and trekkers three days' ride from here, there are recent cart tracks and imprints of slumbering bodies in the loose dirt and fallen ash. It appears they took the west trail out of the Wastelands. I was hoping you could help us find them, coax them and bring them under the protection of Fort Fell before winter cuts off all the roads. Their outcome is grim if they linger on their own. Past experiences with common folk have led me to believe they are not fond of being approached by guards, they hold the same grudge against us as you seem to." The *same* grudge? Was everyone chained to their murdered lover? Were all simple peoples killing and burning their loved ones? "You don't think we are doing enough and haven't been, correct?"

"Maybe it has something to do with the bait traps of warmed corpses luring the wraiths closer to the last of the livable lands."

He was quick to retort. "The actions of select guards will be addressed. We banned that technique some time ago after learning about burning the dead and the wraiths alike."

"And the bitten." Drift spoke up from across the room looking weary and pale beneath his disheveled locks of tangled hair. "Those with significant damage must be tended too. Unless, our dear woodlander has concocted a reversal to the poison that coats their rows of razor-sharp teeth."

"I have not," I confessed. "That would prove to be a tremendous feat. One I'd be inclined to share, I'd much prefer that than amputation." I glanced at the captain and enquired more about the bait traps Gimly set.

Captain gave no inclination to what his emotions were, he was unreadable and his voice unperturbed. "I've much to discuss with Gimly tonight. Since one cannot alter the past, I will hope for a better tomorrow. Scouts are out now searching for the direction of the survivors. Will you be willing to venture out and help us extend our provisions?"

"If you promise there will be no knights in the caravan, you can rely on me to accompany you. Why are you so determined to sway us?"

He pensively mulled over my usage of the word *us* and how I still held distinctions. "All lives are valuable, Ivy. I learned that too late. You could say that I'm atoning for my past inactions." He had lost someone, one need not ask much more fearing the scar would open. "Would you have rode out with us last night, Lady Ivy?"

"Yes."

Drift snorted. "I told you her instincts are different. She doesn't even know how to properly ride and she would still choose that over running for safety."

"That is because I've seen more death than most and despite being a healer, I've a fair share of blood on my hands." I brushed him off and turned to Cultee, yet his hooded eyes traced the lines of unyielding in my brow. He didn't blink. "How are you going to draw the duke's attention to the crisis? Hells, even the king's eyes need to be awakened. If he is on his deathbed, send word to the illusive prince."

Cultee ran his knuckles against his bearded chin. "I'm working on composing a letter to Stegin, one that requests more aid while not insulting his decisional capabilities." I scrunched my face. A letter was a pathetic message, it probably wouldn't be read until after his grand affair. By then, even if it was able to make an impact, it would be too late. "If that fails, I'm considering not attending the gala. My absence would be viewed as an insult by him and his council, but it would draw them to the gate of Fort Fell to summon me for a hearing. When that

happens, reality will be unavoidable and their minds will surely change."
He pulled back. "You don't like my plan?"

"I'm not savvy in politics. Nor do I wish to be. You've already stated your
letters have gone unanswered, this time will be no different."

He shook his head, "That's not an answer."

I wished my tongue would stop flying and allow me to be the docile girl
Keenan asked for on my mission. "I don't like the notion of a boring
letter that will sit collecting dust for months when you are likely not to
survive that long."

Cultee refrained himself. "Before I ask what you'd do to turn the eyes
and ears of a duke, it's your turn to pose a question."

Indeed, it was. "How is Stegin intending on killing Maruc and
Athromancia?"

Drift turned towards his superior, questions filled behind his eyes. This
was news to him, he didn't care to hide how troubled he was. "I'm not
high ranked enough to have that information disclosed to me," he
groaned. "It was Gimly who enlightened me of the outcome of his
father's advisory meeting with the prince's shadows—his body guards
that are never more than a step away. I feel it's relevant to add that I
am opposed to ending the physical lifetime of an Eternal, for I doubt it
will stop a war between races and nations." He fumbled with the gold
ring on his right thumb. "How would you address Stegin from afar?"

"Well, instead of writing in ink, I'd use blood." The captain shifted more
erect in his chair. "And I wouldn't send a piece of parchment in an
envelope. I'd send him the body of a wraith with the letter nailed in its
head. Sir," I added the formality aloofly. My cheeks pinkened as I
became aware of how disturbed I must have sounded to them.

Drift's chuckle grew and grew until the post he was leaning on squeaked
behind his weight. "Definitely, *not* a lady. But, I like her. Sir." He laughed
harder seeing my blush deepened. "We should probably excuse her
before she embarrasses herself even more."

My wide eyes blinked at him across the room. "What a wonderful
suggestion, Drift. Probably the only sensible thought your brain has
managed to construct in years." I rose quickly and pivoted to the

captain. "One last inquiry." He agreed while trying his hardest to ignore the fit of laughter from beside him. "What are you planning to do after Horn's End merges with Fort Fell, knowing how stretched thin our protection will be this winter and how wary we are of men in red and knights in black?"

He sunk into the chair, folding his arms diplomatically on his lap. "This is a recent development. I've formulated as far as reaching out with a small caravan and escorting them into our town, offering jobs, food and warmth. I'd be lying if I said I thought much beyond the first day of their arrival, we've yet to confirm numbers and they've yet to accept our invitation."

Backing up, I blindly felt for the door and opened it behind me. "Gentleman, it's been an afternoon of revelations." The cold air nipped at my spine, I shivered in my skin.

"A pleasure, Lady Ivy," the captain gave a casual dismissive wave. Drift bent over clutching his stomach, the word *lady* triggered another wave of comicality. Eagerly, I shut the door that separated them from me and was left alone with my thoughts and the patterns of rain. The clouds didn't dry up, they continued to weep, occasionally freezing. The young guards kept their chest armor donned and hands readied at the hilt of their swords as they patrolled the invisible boundaries of the land between the beacons. Despite the distance, their tension was obvious. The archers on the towers were a much better defense than the pickets I spent all summer sharpening. With a proper coalminer the odds of succumbing to a respiratory infection were smaller than they had been in the two previous winters. The mushrooms needed to formulate the medicine for pneumonia hadn't been seen in years for they had sensitive growth conditions and their environment had been tampered with greatly. Only the wealthy would have access to it.

The forge wasn't fully ablaze because it had been untended for a day. I scooted Pine's heavy tools aside and plopped myself on his workbench with my back and arms pressed against the clay outer shell to absorb the remnants of warmth. The heels of my boots I pressed to my hindquarters as I hugged my knees tight. I wouldn't be returning to the lady's sleep quarters, there was nothing to do there but dwell on the past or numb my mind with a smoke. And something about relaxing made me susceptible to intruders, Drift to be exact.

I eyed the door which I had just exited. The captain didn't seem the type to mind me barging in to ask one more question—what was Drift's given name? But so long as I remained in Fort Fell, Drift would never let me hear the end of it. I watched the rain clouds roll in and out and the changing of the guards twice before Pine nudged me. He brought me rice and green beans, his method of an apology. "This doesn't mean what you did last night was acceptable." I stated, taking the steaming bowl from his hands.

He hopped up onto the workbench next to me, his feet swinging below. "Yes, yes. You are still livid, irate and fuming that I helped keep your combat skills a secret." I stopped chewing. "That is what you had asked me to do twenty minutes before the alarm sounded right? Or had the drinks already gone to your head?"

"Fine. I forgive you," I choked out in between bites.

"You're welcome," he sighed. Pine watched the darkening sky while I ate. The tactical room opened and closed, out walked two males who seemed surprised to see us quietly congregating on the rickety, sullied table inches away from the bad weather. "Evening," Pine said over his shoulder.

"The storm looks to be picking up." Cultee said under his breath. "Drift, turn in. I'll help Crocker Street board up windows in case the winds shift from the north."

Drift's reply was a gruff affirmative syllable. He wasted no time in obeying orders for his steps stomped quickly towards the fort behind us. The captain tossed his hood over his shoulder and tied down his chest straps. He darted into the rain, his destination the faint twinkling strain of lights off in the distance.

"We can't stay out here much longer. The heat has dispersed," Pine said readjusting his hat to cover his ears.

"You're right." I jumped off the counter to face the wall of missing weapons. "Pine, who decided that you would be better at making swords than swinging them?"

He came up behind me and threw his arm and cloak over my shoulder when we stepped out into the rain. "I did. I am a crafter not a killer. I'd rather change my craft three more times than disconnect with nature altogether and put myself at risk for taking a life."

My heart drummed along skipping beats as pain took hold of my chest. He hadn't intended them to, but his words stung. I was a master in the woodland craft, but I was also an unapologetic murderer of my own countrymen who'd wandered too far into the plague. That night my dreams were soaked in scarlet blood. Innocent blood. As my hands had been a dozen times. Neither time nor the weather could wash the stains away.

Chapter Seven

The storm waned for an hour in the morning, then began pouring again with vengeance. I kept myself busy. Raina waved her chubby hands gleefully as I set an entire basket of monthly tea down on the kitchen table. "Eighty satchels," I stated. "I intend to have another fifteen divvied up to discreetly deliver to Crocker Street if the skies ever stop crying."

Lorelai bounced into the kitchen and obeyed Raina's direction to transfer the basket into the sleep quarters and hidden behind her loom and piles of yarn. "Well done, Ivy," she pinched my cheek. Her worry lines were softened and her touch warmer. "Have you any woolen layers?"

"No. Two cotton tunics, a thin dress and that large rag sitting on my bed," I said, enjoying a bite of dehydrated plantain.

She snorted and picked at the broken hem of her beige rag she fashioned into an apron. "You'll find a scarf and hat on your bed tonight. And a few sacks of preserved fruits and scones for your kind efforts."

"Wonderful," I exclaimed, smacking my lips after a particularly delectable bite. With the teas made and the moisture in the air setting my floral dehydration back weeks, I had to conjure something to fill my time. Pine wouldn't spar with me. The women in the kitchen kicked me out seeing as I was of no use in curing slabs of raw meats, baking hams or defeathering chickens. Rosie was out scouting with her rider and the stables were caked in mud. I roamed.

The common dining and main foyer of Fort Fell were melancholy and the guards on the top tiers were standing astute on the outside posts where rain and snow continued to fall. The extra hands of the town were being used to rearrange sandbags to prevent flooding of the clean water system and redirect mire away from the stables. There were no scribes or ranked men in the captain's corridor, so I permitted myself inside his office. I was eager to know what his troops had found in the Wastelands, I'd wait for his advent. Shutting the doors behind me I skipped to the shelves. I took the eighth book from the right and curled up in Cultee's red velvet chair.

The painting took my breath away as it had done the first time.

My eyes drank in the beauty of the Eleven until the sun went down. Then I learned about my land, the capital names of the four directional provinces and the rivers that separated them. I traced the rough coastline around Numaal and found the coastal cities with ports. South of the large land mass were several clumps of islands, the Crescent Islands and Southern Isles. To the north, the Glacial Split. Footsteps echoed in the barren hallway. I shut the cover of the blue book and rose to wait by the double door. I cleared my throat and tucked my hair behind the row of piercings in my ear.

"I've got to meet with the man first, but deal me in for a game of grabbler!" A horrifyingly familiar voice sounded outside the office. It was not who I'd been expecting, "Pick a woman and we will put them up for bid." Gimly. And he was steps away.

"No. No. No," I whispered while sprinting towards the window. I unlocked the hook and pushed the stained glass window open.

The ledge was slight and the slate shingles slick beneath my boots. I looked down, instantly regretting it for nothing lay below aside from dimness obscured by the heavy downpour. Panic caused my heart to pick up momentum while I side stepped away from the office and around the cylinder roof.

Gimly closed the window. He was wise enough to lock it on a windy night such as tonight.

My soul plummeted. Simultaneously, nausea rose.

I was trapped two stories above the hard ground, in the middle of freezing rainfall. I shoved the book in my satchel, which grew heavier by the second as water droplets weighed it down. My fingers frantically ran across the surface of the roof until they nestled in the biggest groove they could find. I dug my nails into the notch and pressed my stomach flat against the slate. I lasted minutes until my hands and feet numbed. I jumped when lightning struck above and cried an ugly cry when the thunder shook my bones. My salty warm tears were diluted by the icy drops of water smacking my face. I pressed my cheeks onto the rough slabs of tar and stone which caused my cries to come out hoarsely in frantic pants.

Mere minutes in the raging elements had reduced me to nothing.

It wasn't long before the tremors forced my footing to slip. I desperately kicked around with my right foot seeking a hold or the slightest amount of friction to hold me upright for my arms were quickly becoming inoperable.

'I saw the light fade from your eyes.
Yet, your soul begun to rise.
Into the midnight sun, where life then begun, did you finally realize.'

I wept harder hearing the voice that sung Anna's soul into the afterlife. Death was coming for me shortly, I was certain.

'When you awoke to the world of white,
You were startled and fearful of heights.
On the warm winds, when I took you in, did you finally lose your fright.'

"Wisteria!" A voice hammered against the storm. "What is my name?" Somewhere below, I dared not risk a glace, was Drift spouting nonsense. Not Drift. *Him.* The man who had been locked away deep in the duke's dungeons for perhaps than I had been. *Him.* The man who had willingly given me the beautiful distraction of song in my darkest of days. *Him.* Who knew how deeply and fiercely my love for Anna had run and gave me a second chance to live. *Him.* Who offered me freedom and who I had run away from the moment I regained consciousness. Drift hadn't been stalking me so much as he was holding true to his vow of protection.

Thunder cracked overhead, deafening my eardrums. "Zander Veil Halfmoon di Lucent!" I screamed into the whirling wind. Before I had a chance to fill my lungs, a blanket of dense, smokey ether encompassed my frigid body. It was an enchanting embrace of the night. I sighed as it held me.

'Let go,' Zander prompted in his rumbling, honey sweet tone. His voice spoke in my ear, yet his body stood fifty feet below. 'My oath stands as unbreakable as my arms. Let go, I will catch you.'

Knowing echoed in my ribcage.

I stopped clawing at the roof and let my arms sag as heavy as they felt. They dropped to my sides as gravity set in. I closed my eyes as the sensation of falling overtook my body, the seconds stretched on as I plummeted towards the ground. Even after two firm arms intertwined around my body, my soul still felt as if it was falling. Zander secured me to his chest, my trembling uncontrollable even with his warm hands wrapped around my cold, wet frame.

Zander's bedroom furniture was relative to his size. The oversized bed and chair made the unlit fireplace and nearby table seem as if they were fit for a doll. Thankfully, Zander was important enough to have a singular hanging electric light in his room, for when he set me down, I didn't trip over his scattered muddy clothes and boots. I dropped my satchel from my shoulder and with fumbling fingers began to tear at the buttons glazed in ice, Zander was already rummaging in his standing dresser and by the time I made the choice to pull the clingy shirt over my head. He helped pull my arms out when they adhered to the wet fabric and outstretched a fresh, dry grey tunic.

The puddle of water beneath me grew, while I stripped naked.

Desperate to get out of the dowsed attire I started to unfasten my trousers. He balanced me as I took to ripping off my boots and taking down my pants and underthings. "I'll tend to your hair." I agreed. Zander moved behind me with a cotton towel and enfolded the ends of my long locks, catching the water before it chilled my skin. It was the only way for him to honor me with any amount of modesty while seeing that my quivering didn't send me to the floor.

His night tunic fit me as snuggly as the beige dress had, it hung openly above my knees, which were now visibly shaking. Violently. The top blanket of Zander's bed was ripped away in a single swipe and hastily pulled around my shoulders. He brought us level, nose to nose, while he lowered himself to scoop me up behind the knees and place me on the bed, his eyes both shimmered as they never left my gaze. "T-t-t-tell everything, Zander," I stammered into the downy comforter. His tired face lifted into a smile when I said his name. My sit bones felt amazing, for it had been too long since I've had a proper mattress to rest on.

"I will, Wisteria," he promised with his usual undercurrent of humor and stripped his own wet clothes, the light above us offered enough glow to emphasize the sharp angles his abdominal muscles flexed into his low hung pants. I buried my nose away while he changed the remainder of his garments, avoiding a reason for him to believe he was a specimen worth gawking at. The chair from the corner was brought over to the edge of the bed where Zander sat in his fresh undergarments. I inched towards him while he fumbled with his black and white mane. He declined the portion of the blanket I offered to him with a reassuring wave of his hand.

"Do I want to know what the hell you were doing on the roof in a sleet storm?" He asked in a pause.

The muscle in my jaw failed to pause the quaking. I huffed, "Escaping." No coherent words followed.

"Alright, you won't be telling me much given your current condition. Shall I start from the beginning?" I nodded. "My mother was a shieldmaiden of Thalren, a fierce one. She rode along the Numaalian border of the dreamer world, which is properly called the Veil, by the western world. That's not a term commonly heard in the mortal realm unless it's addressing the afterlife. The Veil is another country, another realm with an Overlord, its own cities, own people and all that. Death we refer to as simply, beyond. My mother was a mortal and died when I was in my formative years." I critiqued his face, his bright skin and chiseled jawline. He looked like he hadn't seen his thirties let alone lived through them. "I'm a decade shy of two hundred," he said, watching my expression which was unperturbed. Anna never bothered to tell me her age, she was always dismissive of that topic and found something else to distract my attention when I would probe. "Which makes me a babe compared to the old Ilanthian lines."

He was a mixed blood, the ones Gimly had mentioned. "First generation?" I asked muffled.

His dark brow line snitched above his nose. "Well, that's a bit of a complicated question. You see my father is a resident of the Veil, a dreamer being who rarely steps out of the gateway to the two nations. He did one night to seduce my mother and a few other times to consult the Emperor after I got into significant trouble. My blood got a little more muddied up when I hit adolescence and frequented between the three realms. But, no. I'm not Ilanthian. I also wasn't born an immortal, but now that is what I am."

So many questions flurried around in my head.

My head became a hive of busy bees. I didn't know what to ask first. *An entire nation in a realm?* I hadn't heard of another segregation to our continent Kinlyra other than the Land of the Gods and mortal lands. "What's a dreamer being?"

"Of the first creations the Eternals, the mystical and magical beings Oyokos and his siblings dreamt up before they formulated landscapes and beings of Ilanthia and Numaal. We are a diverse populace. There are elementals–animorphs who are born with an essence of flame or water. Reapers, who guide the souls through the Veil to their destination, the beyond. Sprites who play naughty tricks on your senses. The truth bearing griffins who isolated themselves up in the Howling Hills for nearly three thousand years. Fae, hounds, tunnel worms, pixie, porrigs, kelpies, imps, borhats." He listed casually. "My father, Atticus, and subsequently I, are incubi." That explained *a lot* about his reputation and the persistent passes from women. "Despite what you are visualizing, an incubus's nature does not solely revolve around sex. When it does, the energy absorption is consensual. To keep me in this form while I roam, I need to ingest the sustaining forces from these lands, like fresh red meats–I'm not a vampire, those have never existed outside the mortal's imagination. Companionship is also a passive method regeneration; Fen provides such for me on my harder days. I also need food, because I am half human."

I pushed down the blanket covering part of my face. "Fen?" The man who melted away my cage of iron in the dungeon. He had freed me.

"Fennick has been keeping close tabs on you, whether he enjoys it or not is another question. He highly considered abandoning you in the hot spring after you've taken keen on calling him Nikki." Zander pointed to his white eye that momentarily transformed into Nikki's golden ambered gaze and reverted back again. My jaw gaped. "He hates the nickname by the way. Before you arrived, I was running low on amusement. I suggest you continue the harassment and let's bet on how long he can go without breaking his character's most prominent trait of muteness." He followed his comments with a lazy smile. "Fen and I were tied together after childhood. Where I go, he goes. We loathed it in the early ages, for we didn't understand how precious it was for an elemental to bond with a dreamer and human offspring. A special bond given to us by the Weaver. Wisteria, there is no entity I trust more than Fen, and that isn't because he is bound by instinct to protect me, he's closer to me than a brother and he knows I'd lay down my life for him from love, not allegiance."

My skin began to tingle as the iciness dispersed leaving my nerves raw and exposed. I had no siblings; Anna was the closest thing I had to a sister before our intimacy developed a step beyond familial. What he spoke of, seemed as if the depths of their relationship took lifetimes to forge. "It sounds beautiful. Enigmatic," I said, still unable to comprehend their magically concocted bond. "I assume Fennick's element is flame?"

Zander dipped his chin, a smile consuming half his face. "Yes. A fire fox elemental bound infinitely to an incubus horselord of the Veil and Thalren. Once we stopped trying to murder each other or sever our thread, we got into serious mischief, enough to bring the Overlord of the realm to demand we be publicly reprimanded and sentenced to sweep Oyoko's Temple of Horns during festival nights. Our parents set us to hard labor for years in the fields of somber, to reap cotton without the use of magic and sweep soot off the northern rampart that oversees the rune barrier to the beyond. A lengthy story for another evening," he spoke fondly and finitely. Behind the rickety door of his bedroom a handful of voices echoed off the wall. My head snapped towards the hallway patiently waiting for the men to pass. Zander continued on in a more hushed tone. I readjusted myself on the mattress, nestling closer to him then I had ever wanted to be to the man I knew as Drift. "You're probably eager to know what I was doing in the duke's dungeon."

I felt my lower jaw slowdown in its shivering. My teeth still chattered and clanked in my mouth. I hummed affirmatively.

"Ilanthia and the Veil are facing significant issues stemming from the same source. Every day I see souls of the dead, most of whom were not yet ready to have died, whose strand of life was cut short by wraiths or their infectious bite, stuck between destinations. The dreamer realm is at risk of imploding and leaking monstrosities onto the world from an imbalanced population of dead not moving into the beyond. The White Tower is making fear-based decisions since nine of the Eternals who've passed on had refused to give a blessing over war. Orion didn't want a war. He made that clear when he left his siblings.

"Before Ilanthia and the Veil collectively obliterate Kathra, I volunteered to end the progress of the wraiths and dive deeper into the root cause of their existence. Athromancia does not want a war. She left Maruc to find the best of Ilanthia's citizens to negotiate peace with Numaal. She sent her voyagers to Numaal in order to mend the past and fight against the wraiths. After the ships left, the Empress went underground with her legion of pledged lives. She is trying to convince the people of Kinlyra to see with their heart and map their own truth of Ilanthians and Numaalians. It's taking too long. Her approach has been too passive, if you ask me. It's clear she is at odds with her brother, her lover, her whatever you call him—the Emperor. She has been since Temperance left.

"Dukes Hammish and Satoritu Koi bragged to the palace years ago that they found silver bloods which peaked the ear of King Resig for some time. I came to investigate these claims as a rebel mortal left to die and landed in a prison cell rotting for months listening to the rumors on the estate and waiting to hear a splinter of hearsay from the priestesses who frequented and fucked their way around the members of the council. The only truth and sincerity I heard was in the vow you made to avenge Anna."

Hearing another speak her name caused my tear ducts to burn. He let a moment of reverent silence go by as I collected myself. "Do you know what type of Ilanthian she was? Her blood healed you and sustained you for weeks without water and food, she was probably one of the first or a distant descendant of Aditi, wouldn't you agree?"

I shook my head, feeling a single tear break free and trickle down my cheek. Its warmth trailed to my neck where the fabric absorbed the evidence. "I didn't know there were different types of silver bloods. She avoided any dialogue that would historically place her age. Sorry, I don't have your answer," I choked.

His hand briefly touched my shoulder. "There is no need for apologizing for there is no fault to be owned. I heard the entire exchange between you two, I will be damned if you are to hold any amount of blame for her death. She forced her blood into your body after you vocalized your opposition and gave no consent for such an intimate ordeal. You are distraught, it is I who should ask for your forgiveness in breaching a horrid memory you've tried hard to banish." Zander kept his calloused hand in close proximity to me. "I'll hold my tongue regarding your past, until you are ready to talk about it."

"Thanks," I managed, fighting a wave of self-consciousness. I held back from asking about Cobar, Moriah and Rory locked away in some lord's manor, or worse, the king's palace. "All your practice swooning others with your inflated sense of self has given you the uncanny ability to incessantly talk about yourself, please continue to do so. Fortunately, I'm intrigued to why you stayed in the Wastelands after Nikki freed you. Freed *us*," I corrected quietly.

He was quick to reply. "I made a vow of protection to Wisteria Woodlander." That oaf tried to give me a charming, flirtatious smile. I rolled my eyes to show how immune I was to him. "She was a woman of the Southlands who left our safehouse in the middle of the night to run back into the peak of danger. I swore to protect her or accept death as my punishment for failure." I buried my nose, his voice deepened. "Fen followed you for days. When you entered the caves and he saw a torch ignite, you were assumed safe and he ran back to keep me company. If I went after you, I'd have forced you into safer arrangements. That force, despite my best intentions, would not have gone over smoothly or earn us your respect. So, we let you go." He crossed his forearms on the bedspread and laid his head atop them. "All I knew of you was that you had every intention to return to the duke if not just to kill him for his transgressions. I spent the last two years formulating how to get in his good graces so I wouldn't miss you when you came barging in to slay the bastard. He sent me to Cultee to make use of my swordsmanship on the frontlines with the order to return to him when the captain deemed me ready for knighthood. I hold Cultee in some regard. He's scared, but he is trying. He is the only one with a name and a blade who has put in *any* efforts to preserve humanity. I've set out to make him the next duke of the south after you kill the current one. Residing in Fort Fell has allowed us to explore the Wastelands and remaining woods in search of you."

"Isn't your Overload and the Emperor upset about your hindered return home?" I posed.

"No," he said with a yawn. "They understand the magnitude of upholding a vow."

"Why did you continue searching for me, when the odds were that my short life had ended?"

His eyes softened as he fought sleep. "My gaze sees beyond this world. I would know."

"The same way you knew I was stuck on the roof facing death?" I countered.

"Yes. And how we are able to connect our thoughts. It's all related."

"How?"

"By a bond you deemed, what was that word, oh yes–*enigmatic*." Zander's white teeth gleamed into a devious smile. "I don't understand it fully or enough to explain the details because it is new to us. I have some thoughts, but none concrete enough to confirm. I don't want you scared off before we've had a chance to figure things out." My left hand strummed my fingers.

Scared of a magic thread? Me? "Well, this bond is allowing me to sense a hint of distress and secrecy in your last statement." I inhaled his damp and spicy fragrance. He shrugged like a child innocently avoiding the breaching an uncomfortable topic.

"Perhaps there is an old magic seeped to a promise made in honest vulnerability, that holds a brightness and a resilience to the darkening world. Tomorrow's magnificent dawn may bring clarity."

"Spoken like an immortal," I grunted.

"What's that mean?" he countered.

"You always speak in riddles and of time as if I was allotted the same amount. I don't get to fantasize of tomorrow or a world of peace, when I'm preoccupied wondering how I am going to find food for the day and survive the terrors of nights. If I hadn't promised Anna I'd kill the man who struck her down, I would have taken myself out of this world long ago and met you in your precious Veil."

For the first time since knowing him, he was speechless. There was a panic in his fretful face as he swallowed the truth in my words. "Wisteria," he said my name as softly as a sigh. His dark lashes started to close over his eyes. "There are magnificent sunrises and memorable dusks for you yet to see. I'd have taken you to a place of perpetual peace to live out the rest of your days had you not left so abruptly."

My tone was sharper than intended. "Don't all beings deserve that life of possibilities? Or is seeing beautiful things reserved for people who can take it for granted with longer lives? Should not everyone be striving to create peace and happiness right where their feet are planted?"

"You know in your heart we are not in discord about all peoples thriving and deserving the best of what the world has to offer, I must request you do not insinuate that I am partial to some and not others. If I could have snuck all of the Wasteland residents into my carriage that night I would have, but that is not the case. I intended to leave with you, which was already more than I sought out." The heat from his words lit more warmth in my toes. "Why did you run from us?"

Zander's question took me off guard. I steadied my breath hoping to steady my thoughts. I happily noted that my core was no longer frozen, merely chilly and the shaking had stopped. Peering at his unforgettable features, I willed my recollection to compose itself. My last memory of Zander was him carrying me on his hip darting through the manor of the duke's and succumbing to sleep shortly after I felt fresh air in my lungs.

Never saw his face for he was draped in mantles and scarfs. When I awoke, more than a day had passed and it was nightfall again. I was in a shed, nuzzled contently in a pile of quilts.

My only drive when consciousness descended was my family and friends. I had to get back to Ferngrove, to my home, and see what became of the bodies. "I needed to know the outcome of my homeland. To piece together why the wraiths came for some and knights for others? The rubble didn't paint a clear picture, it made things worse. And Zander, for the record, just because I left you, doesn't mean you didn't cross my mind. I just can't bring myself to dwell much on the past. It hurts." He didn't blink, in fact his intensity grew as he honed in on my words. "We spent four days burning bodies and digging graves once I got home. I wished you were there to sing for them, for all we had to offer were tears."

"I would have gladly sung hymns for the fallen," he stated, before adding. "*We?*"

Air went stale in my lungs. I wasn't prepared for that discussion. "Not yet."

"That's fine, I am a patient creature."

Laying horizontal I fluffed the pillow behind my neck. "Aren't all immortals?"

"Definitely not. Three of my brothers are prime examples. And Judeth, Warroh's Ilanthian partner, she will set a whole match box up waiting for a candle to catch."

"That should be a requirement after one hundred years, give or take," I teased as Zander reached to turn off the lights. My heart rate picked up as my eyes adjusted to the dimness. I was suddenly all too aware that he had given me his bed when he had been visibly depleted and bordering on exhaustion for days. Guilt crept in.

A groggy voice beside me spoke, "Sleep, Wisteria. Fret not about the satisfaction of my slumber for I am quite content, more than I have been in many moons." Tingles crept up my left arm. He spoke the truth. "Unless you are daring enough to invite an incubus into bed with you, I suggest you rest well for I often don't let my prey sleep." Also, the truth.

"It has nothing to do with bravery because even logic is aware that my slender statue is irrelevant to the size of this massive bed. I think it has to do with your cowardliness, for you've not forgotten I hold no hesitancy when it comes to castrating a man for unwanted advances. I'm a very intimidating person, it's alright to be scared to sleep next to me."

A guttural purring sound filled the room, a noise I hadn't heard from a human before. It felt like a warning and yet a pleasurable exhale. My chest tightened. "I'll reiterate it as many times as necessary. I will give you no reason to castrate me." He echoed a familiar phrase. The last time he had made this comment I held a dagger to his manhood, that would be a horrific way to kill an incubus. Probably, the worst, I decided.

Uncertain of how to make use of our mental channel of communication, my words caught in my throat realizing the only way to get my gratitude across was to say it plainly. "Zander?"

"Wisteria?"

"Thank you, for waiting for me." My mouth went dry. "You probably have everything you've ever wanted, but if you dream up something an unorthodox woodlander can create for you, I expect to be told. I don't like to be indebted."

"There is no debt to be paid. None is owed," Zander's heavy head lifted up as he spoke. "But if you insist, I'll ask something of you in the future, don't be surprised if it's eccentric, for I am a dreamer being and we pride ourselves on obtaining the unimaginable."

I rolled onto my stomach, tucking my arms up by my chin. "I accept your challenge."

Chapter Eight

Heat was everywhere, I rolled around on a soft pillow top shedding a blanket that was too large and too heavy for the onslaught of warmth. I had rested gloriously all night without an inkling of nightmares and refused to acknowledge my sweet slumber ending. I squeezed my eyes tight. My limbs stretched in each direction, the edge of the bed nowhere to be found. To my left, there was an obstinate pillow. I glared at the object interrupting my languid morning.

Fennick was seated upright, casually crossing his outstretched legs on the far side of the bed. Zander was slumped over in his chair with a pillow rolled at the crook of his neck. Someone had taken to removing his boots and braiding his hair whilst he slept. Likely, his doting bonded fox.

The covers I had kicked off were bunched at the bottom of the bed leaving me lounging around mostly naked in Zander's tunic. I was grateful for my mass of hair that covered the plunging neckline of the collar.

Fennick hardly noticed me, the morning sun streaming through behind us was enough for him to read a book. He was engrossed in literature. When I did a double take at the blue cover, I caught a flash of a smile. I launched next to him and snatched the book from his open hands. Hastily, I flipped through the pages of unsmeared ink and unfolded that pristine painting of the Eleven and the map of Kinlyra they created. "I thought the rain would have destroyed it," I piped up excitedly in a tone I hoped was quiet enough not to wake the guard in the room or those outside the four walls. "Did you set the pages right?" The elemental gave a short nod. There was reverence in the manner that Fennick ogled the Eternals and a longing in how he scrutinized the map. He didn't noticed me curl up next to him and press my attention to the same parchment as he. Heat simmered at our contact.

Without his soiled attire and smudged ashes typically worn on his face, Fennick's skin shone a shade of browns and goldens that matched his eyes. His hair was cut to make the patches of bright silver less recognizable. I hadn't been imagining things when we rode together on horseback, he radiated heat more intensely than a central home furnace without bursting into flame or breaking a sweat.

Fennick rotated the book and tapped his finger on the back cover. He drew my attention to a signature, that of Captain Cultee, above it was lines of the book's previous owners, including a Duke Michael Monte and King Resig Torval. At the top in printed script, *This Book is the Property of:* A suspicious brow rose at me. "I'm not a thief," I grumbled. "It will be back on his office shelf before the week's end."

He opened back up the widespread centerfold. I moved closer. "Where is the Veil?"

Near the southern portion of the Thalren Mountains Fennick placed his fingertip and moved it up the span of the page, ending at the depiction of Oyokos. Gimly had said the Great Divide was difficult and perilous to anyone who crossed by way of walking. It was more than a blockage of stone and ancient magic, it was an entire *realm*, where the dreamers resided. My mind flooded with possibilities, I tried imagining what reapers and sprites did for entertainment, although I had no idea of what their true nature entailed or even what they looked like. Fennick snapped his fingers, summoning me out of a trance. He pointed by our toes.

The table near the pile of coals was set with water and warmed biscuits. The dry line in front held my trousers, tunic and flimsy bra. I received no further instructions from him, he laid down and covered his face with the open book. "Am I to assume this is your extent of privacy? Why Nikki, you are ceaselessly thoughtful."

My mumbled sarcasm stirred Zander in his chair. "There is a privy with a drawn curtain behind me," sleep coated his voice, the rest of him remained immobile. "You can also use Fen's room, our rooms are connected with the oak door by the fireplace."

I rolled out of bed and grabbed the dried clothes on the line. "Seems irrelevant being as he has seen my nipple piercings already." I placed a large bite of biscuit in my mouth. Crumbs dusted down the neckline of Zander's shirt. I attempted to tiptoe around the bulky chair and found the incubus was no longer a resting statue, he stared at my face which was stuffed full of bread pocketed in my cheeks.

"I figured it out," he stated indolently, a dimpled grin slowly creeping up onto his face. Unable to talk, I chewed. "If you were born a dreamer being, you'd be an elemental. The first earth chipmunk." I choked as I simultaneously pulled my arm back to punch him. "It's the stuffed cheeks that really convince me I've arrived at the most suitable creature for you." I dropped my clothes and threw my fists at his shoulder which sent him howling harder and Fennick, well he was doubled over on his feet biting a towel to keep his silence. Finally, I landed a solid punch that set a brief grimace on his face. That pleased me enough to stop bombarding him. That and my fingers felt as if they had been slamming a wall for the last minute and ached. "A violent, adorable chipmunk," he reiterated.

I strutted over to the bed and yanked the disheveled blanket off and with it I covered Zander's face which remained bright with humor. "For the record, I'd be a squirrel," I hissed at both of them.

I changed attire and freshened up with the basin on the other side of the drab curtain, unable to tame my unruly hair, I let it sway. I tugged the fabric off Zander's head and waved a warning finger at him when he rose to indulge in the platter of ham and eggs his fox friend had scrounged up. He pushed the berries off his plate and with the tip of his fork he scooted them to my side of the table. He tore into the meat, its bloody juices dripping around his plate. Ew.

I muttered, "I have concerns about the lack of variety in your diet."

"The only thing regarding my diet you should concern yourself with, is not becoming part of it." He smacked his lips before raising a glass of water to them.

"I'm a delicacy far too exquisite to be on your menu, Halfmoon," I retorted, leaving out the plain fact I had no desire to court anyone nor the reserves to engage in anything that expended emotional energy. Whatever bond Zander thought we had, I hoped it wasn't draining or requiring tending to. I popped the small handful of fruit into my mouth. The blackberries were soft and tart, harvested too late in the season. I grinded the seeds with my teeth and washed them down with my own canteen of water, aware that the commotion in the hallway meant Fort Fell had awoken.

Zander spoke as if he had read my mind. "The rains have turned to snow and they will return. They tend to cast a dreary spell over the town this time of year. One that puts the shops and pub at a standstill until the sun returns to lift spirits. The staff in the fort will work to can, jar and ready the shelves for the months ahead. The scribes and traders are working on the next import of goods as well as arranging safe transport for the captain when he is called to Landsfell for the gala. If you want to burrow yourself away in my chambers for the next few days with a book and a warm bath while I scout west for villagers, I deem it a wonderful choice. No one is dumb enough to trespass inside and you can take your exit in Fen's shadow when you're ready. The fort no longer finds it strange that we board together, Fen played his part so well I believe he is beginning to enjoy being my male consort," he tossed over his shoulder. Fennick threw a dagger at Zander who caught it by the feather decorated hilt and placed it between us. It was a unique dagger, not in shape, but in the color of the metal. It caught a deep hue of red.

"The guardian dagger, a blade forged with the blood of a griffin. It's a horrifying weapon, those who meet their end by the dagger, never see the afterlife. Their souls vanish before the beyond can ever part for them." He did me the courtesy of swallowing before talking with a mouth of masticated meat. "Fennick's family heirloom is the only guardian dagger I've seen. My father swore he saw another one carried by the Goddess Misotaka on her belt during the war of the Great Divide." My tongue slacked. I didn't know what to ask first. "My dad is old, yes. Old enough to have seen most of the Eleven. I have not, I told you I am a young male to my kind. I've met two."

I tucked my knee up under my chin. "It was... a war?"

"The *first* war. God's took sides, five with the vibrant and five with the blessed—a slightly nicer way of saying red or silver blooded," he educated while I mulled over his words. "One God refused to take sides, reminding his brothers and sisters that despite how long their creations lived, their end destination is the same. They would all end up together and undisguisable by blood, in the beyond."

Zander shoveled the rest of his scrambled eggs into a neat pile on his fork. "Oyokos, the first Overlord of the dream realm, expended nearly all his power to summon Thalren's peaks. It was meant to serve as a reminder for the entire *living* race that the differences between them mattered not. It was meant to fuse the two lands together, which it had done. It allowed the dreamer beings a place to interact and inspire wonder, for that was the sole purpose of our creation in the beginning of time. The Eternals had been reminded of that and called to halt the marching armies. That war ended with a new found fondness of one another. The humans found crafting and immense joy in exploration. The blessed relished their science and delight of preserving history. The dreamers were able to mediate the unseen and tangible with our diverse magic abilities. I hear it was paradisiacal."

Farfetched, but yes, paradisiacal. I couldn't begin to fathom such a blend of people.

"Over the centuries the Eleven dwindled. Context was lost. Memories faded. Historic feats became rumors. Thalren was no longer the seam that held two massive nations together, it was the Great Divide. The ultimate rift teaming with unknowns to be feared and seldom ventured over. There is no blame to be cast on the populations at large, for we are mostly innocent. From the crafters to the estate holders in the capital, the engineers of the White Tower and the pixies of the Glenwynd are not to be held individually accountable for what we simply do not know. Yet, blame must be cast for equilibrium to find itself again. Integrated peace thereafter."

He cleared his plate, quieter and more politely than the last time I saw him hold utensils. "Well, that's a different spin on the tale I've been told. Then again, I'm a rural woodlander who learned most things from plants, seasons and one of Athromancia's convoys that landed on our land before I hit puberty. Mind you the Ilanthians we lived with never mentioned anything that exciting about their nation after the ice melted and the Montuse migrated south." I glanced between the two men in the room who seemed caught off guard with my confession. I disregarded their expressions. "Which one of us gets to tell Gimly he's wrong? I volunteer myself." This earned me a snort from the bed.

"Fen believes you take too many risks. If he hadn't been loitering outside the capt's office last week, who knows how long you would have lasted before chopping Gimly into little chunks after that history lesson," Zander announced.

I shook my head and pointed to my heart. "And to that, I remind you gentlemen that I am a human. I am here for a *good* time, not a *long* time. Don't ruin my fun by telling me Nikki has a soft spot for keeping me alive." Two pillows knocked my head, I was so disoriented I didn't see Fennick leave. The water glasses tipped over. I laughed as small streams of water trickled on my lap and flooded Zander's empty plate. I stood to swat away droplets of water from pooling on my pants. "It was worth it," I admitted.

"Befriending the Empress's handpicked travelers or pissing my woven off?"

"Woven is the official term?"

"Two people wove together by the threads of fate crossed by the Weaver. Woven."

I thought of my two strains of light. "Can you have more than one woven?"

"It's not according to Fen's father at least. He is old and he knows things. He retired as a librarian and architect decades ago, but still frequents Akelis's archives if he is clear headed." Zander mopped up the water on the table with a dirty shirt from the floor. His lips pursed in thought. "So, which was worth it? Taking in Athromancia's comrades or sending Fen on one of his tangents?"

"Remains to be seen. Potentially both if he starts lighting things on fire."

"We are far from home, far away from his main magic source. He can't shift nor detonate things in his normal manner as when his stores are filled."

I picked up the guardian dagger while Zander cleaned the surface beneath. My hands hummed, as if the blade emitted a frequency. No, it pulsed rhythmically. "It is alive. I can feel its heartbeat."

"Your intuition is honed," he paused briefly. "The weapon emits a vibration that if not in tune with the wielder's, will drive them to insanity in a short period of months. Fennick and his forebears have yet to lose themselves to its drive. Even Maruc saw fit that the blade remains within their elemental community. Hidden safely in the fox's hallows."

"Pity he foolishly abandoned such a treasure." It gave a sharp thud as I placed it on the wooden top.

Zander tossed the soggy shirt into the corner and skillfully spun the dagger around his wrist before pocketing it. "Or he remembered I am riding out in a matter of minutes and want nothing more than to end the existence of wraiths for they don't belong in the afterlife either. This blade ensures their total termination."

My chest ached. The names of those I killed burned like ashes in my mouth. I debated whether or not to ask the next question. "What of the soul that inhabited the body before the transition into the undead?"

The horselord wiggled his large feet into the steel toe boots. He tied his hair back before speaking. "Depends on the state of the body. If obsidian has taken their eyes and their motives grow impulsive, they tend to enter the Veil as a haunted wanderer and gather with the rest of their kind at the northern runestone, but never pass into the fields of plenty. Those who are killed and burned before that stage of transformation seem to have better outcomes and are easily transferred beyond."

"That is aligned with our beliefs as well." Internally, I listed off the seventeen names of people I had *murdered* after discovering they had been bitten or exhibiting traits of the restless. This was a list I would carry with me until I could ask for their forgiveness in the near future, when death finally came for me. "I'll stay here for the day. It's alright if Nikki doesn't return, I don't mind being seen leaving here alone." Zander tucked in his red shirt and fastened his belt with his trademark belt buckle I'm sure most here had the pleasure of removing, if not at least thought about doing so a half dozen times. Except me. My eyes trailed up his body as he grabbed his cloak from the hook on the wall. I could admit he was a man, a kind one, an intriguing one, an annoying one, uniquely crafted but I would not be foolish enough to invest. Nor was I dumb enough to flirt back with him. "I will probably fall back asleep," I also admitted to myself.

"Submerge in the bath whilst it's warm. I've tunics a plenty in the dresser, blankets in the chest, books stashed behind the headboard, and the book you *borrowed* from cap's office I would refer to as historical fiction, if you are looking for authentic texts, dig around for the handwritten ones. I believe I snuck some fun scripts out of my father's collection before I left. With the intent to return them of course."

His attempts to pull a smile from me were successful. "Try not to fall off Rosie. And don't forget to fasten the clasp underneath her ribs. Apparently, that's an important one."

"Only if you intend to stay on the saddle, which is grossly overrated," he mocked, opening the door to take leave. "You'll be alright?"

"Obviously. If I'm not, I'm sure you will come storming in with your life on the line, entirely uncalled for. Trying to rescue a girl who never wanted to be rescued." His hood went up. I stepped towards him. "Why did you do it?"

"Do what? Remove you from the prison cell?" I nodded. He tipped his torso back and waved to the guards passing in the hall. "Because, whether you are going to admit it or not, you needed rescuing," he whispered quickly with the door half ajar. His tone left no room for debate.

I debated nonetheless.

"You could have been a sympathetic passing stranger and set me free without making the vow in the first place." Zander moved his weight pensively from foot to foot as guards moved across the hall behind him. I kept talking. "I asked you in the dungeons before you called in the Gods to witness your promise, what had you to gain. To that you coldly stated, *'My motives are my own.'* If you cannot reply, I cannot promise I will be your ally when you return."

"You consider us allies? I'm flattered that my attempts to call your attention have been a success." I gritted my teeth at his overconfidence. A horn blew outside from the encampment. The frantic men began to ready themselves at the doors. "You ask such a quarry now, as I am being summoned to ride out?"

"Do you find the answer difficult?"

He shook his head. "Not difficult, no. Tying myself to you was an easy decision, which is the terrifying part. Outside of reacting to the peaks and valleys of your emotions, I just wanted to. I don't fight fate anymore, Wisteria." His back foot stepped into the hallway after someone called his name.

"You just wanted to."

He spoke coolly, "That's what I said." Zander adjusted his posture to appear innocent. Devilishly innocent. "And lies from my lips will never grace your ears, Wisteria. I'll see you after the storm." He winked and closed me inside his room. Drift's boisterous personality woke up the remainder of the residents who managed to slumber through the horn's blast and ruckus.

I wouldn't miss him. Not at all, I vowed.

A proper warm bath with soaps and oils, however, *that* was a different story. I didn't leave the bath until my skin wrinkled and the waters chilled. Zander had a brush which I helped myself to, my hair shone with volume I'd forgotten it had. Deciding my own attire was too restrictive for a lazy day I lounged around in one of his too big tunics, not bothering to button the front or tie up the sleeves for the fire fox had left the coals and bark smoldering.

Dozens of rolled parchments and preserved scripts were found in the leather case at the head of his bed. I opted on reading pages of poetry and vespers, that depicted a world vastly different than my own in the most elegant penmanship I've seen. These spoke of warm winds, hearty laughing, sensual touches and evoked emotions I've long denied myself access to. The nap I succumbed to extended into the next day. It was drizzling and dark when I awoke in disorientation.

I hurriedly wiped my drool off the pages and glanced around to ensure I was alone. The last thing I wanted was Fennick to have the flattering image of me naked and slobbering in his arsenal to toss in my direction, should he need blackmail. There was a bowl of sprouts with garlic and minced onions left on the table. *Shit.* It was too late. He had already been here.

I groaned, tossing my legs around to feel my muscles stretch and lengthen. I arched my back and rolled my neck amid a plush pile of hair, cracking the stiffness out of my back with a few short movements. An ache grew in the lowest portion of my navel, my mind reiterated the erotic phrases of the author indulging in a woman's nectar, fruit and flower. My hands roamed over my hardening nipples and massaged lower until gratification was eminent. I sighed into the nearest pillow. During climax I tugged the fabric of the bed against my thighs to dispel the waves that shuddered through my legs to my toes. Whatever rampant fears I had about finding my friends in Landsfell dissolved a matter of minutes.

My hunger was the next desire to be met. Then my curiosity was fed by starting another chapter of the bound papers. I read about the humor of the twins, Dradion and Drommal. Their tricks of oceans flooding and skies raining fire upon each other seemed destructive and extreme, alas, they were responsible for the shape of the world. Often, they were spoken of with animal familiars who they bestowed with magic. When they chose to leave the earthly realm, they infused their spirits into several of their familiars, who went on to sire the elementals. Elementals who went on to find their woven, their lifelong comrades.

I found a blank parchment and began to jot my questions.

Do all elementals have woven because they are derived from the twins who had a bond or because that gave their power to their familiars?
How are you going to make Cultee a duke?
What does your real form look like?
Do you know the layout of Stegin's estate?
Why are you and your Overlord continuing to hide the truth from innocent humans, why won't you intervene?
How does your eye work?
Why did they call back the mixed bloods to the White Tower when the king asked for aid?

On and on the catalog of curiosities went.

It was a list I certainly couldn't be caught with for I should not know literacy with my heritage. The thought of retreating back to a cold, hard cot in a room with no lighting or source of heat when a proper mattress and heavy blankets were available here in a room of privacy, seemed outrageous.

Zander did say I could stay until his arrival, which may be several more days off. I was no fool, I knew to accept a safe circumstance while available to me and at no harm to others.

Fennick had splayed my belongings by the white coals, my dried herbs and pipe resting on the far right. I grabbed them as well as the blue bound book and curled up on Zander's chair which could have easily fit two of me side by side. I scoured the pages for any mention of *vulborg*. I was high and halfway through the book by the time Fennick slid through the door with a pitcher of water, lentil soup and apple pie for two. His eyes moved towards the simmering pipe, mine towards the pie.

With a raise of a brow, we made the switch.

I devoured the pastry in the short time it had taken him to slump onto the foot of the bed in relaxation. It was strange seeing him so at ease. Foxes were always watchful and on high alert. "Did you know this book depicts Resig's maternal lineage being gifted the heart of Goddess Anuli? It says she willingly let her cut it out of her rib cage to ingest as her final endowment to Numaal. No wonder the royals think they are better than everyone else, they have fancy blood." Fennick rolled his head towards me so I could see his brows raise. "Is it true?"

He shrugged.

"How insightful," I sighed. There was no point in asking him about *vulborg* if the response would be as irksome. I put the ink pen to the paper and scribbled my thoughts on the ever-growing list.

Why would Anuli, Goddess of compassion and charity, do such an act? Was it pity that drove such a violent end? Were mortals pathetic in the eyes of our own creators that they martyred themselves rather than see what became of us?

Fennick flicked the creased spot between my eyes. "Ouch! What was that for?" Propped up on his elbows he leaned over the table to glance at what I had been writing. It wasn't long before he snatched it out from under my nose and placed an annoyingly devious grin on his face as he read down the paper. His gold eyes brighten with humor. "I'm eating your portion of pie. That's the price you pay for the smug look on your face and invading my privacy." The apples tasted sweeter the second time.

I meticulously licked every remnant of the sauce clean off the fork before setting it down on the barren plate with a subtle rattle. A pie that delectable, I hadn't enjoyed since my mother's cooking. I shut my eyes to savor the arising memories of Lily dancing around the kitchen shaving the apples while my father would come in from behind to steal her away for a lasting kiss when he thought I wasn't watching. I was always watching, they were disgustingly in love, it was impossible to turn away. My sinuses burned at the tender recollection of my parent's marriage. The loss of Anna's companionship stung through my core, any hope I had of a life partner—gone. I held my breath. And only when I came for air was drawn out of the trance. My throat coated in grief, I washed it down with several swallows of water.

Fennick divided up the servings of lentils and he poured me an extra ladle. The thick cuts of carrots and plump kernels of corn were filling, I whimpered with satisfaction falling back into the bulky wooden chair constructed for a giant. "What part of Zander's genetics made him colossal?" I held up one finger and said. "Horselord." A second finger. "Or incubus."

He held up number two. Finally, a fucking answer.

"Is it hard for you to stay in a man's form too?"

He signaled no. His aloof gold eyes crossed over me, the crease marks by his nose pinched up as he debated opening his mouth. His lower lip caught in his white teeth. "I've heard you speak. You don't have to hold up your charade with me."

Muteness persisted. I don't know why I expected anything else. I toss the notion of a normal conversation or getting answers out the window and into the shitty rain.

I laxed my posture and slumped over the pages of the hardcover.

Come morning, Fennick stole away the captain's book and returned it before the fort awoke. I folded away Zander's shirts in his bureau and made his bed upon my exit. I was a far better house guest than he was at upkeeping his own room.

The dampness of the week's rain set the progress of the drying herbs back more than a moon phase. In the low light of the midday sun, I inspected the delicate petals between my thumb and forefinger. Pine strode into the vicinity with his goggles already strapped onto his face, he brought a hammer down on a rough mold of a spear, honing it into a sharp shape with brunt strength. Handfuls of jagged poles were lined up against the wall, waiting to be fashioned into effective weapons. Steam rose from the bucket under his scrap table as he plunged a piping hot tip of iron in.

I paused my work to watch the steam dissipate. "Have you scrapings to forge a jewelry piece? Something small."

The clanging of his hammer stopped. "Haven't you enough rods of metal pierced in your flesh? For each vial of poison on you, there's an antidote, right? That's the law of the master class."

"A ring," I cracked. "With a gap small enough to fit a cliff pearl in its prongs."

"You're tipping the scales," he whispered with more humor than concern.

I gave a shrug. "I am the only master woodlander left in these parts, I've nobody to hold me accountable to the old laws. If I see fit to hold extra resources on my body in a time when we are being murdered by nightwalkers and living in fear with no hopes for a better tomorrow, I'm going to do as I please."

His spear glowed white in the kiln's flames. "Size five or six?"

"Five," I answered cheerfully, wiggling my dainty fingers in his direction.

"I can pour your ring by the week's end. It won't be buffed until I can make time to borrow the smaller grinding stone from Crocker Street."

On his table I placed a sprig of infant fern as a token of gratitude and wandered my way into town, for there was nothing in the storage that called for my attention and my poor ears were ringing with the deafening sound of hammer on hot iron. My mind was too preoccupied with Zander's whereabouts and Cultee's discoveries to properly become acquainted with people. I aimlessly wandered up and down Crocker Street along with several other residents who scanned the hazy horizon hoping to see a team of horses emerge from it or the watchtower beacon be lit signaling the captain's arrival.

The following day was spent in the same manner, scrutinizing the fields for signs of the guard's return. Only this time I brought warm tea and Raina's scarf with me to keep warm as I strode. Perhaps what had delayed their arrivals was them returning with the dwellers of Horn's End, my vagabond comrades, who had to travel light and slowly on foot.

My boots itched as my eyes fell on the western road. I'm sure the small fort town would be in a chatty uproar when their guards arrived, it would be impossible to avoid that as a topic of conversation. I thawed my bones that evening helping Raina in whatever manner she saw fit for me. I mostly kneaded sourdough until my wrist locked. I cleaned the common room's table between guests, picking up conversations that didn't strike my interest.

A horn blowing alerted me out of my rest. The sun had risen within the hour. Partially clean clothes found their way onto my back, my toes crammed into the boots and stepped down the hallway. The stables were full of mounts and the barn hands were tending to the recent arrivals. No sign of Cultee or his seven-foot understudy. I greeted Rosie and offered her a sapling from over the rails. She devoured it. This earned me glances from the workers trying to do their tacks. "Did they arrive in good health?"

"Alone and with no noticeable injuries. They were covered in grime, ordered to bathe before emptying the kitchen of its stocks. We received orders to feed and clip the horses for a fast turnaround, within twenty-four hours I presume. They are leaving tomorrow." I was off to the hall before I registered what had been disclosed.

Cultee was not visibly in the vicinity. Zander couldn't be missed, he was swarmed by nearly every of-age female that worked in Fort Fell, his eyes flirted with them while his hands clutched the utensils which bent under the strength of his grip. I could practically hear the loud chomping of his breakfast in between his coy remarks to the ladies. I snickered under my scarf at the world around him falling prey to his incubus mannerisms.

I waited.

Normally, his eyes would have found mine within a span of several seconds and he'd have risen from his seat to pester me. That was not the case today. He avoided my gaze and even pivoted on his bench to where his shoulder blocked out my presence. A pretty ebony skinned woman took to toying with the ends of his wet hair. I wasn't offended, nor hurt. But, I was confused.

Disappointed, really.

I thought I had a true confidant, one that knew my past and would continue to walk beside me in the present. Instead, I was given an incubus with personality disorders who made a vow to a mortal on a whim *because he wanted to.* After weeks of trying to get my attention, he obtained it. Then proceeded to squander it.

I hated games. I just wanted answers and a plan to get my family to safety, a duke slain and my ass delivered to a place called Opal Lake.

I shoved my list of questions deeper into the pocket of my trousers. My hand curled into a fist around the folded parchment. I sighed and released it, along with my curiosity of what they discovered about Horn's End.

Hopefully, *who* they discovered.

I watched Pine shape, chisel and hammer spears the majority of the afternoon. When he was off the job, there was no hesitation in pulling me alongside him and venturing into the tavern. It was half as full as it had been the week before the most recent attack on the town, people wanted to keep their wits about them. We sat cozily at a table with our rye bread and half bottle of whiskey. Neither of us spoke much, there was a melancholy that lingered. It was audible in the strings of the guitar as well. One of the bar maidens saw our water refilled and upon return she spoke into my ear. "Curtain six." She spun away and onto the next table with a pitcher in her hands. Sage.

Pine looked troubled. "What's that about?"

My left hand rummaged in my satchel. I had basic supplies with me, I hoped Sage didn't have a need for any of it. "I'm in the mood for a brothel visit. I'll see myself out," I said to Pine who motioned to escort me. I deferred and tousled his short mop of hair.

"They search everyone at the door. Try not to enjoy yourself too much," he warned with an amused drunken smile. I was happy to hear the brothel had implemented measures to keep the workers' wellbeing a priority.

The lights glowed a dim, alluring red from the reflecting drapes. The scent of tobacco and perfume hit my senses when the door opened and warmth poured out. The hostess wrapped her satin scarf around my neck and led me into the front room where the eyes of several dancers and a few of its patrons found me. I stripped off my shirt before she asked to pat down my pockets, my thin lacey lingerie revealed the flesh beneath. Aside from my leather pants, my bra was as skimpy as the worker's. I whispered, "I've been called upon." We shared a devilish smile when my hands wrapped around her round waist. I felt her hands search the pockets of my pants and caress the round of my ass. A giggle broke through. "I'll leave payment on the counter after I've seen curtain six."

The affection stopped as she took me by the hands and led me through the dispersed crowd of men eased onto chairs beckoning female dancers who spun gracefully around hanging satins and platforms performing. They were alluring and confident, much like Anna had been. I paused to relish their beauty as one dancer prowled closer. I met her midway in the aisle to show my appreciation for her by means of flattery.

Her reaction to my blunt compliment was a light kiss on my collar bone that felt feathery against my bare flesh. Her dark features and skin was a beautiful compliment to mine, the alternating pattern our fingers made when they locked together was catching. The man on the chaise cleared his throat, subtly demanding attention. I stepped back from the woman and collected myself. *Sage*, I reiterated mentally, banishing distractions. The grumpy man splayed on the seat summoned the dancer without words or coinage. Drift had merely positioned himself upright on the edge of the cushion and sharpened his gaze to where his desires were obvious.

And it was obvious he was pretending I didn't exist.

I was nothing but an obstacle to his meal.

By the time I made it to the stairwell, my own desires had simmered down to a dull roar. Which was fortunate because what lay behind curtain six was enough to mute any positive feeling.

Chapter Nine

Blood pooled on the stone and wood paneled floor, under where Sage stood clutching her stomach in silent agony. I dropped to my knees in the middle of it, the warmth of the fresh blood saturated my pants. She held up her dress for me to see the rivers of red flowing down her thighs. A miscarriage and a hemorrhage.

"Sage," I rose and quietly stated her name to gather her focus. Tears had caused her eyes to puff and swell. "You need to lay down, while I manage the bleed." She numbly nodded and dropped onto the bed, wincing with every movement. I assisted her in lying flat and pressed my index and middle finger onto her wrist, checking for her radial pulse. It was rapid and thready. "Have you passed all the lining?"

She numbly shook her head. "I can't bring myself to look." She pointed to a bundled sheet at the foot of the bed. Reverently, I checked the contents. She hadn't passed the placenta, which explained the excessive bleeding and relentless pain skewing her delicate features. I prayed my expression stayed soft and undisturbed when I looked at her.

"How long have you been bleeding?"

Sage brought her knees to her chest and rolled onto her side. "Hours. The cramping started this morning, grandmother told me it would stop after the clots emptied from my womb. I can hardly stand nor see straight."

"I bet not. You've lost too much blood. I have to extract the rest if I am to keep you alive." Her already pale face grew a ghostly shade as she suppressed a blanch. "We need more support." I rubbed her temple and soothed away the forming worry lines. "Either the bar maiden that summoned me or the hostess of the brothel that brought me here... Raina, perhaps?"

"Chanah will check on me shortly. She works behind curtain five." Her knuckles turned white as she clamped her hands around mine in an intense wave of agony. Precious time passed while we waited. Finally, the curtains drew back. A young woman stood wide eyed in an open robe.

"Chanah?" She nodded vigorously. "I need clean towels and as many basins of hot water as you can manage. Run to the tavern and ask for Pine. He needs to get you stave bark, nettles and witch hazel to bring back here. In the kitchen you'll need to dig around for castor oil. I'll need at least a quart." I pointed to my cloak. "Wear that so you don't draw attention to yourself. These affairs are private and should be kept as such until Sage is of sound heart."

She grabbed the green garment and clipped the buckles under her chin. "Can't you give her willow bark or poppy milk?" Chanah's raspy voice was pitched high with nerves.

"Willow bark thins the blood and the poppy will stop her vascular system altogether. We can't afford either of those. Off with you. Now," I said, feeling my own heart pound in my chest with adrenaline.

I stripped away the rest of the blankets and sheets, as well as the rest of Sage's garments. In the side table I found candles. I lit all four of them, which cast little aid onto the dire situation. Sage propped her hips onto the pillow and opened her knees. I placed a rolled piece of cotton between her teeth so they didn't fracture when she'd grit down. "I am... immensely sorry," my own tone trembled seeing Sage scream without making a sound, all at my doing. I scraped the inside of her uterine lining and removed the last of the placenta. I applied pressure at the portal's opening with my hand and placed my forehead on her heaving chest. "You are strong," I exhaled. "You've battled yourself since conception and suffered today all in silence, permitting the world to carry on unperturbed. You are an amazing woman. I am honored to be called upon in such a vulnerable and sacred moment, Sage." Her wailing began. She panted into the pillow. "The healing can happen. You are both safe just on different sides of the veil."

The bed shook with her sobs, the rags between her legs were saturated but transitioning from bright red to a darker shade, implying the wound was starting to slow. Chanah entered the tiny room, first with the jars of herbs and oils, then with the towels and basins. She wasn't alone, the hostess brought incense, blessing candles and several changes of clothes and bed linens.

We worked synchronized in the dark of night until the break of day, taking shifts to comfort Sage with arms around her, applying medicine and gauze to her portal, wiping up blood and offering her teas to replenish what had been lost. Sage vocalized very little as we formed a circle and offered up the life of the lost little babe to the beings beyond and back into the embrace of the Eternals. It was a heartbreakingly beautiful moment to be a part of. Four women in nothing but our own skin and drenched in another's life essence. This blood didn't bother me. A very different circumstance than Anna's death had been, for in this moment there was a pervasive understanding of cycles, beginnings and endings. Anna's murder was senseless.

Sage standing posed too much of a risk to undo the efforts we had made to stop the hemorrhage. "Bedrest for the entire day. I'll find a way to bring you what you need," I warned sternly. She propped herself up enough to allow me to fit behind her. I pulled her back onto my chest and let her head fall on my shoulder. Chanah brought over a warm face towel to drape over her forehead and eyes. The hostess lifted the red soiled sheet to monitor the saturation of the cotton. She was at peace enough with the situation to collapse onto the bed beside us, Chanah sat on the floor scrubbing the dried blood off her hands.

I dared not move once Sage fell asleep. I happily allowed myself to be pinned to the headboard. The hostess rolled over onto her belly and lifted her chin towards the hall. "Footsteps," she whispered. By the sound of it, several pairs of footsteps approached.

Captain's modest black boots stood under the tail of the curtain. "Lady Ivy?"

The hostess and I exchanged a brief look of panic. "Captain?" I spoke in a low tone to avoid waking Sage.

"Are you decent?" He piped.

I cringed at the man who spoke next. "Does it matter?" Gimly groaned, impatient as ever.

"We are not." My reply interjected theirs, banter-sharp and venomous.

"*We*? Ivy, you tease," Gimly snickered darkly.

There was a hard swat of cane on stone. "Gimlian Monte, you are dismissed."

He hissed, "You can't send me off."

"I can. In fact, I just did."

"My father won't take kindly to your choices."

Captain's heels clicked as they dug into the ground. "Take leave and oversee the cleaning of the latrines. I expect to see my reflection on the shitseat when I return. If there is one drop of piss on the floor, you will relocate your room to the privy," Cultee barked in a firm, even tone. "That is an order. Best you not forget what happens to guards incapable of following simple orders." One pair of shoes scoffed off. Three remained. "Ladies, I can smell the blood and the floorboards are stained. Please, prepare for my entrance. I can't let such a horrendous scene go untended in my mind without confirming peace."

Chanah hid her torso behind one of the pillows she found on the floor. The hostess laid on her belly while I tugged up the corner of the crimson stained sheet to cover Sage's breasts. The curtains slowly opened, Cultee quickly scanned the room honing in on the buckets and basins of scarlet waters, damp red towels and a faint sickly Sage bedridden with towels under her hips. "A miscarriage sir. We've stabilized Sage, but if you have fresh waters and a decent bed, I will request that from you on her behalf. I agree to work whatever jobs necessary to afford her such comforts." I lowered my chin atop Sage's forehead. "She's feverish and bled out, we've barely recovered her to the point of fatigue and consciousness."

Drift and Asher poked their heads into the vicinity and dutifully saw themselves out. Asher's color looked worse off than Sage's. "Whatever needs she has, consider them fulfilled," Cultee stated, his focus fixated on the ungodly quantities of blood dispersed throughout the room. "In return, you will ride out with us at high noon. We congregate in the tactic room an hour before departure and you will wear the insulated gear provided in your sleep chambers. Nights are cold."

I found my arms hugging Sage tighter as he spoke of the frigid, dark nights. I remember all too well how unbearable they could be. "Yes, sir," I whispered, running my lips along Sage's hairline, her sweat left salt on my mouth. "You've found the village?"

His face was stern and pensive. "Tactic room. Eleven. Don't be late." A hopeful little butterfly danced in my stomach causing it to flip and tumble with a foreign giddiness. The three pairs of boots clomped away. We women gave an exhale of nervous energy that left Chanah in a fit of anxiety driven giggles. I dispensed with education on how to tend to Sage the remainder of the day and upcoming week. The hostess rearranged the room with aggression tense in her movements. "None of this should have happened," she cried bitterly, scrubbing the heating pipes.

"No, it shouldn't have," I agreed, sparing Sage a pitiful glance.

"If he so much as stepped one foot in this room, I would have stabbed him in the eye. He isn't worthy enough to see the damage he's caused." She threw the burnt-out candle against the wall.

I steadied myself from a putrid influx of nausea. "Don't tell me her assaulter was Gimly."

"Ay, it was. That man is not fit to father a hoard of undead let alone a life of a human."

Hate coursed in my veins and through the room. "I'll handle him."

"You can't walk up to him and fight. He has ties in the high court."

My mind ran into dark and twisty alleys. I was a woodlander, the ways I could kill a man are as numerous as all the ways I can save one. "No, I can do better. Much better." I was certain there was a smile on my face as I left the brothel and strode into the kitchen. Raina set aside a special hop ale for Gimly. One that would prevent his atrocious tendencies from being active. I gave the bar maiden another dose in the off chance he dined out tonight. He fully deserved what I had set upon his future.

The women's bath chambers were bustling, which I found surprising given the odd hour of the day. Unsurprising, was the cold shower that fell from the spicket above, I hardly caught my breath at the downfall of poorly regulated water. I scrubbed until my flesh was raw and angry and the puddle at my feet a diluted shade of pink instead of thick red. Captain's choice of attire was graciously warm and well fitting. There were woolen undergarments and stockings, heavy tunics and a fleece lined jacket with my own pair of leather riding gloves. The gloves were oversized, yet welcomed. Lorelei came in to dry and braid my hair, tucking away the loose strands that may prove a hinderance on horseback. "You look like a brave knight of Numaal. Except you lack a sword," she said enviously.

"I look warm," I corrected and pointed to my face which was starting to flush under the layers. I kicked the dresser which held my old clothes and dagger. "Keep it safe," I said with a knowing smirk. Lorelei's gaping mouth was covered by her hands.

"I knew it was more than a steak knife," she skipped around the room, retaining a secret of two. I stepped into the hall with my light bag of clothes and as many scones as the seams could carry. "When you get back can you show me how to use it?"

My feet halted. "Definitely not with a steak knife. I'm opposed to the slaughter of innocent animals. However, it has fileted its fair share of restless walkers and disassembled their bodies. So, in that sense, I guess you could say it's cut into meat." Lorelei blinked.

She twirled her hair around her forefinger. "Is that a yes?"

"Keep it safe. Keep it secret. If you can do that, then the answer is not a no." She hugged my waist as I left.

There were ten, including me, crammed into the tactic room. A smell of musky men and fallen leaves met me. Zander lingered outside the main vicinity, poking his head in to hear his captain's strategy for the caravan. "We will set out at eight riders with twelve mounts, four of you will be tethered to a spare and one to a cart. The cart will rest in the chosen location for the first night and be prepared to serve us when we return to it. Devnee, you will see it is kept safe and made use of in the troop's absence. There is fire and oil on it should things go wrong." Cultee made eye contact with a man who had silver in his goatee and scars on his chin.

"We will carry supplies to our peoples in the Wasteland, there are about forty survivors from a village called Horn's End which has recently been abandoned. I've seen this with my own eyes." Cultee held my gaze across the room. I did my best not to cry, only forty remained. "They won't accept our aid without seeing their friend, Ivy, is in good health and in trusted company. Hence, her accompanying us. She too wishes to see our countrymen and women provided safety. We learned they've limited expertise in combat and access to proper weapons. We've been tracking a hoard and estimate if we leave promptly, we will remain a full day ahead of them. Two days, if those on foot are in good condition to make haste on the return and weather stays at bay. Gimly, Ross and the bulk of the guards will remain here to defend the fort in our absence. It will be upheld. The town protected." He calmly glanced around the room. "Concerns or additional clarification?" Nobody budged.

We filed out of the office, conversations among the young and aged men picked up. Cultee pulled me aside by the elbow. "I hear you can shoot a bow. How well?"

I shrugged, "I'm decent."

"Decent is better than not at all." He yanked a full satchel of steel headed arrows off the wall and handed me a tightly strung white oak bow. I took it and caressed the elegant curvature and craftsmanship. "Keep up," he called from ahead of me. I strapped the arrows over my shoulder and locked the bow on my back. My smaller strides had me near sprinting to keep up with the captain who was fast approaching the stables. "You ride alone in the saddle. Drift thought it a good idea for you to gain experience on horseback especially if you are planning on borrowing his mount again." I snorted, knowing full well that the only reason I wasn't sharing a saddle with the horselord was because he was acting as if I didn't exist. "Considering your eventful night, if you find it difficult to stay alert you can ride share. We will fit you to a mount tomorrow if you wish to rest."

I eyed Zander's broad back and half shaved head. "I'm confident that I will be alright." Zander led Rosie out of the stables, brooding as he hulled the saddle atop his shoulder.

"Okay yes, fine." Captain spoke, dismissing my fluffy words. "Drift will see you squared away and fit atop Nordic. Copper will ride ahead of you because Nordic fancies his mount." He pointed to a brown steed with soft blonde spots scattered around his muzzle and neck. Nordic was a beauty. And gentle. He set his muzzle in my outstretched hand, the fuzzy hairs on his nose tickled my palm. The same stable hand that reprimanded me for running off was the same one who plopped Nordic's reins into my left hand and pointed to the dreamer being who was crouched over fastening that important buckle under Rosie's rib cage. Nordic clung close to me as we walked in stride out the barn.

"You are ignoring me," I said flatly.

He massaged his knees as he rose off the ground. "Yes." Zander tied his sweet-tempered mare to the post and walked around to the left side of Nordic, directly behind me. He busied his hands securing knots to my bag and the saddle.

"Can you at least give me the courtesy of explaining why you are upset with me?" I shrugged. The arrows on my back clamored with the slight movement.

"I am avoiding you. I never said I was upset with you." His piercing eyes peered down at me, there was undisputable fatigue in his face. No anger plagued him.

I crossed my arms. "You've not *said* anything. That's the problem."

"Up in the saddle," he directed, as two more guards led their mounts by us. One was my father's age and the other roughly mine, that was Copper. They each returned my smile. "Wisteria," grumbled an intolerant beast. I glared at him, placing my left foot in the stirrup and swinging my right over Nordic's back. The weight beneath me shifted, I clutched the horn on the front of the saddle trying not to appear uneasy. Zander stroked the long neck of the horse until he settled. "Shall I tell you what the real problem is?" He asked, measuring the length of the stirrups against my short frame and readjusting them accordingly.

"Tell me," I exhaled, bending my knee to the angle Zander deemed acceptable for riding.

"I told you not to become my meal and you've gone and made sure your scent is on every damn piece of clothing I own. And my sheets. And my pillow. You've sent me so close to a frenzy where I can't feed unless it's from you. As if I didn't have a difficult enough time in this realm already, I've gone lusting after the forbidden woman. Being in the same proximity strains my self-discipline." I shook my head at his serious tone.

"I've done no such thing," I defended myself. Zander laughed as he walked to readjust my right leg.

He put his hand on my knee. He squeezed tightly. It was warm. I didn't mind when he inched it up to my thigh to secure me upright as he removed my foot from the brackets. "What part about pleasuring yourself in the bedroom of an incubus seemed like a brilliant idea?" I felt faint. The slow turn of his head left me blushing. "You weren't kidding when you said you were a delicacy. Exquisite indeed." Zander raised his head to watch my face flush, smiling at my discomfort. A handsome smile that youthened his near two century old wisdom lines in his face.

"I did that. I didn't know... you'd... I'm sorry..." I squeaked out. "Is that why you look so haggard? You didn't eat last night?"

"Firstly, I'm not haggard. I'm rustically handsome. Secondly, my intention was to attempt to feed last night, then who shows up naked and strutting around the brothel smelling like the most luring nectar of the lands, but the very woman I am trying to avoid."

"I wasn't naked," I defended. My leg was pinched tighter as he steadied his breath. "I'm sorry," I swallowed again.

His tight squeeze lessened. "You didn't know. Hence, I'm not furious." He placed the reins in my hands and jumped into Rosie's saddle in a swift hop. "We have to discuss you being friends with an incubus and the nature of my habits to avoid predicaments in the future. You'll do good to remember we are highly possessive creatures. Once I have a scent, there is an inexplicable need to chase it. To obtain it. Irrational really. Luckily, there is only one of us here. The thought of you around my brothers makes me... *uncomfortable*. I was already chasing you, but now... " He shrugged off his thoughts on his behaviors. "During the trek we can strengthen our mind link. We can communicate by syphering while keeping our distance until I've found a way to feed. I'd hate to be useless in battle." I nodded, but I hadn't a clue on how to access our mind link or what a syphering communication looked like. "Then we can conquer that long list of questions stuffed into your pocket."

"Are you going to be alright without sex?"

His lips curled up revealing a straight white grin. "As I have said, it's more than sex. That is not to say I don't crave it and question my choices about remaining in this form. I've been celibate over the last two years which leads me to frequent the brothel to drink in the pleasure of others, that fills me enough to get by."

I tilted my head. "You'd lose your form if you were to engage in your own pleasure?"

He chewed his cheek in thought. "Yes."

"You are not alright and should have stayed back in Ross's place since I'll be gone. You're even *hazy* as if you were a painting with smudged lines and blurry details."

He made a noncommittal humming noise through his lips. "Alright. Riding basics." Zander went on detailing positioning, steering and safety measures to take for extended excursions, such as the one we were embarking on. I was warned about soreness, fatigue and maintaining myself upon a spooked horse. I was less than thrilled to hear almost anything and everything can spook a horse or cause skittishness. "These mounts are accustomed to riding together and follow each other's noses to rump on tight trails. Don't worry about him deciding to stray away."

"How many nights are we expecting to camp out?"

"Four to seven. The first two days we will ride hard. After we make contact and if they choose to join, our pace will slow with the extra company and the dangers of travel exponentially increase." Nordic's breath stalled in a frozen cloud as Cultee trotted into view, riderless mounts and carts of provisions followed him. It was time. I felt more excitement than fear pushing my chin up. Grey swept over the black stalks of dead trees in the distance. It was going to rain. Sleeting rain by the looks. I pulled my leathered gloves on, buttoned the large cuffs on my thin wrist. Raina's scarf I wrapped around my neck a second time. I rode in the middle, Copper in front, Asher directly behind me and Zander rounded out the back to keep an eye on the cart. Both quickly fell out of vision as our strides picked up into a canter.

Without another body to hold onto, my boney hind quarters repeatedly smacked the hard saddle, the bruises would not be pretty nor the recovery quick—not with several more days of horseback riding ahead of me. Once the sun set, I figured we'd slow to be more mindful of the ground beneath the dozen hooves, the opposite was true. Cultee drove harder into a wooded clearing, leading the way with a soft, portable electric lamp. Asher dropped in stride with me. He covered his freckled face which was chapped red with the wind whipping it. "The electric light doesn't give off heat like a fire would, nor a smoke trail," he educated. "At the top of the next hill we'll arrange the bedspreads and set sound traps to defend the cart when it comes. Are you feeling alright, you haven't touched your waterskin?"

I licked my lips. "Being the sole female on the trek, I didn't water to be the reason the troop stopped for respite."

"You are seriously starving yourself just so you don't have to pee?" He laughed so hard he snorted.

"Yes. I'm not tagging along as a burden. I'm here as an asset and want to be perceived as such."

"You're a master of a craft, no one here looks down upon you." He watched me reposition my hips and tuck another blanket under them. "Your ass sore?"

"Very. Please, tell me it gets better." I groaned, straightening my stiff legs in the stirrups to relieve pressure on my tailbone. My nose buried into Nordic's mane as a distraction.

"No. But your tolerance does, that's my experience anyways." Our mounts hastened, following the lead of those ahead of us. "Hang in there, Ivy. In a short while you will be lying flat on the ground." Asher prodded his horse and fell back into line. I pulled my chest low on the spine of the horse to balance myself atop uneven trotting, the tip of the bow knocked the back of my head with the jostling movement leaving yet another bruise.

The Rage of the Woodlands

I was grateful Zander wasn't there to watch me slip clumsily off Nordic and fall onto a patch of dirt. My legs felt detached, as if they hadn't belonged to me. My lower limbs didn't cooperate as I puddled onto the floor. Nordic circled me with curiosity, patiently waiting for me to lead him with the rest of the mounts to the creek and remove his heavy saddle for a few hours of respite. The minutes dredged along as slow as hours while coordination and sensation returned to my muscles.

Asher removed Nordic's saddle after he tended to his own. I thanked him and copied his movements on how to tie the reins into a loose slip knot—something very difficult to accomplish when there was an absence of light. Cultee watched from across the clearing his dim lantern shone just enough for shadows to form in the small space. I was beckoned once Nordic was good for the night. I grabbed a scone and my woolen blanket from the saddle bag and treaded to the light. "Your horse did well," he said, his gruff mustache hiding an awkward look of pleasantries. Perhaps that statement was meant to be a compliment. Unsure how to approach it. I agreed.

"He did."

"The rain is light tonight and our interval brief, we won't be spiking tents, however, I do ask that you leave space between your bedroll and these men until better arrangements can be reached."

"That was my plan as well, captain. If you have spare rope, I can sleep in the fern." I pointed behind him to a needle shedding tree whose branches were plenty wide to hold me comfortably for the night.

"Afraid the rope is on the cart, miss Ivy."

I shrugged. "I'll settle for sleeping under it. I've always enjoyed the scent of seasonal transitions and a cool ground holding moisture from recent rains. Saplings sprout around now too, their roots are tender, like cooked carrots, only not as sweet." Cultee adjusted his stance, his odd sort of smile remained under his uneven greying beard. I held my tongue from ranting.

"You're much like my sister; she had a knack for finding delight in life's simple things. And also, a brave and kind heart."

"I would have loved to ramble on to her. Is she at peace?"

"I hope so. Enough of my story, you need to retire for the evening. The morn will be here in two blinks of an eye." He walked off taking the glow of an electric bulb with him. The trunk of the tree was girthy enough to block the change in winds, the mounds of needles and fallen foliage I kicked into the shape of a nest around me and settled my body against the quiet ground and began to nibble my first meal of the voyage. The stars were blocked by a wet haze and tree branches. I craned my neck around hoping to catch a glimpse of a far-off world shining against the black velvet night. *The southern tip of the Storm Warrior constellation will be visible to the north just before dawn if the weather is in our favor. I smelt the winds. Storms are coming.*

Nosey. I rubbed my brow as I replied in my head.

You've not bothered to reach out to me and that offends my tender disposition. I gritted my teeth with his echoing sarcasm. *I can practically hear your eyes rolling.*

I rolled my eyes for real this time. *Because I don't know how to connect with you, you giant oaf! You gave no instructions or guidance, only a vague recommendation to strengthen our mind link, and used the word sypher. Whatever that is.* Humor pricked up on my left palm. *Stop laughing.*

Feisty. I enjoy it when you are fired up.

I don't like you at all.

We both know that is a lie. I choked on the dry crumbs of bread.

Take your time showing up so you don't infect the camp with your personality.

I'm conserving what little energy I have left. I'm not as optimistic as Cultee, I believe the wraiths are getting stronger and faster the more they grow in numbers. When they catch up, I want to be ready. Even after Zander burned down the entire plot of forest with over hundreds restless walkers, he believed it had done little good.

I'll protect you.

I know you will. Because you like me.

I tossed in under my blanket, hiding the anger and pestering he stirred in my bones. *You are the only one who can answer my questions. I need to keep you alive until it's convenient. Let's start: How do you plan on making Cultee duke of the south province?*

I'll answer that one after I, the giant oaf, explain accessing our mind link, which is one of the many manifestations of a bond granted to two people by the Weaver of fates. We are woven, this links us together in ways that the physical realm can't fathom. It's magic older than the earth itself. It is the same unseen force that continues to group the Eleven Eternals together world after world, infinities after infinities. The link allows us to deepen our connection and is opened first by acknowledging its existence, second willing it to seek me out and lastly securing it on both ends.

You came running to me every time I felt uneasy, but I never said one word out loud or in my head. Why can I feel your emotions and you mine?

Another manifestation of our bond, I reckon. Emotions transmit before words.

I've seen our bond before, it is a violet line. I saw two.

His intrigue grew. *Tell me more.*

When you made your vow, a ribbon of light shot directly out of my left hand towards the back corner of the dungeon where you were captive. It is in the same spot where I can feel your emotional state and that tingling of electricity when I interacted with you by the creek, as if it was reawakened. And the gold one was angled just a bit differently, enough to where I could separate them. Does that help you narrow down the type of threads of fate that are wrapped around us?

Yes. I'm surprised you saw her magic, when it was so brief. I blinked and missed its form.

Humans and magic were hardly used in the same sentences. Unless they were priestesses of Misotaka who were granted visions of foresight and premonitions. *I remember Fennick very clearly mentioning something about threads fraying and anchoring. He felt us. He sounded a lot more confident than you do in discussing this. Should I just talk to him about it?*

Eventually, we can. When we are comfortable. We have to wait until he stops being a mute. He is dedicated, we made a bet you see. If he can sustain silence until we fake the death of his persona, then I owe him a renovated room in my family's house. One that suits his taste and nature. I briefly wondered what a fox's sleeping arrangements were.

I deserve to know my own fate. You will tell me when you figure it out, for if I find you hiding such secrets from me, I'll make a new course in life to sever this thread.

I've never planned on keeping anything in my life undisclosed to you. We just need more time to explore it. The purpose of all threads is to bring people together, that part is simple. What is trickier is deciphering how we work in each other's lives. What roles to take.

You immortals always need more time. My knees drew to my chest as silence rung. *Fine, keep your secrets under the condition of giving me more aid in Landsfell. For my agenda is greater than murdering the duke, I also need to confirm the whereabouts of three silver bloods taken captive two years ago during the attack of the knights on our farm. I promised a man, a dear family friend, a reunion with his family. I intend to keep my word and see his wife and children freed from harmful hands. We are fleeing the shores the last week in December.*

That was an ambitious promise to make.

I practically snorted out loud. *So was a particularly spontaneous vow of protection from an oversized incubus to a half dead red blood.*

I can't wait to see your face when you realize this form is tiny compared to the form I take in the Veil.

Impossible, unless we are talking about your grossly inflated ego.

His humor moved through me, it failed to cover the sense of great wariness. I closed my eyes and dug into the unknown between him and I. It was dark and light, heavy and soft, jagged and welcoming.

I kept digging until I found him, a formless mass that resembled a midnight rainbow, dark and colorful simultaneously. He smelt of cool mint, sugary honey and freshly fallen rain in the deep of a green forest. I inhaled deeper. His wariness took the form of a rust-colored cloud that festered and ate away at him. He cleared space for me to move inward.

The wariness, however heavy and sticky, was nothing compared to the bright, alluring core that was kept in a cage on the far side of his consciousness. Whatever it was, it was breathtaking.

Down I dove.

Moving through the currents between us, time and space—I swam over to it.

The bursting sphere rattled the bars and called to me as I approached. I reached out to the ball of brilliant sun locked behind Zander's iron will. It rippled as if to wave a greeting to me. I smiled, my own green colors of contentment wrapped around the prison that held it.

It was earnest and enchanting. It wouldn't hurt me. It danced for me and flaunted its array of shimmers and countless forms. For a long time, I rested in stillness, enamored by the sun. I swore it winked at me. That was all it took for me to slip my hand between those iron bars.

No. No. An abruptness hit me as our bond was closed. *You're too brave. You're too confident, too curious. Admirable qualities, but you prompt your own demise.*

I felt cold.

Too cold to attempt to reconnect the two of us I curled into myself.

Chapter Ten

My shoulders shook so vigorously my head almost snapped off. "What in the bloody hell was that? Are you trying to give away our location, girl?" Someone screamed at me. Loudly. It didn't help the waves of nausea or the spells of dizziness. I clenched my gut and dry heaved towards a rough, flakey pillar.

It was a tree. A fern. And around me my nest of foliage. Beyond that, Captain Cultee and his guards all peering in my direction. A middle-aged man with a scarred brow was the one who had shook me from my nightmares. With his gritted teeth, he placed his hand on my shoulder as an apologetic act while I heaved up nothing a second time. "If you are visited by terrors in the following nights, I fear you either have to retreat or abandon sleep altogether. One more outburst like that and they will descend upon us as crow scavengers circle the dead."

Cultee moved forward. "We will have no chance of saving our stranded kin if she's leaves. She is to continue on without debate, Hades," he grunted, finishing the last of his water sack and refilling it in the stream at his feet. "You lot have a quarter hour to get refreshed and your bones atop readied mounts. If the entire sphere breaches the horizon and we are not moving, you will get left behind and fed to the leeches and the scavengers that Hades mentioned." Hades' silhouette blurred as a bead of sweat fell into my eye from my damp forehead, which couldn't compare to the saturated layers of tunics and scarves. Once in relative privacy, I stripped my cloak and the first of the three layers off my back and shook them into the wind. Asher walked up to the tree holding my arrows and bow.

"The water you've been avidly avoiding will help settle your queasy stomach and clear the demons from your mind. Besides, someone should mention that this is the last water source we will have access to until we pass through here on the return, it is rock formations and cliffs from now on. If you faint off your horse, that will tarnish your pristine reputation far more than requesting to stop and relieve yourself away from us," Asher said, nonchalantly leaning against the long trunk of the fern.

"Thanks for the consideration. Fainting would be far worse than violent nightmares waking up the Wasteland, right?" I whispered with a sore raspy voice.

His youthful freckled face grinned. "Absolutely."

I finished a full liter by the time Zander waved me down to watch the proper way to lift a saddle off a tack and place it on the blanket covering the horse's back. "I can do it." I motioned for him to take two steps back while I steadied the hard leather on my shoulder. On my tip toes I jumped and at the same time pushed the saddle above my head onto Nordic. I remained under his close supervision until he was satisfied with how tight I secured all the miscellaneous straps and buckles. Our bond wasn't as cold as it was last night, but it was barren.

We both had isolated ourselves in closed doors on opposite ends of our thread.

Captain was atop his mare chatting with Hades, who readjusted his scabbard on his hip, the tension between them had long been resolved by the looks of their cheerful dispositions. The rising sun was half awake, I placed my foot in the stirrup and kicked my stride over Nordic. Drift gave a harmless chuckle. "You forgot to untether your reins from the fence. I'm afraid you are not going anywhere."

I groaned as I slid off and stomped toward the fallen timbers that were made into a fence. "I would have happily assisted you, if you'd all but ask just a simple request from me," Zander's white portion of hair glowed translucent with the halo of sun creeping up behind him. He opened his connection a little, well unlocked his door.

"Which is exactly why I did it myself, Drift." I tossed my reins over the horn of the saddle and prepared my footing. Up I went. Out we rode.

The coal and copper mines were far more serrated than I remembered, granted I haven't explored these specific lands for they were out of my community's reach and lacking in plant growth. The guards and I had fallen into single file formation while trekking inclines, I opted to keep my focus ahead for if I peered downward I'd see everything that could go wrong.

On even fields, I closed my eyes and tried to find Zander in my mind. "I shouldn't have to mention that shutting your eyes while on a half-ton animal is an unsafe idea. Highly frowned upon."

"Noted. And I shouldn't have to mention that throwing my soul straight from the cozy connection into fucking cold, icy darkness last night was bullshit." I muttered aggressively to the man trotting side by side with me, the same one I was trying to link to. The clopping of hoofs on stone rubble was loud and constant. I couldn't vocalize anything more.

Knock, knock. There it was. A polite tap on my mental walls. I opened myself just enough to see a flurry of colors patiently standing in the abyss of our connection.

It was complete bullshit. I fucked up. I opened the door a little wider, happily accepting his apology. *Jilting you in such a harsh manner was incredibly rude, uncalled for and undoubtedly the reason your night terrors were sparked.*

You are right. I agreed, knowing I had terrors long before our syphering.

I permitted you to wander too close to my unprideful nature thinking you'd turn away in fear or disgust. You flocked to my darkness and reached out to it, practically gifting it keys to its enclosure. In a moment of panic, my consciousness did what it thought best to protect you and everyone in our company.

I stepped out of my mental compartment and met Zander halfway, his colors swarmed around me. He was comfortable. *I was pulling back your many physical layers and emotions, I didn't realize I trespassed.*

I let you in. I wanted you to see not knowing you could see so well in the dark.

This man had no idea what he was talking about. Had he such little insight into himself? *Can I tell you something about your imprisoned nature?*

It's horrendous, isn't it? I raised a brow. He sighed. *If you must.*

You called it darkness, but it was a blinding brilliant light. As if you captured the sun, swallowed it and kept it. It was alluring and sincere and practically spoke to me.

Zander made a clicking noise with his tongue and maneuvered Rosie around a red rock. *What did the luminosity seem to say?*

That he would protect me, be my sword and shield. That part of you would never hurt me—in fact, I bet my life on it. If you let me get better acquainted with it—I'm sure I can mediate peacefully between the two of you.

It horrifies me. That magic has done terrible damage, I can't let it out. You're not scared?

I reminisce fondly over the desperate and friendly 'nature' as he called it. It was energetic and powerful, but not dark and petrifying. *Are we talking about different things?*

It would be easier if we were. What question shall we tackle next? Cultee as duke?

Yes.

Gimlian Monte is Duke Stegin Monte's bastard son who the duchess wanted exiled. Gimly is his only male heir and Stegin would not banish him from the family line nor the province, Duchess Kacey sought a compromise, and Gimly was sent to live and work in Fort Fell until he proved himself wise enough to either be welcomed back into the family or strong enough to pass as a knight in Kathra. Cultee Monte is the son of the previous Duke's fourth marriage, which makes him a half-brother to Stegin, but legally and politically able to take the chair of power over the Southlands without stepping over lawful lines.

Stegin is detached from the frontlines and so far up this mysterious prince's ass he won't ever see flaws in leadership. Cultee was raised outside of Landsfell, he learned to love the land and its people and recently when I had met him, he battled his own difficult choices to see the fight against the wraiths through to the end with his allocated resources. Captain's red cape flew wildly in the strong winds as he led us straight down a cavernous dried river bed. The darkening clouds ahead a looming threat to our travels. *The wraiths won't stop. They will make it to Landsfell and when they do, the citizens need to be ready. Cultee can save lives if he sits in that chair, he is the only one in his family equipped with the painful reality and experience to fend them off. If the dreamer realm is to survive, reckless killings have to stop. I need to get Cultee to Landsfell for that winter gala and be sure to distract Stegin enough to let his guard down.*

Didn't Stegin recognize you as the same man he placed in his dungeons when you came to him as a wandering horselord?

I altered my appearance significantly by striking a bargain with a fae to glamour me well beyond my own abilities.

I couldn't stop my eyes from glancing at him between the quickening horse's canter. His appearance was pretend. His name in this realm, created from the context of a make-believe story. If it weren't for our bond ensuring me the truth behind each word, surely, I would have written him off. His bare hands loosely held the reins despite our hastiness. *You are staring.*

You are fading. I nodded my chin at his paleing hands which were as his hair had appeared this morning, translucent. He grabbed leather gloves from his haunches and donned them. *What's the longest you can go between feedings?*

I won't starve to death if that is what you are worried about. Not like a certain lady in the caravan who refused a proper meal all afternoon. He skillfully avoided the question and shifted the subject of the matter. Another tactfully placed grin pulled his eyes up. I ignored it and led Nordic too close to Asher's mount who nipped recklessly at me.

"Sorry!" I shouted to Asher, who didn't hear me with the wind and hooves pounding around us. I buried my chin under Raina's scarf and held my breath so it didn't freeze my nose. Icicles formed on my eyelashes.

What kind of magic can incubi cast?

Nothing fancy like fae glamour or pixie spells. Incubi are physically strong specimens and our magic—if you care to call it that—enhances the sentiments of those around us, some have learnt to sway the thoughts of a room. There is a 'charm' that befalls most weak minded should they find themselves in front of a partially hungry or ambitious incubi pursuing a meal.

Your form now, it is a lie too, right? Magic you spin to appear this way to red bloods?

I am red blood, born in this realm and of this realm. This is the human form my mother birthed and loved, even with all my spatters of missing colors. When I was fourteen my father led me to the dreamer realm for the first time and I transitioned to my dreamer self. Both are me, however, only one form is acceptable in this corner of the world. So, to answer your question, how you see me is not a mirage I concocted to match a story of my being descended from a shieldmaiden. It is a lot less effort to just allow my dreamer attributes out in the open when they see fit. We can't risk that now, can we Wisteria? So, I work hard, with whatever magic the Eternals spiked my blood with to hide my horns and restrain my wings from unfurling.

My eyes glazed over while my imagination took control of depicting Zander as a dreamer being. Horns would suit him and his long mane of hair and shaved designs on the sides just above the curl of his ears. Wings? *Was Oyokos an Incubus?*

He was.

Are you his kin?

That's a complicated question. Oyokos and his siblings created us in his image; however, are you aware that the Gods and Goddesses can't have children in the manner we can reproduce?

Anna, Moriah and my parents used to chatter about the Eleven over tending to the garden or night caps. *I vaguely remember something of that sort. They can either empty a piece of their soul into an already living person or be made into an object as a means to carry on their gifts when they choose to depart back to the beyond.*

Correct. Incubi are not his descendants, only his image. He intentionally gave his blood, and coincidentally chair of power, to a reaper of souls named Malick.

But you are somehow tied up in his blood. The energy up my left arm pulsed. I couldn't identify the message conveyed. *If it's too complicated or private, don't feel obliged to share.*

Nothing I am will be hidden from you. Except that ball of sun in the cage, as you described it.

My core heated up at his honesty. *Wings and horns sound exciting. I'm looking forward to the day when you don't have to hide yourself from me or the rest of the world.* There was a pause. Internally his rainbow of colors pulled back coyly. *Are you blushing or at a loss for words?*

A little of each. Would you like to hear the story of my blood lineage? It's lengthy, I must warn you. I'll trim down as many details as I can to make it bearable.

My frozen lashes widened to observe why the sudden change in pace was implemented. *Wisteria?* Snow began falling two leagues ahead. It was fast approaching. Heavy, wet snow blew in and our destination was straight through it. I weighed no more than a sack of rice. I'd blow off the saddle. "Tighten your thighs and lower your torso along Nordic's neck!" Zander shouted, feeling dread freeze me. He galloped ahead of me and shouted the same thing at Asher, Copper and the guard behind Hades. They paralleled their bodies to their mounts.

"You are scared," Zander stated, eyeing me closely. "I'd never thought I'd see the day."

"I am not!" I lied through my fear clenched teeth.

I heard his annoying, hearty laugh even through the storm.

"Push on!" Cultee yelled, his voice carried meekly on the strong gusts of wind. "Push! On!"

Zander dropped back behind me. "Lower! The winds will soar over you!" My breasts flattened themselves on Nordic's back, the horn of the saddle jammed up into my ribcage making it hard to breathe. "We won't stop until after we pass the thick of it. We need to be fast to make it through before ice and snow pile up!" Around me our line formation began to fall apart as it turned into an all-out sprint into the eye of the storm, even the riderless horses broke free and galloped until their tethers threatened to snap.

Push on we did. Hours of it. It was awful.

Men were screaming commands, I heard none of it because the winds were whipping violently. I feared tearing my eyes away from the hindquarters of Asher's horse for that served as a reminder I hadn't gotten lost in the dense wall of white or fell into the chaos of an ice storm. My knuckles froze around the reins and my legs held an observable and embarrassing tremor, not that anyone could see more than three yards ahead of their nose. It mattered not. "Ivy!" A familiar voice boomed. "Can you last until nightfall or do you need to join me in my saddle?"

In his saddle, was he serious? "Stop assuming I need help!" I shouted over my shoulder. That slight motion caused me to shift wayward and my fumbling foot became dislodged. "That was your fault!" I added, kicking around for balance.

I nearly wept when I secured myself back in the stirrups.

"It was," he owned his mistake. "Less than an hour to go. Stay strong my fierce flower!"

I turned to shout but thought better of it for I had finally gained a scant sense of control. Instead of clever rebuttals, I narrowed my attention on my positioning. My taut muscles, aching back and stinging legs were on the brink of failing when the captain dropped to his feet on an inch of powdery snow. Cultee ran to my still trotting horse and snatched the reins to cool Nordic to a walk and eventually halt. "We made it. Twelve mounts and all riders." He knelt on one knee in an exasperated motion and prostrated himself to the Eleven, even going as far as to spill a portion of his water out as a gratuity offering to them for our safety.

Asher, extra red and cherry ginger in the cold, hustled to my side. "Did you want assistance getting off today or were you planning on falling to the ground a second time?"

My stiff fingers managed to form a crude gesture that sent the troop of men into a hushed laugh, their relief was palpable. Two hands firmly encircled the entire circumference of my waist. Zander plucked me off

Nordic as easily as if I were a daisy in a summer field. Asher opened his stance to receive me, I fell into him.

My legs refused to straighten, they buckled time and time again. Asher didn't laugh, he held me upright until I gained control of my lower half. Zander oversaw responsibility of the dozen mounts while the rest of the men carried out Cultee's orders and began to organize oiled sheepskin and a tarp to repel water over their heads.

At my feet he laid a small skin and a deconstructed tent. "We will round on you while you sleep and wake you before a fit befalls you. I see a decent plot to pitch your tent on the leeward side of that rock. Should block the winds from sweeping you away in the night." He pointed some yards away, on the other side of the huddle of horses. The moon light reflected off the settled snow and brightened the landing, we all moved about with awareness.

My jaw was rigid. I agreed with a short dip of my neck. "You are off to a fantastic first excursion, Lady Ivy." I repeated my previous gesture.

Asher carried my designated camping supplies and wordlessly assisted me in aligning the poles to keep the triangle shape symmetrical on both ends. We walked to my saddle bag, then separated ways for the night after we ate a light meal. I hovelled back to my tent, opting to crawl on all fours when I neared the low flaps of the tent. I rolled the thin sheepskin out on the gravel and mud, a thin barrier from the frozen ground.

The horses settled, the guards slumbered, the quiet of the night disturbed only by the pattering of rain on my tent as the weather warmed just enough to turn snow and ice into a dreary rain to soak the soul in misery and bones in chill. Darkness set in fully. My lengthening legs trembled when I flexed my toes, the ache and tension of my tight body searched for relief.

Finding none, I groaned.

The wind rocked the weak set poles, dislodging one from the ground outside.

I'd have to get up and fix the damn thing. I muttered curses as I got on all fours. On hands and knees, I tore open the flaps and moved into the rain. The fabric of my pants grew heavy, absorbing water. I found a rock to hammer the spike into the rocky soil, I fumbled around for the pole to discover it had been fixed and set straight. Zander's voice was in my ear, "Captain agreed it is best to let the others sleep while one of us, me, ensures you don't scream murderously in your dream state. I'll rest outside your tent for the night." He was close enough to hit. If only I had better night vision.

"That's stupid. It's raining."

"I like rain."

"Get in here."

"No," he hissed.

I shoved him. "You will get sick. I don't have enough herbs prepared in the fort to reverse pulmonary inflammation and infection should pneumonia befall you, which it will."

"I'll take my chances."

"Get in the tent!" I yelled. "We will stay on opposite sides."

"My body is bigger than this tent. There is no avoiding each other unless I'm outside."

"Wrong. I'll stay outside and you go inside."

He pulled my belt loop backwards sending me to land on my ass. With his face next to mine he pushed me back into the mild protection the hanging fabric offered. "Don't fight me on this."

"I'm going to win."

"It's not a competition. I am starved and weak and—"

"—and need a warm place to sleep and recover your fancy blood next to a pathetic, scrawny mortal." He closed the two triangle flaps. I heard his bulky shadow lay down, his back faced me, his decision was finite.

But it was a dumb decision.

I had limited knowledge, but I assumed there was only one way to lure an incubus with absolute success. He might be livid, but he wouldn't break his vow and leave me without an ally.

I removed the wet layers of tunics and eased myself onto the sheep skin, focusing on the tension strung in every extremity and their only hope of release between my legs. Behind my closed eyes I envisioned roaming hands caressing the swells of my breast and lips around the pierced peeks of my nipples. My shirt unbuttoned and my skin rippled in the cold. I feathered my navel lightly with the tips of my fingers and let a much needed sigh escape when a fire ignited in the low of my stomach, slowly burning its way between my legs.

"Fucking insane you are!" Zander barked, tearing open the tent. Our connection came to life with desire and thrill. There was no dodging the pulsing that shot down my arm as hot and inescapable as midday summer.

Hunger and lust. Lots of it.

I didn't close him off.

Warmth cocooned me while he settled himself alongside my body and pulled the back of my head up onto his forearm to use as a pillow, after that his spare hand tucked into a white knuckled fist which stayed firmly at his side.

I'm not going to stop. I sent down our thread while sending my hand into my leather pants where I was met with slick wetness of arousal.

He swore and matched his panting to my own. *I don't want you to.* "I need to have you. So much need. So much want." His breath rustled my hair and warmed my exposed neck and breasts. No other part of him made contact with me. He was vigilant in remaining a gentleman. *Fuck.* I made long lazy strokes up my inner thighs, which were sore from two days of being jostled.

I rested the heel of my left hand on my pubic bone and spun small circles around the bead atop the folds. My right hand groped my breast and pinched my nipple until my yearning doubled. Tripled. My hips shifted without my permission. *I'm afraid I don't know how to feed you.*

I'll guide you. My mouth will hover above yours when you are ready, that will be my only active contact with you during your escapades. I will not partake. My circles hastened, my body flushed as if it were undergoing a fever.

Will it hurt? I flashed my eyes open and found his to be fixated on mine. He shook his head no.

"I have something to show you," he posed breathlessly into our warming tent.

Yes? I sounded back. He pointed to his head and atop the crown of his hair where two crescent moon shaped horns emerged, one with a sizable fragment missing off the center.

Reflexively my right hand left my breast and reached up. "Can I?"

"Wisteria Woodlander never needs permission to touch me." His anticipation rang down our line. I stroked his damaged horn, feeling his eyes searching for a reaction.

His horns were ribbed with smooth grooves and felt denser than human bone. Their length extended my hand and their color was that of Zander's hairline, jet black and freshly fallen snowy white. *You've probably heard this a thousand times from the countless who've caressed you, but your horns are stunning. Pretty.* I sent him, surprised at my own openness to a man who thrived off compliments. My right hand fell to his face and cupped his strong, scruffy jawline which was brought close to mine, angled just so his thick, heart shaped lips were open and hovering eagerly above me. Fangs. He had pearly white elongated canines and his excitement stoked the flame in my stomach eager to be engaged. My left hadn't stopped grinding into my clit. It moved faster now.

The only opinion I value is yours. He was relieved, immensely so, the bottled nerves he held onto were released as he tapped into my mind and began to stoke my pleasure. *Your fragrance is compelling enough to seduce Oyokos himself and if he was fortunate enough to hear you whimper at your own self pleasure, he would be on his knees worshiping you for centuries on end.* Two of my fingers plunged inside me. I gyrated, pressing into my own hand. *You are wet, I can taste you in the air. Dripping, ripe peaches with a hint of vanilla. Fuck, you are sweeter than my wildest dreams. I'll be drinking your scent for lifetimes to come and craving you in all your human perfection.* I moaned in a hush tone.

In a knowing, Zander's hand tucked under my chin, tilting my lips up to his. They were a hair's width away from brushing in the space where his panting and my rapid moaning mingled. The tip of his nose touched mine, bringing his glowing gaze level with my green eyes. "Wisteria, I need you. I want you," he muttered into my mouth, his fangs not interfering with the way he said my name. My unruly right hand wrapped around his horn as a means to steady the rolling waves that moved through me when I unleashed my orgasm. He stifled my cries of ecstasy by covering my mouth with his and inhaling so intensely it pulled my toes into a curl. Not a kiss. No, it was a proper feeding.

My knees shook and struggled as I forced them to bend. "We're not done yet," the dreamer whispered into the quiet of the night, his mouth slacked and so close to mine.

My body still hummed in the glorious afterglow of a climax. My hips and knees hadn't stopped quivering, when he tugged my left hand out from my undergarments and inserted the fingers that had just been inside me into his mouth. His slick tongue sucked and stroked my fingers, he even bit a playful nip on the soft tips, his way to lighten the situation. His thick eye lashes shut as he regrettably released my hand. His head fell back as he swore. "Fuck. I was right. Peaches. Ripe, luscious peaches." His lips shone glossy, coated in my juices.

I giggled.

"I like peaches," he confessed, slowly turning on his side to view me laid over scattered piles of clothes. "I fear I may have an addiction alongside my obsession, you are owning that responsibility, Wisteria." His eyes didn't roam lower than my chin when he drew my tunic closed and brought the wool blanket up to my nose. His gaze sharpened. His body loomed. Feeling small, I buried myself a little more, holding my breath in anticipation.

Here it came—the scolding. "If you pull a stunt like that again, the consequences will be dire. Am I understood?" He growled in a feral manner, which resonated against my frame.

"Don't expect an apology because I am not sorry," I piped up.

His seriousness was palpable. "Despite how distressed I am over your ability to make sound decisions; it is with deep gratitude that I ask the following question. How can I begin to repay my debt to you?"

I raised a shoulder to my ear. "Consider us even. No, more outlandish woodlander gift for you."

"Fair enough. Stop biting your lower lip, it makes me want to sink my teeth into you." He snapped his jaw and canines.

I had been biting my lip. I released it, but locked my gaze on him. He was solid without blurred lines or translucent flesh. I dug down mentally to see his cloud of weariness had lifted significantly and the wisps of his colors swarmed around me in a sphere, caressing my neck and spine delicately.

"I feel loads better. Much more myself than I have since I left the mountains behind. Stolen orgasms don't feed me the same way ones given to me do, the ones meant for me satiate better."

His white eye held more blue than I had seen in it before. They both began to glow, I practically saw his imagination rampant as if they were glass windows to his thoughts. "You are still hungry, do you need—" An animalistic guttural purring silenced me. Zander's body tightened as he brought his lips down to my collar bone. The light behind his eyes cast enough glow onto his face which was twisted with conflict.

His tone dropped an octave, saturated with lethality and lust. "I strongly advise not posing the question about to fall off your lips, my flower," he stated, watching my hands return to examining the large crescent moons atop his head. I stayed quiet. His half-hinged jaw slacked further, but only silence escaped when I stroked the subtle ridges on his horns. My thumb stopped to graze over a jagged edge. "It's not painful anymore. One of my brothers tried to remove it with an ax when I was a kid. Mine are bigger and threatened his influence," he said casually. I didn't bother to hide my horrified disgust. "We are on good terms now, all seven of us get on well most days."

"Men are barbaric and entitled," I sighed, reliving the raid of knights on my family's farm and business. My stomach twisted with revulsion. "No matter which realm you reside in, violence and vengeance are ingrained in your bones."

"Says the girl hell bent on murdering someone for revenge."

"You make a good point." I pouted, retracting my hands from his horn and shoving his chest to heave him off of me. He didn't budge with my strength, but understood the message conveyed. Zander provided distance between us, as much as he could given the size of our tent and him. Our legs still touched and his arm remained as my pillow. Over the minutes our breathing evened and slowed, chills found their way back into my body hearing the icy rain continue to fall on the ground outside. "Will you wake me if I seem restless?"

"Yes, Wisteria," Zander confirmed. It put me at ease. Cool mint filled my nose and a lullaby in my ears, one of foreign familiarity.

The precipitation from the sky had stopped, leaving a coating of ice on each blade of grass, stump and stone. Judging by Zander's spry energy and the preparedness of the mounts, he had been up for seemingly hours, leaving me alone for the duration of my sleep. The clouds held a touch of pink, which was reassuring to the soul. I walked in the opposite direction of the guards to find a private location to relieve myself and readjust my top two woolen layers after last night's pleasant debauchery. Asher had disassembled my tent by the time I returned and motioned for me to eat my bag of dried cranberries and bitter walnuts. With my mouth full, I thanked him.

Alright, I've decided that I am in agreement with you. Zander's voice rolled down our bond. *You are an earth squirrel, for you are far too resourceful to be a chipmunk even though you are about the same size.* Zander's mockery grew when I turned to him with my cheeks full of nuts and berries. He was quick to turn away to bury his mirth beneath a horse blanket and avoid Hades' scowl.

Cultee tightened up the murky laces on his boots. "Two hours from here is a granite overhang standing from an abandoned quarry. Our comrades have settled on the highest mound to keep and retain a vantage point from guests wishing to pay them homage in the night. It will take us another three hours to trek up the back route with our hooved mounts to retrieve them. Anticipate injuries, although I can't fathom the extent. It's been over a full moon phase since the restless darkness crept into their village to steal lives, wreak havoc and dismantle hope." I tapped my trusted satchel that swung at my hip ensuring it was ready to be raided for healing work. My supplies were nearing barren. I huffed into my hands prior to placing my gloves on, scant warmth clung to my fingers. Gripping the reins was cumbersome as was trying to keep myself atop Nordic, for frost coated everything in slick layers of ice.

Zander, Hades and another guard with experience were given responsibility over the riderless mounts and coaxed them behind the captain. We traveled at a conservative pace. I wasn't the only body struggling to remain upright. The hooves of our horses lost traction on the large slabs of flint, limestone and granite. *You're spritely.* I said, sensing his presence prancing around, reminding me of a puppy seeking its master's affections.

And shall remain so for weeks to come, thanks to a marvelously unexpected late-night feast, Zander educated. He tugged the off-white mare that was meant to follow Rosie but got sidetracked by a thicket of bramble berries.

Peaches are hardly a feast, I retorted. *How much more intricate than dreamer and Numaalian is your descent?*

I related primarily as a red blood until fourteen when my mother died from a sickness that caused her bones to grow brittle and frail. My mother was always open about who sired me, the night of my conception and the fact it wasn't consensual, this alone founded my personal code of obtaining consent as a requirement prior to any action. *Because of my genetics, I physically aged as an adolescent you'd recognize as a teenager, not the Ilanthian aging of appearing as a kid well into one's thirties. I went into the seam for the first time, guided by my desire to find the other half of my family. My father, Atticus di Lucent received me, along with my six older brothers, most of them were against my advent, none more than Kailynder, the pure blooded dreamer being first born of my father, the sole heir of the last succubus.*

My lips dried the more I licked them, I tucked my chin under the wool so all that was visible was my lashes and brow. *He's the one that tried to hack off your horns?*

Yes. I was held down by Wyatt the first night of my arrival. Clavey heard the screams and splintered Kailynder's face so badly that his jaw had to be sown up for weeks in order to set into place. For such a morbid detail of the story, there was a lightness in the manner he spoke.

Why do I sense fondness as you recollect such a horrid thing?

Because hearing him apologize in front of the city of Veona through steel wires with a lisp on his knees the following morning is something I can hold against him for eternity. One glance at my damaged horn sparks compliance, which is far better than igniting guilt. I've grown fond of him over the decades, I don't wish him or Wyatt any malintent. A year into becoming acclimated with my changing form and new found strength, I encountered a nine tailed fox following me to the leap—*a ledge where winged creatures learn to fly.* My imagination concocted a young Fennick as a fox sneaking up on a tall, gangly Zander Halfmoon, but nine tails on any creature seemed too farfetched for my mind.

Days passed and I grew sick of having someone witness my failure to catch a wind current. Fennick laughed as I hit the valley floor time and time again. I confronted him. There was nothing but potent hate the moment our eyes met, he laughed harder seeing how bruised and scrawny I was. I punched him thinking that would shut him up. He bit me. I kicked him. He shredded my juvenile thin wings with his claws. I couldn't even attempt to take flight for a month until they mended. I spent every minute of that month thinking about skinning the silver fluffy fur off his body without getting burnt and I know he was imagining all the ways to cut me out of his life.

No sooner had I received the healer's blessing did I dart out the doors and go straight into the fire fields screaming with uncontrolled rage, I now understood that to be hormones, pride and our woven connection. He met me amid the growing flames in the form of a boy not much different than I, red threads spun around us. Neither of us wanted this.

We both tried sprinting in opposite directions and used our strength to fight fate instead of murder each other. United against a common enemy, we kept at it for days and nights on end. There were a few times I thought we succeeded in severing the threads and outran the Weaver's reach, just to be drawn tighter together.

A small crowd had formed and when neither of us had strength left enough to fight, we were like two magnets pulled into one another, colliding so hard we crashed unconscious and lay side by side face down in the dirt and ash. Even souls in the beyond peered across the runegate barrier to watch.

My father flew down as Fen's family emerged from their tunnels to inspect us. We had no energy left to acknowledge anyone or each other. I didn't even get his name until days later when I found myself waking up at odd hours to search for him in his family's burrow—just wanting to be with him. When his kin would inquire or get curious, I found myself angry that I allowed myself to be drawn out against my will to be with a rodent I detested. What was even worse was the lack of control over it, some days I awoke and found myself not even in my own body, my eyes saw his world. He experienced the same phenomenon. When we inquired about it, we learned about our own type of mind link. The elders told us the basics of fate threads which were having to live out our lives side by side. The elemental will undertake any burden to see his bonded, I, well and alive. That sat as well with me as swallowing hot embers. Fennick hardly batted an eyelash, he was suddenly far too content with the arrangement. I wanted better for him. For the both of us.

I've not been with them long enough to see many interactions, but from what I know of their temperaments, this was humorous. *This whole arrangement seems unfair to Nikki.*

That is what I thought too. I thought I knew better than the Weaver so I left to explore the world alone. I made sure I was untraceable; elves hid any track I may have left in the Veil and I took on my human form as I entered Ilanthia. For eleven years I dodged any invitation to return to Veona and dismissed any inkling of Fennick pressing in on my forethoughts. Percy, yet another brother, intercepted my travels. He lacks the ability to change skins and holding true to my father's view that dreamer beings shouldn't have to adapt to make others comfortable or fit under their door frames. He arrived in full incubus form.

I interjected. *Other than the non-consensual sex thing—I think I am inclined to agree with your father.*

I'm sure you two will hit it off nicely. At least, on occasion, he sounded honest. *This particular caravan I was travelling with wasn't keen on having attention drawn to them, for we were hunting down perpetrators of an underground slave trade of children to be sent to the Cresent Isles, a very sensitive market with easily frightened cliental. Percy was welcomed, however; an ambush struck us in the night. The masked swordsmen took almost everyone's lives. Including mine. Two swords cut through me, I can still feel where the blade pierced my sternum. Percy flew off to retrieve help. I knew he wouldn't arrive back in time with aid, blood poured out of me. I felt myself being pulled into the beyond and yet a stronger compulsion was beckoning me out. I saw the red rope and gripped it tightly.*

Fennick had me cradled on his lap and streams of his blood were mingling with mine. He carved out one of his three immortal fox hearts from his chest and replaced my punctured heart with his. We were taken to the White Tower to heal. We were inseparable and given the same recovery chambers although we've yet to speak a word to each other at that time. When I suffered, Fennick would suffer. I wasn't healing well with my mortal blood and if I were to die then, his lifespan would be significantly shortened. Few woven prefer to exist without each other. It broke my new heart to watch him in tormented with pain, all done because of my stupidity of trying to dodge fate. The Veil's Overlord, Malick the Reaper, came to the bedside when the Empress and Emperor called upon him, informing him of our poor recovery rate.

In the same manner God Oyokos chose Malick to be his son and carry his bloodline, Malick chose me to be Oyokos's grandson. The same blood, although diluted, that once coursed through Oyokos entered my body and healed the gaping cavity in my chest. I wept when Fen finally took a breath without pain. His wound became a scar and I became a happily woven immortal to Fen. From that moment on, we honored our bond and I pledged myself to him as he had done to me that night when death came for me. I wept harder when I realized Malick was transiting to the beyond and my selfish actions led the Veil to grieve the loss of its great Overlord. My father stepped in as steward to the chair of Veona, voted in by a consensus before I left to come here. He is thriving in his role, while I am attempting to right some of the damage I inflicted on the dreamer realm by lessening the influx of souls and soulless beings pushing us beyond capacity. That is the jist of it! He exclaimed. Nordic's hooves clomped rhythmically with those around me, we sounded more of a band of drummers than a troop of guards.

That's quite a story. I'm afraid to say anything because whatever I share about myself will sound dull and pathetic now. Not that it didn't already before his extravagant tale of his first three decades of life. I pulled my chest lower to the steed's back to maneuver a particularly harsh gust of wind that whistled as it blew fervently around the pit of the quarry.

You could never speak to me again and I'd still find you irresistible and intriguing, even if you have yet to tell me anything about yourself.

I tiptoed backwards on the line of our connection. *You are old and have traveled the world, you know more than I do.*

I don't know anything important. Like what haunts your dreams and what makes you laugh the hardest. I don't know your favorite foods or colors or season. How does one become a master crafter, what abilities have you unlocked and what does the tattoo represent? I don't know what you want to do in the world after you set it right and find peace. He smiled on his horse, peering into the distance. His gaze moved upward to a large wall of marbled granite. Smoke rose atop it. *Your awareness and the way you eye every guard's sheath and critique their footing when they enter a room makes me think you've practiced with blades bigger than daggers and have a honed warrior's heart. I want to know what makes you so confident when you step into a brothel and what makes your actions so precise and self-assured when you address life threatening bleeds and surface wounds alike, when most would faint or stumble.*

I like spring, I offered before changing the subject and noting out loud. "They've lit a fire, I don't smell flesh in the smoke, but why would they be taking such risks?"

"I can't answer that," Cultee replied, dropping back on his mount. "Yelling for them to douse it from here would reverberate too greatly. For now, let us take this as a sign of life and hurry up the back."

Hades gave a frustrated groan. "They are attracting more than our eyes. The sooner it is stifled, the better."

He was right. "Captain, may I try to flag their attention?"

"If it is subtle," he permitted with an uncomfortable way of encouragement.

I slid off Nordic and found my feet, it was a nice change from landing on my ass or needing help. Hades was muttering something out of aggravation when I stole a lengthy rope from a spare mount and dashed over and up to the sturdiest whitewood giant I spotted. I whistled a sparrow's song while climbing the trunk of the tree, twice my cloak snagged and I ripped it free. My whistling changed cadence and volume. In a matter of minutes a pigeon cooed a reply. "They know I'm here," I said to Cultee, the rising excitement caused my voice to squeak. Two male shapes appeared atop the overhang, one with a heavy stagger.

Brock. He had made it out alive! Goddesses, I could have wept.

"Good. Get down before you break your neck." My weapon and bag clamored as I lifted myself higher in the tree. "Wrong direction, lady." I had an idea.

"I can get to them faster and put out the fire. We will be all packed up and ready to return to the fort by the time you make it up the back." The wind, thirty feet up an isolated tree, prevented his orders from reaching my ears. Brock waved ecstatically from atop the sharp hill, more shapes were beckoned closer to the edge. Perfect for what I was about to do, I needed all the strength they had available. One end of the rope I secured to the top of the whitewood, the other to the tail of an arrow. Disregarding the warnings below, I shot the arrow twenty feet above me, where it grew taut. When Brock's distinct chuckled made it to my ears, I set my boots onto the rope. *Like I said, you don't need to talk for me to find you intriguing. Is this mortal danger ingrained in your daily routine?* Zander mocked briefly before my own bold voice took over.

It screamed at me to run.

I ran. And when the incline grew too steep, I jumped and clung onto the twined rope, which tore at my skin.

My forearms and biceps burned with exhaustion as I hauled my body weight behind them. Brock reached over the edge and grasped my hands. My sweat slicked cold hands were frictionless in his grasp and slipped free. We both huffed and tried again. This time he clutched my wrist guard and another joined him in lugging me up with ease. I rolled onto my back and was quickly mulled with an embrace. Brock pummeled me with eager hugs which softened into heavy sighs of relief. "I thought I fucking gave you intel that sent you to your death. You had me believing I done killed you off!" I laughed as he pushed me against the hard stone, he pulled back to examine my face and new warm garments. "They gave you knitted wear? Are they reasonable people or are they like the knights who burnt down the docks with the wavedrifters inside the ships?"

"There are only guards of Numaal in Fort Fell, I've yet to see a knight or hear their captain speak poorly on our people. Is Rodrick alive? I bet he has questions."

A firm grip laced under my arm and brought me to my feet. "Ay, I've plenty of concerns," Rodrick's thick leather collar protected his ears and neck from the cold, but his bearded chin was hardened with skepticism. "Good to find you in good health and better spirits." He released me and offered his right hand to Brock who accepted it and was brought to his foot, shifting over to his wooden crutch for stability.

"You need to put out the fire. Wraiths will flock to it," I stated, turning to view a collection of tents huddled around the stone firepit. Madam Tidal was the first of the faces I found, she couldn't form a smile. Her eyes were empty, for her mind was haunted. I could empathize all too easily with her. "Rodrick, we've got to get everyone packed for descending the back trail of the quarry. And the fire–"

"The fire stays lit until the coals are hot enough to heat my blade. My left hand needs to be removed," he muttered, swinging his left arm in front of me. I degloved it to find his skin blackened and the shadow of a wraith's venom trailing up his forearm. He had been bitten. "Well, Ivy, your timing is impeccable. I thought I got out of the cabin scathe free.

One of their fangs must have nicked my knuckle in combat and now, well, I need someone to lop it off for me and cauterize the bleeding."

"If you've a small blade and liquor, I can do it without a fire. And without pain," I ensured.

Rodrick turned to my old friend. "Brock, smother the coals and fetch the last of the rum. Your parents were the best in their craft and made a name for themselves that drew all ill windriders and wavedrifters to their apothecary back when you were a whisper. I remember helping your father nail up the shelving when he first opened it, Lily was round with you in her belly. Yet, she still danced. Ivy, the prodigy child of the Southlands, I hope you live up to your reputation, for not even your parents had to be trained under the conditions you have. I doubt they would even know what to do with a decaying bite." I had not known Rodrick to have been acquainted with my parents, hearing him mention my mother's name made this encounter more personal than I would have liked.

"I intend to exceed it, sir. Let me signal to the caravan to continue their trek up and then we will get to answering your questions and addressing your arm. I can only speak to what I have observed, Captain Cultee himself is leading the excursion. If you've political or historic questions, best address them with him." I would need the rope to use as a tunicate. I pulled an arrow from the satchel on my back and approached the ledge. Despite the distance, Zander managed to look twice the size of his comrades. I wiggled my arrow at the guards and locked it in its notch. Aiming at the tree's tip I found the knot I tied, pulled back and released.

The cord under my feet went slack as I severed the knot below. By the time I had collected the rope's length, the guards were on the move. *Better than decent aim.* Zander humored.

Rodrick and his son led the way to a small wooden chest of supplies. They had hammered nails into planks of wood to ease transporting such a bulky item. Tidal dozed in and out of slumber, eyeing me under her drooping lids and frowning as Brock turned off the only source of heat. Rodrick handed over a sharp knife, a small wooden saw and a half empty bottle of alcohol, he didn't bother to hide his dread. "Flint, help take down the tents and stack the cots. Ivy, where would you like me to lay?" He fidgeted his good hand, cracking knuckles and tapping his thumb and middle finger repeatedly.

"I will need sunlight and it's best we move away from anyone with a weak stomach. That rock slab over there looks nice," I grinned at Brock who had already begun to collect a mound of blankets and a handful of towels. He was planning on assisting me. "You up for this?" I posed.

"I have come a long way from my nights of phantom pain and thoughts of ending my own life. If you are still fighting, then so am I," he said, giving a firm pat on Rodrick's shoulders and easing him away from the crowd that began to stir at Flint's prodding. He whispered in my ear, "That and I'm not on the other end of your saw and stitches this time." I elbowed him. His commentary was not helping Rodrick.

Rodrick did not wait for my queuing. He tore off his trench coat and cuffed the sleeve of his left arm. "The captain is placing himself in danger to see us rescued? He has got something to gain."

"He left most of the guards to defend fort fell, a town population over four hundred. We brought a cart of stews, blankets, provisions and it's camped out a day from the fort, waiting for our return," I said, covering his arm in cotton prior to wrapping the rough rope around its circumference. He grunted as Brock and I took either end and pulled it tight.

He huffed, "No knights in Fort Fell? Seems odd."

"I've begun to think maybe the duke and royal advisors don't see value in sending their strongest forces to the frontline, it sounds as if there are strained family ties guiding the decisions being made. Whoever led the knights' charge is hiding something and protecting themselves. Cultee isn't that way. He was raised out here and most of the guards he is training were crafters. Pine is the smithy there. He's Elousie's son," I added, watching his pallor change. "Any other major concerns before I send you off into the twilight?"

"I don't trust anyone in red," he confessed. "I'll walk back to the fort, but that captain will be getting an earful." Pulling off my scarf I exposed my earrings. "What's that?"

"Spotted blue cap spores." I gave him no time to have concerns. I placed the small vial under his nose and he inhaled the essence. Brock snickered at the aloof expression that befell the village leader.

"Ivy!" He yelled, a slur apparent. "I can't feel my body!"

Gripping his chin, I turned his head to face the right. He lost coordination to move it on his own. "That's the point, sir." I felt for his pulse at his carotid. It slowed.

It was time to act. I pulled my own layers off to work as quickly and efficiently as I could. It wasn't long until the cold robbed me of my own sensation in my toes and fingertips, luckily the warmth of Rodrick's blood restored my nerve endings and allowed me to maintain control over the tip of the blade as I cut through tendons. I used smaller cotton threads to hold the veins and arteries closed so I could sew up the vascular system with fishing threads. Brock and I gripped each end of the saw to make a clean cut through the radial and ulnar bones, he found a pumice stone nearby we used to buff out the sharp edges and smooth away the chips of bone. Enough skin had been saved for covering the stump of his arm which the last of my stitches and salve had been used on. Someone came behind me and wiped beads of sweat from my forehead with a chilled, damp cloth. Next to me a clay cup of fresh water was set.

Her brown hair was shorter than I had last seen it and her feminine curves were replaced with a gauntness that was frightening. "Fauna?" Her name fell off my lips.

"Gods, I've miss you!" She kissed my hairline, then my cheeks, then my nose. "You have gotten a gathering over there; I've told them not to disrupt you until you bring out the salve. That's when I know you've almost finished on your patient, having been one quite a few times myself." She beamed and pointed to the guards who were off their mounts and striking up conversations with the remnants of Horn's End. Flint and Cultee were busy divvying up sacks and trunks to carry. Drift was helping the women roll up their blankets and garments, he even fashioned a carrying sack for a mother and babe that would disperse the weight off her lower back and allow the fellow to feed liberally. Fauna lifted me and began to wipe off as much of the blood as she could with the thin rag. Most of it was dried and sticky at this point, only a proper scrub in a creek or tub would get it off.

"Fauna, tell me about the nightwalkers," I said, meeting her sunken eyes.

"They came two days after you left. We all thought you went to gather, but Brock told us about the guards scouting closer to Horn's End. When you didn't return, we assumed the worst. That what happened to Horn's End also happened to you." I squeezed her hand for encouragement. "I didn't know how strong they were. They tore the doors off hinges and splintered spears with their hands. They peeled back ribs with one hand and with a vacant black hole in their head they moved around the village sucking the life out of us. Rodrick, Flint and Brock had some of their wits about them to know when to flee. They collected as many of us as they could and lit the entire village up in flames before we set out. There was smoke rolling in from the northeast that day, we could hardly see where we were going, honestly, we thought we were heading due west. Apparently, not."

Brock interrupted, "I told you we weren't, but nobody listens to the cripple." We shared a weak laugh and I allowed Fauna to wipe her tears on the scarf Raina gifted me.

"Keep it for the journey, there is ice and wind turbulence up ahead." I wrapped it around her neck and tucked it into her jacket. She hugged me one more time before realizing my bloody hands were not able to hold her back due to their filth.

"I'm so glad you're both here," I said, moving my attention between the two of them. I had chosen not to think about them or just better assume they had died so as to not get my hopes up for a reunion. Now, here they were, within arm's reach.

Brock swatted sentiments away and picked his crutch off the rocks. "Looks like the captain was considerate enough to bring extra four legged bodies. I'll go discuss my situation with them, so they aren't surprised when I have to partner up in the saddle."

"Rodrick will be lethargic and limp for the days ahead. He will need a mount too."

Brock winked and left to convey our messages. While I covered Rodrick with his coat, Fauna covered me with mine. Her touch lingered. I had forgotten what it was like to be tended to, not in the sense of having needs met or being protected, but just a body to remind me I wasn't alone. I pressed my forehead to hers. Staying near each other's warmth, we waited to be summoned. Cultee and Flint walked over when the rest of the camp had risen and prepared to move out, behind them they led a mare. Flint readjusted the arm sling I wrapped around his father, and hauled him upright with Cultee on the other side. "Thank you, last master," Flint commended. "Let's hope the journey to Fort Fell is uneventful, I fear most of us can't afford another battle. Hope is as fragile as our bodies. Trust is as thin as freshly frozen ice." Flint mounted the mare and pulled his father up by his waistline to rest in the saddle. Cultee helped arrange them before deeming them safe enough to ride off behind Asher, who Tidal had wrapped in her flaccid arms.

"How fares your strength, ladies?" He asked, assessing the astuteness of our statue.

"There are mothers, newborns, and frightened young and old among us. I will walk, captain," I said buttoning up my tunics. "I'll just snack on my scones sir and I'll be ready to trek."

Scowl on face, Cultee crossed his arms. "The moment I sense weariness or you are unable to wield your arrows you sit in Drift's saddle. You are the only one petite enough to ride with him without inflicting Rosie's stamina."

I debated a rebuttal about my size. "Rodrick has valid concerns. Everyone here wants to know why knights do not reside in Fort Fell and what your relationship is with the knights who attacked us two years ago."

"To my knowledge knights haven't ridden this far south, they'd no reason to. But, if you say they have, then I believe you." Rivers of betrayal swam behind his eyes, as he faked a pleasant grin for us. "We need to head out now if we are to stay ahead of the horde." He hustled back to the villagers and rallied them for the days and nights ahead. No one would have known he was wounded and perplexed seconds before he spoke passion into them.

"Scones?" Fauna's eyes widened with joy.

I snickered at her appetite. "Blueberry, with jam inside." My friend smacked her lips and we ran off to the mounts hand in hand. She licked the crumbs off her fingers and jumped up and down with giddy joy as Cobar would have. Cultee spearheaded the voyage down, Hades and another scouted the trail miles ahead and returned every hour like clockwork. Zander rounded out the rear, knocking on my mental walls several times before nightfall, requiring reassurance of my wellbeing in order to focus on his job at hand, which was to remain diligent in spotting wraiths.

Camp was made in the same clearing as the night prior, it took all afternoon to make it that far. I bit back a smirk as I recollected what had happened on the wayward side of the rock–the same location where Zander rolled his sheep skin out for the night. He protectively defended the patch of dirt when two male windriders sought to claim it from him. I sent amused giggles down our bond. He opened his stance.

Are all incubi so irrationally territorial?

This little demonstration is nothing. You are welcome, by the way, for not tackling Brock when he hugged you on the ground. And Fauna for that matter.

You need to relax.

I am. He lounged across the patch of dirt and sent me a devilish wink.

Fauna had to lure me away from my fond memory of sharing that patch with him by promising warmth among the females who had organized themselves with their backs against two fallen timbers, good protection from wind. The comradery of ladies was wonderfully uplifting. Tidal was given the baby to swaddle and soothe, which instantly added a spark of joy to her melancholy cheeks. Fauna settled on my chest in a fitful slumber. I wondered if I was such a hardship to sleep next to.

Fauna's ragged breathing evened out as I repositioned onto my back with her in my arms. All too soon, she whimpered with clenched fists. This is karmic retaliation for all the nights I shared her bed in the brothel and awoke with her frantically trying to calm me down. I grimaced as someone nearby shifted, causing the pile of us to reposition our extremities. My nose was exposed and numb. It was probably dripping. Wonderful.

My arms were locked down, my neck crooked and locked in an uncomfortable position. It was a long night. I hadn't shut my eyes for longer than a few cycles of breath at a time.

When the camp stirred, I slipped away from the females and walked a few yards down the rock-strewn road that would be under our feet shortly. Leaning against a wet rock, I rubbed out the kink in my neck and emptied the small pebbles gathering in my boots. Under my elbow, I felt the rock soften. Moss. A sign of a good day. It filled my stomach enough to take away the gnawing feeling.

Captain's lantern traveled from the bedrolls towards the heap of saddle bags piled on the floor. I walked closer, to avoid giving him a fright. He placed tobacco in his mouth and began to stroke each mare, gently waking them up. One by one he lifted the saddles, he flagged me over to demonstrate the safest way to place the blanket and fasten the straps. We fell into a rhythm. Pride simmered, for I felt as if I contributed and learned a new skill.

I stepped around Zander's sleeping form, and knelt next to Flint who watched over his father. "Any fevers or spreading redness?" I asked, running the back of my gloveless hand across his forehead and down the side of his flanks.

"None. He is starting to arouse."

I looked at him sternly. "He shouldn't be fully alert for one more day at the earliest."

"He will be in pain when he comes to," he voiced, wiping the dirt off his father's worn leather attire.

"I understand that you are worried. I'll ensure it will be tolerable." I tried comforting Flint. "It is hard to watch someone you admire suffer. I don't intend for you to witness such a thing."

"You are kind," he confirmed. "He never second guessed the need to cut off his own arm if it meant protecting us a day or week longer. I doubt I would have reacted the same. He is a better man than I."

"He has attributes that you can aspire to obtain. That doesn't make his pedestal higher than yours. Surely, each generation strives to lift their young higher than themselves. Your father will see you surpass whatever expectations you have set for your future self."

He leaned into my shoulder. "Even your words mend, whether that is their intent matters not. It does provide insight into how much of a master healer you are in your truest nature, woodlander. One of your many traits I've long revered since you stumbled into the wreckage of Horn's End two years ago." I moved away from his shoulder sinking into mine. Perplexed to see his gaze lingering on my exposed neck. My hands reflexively left Rodrick's flesh and covered my own. "You must grow tired of hearing how your loveliness rivals your wits and valor."

"With the end of the age of mortals fast approaching, I have no time for courting, nor flattery, Flint," I cautioned.

"Wouldn't you rather witness the end of days side by side with someone of dear importance?"

"Quite the opposite," I stated flatly. He rested onto his hindquarters; his focus returned to his father's latent condition while I hopped to my feet. My boots nestled into the melting snow leaving imprints as I tracked back towards the women, bringing with me the sun rising over my statue. I found Fauna before she could complain of my absence. We discreetly ate one half of Raina's sugar coated orange slices and sparingly sipped water from my waterskin.

Rosie's mauve brown hide approached from my left, Zander's black leather pants draped down either side of her belly. Fauna looked up at Zander with outright wonder. I kissed her knuckles as I pried them off my arm.

"Sorry, friend. I need to ride on horseback in order to be of any use." I turned my attention upward. "I am tired. I have dreaded this moment, but I need your arms and saddle, Drift." Zander extended his hand to me in his all-knowing, confident manner, while offering Fauna a chipper smile.

I took it and was hauled into the air. Fauna gasped at how quickly I was lifted into the saddle and how effortlessly he removed the arrows off my back and spun the belt around my waist to where the satchel hung at my left knee, entirely accessible. *Honestly, Zander. Your pride is insufferable.*

I knew you would need me eventually.

Fauna smirked modestly, not enough to hide the sadness lining her face. "We hardly slept when we shared a bed. I didn't expect that sharing a frost covered rock to be different. Sleep now so I can make use of you later." Zander let out an audible laugh. I elbowed him in his ribs. Twice. It did little.

Are you absolutely certain you're not part succubus? A female incubus.

I enjoy sex. I did not know that was a grievous sin that would ban me from entering the afterlife.

Hardly. Definitely not with an incubus Overlord monitoring the souls to their destination. He brought my head under his chin and wrapped his large cloak around my body. Heat and spice rose from his steadily rising chest. He took off his thick glove before sliding his left hand around my naval. He secured his grip on my hip. It wouldn't wander away from where it affixed, that much was certain. *Wisteria, I have my own list of questions that you can answer once you are feeling up for it.*

I sent a soft affirmation down our connection. There was so little I knew compared to his vast knowledge, yet I agreed. Somehow, this godly creature believed I held information deemed useful, or probably just interesting to keep his immortal mind busy. Sleep would have to come first.

I hardly remember setting off and I certainly did not recollect being rearranged a top Rosie to where both my feet were draped over one side in a side-saddle position. Zander held me snuggly with my head firmly against his chest. His harsh whispers are what stirred me awake after midday. "Break away and unsheathe your blades!" He shouted into the open woods. The ring of steel retracting from belts was loud, causing the entire lot of us to hold our breath.

"They've never attacked during daylight," Cultee spat nearby. Zander did not react. His heart hadn't skipped a beat or sped up. His jaw remained laxed, his lips parted. His eyes scanned the woods and when they found nothing, he turned them down onto me, cozily cradled in the pocket of his arm.

Admiring the view? I pinched the sensitive skin by his ribs and straightened myself, swatting off his grip. He lifted my bow off his back and pressed it into my right hand. "The horde knows we are here."

"Why aren't we moving forward?" I asked, stealing a peek at the men and women huddled together with wooden spears pointed at the devastated tree line of the Wasteland. They were petrified. "If we run–"

"If we run, we will exhaust ourselves. Even if we drop everything lacking value and never pause for respite, we still wouldn't arrive at the cart until tomorrow early morning. When they come for us, we can't be fatigued."

"When they come for us, let's be closer to our destination to give half of us a fighting chance at surviving. Those who can't pick up arms need to run to Devnee because he has that excess supply of oil and fire that we could use to burn the wraiths down. We could at least hold them off until the next sunrise or until the watchtowers of Fort Fell send help," I retorted.

Zander squinted at me, debating the weight of my words. He looked up. "We could chase them down in the light. Captain, don't you have a theory about them regenerating strength at night and weakening during the day?"

"A theory, yes. One we do best not to test now if it means putting so many lives in danger. Let's send Hades off on a sprint to the cart, he will back track with as much ammunition as he can carry and help Devnee burn oil," Cultee spoke orders to his men.

I inhaled. "Hades should take the mother and babe with him. They won't weigh his mount down and if any one deserves to survive this, it is the infant." Everyone's eyes bore into me. It was as if Zander's dense form was no larger than a speck of dust or translucent window. They stared through him and onto my back. "That's just my opinion, sir." My ears burned under the unwanted attention.

"It is justified. Hades, kindly collect Mauve and Agate. Be sure to strap the babe tight so the cantering doesn't jostle the little one." Cultee surrendered his waterskin to Mauve, who accepted it without hesitation. Captain and Hades adjusted her seated position and they took off down the snow covered hills. "The rest of us will set out with haste. Consider this the last relief point until this time tomorrow. The night will be... eventful. The guards will alternate fatiguing persons and those with setbacks on the mounts. Remove anything of value from the chests and trunks, being light and agile on our feet is a priority since we highly regard each other's lives." It was not a convincing speech, but an honest one. I could not have been the only one to sense the absoluteness behind it, should we fail as a collective. "Guards of Numaal, your swords stay vigilant until Fort Fell is within sight. Villagers, your feet remain moving until a fire disbands the darkness." There was a firm mumble of obedience. His horse clomped over to me. "Woodlander, you are the singular ranger among us. Don't waiver." His broad nose flared as he called his mount onwards. Panic arose among the residents of a fallen Horn's End. They distraughtly abandoned their goods, sentimental valuables and even necessities of warmth and food to keep pace with the rapid strides the captain had set for the caravan.

"Drift?" I called the guard. "Do you think it best I ride behind you, to have my bow at arms?"

"It's a fine idea. I've been waiting years to be held by you," he whispered back, not hiding the upturned half grin. I dropped to the ground to rearrange my personal belongings and enjoyed the heat returning to my toes. He moved his cape aside and pushed his hips up to the horn of the saddle. My hand felt petite as it disappeared in Zander's grip. I plopped behind him.

"You've baited your time well, old man. I'm sure you've been coddled by countless to pass your days," I stated into the fabric of his back. His left arm reached behind him and brought my arm around his thick waist. He left it there. Zander reared Rosie west and the jostle led me to cling tighter to his hard torso. Was he flesh or stone? "You do seem the type to need extensive coddling."

If I admit to it, you must swear to keep it from Fen.

Fauna's hand grazed my knee as we set off. I watched her and the others hike up their trousers and blankets to trek into the snow. I should be along them, not resting atop a horse. *I'm not getting between the two of you and your woven blanket thing. Besides, your need for cosseting is likely not a secret from him, given what you told me, I safely assumed you have none.*

That is true. Very little we keep shrouded, although it never feels as an intrusion of privacy. But Fennick doesn't know the extent of the patheticness I am willing to sink to if you are the one coddling me—to have my needs and wants satisfied by you. I will be wrapped around your finger. Happily so.

His midnight rainbow shone the brightest and rang the clearest I'd ever felt it. His words took the truest form, there was nothing but truth in what he felt. *That is forward.* My lungs stalled trying hard to ignore the grating his flirting caused on my core. Was this him flirting or merely stating facts? Internally, I wavered in the space between us.

Your scent is heavy here, I cannot think clearly. I felt him reach out and touch our bond. He retracted, feeling me step away. *You aren't fond of my forwardness.* I stopped my energy from flowing to him and contemplated how he perceived me on the other end of our connection.

You are not special, I don't engage in relationships. I'm sure you heard Flint and my dialogue this morning.

I did. It pleased me to know that I am not the only one who you react coldly to after a compliment. The snapping of twigs far off took the moisture from my mouth. *I'll take a page from Fennick's techniques and tame my forwardness. Mildly and temporarily. Until you have grown accustomed to it.* He corrected his behavior before I had a chance to reply about Fennick's techniques.

Impossible, but appreciated. Zander called to the nearest guards to flank the crowd and set the fast pace. *I'm sure all of my boundary crossing with my self-pleasuring blurred the friendship line. It was probably unwise, but it didn't feel wrong. Strangely, I don't regret it.*

It was not wrong. We are still trying to understand the roles the Weaver wants us to play and we both learned a lot that night about the complexities of you and I.

I waved at Brock who rode with a villager that I didn't know by name but recognized as the apple strudel lady who sold baked sweets. Her hands were swollen with the ache of arthritis. Certainly, her other joints were too. I rummaged in my trunk for the last of the willow bark. I tossed it to Brock who knew what to do with it. *You were scared to see my reaction to your horns.*

A little curious to see what your reaction might be.

Why?

As you know, the blessed and the vibrant physically look the same, honestly, if they didn't out live everyone there isn't much of a difference between the two lots except residing on opposite coasts of the continent. That's why without a priestess descended from Misotaka's bloodline it is tricky to find silver bloods among Numaal. Even to those who frequent the Veil or see me in the temples of Akelis, an incubus can take people off guard more than an ice scaled serpent with butterfly antennas and two heads. He must have heard my inhale. *Yes, there is such a dreamer being, it can wrap around the White Tower thrice. It's called a morrat.* I blinked. *That is not the point I'm trying to make. People don't grasp our abilities of charm, the insecure relationships tend to flee fast when they see the seven sons of Atticus arrive in Akelis for holidays, temple prayers or grocery shopping. I honestly don't know what I would have done if I sensed any hesitancy or repulsion from you.*

You would not run off. That is not in your nature.

A pensive moment passed. I knew he wouldn't have. *I would have tended my own wound as I am accustomed to and stayed by your side, as I am now, in whatever capacity you need me.*

You would have closed off. And we can't have that because I still want the sun out of the cage. My brows stitched together at how silly my words echoed in my skull. There was no taking them back. Zander heard them and cleared a laugh from his chest discreetly.

For someone who has no interest in engaging in relationships you sure pry a lot.

Until the glorious day I finally get to leave this world behind, my reckless mortal self is stuck next to your exhausting godly arse, so I am attempting to make it comfortable and not strained. My palms started to sweat. Heat burned from my hand onto his naval. "There are five hours of sunlight left. They will creep alongside us, closing the gap and striking when night the moon peaks. Is there harm in lighting a torch or twenty? It will help foster a sense of control and safety."

Cultee hollered, "Any salvageable wood that is not scorched is wet. We need our garb for warmth and can't afford to burn it."

I looked around the sparse foliage and a few trees. "You can always use eroks." I shrugged, pointing to the thin shoot with wide roots. "The bark is wax covered, if you peel it back you will find dry wood and roots saturated with oil perfect for a flame. It is fragile, but it works in a pinch."

Fauna and one of her female colleagues sprinted ahead of Copper to dismantle the nearest eroks. Flint tossed his lighter to her and within seconds the small first flame formed. Within minutes each member of the party had a branch or a full torch in flames. A villager pressed a thick branch into Cultee's hand. He examined its coated bark. "Ivy!" Captain shouted. Startled, I spun in my seat.

"Yes, sir?"

"Remind me to never travel without you again. You're outlandish, but surprisingly resourceful," his leeward compliment was lost under his horse's clomping hooves. Pink warmed my cheeks as I pressed them against Zander's back. What would my parents think, blushing at the praise of a captain? "They're moving ahead of us to intercept the shortest distance; we need to increase our speed I'm afraid." There was no complaining, only action.

Those on the ground were hustling at a jog, sweat warmed their bodies, temporarily fending off the bitter cold that accompanied the all too soon descending darkness. My hairs stood on end. My breath was no longer visible for night had robbed most of us of our vision, save what the flame offered.

A confident hand grazed over my left arm and laced their fingers with mine. I calmed under the strength and warmth. "Arrow in notch," Zander whispered as he turned Rosie directly east. We stilled. I left our hands where they were and peeked my head around his tall wide form to see the pitch-black night splayed out. I think my grip slightly tightened because his thumb stroked my wrist in a comforting gesture. He eased his hand and reiterated, "Arrow in notch, my flower."

Flowers were delicate. I was not a flower.

At his exasperating words I swiftly pulled my touch away, which may have been his objective, and set an arrow ready on the bow. Not able to see behind his form, I knelt in the saddle. Zander, clearly unfond of my positioning, tried to pull me down on my hindquarters, I buried the bond so I did not have to hear him boss me around telling me to sit properly. I was far from proper, I assured myself turning to see a guard and Copper flanking us, alone in their saddle with fire and blade drawn. "Onward!" Cultee hollered loudly, full of determination. Most of the crowd followed him. Not us. "Run until you see a bonfire. Continue to run west on the main road until the fort is within sight if you do not see any more survivors by noon tomorrow." The villagers sprinted into the night as a glowing mass chasing the captain's lantern.

The able bodies guarded the moving parameters, the night quieted.

Copper exhaled, "How the damn heavens are we supposed to see?"

"They have got to make the first move. The light from the eroks will illuminate their forms when they get close enough to us. We have to act fast, their proximity won't allow much room for error or tentativeness. Go for their heads and the vulnerable tissue on their necks," Zander stated assuredly. "When we last counted the horde their numbers were about the size of our current caravan. That has probably tripled or more since we've lost Horn's End."

My teeth sunk into my lip. Nearly two hundred undead were out there. Yards away. The most I had fought was twelve. And Keenan was always at my side. "Fuck," I said, letting my guard down in the familiar company.

"I've always enjoyed it when you talk filthy," Brock snickered, lining his horse up with Copper's. "Since we are probably going to die, might as well confess that I had a thing for you, Ivy."

I giggled, pretending to be flattered. "You never stood a chance."

"Whose fault is that? You cut off my bloody leg, I can't stand at all!" Brock countered. Our company laughed. "Note the past tense. I am more than honored to call you a friend and happily remain indebted to you for saving my life."

"You are so dramatic," I said, locking my gaze on a dark shadow I swore stirred. "Cut the shit and be ready to strike."

He exhaled a moan. "Ah! The filthy talk continues."

"Fucking hell," I whispered.

Zander purred. *Your vulgarity openly enthuses them, try to be more tactful.*

I punched his back. My eyes watered because my fist bruised as if it hit a wall. *I am not a fragile creature!* In an afterthought I added. *And they are harmless, Brock is a brother.*

True enough. A long minute passed as more and more branches cracked in the near distance. *You told Cultee you were decent with a bow, I expect that you were down playing your abilities.*

I was. *I can mercifully kill from seventy yards with an arrow and with the right blade, I can decapitate and disembowel in three steps and two bats of an eyelash.*

Who taught you?"

Ilanthians, Anna and Keenan. They were on the ship. I stated finitely as if that was explanation enough. Spinning in his seat, Zander pulled a ten-inch blade from his belt and slipped it into my tunic's front pocket where it punctured the fabric. The guardian dagger pulsed loudly. *What are you doing?*

All that I can to keep you alive. Go for their hearts if you fall into hand-to-hand combat.

The woods groaned.

An eerie clicking echoed as the wraiths formed a long wall of decaying bodies encroaching in unison on our party. Unable to withhold my reactive nerves, I stole the spear of flame from Copper's hand and shot it into the woods where three figures frantically moved in front of it, dashing on four protruding legs towards us. The first one lunged at us and was met with a dull *shink* of metal through its skull. It seized and fell limp on the end of Zander's sword like a ragdoll in the wind. Moments later two more attacked Copper and Brock and met a similar fate. The horde collaborated with their strangled screams and odd clicks. "Brace yourselves!" Zander hollered, seeing countless claw their way across the frozen tundra and launch themselves at our mounts. They weren't aiming to take *us* down any more, they aimed for our advantage. They meant to slay the horses.

"No!" I heard myself scream as Rosie stumbled backward, narrowly avoiding the lengthy claws swiping at her neck. Zander and Copper slid off their mounts to defend them on their feet while I locked and launched arrow after arrow into the thick black flesh of the rotting evils. The pile of bodies grew high enough to where we had to digress several feet to make room for more crumbling wraiths.

"That's nineteen in total! I'm taking credit for four of 'em!" Brock wiped dark blood across his face in a sad attempt to remove a splash of it.

"I'm at eight," Zander countered. "The rest of the undead watching are opting for a different fate. They are moving towards our vulnerable travelers. We should too!"

The horselord returned to the saddle, his weight and momentum caused me to fall into him. "I'm going to sit backwards." I stated, fumbling around with much less finesse. "I don't want them to come for our open backs."

He didn't fight me. "I won't bother trying to stop you." He blindly reached behind himself and knotted his hand in the fabric of my cloak. Another precaution for my safety. No sooner had we trotted off away from the mound of wraiths, did a dozen more chase after us.

I struck them down. Most square between the eyes and many through their windpipe and jugular. "Drift, I've taken you out of the lead! Brock, add thirteen to my personal headcount!" I shouted as the last of the chasing wraiths merged with the icy night.

Copper joined the banter. "This is a competition?"

"Yes, one you are going to lose by the looks of it," Zander offered, digging his heels into Rosie.

"What are the stakes?" To my shock, it was sweet Copper who posed that question.

My fingers clutched into the edge of the saddle to stabilize me upright. "Bragging rights!" I shouted, my voice slipped up an octave as the holder of my cloak tugged me into his spine as we climbed up a hill. The other two mounts found another path up the slope. I held my breath until I saw them again at the top. Nervous sweat broke out along my hairline as the minutes passed.

Brock was breathless. "I was hoping for something more exciting like a kiss from Ivy!"

"So long as when I win, I expect a pint of whiskey from *each* of you!" Their laughter was agreement enough. Screams ahead beckoned our haste. I had to lower my weapon and press my spine into Zander's for the remainder of the time it took to arrive with the rest of our convoy who were scrambling in groups of torches and spears. Long contorted black limbed entities edged closer, we were surrounded on three sides which shortly became four.

Cultee grunted, observing the restless thwart our progress and send most into a frenzied upsurge of dread.

The young children wavered as blood left their round faces, I saw Cobar in all of them. *Release me.* His hand stayed entwined in the fabric. *I need to go to them.* My heart ached at this point.

It doesn't feel right to have you leave my side amidst a battle with imminent bloodshed.

I reached down into myself to where I felt Zander's strong warm presence rooted into me. I spun myself around our bond, snaking down our connection. *I can handle myself.* He was quick to swarm his colors over me. A hug he was resistant to disengage from. *Zander Veil Halfmoon di Lucent, you will let me go.*

This is the last time. Don't make me regret it. The moment his hold opened, I dropped to the ground and ran to the closest child. Small arms hugged above my knees and another pair around my waist. I held my bow string taut. It cut into my fingers. Cultee was barking orders, none of which I comprehended because I was focused too intently on the cracked configuration of the nearest wraith. Its movements were unnatural as if its limbs were dislocated. Fauna covered the eyes of the nearest child, who proceeded to faint in her arms.

The clangor of iron and steel combined with the putrid scent of death infiltrated my nose, alerting the rest of my senses to the danger around me. My heart skipped along as my eyes absorbed the scene.

I shot one arrow into the equivalent of a wraith's thigh to bring it down. I shoved the guardian dagger into its chest cavity right after. The blade thudded in my hands when it tasted the blood as if it was screaming to be further quenched. I obeyed the call and sprinted to where Rodrick was draped unceremoniously across the rear of a horse. I took out another wraith and shouted, "Sixteen!" It took tremendous effort to not reach for the glinting swords and put my years of combat training and wraith hunting to use. I stroked the feathered ends of the weapon supplied to me.

Copper pulled his sword out from a decaying corpse and grinned at me. "Seven!" He sliced off the arm of the next restless who did not notice pain or the fact it was missing a limb. "Eight!"

"Step it up men or I'll have your coin purse empty buying me rounds!" I hollered, shooting two arrows in one release taking down a soulless thing inches away from closing its gaping teeth around Cultee's calf. He and four men linked together against a wall of incoming wraiths. I winked as I ran by him to gather up the wandering children who moseyed far too close to the edges of danger. I corralled them away from drawn swords, unfortunately I could not erase their memories of this night.

Flint hit the floor, his weapon had fallen inches from his grasp. The man next to him was dead, bled out from the gash across his abdomen. Flint was in a scramble, tied in a blur of legs and punches. With Fennick's family heirloom in hand I ran and toppled over the creature, stabbing just below its scapula. It turned on me. Chasing me as I ran away from the thick of the fight.

I sprinted down a path of snow and slush. Flint caught up in the dark of the tree tops and tackled its legs. I killed it while a distraction pulled its black eyes and skull face off me.

A pestering rattle in my left hand demanded to be met.

It was my woven who eagerly waited for my reply.

Seventeen. I sent to Zander, who was impatiently and energetically hovering. The overbearingness did not end. He called me to him from yards away in the main battle.

I hear him yell across the clearing. "Woodlander! Shield my flank!" Zander was off his horse and spun two long blades, one in each hand, ones that would take all my body weight to even lift parallel to the floor. He had tied torches to the nearest charred tree trunk and stepped into the light, summoning the monsters to approach him. Daring them too.

They came.

Chapter Eleven

He sliced through them like a hot knife through butter. Bodies fell. His vigor strengthened as time passed. "Twenty-two!" Grey drab entities jumped over Flint and me. We sprung upright after finding a break in their horde. Flint staggered and worked out kinks in his back, I ran and rounded on Zander from the left. Standing atop a boulder, I launched arrows that slayed the wraiths before they could meet his blade. He spun around in confusion.

"That's twenty for me!" I boasted, launching an arrow that whizzed right by his ear and plunged into the chest of a wraith. The horrific gurgling sound escaping its pierced lung was nauseating. I sent another to end it.

He roared. "Stealing my chance at a victory, are you?"

"You must not want the prize bad enough."

"I've never desired anything more in my entire life," he shouted over his shoulder after ensuring his double strike brought down the gangly form jumping at him from the nearest tree. More emerged and tag teamed each person armed with metal. They went for our ankles and simultaneously our hearts. I kicked the disfigured head under my feet and fired an arrow at the wraith swinging its open claws at the children in the middle. A woman was swiped down and feasted upon. Cultee ended that one with painstaking anger that we all felt, the screams of terror were laced with sadness and disbelief as more blameless blood spilt on the ground.

The adored hilt of Fennick's blade was drenched in a sticky, necrotic blood. I kicked the dead off me in order to remove the dagger plunged in its stomach. It took me too long to reorient myself, they had swarmed a mount and silenced its whines all while I had barely retrieved an arrow from my back. My comrades were still fighting, all as worn down as I began to feel. "Twenty-nine!" Zander shouted while rolling on the snow dodging an attack. Captain was on his way to his aid. My numb hands familiarized themselves with my arrows. I pierced the wraith's skull and the one behind Cultee. He hardly had time to process my shot, it was far better than the average guard, as he pulled Zander off the snow mound.

"I get credit for those!" I hollered across the battlefield, a young boy shot me a toothy grin as I ran to help Brock off the ground. I stabbed the twitching nightwalker twice for good measure and looped my bow around my torso. Brock wrapped his arm around my shoulders as nearly all his weight shifted onto me. I scanned the chaotic scene for Rodrick and his mount for that is where my old friend would be the safest.

He hopped along openly bitter about the destination. "Where is my crutch? My brace?" He spat tripping over gnarled roots.

"Next to a dead man. Go after it and you will join him in hell, or stay here, recuperate and let me fetch it." I shook him off my back. He arranged himself on the floor amid frozen foliage.

He caught his breath, "Sounds a bit more promising when you put it that way. I can fight." He grabbed my wrist and pleaded with his brown eyes.

I crouched down. Pressing our hands together I said, "You will fight. You are irreplaceable. I'll see you back out there to slaughter a few more of these fuckers tonight or in the weeks ahead." His laugh fueled me with enough purpose to slide my way back into the heart of the clash of the undead and living where Flint had managed to pull himself off the floor, the women of the circles were covered in entrails driving spears into damaged wraiths. The remaining guards, along with their captain, forced their way west and pulled the chaos with them.

We were making headway to our destination. The darkness followed, bringing death.

"Ivy, get down!" Complying, I hit the floor as Copper flew over me to tackle a wraith. My flat stomach groaned as my ribs contacted a jagged rock. I winced as I rolled and found Brock's warped metal brace. I scurried back to him and strapped it to a mount.

"Go west! You need to keep yourself and Rodrick alive and on that mount. Flame and sword high! Cultee will send the others behind you." I helped him into the saddle and arranged Rodrick to where his neck would not snap with the haste. I left him as he began shouting names of the villagers to trail him. I ran to disengage a few of the wraiths in combat, all too aware my steps and stamina were twice as good as any decade trained guard of Numaal.

Keenan would want his years of efforts to go unnoticed until the time was right to unleash them—that time was not now. Stegin wasn't here. The ache in my chest grew. I intentionally slowed and stumbled, allowing a gangly fist to slam into the side of my head, knocking me to my knees.

Copper rushed to help me fight the wave of evil. One mighty swing of a sword behind me severed the body into two clean halves. Blood trickled from my ear, the ringing didn't stop. "West?" I shouted, unaware of the intensity of my tone. Could have been a whisper for all I knew.

Luckily, Zander could speak to me under the deafening pitch sounding in my head.

My head felt faint—I should have taken a blow to my leg and not risked the strike on my mentation. *You've been compromised.* I knew what was coming, him wanting me within arm's reach. That possessive incubus trait made an appearance. I made a dash away from him, his arms folded around me. I kicked when he tightened his grip around my waist and chose to fight single handedly with only one of his swords—putting everyone at risk. I punched him square in the chin. "Put me down!" I screamed, causing the blood to rush to my head.

"I am not your enemy. Stop fucking hitting me!" he gritted, spitting out blood. I grunted. "After you prove to me you can shoot an arrow with accuracy—I will release you. I guarantee you are going to be seeing double or blurred vision after that last hit. I've taken that same crush too many times to recollect."

"I do not have to prove anything to anyone! Especially not you nor do I have to obey your word," I fussed as he calmly placed the bow into my hand. He pointed to a wraith swinging from a low bough. An easy kill to make as he kept me safe from oncoming attacks. I raised my arrow and focused my left eye. My peripheral was dim and hazy. I opened both eyes and watched villagers run by. I didn't trust my aim not to waiver and hit a civilian by grievous mistake. Lowering my arrow left me feeling defeated. "I owe you an apology," I swallowed the bitter taste of fault.

"I'll collect it when I come to collect my victory kiss." I felt his lips and cool breath on the back of my skull where contusions had started to form. Humor sounded between our tie of fate.

"You assume that I and the others are out of the competition. Arrogant of you." Zander gave my bow and arrow satchel to a guard who had thrown his body atop Nordic and rushed to find the reins. It hurt to have them leave my side. In return for my bow the guard offered up his guard's sword, which was smaller than the horselord's, but far bulkier than Orion.

"You assume that Copper or Brock ever had a fair chance to compete for a prize I would die twice over to obtain. I was merely humoring them." The bluntness didn't match the serious tone which he spoke.

"So much for taming the forwardness."

"That was before you agreed to offer your mouth up to the victor despite whom that may be. If I am exceedingly jealous or possessive or wanting more, it's your fault for feeding me such addictive substances."

"Peaches are hardly addictive," I gritted.

His spine straightened and he gained another four inches in height. He saw into the depth of the night. "Your fault," he bluntly reiterated.

It was. I doused first his room and then him with my scent. There was only one way out of this predicament. "I can beat you. I'm only behind by what? Three?"

"Eight," he corrected, a rustically devilish grin appeared.

"If you place that sword in my grip, I'll embarrass you and every guard here." I pointed to the Numaalian sword he presented me. I spun Fennick's dagger in a way that earned me an impressed brow raise from the two-century old mixed blood. "This will suffice until insanity consumes me."

We turned away from the rider. "You're remarkably arrogant for a girl who just got her skull kicked in."

"Good. Let's hope others are underestimating me too," I murmured. His face dropped.

"That was fucking intentional, wasn't it?"

I brushed him off. I ran towards the dividing sentries at the rear to protect the slower paced and injured. I evaluated the rest of the cautious horde. We had made great progress in lessening their numbers. I didn't have much time or bodies to close the gap between our kills, I had to make every strike count before cold sweat set in. Waiting for the wraiths to grow confident or for the captain's blessing for my recklessness was burning away my precious seconds, I darted straight into the darkness without a torch knowing they would be caught unprepared.

At the first slight shift in the night, I stabbed. The warm liquid pooling in my grip told me it was a success. I withdrew and swung at the creature, pulling my feet out from underneath me. "Twenty-four. I can taste the burn of liquor already, old man!"

"Thirty-one. Thirty-two," he huffed, ripping a spine out of an elongated torso. His swords he left at my feet. He went forth unarmed. He tore through the horde ripping heads off with his bare hands snapping vertebrae. The man could see in the thick of the dark with precision. His brute power was apparent and beautifully terrifying.

Maybe his dreamer being strength and godly blood, did set him apart in an animalistic nature, an attribute very different from my common blood? My filthy boots stayed planted firm as he single handedly destroyed the remainder of the many, many monsters mobbing him. He must have stopped and finished the job because a large black leather boot kicked my toes and stole my attention. "Are you afraid?" His chest heaved, the exhales rustled my hair. His hands and forearms were slick with decay, and the white portions of his braid shone under the small glint of the moonlight. "Say something, Wisteria."

I was in a daze. "I am a little envious," I admitted. "I also stopped counting after fifty crunchy noises, which I presumed were deaths. I lost the competition." He patted my shoulder with a gentleness one would have assumed witnessing what I had just did, an impossibility. Yet, his touch was as reassuring and soft as it had been with me in all our previous interactions.

A man of precise control.

"Let's linger," he said, taking the dagger from my slack hand and shoving it into one of their hallowed skulls. We must loiter a fair number of minutes to make them believe our victory was a prolonged struggle. Well not *our* victory, if in fact did very little. I placed my hand on my hip bones while he stabbed each evil with his woven's blade.

"Ouch," I yelped, realizing my rib cage was more than bruised. It was broken. Four of them by the feel of it. Zander was within my personal space before I had time to register any movement. "I'll tend to it back at the fort. It's nothing," I pledged before he inquired.

"*Nothing* doesn't make Wisteria Woodlander shriek in pain," he responded in a tranquil cadence.

I handed him his long swords off the ground and reiterated, "I'll tend to it once I am back at Fort Fell."

He was skeptical. "So you said."

"Yes. Twice now actually."

"Do I need to carry you?"

"Do I need to punch you for even suggesting such a stupid thing?"

He chuckled, "You have already done that several times in the span of the day. I fear your hand will break should you decide me deserving of yet another knock in the skull."

I groaned, "Most of those were warranted."

"You are violent. I quite like it." I shook my head in disbelief at his bizarre flattery, at the same time I shook off the aches that tried to creep into my body. We had several more leagues to run, there would be no resting until the sun rose.

I dipped my head towards the distant end of our caravan. They were completely gone. "You can see in the dark, right?"

"In the dark and into other worlds, yes. I will guide you." He put one of his swords away and with his free hand held mine as a means to guide me.

I took it. The sticky blood coagulated on our skin. "I need to stay awake. How about you ask your questions now?"

He squeezed my hand as means to agreement. "The people of the Southlands seem to cringe at the mention of knights. Even when I told you that was my projected course in these lands to get into the duke's graces, your hate was blatant and earned me your cold shoulder on the first day of our reunion. What happened the night of the attack?"

It had been years since I had vocalized anything about that night, it only resurfaced in my dreams to haunt me. "An armed carriage came to Ferngrove after it raided every homestead within a full day's ride. There was a man barking orders from inside its black curtains and a priestess covered in rubies who relayed the messages to the knights. They slaughtered us, but not before they raped my mother and made my father watch. They gutted my mom when they finished, Anna tried to pull me away from the house. I couldn't move. When they killed my dad who stood unarmed protecting Moriah and her infant, Rory, and her young boy, Cobar, I jumped out from the pantry and charged at the largest one." I tiptoed over a root, recalling his appearance.

"With his black, spiked armor and pleated steel, he looked your size. There were even horns protruding from his helmet, two out of each side, not your crescent shape." I gestured on my own head. "He spotted Anna behind me, the priestess shook her head at us. They believed both of us were red bloods. The knight promised to save us for later since he already... *my mother*... Tweed sacks were tied around my head, Anna's too by the sound of the struggle. The man in the carriage ordered the three silver bloods to be taken to Landsfell and to kill all spares, outside of the two whores to join Stegin's brothel, as they were a gift for allowing him to hunt on his province. The *whore* reference was for Anna and I." I added to clear confusion.

He was slow to reply. It was a quiet affirmative hum. His white eye was Fennick's gold, I waved to him as if he was here among us. Zander blinked at my greeting to his woven, yet his face was still taut with my heavy story.

"I can't help but feel somewhat responsible for the other villages torn down by the knights looking for the Ilanthians we sheltered."

"You can't say with certainty that the rest of the provinces weren't hiding blessed blood or that they weren't going to get pillaged regardless. Your parents and the elders who raised you knew the risks they took when they extended their hospitality to the blessed," he reassured. "They had their reasons too, which they deemed more valuable than death."

"I do not know how accurate or well-trained the priestess was for she didn't seem to think Anna an Ilanthian nor register Keenan running back from gathering luminescent blossoms from the shore. Maybe, she was trying to be helpful or kind, wanting to keep people alive."

"Doubtful by the sound of your narrative thus far. She didn't know about Anna and Keenan was too distant from her vision, perhaps Anna had a generational magic that allowed her to shield herself. It is not uncommon for the old families who descended from one of the Eleven or were of the first created from Korgi Dunes or Montuse." Zander offered in a contemplative tone. "Sorry, to interrupt."

"There is not much left of the story you don't know. I was hit unconscious for kicking the guard in his loins the moment he tried to toss me over his shoulder. There was plenty of screaming and crying from the babies and a protective mother. They were gagged. We were separated. The broken family to the upper chambers, Anna and I to the dungeons. The rest you can assimilate."

"Those knights were from Kathra. Did you happen to pick up any names or details of the man behind the curtains?" I shook my head. My gut twisted as if I had disappointed him.

"I'm sure if I dare to dwell on it, names and details would arise. If I didn't fight my dreams, maybe they would tell me something more."

He stopped in his tracks. "If it causes you torment, it's something you will forgo." Appreciation simmered down our line banishing all notions of my disappointment.

"Can you enter my dreams and fish around for your answers?"

"That would be convenient. But dreams and dreamer beings aren't linked, but through our bond I can guard what energies flock to you in the unconscious state. Not that you have granted me permission for me to do that yet."

My sweat chilled on my body in the next gust of wind. "Do you have nightmares?"

"Occasionally. They have run their course over the last century and have diminished with passing years." He continued his wonderment, "Why do they call you the prodigy child?"

"Because I was concocting better than my parents before puberty. I had an unfair advantage, I grew up with Ilanthians and could properly read and write; therefore, properly study and memorize all the herbs and uses in Numaal and even in Ilanthia should I get lost in their woods. Moriah was a physician. I can remove septic organs with the proper tools, sedatives and cleansers. The other crafting clans heard of my progress via seadrifters during bartering season—when we would gather to exchange goods before winter. I didn't get my master's ink until weeks after I left you. Keenan performed the ceremony and at my request added a spray of lilacs in memory of Anna."

"Just how dangerous is a master woodlander?"

I couldn't stop myself from thinking of how much torment Gimly was going through, and smiling. "Plenty dangerous. I have enough toxins on me at any given time to sedate and or kill anywhere from thirty to forty men. Closer to twenty if they are your size. I can also inflict passive long-term damage. For example, prior to us disembarking I found out that Gimly was the one who raped and impregnated Sage months ago. I remedied his behavior by promptly making him impotent and to further grind salt onto his wound, I killed off his seed. He will not sire any heirs nor bring life into this world to continue his name."

I heard Zander's mouth open, stuttering noises escaped. His one golden eye and one blue eye blinked. Fennick lingered in his mind.

"Cultee warned him not to piss off a woodlander, he ignored that warning. It is his own damn fault and I don't feel one ounce of guilt.

Come to think of it, I can't think of anyone more deserving of a desolate future."

He swore. A lot. I think it was a happy bombardment of curse words. "Remind me never to get on your bad side," he stated. I wavered and stepped over a lumpy object that I soon realized was a body. My bowels twisted and clenched. "Let's stop and light a fire for her. There is a man not too far off. I'll collect him too."

"I agree." Being as I couldn't see in the dark, I stood where I was left, my heart heavy. Zander returned with a body draped across his arms and laid him next to the female he arranged with her eyes shut and arms crossed her chest. Then came the honey voice that I first heard back in Stegin's dungeons; it was as comforting as it always had been. It was sweeter than ever and full of hope instead of sadness. I held my breath to hear the conclusion. That and I knew my empty stomach would be sick if I inhaled the scent of burning flesh that begun to invade the air as the erok's flame caught on their woolen clothes. He spoke a language that Anna would whisper in her dreams and rested his palms on their heads before departure.

We took a flamed branch with us. "It's the language of the Eternals. I started jabbering after Malick emptied his blood into my vessel. It's a dead language now and I've no need to speak it to the Emperor and Empress, when common dialogue works easily enough."

"It's exquisite," I admitted. He had enough decency not to make an outrageous self-inflated comment. Who would have imagined? Over my shoulder the bodies smoldered into ash and flecks of hot soot floated into the dark night, illuminating the small woods. We made it up the next hill. I pointed at a small glowing oblong shape just over two miles away. "They are making great progress."

Zander took my wrist and moved my pointer finger to the left a few centimeters. A few more leagues beyond the caravan a bright burst, which could only be a fire, raged. "Hades made it to the cart. Devnee lit the pyres." Our chances of survival significantly increased. I practically collapsed in relief on the downhill and again denied Zander's offer to carry me. "All that's left to do is arrive before noon tomorrow so they don't leave without us."

"We will make it an hour. If you are implying, we rest for my sake, I may revoke all and any unmalicious feelings I've come to harbor for you." I waved a finger at his widening grin. "None are starry-eyed, I've merely started to tolerate the way you grate on my nerves. Which is a lot, I'll have you know."

His eyes twinkled with mischief. His woven eye was a lustrous, milky white. "No racing?"

"No," I hastily replied. We both knew I couldn't afford to lose another bet, not that I had anything left to offer up. "I'll meet you there. I've a torch, blade and a destination. I'll be fine if you run along ahead to inform your captain of your success."

"No chance I am stepping out of your five foot radius. Do you have rabbit food to eat? You're looking faint."

I checked my breast pockets and satchel. My movements were stiff because the blood had begun to dry and freeze onto my flesh and fabric. "My scones are on Nordic. It's just up ahead at the bend of the creek." I wondered, "Is there any way to reverse incubus energy?"

"How so?"

"Instead of taking from me, can you *give* me some of that *pep* you've absorbed?"

He pondered a moment in silence. "No. My nature is extensively selfish despite how I would enjoy little else than to replenish your stores."

My asking was worth a try, I banished all thoughts of magically reviving myself. I conserved my energy and focused on placing one foot in front of the other, Zander seemed to be doing the same with the addition of holding steady his right hand behind my shoulder, hovering inches away should my footing slipped.

Which I can proudly say, it didn't.

The putrid and familiar scent of death revolted my stomach. I had little choice but to remove my gloves and first layer of tunics, which allowed the cold to permeate. "You look ravishing in my tunics, do you need to don mine to prevent your bones from shattering in the brittle cold?" I glared at him. He knew damn well his comments were cheeky.

Two could play that game. "No, I prefer heat in the form of bodies making friction. Worry not, ahead lies my friend Fauna."

"Can you accept my cloak? You can rid it before we enter camp, no one will know you needed aid to remain alive. Another one of our secrets, not even Fen will know."

"I will remain alive without it. You forget I have been surviving off of frozen tree moss in a brothel gown and *alone* for the last two years."

"You consider yourself alone despite living in a village. That defines emotional distancing. Was it self-imposed solitude?"

I had one true confidant in these lands and he buried himself in a cave seven miles away from Horn's End, rarely allowing me to visit which rarely allowed me to let my guard down. "It's complicated."

"Say you accomplish your vow to Anna. Kill the duke and tell the Emperor about these *vulborg*. Would you still want to be alone?"

"Being alone is not the same as being lonely."

"Forgive me, Wisteria, I've misspoken. Do you not form intimate relationships because of your history of having them ended too soon?"

The sensation rising in my chest was as constricting as the weight of a ton of rocks crushing my heart. My parents. Anna. Moriah, Rory and Cobar. And the seventeen...acquaintances, friends... I murdered. Brock was almost one of them. I lashed out defensively, "You trend too far into matters that will never concern you. If you were considering breaching this topic in the future, I recommend holding your tongue or risk me cutting it out of your mouth."

"I understand that this subject of conversation has concluded."

Silence festered. Distress blossomed and climbed up my legs and spun around my chest as comfortable as a thicket of thorns. Gods did this man know how to aggravate me. The thorns choked out any warmth of happy thoughts. When the fires of our caravan were roaring within ear shot, a second wind of motivation strummed through my feet. I ran to the break in the flames and shot through to the other side. "Fauna!" I called nervously. A meek brunette popped her head up from a bed roll. She was on her knees when I fell into her arms. I was fairly certain I was asleep before gravity took me all the way to the sheep skin.

B.B. Aspen

Chapter Twelve

"Wake her up," A male said. He sounded not too far off. I turned to my side and continued sleeping.

A female defended, "Can't you see how swollen the side of her head is? She needs rest!" Now, that someone brought attention to it, the right side of my skull ached. My gums bled. My heartbeat thudded in my ear and flooded my mind with a high-pitched ringing. I swallowed. My jaw hurt too; I ran my tongue along the ridges of my teeth to ensure I had them all. I did. And blood in my mouth.

"She promised my father the pain would be tolerable. Don't make her a liar by preventing her from carrying out her word." I moved my fingers and toes to dissipate the sleep. Flint was the male voice that stirred in my half slumber. Fauna the female.

"Take me to Rodrick," I muttered, pushing myself halfway up on an elbow. My hair broke free in the night, it was a dirty disaster. I rose slowly. Every twinge and ache made themselves known to me, my flank and side body stabbed me with each inhale, I kept my breaths shallow to manage the pain. I ignored Flint's extended hand and cautiously rose upright from all fours, following his steps to the cart where Rodrick laid under a decent amount of blankets next to Hades, Asher and Devnee who were heating up the morning oatmeal in a large iron cauldron. A reasonable amount of softness was hidden behind their scars and overgrown brows. Rodrick's eyes shut with relief when he saw me.

"Good morning, Rodrick," I said, peeling off his covers. No body sweats, no fevers. Excellent progress.

He unclenched his jaw to reply. "A fine one it is. However, I'd much rather be in one of your drug induced comas than awake with this harsh pain." His jaw tightening again, his proud eyes moved away from his son's.

"Naturally." My own hands were atrociously filthy, there was no way to do a proper assessment on his wound without risking infection. I'd have to keep him at ease until I'd more resources. Untucking my shirts from my trousers I lifted the last of my layers until the skin on my navel was exposed. I pinned the fabric under my chin and began to untwist the white dangling jewelry from the piercing in my navel. The few who were awake stared. "Poppy milk," I educated the nosey crowd. I dropped my clothes and brought the vial to Rodrick's lips. "Three drops now, two more in an hour. You'll need to eat something if you want to regain your strength."

"Do you want to take some?" He asked with his upper lip twitching.

My head shook. "Why on earth would I need this?"

"You flashed your purple molting contusions to the camp. Was it two broken ribs I saw?"

"Four," I corrected. "And a strained psoas muscle, a concussion, a ruptured eardrum, misaligned jaw and my ass hurts from sitting in that Gods' damn saddle. I have done far more damage to myself in my youth, these are merely scratches, so stop worrying."

"Your parents were martyrs too," he whispered, dozing off. If my father had his sword in hand and half the aggression I was endowed with, he may have been able to stop the knight from defiling his wife and murdering her thereafter. Rodrick's pupils constricted and glazed over as the poppy plant went to work on his sensory system. "There is room on the cart for you to ride with me."

"I will walk. Save these cushions for the children," I pulled his cover back up to his chin.

Hades pushed over a wooden bowl of oats and a flat stick to use as a spoon. "Eat," he said.

Bland, but filling. My stomach rounded outwards, my pants tightened. Fauna brought over my waterskin and we split the last jam scone. She was quiet. Unusually clingy. She linked her elbow through mine and rested her heavy head on my stiff shoulder. We stayed stationed here until peak noon when the fires fumed and the wary scouts confirmed the absence of undead on the road ahead. I medicated Rodrick and slid off the wooden platform and onto my feet. My boots felt too constricted, I unlaced them for breathability and somehow persuaded them to fall into a stride. *There is room in my saddle, Wisteria.*

Riding knocks me around too much. My bones are skewed as it is. I'll settle with bloody ankles.

I grow tired of your refusals, but your stubbornness will never deter me from asking. When I see the fire behind your emerald eyes it only makes me try harder.

I have noticed. My refusals and acts of violence motivate you to be more of a pest. I pointed ahead of the cart. *I spot an envious child.* Rosie passed us, her rider off to escort a young boy, perhaps eleven, in Zander's front saddle. He was beaming when learning about the reins and horns. Zander's boisterous booming laugh spread over the people when he blamed the boy for almost steering them down a cliff. The slight hope was contagious. Almost distracting enough to pass a full ten minutes without registering distress from almost every joint of my body.

Unable to rally speed and strength, the lot of us camped out one final night just four hours outside of Fort Fell's watchtowers. There was venison stew and wild rice. "Care to barter?"

It was Tidal. Her full waist was less flattering without her lavish silks and belt to draw the eyes to her bosom and normally heavily painted face.

"Please," I jumped at the offer. Her serving of rice was dumped onto my bowl and Devnee gave her my scoop of deer meat and bone broth without so much as batting a lash. "There aren't many of us left. I'm sorry about your ladies, Madam. We all relied on your compassion and business to stay in good company and good spirits."

"Taking you in was no problem at all, darling. You hardly took up space and your services were vital to conducting a safe brothel," she brought the steaming bowl to her face and inhaled the hearty scents.

There was not one grain of rice remaining in my bowl when I dropped it off to be cleaned in the creek water. Fauna, who claimed she was too tired to eat, neglected the meal and snuggled up to a distant tree stump. She didn't stir when I took a seat next to the rotting, wet bark. Nor did she recognize me when I wiped the cold sweats from her forehead and blotted the heat from her neck.

That moment was a harsh reminder that this plague of restless undead robbed Numaalians of far more than our lives. Death may have seemed a better option for many, I knew several who had chosen that route for themselves out of grief or disparity. I lay prone on my stomach, allowing the snow to decrease the moderate amount of swelling on my right rib cage and along my hip bones. I longed for willow bark to relieve the sting, what little I had left was stuffed away in a glass jar in the stock pantry. Just a day away, I told myself to prevent a whimper from escaping into the night.

Zander's cloak was spread across me when dawn cracked. *Cultee made me do it.* He defensively sounded in my head before my glare spotted him shaking out dirty linens and beating the dust from the saddle blankets. *No one else saw you warm under my cloak except Brock, you have time to drape it across your friend there. She seems a bit more fitful than the last two nights, it might help her.* She did look a pinch more well-off under the weight of his thick outerwear. Rodrick, however, was heard softly moaning like a ghost haunting the grey foggy woods.

That was his call for my aid.

I dug my knuckles into the frosted mud beneath me and braced myself as I attempted to rise to my feet. A spasm came and I crumpled. My sinuses burned as I held back a floodgate of tears for my body was desperate for a release. *I saw that.*

My temple hit the mud. The mud stuck in my hair. *You saw nothing.* I felt paralyzed for no matter which way I rolled or pivoted my back and body, the spasms along my body struck me down like lightning bolts. *Can you come get the vial for Rodrick? I am briefly incapacitated.*

He was light on his feet, I didn't hear him arrive on the female side of the camp. "Two drops and make sure he stays hydrated," I stated, watching his large figure crouch down to where I lay contorted with both hands behind my neck to stretch the intercostal muscles of my ribs. *You will have to fetch it. It's the vial on my navel ring.*

I felt his breathing slow as he took off his gloves and set them aside. With the tip of his pinky finger, he lifted the two layers of shirts. *Is there harm in taking one drop to enable yourself to function for the morning?* With a high level of focus and precision he managed to unhook and untwist the pearly white glass without contacting my skin. He reverently pulled my tunics down. *One drop.*

There are bound to be other injuries here.

He placed his hand on my knee. *Did you get hit in the head a little too hard or have you always been this bull headed?*

I thought about our first dialogue in the cells two years prior. *Fucking stubborn, I believe were your first choice in words.*

And by fuck's sake I had never been more right about anything in my life. Take the blasted sip and be done with this.

I counted my own respiration rate, it was above thirty. Too high to maintain for the entirety of the day. *Okay. One.* I stressed. He used his nails to unfasten the miniature lid. I smiled as I watched his frustration. It reminded me of when he attempted to clasp the little straps on the back of my brothel gown. He must have felt my amusement for he stopped and returned a reminiscence smirk.

Zander moved the open vial closer to my face, I parted my lips as his hand slid behind the nape of my neck. It was a liberal drop I noted swallowing the creamy bitterness. Serenity found me as did my first full inhale and expansion of my lungs. My diaphragm lowered without spasms. I relaxed my head in his hand and floated to my feet on the giant cloud of Oyokos's grandson. My body levitated and glided in his wake as he made large strides to Rodrick's bed on the cart and administered the poppy milk to the middle-aged man, holding his elbow out of his sling.

Flint crowded around the cart, along with the mother and her infant in the body wrap. The guards had already started to dissemble the camp in the dark hours of the morning. Their eagerness to return to their homebase was apparent. Hardly anyone slept. Fear kept them awake and drowning in adrenaline.

I squirmed out of reach when I was tapped on my shoulder. My eyes widened to take in Cultee standing unarmed with his two hands warm in his leather pockets. "You startled me," I said, finding my words.

"Lack of sleep and too much excitement frays the nerves. It's normal after such close encounters with death and much physical exertion." He glanced around the cots, firepits and laundry. "Also, there is little else besides fighting against a common enemy that can congeal two groups together so cohesively."

"That appears to be the truth," I watched two guards teaching a windrider's son how to hold a sword. "Rodrick will have concerns when he comes to. I'll admit, I'm more perplexed about our nation hearing you knew nothing of the capital's knights. They murdered my family at the single word of a shrouded man and a priestess in finery." The poppy had loosened my tongue.

"Do you know what they sought?"

Wisteria, do not give him reason to doubt your trust or the innocence of those he is bringing into safety. I willed my lips to seal or at the least demonstrate control. Shaking my head, I said, "A story for another time. I fear speaking about it will cause me to lament over things I cannot change about the past and remind me of what little control I do have over the future."

"I respect your silence and I will also honor your privacy should you confide in me. You may find I am a man of many allegiances, none greater than a supporter of life itself." He lit his lamp and walked away.

Did you hear that! I frantically tugged at our line. His presence nonchalantly came out to rest with mine, like two comrades sitting side by side on a bench.

I did. This is promising, yet you must continue to use caution.

I danced a little with my feet. *I do not get to live long. Caution is for patient immortals without a ticking clock set on their hearts.*

How about a ticking clock for the start of a war? The Emperor is less than five years away from marching across Thalren and erasing any trace of Numaal, despite the purity of the crafters and misinformation spread to the nation by its superiors.

That's a bit heavy for me to comprehend given the current state of my brain. The wise Empress won't let anything happen.

She is underground, rallying against her Emperor. My father said she outsmarts him or brings him to enlightenment before he acts brash.

I'm brash. That's what I've been told.

You are unfiltered and pointedly aggressive. It's refreshing.

I left our conversation to binge on dried apricots I found on the back of Nordic's saddle bag and wasted little time in bringing the last of them over to Fauna. She was one of the few in the camp yet to awaken. I rubbed her back, stroking her spine until she flipped over to greet me. "Hello, gorgeous!" I piped happily feeling the effects of the plant. Her brown eyes seemed darker in the dim light the sun offered. When she finally found me and focused, she leapt into my arms. I yelped and tumbled onto my back. "I am sure that hurt," I moaned, rolling around with her in the mud.

"Good morning, Ivy," her head nestled on my chest, against my broken side. I moved away. "I need another decade of sleep. I can't bring myself to face the world today."

"I have apricots." I pushed one into her mouth. "You can keep your eyes shut on the walk back, it's relatively obstacle free. Just lean on me." She nodded in agreement and opened her mouth for me to place the final fruits in it. Lean she did. All her weight I carried on my back for the last half mile. Her arms wrapped around my neck and her knees clamped around my waist.

I was one weak thought away from crumpling.

A guard from the fort's watch tower rushed to pry her off me and was rapidly dismissed by my unrestrained mouth. I lugged her through the dining hall and into the far back of the stone, poorly lit women's chambers before collapsing next to the cot she occupied. Fauna waved me away when I offered for her to accompany me in the bathing room. As tired as I was, a bath was not something I could forgo. I could hardly stand the layers of filth and decomposition that caked me.

I fell into the tub from fatigue, bruising my shins and somehow not giving a care about the chilly waters.

A cold soak was necessary to allow the water to penetrate the thick mounds of blood and grime that built up on my skin over the last week. The amount of mud in my hair could have fertilized Conrad's entire herb garden. The tub was opaque when I left it. A filthy rusted brown. The water that fell from the shower head was a few degrees warmer than my skin, any warmer and it would have felt akin to boiling water melting my flesh off my thin bones.

Rowdiness broke out in the main hall, scents of a proper meal wafted down all corridors. Ronan found me struggling to bind my splintered ribs with a tight wrap around my breasts and diaphragm. She drew the ends firmly together and tied them between my scapula, failing to keep the shock of my appearance off her face. She followed me to my room where Fauna had taken the liberty to change into clean clothes, the billowy beige staff attire of the fort. "I'm Fauna of the Wastelands, a nomadic windrider who no longer has goods to trade and therefore is no longer deserving of her crafting name." She held out her pale hand to Ronan who took it and warmly held on to it after the greeting ended.

Ronan's almond eyes rounded. "Ronan Underhill. I have not been to the cliffs in thirteen years, but I'll never abandon the surname. It reminds me fondly of my brothers and parents who are hiding in the caves of the sound."

Fauna's face held the same pity and respect as mine had when first hearing her hopeful words. Her sunken eyes fell to the floor and didn't rise. Neither dared speak again. "Ronan, do you mind slathering my back and jaw with salve? It should hold me over until I can retrieve the willow bark or whiskey," I interjected between the two somber women, my energy no livelier than theirs. More liveliness could have been found in a graveyard. She agreed and delicately rubbed my bruises and lacerations with her fingertips. I buttoned the small green tunic and turned to Fauna who had hardly put any effort into taking away her dreary appearance. "Have you a need for this?" I held out the unlidded jar.

"No," she stated, moving her eyes up my buttons to my face. "That tunic brings out your eyes. They look like merchant's stones."

"Too kind," I took her hand. "To the showers then to Raina's feast, the kitchen prepared something glorious for everyone's safe arrival."

"Skip the showers." She insisted. "Let's get some wine and dance."

My eyebrow rose. "You've barely been conscious or on your feet the last two days and now you want to go *dancing*?"

"I have conserved a lot of energy. Now, I'm ready to expend it," she told me, hopping swiftly by Ronan without so much as a pardon. "Is that ham I smell?" She was now skipping down the dim stone hallway showing no sign of stopping. I grabbed her and spun her around my arm as she burst through the oak door to the common room, almost knocking over Mauve and Agate with her inattentiveness.

With the promise of a hard cider, I coaxed her to follow me up the steps and fall in line at the serving table. I held her plate and mine for she was too busy peering around the tall stone room and at the posted guards in scarlet Numaalian uniforms. Raina pinched my cheeks when she spotted us in line and put a heaping pile of pasta on my plate with several carrots. Her maternal touch retreated as she scowled at the cuts on my face. Her eyes fell to my molting wrists that my arm guards had cut into. "It was worth it," I said quickly. "Meet my friend, Fauna." Fauna managed to reel in her tapping toes and depressive attitude to introduce herself. Even thank Raina for the scones.

That appeased the chef to remove her gaze from my bloodied face.

Copper, Flint, Asher and Brock all seemed to be getting on well. They seated themselves together at the front of the hall, acting as a rowdy welcoming committee to anyone within earshot. Brock fussed with his posture and tenderly rubbed the right side of his head. A migraine. They often plagued him when his back muscles overcompensated for his attempts to keep his back erect and limp to a minimum. I would have to do an adjustment.

Near their table, Fennick was arranging a mobile fire pit and spigots, I assumed to heat the water we would all be needing to bathe in and consume. His soot covered skin was as in need of a scrub as any of the newly arrived villagers. His woven had changed his attire and stood conversing with his superior next to Gimly, Ross and a quiet Rodrick. Hades ushered them in rounds of ale which they clanked and guzzled.

Fauna's eyes went straight to a man in passing and with a swing of her hips she persuaded him to give her his glass of wine, it was empty by the time I turned to reprimand her for drinking, having not eaten properly in weeks. "Relax. Can't we enjoy the rest of the day?" She kissed my lips gingerly.

"We can. And the next as well," I replied as I caved and sunk into her. I waved down the nearest available ale and followed her suit. The empty glass echoed hollowly on the table. "Let me tend to Brock, I'll be back before you miss me."

I snuck up on Brock. Asher and Copper did a better job of concealing my sneaky approach than Flint, who just shook his head at my attempts at stealth. My hands grasped either side of his shoulders. Brock's head fell back onto my stomach. "It hurts." He told me.

"I see that. Let me find it," I said, beginning to inch my fingers down either side of his spinal notches feeling for the strung tension or displaced vertebrae. "Arms up," I announced once I found the misalignment. He raised his arms over his head and I laced mine through them, my right knee cap angled in his lumbar spine. I pulled his arms up, dug my knee in and twisted his torso simultaneously. With no prior warning, I jerked him. He cracked too many times to count. The table gawked, mostly in disgust. I heard one of the young guards mutter, 'Ew.'

I released his arms and wrapped mine around his neck. He eased into my right hand, where I cradled the weight of his thick skull. "More," I urged. "Don't you trust me?"

Brock went limp in my hold. "With my life, Ivy." He gave a lazy grin. I had him inhale and on his exhale, I spun his head. Too quickly for even Fennick, his eyes shot over hearing the loud pops of a man's neck. Probably a similar sound to his woven tearing the spine out of a body. My manipulation was instant relief for Brock's headache and the strain of holding his body upright softened. "Thanks, buddy."

"Yup."

I left him with a pat on his head to devour the plate of pasta. Each fleck of sauce on my face I ensured I licked up, and I drank the sweet glaze from the carrots. Fauna hardly touched her meal, her attention stayed fixed on the highest stained glass window, she was far off. My hand found hers under the table, she was cold. I wrapped my forefinger around her wrist, her heart rate was rapid.

"Stop assessing me, I am not one of your infirmary patients. I am your friend."

"Or a slow morning pursuit." I remembered fondly the mid-afternoon sun trickled in as clouds parted briefly above us.

Her cheek wrinkled upwards. "I don't think I can stomach food, Ivy. Not when I know the fort will be running out in the months ahead. It's only time before the roads to Landsfell are blockaded and the undead feast upon anyone dumb enough to transport goods. They will stop sending them." The conversations around us paused to allow the darkness of her words seep in. Fauna pushed her meal towards the center of the table. "Is there a pub with a fiddle and hard floors?"

"Yes," I stated, watching her pull herself out of her own mind of misery. The tavern was likely vacant this time of day. "We can find trouble to get into while we wait for the doors to open."

"I do love trouble when you're involved," she bobbed in and out of the growing crowd, toting me behind her. My body strained with discomfort every step of the way. I pardoned us as we crushed several sets of toes on our way to the main door. She stopped at a spearman, "Guard of Numaal, my woodlander friend has a need to get to her stockroom, but we've no suitable coat for travel has worn on us. May you be so kind as to lend us your cloak for the evening?"

He leaned on his spear head, he was of the last men to stand astute inside the entire fort, the rest had given in to the new faces and conversation without any reprimanding.

"You wouldn't want two ladies to freeze out there in our delicate flesh, would you?"

Biting a remark back he sucked his cheeks and with a roll of his eyes tossed his red cloak at Fauna, who roughly brought me to her side, her fingers collapsing my floating rib. I swallowed the pain so as to not ruin the good times she was set on having.

We scurried to the smithy's and pressed our backs against the kiln for warmth. I hopped over to retrieve the container of willow bark and slipped it in my satchel after placing a flake of it in my mouth. Fauna's doe eyes were on the eclectic weapons and armor on the training wall just around the corner. "I always thought the sword dance was elegant. And when you did it... it was outright magical." Across the room our eyes caught. "Don't bother lying to me. I saw you practicing on summer nights with a curved sword as your partner."

My chest felt hollow. I held my breath wondering what to say next. "Perhaps the hazy summer heat had gone to your head and gifted you fanciful hallucinations."

She shook her head. "After the hell we've survived, you still can't confide in me? I bet if Anna were here you wouldn't be hiding things."

"Don't," I said, dropping my tone. She pursed her lips.

"Anna fills your dreams at night. You scream for her, cry for her, reach for her. Tell me, what do I have to do to get you to move on from a dead girl and invest in what we have? Do I have to be dead to gain your affections?"

My own head started to ache as the blood left it and fell to my toes. My hands curled into themselves and my nails dug into the skin on my palms. Her eyes challenged mine as her unknown cruelty greeted me off-guard.

"Is everything alright?" I probed, keeping three feet of distance, holding myself back from lunging at her.

"Well, if you only give attention to dead girls, I am well on my way to receive yours." Fauna lifted her dress and revealed a foul black bite mark that turned her skin a dangerous murky black visibly trailing up the veins of her neck. She would not make it to the morning without transforming into a wraith. I gasped as she plunged her fingers into the wound. "I can't feel much," she wept from fear. "No hunger. No warmth. No sympathy. I want to feel joy before you kill me. *Please*," she begged. I stuffed my nausea down and realized my head was nodding to her words in agreement, despite each fiber of my being protesting. I knew tonight would break me. More than past killings. But her soul was far more important than my never ending misery. I could live without a friend, she couldn't live an eternity on the wrong side of the beyond as *one of them.*

I choked out, "First stop is the tavern. I'll steal port wine and bribe the lyrist to play folk music until your heart's content and your face hurts from smiling. Then we are overdue for a gallivant in the rain in our lingerie and woolen socks. We can store our clothes in the stables and run down the back half of the hills, there are no watch towers west, we can ramble till the sun rises in warm hues of pink, rose and pale violets." I did not speak of what would come next. There was no need to give voice to the sins I would commit. "If that is what you want."

"Yes," her finite words of confirmation further damned my soul.

The side gate to the tavern had rusted locks, easy to break. I took a short knife off the butcher's block which I used to pry the cork out of the aged cherry port. I slipped it into my boot for safekeeping. We'd no need for glasses, Fauna drank two thirds of the bottle and offered me the remainder. It warmed my toes. By the time the tavern's front door opened for its customers we had already helped ourselves to the front table nearest the dance floor. We casually greeted Joshua who studied us as we drunkenly began to two-step without the rhythm of the banjo or lyre.

When they did start playing some minutes later, the establishment filled up and the bar maidens were kept busy with the largest crowd they have tended to in some time. "You sure you won't get sick?" I hollered at Fauna who insisted on spinning clockwise and reversing it each chorus. It was dizzying looking at her.

She reached out and pulled my lips to hers. I tasted not one drop of fear, just elation and alcohol. Her hug was too firm, the softness nearly gone from her limbs. I managed to squirm out of her embrace with a back step that was part of the dance. I toppled into Pine. "You've managed to snag another dance partner. Mind if I join?"

"Not at all," I celebrated, mindfully moving to the parameters of the dance floor to be a spectator while my ribs and flank protested the decision to fling my body around so irresponsibly given the acute state of my injuries. It was difficult enough to stand upright. I contemplated fetching tea as the two of them stepped seamlessly into the next song. I shoved more willow bark into my mouth.

Night had descended fully now, the wax lamps and flimsy electric lights were lit to ward off the grip of darkness. Unfortunately, there were no plants, magic or potion to reverse a bite and dispel the darkness that had begun to consume Fauna's soul. Her eyes held very little of the warm chocolate I remembered. Time was against us and the balance of providing her a fulfilled last hour of life and ending it before her soul was lost took precision. I drank water the rest of the evening while the blade in my leather boot itched watching her actions become less and less her own. Her normally flirty requests became forceful demands. Her movements were less graceful. Her gasps for air were more dire.

I lingered so Pine's warm laugh and rough hands stayed in the forefront of her night's memories. Before the cold came. Before eternal darkness introduced itself. Off of the high-backed chair, I removed the red cloak and moved to steal away Fauna from the dance floor. A round of applause sounded for her performance, even as we strolled down Crocker Street we heard chatter of her enthusiastic dancing. Fauna's cheeks were lifted to her eyes. Her lashes closed around the simmering coals that stared up at the street lamps.

I moved the hood of the cloak back so she could feel the water drops hit her face and trickle onto her scalp. To me it felt like cold fingers combing through my hair. I shivered as they trailed down my spine. Gaging her ability to sense her human self, I observed how she hardly reacted to the icy rain fall. "The stables are next to that watchtower," I said, pointing at the stone and wooden scaffolding with a decent sized pyre atop.

"He looks warm," she noted, staring openly at the guard armed with a bow. "I'm covetous he can actually savor the fire." Fauna looked down at her pale open palms, her face started to turn downwards. We could not have that.

I moved to face her, clutching both of her hands in mine. I brought them to my cheeks and guided her to look at the smile I put on my face. We climbed up the steps to the watchtower's flat roof, I used my elbow to pop open the trapdoor that led to the stone firepit above us. "Excuse me," I grunted, hauling Fauna up by under her arms. She lost footing at the top when she opted to continue dancing on the slick wooden planks. The guard was too stunned to help us. "You will not mind sharing the tower tonight, right? Consider us an extra pair of eyes! Granted, one of us is seeing double and the other is about to faint into exhaustion." He returned my upbeat chatter with a bemused brow. We crawled to the corner and buried ourselves under the red blanket of fabric, tittering as we linked ourselves together. "Sir, do you mind giving us privacy?"

"I'm entrusted to alert the fort at the first sight of danger. The most privacy I can offer is ignoring the pair of ya."

Fauna pressed me into hard ground, she meant to make advancements towards me yet succeeded in crushing the air from my lungs and further damaging my bones. Spasms started. "Ease up, Fauna. I'm not going anywhere," I whispered, pressing her shoulders to roll her off me. "I won't leave you." The pressure lifted, not before the tears burned from the corners of my eyes.

She tore at her neckline. "I want you to want me and if that's unobtainable, end it swift and sweet my friend." The man with the bow could not hide the baffled look of uncertainty behind his falling, water drenched cap. Fauna's lips sought mind out. She sucked above my clavicle, her teeth grazing my damaged skin. For all I knew they could have been lethally infused with venom at this stage of her transition.

A grunt escaped when I clutched her jaw to move her face away from mine. "Ease. Up." Her features no longer held a feminine softness. No longer were her lips pink and plush, they were thin and dry. Her sun kissed flesh retained not an ounce of rosiness, the black poison crept up her collar draining what remained of her personality.

The guard caught sight of her clenched jaw and blackening flesh. "She's turning into one of them." Disgust sent him steps backwards. Fear moved his hand to the horn.

"Don't! She will not be a threat," I pleaded with him while unhooking my earring. Spotted blue cap spores made their way into her lungs, shortly after she became limp in my arms.

It took a full minute for the guard to grow confident enough to approach us. "Is she dead?" He dropped to his knees and positioned her reverently across my lap. I shook my head to give him his answer. The flood gate of regrets I held at bay telling myself her last glimpse of this world should not be one of tears or sadness. She had seen enough of that.

I swung the red cloak around her decaying, limp body. The rain pattered harder around us, the runoff pooled under us. "What a blessing in my life you have been."

The bystander froze as the magnitude of this moment sunk in. Fauna's lips parted. "The joys you gave me are fading." Panic filled her lungs. "I can't see colors. I can't recall the taste of food."

"Here I thought my company was unforgettable," I humored. Pressing my forehead to hers.

Her eyes shut. "Remind me, Ivy."

I cupped her face in my hand and painted the images of us with our golden skin warmed by the sun and basking under the willow next to the abandoned berry fields. I told her of the sweetness of the raspberries and the tartness of rhubarb pies the village clamored over, I never enjoyed them. The few times I did were when Fauna and I were allowed back in the kitchen to help prepare them. We spilt the flour and continued to make a mess of things by snogging on the baker's counter—I gave explicit details of that particular encounter which left the guard blushing and Fauna smiling at his discomfort. When the twitching started up her legs, I knew I had to be quick.

Under the downpour of icy rain, I leaned in for one final embrace. I was hardly breathing to stifle the screams that wanted to erupt from my throat. The knife in my boot found itself buried in Fauna's chest. My hand shook when it released the hilt. I grabbed at the solid ground and discovered wet stone—a revolting blend of rain and blood.

Unlike, Fauna who had felt nothing, I had felt everything. There was no stopping the painful remorse and loss that clutched my heart and dragged it down into the depths of sorrow.

Chapter Thirteen

Enough time had passed for the corpse on my lap to have gone rigid, all the lifeforce had drained out and stained the stones an ominous scarlet-slick under the flickering fire. The guard on the watchtower had been yelling words—all unintelligible to my dazed mind. He left his post in a huff, dropping down the trapdoor to the chambers and steps below.

By the time Cultee and his primary two guards appeared at the scene of the murder, I was half way down the stone scaffolding. A large male figure peered down the steep side of the watchtower, his unbound hair the shades of night and starlight hung heavy in the rain that fell from the weeping sky. I firmly blocked out whatever messages he was sending down our bond, just as I tried desperately to shove down the biting word that echoed in my head. *Murderer.* Gimly's silhouette leaned next to Zander's, they both watched me jump the remaining single story and land on my feet. The impact rattled my knees and ankles enough for me to stagger the first few leaps of sprinting towards the barn's dim light and promise of warmth.

The piles of straw in the upper hay loft drowned out the whinnies of the horses and filtered the scent of their excrement. I buried my still trembling hands into the golden weeds and dug out a safe place to rest. When heat began to creep over and into my flesh, it brought with it the pins and needles poking at my skin as well as the harsh reminder of the warm trails of tears rolling down my wind-chapped cheeks. *Poppy, Dirk, Rusty, Raven, Flora, Josafin, Citrine, Rapplin, Adar'da, Maple, Serpentine, Tides, Venus, Titan, Coral, Lucinda, Evett, Fauna... eighteen.*

I recited their names. Accounting each of their faces, ages and how exactly I had ended them. Each time their names further engraved themselves on me, bleeding unseen scars.

The blurry world spun when I did manage to open my eyes, there was blood soaking my every garment. I closed them; tears welled behind my eyelids. *Poppy, Dirk, Rusty....* "I can either come up there and risk breaking my good leg or you can come down here and talk through this." Brock. Brock had braved the weather on his rusty brace and crutch to seek me out.

"Neither," I muttered into the dry hay.

The wooden plank bounced as the ladder toppled against the main plank. "You have a knack for making things difficult for me, you know that?" Brock bantered as he initiated his climb up the prongs. His brace caught on the second step. It rattled, unable to break free.

A quiet, but violent stream of curses followed.

Scooting to the edge, I dangled my feet and watched his struggle. "Don't bother, you're just going to make more work for me when you snap your neck for real this time. I don't want to be responsible for killing two friends tonight, one is plenty." There was no particular tone in which I spoke as if my world was suddenly stripped of color. A drag monochromatic dimension. "I'll come down if you bribe me with the whiskey."

He rattled a full glass bottle and extended a dirty hand towards the ceiling on which I perched. On the last step of the ladder, I accepted his hand and no sooner did I grab it was I pulled in for a soft embrace. "She was bitten," I said, his worn woolen shirt scratching my chin.

"I know. I heard," was all he said in reply. But, he truly knew for he continued on as if my scars were plainly written on my forehead. "She asked you to end her life, as many have before her, because you are the only one capable of ensuring the last moments are ones of laughter, love, honor and humanity. You do not fear the fallen as we all do. Rather you help them cherish the person they were and remind them all of what they have offered this world before they leave it. You walk them to the darkness with a steady hand and a bright light." A sob unleashed on his chest. "I'm sorry for this weight you bear for all our sakes and I wish we were all as equipped with bravery, compassion and decisiveness as you are, so we may take some of the responsibilities away from you, my friend."

"I'm a murderer," I cried.

Arms tightened around me, I cared not for my broken ribs, I relished the solid gesture of a companion. He held the pieces of me together. "No. You sent her off with grace and saved her soul, and perhaps the souls of many others, from falling into the shadow beyond the veil. It was a necessary and final act of love, Ivy. We all perceive this, even the captain after sending Fauna off to the pyres, commanded the tall fellow, Drift, to check on you. I stopped him and volunteered. I doubt he or anyone here is aware of the many roles you played in Horn's End."

My neck stiffened. "Whether they begged me for death or not, I'm *tired* of having to kill people I care about. *Children,* I have killed *children!* There is a special place for me in the deepest hells. It festers and eats away at my soul. A part of me dies every time I agree to spill their blood or stop their heart. I fear there won't be anything left of me when this is all over. Empty. A remnant of the woman I was. The wraiths will celebrate for they would have claimed me without a bite for I'll merely be a hollowed-out shell, dead and useless to the world. I'm a murderer." I pulled back enough to see his own grief flash in his eyes. Eyes which moved to the stable's gate to see a spectator silently lurking with his hood dropped and his handsome features made more prominent by the absence of soot that typically covered Fennick's face. His hard gaze softened, telling me that he had been hovering long enough to have heard the exchange. My confessions. My sins.

I turned towards Brock. "I'm not okay."

"What can I do to heal the healer?"

I swiped the bottle from his hand and spat the cork out onto the musty aisle. "There is no remedy, not time nor new attachments." The amber liquid burned my throat and settled in my chest, taking the edge off the physical pain from combat and sleeping on rocks. "Vengeance seems to ease the sting." Brock swallowed an ounce from the bottle and set his taut, concerned thin lips towards me.

He was already shaking his head when he spoke, "I pity the man who is on the receiving end of your fury."

I helped him slide the stump of his knee into the walking brace and rose to find myself wondering if the duke deserved anyone's pity, either now or after I ripped his title and throat from his disemboweled body. Fennick didn't run off to his woven or to the captain, in fact, he did something against his character's nature. He approached Brock and I with his rattling wheeled cart.

"A fort coalminer?" Brock posed.

"Yes, a mute. Typically, as unsociable and skittish as a fox." Fennick's eyes glinted with weak humor as he walked closer. From his cloak he retrieved three shot glasses that clanked as he offered them to us. Brock was grinning wolfishly seeing each of the glasses filled to the brim with bourbon, he introduced himself to the elemental who stood watching the tears roll down my face from my puffy, reddened eyes.

My right one was swollen shut, my lips were cracked and bleeding. Fennick reached for my free arm and ran the tip of his index finger along Fauna's blood that soiled me and smeared it on each of our glasses. He raised his and we followed suit. The tears flowed more liberally as we drank to another life lost. We tossed the drink back and Fennick promptly went back to ignoring us. "Let this be our secret," I called after him. The *please* I held in my throat as he turned on his heel surprised at my request. He dipped his head. The small gesture led me to believe he would grant me the favor of concealing my horrible sins.

Once the coalminer had been enveloped by the rainy dusk Brock sputtered, "Odd man, that one." I agreed and we drank ourselves incoherent for the rest of the night.

I believe I loitered in the captain's office for a good portion of it and even ran errands up and down Crocker Street. I stole receipts from a grappler table and found bird feathers in my pockets. Drunk me was angry and on a mission.

The details of that night blurred.

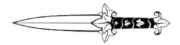

Several hands tried to halt me as I staggered my way down the ranked guard's hallway, Asher among them. I lost Brock some stairwells ago, none of the guards that were on duty bothered to stop me after they spotted the frozen, glops of blood on my every inch.

Cultee was not in his office, the next best place, given the time of night or morning, would be his sleeping chambers. The first four doors on the right yielded no captain, several disgruntled men barked at me to go back to the western wing to which I told them, '*Fuck right off and take me to the captain*'.

When the fifth door swung open, I was prepared to give the captain an earful about his cowardliness in confronting his family. I frowned seeing a chiseled torso with a massive scar down the center. Muscular arms which drew me into the room before I could gripe.

The door locked. I leaned against the dresser to stop my feet from swaying all while shamelessly admiring the way his hair draped down the center of his spine accentuating his sculpted build as he moved to the bathing room. Had he always been so... so striking? My drunk self found Zander remotely attractive. Intel I would not admit. Not ever.

Nope. Never.

He left me wobbling when he went to the washroom. The water ran. The pipes moaned as heat stretched them with water barreling out the faucet into the porcelain tub. It sputtered before flowing consistently.

The raise of his brow and wave of his hand was a question of whether I could manage the rest from there. I felt a smug grin creep up my face. The floor was hard under my bum as I pried off my muddied, crimson coated boots. I gaped at how resilient Fauna's blood was for it stained my skin after the wet clothes were peeled from my limbs. My palms took on a cherry hue, my nails held dark droplets and damage from scaling down the stone watchtower. My pale winter skin was unrecognizable beneath the bruises and streaked blotches of scarlet that lead to my chest, neck and navel from when I had held her on my lap and drove the knife into her most precious heart. The stillness that followed the final breath consumed me. Tears found their way to my eyes, blurring the view of my hands. Minutes were fleeing by and I was still gaping at my hands.

Paralysis struck. No progress had been made to get my naked self off the floor and into the awaiting tub. I pressed my palms into my skull, banishing the guilt and anger rising to destroy any pleasant memory I had with Fauna before... I *murdered her.*

Atop my bloodied hands another set of large rough hands moved into place. "You are not in this dark place alone, Wisteria." Zander's breath fanned over my eyelashes. My eyes squeezed shut as my diaphragm tightened around my core. Sickness wasn't far off. "Nor have you been the first to dig your way out of the suffocating pain that seeks to consume you at every turn. You can make it out. I made it out. I am here to help you in whatever capacity you require of me." I registered where his hands left my face to move to my neck and coaxed me off the floor. He repeated himself. "You are not in this dark place alone, Wisteria." I looked at his lips, vacantly shaking my head.

Names flooded my mind. Like demons refusing to sleep, they haunted me and filled my head. Zander's lips moved, but he didn't make a sound. I wasn't sure he was talking at anymore.

He mouthed my name. *Wisteria.* I leaned into him, a solitary anchor keeping me from drowning in the swirling dark thoughts and memories. The manner in which he lightly held my fingertips to lead me across the floor suggested he believed I to be breakable.

I was fragile like a bomb, not fragile like a flower, I told myself.

Zander kept speaking, or rather, his mouth kept moving, though nothing he said was louder than the voice in my head. *Poppy, Dirk, Rusty, Raven, Flora, Josafin, Citrine, Rapplin, Adar'da, Maple, Serpentine, Tides, Venus, Titan, Coral, Lucinda, Evett, Fauna.* It was a miracle I hadn't slipped stepping into the tub, not that Zander's hands ever left mine to let that happen. He stayed at the bath's edge to wash and rinse my hair, to ensure I wasn't tempted to submerge myself under the waters for too long then saw me dried and warm in one of his blue night tunics which he pulled over my head.

The seat cushion from the wood chair made a fair pillow. After a week of horseback riding, freezing weather, wraith fighting and death—a burning fireplace, a rug and an old pillow were luxurious. As time drew on, he realized the only response he was getting from me would be silence, I would not be moving off the floor or arguing for him to sleep in his own bed. I dozed into a dreamless state.

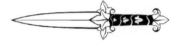

The sharp pain in my sides and cramping legs woke me with a rude jolt that crumpled me on my knees. I whimpered and readjusted on a hard surface. I didn't know how, but there were still tears to be shed.

My eyes found the short flames of the fire flicking up from the pile of embers, they danced and entranced. Their beauty stopped appealing to me when I pictured Fauna's body, once so full of life and warmth, swallowed by the pyres outside the fort in the rain. Moping around would not stop me from having to kill another infected innocent person. Dwelling on my sins would not stop another's blood from staining my skin. I had to *do* something—anything.

I sat up, the blanket atop me fell to the floor. "Cultee," my voice was hoarse.

"That's the first name you said that is of any relevance to me," Zander whispered far off. A chair joined me at the fireside. His tone was worrisome and a tad aloof. "If you sober up and get a few hours of decent shuteye, I will take you to him, I'm sure he heard by now you've a bone to pick with him. You're not nearly ready to present a case in your stupor, your shirt is unsalvageable and in the trash, your pants are soaking and my Gods and Goddesses your body and face are a horrendous shade of putrid yellow and maroon. You cannot stand straight without wincing and your words are... names. If those names are what I think they are—then I have failed you. You should not have been forced to endure a life of self-hostility. I should have thrown you over my shoulder and taken you to Veona two years ago." I turned to him, his face was stitched and scrunched and tired.

Zander leaned over his knees, his knuckles combing over his unshaven scruff on his jawline. He did a double take, watching me examine the finer details of him, particularly the webbing of the white scar on his sternum that held his woven's immortal heart. "You can hear me now?"

I nodded once. My head was distracted by the ringing in my ears and headache creeping in.

He caressed the outside of my mental door, not barging in nor retreating, just resting on the cusp of our bond. *How about in here?* I nodded, he clasped his enormous hands around my forearm, his forehead rubbed against the skin on my wrist. He looked drab. "I feared you might have been too far gone. I did not know when I'd get you back. *If* you'd come back."

"I am not completely *here* nor am I *alright* after killing Fauna," I rasped, eyeing the containers of salves, splints and water pitcher behind Zander, who had yet to lift his face. I doubt I would ever truly heal from such deep self-inflicted wounds or live long enough to cope with the grief in a healthy manner. My gut churned, I pulled my hand away from Zander and reached beyond him for the water. Seeing my intentions, he brought the cool glass to my lips and refilled it when it was empty. "I didn't intend to disrupt your rest." He'd been wearing himself out for weeks plotting against the hordes and scouting for Horn's End. I pointed to him caring for me on the floor. "This isn't reasonable."

He gave a light grunt. "You strutted down the halls screaming profanities. Everyone's slumber, myself and the captain's included, had been disturbed. You did us all a favor by knocking on my door–saved me from a belligerent fight with you down the hallway hauled over my shoulder. Cultee will anticipate a friendly visit from you in a few short hours once the sun sets. Rodrick too, per Flint." The more I settled into my body, the more it ached. "I had every intention of following you down the watchtower's ledge and tending to your broken bones and spirit here for the evening—Pine gave me jars and instructions for setting your bones, but Brock convinced me you'd be alright under his care—that he had seen you though similar circumstances before." His words came out dryly, the irritation and struggle in his tone undeniably surfacing. "Seeing as you stumbled upon me, you will obey my every word until I am satisfied with your mending."

I sucked my tooth to distract from the predatory pacing pounding down our bond. I sent back vivid annoyance at his determination. "I believe I was warned about your illogical attributes."

He pushed the chair back to the corner and opened the comforter on his mattress. "You will let me bind your fractures, you will eat every morsel of food brought to you, you will get your ass into the bed and stay there until you are on the moderately restored. You will permit my accompanying you into the captain's office *after* giving me a summary of what exactly you plan to say and gain from this impromptu meeting. You will not leave my sight nor venture from my side." He reached down to scoop me into his arms. I waved a stern finger.

"And if I refuse?"

"Unwise." His gaze smoldered more fiercely than the crackling embers.

"You're being ridiculous."

He bit his lower lip in a challenge. "You think I am being ridiculous? Flower, I have hardly begun to indulge myself." I was nestled in his chest one moment and on the bed the next. Zander's motions were too fast to retaliate and my strength had been depleted, I jabbed at him, hitting air. "I expect a harder hit when you are fully recovered." Covers were drawn over my legs. They felt glorious on my exposed flesh.

Zander tossed another log into the fire and brought my black trousers out from the red waters of the tub. He splayed them out in front of the bricks, my tunic was rightfully in the bin in the corner. He lifted my legs aside and sat, the bed dipped at the added weight. On his lap, Pine's remedies were collected. "Do I need to refresh your memory on which of us enjoys coddling?"

"No need. Fen may stumble into his room and overhear. That would tarnish my reputation beyond repair," he added a wink to his hushing. I shook my head in disbelief that someone so *overbearing* could be so playfully serious. Fennick. He had actually displayed empathy towards me, a notion perhaps best kept from his woven. "Should I massage the salve on your back first?" The lid popped off the yellowing cream.

I swallowed, trying to wrap my head around the situation I was trapped in. "Ronan saw to my back earlier. My flank and the circumference of my ribcage need the most tending too. And when I'm upright, I'll need a wrap around my torso to keep the bones set for fusing." I kept my focus on the glow of the fire while he finished unbuttoning the long shirt. He arranged the blanket to cover my navel and below, I used my hands to shield my small swells and peaks from Zander's eyes. I had no decency left to blush.

He hardly batted an eyelash at a naked girl in his bed, he was immune to immodesty, his attention was fixated on properly blending the salves and creating the right consistency before application. A curiosity filled my far mind, wondering how well he'd fair if he was raised as a woodlander with no immortal health, sight, speed, strength and under my father and Eloise's strict discipline. The pillow absorbed the strain from my neck as I lay flat, peering down at my marbled black body. I grimaced at how wholly unflattering it was.

Our eyes locked, exchanging permission. He was considerate enough to warm the salve prior to applying it. The pressure was tolerable and his hands remained steady as they worked the medicine into the tissue moving up from my left hip to the sensitive spot under my arm. My breath caught knowing his next surface to cover was over the jagged edges of my four severed ribs, and a displaced floating one from Fauna's advances, his touch was hardly heavier than a brush of a bird's wing. *Half way done. You holding up?*

I hummed, unable to ground myself enough to grasp at the cord between us. "You're doing wonderful." I believed the crease in his brow lifted and his confidence grew as he started on my other side, paying close attention to the strain in my neck leading up to my jaw and ear. I made a mental note to thank Pine later for such thorough teaching, for Zander even switched the mint salve for the mildly scented calendula when he applied it to the cuts and contusions on my face to spare me from burning eyes or stinging scents. The blanket at my hips was brought up to cover my breast, I eased my hands to my sides as he finished up the balm on the corner of my mouth.

"Thanks," I whispered as he smeared the last of the calendula on my chin, his gaze still intently locked on my lips.

"Sleep," Zander ordered, capping the jars, his eyes roaming the details of my injuries. Displeased with the severity. The light above was turned off a moment later. He must have deemed his job satisfactory—to that I agreed, it was well enough done and my body had begun to relax. He was rising to don a shirt and a spare set of blankets from the chest at the foot of the bed when I heard the faintest click of a nearby door snapping into its frame. The fire twinkled brighter with the elemental's arrival in the adjacent room.

"Goodnight, Nikki," I whispered against the pillow. A male's outline leaned on the brick fireplace, the flames reacted to his presence which caused the coals to glow white. On the furthest side of the bed Zander lay, watching the same shadows upon the ceiling beams shapeshift and flicker. The two men nodded at each other. The door between the rooms shut.

"I'm sorry about Fauna and the pain of grief that sits upon your heart," Zander said. The notch in my throat bobbed, sobering up brought back my horrendous crime and flood of *feelings*. A throbbing headache too.

Whatever else he wanted to vocalize was stifled by his restraint to do so.

Not that I would listen to him anyways. Muteness clouded my ears, sleep shortly after.

Chapter Fourteen

The spread of steaming oats, broths, crackers and cheese took over the surface of the side table. A fair majority of it resided in my stomach.

Zander was fussing over everything.

If I pushed a spoonful away, it found its way back to my plate moments later. "It pains me to say this, but one more bite and I'll be sick." The bowl left his grip to snatch up a glass of apple juice. I stretched my neck and gently worked the tension from my aching jawline. I'd a new scar. Fennick crossed the room, tossing a clean tunic on the edge of the bed, not attempting to hide his delight with my persistent swatting away of his woven, who was as disgruntled as a pestered nitpicking mother hen when I set down a half-filled glass of tart apple juice.

Zander huffed, the spoon in his grip bending slightly as he set it down. "You'd feel a lot better had you not chosen to deliberately get your face smashed." His statement was both factual and brimming with accusation. "All this just to be considered ordinary by Fort Fell's standards?"

"No one can know until I get into Landsfell," I whispered, limiting the movement of my jaw.

"It was stupid," he retorted.

I forced half my swollen face to raise into a cocky grin. "Maybe I wanted you to win." He shook his head gravely, not remotely enjoying my attempt at humor. The mute sprawled out in a feline manner, his strong, lanky limbs hanging over the armrests. His piercing features mimicked Zander's sentiments when he caught on. "I intentionally got injured, so what." Scoffing, I said, "I really don't care what either of you think about my decisions. It is done."

The fox reverted to discounting me which left me no choice but to turn my attention to the man adding brown sugar to the bowl of oat mush. The sight of more food was exhausting. It did smell wonderful though. The griffin blade was back in his rightful grip, Fennick cleaned his nails with the tip of the steel whistling nonchalantly as if replying to the song of the birds chirping on the gloomy morning. The first sound I heard from him since our prison break. He stopped when he caught me observing him in his casual recline instead of eating the mounds of food.

Zander fluffed the pillow behind me. "You better be fucking decent or so help me Gods I'll be embarrassed for you," he sighed. "Were you going to tell Cultee about the Ilanthians his brother and a mystery noble are holding captive?"

I shrugged. "If it came to it." Silence was left for me to continue talking or to eat. I left the spoon on the table. "I'm tired of killing people." He put the lid on the sugar jar, his eyes, round and penetrating, held mine. "Landsfell's inactions are ensuring the demise of all living beings. It can't continue. Every nation deserves answers and swift retribution. Cultee needs to go to that frivolous, gaudy gala and bring a gift. A gift that will send a message, beckon those to their duty to defend the populace and pose the hard questions to those in power. I have several suggestions for him. I was going to offer him my thoughts on what would be the most marvelous display for the duke and his pompous aristocrats.

"In fact, I have already been into his office and drafted two letters to send to Stegin on his personal letterhead. I found Gimly's wax seal and I vaguely remember arguing with the bird keeper to send his fastest white-tailed hawk. A letter may be on its way as we speak." My words stopped as my memories pieced together what happened between the stables and Zander's room in the fort. A definitive answer broke through the hangover and fuzzy flashes. "Correction. One is *definitely* on its way. I doubt Stegin is interested in his brother's advice so I forged Gimlian Monte's penmanship that I found on a gambling note and sent it off."

"Creative," my self-assigned guardian complimented. His companion in the corner slacked his gruff chin. "Can you recollect what it said?"

"Let's just say, if Fort Fell receives aid from the duke this week, he read it and values his son's life. If we are left to fend off the growing masses of undead restless with what little means we have here, well, that could say a variety of things—all none pleasant," I admitted. Stegin may realize the letter as a sham, *if* he bothered to break open the seal. He may also default to ignorance and safely assume his province is safe at the blood and trials of his kin. Or high influence from the capital lords may be luring him to stay the current course. My train of thought was disrupted by a hot bowl placed on my lap and a firm suggestion to eat it. "You're annoying," I managed to say in between bites.

The meal was begrudgingly delicious and sugary. Just the way I preferred it.

"I've been called much worse," he said proudly. "Gimly can't be present when you divulge all this to the captain. We will have to be tactful. No more drunken squawking or threatening to decapitate people should they not escort you, hell knows where, an hour after midnight."

My green eyes glared. "I'm not going to mention anything about the mail already being carried on wings, Cultee has bigger things to mull over. For example, how to move the people in Fort Fell to the nearest safe city with high rise walls before the Wastelands evolve into the Deadlands. The Sanctum should have plenty of room to harbor refugees in their silver temples and a fair warning of the arrival with their gifts of foresight. Pine has studied three of the crafts, well I might add, he is the obvious choice to lead them north along with Hades, Rodrick and the majority of the guards. Together, they can keep the group cohesive and safe. Cultee must be persuaded for them to depart before we accept the duke's early arriving carriage and escort to the gala, just after the waning moon. He may be more receptive to abandoning this stone box if you, his trusted second, plant the idea in his head."

"Early escort arrival?"

I nodded and swallowed. "Numaal is a patriarchal monarchy. Fucking selfish men are everywhere. Gimly and his father are cowards. You can't possibly believe Stegin will send troops to fight. No, they will preserve their blood line and run behind their walls and catapults. And I will be going with them to ensure I end their line. Captain will want you by his side. Very few others because he will want the citizens safe on the trek north—that is if you can manage to convince him."

The way I was being studied by the pair of them was unsettling. "You are devious with frighteningly close attention to details. You would excel in political affairs."

"Disgusting. The thought of politics is nauseating. I am an entirely selfish girl craving revenge. I was also drunk. I still might be. Besides, if people stay in the fort, they will fall and I will continue killing and burning those who meet an undeserving fate—I lack the emotional stability to keep doing what I have been doing. You do not want to see me unhinged with a sword in my hand unless you put me on the frontlines against the undead or criminals." Zander simply hummed, taking to slicing the wedge of cheese. He reprimanded my refusal of a second bite. Yet, I found a third and fourth mouthful settling in my stomach before I spotted any satisfaction in his blue eyes. The milky white had cleared greatly in the last few hours.

The bed lifted without his weight. He tossed washed trousers to me, Nikki already had his eyes diverted. Zander plucked the cotton wrapping off the mantle, examining its elasticity while I shimmied into my bottoms. I rubbed my belly button, feeling more naked without my vial of medicine than I did without clothes. Hopefully, Rodrick was at ease because that was the last of my provisions. My jealousy spiked when I strode towards Zander at the fire pit. I lifted my arms above my head and locked the air out of my lungs, I sighed and wished I had stolen away a half dozen drops for myself.

"Tight is necessary," I reminded.

He reached around me, spinning me in yards of fabric. I kept the wince off my face during the last of the treatment. A shudder panged through my body when the final knot was set and I lowered my arms to my sides. There was a significant restriction in my range of motion that didn't hinder me from dressing into the grey tunic without asking for help. Zander motioned to a cushioned stool, twirling a hair brush as he did. "Why do you don the same style day after day?" I pointed up to his three rows of braids he rebound after his shower.

"To make myself presentable. Something you hardly invest in."

"I have no one to impress."

"Sit and I'll tell you their significance." My throat tightened feeling the pains of my aching innards while my knees bent to comply.

His hands moved gracefully and fast. "One braid for each of the three nations of our continent, Numaal, Veil and Ilanthia, united into one." He flicked his long pony over his left shoulder taking the comb through my dried locks.

"There is complete peace in the Veil?"

"Mostly. We nearly obtained it just before the spawn, which I can only describe as dead wraiths, began to attack the boundaries from the beyond. Approaching the topic of safety for our peoples is difficult, each of my brothers seem to have a different resolution in facing an unknown enemy. Outside of a few unorthodox groups, peace is ample in Ilanthia, they are looking into expansion by settling on the Southern Isles as they are waiting for a trilogy to be chosen."

The fringe of the comb massaged my scalp while I thought just how close the south province was to the Southern Isles and a shot at peaceful living. Maybe we should not have burned the white wooden raft Anna sailed upon all those years ago and sent ourselves south. "My hair is fine down," I swallowed. It covered a large portion of my molting face and hardly healed lip. "Anything else you feel compelled to fuss over or are we ready to go yet princess?" The handle of the brush thwacked on my skull, not hard enough to cause any real damage, but enough that I spun to him and scowled. "Are you always so sensitive?"

"We are not finished discussing what else you intend to request from the captain. Frankly, I'm not comfortable with you owning the plot you've already set into motion. If the wrong people suspect you've any involvement with illusive silver bloods, you will be hung and left on display outside the capital. Not even Rodrick, Pine or Brock can know you're versed in literacy."

"Pine knows. Well, he suspects I am familiar with Ilanthians." The calm crackling of the fire became the most audible sound. Fennick and Zander were holding their breath. "He won't say anything."

"Can you be sure?" Zander rose in no more than a concerned whisper.

"He promised," I stated as if that was enough. "He has seen me with strangers over the years of his various crafting. He doesn't know their names, but if he saw Keenan's face he'd be able to point it out. The way he moved during our sword training sessions, well, it is quite obvious he wasn't from around these parts or trained with a bulky legionnaire sword. Anna had prominent traits, but she is dead." Her vibrant red hair was slow to vanish from my memory.

"He's seen you combat training with an immortal warrior from Montuse," Zander sounded more jealous than anything. He sat on the edge of the bed with his milky eye fading deeper into fog. His knuckles ran over his chin, his toes tapped on the floor.

I banished his anxious energy with blunt words. "Yes. He has also seen me fuck women on the hillside and jump naked off cliffs. He will not say anything," I pleaded, wondering just where Zander's thoughts were heading. I felt for our bond. Fatigue prevented me from grasping it fully. His thoughts slipped away. "He doesn't even care that I'm tipping the scales of nature. He is making me a ring so that I may push the odds of escaping the duke's manor alive, granted he is smart enough not to ask questions about the content of the bead the frame is fit for." The fox took to munching on the leftovers, mulling food and thought over in his self-imposed silence.

"Does he blindly support you from his own guilt of having already turned you into a higher authority? A hard life of losing one's wife, child and home many times over can lead people to betray their own relations. I hope you are right about him."

"I am," I sighed, settling my sights on my scabbed knuckles that I hadn't known were in such a condition. I made a fist and watched the skin around the scabs tear open.

Minutes passed before the horselord's spine straightened. "What of this gift you wish captain to bring Stegin?"

"A living wraith. Potentially, two. We can transport them in a reinforced iron box. I've spores in excess to sedate them so people do not get suspicious on our carriage ride to the capital. Nobody will be aware of such a beast when we enter the city or an estate. Sage told me Stegin loves to be entertained in the most extravagant ways, it is best we don't disappoint the fool."

Zander groaned. "I should have known you'd concoct something so bizarre the moment you told the captain to write a letter in blood and send it on a corpse with the parchment nailed in its skull." His woven stopped chewing to evaluate the seriousness of the conversation and appeared both impressed and horrified when he discovered we weren't playfully bantering.

"I'm not hearing you disagree with me."

"Because it's a lovely idea. One I will support when you mention it to Cultee. The gift of the undead and the notion of moving the people to Sanctum are the only two ideas you will take credit for. If you run your mouth anymore I'm afraid I'll have no choice but to expose our open alliance and final goal which will be Stegin's death and Cultee on the seat of the south province."

I rolled my eyes. "I think there is more support for his assassination among the people here than you realize. And Cultee mentioned he had many allegiances, none greater than to life itself. I bet a bar of chocolate, he will act on our side *and* once I tell him about the Ilanthian children being held and likely tortured, he will help me find a way to free them too. Silver blooded or not, he has a moral compass."

"I'm not risking it." Zander's words held a sense of finality.

"You old guys really have no sense of fun," I grunted, getting to my feet.

"What part of being arrested for planning a high lord's murder or publicly slaughtered for conspiring with his enemy sounds *fun*?"

"I'm tired of *just* surviving. Sadness frequents too much so might as well dodge my old friend Death for delight before he really does come to claim me."

"Bloody hell," he rubbed his tired scruffy face with tense hands. "I know you want to do something impactful to stop the blood from flowing on your hands and lands, but this needs to be done strategically so when we do act it is done confidently, thoroughly and without fault." He reached towards my wrist. I let him take it.

His warm palm steady on my skin. "I will not live forever. I will be dead by the time you feel things meet your safety standards to make a move. You will be doing it without me. You better avenge me with style." The dreamers kept their gazes downward, as if they felt pain from being reminded of the facts. It was doubtful, sure, but they did recoil from the bluntness.

Zander hissed. "Fuck. Fine then, twenty-one days." I blinked at his gritted teeth as he spoke. "Give me three weeks to set the stage and gauge how dangerous the court members inside Landsfell are before you approach the captain with your truths. Keep mine and Fen's name from your mouth. Remain inconspicuous, but not emotionless. Your passion is what will persuade the world, Wisteria."

"Alright," I surrendered, pulling my arm back to my side. "Let's go check up on Brock before corralling Rodrick and Hades into the captain's office."

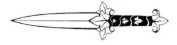

Overall, the meeting went decently.

If I had managed to get through Rodrick's condolences without crying, I would have said the exchange went very well. But, alas, with Fauna's death so fresh and my guilt throbbing beneath my skin, I cried.

It didn't make me feel better. I used the backs of my wrists to wipe the last tears and snot away, peeking in at the guards who were now summoning Gimly into the cozy office to work out the details of dividing themselves up for the tasks ahead.

Gimly's normal scummy swagger had been replaced by a defeated man who stayed up all night gambling his jewelry away, since the brothels could no longer serve him. "Gimlian, come." Captain beckoned. "We're discussing arrangements to the capitals." A glimmer of an answered prayer shone behind his dark eyes. He scurried into the room where there was ample support for moving everyone north to the east province's capital of Sanctum. It sounded as if it were to happen no later than week's end and provisions were to start being crated off tonight.

I was politely sent from the room, not in a dismissive gesture. Cultee wanted me to work with Pine to construct an iron coffin that could fit under the seat of a carriage while his nephew was distracted. I believed he felt I would mend better under friendly company, the horselord's gut hardly clenched at the orders hearing the more difficult task of capturing a wraith being assigned to him. He demolished countless in the pitch of night with nothing but his bare hands, I felt comfortable he would succeed in obtaining and restraining one measly wraith.

As he assured me, Zander hadn't fallen out of my arm's length radius and if his eyes ever left me they were surveying my surroundings. Stairwells apparently posed a significant threat to me, he crowded my space with his hand ready to catch me should I suddenly become weak in the knees. Nor was he going to let me starve. We went right from the office to the kitchen. He insisted Pine could wait a quarter hour while he rummaged for more snacks in the back pantry. I found a basket of rosemary crackers and emerged to find him helping himself to a pot of hot coffee left on the irons. The more he sipped the more his brow softened. I jumped up on the counter next to him, grabbing my own clay cup of warmth and earthiness. I stirred the sugar in with a cinnamon stick.

"When were you hoping to give me that victory kiss?"

His overconfidence pulled my lip into an unsavory snarl. "When the moment struck me." I crossed my arms, careful not to spill the contents swirling in the cup.

"Are you feeling stricken?"

"Yes, stricken by a monsoon of irritation that plagues me when you speak."

"We have solitude and privacy. I'll let you take advantage of me if that stirs you to feel any emotions other than sadness and rage." He tilted his head to the side and licked a rogue droplet of coffee off his sensual lips. I pulled my eyes away insisting it was the steam from the cup that warmed my face.

"I murdered my friend last night and hardly finished wiping my tears. Yet, now seems like a good time to ask for a kiss?" I felt my head shaking.

"Yes," he stated, setting his empty cup down.

"What profound emotion do you think a kiss with *you* will instigate in *me*?"

"Frankly, I don't care as long as it is not of the two I previously mentioned. You deserve to chase after other emotional highs, to feel something different and uplifting for once."

"Do not hold your breath." Air left me as I shook my head and latched onto our connection. He was already there waiting for me. "No, incubus or Oyokos magic?" I asked, holding his gaze.

"Just me, in all my glory."

He was readily awaiting me on our thread. *You really are insufferable.*

"I would like to point out that the exact wording of the bet was '*a kiss from Ivy*' and I did promise to tame my forwardness and fondness. You will be doing all the initiating, just so we are clear."

Grabbing his collar, I tugged him until his hips were set between my knees. One arm leaned on the cabinets above me, his other stayed loose and casual at his waist. I studied his untucked tunic and how all ridges of his chiseled torso and scars alike were subtly perceivable under the taut fabric. His neck muscles flexed as he dropped his chin within reach, yet far enough to where I would have to make an effort to reach his mouth. The salt and pepper colored stubble scattered along his prominent jawline and down to the bob in his throat aged him into his late twenties, the age he would always appear even after eons cycled through. *Your eyes are clear. What does that mean?* A blue halo glowed around the rim of his eyes.

That I am fully present, invested in this moment.

I inhaled his cool coffee scent and the hard taste of spice behind it. His jaw slacked and mouth parted when my thumb brushed over the plump curve of his lower lip. The unfamiliar texture of his face was pleasantly scratchy beneath my palm, a stark contrast to his smooth lips. His eyelids shut as if all his focus went into remaining eerily unmoving. Predatorially still.

A trait that was not human.

The steady calm between our thread hummed with a light blue and green telling me Zander was fine. *This* was fine.

His hair of raven black and snow white was incredibly silky. I ran my hands up the shaved side of his head and locked my left hand on the nape of his neck and pulled his lips towards mine. Our lips brushed briefly. I took it upon myself to explore the man bound to me by the Weaver. So, I met his lips again with more fervor and took to cupping his face with my right hand. The slow lapping of his tongue meeting mine in his mouth stirred my inner Goddess, he smiled sensing my metal bar twisting around his tongue. I eased the pressure against his mouth only to suck his lower lip into my mouth and nibble it with dull canines. My hand wrapped around his throat. The escaped purr of delight and surprise brought Zander's eyes to sharply open.

I continued to catch him off guard by drawing his hair to the side giving me full access to his neck and the erogenous zone behind his ear. My slick tongue danced atop his vulnerable arteries and curvy bones. Heat rose from his back, warming my hand that gripped his neck. From his ear lobe across his jawline to his awaiting mouth, I slowly dragged my open lips.

I sunk into him, or rather brought him firmly onto me, for the last of my owed bargain to the victor. An eager tongue flicked into my mouth and slipped along the roof before slowly retreating into its owner, leaving me distracted and dizzy. Our breathing synced together in a dance that came naturally.

Inches separated us, Zander smiled wide and white. "The verdict?"

I shut my eyes to identify it. No thoughts of death or revenge. Something new was spurred in the last interaction. It was not a romantic feeling. If I had to give it a label, it was curiosity. "You need to shave."

"Wisteria," he sighed helplessly.

I patted his shoulder and hopped off the counter, coffee in hand. "And what about you, oh great one? What sort of emotions flooded through you at my bestowed kiss?" His brow creased at the name calling. Crackers found their way into my mouth, I needed anything to remove the lasting sensations of Zander's tongue that set me off kilter.

Zander peered down at his imaginary watch on his wrist. "Afraid we don't have time for that, Pine is ready for us by the kiln. Come, we are going to be late." I sent fury down our connection to which he hardly reacted. With aggression I shoved two crackers in my pocket, snapping them into inedible crumbs, and finished off the coffee while he paced the span of the kitchen, his mind elsewhere. When he did pause, he looked up and absently stated, "It felt nice."

He was a sexual being, of course a tongue in his mouth would make him feel *nice*. Hell, a bat of an eyelash in his direction would have his gaze following a lady's ass out the door. He had his mouth over every male and female in the brothel within the first two weeks was my best guess. He would be content with any amount of flesh offered to him. But *nice?* I grunted, "I expected a broader vocabulary for an old man who keeps exquisite poetry in his briefcase." Zander opened the doors, his tongue slowly tracking over his lower lip as if in a fond memory.

When your eye is white, where are you? I asked, jogging to catch up with his stride, he slowed down seeing the effort it took to match his pace. My ribs were already protesting leaving the bed.

Overseeing affairs in Veona or seeing the world through Fen's eyes.

What types of affairs?

Personal and public alike. It's called, tranplacency. It is a perk of being born of blood from two worlds and granted the blood of the third. I am technically a man of all three nations, though I identify primarily as human and dreamer. Fennick is a man of two, Ilanthian and dreamer. We cannot hold conversations and share emotions through our bond, but it allows us to adapt perspectives and me to settle things back home.

Home. He was far from home. Yet, he remained here. In this magicless quarter of the continent because of a dumb choice he made. *Do you miss it?*

Yes. Nothing more than the perpetual weather of late spring that encompasses the realm, the long days and warm nights lit by champagne galaxies and orbs of Eternal essence. More flurries of snow and slush greeted us when we exited the fort, beyond that, gloomy skies of grey and dirtied paths of mud. A world vastly different from his paradisiacal Veona. Recently, this bleak world was all I knew. Gone were the glorious seasonal celebrations in the garden patch, the muggy summer nights dashing around Ferngrove barefooted and naive. Gone were the family and friends that stood as the pillars of my joyous childhood and prospect of having a home.

"Soon you will get your answers in Landsfell and return to ensure your home survives this awakening madness. Redeeming whatever wound you feel you inflicted upon it." I interjected, numbly waving to Pine whose image popped out from the brown kiln as a familiar sting of detachment nestled in my heart space. "Seems Asher is enthusiastic about the plan." We arrived under the shelter to hear the young guard eagerly whispering the lanky dimensions of a wraith and detailing the damage it was capable of inflicting. Pine was sketching with a scrap of charcoal on the counter top. A twice over welded iron box with scarce holes for ventilation, just enough for me to waft spores or fumes into for sedation.

"Jaw traps? Arm and leg shackles?" Pine posed to his growing audience.

"All of it," Zander said, admiring the clean lines of Pine's design. "And feather stuffing between the layers of metal to suffocate its shrieks and shrills. We want heads to turn the night of the gala, not a moment sooner. And hauling this monster into the city center will do just that if we are simp on precautions and are flagged for suspicions. I don't intend to draw the bastard son of the duke's attention either. Pine, I'll be training Asher in the open space, signal for me when the draft is complete and production commences, I'll send the mute for welding efficiency. From that moment on you have twenty-four hours to construct it, for by nightfall tomorrow I'll have a wraith in need of a coffin." His boot pivoted towards me. "Ivy, collect willow bark from the shelves, a blanket from the racks and follow me. It's in your best interest to watch how to properly disarm a soldier, it is important for a novice, of young, infallible beauty, to learn maneuvers such as these.

Asher will practice offensive stances until he pulls me flat on my back."
Zander's eyes were not on Asher nor I. But on Pine's reaction to his
commentary on my novice-ness. Pine seemed more interested in
calculating the width of the box and hadn't heard much of Zander's
domineering monologue.

I did nothing to bite back the *I told you so* slant in my eye that pinned up
the corner of my bloodied mouth. Pine was trustworthy. I'd bet my last
cone of honeysuckle he wouldn't stab me in the back. *Stab.*

Fauna. My heart sank.

My face turned down as darkness swept up from the vibrant memory of
the corpse I held in my arms that dreadful night. The body of my
courtesan friend. Each bite of food forced into my stomach that
morning threatened to reemerge as guilt boiled up. The nausea was so
strong, the willow bark never made it into my system. I slipped it into
my pocket and blindly followed the red tunics of the guards over the
wooden fence into the training field.

The cold drizzle soaked my spirits further weighing me down. The dull
clangor of Asher plowing into Zander's side was repetitive enough to
ignore. Asher's stamina only grew with each failed attempt as did
Zander's. The morning stretched into the afternoon, the glum hadn't
dispersed. My eyelashes caught the raindrops which gathered into thick
drops of ice water and trickled under my collar to trigger chills. Behind
me hammering had begun, I gave a longing glance at the raging fire
Fennick fed and the steam coming from the buckets nearest Pine.

Zander intercepted the view of high flicking flames with his dense build.
He ordered Asher to call the patrolling boys to the yard and take turns
breaking stances and disarming. Anticipating his next actions, I got
myself upright painfully stacking my bones atop one another. Damn
everything if I was seen as a distraught damsel needing the assistance of
a lady's man. What I really needed was a tonic strong enough to put a
halt to my spinning dark thoughts that were quickly becoming a tangled
web of grief. "A warm bath or midday rest?" he offered.

Those would not knock me out. "A swift hit to my cerebellum isn't an
option?"

"No. Neither is whiskey," he said, watching me hold my sour stomach and stitch in my side. "You didn't consume the bark?" I shook my head and the droplets from my hood scattered.

"My stomach and heart hurt," I whispered. His shortened strides were assured and emitted a non-approachable aura as he led us back to the ranked guard's hallway and into his homely bedroom. Zander prodded the white coals until they were lively enough to catch the dried paddies and splintered logs he placed atop the ashes.

Boots off, I slithered into the bed. It was impossible to ignore the sharp pain hammering into my flank, I buried my groans into the mound of blankets. Pillows over my head, Zander's orders to remove my bindings and chew the bark were muffled. Ignoring him, I played it off as an unheard statement. Curling into myself as if to embrace the darkness of my own soul, I dozed off.

"I love you, Ivy. I need you to drink my blood."

I shook my head. "You said you weren't that kind of immortal. I don't want it."

"It's too late to explain," Anna pinched my nose leaving me gasping through my mouth.

"I don't want this! This doesn't feel like love!"

The light in her eyes had almost dimmed, a stray tear formed and trailed down her high cheekbones. "This way I will always be with you. Fear not the path beneath your feet, for the courage of your heart can overcome even the most impossible of tasks. My brother will not forsake you." What she meant at that time went unregistered. Anna had bitten her own wrist and sucked the last of her life force out. She descended on me, her cheeks swollen in holding the precious liquid, then pressing her lips onto mine she demanded I drink and wouldn't release my breath until I had all but drained her. There was no fighting her...

Air ripped out of my lungs as the taste of her blood drowned my ability to distinguish past from present. A scream was building, I felt it in my frantic chest. I clawed at my surroundings, which were unrecognizable shadows of a deep night. A heavy bar fell across my abdomen, I heaved it off. It came back and hooked softly around my waist. A familiar left hand secured around my hip.

It was him. The man with the voice.

He was in my nightmare. And he was *here* in this tangible world, the furthest thing from frightening. "Sing," I exhaled, my clammy hands examining the callouses I have grown accustomed to. The pillow shifted as a body moved closer to mine.

A dead language hadn't sounded so lively nor lovely. The intricacies and cadence of the tone he carried were as varying as the wind itself. Their calming capabilities were much more effective in a close radius rather than down a dank corridor of a dungeon. Turning towards the voice of velvet, I clung onto it and let it carry me to faraway places.

It was strange waking up next to a man.

Not as uncomfortable as I had been picturing all these years. The same could have been said for kissing one. I pried his grip off me only to battle the dead weight of his limbs which felt like steel binding me to his chest. Rustling in his sleep, he rolled closer. I swore as I sprained my side while scooting down to the bottom of the bed. The mending was well on the way, the intensity was dulled.

I was quick to stuff a pillow into Zander's now empty arms to dissuade his mind from recognizing my absence. A prideful smirk spattered my cheeks when a full minute passed without him rousing. I hopped straight to the privy and drew the curtain. My breasts hung freely when the wrappings gave way and were soon eased by the lukewarm waters from the rusted shower head. The pipes were fast to run cold. There was only enough time to wash the important bits and savor a half minute of warmth on my fractures before succumbing to hypothermia. Hopping over the draining tiles, I wrapped myself in the nearest towel and crept out of the washroom.

Zander crushed the pillow, his knee bent searching for a resting place and finding none. Groggily, he flipped onto his stomach. His long hair nestled down the center of his spine, his back and shoulder muscles protruded from under the shirt like thick cords.

I stopped tiptoeing towards the dresser to imagine what he would look like with *wings.* The muscle and skeletal structure alone would be phenomenal and occupy my admiration for days, but to see the way the wings protruding from his back *functioned.* That would be a real treat, for it seemed unfathomable. Birds had hollowed bones for flight. Zander was *dense*—for lack of better words. His wings in proportion to his mass would have to make them *enormous.* Gods, my head hurt imagining them.

I slathered my torso in salve and pulled the smallest tunic over my head. Belt and bootstraps buckled; I crept to the door. The door hardly squeaked as it shut behind me. I had slept the remainder of the previous day and all night, the sun had just begun rising. Its tamed hues filled the low clouds with a yellow undertone. I followed the morning glow out the nearest archway, with casual haste after I noticed the figure with silent steps striding beside me. He would lose his stealth in the open space. The fort with all its stone crevasses and nooks was a hazy block at the backs of my heels. Movement scurried into the distance. I diverted from the stables to the end of Crocker Street.

The glassblower and the bakery were the only shops with lights on and candles lit. Despite the clutter, it was welcoming inside. In an eclectic sort of way. Mr. Crest looked as if he started his day many hours ago for he was sweat drenched and midway through a project which looked to be a simple lantern. "Pine said you'd meander in, crafter." The thin, grey-haired man called over his shoulder. "Scrapings and shards are in the back. Take what suits your needs, but nothing with a tag or signature from the shelves." His focus stayed on the molten blob of sand and glass he was scraping off his blowing stick.

"Thank you, sir," I called, not wanting to distract from his delicate workings. I kicked the splinters of glass and metals away from the doorframe and stepped under the lopsided construction. What little light entered the vicinity came from a rectangular window at the top of the wall. Stationed outside, in clear view, a pair of boots. Standing on a crate I pulled the window down and in the same motion swiped my hand out and grabbed Fennick's ankle. A hot grip reached down and tightened around my wrist. "I don't need a chaperone," I hissed.

He crouched lower, nose to nose with me, his eyes glazed milky in an instant. Zander and he were sharing those eyes. Sharing his point of view of staring me down through a dirty window well. I bit at the both of them, "Zander, call him off. I'll come back to you safely, I swear it." Fennick blinked. "Let Nikki have some fresh air, I'm sure he loathes me after two years of hiding in the Wastelands and having him trail my ass while you get beauty rest is punishment for the both of us." Fennick's eyes befell a red and golden glimmer. He removed his hand from my forearm and gave a singular shake of his head which was answer enough. And for the first time in my knowing him, a broad devious smile plastered across the bottom of his face. He caught my stare and vanished beneath his scummy hood, shaking loose my grip with a kick of his leg. "It will be a few minutes, *darling*," I mumbled beneath my breath, earning me a low growl from the stalking creature who stayed in a man's form.

The size of the vials varied, but none of them extended longer or wider than my littlest finger. They would all fit into charms and jewelry pieces exceptionally well and remain understated. Mr. Crest did not acknowledge me as I saw myself out with words of gratitude. The cold nipped my nose and encouraged me to hustle. The faintest clicks of slate above me told me all I needed to know. I reached behind to adjust my long hair and gave a crude finger to the entity hounding me from the roof.

He gave a challenging grunt. One I happily accepted.

Rushing towards the main gate and into the thick of the fog, I dodged the outpouring guards and pivoted to the right. Fennick didn't miss a step and steered us to a ravine where we went unseen. We entered an outright sprint aiming towards the northern watchtower. Side by side we ran, his hood blown back revealing the same wicked expression as I. Coldness was replaced with competitiveness. Discomfort with eagerness. We had another half mile to go. From the way he glanced over his side, it was clear he expected fatigue to hinder my steps. I took advantage of his distraction. "Being Zander's husband you must not get too many opportunities to admire many women from behind. Go on, take a good look!"

I didn't expect his laugh to sound like a lion's roar. In all honesty, I anticipated a piercing glare or spit on the ground for my commentary. But, an uninhibited laugh filled the air around us and warmed my flesh like dousing in a hot spring or a hug from my father.

Fennick gained on me and was far more agile in jumping over the gnarled roots and overturned rocks. I managed decently, narrowly avoiding a thicket of withered thorns. It felt liberating to put all of Keenan's training to good use, I pushed on. He was smiling wildly when I entered his peripheral.

He was five feet ahead when his right arm flew out and barred across my abdomen. Using my momentum, he spun around and stiffly hopped backwards into the small carved out line of earth all while keeping our eyes on the approaching figure.

The hulking form hadn't bothered with shoes or to button his shirt. His knuckles were white as he balled them into fists at his side. He stomped toward us. I swore the earth shuddered under his steps. "Nikki, what do you say we race to the stable instead?" The twisting of his feet told me he agreed. We started to run again.

Zander leapt into the air and landed behind us, obstructing the route to the stable beyond the rolling fog. Not falling scared or frazzled under the angry gaze I tapped Fennick's arm, a signal to lower it. "Did you want to join us in our morning exercise? We were just getting started, I was about to completely dust your man here before you showed up— and in a fabulous talkative mood I might add."

A flash of his canines and a huff of his bare chest were his response. He planted himself right in front of me, towering over me with the unbreakable stillness of stone. I gave a frustrated grunt and mumbled to myself, "Your fucking audacity!" To my right a large chunk of a log lay. It was easily displaceable. I collected it and dropped it at Zander's feet.

I stood atop the stump and leveled out the height difference between the two of us. "Do you have something to say?" I shouted at him then waited for a reply.

Fennick's eyes smiled at my new stance.

Zander's shoulders were squared and erect. I molded my posture to match his. He let a gritty scream escape, one I returned with more robustness than his.

"You don't intimidate me! You don't scare me!" My mouth was dry. The veins on my neck budged. "If those are your tactics to enforce compliance then you have lost me and I will call upon the Eternals to witness that you have held your vow fulfilled and banish you."

His jaw tightened to the point I feared his teeth would shatter. "You. *Left.*"

"Controlling lunatic!" I shoved his chest. He did not budge. "You damn well heard my promise to return to you safely. Apparently, my word means shit to you if you scrambled out of bed to retrieve me yourself rather than wait until your obedient friend dragged me back to your almighty presence. I would have walked freely back to you had you not been so bull-headed, and here I thought I was doing a courtesy by letting you sleep in after I kept the whole damn keep up with my *nonsense.* You are impossible and your personality gives me whiplash!"

A growl.

"I'm safe. Your friend is safe. We were having, what I thought to be, a bit of harmless fun. A needed distraction."

Remorse struck across his face like a slap of honesty. His shoulders slumped as his eyes diverted from mine. The male submitted with a hinge at his waist and remained in prostration until a surprised looking Fennick cleared his throat.

I continued to spit the rest of my rage as he rose. "By the way, pissing competitions are for idiotic men. Try to overpower me like that again and I will cut you down where you stand to where even the wraiths wouldn't know what to do with your severed body parts." There was a reflexive bark from Fennick, not appreciating the threat to the man he was bound to protect.

My adrenaline stopped flowing. My joy had been zapped.

I jumped off the stump and began the slow and chilly walk back to Fort Fell. "The last woman I trusted led Fennick into a river labyrinth to be slain and drown," Zander muttered under his breath. My boots were stuck in the frosty dirt. The heaviness of his confession settled on my mind. I turned to watch Fennick put his blade away. Zander was closing the gap between us, his arms out and hands open in front of him. His emotions strumming across the unseen line between us.

I tucked my hands under my elbows. "I harbor no malintent or ill wishes towards Fennick." I looked past Zander and unto the elemental in burnt robes. "You broke the chains that held me to my lover's rotting carcass and melted the bars that held me in my enemies' grasp. Despite your annoying silence and sluggish pace as a running partner, I hold you in high regard. I owe you more than I care to admit." Fennick dropped his chin as a means to recognize the sincerity of my words.

"As for you," I locked eyes with Zander. "You have poor taste in women."

His chuckle ridded the last of his tension. His deltoids and sternum relaxed into a heavy posture. "Historically, that was the case. I've grown much over the last century, but as you know, some scars remain with a mark that is not easily forgotten nor forgiven. Losing my brother is not an option, Wisteria. Nor is losing you. Sorry, to have disrupted your morning in this foul manner, it seemed you were both enjoying yourselves."

"Apology accepted." Zander pursed his lips with obvious relief. "Also, it was stupid to give me a chaperone who you don't trust me with."

"I trust no entity, myself included, more than the man beside us. You make it sound as if I forced him to be with you when I could not. I had nothing to do with it." I raised my brow, seriously doubting what he implied. "Were you actually thinking you were going to win that sprint? When I arrived, he had you beat." My mouth went into a thin line. I walked away from the pair of them who were donning boyish grins and settled into walking side by side with their arms brushing against each other and holding hands.

I followed the slope upwards, the fog lifted to reveal two carts unloading empty crates to be filled. Plans were well on the way. "Speaking of arriving. How the hell did you get out here?"

Zander did not follow me out of the ravine, he'd be spotted. "Being Oyokos's grandson has *some* perks." He shrugged his shoulders which engaged his stomach muscles into two firm lines which guided my eyes downward towards his undone buttons. I waited for him to divulge more and tore my flitting eyes off the sharp angled 'v' leading into his pants scattering my thoughts. "I can turn nothing into something, sometimes."

Vague. "Again with the excellent vocabulary. What the fuck does that mean?"

He shrugged again, slowly releasing Fennick hand.

"Fine, you dusty elderly man, keep your secrets. But, if they start interfering with me, I'll demand answers and you will give them. Fair enough?"

"Yes, sweet blossom," his honeyed voice rumbled.

I turned on him with a fist already formed. He was *gone.* Evaporated into the morning. Fennick stepped back with his arms up, not wanting to be on the receiving end of my scabbed knuckles. There were already too many disagreements for the day. I lowered my fury and put my hand back under my elbow. "Feel free to go about your morning without the burden of me," I said.

He put his hands in his pockets and chose to usher me as close to the fort as the fog allowed before heading to the smithys, doing all he could to stand against my words. To him I was not an inconvenience. When I turned towards him, I watched back darting towards Crocker Street.

I would not understand anything more about the strange duo until he agreed to converse with me.

I received a lot of looks from the ranked guards as I strolled to Zander's room. None of them were crude. His door knob twisted easily. He was arranging food on the table next to the bed. "You know," I harped on him. "It is not safe for a lone man to keep his door unlocked in such a place. What would people think if they knew you didn't take any precautions or mind your own safety?"

"Luckily, you are here to protect me," he countered, moving the bowl of granola and oat milk towards the empty stool. I seated myself across from him and his coffee.

"Ha," I offered dryly. "You're not eating?"

He patted his stomach. "No room, I am afraid. I'm to the brim with peaches."

The spoon never made it to my mouth, it slacked back into the bowl with a clumsy clatter. "*Really?*"

"Really," he said, watching me take to stirring the raisins into the cold cereal.

"Have you no shame?"

"You do not. So why should I?"

"I see your point." I chewed a cluster of oats. "You've reverted to being loquacious."

"I have. And, please note, I'm not challenging you to a pissing contest."

"How mature of you."

He leaned into the great wooden chair, waving a hand nonchalantly. "It was bound to happen at some point."

I finished my meal before I felt like speaking again. Even then, no words left my mouth. I rose from the chair and stretched my limbs. It felt wonderful to have exercised so impulsively this morning, my splintered ribs hardly called to me until the walk back.

"Do you want help with the salve?" A tender voice piped up.

"I applied amply this morning. I notice great improvements already."

Zander cleared the table and set the cutlery aside. "You'll kindly comply with receiving another layer of ointment before I head out to capture a wraith, correct?" His effort to make a demand sound as if it was negotiable was humorous. I laughed but agreed in the end.

"How will you be capturing a wraith?"

"By beating its skull until it fades and tightening chains around it until its innards implode."

I've seen too many infected bites not to vocalize my concerns. "And it's mouth?"

"I'll place the gag or muzzle *after* rendering it unconscious. I'm touched to find you concerned about my wellbeing. I can feel you *here*." He motioned to the invisible space between us.

I scoffed, "The thought of a wraith occupying and modifying *your* body is terrifying."

"Because it's beautiful?"

"No, you conceited fool. Because it would be an unstoppable force demolishing every bit of greenery in sight." His eye mimicked the terrors my mind foretold should he be lost to the darkness.

"Fen would burn me long before my transformation. No matter the cost, he will not let me unleash the chaos of darkness upon this world or any other. Worry not," he concluded the topic by rising from his seat. He pulled out leather luggage from behind the headboard and rummaged until a notebook caught his eye. *Malick, the Reaper.* "If you are ever interested in what an open table democracy of diverse beings looked like, it's a decent read. Frank with the true hardships and rewards spelled out in easy terms."

I skimmed through the first few pages of handwritten ink. It was written in first person. "An autobiography," I muttered. "A treasure from someone you admire, you must be tickled he left it in your care."

"More than an honor. Although, I have never needed his journals to know of his talents—his might and wits were legendary, the tales the storyspinners speak of over fires. In many ways he fathered me, by blood and advice, he built me up to overcome a world of diversity."

"Keenan suited himself into that role for me." My reservations gnawn at my belly. I admitted, "I am upset he didn't teach me more about the realms beyond Ferngrove or bother to divulge the agendas that are now large at play. He knows far more than he told me." I bit my lip wondering if he had packed up and secured a ship at the southern port by now. I would see him soon enough and ask.

Zander handed me a wet cloth to wash my hands and face. "He has his motives; you may still come to receive them before the end of the age. Your family would have expressed reservations if they existed, you have sharp observation skills and you'd have been hesitant from early on if you sensed true betrayal." I nodded from behind the rag and let my thoughts fester in the silence offered.

We took an early dinner in the dining hall to meet Pine. Asher pulled us down the hallway, his red hair catching the torchlit glimmer with the bounce of his steps. Not only had the box been completed, but so had my ring. His enthusiasm was endearing.

Pine had buffed the thin band of iron until it shone like pure silver despite being crafted from scraps of spearheads. I was gawking when he grabbed my hand across the table and slid it onto the right middle finger, the kiss on my knuckles that followed sent the both of us laughing. I'd much rather be caught in a course of nervous giggles than crying *again*. "Chivalry is not dead."

"No, you look absolutely absurd," I chuckled, pulling my hand back from his. The light caught on the gemless band. "It is the prettiest thing I've ever owned. Thank you, Pine."

He, admiring his craftsmanship, agreed, "Ay, made more beautiful by the lady who wears it. It is the least I could do for you after what you did for my mother and the commune." His head dipped in gratitude before his words flooded out. "You used to eye merchant goods like a hungry wryven wanting to hoard all the treasure behind your golden scales. Expensive taste, never any trading money." I was six years old when I wrapped myself in spools of silks and satin. I would never forget that dreamy texture against my skin. Heavenly. My family never had a need for such a commodity as money. Many crafters made a living from those who coveted the stones of the underhills and ironsides or transport such frivolous rocks by means of the windriders and wavedrifters to city ports. They'd been forced to become acquainted with coinage and pastels.

I spun the band with the soft pad of my thumb. My molting face reflected back at me with a hint of a smile buried under the scabs on my lip. Pine was assessing the scabbard Zander wore next to the gold embedded horse on his front buckle. Zander adjusted his waistband well aware of the scrutiny.

His large hands interlaced atop the table as he leaned in. "Captain has already sent snow owls to secure rooms in a quaint inn for whoever decides to trek westward. It is in a safe district of the city, predictably set up with plenty of protection for the influx of visitors and gala attendees."

Pine tapped my elbow. My eyes moved from my plate onto his weathering face. "You still wish for me to go north to Sanctum?"

"I do."

Zander hardly ate. His breath was as steady as his hold on our bond. I sent reassurance to him because I felt oddly unshakable with my newly rekindled relationship with my old family friend.

"And after I've seen the villagers to safety, what would you have me do?"

I swallowed and adjusted my softening gaze. The allegiance he offered was unshakable and... *mine*. I knew it was and I replied as such, but not without kindness. "Explore the east province and gather a beige tinted understate flower called scalic that grows in dry dunes bordering the north. It has six leaves and raises no higher than your ankle. Reduce several the aged buds into an extract and compile them. It's the residual you'll want to bottle. Disguise it as baking goods, as flour. Don't sample or smell it. Kindly, have it stored away to be easily accessed upon our next reunion. As much as you can."

"So, you shall have it." He agreed behind his water goblet not daring to ask what the scalic was for or how a girl whose family had never been to the east province came to know of their plant growth.

A pensive energy beckoned me into my head. *Did his mom welcome the Ilanthians or was he raised with prejudice?*

Elousie was the first to offer her home to them and nominate herself to serve as a midwife during an imminent birth of one of the travelers. Pine had already moved out. He never met them.

"Drift," Asher commented, plainly worried about his commander's choice. "You'll be wanting your strength." He awkwardly whispered in passing after witnessing him not take one bite of food. Hades had called him from our table and was making good use of youthful guards in the fort. His commands to pack the trunks and barrel off clean water were heard in echoes around the spares dining hall. Even Gimly heeded them, for with each completed carriage and cart, he was one step closer to returning to his spoiled life in Landsfell. I doubt I would ever get the chance to savor my enemy's son matted in horse shit and taking grunt orders to trim the hooves of the mounts. He swallowed an ale and stomped back outside to carry out his tasks.

Dismissing the notary regarding his appetite, Zander asked in an edgy tone, "Where shall I find it?"

"The launderer's well," Pine stated.

I tapped the waxy, leathered forearm that rested across the table. "At what point will my skills be required?"

"Midmorning is my estimate. Your roommate has enough decency to let you rest your bones until the spawn stirs," Pine said while watching his ring glinting off the candelabra. "I'll send a prayer to Orion, that Drift is swift and the captain's confidence has been correctly placed."

Our bond was taut then lax. He gave a lazy youthful grin to Pine, "I'd appreciate any Gods' guidance. You are kind," Zander said with soft reverence. The staff in the kitchen exited with three guards maneuvering dry grains by the sack from the pantry, Raina barked at the salt being hauled out of her work station. Sage folded her apron and emerged behind her grandmother.

I stood. "I'll bequeath the Eleven intervene tonight should you dare start to drool on my pillow. Keep your slobbery jowls on *your* side of the bed or I will smother you with the pillow." I left the faint chorus of laughter to find Sage and bury her in a hug. We stumbled backwards, the hold never dropping. I pinched her tinted cheeks and planted a kiss on them. "You look well, Sage."

"Cultee upheld his word. The entire brothel has been granted meals whilst you were out with the excursion. We are all preparing to leave." Her thin elbow linked around mine and we strode left down the dimly lit hallway, passing the shower pipes and coal warmed commune where some survivors of Horn's End gathered to brush each other's hair and do a fair bit of wallowing. We increased the furnace pressure and nestled ourselves nearest one of the steaming pipes.

My knees cracked as I dropped onto a low stool. "Gimly hasn't been a bother recently?"

The joy that filled her painted little crow feet by her eye. "Not I nor anyone with a pulse. Whatever witch's brew you concocted worked." Her feminine hands patted my shoulder. "My bleeding stopped, my appetite returned the night before last. I'll be able to hoist crates with the rest of the fort in no time. Grandmother says we will be on the road north before the darkest night, I've been trying to retain as much cushion on my legs as I can. But if she cooks me one more pork liver, I might just hurl." A valve from the boiler popped in the distance as the shower in the adjacent room was turned on.

"Sage, do you remember much about Landsfell?" I said, running my fingers over the lapel of my current tunic.

She whispered, "All of it. It's my birth home."

"Landsfell was always my destination."

"Yet, you know nothing of it?" she accused.

I let out a steady exhale. "I am a survivor and will continue to be that. However, if fortune struck, I was hoping to learn the city's mysteries and layout prior to arrival from a local who knows such information."

"Fortune is on your side, Ivy Woodlander for I know the gladiator competitions of the Pits and the perfumed streets of the Crimson District alike." The light on her face transitioned into that of an animated narrator as the night passed on and the common room emptied.

Chapter Fifteen

Sage, having grown tired of sketching the streets of Landsfell on the humidified mirror, took to sleep in her chambers. I scoffed at the suggestion of dozing off. The thought of me in a city of a half million people was both nauseating and exciting, Fort Fell was the most populated plot I'd ever explored. I would have to be ready for anything, and with time to burn for the evening I rolled the pillow and cot into a reinforced punching bag that I hung from the ceiling using the scraps of the hideous gown. I had much strength to regain after my time in the fort laying low.

I stretched my sore limbs then rounded on the bag in a series of uppercuts and jabs. Bobbing and weaving, I sparred until sweat broke out on my forehead and my thighs burned. I was nowhere close to being finished. I flung my body across the room in a series of Montuse maneuvers, the acrobatics left me dizzy and the walls dirtied with the imprints of my boots. My bloodied knuckles decorated the dilapidated fabric.

My chest fluttered with unsettledness as I fought the urge to scream down our bond asking for a reply or retire to sleep. Then it came. *I've returned.* My shoulder slumped as tension dissipated. *Bastards have grown their horde already, by means beyond my understanding, it took longer than I would have liked to pick one off. I ended a hundred more in my spare time just for fun.*

Captain will be pleased with half your report, terrified of the other. The words did nothing to transmit the ease that washed over me and caused my eyes to water. I didn't want them to. The warmth trickling down my forearm and spreading over my palm told me he felt it. What I had tried to keep from him. I sagged onto the hanging fabric enjoying the way I felt weightless with relief.

You're not in my room.

I've been busy.

Oh?

Seeing as I destroyed the humble sleep arrangement and the singular sheet paired with it, I collected my dagger from Lorelei's bedding whilst she slept replacing it with a green fern and tiptoed down the ranked guard's hallway until I stood outside a scarred wooden door and shabby frame. It opened without me having to turn the knob. "Busy doing what?" Zander said, pulling the door open for me. He had already washed and readied himself for the night in a thin tunic and gauzy bottoms.

I pivoted on my heel. "Who. Not what," I tried. "I was occupied with another's desire for distraction from the end of the world."

His eyes fell under a shadow and his tongue flicked out to wet his lips like a Gods damn serpent. He tasted the air. "Lies, I smell everyone's arousal and if you were busy *doing somebody*, I'd scent it on you across the nation. Although, you are drenched in sweat and unbound which makes me concerned you finally cracked and landed yourself in a fight." He spun me around in a delicate dance searching for new scratches and welts. He found none. "Your knuckles are bloodied and there are fabric burns." When he stopped, I pardoned myself and went into the privy to change into a long tunic as a way to avoid a smug retort.

"It is disheartening to hear the wraiths have multiplied," I confessed from behind the curtain. "They don't reproduce like the rest of us living creatures, which leads me to wonder if they have infiltrated the eastern province. Hells, maybe even the northern province along the sand dunes." No matter how I viewed the situation, it was bad. I placed my toothbrush down and washed the dreariness from my face. A sad attempt to make myself more lively.

Half of the comforter was turned down, Zander was motionless by the dying fire pit. "Have you more of those paralyzing spores on hand? I want to limit other's potential exposure, until we secure the spawn in a closet. Iron box or no, it's... I tried interrogating it, Wisteria." He watched me walk to the bedpost and to his side. "I think it knows how to communicate. But, not in any language I recognize. Maruc would know."

"Shall we ship it to the White Tower? A boat will be awaiting me at the southernmost port the days after the orca moon. I can sail it to the Lands of the Gods and deposit it there for the Emperor to... observe. Do you think it will inspire him to fight for our cause?"

"I do not know what he will do nor do I claim to understand the reach of what he sees and knows."

"Do you think he is aware of the horrors devouring these lands?" My heart grew heavy.

Zander repeated without confidence, "I can't speak for him nor the Empress."

"Fantastic," I gave a sarcastic grumble and took off one of my left earrings. "Uncork and blow the cap, not the vial unless you are eager for me to resuscitate you."

A familiar dimple appeared when his smile did. Anxiety of the unknown softened and began to dissolve. I left him where he stood to slide under the heavy, warm blankets. Reaching across the bed I clutched the corner of the fabric and tore it down.

He asked, already knowing, "An invitation?"

"No. A reminder that this is your bed and I'm not cruel to insist you spend another night in that wretched rickety chair."

He surrendered his arms in the air. "My slobbery jowls shan't stain the pillow you rest your head upon for Fen would not be happy to wake up knowing I've lost mine." Zander rolled into bed and onto his stomach.

"You'll lose more than your head," I promised, pointing to my Ilanthian dagger I was recently united with that lay resting atop the nightstand.

"Then should I beg the Goddesses to torture you with a nightmare so I may be blessed with you wiggling your way into my arms?" A hissing came from my parted teeth and a heat built up from my core. The light was switched off in reply. "It was a joke, loveliest Wisteria. Watching you relive your past torments me, I promise if I could sway the last two

Eternal to banish grief from your mind, I would give my blood to do so. I'm far content knowing my hymns soothe you."

"You're an ass," I grumbled, rolling onto my strong side. My new adjustment permitted my fractures to heal without compression. "You're familiar with bad dreams."

"Neither of us are special in that regard," he admitted. A fair amount of guilt crept up my chest. "Over time they've diminished. I'm certain that will prove the same for you."

I humored dismissively, "I'm a red blood. I don't have time nor do I want it." I fluffed the pillow under the crook of my neck. "Should you find yourself in need of soothing your frights, you know where to find Fennick. I expect he is an expert by now."

"He pulls me back to reality by whatever means he sees fit. I reckon he'd do the same for you."

When I awoke far into late morning, Zander was half buried under pillows, hidden below long strands of hair and a rough, short beard. Unaware of the risen sun and my slow observation. His black eyelashes amplified the sun kissed and albino skin spattering down from his hairline to the straight bridge of his nose. I stretched and nestled deeper into the divot my form created on the mattress.

My stiff hand reached for the poetry book on the table, I didn't want to risk leaving the bed for him to find it empty and endure another horrid display of control. I read a chapter titled *Opaline Ocean* where imagery of black lotuses on a violet lake were painted in my mind with words of such precise detail they sounded more of a song. *Eternal Elm* spoke reverently of charred plains that encompassed a burning tree. A tree planted on the edge of the darkest depth of obscurity whose millions of seeds caught fire and rained down upon the lands every turn of the century. I swallowed the fear invoked and shut the cover of the book.

Four knocks tapped on the door, followed by a soft spoken, "Woodlander?" It was one of Cultee's men from the trek, whose name I'd already forgotten.

"Ay?" I replied, hustling to fasten my trousers. Zander remained statuesque as I opened the door and spared the vaguely familiar man a few safe inches.

"I hope I'm not interrupting. I beg pardon if I have, Lady Ivy," he stated uncertainly. I ran my fingers the length of my hair and covered the open buttons of my tunic.

I shook my head. "Nothing to be interrupted. I've been awake for some time now." He was wise not to challenge me with insinuating commentary. "What needs do you have that are a cause for calling upon me during recovery hours?"

His thumbs tapped a burgundy leather bracelet around his left forearm. "Rodrick's son bequests you tend to his father and Raina offers you her pantry to rifle through before it's crated off."

"Rodrick will be seen first. Take me to him," I said. *Stay in bed.* I demanded down our line.

As you command. A lame resistance. Fennick wouldn't be far off, was my assumption.

The guard glanced at my feet. Shrugging, I moved around him on my bare feet. We trodden up a half flight of stone stairs to where Flint greeted us in the hall and ushered us into a small room. Rodrick was sweat soaked. His pallor was a far cry to envious. A complacent, easy grin found its way on my face. Flint immediately relaxed when his father mimicked the weak expression. "Has he been showered with lathering soap?" I asked, quickly unraveling the shreds of fabrics, ignoring the exudate of a budding infection.

"Yes," he responded, biting the knuckle of the fist holding his head up and off the table.

I called over my shoulder. "Flint. Kindly, go ask Captain Cultee if he has incubated penicillium fungi. Rodrick will need two tablespoons daily for no less than a week." I heard him scurry off. "Guard," I failed in recollecting his name. "I need nothing from Raina's domain besides a gallon of boiled water and four ounces of distilled liquor."

The infection wasn't yet systemic. To prevent it from becoming so, I used the head of a needle to puncture the abscess forming in a pocket below the tidy stitch work. Under the scrutiny of the patient's eye, I irrigated it with the sterilized water brought in from the kitchen well. I packeted the small wound with a poultice and wrapped the nub loosely to avoid restricted blood flow. "No submerging this in water," I instructed, rising off my stiff knees. "If you feel lethargic, double the penicillium for the day. Flint will be sure you are getting rest and hydration to move the illness out of your body. When you travel, place it in a sling." I washed my hands in the warm basin noting the brow crease on the younger man's face.

"You're not destined for Sanctum?"

I eased my features to hide the surprise of Zander's low drumming slithering deeper into my consciousness. He woke up and I felt him sorting his own thoughts. Taking the towelette, I offered sweetly, "My aptitudes will be used fully in Landsfell. Cultee agreed to the arrangement."

"These red guards are filling your head with foolishness."

My eyes shut, begging calamity to settle in me. I retorted, "I've always been foolish. Just as I have always retained the ability to form opinions of my own regardless of what those around me believe."

A mere half second passed. His tone was sharp. "You forget, I was raised in Brigade Castle in the capital before my father removed himself from his position and chose the life of a vagabond." His eyes hardened. This was the first time I heard him mention his upbringing. I couldn't determine if his sentiments were regret or anger. Or both. "There will be no place for you among the ignorant, refined and those who have the sense to wear shoes in winter. You belong with the rest of the crafters."

I threw the towel into the bowl. Now, I was angry. Again. "I belong to myself."

Flint dug his heel into an unstained knot on the floorboard. Heat spread across my chest. "That place of pompous scholars and parties, is not your world. The sooner you realize that the better."

I stepped next to him so the venom of my whispered rage clung to his collar and suffocated his air. "You're quite right. That place, as well as the Southlands, Northlands, Plains of the Horselords and even the Land of the Gods is not my world. It is *our* world and if I wish to see our world, forsaken or not, I will." I bid no pardons or excuses as I left behind Rodrick nursing his freshly prodded wound and his sour son shooting glances down the hallway at my back. I laced my boots tight and my cloak tighter.

A bit too early in the afternoon for such a large amount of anger to settle in that tiny statue of yours, isn't it? Zander commented as I walked past him in the dining hall on my way out the front gates. I'd business to finish on Crocker Street. His company of men and village women seemed to be enveloped by his words and animated energy. He told a colorful story of his years as a stable hand and the gypsy caravan that roamed by with mysterious guests. A story I would have enjoyed if I had been in a better mood.

I stepped over a snow drift. *You'll get used to it. I find anger a productive emotion and see no need to banish it.*

I've no grounds to disagree. He wavered on our thread, preparing his thoughts. Eventually, he called out. *You've the intention to return to the fort?*

Flint stripped me of any creative remarks. *Yes.*

Soon?

Unforeseeable.

By the time the Chanah laid eyes on me, I managed to mute the rest of my thoughts, and the thoughts of a determined incubi. "Curtain six," I stated, readying to unclasp my layers.

"No need for a search. See yourself around the establishment as you see fit." Her warm palm grazed my cheek where I knew an unsightly bruise existed. She investigated my split lips and swollen hairline before shaking her head. "I'll bring you both some warm refreshments." Her bare hips swung as she walked behind a heavy curtain. Sage's work area was barren save for a cushioned chair and a wooden box of belongings.

"I retired from my line of work. We all have," a soft feminine voice spoke behind me. "Chanah had the floor and bedspread scoured clean. The room will always be sullied crimson in my eyes." I turned to Sage while I loitered in the hall. "Come, let us chat in the lounge. I've thought of a few more important details that may come to serve you." Her outstretched hand took me in. The hostess found us coiled up on an old chaise and poured rice water. The starchy sweetness reminded me of sparse harvesting seasons when the fields had not yet come to fruition and there were mouths to feed. I took it with thanks and relished the uprising memories, for my mother was in most of them. Her wide smile and open arms are an engrained childhood vision.

Sage tapped my wrist. "I failed to mention my parent's employment at the Monte's winery and the arrangement with my sister, Yolanda."

"Is that so." I hoped my craving for knowledge didn't come across too eager. "A winery is a sensible conclusion knowing that your parent's dreamt of a simple life. Fermenting the fruit of the earth is a marvelous craft and not too off the mark from a woodlander's." It was nice to see a touch of joy hold her cheeks high.

Sage carried on. "*Forlorn Label*. It's the only brand of wine offered to the lords and the royal family during festivities to avoid any unnecessary risks. Its distribution is monitored. It's served sealed. Corked, foiled and waxed. Three signatures mark the final product ready for their lords and ladies. Those are also the names, should something go wrong, who will be held accountable. Any sign of tampering will get the servant and their master flogged openly in the slums by an inbred brute named Crosby. He's foul." My breath caught as I buried my desperateness for details under a fidgety hand. Few reasons existed for her to confide such information to me. All of which made me uneasy. If they made me uneasy, then my protective acquaintance would surely hate it if I accepted the intel she freely offered.

I treaded lightly and kept the conversation elusive. "Have the Monte's always been a fan of public retribution?"

Her eyes traced the small wooden window still behind me. Her head cocked as she pondered her reply. "The captain of Fort Fell has been the most reasonable, unlike his kin."

I sipped the rice water until the cup sat empty on my lap, allowing her words to sink in. "Which process do your parents oversee? I envision them much preferring to be harvesting the crops rather than the tedious task of tempering sugar, temperature and bacterial growth for a balanced wine."

"Martin and Lena a'Loure are assigned to the oak barreling and bottling of Forlorn. The season before I left, Crosby caught my father, who overlooked a too-porous cork wood on the Pinot Noir. The vendor on 5th street who supplied the weak cork was never mentioned. My father is a good man and could not watch another's livelihood be stripped from them. He was crippled on his right side after that and threatened to throw himself off the ramparts when he found out his daughters entered the life of a courtesan to relieve the debt Crosby wrote on my family name. I'm familiar with all the ways the high lords sneak their consorts into the manor's private chambers, having used them many times myself. The tunnels are also used to store goods before major events including the winter masquerade, and to house extra security measures, such as weaponry and capitol knights." Had she any idea of what carrot she dangled before my greedy eyes?

Glimpses of a long silver haired Fennick melting the bars and chains that held me and the rotting corpse of Anna. Then there was the fog and frantic footsteps sounding above the dungeons. My arms and legs wrapped around a tall stranger who wove in and out of passageways in the night. I didn't want to recollect anything of the turns and twists that led us to the open air that night. But, now? I wanted to know. *Needed* to know. The fate of a family may be determined from her insight. "Tell me how to navigate them."

"My older sister, Yolanda, is working for Madam Marmacient, the primary supplier for the wealthy. She is favored among the courts. When I last saw her, those sentiments were not reciprocated. Far from. If she is still there and in business, she may be your best ally if she knows you too have helped her family. She will be difficult to win over." Sage moved hair off her neck line to unclasp the brass link. A light necklace and charm of two suns fell onto my palm.

She began again. "The guards moved most valuables from the premises yesterday. Curtains three and seven are boarded up as all the rest will be this time tomorrow." She sounded short and unsurprised at the rapid turn of events in the Fort. "The most pressing thought occupying my consciousness is wondering what sort of life lies ahead for me in the east province since the only skillset I excelled in, I refuse to partake." She swallowed air before her words struck me. "The guard on the watchtower told the tavern what he heard, what he saw the night you and Fauna climbed up. I do not wish to rattle myself over the future, talking about my past feels more grounding. Sentimental even. It is selfish of me to want to consume your time, yet if I can help you as you have helped Fauna, and those before her, I want you to listen and ask questions. So, in the end, if I am lost, I will not be forgotten and maybe my family will be better off for it."

"Sage d'Loure." Life filled her cheeks hearing her name. "Speak your story to me under the white sky and let your tale become immortalized by the Eternals."

And so she did.

Night came. I wasn't ruffled to find Fennick running errands up and down the nearly abandoned Crocker Street, hovering close to the building I stepped out of. I watched him under failing, dim lamps as he hauled sacks of manure and straw from stores. He loaded them onto a wheeled crate to be the source of heat and light for those walking north. Heading into the season's darkest days, his crateful didn't seem enough. He scrambled into the bakery. Out he came with a cinnamon loaf and a square of hard butter. I stared dumbly at him when he poked my hallowing stomach. That was the warning I received before he shoved the desert into my chest. Pain clenched me. I swore at his back while shoveling food into my mouth, savoring the salted butter on the roof of my palate.

Zander replaced Fennick at my side and hounded me down the hallway when I re-entered the gray stone slab of rock. "How does one forget to eat on their recovery day?" His voice carried, causing the archers on the second floor to peer down at us. I felt like I was sprinting and making no progress to escape his pestering. Damn his long limbs. After we made it up the stairs in the captain's hall, I turned on him.

"Drift," I gritted loud enough to bring several of the scribes to their doorways. "Not everybody here eats an entire pork belly in one sitting!" Snickers arose. Zander crossed his arms, thinking twice about puffing his chest out at me. "Nor are we all fortunate enough to grow up with consistent meals, least not in winter. I've gone without far more often than I've gone with, as of recent years I've settled for a small meal each day, or every other."

No longer. He sent before saying out loud, "Never again. This misfortune has been far too normalized. I'll find you some bushes or berries...squirrel food..." he mumbled under a firm scowl.

"Your consort managed to scrounge up a treat from the bakery during his work hours," I retorted, passing Hades who stepped out of Cultee's office. Few brows were raised. I bid the gathering of men a fair evening and hurried off around the last corner. Silence lasted roughly fifteen minutes. Zander brought yogurts and what resembled a dehydrated fig. Whatever it was, it tasted decent enough.

Zander closed the curtains to the solidary window above the bed. "In your haste you missed the news," he started. "Captain received word from Stegin the carriage and armed riders will be arriving tomorrow eve. He did not offer further aid to the fort, just his family, you were right."

I spun in my chair. "I am a persuasive writer."

Zander untucked his tunic from his trousers, I diverted my eyes at the flash of scarred skin. "Gimly basked in the praise tossed at him for his forethought on the heavy matters at hand. At the present moment, he may not have the wits or care to hunt down a clever imposter or suspect a literate crafter; however, when he returns to his father's city many shadows will be assigned to his protection. They are trained to keep their wits about them at all times."

"I don't plan on conjuring more letters in his sloppy penmanship," I insisted.

He sat himself in the chair across from me intentionally placing salve and cotton wraps in my direct line of sight. "What are your plans?" Zander cuffed his sleeves, his forearms flexed as he rested his hands on the table's edge.

"Sightseeing."

His lips pursed, "Unlikely." Zander blinked. His eyes now a matching shade of clear teal topaz. "Whatever mischief you'll be doing is bound to be more appealing than being stuck under a homicidal lord's scrutiny. I anticipate him to proudly display his dungeons, to which I will scour for your friends just as thoroughly as I will each guest room and private chambers of that estate."

My appreciation is beyond words. I emptied my mouth. "Do you have formal events in the Veil?"

"Formal in the sense of flaunting ideas, but we've no hierarchy of lords and ladies, evolving fashions or need for excessive wealth. Events are for upholding traditions and socializing, which we do a lot. Revels are frequent. The Overlord holding the seat makes decisions for the good of the land but always with a crowd of three or more persons. Anybody can question an Overlord's judgment and call for a reevaluation with the city if they have disagreements. It's humbling and levels the notion of power." He filled his water cup, making an exasperated face. "The fact that everyone is ancient and holds no value to finance nor the diverse magic of each race leads to a very balanced, hardly boring, existence. But, yes. We party."

The spoon in my laxed hand swirled the clumps from the vanilla yogurt. "Numaal must seem archaic to you. Do you pity us?"

He leaned forward, arms flexed. "I've never pitied the vibrant. I love my lineage. The longer I reside here, the more I find myself envious of your ability to take risks and choose the paths of most resistance. True to your name, your mere existence inspires one to make the most of every moment."

Coping his actions, I filled my glass and clacked it on his as if it were a fine champagne. "To risks,"

"To calculated endeavors." He countered, raising his water in the air then to his mouth. My side hurt from holding in a sarcastic laugh. I splinted my ribs as humor shook them. "I promise you, if you'd have met me in my early years you would have been *appalled* how foolish I was. And the two of us together, destructive. Add Fen to the mix, explosive." He flared his fingers at the last statement, his white smile mirroring mine.

"But fun," I managed to say.

He gave a fond sigh. "Indisputably fun." I picked up my spoon and spun the food in the bowl.

"Why did you decide to become cautious if life in Veona was all you dreamt of?" His lips pursed into a thin line, I could have sworn the room darkened. "It was the woman you loved, wasn't it?"

"The world is better without her in it." He said by way of confirmation. Shadows regressed. Whoever she was did a number on him. "Hand me that list tucked into your undergarments. I'll speak to what I know if you finish that yogurt and promise to stay resting until the carriages arrive." My handing him my questions was confirmation of the deal.

His eyes combed over the small parchment that was dwarfed by his hand. "Anuli, the Great Mother." Zander started. "We have temples to her kind heartedness in both Akelis and Veona decorated with the most delicate blossoms tended to by stray children and adults needing a home. Anuli mothered the first vibrants and adopted each one into her family for many generations until Numaal expanded beyond the capacity of her lap and arms. At the time of the Great War, she wished her beloved kin to see past prejudices and bloodshed, to see with their hearts even when the Eternals hadn't accomplished that feat. When they couldn't, she emptied herself onto the lands and departed. The country itself was her chosen vessel. Her blood nourished the soil and gave seasons to the country.

"Taite, our nefarious God who was hardly rattled by the actions of his creations, saw his sister's death and took to the skies as quickly as the Twin's wind carried him. He called for the triple throne and Oyokos to put a stop to the madness. Thalren was born. The war stopped to grieve the loss of our earth's first departed Eternal. No one grieved harder than Taite who indulged in his infamous vices of pleasure. In his stupor, he was never able to speak again. His bloodline is surprisingly normal, many of them tend the vineyards north of the dunes and southern groves of the Akelis. All are exquisite wines."

I said, "According to your story, it was love not disappointment nor pity, that lead to Anuli's suicide?"

"I know not what led to her final choice," he stated carefully as not to cast blame. "What I do know, is that I specifically mentioned to you that book from Cultee's office was historical fiction." I turned away so he could not catch my eye roll.

"There are drawings of people eating Anuli's heart! Drawings of a barbaric feast taking place in Kathra's palace walls with red flags and dual headed raven seals drawn in precise detail." I exclaimed in a loud whisper. That was evidence enough even to rural folk like me. "If I was Taite watching my sister get their heart chewed on by civil beings, damn straight I would try and wipe my mind blank with whatever I could get my hands on."

Zander lowered his chin debating his next choice of words. "Suppose you are right. The royal family's line was tinged gold with blood from a Goddess. What does that change for any of us?"

"It has significance," I grumbled, somewhat defensively. His blue eyes shone with intrigue. I'd ask Maruc when I met him along with Anna's odd request to have him take me to the Opal Lake. "Do you think the people here will be safe in Sanctum? Welcomed, at least?" My stomach grew heavy thinking of a shunned Sage and isolated children who have survived horrors most can't fathom.

"Relatively speaking, Sanctum is a friendly place for the faithful. Their mission is to grow their own, their righteousness will ensure the refugees are brought into their customs and given necessities." My hands knit together. "If they make haste, they will be fine, Wisteria." I looked everywhere but at him. "Do you want to discuss the unspoken rules of Landsfell you'll be expected to follow?"

My stomach tightened at the notion of any regulation me as a woman would have to follow. "Sage told me enough. Some shit about manners, walking in groups and clandestine weapons on women."

Zander stretched his long torso over the back of the seat. "Are you going to comply?"

"Are you going to use your incubus sway to compel me if I refuse?"

"Never. Although I may have to get persuasive if I catch rumors of a rogue woodlander running off to instigate trouble during the province's most attended and guarded festival. Fen wouldn't be happy about busting us out of the duke's prison cells twice in one decade I presume." He shook his head imagining Fennick's fury. "If he had an ounce of his true power, he'd burn the damn place down just so he didn't have to go back in and fetch us a third time." There was a twisted hint of a smile that set on his upper right corner of his mouth.

I certainly was not opposed to that last scenario. So long as Moriah, Rory and Cobar were back with Keenan and I sailing to the Lands of the

Gods, I couldn't care less what happened to the duke's manor. "The fires could ward off the wraiths, at least for a day or two while the rest of the city evacuates to Kathra. Or it may draw them in."

"It was hypothetical, Wisteria. You will never be in chains again." His low reply was a promise that sung down our connection. My left hand itched. I shook it out under his gaze. "The more we sypher, the faster we will get acclimated to it. As for the *knowing* accompanying our ability, it seems that when we are feeling sentiments strongly, the other is made aware. I am as sure of your emotions as my own." He moved his attention from me to the fire. Dull crackling filled the room. I stared at my hand waiting for the blue and golden threads to shine from it. Nothing.

I finished the meal and readied for bed. Zander had the balms heated when I stepped out in his nightshirt, they were mostly melted when he brushed them on my skin. The medicine was heavenly. The sharp pain of several splintered ribs drew me back to the rough circumstance of my body, reminding me of how human I was and how slow the process of healing.

When Zander's hands left me, I buttoned up the remaining clasps. The covers were brought up to my chin before Zander lay himself atop them on the opposite side of the bed where we laid until the captain called for us the following day.

Chapter Sixteen

The snow that fell was graciously light, were it another degree above freezing it would have become heavy enough to weigh the transport cart down. The duke's selected guards were already in a foul mood having been ordered to trek away from the city walls during the festivities to collect a bastard son and his disowned uncle amid a winter storm. The six men in mink fur and red cattle leather boots said nothing as an iron box was set just under the passenger side seat of the carriage. Zander won them over with some distasteful comments about the northern province not being fit to survive outside of their desert oasis of privilege and spoils.

I tugged Raina's knit hat down over my face to hide my disgust. My satchel was filled with whatever the pantry had left, it hung heavy around my neck as I stood there dumbly in the snow waiting for directions and trying not to stare at the trunk under the seat or wonder when the plant elixirs would wear off.

I had already said goodbye to the few people who braved the weather to see me off, Sage and Loralei just re-entered the fort when Brock headed towards Captain Cultee. He was smiling and a tad breathless when he arrived at the carriage. They exchanged words before Brock swung off his pack and threw it at Zander who caught it and gave one of his boisterous showmanship laughs that managed to bring warmth to the gathering group. "You can't get rid of me that easily," he smirked before boarding into the yellow oak carriage, seated just atop the wraith. Zander gave him the hand satchel before lifting two custom engraved trunks onto the totting cart. The *M* the same font that was on Gimly's signet I used to seal the red wax for the letters.

A few more travelers sauntered in; among them an elder scribe, Asher and lastly Gimlian Monte. He had cleaned the horse shit off his boots and pants, washed his crimson cape and by the looks of it his greasy cropped hair attempted to put himself together for his return home. No amount of snow and rain could rid the potent scent of musk cologne he bathed in before strutting around the six men his father had sent. The emblem square ring on his right hand prominently displayed. Asher glared at that ring. "We set out tonight and make haste through the dark. The way has been cleared extensively and the city's lanterns can be seen even on nights such as this," the lead guard spoke. Cultee looked as if he had something to say, but thought better of it, opting to dip his chin in compliance. "The girl, the gimp and the scrivener can ride in the shelter. The rest with able, strong bodies of us will be atop mounts."

The scarf around me heated up as my face burned. *Gimp? Able, strong bodies?* This prick. Gods I wanted to prove them all wrong. Zander moved Rosie's reins away from my reach. And a satchel of arrows for good measure. *Timing.* Zander spoke. *They will reap what they sow, my lovely woodland flower.*

Now anger pulsed to my head. I walked away from the mounts to the carriage, distracting myself by admiring the large pine trees sagging with a foot of white snow on their limbs. The branches touched the ground, few green sprays peeked out from under the evergreen's winter coat. There was a grip on my shoulder. I spun around so fast I made myself dizzy and in the slick snow I almost toppled over to get out of reach. "Lady," Gimly said uncomfortably. I adjusted my stance and wondered how fast I could get to the dagger buried under the apple slices in my bag.

"Gimly," I stated, more sour than sweet.

"You leave your identity here at Fort Fell. You are not to mention your craft, status or name to anyone. You are to stay in the Gooseman's Inn and Tavern keeping that tattoo on your back covered until I come for you or I will skin it off your back. Am I understood?" From our first encounter it was clear he had plans for me within his political schemes. And for himself.

"Why?" It came out as a whisper.

He snorted his wet nose and tilted his chin down to my short stature. "Do you always ask so many questions? Get a new name. Stay put. If I so much as catch a rumor there is a woodlander in Landsfell, I'll finish the job the wraiths started on your pal Brock. The company among us will be receiving a similar message, but a different threat if they are to mumble about the crafters in Fort Fell." He didn't wait for a response, he moved on to prep his mount for the night of travel.

A new name? A new identity? My rage was met with a new emotion of apprehension. I was never any good pretending to be someone else. If Fort Fell was my test in restraining my opinions and hiding my emotions, I would have failed quite significantly.

I swallowed and pressed my back against the truck of an old pine I had been eyeing and inhaled the sweet crisp scents of the pine needles and fallen snow. I let them chill my lungs and center me a bit more, before I had to shut myself into a mobile box that would be transported onto the lands of Stegin Monte. I permitted excitement to trickle into my heart and douse the rage burning. I could do this, I told myself. I could be anyone but when the time came to kill my enemy and avenge my love, Duke Stegin Monte and his superiors would know *exactly* who I was. Another breath went by before I moved aside the low hung branches and stepped out of the tree's shelter.

Branches cracked behind me under the weight of my watcher hidden in the distance.

Captain Cultee hollered for a lady. I ran towards the beckoning and slid into the small carriage next to Brock and his weakened metal braces. His crutches were twisted and probably painful. He snapped his fingers and motioned that I sit next to the scribe, Adious, a lifelong student of dialects and history. He talked our ears off about flood dams over the Ticck River four centuries ago.

I was jealous when Brock began to snore so much so I sought Zander out for entertainment when Adious went on to describe the mechanisms of proper irrigation from a back flowing riverbed.

How much longer exactly? I asked Zander while finishing yet another muffin in my attempts to avoid the interaction.

We are three hours in with another full day and evening to go.

I swallowed my sigh. *Be appreciative of the weather blowing about, at least you don't have to engage in ridiculous conversations. This scribe is making my ears bleed!* Adious casually tightened the doors as our cart clanked down a steeper drop in terrain. *Are these men familiar to you?*

Some I met two years ago. The rest know me by reputation as a partial pale horselord eager to become a knight. I doubt they've met another of my descriptions. He opened up the door on my end of the bond and pulled me out to meet him. I used caution when he permitted me near his aura, I didn't intend to dive down into his abyss.

I wanted to. It called to me still as I tried very hard to ignore it, the angelic sound and taste of trust radiating from his center.

Your caged core still wants me.

I know. It never stops. I readjusted my neck on the cushions provided in the small quarters. *I've learned that all of Numaal's dukes and the vizors of the royal family arrived already. Duke Satoritu Koi manages the north, Duke Hammish Hetterstud the west and Duke Roland Verdain the east alongside the Resig's influence. I'm willing to bet one of these blokes transporting us has already had the privilege to transport other anonymous guests into the city and with a little coaxing I may come to find the undisclosed whereabouts of Numaal's high lords.*

Do let me know if they've committed heinous crimes against the living and blameless. I'll happily see them in eighteen days once I've had my way with Stegin Monte. Unless an opportunity presents itself sooner...

We made a promise, Wisteria Woodlander. Do not strike down your target until a plan is in place. A plan you've given me three weeks to construct.

I sighed watching Adious tie his scholar beads around his wrists in a ritualistic manner. *I haven't forgotten.* He was relieved. *Gimly has plans for me. Not good ones. If you hear anything, you will tell me.* There were no words to confirm he would comply, only tight caresses on the shell of our syphering. Outside I heard his booming voice get to work on softening up his company. A gentle reminder of his time restraint was all it took to light a fire under him to seek details more aggressively. Our bond hummed after I laughed.

What? He found his way back to me.

I make you nervous. I smiled to myself in the darkening cart.

You are unpredictable in the most delightful of ways. You terrify me.

Good. At least when I die, I have peace knowing I've tormented you for some years and made your boring eternity fun.

If you manage to be a pestering thorn in our side when you die, Fen and I may hold you at the crossroads and take revenge. You forget which of us here has a certain amount of sway over the souls that pass on my feisty human friend.

This is hardly feisty, my overgrown pigeon guardian.

My wings are leather, not feathered. If you are going to insult me, at least choose a more realistically relatable animal, like a bat.

Your most relatable animal is a wild boar. Loud, aggressive with pungent pheromones and none too intelligent.

My brothers are not going to know what to do with you.

I wrapped a blanket across my lap. *You seem to think we are going to Veona after this. My next destination will be the White Tower by way of ship and sea. There is no time to waste trotting over and around the Thalren seam. Get back to schmoozing, midnight has come to pass and we are no closer to setting a plan in motion.*

So domineering. I do quite enjoy it.

Per Cultee's recommendation, we did not stop for respite during the night hours. Once the sun had risen we were permitted respite. Brock and Adious took the sliced meat as a meal while I hurried off for some privacy. The guard was correct in saying the territory had done extensive clearing, finding any amount of decent shrubbery to squat behind was a challenge that took me a quarter mile away from the men. The walk back was nothing shy of embarrassing with most eyes on me making my way through the barren bean fields. Stalling for time, while Brock emptied spores into the vent of the iron box I assisted Asher in filing his mare's front hoof of the implanted stones. "In you lot," we were addressed by a heavily insulated guard and told to squeeze into the carriage. The scribe hustled in as I handled Brock's crutch. "I've never missed the lantern lighting in thirty years and don't intend to do so now." His tone softened. His eyes longing gaze up at the dim barren sky, reminding me once again that we were humans, born to be the product of our environments, but nonetheless emotional and desiring the same basic emotional needs to be met.

The carriage gained speed and prattled my healing bones. As a distraction, I built up enough courage to ask Adious a single question and risk him ceaselessly rattling on. "Do you know much about the lantern lighting?"

His aged face lifted into a smile that pulled wrinkles into the corners of his eyes. "Why, yes! Many of my childhood's fondest memories came from the lanterns spoke of." Joy tumbled off him. "From the onset of autumn to the day the lanterns were lit, my neighborhood would be busy collecting reed parchments, wax and wicks, venturing out as far as we are now to beg the farmhands for their honey hives." All gazes went to the flattened, seedless dirt and outside our carriage's window. "You'll have to take my word for it young bloods, this was rich soil with succulent flowers as far as the eye could see." He pushed on through the swell of sadness. "The lantern festival is special. In my early years, my family's hovel bordered the literacy department of the university. When it came time for us to write our wishes, messages and prayers onto the domes of the flying lights and the sails of the paper ships, the scholars would flock down the streets offering aid to those who weren't educated. I may go as far as to declare this was when I chose my life path of learning, for the professors and students of the school always appeared to have a manner of wisdom and grace to them as they happily sauntered down streets of sewage and poverty; not thinking twice about the state of their violet robes soiled from the gutters or their practiced hands holding children of all ages.

"The festival united the city's sectors, brought families together and set hope and light back into the dark days of winter when we all would dream about our transcribed dreams and prayers making it to the ears of the departed Eternals. We need this festival now more than ever I dare to say." His statement had Brock nodding in agreement.

Brock cleared his throat. "Those who have died, can they receive messages too?"

"No harm can come from trying. I promise you that, should you write to those who have moved beyond that you will not be the first or the last to do so." Adious narrowed his grey eyes across from him and leaned across his knees to whisper. "Those who were taken into darkness when they died will need a light to be able to find their way home. Stay alit, for it is imprudent to do otherwise when we haven't learnt all there is to know about the destination of a journeying soul."

I hadn't a clue if he believed that himself or if he was trying to keep the dimming optimism in our heart burning longer, that a soul taken by a wraith had a chance of a peaceful, painless afterlife, was a notion I gave up on years ago. And yet, the way he said it with such fervency and reverence... He was an academic man; he knew many things that I didn't. For a longtime he remained silent, I spent thinking about eighteen particular souls and the messages I would write to them.

"Whatever name you give as your own, Ivy, I can guarantee will be more easily forgotten when your face is less memorable. Landsfell is likely to be intrigued by your piercings." Adious gifted me a small velvet purple satchel no larger than my palm's width. I filled it with metal studs, hoops and a good portion of my dangling earrings and nose ring. Three I had kept on and would take fate into my own hands if it came to it. I refused to be tortured or left to rot if taken captive. I thanked him. His face wrinkled with understanding.

Landsfell reminded me of a worker weaver bird commune, whose nests were built to hold an entire flock. The rises and walls encompassed the city like the unsuspecting cocoon of sticks around a busy and bustling inside. Captain Cultee headed to the wall's sentry lookout and slowed the pace of our convoy to a crawl. I heard the clicks of iron moaning as they had been released, Brock and I fought to press our face against the window as the dense tall doors opened for us. The monotonous humming sound became a collaboration of music from what sounded like one hundred different directions, conversations and arguments of countless running up and down the streets with squeaking wheel carts and blissful children. I had not seen such life in what felt like ages.

Guards were on each side of the tower, twisting the mechanism that sealed the weighty doors behind us. I spotted pyres and gongs stationed in quarter mile increments on either side of our carriage. A bold alerting system, armed with two men and two archers per turret. The guards that lined the streets were red faced, stumbling around in decorated formal garb. Street vendors of powdered cakes and steaming pork pies were shouting at eager passersby. Brock and I shared a turmoiled expression for neither of us had a coin purse. My stomach sunk into my damaged ribs watching the full-bodied women spinning around the ribbon pole with candied lollipops in their hands, their skirts dizzying any onlooker. Amongst the chaos of the late night and thick crowds of bustling bodies was a palpable theme of ease. The different dialects of Numaal blended into one as the masses moved towards the center of Landsfell, towards the brightest bell tower, nearly everyone carried a lantern with them.

Captain's voice approached on our right. "Gimlian, take two men and assume the responsibility of escorting Drift onto the estate. He boards near my sector. I will congregate with my brother shortly once I've seen to our guests' arrangements."

There was an abrupt knock on the top of the wooden and metal roof. Zander. "Don't miss me too much, flower."

"Don't count on it, princess," I shouted upwards. He snorted a laugh.

How are you feeling? Zander's energy swarmed around me, scouring for any sign of a frayed emotion or worry.

I have reservations all of which are buried away for the time being by excitement. I'm sure when I am sharing a room with a wraith tonight I'll have different thoughts. My throat dried at the mere idea.

The first opportunity I have to assess your safety, I will do so. Don't take risks. Over medicate it, even if it means emptying your supplies. These festivals are not known for their shortages of resins, sedatives and psychedelics. His horse trotted off. The slack, relaxed connection suddenly tightened as we both grabbed onto our respective ends. *Please, do not get yourself killed.*

He was more than two blocks away now. Three, almost four. *Such a fluffy request from a demi-God. I'll try to accommodate it.* I stared at the masses, too dazzled by the shapes and colors of the paper domes they held to recall the exact moment I felt the sypher bond dissolve with the distance set between us. Alone with my own thoughts, I welcomed the mortal magic of the night and let myself be lifted by the beauty floating in the sky and along the river that cut through the city. It stifled the nerves that threaten to rise. Cultee said nothing when our carriage came to a halt, for he too beheld the same sight as I. His eyes marbled over while his sadness emptied out of his composed stature in the form of a deep sigh through his nose.

A tug on my arm. I allowed him to escort me off the steps and as far at the front desk at the inn. An inn that was not Goosemen's. On the shelves and the beams above was etched *Arborist Rentals.* Adious stayed behind while Brock and our trunks followed with the spare guards from our journey who set them down on the steps and were then given orders to disband for the night. The couple behind the desk were lost in the evening as well, neither thrilled to be interrupted by new guests claiming their reservations.

"Captain Cultee Monte of Landsfell and Fort Fell," he stated coolly, no hint of distaste for his family name anywhere in the air in his demeanor. "I've two rooms reserved for the boarding of my guests paid in full until spring. Provisions and meals delivered upon their requests." The inn owner peeked her head around his chains of finery and took in the sorry sight of his guests who had been gifted such kindness. Brock's eyes widened at Cultee's back, I kept my stunned gaze on his collected features.

"Yes, sir. We've booked two adjacent rooms on the second floor," she hushed.

"We were to have the top floor."

"Captain Monte, that was before a wealthy count from the Southern Isles offered to pay triple the rate and secure it with a bank note days before his arrival. I've yet to greet this Count Hilderbrand, he has not come to retrieve his key." The owners shrunk under Cultee's intensity.

"How have you planned to compensate me for this inconvenience?"

Two brass keys slid across the counter. "Both apartments on the second floor belong to your guests. The accommodations are just as remarkable and private as the grand suite above them. I've already stocked one room for the miss and one for the fellow with the clothing you requested. Three meals a day for each."

Captain cleared his throat. "You will honor them with your best hospitality and ensure they are unbothered by the curious public who've by now seen my arrival. You will not be bribed by any shadow."

"Understood, my lord." Their heads lowered. When they rose, they met my eyes and readjusted their attire. She slid two gently worn brass keys over the table top while her presumably husband opened the log book and dipped his feathered pen in a pool of black ink. "Names for the Arborist's records, Captain?"

The captain stepped back and gave an honorable gesture for us to move closer to the owners to speak our names above the noise of the night and the tavern in service behind the couple. "Sage d'Loure," I stated with a calm smile. On the off-white parchment went the name I promised its owner would not be forgotten. When the scribbles finished the man looked up at Brock who straightened himself upright with pride.

"Rhyolite Stout," he said, watching his name of stone and beer become concrete.

A key was handed to each of us before we followed Cultee around the bar and up two flights of stairs to where a few well-kept apartments, outstretched from the landing of the stairwell. My fingers examined a preserved knot in the wall's panel, below the inscribed number 'two'. The lumber workers had completed a marvelous job in filing down the long boards and maintaining the wood's distinct character just as the architect made sturdy the many alternating rows of cedar, oak, maple and pine. An assortment of reminders that held alive the roots of my past. Perhaps when the city was not to the brim with people, food and industry the earthy scents of Ferngrove would fill these halls on a rainy day. "Miss d'Loure, I knew you would be one to appreciate the artisanship of these apartments. They are not the most grandeur, but the quaintest in my opinion—if that counts for something." Captain led Brock into the first room as I entered into the second.

Save the stone masonry on and around the fireplace and small cooktop, everything else was glossy wood decorated with auburn orange blankets, curtains and towels that gave me a sense of home among the unknown. A soft knock came from the back right closet. A section had been removed between our rooms and some floorboards loosened. Reaching through the gap I tapped a red sleeve. "You are right, my Captain. I very much like it here." That was the first time I referred to him as *my* captain and I had done it intentionally so. Firstly, to show my gratitude. Secondly, to reinforce that we were a team and that despite my initial judgements, I needed to trust him. And him I. "A lovely place, the Arborist seems a bit more my pace. Your nephew expected me at Goosemen's Inn. I suppose I'll be granted a bit more freedom and privacy away from the center of town." Our eyes met as we came to an understanding.

Brock got on his knee and decluttered the space between us, emptying the cobwebs and trash that had collected under the boards. "All ready," he said, motioning his chin to Cultee and I who each lifted a handle of the iron box. We set it down softly, some part of me feared a minor disturbance would aggravate its pitchy screaming, even after a bumpy carriage ride and the raucous noise of Landsfell. Alas, the box did not stir under our noses. Brock realigned the floor and tossed a heap of linen over the seams for good measure. He took a hanger off the bar and tied to it a satchel of various medicines used for keeping the wraith silenced. Cultee assisted him in rising off the ground. "We will take turns. I can take the first night watch and we can divvy up the hours after breakfast."

Behind me lanterns took to the sky like phoenix birds of myths, elegant and disbelieving. "Of course, the man who chose his name after a rock and a type of beer would choose tonight for his watch." Turning back towards the closet's tunnel I raised my eyebrow. Brock smirked guiltily. "I'll admire them with you from the balcony and your shift will stretch into midday." We all gazed at the lanterns drifting across our windows.

"You'll make me tea then?" He asked, shouldering his fate.

"Black or green?"

"Green. Easy on the honey," he reminded. Captain's cheeks rose to his eyes temporarily before a vacant, stoic look displaced his features making him appear cold and detached. Not even the lights reflecting his round eyes thawed his new, rigid composure.

"Sir, will you be staying for tea or perhaps you'd enjoy a warm cup on the ride to the duke's estate?"

His heels clicked as they moved together, straightening his posture. "Neither I am afraid. I've to deliver Adious to the academia campus and greet Dutchess Kacey no later than midnight on the patio gardens." He blinked twice. "We will keep in touch." He hurried off, managing to check the lock behind him.

Brock had a better view of the city center from the window above the dining table. A view I'd never thought I'd see. People by the thousands, filling up the streets with unbridled joy, clamoring about without a care in their world. Life seemed unfair. Perhaps I had already used up my allotted amount of happiness the Eleven granted me at birth and left to now suffer painfully for the rest of my short days yearning for the ignorant bliss that enraptured the lands. Dwelling on it dampened my mood. The estate was easily spotted two full leagues away for its inhabitants had sent up crimson lanterns. Assuming Sage's directions had been correct, the finance district and the slums known as the Trench were directionally out my window to the east. And in the direction of the red sky were the courtesans, fine eateries, shops of satin and the entrance to the underground tunnels. Gods save the world from my wrath should I discover Anna's fate had befallen Moriah, Rory or Cobar. Anna's blood hummed with affirmation, mine with revenge. My ears burned.

The owner, who introduced herself as Coraline, brought tea kettles up at my request to which I concocted a strong brew for Brock and a soft chamomile for myself. The night quieted gradually while lanterns swam high against the stark night sky. So high and distant that they lifted and blended into massive constellations in the starry, winter night. Were it not for the low haunting groans rolling out from the closet, I would have finished my prayers to Oyokos for all the lives I sent to him before their time.

I helped Brock pull the layers of linen off the box. The moans turned into snapping snarls after we exposed the ventilation filter to the fluorescent lights of the apartment. Its foul breath filled the closet as it hacked violently, wanting to escape the effects of spores Brock wafted in. It stilled and yet I found myself clutching the wire of a hanger fiercely. As if that choice in weapon would have been effective against a wraith. Brock laughed and dropped the sharp end of his crutch he had been holding onto. I eased into his nervous laugh and together we sipped our tea pretending to be oblivious to the evil festering on such a beautiful night.

Zander? I reached out as I left Brock's chambers for my own. Our strand tightened. He gripped his end and tugged back. It went slack. We were too far apart to uphold our syphering and he was far enough away for me to scout out Yolanda and Sage's mutual connections before day broke.

The dressers were beyond adequately stocked. I chose a cotton navy blue skirt and a fitted shirt which I covered up with a pleated sweater. Although, after a quarter mile of walking west I decided next time, I would opt for a cloak to aid me with blending in with the rest of the women my age. I tied my hair into a messy knot as I watched the other's do and even placed a red carnation flower under the hair tie to appear part of the festivities.

Keeping my gaze down and my destination fixed on Madam Marcamient's brothel, I endured the thick crowds of hasty bodies bumping into mine. Eventually, there was no avoiding people in touch or conversation as the locals and visitors alike were hustling one direction or another, too involved with their own agenda to be cognoscente of another. My skin felt itchy around all the commotion and electricity.

The bordello was as Sage described it. A sprawling brick estate to the brim with occupants and clients lining up outside the adorned iron fence. I appeared to be the humblest dressed person within fifty feet seeing as the male courtesans were doing a wonderful job of weeding out those who either could not pay or would pose a threat. Around the parameters I trekked, scouring the establishment for a way in. A cold sweat broke out on my forehead when I succumbed to the reality that there were no flaws in its design nor the security formations. The city sounded louder causing my brain to go fuzzy.

I told my feet to move and wound up leaning against a wine barrel on a stone patio.

A tall man who wore the gold chain of servitude around his forehead spotted me pondering in the shadows, just beyond the end of the line. I turned my gaze onto the flooded streets and skies and slowly meandered it back to the man hoping I remained unsuspicious in my endeavors. With a long finger he called me forward to the fence. I dumbly pointed to myself. He nodded. As I moved forward, I placed a strut in my sly walk. I passed a row of men caped in wealth and perfume. The scents were unnaturally potent. I held my breath and wiggled my way around roughly one hundred people to stand in front of the courtesan. "Sir, I'm flattered you've called for me. How may I, a commoner assist you on this heartwarming evening?" His gold band glinted among his shaved brown locks as he rose his baffled brow.

"I am as much a refined sir as you are a blameless commoner. Only those with appointments are to be tolerated loitering. Have you an appointment?" He spoke disinterestedly. This was not his first time reiterating his speech tonight.

"I didn't know I needed an appointment to see my sister," I stated, crossing my arms across my ribs. "Although, I suspect she is entertaining elsewhere given the influx of highborn visitors."

"Most of us employed here do not have family—none that associate with us. Certainly, none that care to visit." He scoured my features trying to place me. "What's your name?"

"Sage d'Loure."

His painted handsome face rose a thick brow. "I have known Sage for many years. You are not her."

"Wonderful. Then you must recognize this." I help up the necklace holding the charms of two suns. His hands that intended to redirect me away hesitated. He licked his lips, not breaking my gaze. "She sent me. I need to meet with Yolanda."

"Your agenda?"

"Her family's safety."

He made a *tsk* click of his tongue and took the bait. "At the current moment, she is beyond our reach in fortified walls. Yet as fate has it, a northern lord has arranged her escort at Bjorn's Luncheon for his political meetings just on the edge of the Crimson District. She will wear a pink fur scarf and her headdress of debt. This conspires the day after next at promptly noon. At most, what I am capable of is delivering the message that her sister *may* have sent a stranger who bears the twin to her necklace. What shall she keep her eyes keen for? Will you come as a beggar or perhaps a servant in her presence? She is quite a sought-after item."

The use of the word 'item' put a scowl on my face. "I will come as a friend bearing the sigil of two suns." I bowed my hips in gratitude. A firm hand stopped my shoulder. Something small and weighted slipped into a side pocket.

"An outsider who sinks to the level of minx and coquettes? A stranger to the city is the girl who calls herself Sage."

"So removed from humanity is the man who turns his nose at a whisp of appreciation."

He grunted. I used the momentum he pushed me away with to dart around a drunken party of boys, years shy of calling themselves men. I dodged much of the mayhem, toppling only twice into elated locals, who hardly batted a lash at my frantic pace. When my palm started itching, my nerves didn't improve. The mere thought of the unreasonable incubus hunting my agenda down all while analyzing the inner workings of the high lords and ladies of Numaal was irksome. I scratched my left hand and shimmied into the Arborist. The muffled moans from the closet stopped after Brock's interventions, but the persistent droning roars from the city ensured my sleep was fitful. And when I awoke some odd hours later, it felt as if I had stayed up on watch. My mending body felt twice as heavy. Coffee remedied the pressure in my skull, ointment aided the softening ache in my ribs.

Brock's knuckles pounded four times on the back side of my closed closet. "You're on, Sage." I saw him briefly in our exchange, when he came to close off his room and open mine. I tossed on wool lined trousers, a pair of plush socks and the largest top in the dresser drawers. I refused to acknowledge my sudden preference for oversized shirts, but danced around the kitchen nook with the flowy train of my shirt whipping behind me with my long strands of loose hair. Coraline rang a petite bell in the hallway. Our first meal had arrived.

Toasted rye, marmalade and a full platter of sliced ham, which I promptly shoveled onto Brock's plate. He grumbled out of his doorframe, eyes swollen slits, and rolled his food cart into his chambers. I took the warm porcelain dish and spread of toppings into my apartment, enjoying them as I watched the sleepless city below from my window. There were half as many people meandering the streets the night before and yet, there was hardly any distance between those passing each other. To live, work... exist... so cramped together. It wasn't a life I would have chosen for myself. Then again, if I had been born into such a lifestyle and not as a crafter of the Southlands, my sentiments would likely be the other extreme. I spotted a lovely couple, strolling arm and arm down the cobble road. The laughing lady had a petticoat and he a taupe overlay, neither appeared wealthy enough for a full-length cloak or warm head wear. Such things did not appear to dampen the way in which her partner coveted her as if she were dripping in gems and starlight. Mixed feelings of envy and loneliness flooded through me.

Anna frequently enforced how fortunate I was to be raised around affectionate and devoted parents, encouraging me not to roll my eyes at their mushy dialogues or turn away at their tenderness. Moments I never knew I would miss. A hollowness reverberated as I struggled to remember my father's corny jokes or my mother's flirty retorts. Finally, I recalled his laugh, her smell and Anna's hair. I emerged from the onslaught of panic, shaken on how easily my past slipped my grasp. As if I was reading a book watching the writing on the pages vanish before my eyes.

Hours of that day I spent reflecting on the trivial details of my childhood and adolescent years, reliving moments as profound as Rory's birth on the homestead to the subtle sound of breezes rattling the drying corn stalks on the last warm days of autumn. I didn't want to forget all the things I was composed of.

Vocal fussing came from the wardrobe. The sides of the box shook with limbs searching for freedom. Its frustration intensified each passing second. I was quick to snatch the powder and dump it into the box, even faster to snap the vents shut. My hair stood on end. Listening. Low, disoriented grunts fizzled into silence.

I released my rigid posture, backing away from the corner inlet into the seating area. My hands fell from my chest to my hips as adrenaline left me. The wraith's limbs went limp, a faint noise that caused me to slow my actions and stare at the broom closet. A dinner bell sounded, it went unheeded. Unable to eat, relax or partake in vigorous exercise; I examined the bronze, rusting chain the male courtesan dropped into my possession. A low-quality headdress of debt. My means of entry into Bojorn's Luncheon, into Yolanda's line of sight.

Chapter Seventeen

It came as no surprise to find a towering Zander and hustling Captain, carrying up the next morning's first meal in lieu of the owner. I felt the dreamer approaching well over a quarter hour ago, when he must have left the duke's premises. I crawled out of bed and unclasped the door to greet them silently with a sleepy nod. Brock motioned for us to enter his chambers, which were nearly the mirror image of mine. My bare feet were soundless as I hopped down the hall just behind Cultee. "You two look awful," Zander commented in his typical frank style of commentary. He was staring at the dark circles under my eyes, all while I examined his fresh red and gold shirt which was tailored to properly fit him. He was getting on nicely with the duke and his company if he was garbed in his money.

A short-tempered Brock bit back, "You'd look worse for wear had you been up for two nights straight with *that*." He collapsed in the armchair and pointed to the closet behind him. "Between *that* and an inconsiderate lord who moved into his apartment after midnight to rearrange his entire collection of furniture at an unholy hour, genuine rest is unobtainable. How is the fluffy palace bedding, buffets of food and scented spas? Or are you also sleepless from the harem of women the duke has at your disposal?" Zander snorted, placing porridge in my hands. Too drowsy to eat, I set it on the side table and took a seat on the floor, leaving the remaining couch available for Cultee who paced, fidgeting and unable to pause. Zander simply wouldn't fit. I sent silent ill wishes to the lord above us. The ceiling was silent now, he was probably snoozing after his busy night of dragging cabinets around his floor.

Cultee poured a glass of chilled water for Brock who took it, diverting his eyes. "I'm here briefly to deliver what updates I've obtained. I can't speak to Drift inside the estate, he is in the center of my brother's affections alongside my nephew. I had the advisors clear Drift's morning schedule, he will stay until midday, on duty, so you both may rest and repair your frayed ends." I whispered gratitude and pushed away the bowl Drift tried presenting me again. "There is smoke rising in the east. A surplus of it," he carried on, looking as faint as I felt.

Fort Fell. My chest went heavy. I blurted out, "Do you think they made it far enough north?"

I noticed Cultee's boots did not shine with polish as Zander's did when they turned towards me. "Neither I nor my informants can say for certain if it was the Fort that went up in ashes or the Wastelands. The winds blow debris around Landsfell, which does not aid our cause that danger is active and so close to the gates. If the black soot laced with the flesh of the dead wafted through the city, more would be swayed to pick up arms. That is not the case, so in disparity I've convinced the dutchess to post another hundred guards on the ramparts. The restless are running out of life to prey on. They will migrate. Send your prayers to the Anuli that the lanterns didn't catch their fancy." He reached his hand out to me. I looked up at it.

"Honestly, my bones are comfortable here." I deferred his hand, just as I had done the bowl of porridge. "Is there any chance the lanterns disoriented them and led them wandering scattered? If they arrive here maybe, it won't be the whole swarm or not until later in the season, giving the city time to empty several thousands of its visitors out. More if we can bring its leaders to the light."

Captain did not bother to fake optimism. He merely nodded. "Drift, what have you gathered?"

"Gimly spoke not one word when we were brought together with a small audience to speak of our endeavors at Fort Fell. I was asked not to describe the devastation with any gruesome adjectives, for it would displease several of the duchesses and high ladies at the conclave of advisors. Oddly enough, that meeting was postponed for the announcement that the Stegin family's favorite priestess is coming.

Typically, meaning a royal family member will be arriving as well, if they are not already among us in this sea of chaos. Colette has been rumored to be the woman of choice for our young, veiled prince. Either Stegin does not want the rest of the country to know how much his territory has crumbled or the council is already aware of the happenings and share a similar circumstance. I fear this sickness may have been planted for years now and intentionally left to fester for reasons I have not yet uncovered."

"Colette plays your game, horselord. Don't be dumb enough to engage with her flattery. She is a snake. One designed to allure. You will get bitten, not gain intel or favors from her mouth." Cultee was walking to take his leave. His pallor is that of a sick man. There was a lot to stomach and a lot more at stake. "I can't be seen frequenting here. Nor can Drift, he will be followed. In one week, either of you," he waved at Brock and I, "will need to meet me to discuss the developments of our plan and what each other has learned. Eight in the morning, on the bench outside the print shop. There is only one in the city. Don't be late. You hide your face and you hide your limp." He directed accordingly.

The door shut. I muttered into the drab atmosphere, "Inspiring."

"Bleak," the underhill took a full bite of food and readjusted his stump on the cushion. "But, if you're set on staying here Sage, then I'll happily die for the cause."

"You are free—" I countered quietly.

"I am free to do as I please, yes I know. We've had this chat. However, what I will not be doing is sleeping with Drift in my bed. I hear he drools and the frame of the headboard will shatter if he so much as sits on it."

The pair of them laughed. Zander bent his knees with his arms open causing me to wave a cautionary finger at him. "I don't need help getting up." I popped upright, cracking my joints as I rose. "And I'm not eating until after I've slept, so don't pester me with food."

Zander lowered himself into a bow. "Anything else, your majesty?"

"Yes, actually. Don't rummage through my belongings while I'm sleeping. And I'll need games and trinkets to occupy my mind when I'm fretful or bored locked away here. You'll have to find a way to get them to us, I'm sure Rhyolite feels the same." I pulled open one side of the closet and pushed on the other until I saw into my chambers. Zander squeezed through the opening behind me and softly closed off the passageway between the rooms.

I glanced at the bowl in his hand. "The porridge is for me," he interjected before I hounded on him. I was too tired to feel our bond and check if that was a lie. "Also, don't expect me to believe you've been locked away here. You told me you would be doing some sightseeing and I felt you moving about holding true to your words." He touched the center of his chest. I examined my palm and found our connection with more ease. *Yes, I spent time along the streets at the lantern lighting. I'm paying for it with fatigue.* I found the end of the single bed and stretched back onto it before pulling my head onto a pillow. *Did you find any of them?* I asked.

Not yet, he replied keeping what hope I had alit. *I would love to hear about your first experience in a city just as I am sure you'd love to hear all the ways aristocrats have designed to torture me with nonsensical traditions I must comply with to gain their trust, but alas Wisteria Woodlander your time to rest has come.*

My chin lifted. Fright gripped me.

The wraith is stirring. I can hear its breathing start to quicken in the walls. His eyes grew wide, when he focused his keen senses on the iron box. *In less than a minute it will be groaning, scratching its nails on the lid, kicking the sides or wailing.* I shivered as the high-pitched sounds of fingernails on metal begun to vibrate in my teeth. Zander had the closet open and powder blown into the box beneath him before the wraith had time to unhinge its jaw around the device it was gagged with. His brow was stitched when he came back.

I don't like it either, Zander. There is nothing we can change about the standing situation at the moment other than seeing how it unfolds. He lifted the stool from the kitchen and carried it over to my bed, his eyes not once leaving the brass knob. Once silence fell, I closed my eyes. The floor gave slightly as Zander settled in.

Can I sit here?

I nodded. *Did Nikki start the fire?*

He sent me no visual insight, but I know my brother is alive. You can ask him for us both when you see him, I reckon he had something to do with it. I don't know what he exploded or why, but the smoke in the air forty miles away nearly singed my nose. I took a deep inhale and caught no hint of ash, nor had I during the lantern festival and there was fire literally all around me.

My human senses must make you laugh.

Incubi survive off our ability to smell. No human, no Ilanthian and very few dreamer species even come close. We all have our strengths; I promise smelling when partners are cheating in their marriage or knowing how poorly one's personal hygiene habits are is not a blessing. He made a gag sound. I smelled my wrist and inhaled the soapy vanilla residual from last night's shower. *You should have put a salve on to speed up your recovery.*

I'll heal up in time for the gala, don't worry.

No. He was dead serious. *You're not attending.*

Yes.

Maybe.

That's better. Not that it matters because I'm going. You don't have to dance with me or acknowledge me. You may not even spot me with my gown of fancy fabrics and a mask that hides my identity. I imagined how lavish I would design my gown, should I ever be able to afford such a thing. The only dress I've ever owned was a shanty brothel garb which was beige and scratchy and hardly contained my breasts.

I will always find you.

We shall see. I'm innovative. I will find a way right under your nose.

If it compromises our plan, then no. I rolled to the side and let a deep sigh escape. I paused between inhalations, waiting for the wraith to rouse. *You are not reassured enough by my presence to rest?*

No, but I will sleep nonetheless. Don't allow me to become fretful.

Yes, my domineering little lady.

I am not yours. There is no need for such possessive pronouns.

There is some *truth in that.* A quirky smile laid across his shaven face. At a glance it was apparent he wouldn't elaborate; I was too weary for his immortal riddles, emotionally too, for I had depleted what social reserves I had by avoiding people in a packed city. I was not meant for a life among crowded streets dodging parties by hopping gutters and vendors, that was my final conclusion prior to sleep.

A heavy hand laid on my deltoid. My mind was pulled out of one state and into another. I felt as if I hardly rested. *I left a few books for you to peruse. From what scent I gathered, you enjoyed the poetry of feminine flowers the most.*

"Fuck you. And yes," I yawned, squinting at the drawn curtains which did little to filter out the midday sun. I looked at the closet. "Any disturbances?"

"Twice in five hours. The last dose was hefty, hopefully I bought you a few more moments of peace." I propped my elbows under my back, grimacing less than I had in prior days. Improvement. Splayed across my comforter was a meal, water and salve—uncapped. "One application today and another tomorrow, your bruises will have reabsorbed entirely and the swelling will be absent by the weekend. Even your lips are soft and intact, the scar on your jaw is hardly visible." Whether he was aware that his gaze settled on my lips or not, I reacted dumbly by shoving his arm off my bed. Only then did I realize he was dressed to take leave in his leather gloves and coat.

"I'll put the salve on," I grumbled a half-ass whisper of a promise. "That was nice of the captain to order you to babysit. I'll have to send him my thanks." Zander made a panicked grunt because his head smacked the ceiling when he rose. He massaged the crown of his head. "You've grown." My eyes got wide. "You're losing shape."

"I was distracted by thoughts of the Veil and I may have let some physical molding slip." I watched him bend his knees and shake out his limbs, as if that would help him fit through the door. I shot out of bed and stood next to him. "What, may I ask, are you doing?"

The top of my head came up to his mid chest. Somewhere between his nipples and navel. "Measuring." I grabbed his hands and pulled off his gloves. "And now I'm making sure you are not becoming blurry again."

He gently flicked my nose and backed towards the door. "No blurry lines. Not yet."

"I will take leave before you conjure up any ideas." He no longer met my gaze and dipped out the door frame.

"There is no need for peaches, when you've an all you can eat fruit buffet at your beck and call," I stated, remembering what Brock mentioned. I stared at his back; he did not turn around but he did shake his head in irritation sending his black raven hair shimming across his broad shoulders as his steps were heard in the stairwell. My stomach growled. I fed it roasted winter squash seasoned with rosemary and rummaged through the books and scripts Zander left for me. I scarfed down the custard that was desert and yearned for more. My hand sprung directly for the leather bound poetry book where I read and reread hymns to Oyokos attempting to grasp the author's confusion and pain laced in the phrases. A grave sin was committed, there was a need for redemption and forgiveness that saturated the ink stained lines. I would need to ask for clarification on that matter as well as the black ocean of lotus and fiery rain from the Eternal Elm. It was all too abstract for my non-dreamer mind.

"Why didn't you prepare for me Anna?" I sputtered out in quiet anger. "None of you did." I half expected Keenan to appear and offer a quick, logical reply. No one responded. The silence stretched a little longer. When I could not sit with my own thoughts I opened the window, the slightest of cracks, permitting the outside rumbles of conversations and partying to seep into my second story room, a pinch of commotion to offset my spiral.

So, I thought. It heightened my loneliness. The quivering iron box rattled. Ah, yes. I was not alone. It hollered briefly, its razor teeth clanking on the iron bit. It was chewing through the bar and ball. Brock's face peeked across the passage. He looked rested and offered a goofy grin. I let him know what I assumed. "Do you think Drift could wrestle another one into its mouth?"

I shrugged. "Risky, given we've company above and below. Besides, we don't know the next time we will see him. Cultee stated his visitation policy."

"In the meantime, we maximize the stash."

I shrugged at his statement. "I can't come up with another alternative at the moment. Drugs can be replenished and sent via discreet packages, let's try to spare what's left of our peace of mind." Brock's gaze moved behind me. Out the windows to a lively nightlife. "Go explore the city and drink some imported port wines. Report back to me with your favorite, so I might try it later."

His eyes shone. "You'll be well off for a few more hours?"

"Definitely, go on. Hardly, anyone in the city deserves a night of untroubled exploration than us simple crafters who managed to survive the last half decade."

"I knew you would not resist the lure of the lantern festival." I smiled. "How was it?"

"Hectic. Entertaining. Loud," I paused and redirected. "Dress warm. Take notes of the landmarks around here, I used the view of the university's library dome as mine." I offered so he wouldn't have to ask for directions or imply he was unschooled.

"I memorized the letters on our building. The stables down the street are a good indicator of my location given they reek when the wind blows just so. I'll be back before midnight, eat my portion of food if you want so you don't lose the weight you put on." In all our years, neither he nor anyone in Horn's End have seen me weigh more than a sack of rice. I was just lean muscle, bones and surprisingly decent breasts. A sarcastic shake of my head and I closed the closet. I took his portion of potatoes and desserts to my bedroom and when the plate was clean my stomach demanded more. I hadn't much else to offer besides water.

I took to the mirror. Zander's assessment was accurate. Excluding my ribs, I would be healed with a half dose of salve. I stripped my tunic and applied a liberal coating on my torso, neck and parts of my face. My hip bones were prominent, but not protruding grotesquely. My shoulders were sculpted as well as my legs, yet there was an inkling of femininity exuding, especially when they were bare, unbloodied and unbruised. I brushed and braided my hair in preparation for tomorrow's luncheon. I would portray a meek and low level courtesan. How did Zander and Fennick pull off characters so easily? If they were nearby I would have asked them for advice, but that implied that I needed help and that I valued their opinion enough to ask for it. Two things I would not dare to admit. Besides, who knew if Fennick had found his voice and wanted to use it with the likes of me?

Twenty-two years ago, I was named Wisteria, followed by Ivy and recently Sage. After sunrise I would be... Mildred Mcgaffer.

I do not know how the name came to me, but I was fond of it. I practiced saying it what felt like hundreds of times and in all sorts of tones and manners. Mildred would be clumsy, orphaned and sweetly daft to avoid deep questions about her past or suspicions of her intent. I found a dress, tore at the neckline and neatly sowed the frayed edges as Keenan taught me in my youth until it was suitable for a whore with a rusty headdress who needed attention brought to the necklace she would flaunt.

Flaunt I did. God's damn it was cold with a shallow morning sun! The ball in the sky was hardly visible under the layer of bleak clouds.

The light coating of makeup I dusted on my face was all but wiped away by my runny, wet nose. I politely dabbed my upper lip with a kerchief I folded and stuffed into the pair of long gloves. The cold wind added a blushing of color to my features. The unfamiliarity of a long dress and a formal situation caused my lungs to quake in my chest. I swallowed it. I slowed my pace, my narrow toed boot tapping on cobblestone, then composed myself when I approached Bjorn's Luncheon. The door attendant peaked his interest at me, tilting his chiseled fresh face in my direction. "Well met," I grasped the hem of my pleats and softly bent my knees. A small curtsy.

He exchanged no formalities or day blessing. "State your name and to whom has called for you."

The nerves in my throat were of aid for once. "I am Mildred. I do not know who is to receive me, sir. Madam Marcamient sent me, for the other ladies are *occupied* at this time. She assured me that my socially wise colleague will have arrived on the arm of a high lord and would give me guidance. I'm in my formative, training years." I lowered my gaze and my head followed.

"You've yet to have your virginity auctioned off? Well enough," he said without a whisper of discomfort as if auctioning off sex was a casual topic at hand. I shuffled my feet uncomfortably, stepping on the hem of the canary yellow dress.

The door opened. I straightened myself, removing my cloak to place his attention elsewhere. "Madam has sent us quite a spectrum of debtors this morning. If you are not claimed by a lord or threaten to tarnish the establishment's reputation with your homely mannerisms you will be removed. You've much to learn by watching the city's jewel." My head shook vigorously in agreement. "Your colleague is upstairs."

Mildred soothed the rousing around her flat stomach and tossed her thick wavy hair away from her exposed neckline. Strands of hair got stuck on her lip gloss. The door man rubbed his brow. Mildred stepped inside a grey stone manor decorated with oil paintings and chandeliers to provide lighting since windows were reserved for the upper loft from which cigar smoke wafted. The few scattered parties below hushed seriously over porcelain tea sets and servings of garnished hors d'oeuvres. One person cared to notice my arrival, she quickly turned away and vanished behind a red pink feathered fan and a conversation with an aged, well composed man. Perhaps a thirty-year age gap between the two.

I placed the clasp of my cloak onto an extended finger of a butler and casually wrapped my fingers around the stem of a crystal champagne flute and began missing the gemless piece of jewelry Pine has crafted in the fore weeks. Realizing I had no means to pay for food and beverage, I was quick to set it down on the buffet cart that rolled by. My face blushed when the servant girl removed the flute I touched and emptied it in the back. Tiptoeing around the seating arrangements and pampered guests in finery, I found the stairs and went upwards into the thick haze. Down the hall I trod, palms sweating beneath the thick fabric.

A dark mahogany door was left ajar. Laughter and quick wits sounded from the other side, along with the *clank* of bottles and glasses rearranging on a wooden surface. My gut clenched as I waited for the smoke to settle around me, for my surroundings to be made clear. But even in the dimly lit room with plumes of tobacco, Yolanda shone like a diamond in a coal quarry. Her headdress was brilliant platinum and her smile was dazzling enough to rival it. Her cascading diamond earrings and dangling necklaces failed to outshine her skin's pale glow and her long strawberry blonde hair. "Next round is on my tab. Find me something aged in oak barrels, no vanilla currents!" A hoarse voice garbled at me from the corner.

"Kind Lord," I replied with another curtsy, not that anyone could see the gesture. "I am not the maiden of the Luncheon, I am sent by my Madam to offer companionship and learn from the Landsfell's finest company, Miss Yolanda." Yolanda asked permission from my man at her right to rise. He permitted it. Her pink dress swept around her curvy thighs hung high enough to where one could see her silver embroidered shoes and smooth ankles. Her painted brown eyes caught on the two suns. "I am Mildred. An understudy, not yet auctioned. Madam saw promise in me and has assigned you to my cause so I may emulate your grace."

"She mentioned I would have an orientee, I wasn't expecting you to show up. You've got guts, a rare trait for today's world," Her voice matched her demeanor. Radiant grace and sophistication. "Unfortunately, matters today are intimate and I must defer and further delay your education." She pivoted back to the table of what I counted to be five men and two women, all in red silks and black onyx. Yolanda casually fondled the collar on the man nearest her while keeping her gaze across the room at a man with a rolled cigar tight in his lips. "Mildred will need to be escorted by my status to save face of those gathered here. You understand, Juanan." Such confidence and collectedness, exuded from her in the face of the free high lords and ladies.

An affirmative hum was our queue to leave.

An arm laced through mine. The moment she opened the door she said, "Speak, thief of names." My eyes watered when fresh air washed over us. I suppressed a cough. Yolanda's red lips matched the faint copper in her hair. I tried not to stare or scream for Anna even though it was a far cry for the flaming red boldness of my Ilanthian friend.

"I sent your sister to the north in good health and in good company with Raina." Her eyes remained unstartled and her footsteps unroused. Her grip around my elbow tightened. "I say this not to hold above your head, but so you know she and your grandmother are on their way to finding contentment. May you find joy in that." With any number of prayers and divine intervention may she and the three realms all succeed in our peaceful endeavors. "I know about the porous corks, Crosby and the fate of the d'Loure family. I also was told you are familiar with tunnels beneath the duke's estate. Sage said you are difficult to charm, since you are indeed the most charming lady within two hundred miles of here. I say I must agree."

As I had seen other ladies do, Yolanda whipped out her fan and cooled herself from the flattery. She gave an audible ladylike giggle. Her lips didn't move as she spoke softly, "I was *very* clear last time I spoke to Bastion's slackies."

"I am unacquainted with a Bastion, but I do know of a Martin and Lena. Would they like an escort north? Would you?" Her delicate throat bobbed.

A polite snort and conversational pat on the wrist. "You are offering me my freedom? You have seven hundred thousand and forty-three hundred in pastels on hand?" That sounded like a decently sized sum of coin exchange. I had nothing to compare it to, so I said nothing to avoid looking more foolish than I felt in this ridiculously itchy gown and oversized gloves. Food trays passed us heading up stairs. My stomach was growling with more hunger, it twisted. The twisting morphed into a sharp sensation.

"If I paid off your debt with Madam Marcamient, will you show me through the tunnels?"

Her body trembled with honest laughter. "Alright, yes."

Again, my stomach cramped. This time my lower back twinged at the onset. I ignored the discomfort. What I could not ignore was the warm trickle of blood running down my upper thigh or my racing heart when I realized my cycle had chosen to resume now for the first time in over a year.

At the breech of the door, I pulled her hand into mine. My thumb has a firm lock. "Once you are free, come to the second floor of the Arborist asking for Sage." Her hand was shaking when it clasped mine in sealing our agreement. There was a fool's hope in her eyes when I left her that day. The doorman all too willingly ushered me out once Yolanda left my side. My hood was up, my head chain was off and I was sprinting on the main streets to get to my room before my cramps caused me to double over in public.

Coraline was delivering lunch when I arrived on the second level. I saw she had another tray kept warm on the trolley cart for her new tenant. "Good Day, Sage," she greeted, arranging the cutlery for us in the hallway.

"Same to you, ma'am," I leaned on the nearest wall, refraining from clutching the lower part of my abdomen. "Could I burden you for some extra firewood, warming bags and anything that has chocolate in it?"

Her middle aged face smiled and showed small creases by her eyes. "Have you cotton strips and inserts or shall I bring those too?"

I had absolutely nothing in stock for the matter at hand. I smiled back, "I will appreciate anything and everything within reason."

"I will heat up the pipes so you can take a hot soak and leave supplies outside your chambers after I've tended to Count Hilderbrand." Ah yes, the merchant from the Southern Isles who doesn't sleep.

"Your kindness is appreciated," I quickly pardoned myself after accepting the meal tray. I shoveled the bread and rice into my mouth all while lighting the stove top and boiling two simultaneous pots of water. A tap on the closet. Crumbs decorated my face when I swung open the door to find Brock. His eyes widened at my outfit, the long white gloves and narrow boots more than anything else.

"Should I be concerned about you wearing the urban clothes of a lady?"

I matched his whispered tone. "It was a one time thing, won't happen again. Sage has a sister in the city, a high society courtesan, I wanted her to know her sister was well and sent north the last time I saw her." An odd huffing sound came from the box between us. Brock talked over it.

"Did you find her?"

"Finding her wasn't the problem, she seems rather popular. Speaking to her was. I had all but twenty seconds to tell her Sage and Raina were caravanning out of the province before I was disposed of off the premises of a ritzy eatery. She won't come after me, she hasn't time, her own money or freedom."

My bowels cinched. I winced and lowered myself to the floor, Brock reached across the way to help me down softly. He was about to say something when the huffing and sniffing from the wraith continued in slow drawn-out inhales.

Brock readied the powder. I scooted away.

"Mi... Mi...gouri...Migouri...?" A lengthy inhale. A lengthy pause. Words. The wraith had words. It smelt something it recognized. Fresh blood. "Migouri." This time it spoke it sounded confident. As if it knew exactly where I was sitting, it tapped a claw in my direction. I scurried across the flood, getting tangled in the hem of that damn dress.

It stayed quiet. The soulless shell smelt its next meal and remained completely calm. No tremors. No clawing. No screeches or screams despite having chewed its way through an iron gag in a half week and freeing its jaw. Was it going to enter a starved frenzy with its meal unobtainable and in close propinquity? "Yes, Migouri," I said, surprising both Brock and myself.

It purred in approval. We listened to it reposition itself. Two more taps in my direction. With the backs of my knuckles I tapped the flooring twice. Another content snarl and then... nothing. I shrugged at Brock who crouched into position to open the vents and insert the spores. With my heart still racing, I urged him to do just that. Drug that thing into oblivion.

"It smelt my blood."

He agreed and walked over to my room to help me off the floor. He saw the steam rising from my kitchen and took the kettles off before they whistled. "It responds to you, to whose blood it smelt? What is terrifying is that it *calmed* him down."

"Or her," I said aloofly.

"Let's agree on 'it'. *It* is no longer human. It does not have the privilege of being identified with the blessing that comes with being a man or woman or someone in between. Speaking of the blessing of being a woman, are you... alright?" His cheeks pinked, but his gaze was firm. "I had sisters. I heard you asked for chocolate and heat packs. Do you need more pillows?"

I shook a flattened palm at him. "I have a few comforts here and being delivered, it's just painful when it restarts so abruptly as if it is making up for the last months with vengeance." I stopped myself. He didn't need to know details. A no would have sufficed. "I am still starting my watch after dinner," I reinforced as he rummaged through the provided assortments of teas. "Nettles, please," I said, catching him in his moment of indecision. I unlaced the shoes and kicked them aside. My cloak I tossed in the same corner.

I walked to him in the kitchen. "Have you heard the word *migouri* before?" I asked.

"No. Adious might. He knows a lot."

"He talks a lot," I recalled. "Is he aware that we brought *it*?"

"He was not fazed when we pulled drugs from a satchel and paid suspiciously close attention to our seat. Cultee brought him along for a reason and he offered unprompted insight to help you blend in as much as a crafter could. He seems too *nice* to be fraternizing with the enemy."

"Do you think you can find him?"

"I am confident in stumbling across the most impoverished road nearest the university and starting there. I will fit in with my shortcomings." He gave a prideful smirk. "You will have to be the one to meet outside the print shop if I am to be seen on any repetitive nightly excursions in the future. I won't breathe a word until you meet with Cultee. This plan is fragile regardless if Adious is neutral or otherwise." I groaned curling into a rigid shape. Brock tapped my forehead in passing. "Don't hesitate to ask for anything," he added in regards to my cycle.

I hovelled to the bath; it was near boiling when I stepped into it. The perfect temperature. With my hair pinned up, I soaked to my shoulders. The steam turned the tight room into a sauna. There was some release in my sacrum with the weightlessness of the water. I popped my joints and vertebra until I felt more aligned, not that it mattered, for I was curled over into a ball within minutes of getting out of the bath. The blankets were torn off the bed and dropped in front of the firepit, which

I lit and fed the dried logs Coraline left outside my door. I filled the rubber heat sleeves up with scalding water and nestled myself around the fire with blankets, tea and several chocolate muffins. One would mistake me for a heaping pile of laundry were it not for my green eyes poking out from the sheets I spun around my head.

There would be cramps, back aches, chills, fatigue and hunger. Hopefully, I would avoid anemia this turn of the moon, for in the winter it made my stamina weaken. Keenan and Moriah always balanced my combat lessons with breaks for self-care and acknowledged the needs of the physical body to promote not just self-healing but optimal performance. To know your own weaknesses was a strength and the prevention of ailments was preferred over the treatment of one.

Women's cycles, as cumbersome as it may be, were revered by both my woodland culture and Ilanthian friends. Moriah would always go out of her way to massage my low back with hot oils and set aside her time to comfort me with extra stories from her childhood and how the cycles of the moon and our bodies were so powerful that they forged the seasons themselves. Not the other way around. Anna and my mother also enjoyed these moments for we would all gather in the kitchen or around a pipe and share intimate secrets of marriage, motherhood and whatever was on our minds. Such fond recollections allowed me to survive the subsequential stabbing in my uterus.

"It has not moved. Not in the slightest," Brock said when we met to switch roles. "It's not the drugs. It must be your blood."

"I doubt I'm that special. When my flow is over, you should cut yourself and see what reaction you get," I posed.

He held up his forearm. A bloody gash marked his inner wrist, irritated and leaking red. "Already did. I opened the vents and my vein." I rubbed my nose hiding my reaction to his foolishness. He was likely bored, curious, and wanting answers. I could not blame the man, I felt the same. I walked to the bathroom and came back to give him some salve for his cut.

"Try knocking," I whispered, succumbing to his experiment. He did it first twice, then once. No response either time. My turn. I knocked twice on the wall. *Tap, tap.* It replied softly from below our feet. I put greater distance between us and knocked twice on the kitchen cabinets. *Tap, tap.* Three times on the side of the bed frame. *Tap, tap, tap.* "Well, fuck," I said, not bothering to hide the string of panic and distaste for the unfolding situation. I tightened the layer of blankets I was holding around me. "At least, you can get better sleep. Maybe we both can," I offered the one positive angel I found.

"If its teeth can break iron, I imagine it's capable of loosening the shackles in there too," Brock countered.

I made a sour face. "I take back what I said about sleeping well," I muttered.

"It is a well reinforced iron box, I'm not saying that it will get out. What I am trying to get at is that it has been awake and has not *attempted* to free itself, not even a clank of its wrists against the chains or squeal of distress," he rubbed his scruffy beard not covering his wide yawn.

"It decided we are accommodating capturers and ran out of things to complain about." I waved him goodnight, for I no longer wanted to discuss this topic. What consumed my mind was getting comfortable side-lying on the floor so that the heat of the fire radiated on my back. I nibbled the muffins, eating the sweet parts first, and washed every crumb down with tea. The blankets were on a rotation schedule. The one folded on the hot stones nearest the flames would be the one to be tied around my shoulders once the water in the packs went lukewarm or cold. My jaw shivered. Menses in the winter were never my friend. My menses anytime of the year taxed me, but when food was scarce and the iron in my system dropped, it took a significant amount of rest to feel remotely human.

Midnight had passed and the fire needed to be built up for effectiveness. In the hall, I tugged the rope that inconvenienced the owners with a pleasant-sounding chime of a bell. Minutes later, a male came up in a nightgown and forced an affable look on his face when he asked. "What needs have you at this hour?"

"Fire wood. And another bundle at breakfast will be delightful," I said. He moseyed off before any amount of gratitude could be spilled. I made spiced ginger tea with cardamom and cayenne while I waited for the wood. The wraith was undetectable, by ears anyways. I held the dome of my ear against the closet—not even a quivering breath escaped. I tapped twice to ensure it was alive. It echoed back promptly.

The fire thrived for short hours, ash collected on the lip of the chimney. I could not get close enough to the flames without singeing the hairs on my arms. That did not stop me from trying to wrap myself around it during the periods of cramping that left me a disaster on the floor. I garbled loads of profanities when I was granted a moment of respite. I watched the clock, counting down the minutes until sunrise. Until I could close my eyes and sleep through these torturous first two days of my cycle. The initial days were the worst. Once I was able to stand up and socialize, I would be back out in the city, working on ways to earn money.

Asking Captain for *any* sum of money was an absolute no. I would find a way outside of healing and diagnosing ailments to serve the community for coppers. Thanks to Sage's details of Landsfell, I knew how to find the Pit. Gladiator games were barbaric, but it was lucrative and most of the fighters were prisoners, enslaved to their crimes and bought by a master to avoid execution or an overcrowded, infested foul cell of the city. They were deserving of their path of fate, right? And for those who choose the gladiator life, who represented themselves without a master or sponsor, they had to have weighed out the risks at some point before entering the commitment. I talked myself in circles, looking for a way to earn coins that did not dampen my spirits or stain my clothes in blood.

Ring, ding, ding. Coraline.

I hoped she brought something syrupy and warm. I paused. Listening above the slow crackle of a low flame and the wobbly wheels of the cart was heard a second set of feet. A male chattered with her about the cumbersome bundle of logs, likely her partner who I had woken up earlier. I was in no condition to greet them both in daylight with my sweat slicked hair a mess over my shoulders. I'm sure my pallor was dreadful and my attire sloppy, but I knew the inconvenience I placed upon them when I asked for a third delivery all within a half day.

I ought to help.

I released the deadbolt and key lock. The tiny gap of ajar door left in a shockingly large amount of cool draft. The abrupt difference in temperatures stopped my beads of sweat in their tracks, I shivered when I opened the door up the rest of the way. "Sage, good morning." Coraline cleared her throat. Her distressed eyes left me reverting to the man she was having a discussion with. Under the black and bright teal silks hinted at a well-built physique and wealth. His hat rose towards the ceiling, a fashion of foreigners and influencers. His pale hair was trimmed and gel sculpted to define his impeccably well put together presence, a bold contrast to my current state. In retreat, I slipped away from the interaction. Imagine my surprise when he set down his sapphire encrusted cane to unburden Coraline from the dozen logs of splintering wood.

"Count Hilderbrand!" She sputtered, frantically waving her hands, unsure if she should claw the bark out of his grip or allow him to do as he pleased, offending him wasn't an option. The count turned his golden eyes in my direction. I found myself grinning in the doorway and went so far as to usher him inside. Coraline would have hit the ground in a faint if Brock had not stepped out and intervened.

"Hauling around fire wood still, little fox?" I whispered, watching him pile the stash on the tiles next to my linens. He straightened the pleated cummerbund under his vest, dusting off imperfections as he did so. His keen eyes danced around the room, absorbing miniscule details. When they fixed on me, they glinted with amusement.

"Against all odds, you have managed not to turn into cobbler or cake. There is chocolate on your face, by the way, little vixen," he commented with a faintly noticeable accent, not native or from the Southern Isles. He kicked one of several muffin wrappers and pointed to the smudge of chocolate on my cheek. I was too busy admiring his attire to move away. The blue details on the boot laces matched marvelously with the underside of his cape and his lapels. Of the infinite remarks he could have chosen, chocolate on my face was the kindest.

I meant to retort. To blink. To comment. To question. I stared at his mouth, baffled that it produced sound. He was smooth faced and dapper. Stylish in a youthful, refined way. He didn't hide his lean body in baggy clothes or his bright foreign features, he flaunted them. He was chiseled and confident, all the things the coalminer was not. The combination of all of his attire and attributes made him distractingly handsome.

The count's arms extended towards the open door where Coraline and Brock stood observing everything beside the cart. Coraline was a bundle of nerves. Fennick trailed me into the hallway, collecting his walking cane in a twirl of his wrist. Radiating sophistication and finesse. "You are Miss Sage, yes?" I nodded. That was all I could do. He sounded so regal, yet considerate in the way he addressed those of lower status—the manner he addressed me. "And Mister Stout?" He removed his glove for formalities. No bleeding calluses, cuts or burns on his well-manicured hands.

"Rhyolite Stout," Brock confirmed, wiping the condensation off the water jug, his eyes scouring my face for any sign of mistrust of the man I led into my private chambers. The subtle dip of my chin, an affirmative nod of no foul play. The two men shook hands across the meal trays. "Count Hilderbrandd, was it?"

Fennick mastered a greeting that I had heard in my childhood on the southern docks when islanders reached lands after days or weeks on the rolling waves. It was lengthy enough to demonstrate his proficiency of the island tongue and magnitude of his travels. "Nicholo Hilderbrandd, Count of the seafarer colony on Septar. Pleasure to meet your acquaintances." His smile was well executed. He even carried the pride of the isle in his strut. "If you have interests in the world's strongest mounts, richest tobacco or fastest ships on the open sea, stop by and I will pour you the most tantalizing ambrosia that has ever graced your lips. Our bees are unlike any other. They populate and work year-round in the hot climate, bringing in nectar from cross pollinated plants among the span of the four hundred isles!" He softened his enthusiasm. "It's delightful and I'd be willing to share," he ended his chatter by placing his glove back on. "Consider it as an exchange of cultures. Winter festivities for summer wines."

Brock casually made his way to my side, his pride so full I forgot he had limp. "You will have more than one of us knocking on your door in the days ahead, of that I am certain. Your aid was appreciated, Count Nicholo, do have an exciting continuation of your day. May it be prosperous and joy filled," he said as means to dismiss him from our hallway.

"Same to you all." Fennick tipped his hat and looked each of us square in the eyes when he bid goodbye. His garments swoosh behind him as he rounded the corner and ambled up the stairwell. Coraline looked relieved by his absence for those remaining were not renters she had pressure to impress. I took my tray, which contained an additional pot. I removed the glass lid.

Steam and savory scents burst out to lick my face. "Bone marrow broth. I figured you may require it. Thomas said you were pale and I will not have a lady fainting in my home from a monthly flow."

"I'll find a way to repay your thoughtfulness."

"Your Captain was generous with the first two payments," she settled the qualm.

The bone broth, as thoughtful as the gift was, would go untouched. I would not be consuming the wet bones of dead animals simmered with their fat and salt. It was left on the cold iron back burned while I took to refilling my heating packs and mug of tea from my nest of blankets on the floor. A noise stirred from the adjacent room. Not the wraith. Fennick chatted with Brock. When my eyes were shut and head floating on a feathery pillow, the closet creaked open. "Are you decent?" The underhill asked.

"Yeah," I groaned. The pair stepped in.

"Drift sent him to deliver goods. Apparently, the horselord met the count years back on the foothills to the east and owes him some favors. Including his silence and reach of resources," Brock lowered himself onto the chair nearest me, lifting up a cover that was over my face. His hand brushed mine. "How are your fingers icicles and your face feverish?"

"I'll be better tomorrow." I should be. I rolled onto my side to face my friend. He scrunched his face out of concern.

Count Nicholo stepped over the yellow dress that had been there for a day now collecting wrinkles and smoke. "I do not know the full extent of the story or what disclosures you share, Halfmoon said he must speak to his captain before I can be brought into the circle. I will attend my duties and events of the celebrations as planned, intervening on intimate levels only when asked. Neither of you are local, I will keep watch over your reputations and circumnavigate rumors should they arise if you are ever to make a name for yourself, or accidently step into the complexities of Landsfell." His eyes squinted to my side table. The headdress of Madam Marcamient lay tangled there. "It is quieter on your floor than he said it would be. Is all well with the luggage?"

Brock stroked his chin. "After your pal Halfmoon talks to his superior, come back for that discussion."

"Understood. I would like to point out that my work takes place at night and late into the mornings and when I am available, I am what is referred to as an insomniac." There was an echo as he hit his cane on the floor. Up from the jewels shot out a long blade. "I will happily oversee the night shift." Brock was impressed and relieved to divide the long hours. I was too, but I didn't say anything. My brain was trying to comprehend my two worlds of secrets colliding and melding into one.

I stared up at Count Nicholo who managed to exude the right amount of pompousness and humility to lace in his pretend story with enough facts to make it believable. Brock was already contemplating trusting his character to some extent. What a great liar. He had centuries of practice.

My knees scrunched up to my chin. "Whatever Drift had him bring, just set it on the table. I'll find time for it on a later day. Unless it's candy, then I will have it now. Take that broth with you, buddy," I spoke to Brock. My teeth gritted when the cramps interrupted my brain neurons. I vaguely overheard Brock apologize on my behalf and send him out of my room. The fire licked my back as what felt like the elemental's sendoff. Above us a door open and closed, steps softened as he either took off his boots or walked on carpet. "When I wake up, I will have reverted to my amiable self. I'll pay him a visit so the fellow doesn't believe I'm neglectful nor exclusive."

Brock left me snoozing.

Chapter Eighteen

The sun was gone when I stirred. The firepit was hot with white ashes, yet empty of any fuel. I spun around the room searching for the source. There was a bowl of freshly whipped sweet cream and a grand slice of red velvet cake, wrapped in a paper chef's box. A lone fork set beside it. My bedroom door was open. The figure of a man lay in disheveled sheets on the foot of the bed. Sleeping. Not the most useful insomniac for night watches, but at least he brought desserts. And heat. I crept into the bathroom powering on the electricity so I could tame my hair and find clothes.

When I deemed myself presentable I stepped out.

Fennick was upright, his eyes mere slivers of sleep. His sleeves were rolled up past his elbows, busy lines of tattoos were discernible starting at his wrist and ending who knew where. His silvery blond hair caught the sheen of light from the hallway and a recognizable white halo appeared around him, the one that was present around his much longer hair the night of the duke's prison break. I was feeling uneasy about his personalities and how to approach this version of him. I lead with a short, "You don't need to be here."

His eyes snapped alert. He managed to speak with restraint and quietly, "Ilanthians do not leave a woman alone on her hallowed bleed. I am not leaving you tonight. Maybe not tomorrow either." I shook my head at his obstinacy. "In fact, you are going upstairs for a proper meal before I let you binge on sweets. We can talk about why my presence distresses you." I shook my head in agreement.

He left me to tidy up my clothes, douse the fire and remake the bed. The bottom of the mattress was still warm to touch when I tucked in the covers.

I left my boots in my room and locked my door. On the door frame I knocked once. *Tap.* It was odd believing the wraith to refrain from outbursts. I felt confident it would.

I tip-toed up to Fennick's apartment which had two dark maple doors and a service bell made of what appeared to be solid silver welcoming tenants directly out the stairwell. The doors were left agape, candles were lit sporadically and a dim lamp glowed in the kitchen.

I stepped in. Bleary eyed, I spotted steam rising from the kitchen counter, the aroma in the air I was unaccustomed to, but found it pleasant. Fennick's back was towards me, his silhouette easily viewed without the layers of formal wear, only one cotton shirt he wore, he was even barefooted. He held tongs and a pair of wooden sticks, easily maneuvering the utensils from pot to pan, sampling as he did. He clicked on the kitchen vent above the stove top, the potent fragrance of sauteed herbs was sucked out of the room.

His living space stretched directly into his kitchen, the length of the complex. There were no sofas or chairs around the hearth.

Come to think of it, nothing was in its expected place.

Blankets and towels covered the windows. Pillows, coffee tables and dressers were then arranged in front those windows making his chambers impenetrable to light and eerily quiet. It was prime evening hours for drinking and dancing, neither of which were audible. Not to me at least.

I veered left and using my hands found three standing racks of clothes. All materials felt delightful on my skin, light satins and heavy velvets. I lifted the sleeve of a maroon tunic to my nose and inhaled deeply. It was artificially perfumed, masking the scent of cedar, pine and smoke I started to associate with him. Beneath the racks of fabrics were just as many shoes and accessories. I made a choking sound of disbelief.

If he noticed me, he did not say anything.

A table and its surrounding chairs were spared from his unique interior designing. I sat in one, crossing my legs on the seat. Fennick took the eight dumplings out from a steamer and placed them on a towel using the wooden sticks. Garlic and green onion fried rice were scooped into a bowl with sesame oil. Everything was tossed together and brought over to the table, along with two place settings and a variety of utensils. The vent was turned off. He sat down across from me, eye contact was unavoidable, as was acknowledging him. "Hi." My gaze was down and attentive on holding the two wooden sticks in the same hand as I saw him do.

"You are uncomfortable around me," he said plainly, his tone void of the count's excessiveness and any notion of Fen's annoyance.

"Unexpectedly, yes." He motioned for me to continue. "I don't know who *you* are." I pushed a doughy dumpling around the edges of my plate, it left a trail of soy sauce. "You are a fantastic performer. A well-practiced liar and deceiver, fabricating entire life events of imaginary characters you turn into in a matter of minutes. We have never spoken before, not really. How am I to know when it is on or off? When you are telling me half-truths or playing me like the rest of the world? I don't enjoy being lied to or taken as a fool from Fen, a coalminer, Fennick nor Nicholo."

His smooth face was more visible under the light when he cocked his head to the side. "You view them differently despite them all acting in your best interest?"

I pressed my fingertips into my temples, gathering my thoughts. "That's just it. It was *acting*. Fen, who I met in the dungeon, thought I was a chatty thief. He disliked me from the beginning and regrets freeing me. The coalminer tolerated me, as reckless as he believed I was. Nikki did not care how sloppy I grieved or how I broke the rules. He surprised me—in a good way. I felt stronger, brighter. Fennick is who I imagine you are when you are home in the dreamer realm, using your given name with your intimate lovers and family, going about daily life in your world. Nicholo is a farfetched persona." I threw up my hands in defense before he felt the need to educate me. "Do not believe I am entirely idiotic. I understand that 'the count' had to be a man to match Zander's travel history and have the means to gather, cart and ship stallions off to the Southern Isles. Nicholo had to be learned, extroverted and excessive, but how am I to truly *see you* when you wear personas and fancy fucking silks. Unless, that is who you are—a someone who enjoys fancy fucking silks." I sighed. "My head hurts."

Fennick strummed his fingers on the table's rim, chewing his cheeks subtly in thought. His eyes the color of melted coins pooled as that bore into me. I gave a long exhale and diverted my eyes elsewhere so the intensity of his eyes didn't melt my emeralds. "It is not a dilemma easily remedied for I cannot shed my own shields of self-preservation to roam Numaal as a fox whose fur is one of silver and gold flames. Zander, inevitably, will lose his shit when I am put to death for being what I am and start a war of the realms. Numaal will be wiped clean off of Kinlyra if that happens."

I stabbed the dumpling, liquid poured out. If Zander was capable of that, why were there restless souls imploding in dreamer realm and wraiths amuck? If he had the ability to end this, why wait for more to succumb to the plague all because he is frightened of his own power? Fennick spooned rice on his plate. With a tilt of his head, he referenced my plate. I pushed it closer for him to fill. Something must have happened when he lost control. "You aren't going to tell me why he is so afraid to unleash himself and end this are you? This shit could have been over years ago."

He shook his head no. "See, you know more about me than you thought you did." The start of a grin was appearing at the corners of his mouth.

I rolled my eyes. "Let's see if the count can cook." Skinny cooking sticks aside, I grabbed the spoon and ladled a dumpling with the fried rice.

"I'm sure he could with his extensive pantry of spices, but he did not prepare this meal for you. I did."

"And you are?"

"Suppose, you will figure that out. If not over dinner maybe when you tell me about how you silenced the wraith? Or why is there a prostitute's headdress on your side table?" Time. He meant time. He arranged his first bite, picking the pursed dough with the tip of the two sticks. He blew on it and scarfed it down in three bites, not spilling one drop on his upmarket shirt.

"Or while you tell me about the massive fire you started east and how the caravan of villagers fair." The bite in my spoon cooled. I sampled it, adjusting the ratios of rice and vegetables with each bite until I found the most delicious combination. "It tastes really good. Thank you for dinner." A wrinkle in his forehead lessened.

"It's my aunt's recipe. Aunt Marissa is Ilanthian, living north in the humidity and rice fields of Havana–old Montuse. The land of your family's friends has changed drastically over thousands of years. If Keenan remembers the ways of the Ice Jungle he is *old*, probably of the first Ilanthians the Eleven created from enchanted clay." I kept eating. "I spent a lot of seasons working to perfect dumplings with my cousins. They were pups at the time, people pups. That kitchen was a complete disaster when we were done, add my infant fire magic to the mix and it was unrecognizable."

"Which of your parents was raised in Ilanthia?"

"My father, Honri. He was vivacious in his youthful years. My mother, Fedora Feign, was a single vixen and loved all the far-fetched ideas my father had for expanding the Burrows under the Eternal Elm. They did it. Together they dug tunnels and established a community where once were separate homes. Now, age has my father handicapped at three hundred and four years of age and the steps to the Burrows have become too steep for his knees. He rests at Veona."

"That sounds young for Ilanthians."

He shrugged. "Long before the Great War all peoples mingled, silver ans red bloodlines were mixed and over generations mixed and mixed again. It is not old nor young nor immortal. It is what is. No matter the quantity of time spent with him, it was and will be cherished. It is not unusual for offspring to outlive their birth parents when they are a blend of races."

When half my plate was emptied into my stomach, I stood to collect water from the tap. I set a full glass next to my dinner date, whose name I hadn't decided on. "Did you set the Wastelands or Fort Fell up in flames?"

"The Wastelands," he swallowed. The muscles of my gut tensed. Sadness befell my body. I could not force myself to sit down. My home land, my family's graves, Keenan's cave. "Wisteria, the convoy was almost taken a day into the trek. By not several hundred, but *thousands* of wraiths roaming the terrain." He swiveled in his chair, standing to comfort me. I stepped backwards. "The coalminer needed to die to be born as Count Nicholo, what better way than giving your friends, the fort staff and guards time to pass into the boundaries of the east. To keep the living alive. It was all I could think to do, Wisteria." He said my name again, heat broke in my chest hearing his plea for understanding.

"I would have done the same. Had I, you know, fancy magic and resources to do it," I confessed. The man across from me shook his head in a somber knowing. If I had the power to ignite the Wastelands... the Blacklands... the Deadlands...I would if it meant keeping the last of the crafters and innocents on this side of the Veil.

My home. My *home* was *gone*, forever. I was a nomadic lost girl. After I completed Anna's requests, I would return to nothingness. Alone. Feeling faint, I set my glass of water down on the counter top. "It's my cycle," I said, searching for reasonable excuses to the emotional influx.

"It is horrendous that this is the reality of our world and these are the choices we have been forced to make. Your cycle aside, this news is tragic. For my role in desolating your homeland, I am apologetic."

He did look devastated when he apologized. Sadness wasn't a good look on him with his bright features and inked skin. "It had to be done. Tell me you went around with your red dagger and further ended them?"

He lifted his shirt to reveal more tattoos on his skin, webbing of a scar and the feathery hilt of a dagger protruding out. "Happily so. But do not be fooled, they will regroup eventually and they will find their way here. Let's hope Zander can get Cultee sworn in as duke before they come or at least make enough friends with weapons while highborns scrap for titles. We need an army to defend these walls. I've been watching their rotations and find their preparations lacking."

"Does Veona have an army?"

"Yes, there are military sectors to make use of the various magic or physical skill sets of each dreamer. After Thalren became viewed as a wall, it has not been cohesive, but it is a formidable force. Kashikat runs the flight division. Kailynder oversees combat training for steel and swords. Dagressa works with engineering feats and berserkers. The fae, nymphs and elves are reclusive but take ownership of the city's mighty defenses with the spellwork, traps and illusions. Fire foxes mesh where we are needed on the offense and the water wolves patrol the river runs and frozen glaciers. The Overlord has the ultimate say in military matters, in the current state that would be Atticus, Zander's father."

"Has Numaal's walking dead been brought to Atticus's attention?"

He dipped his chin agreeably. "For many years he has worried about the wraiths. Their physical bodies cause destruction here and their dark souls gather in the beyond, just outside the protection runes, we do not know what force they wield. It is clear their intent is disparaging. His sons have built up the ramparts next to the Eternal Elm and rune stones. War is imminent for our lands too," he said calmly, offering me a chair to sit on. "Sit. Eat the damn food before I take it away." His patience was crumbling.

I sat, so did he. I watched my water level out in the glass while accepting the hard facts, no help was coming with aid for Numaal. No outside help at least. I had to get access to the tunnels, maybe people would be safe hidden underground or led outside the city. I had to see how large they were before gauging the volume of traffic they could handle.

"What's that look on your face?"

"Constructing a plan." I pointed to my head. "I'll fill you in as I see fit."

His jaw noticeably gritted. My throat constricted under his firm focus. "Does Zander know your meddling?"

My tongue left the roof of my mouth and hot honesty left me. "He expects me to meddle and if he is stupefied by my independent efforts then he is a daft idiot. Of course, I am going to try to come up with my own solutions and plans in case his plan is an epic failure. Which by the way, neither he nor Cultee have proposed a strategy yet, so there is no formal, solidified plan to meddle in." He flexed his arms above his head, his silk shirt lifted with him. More whorls of tattoos stained his waistline and downward.

His voice dropped, his outsider accent was more prominent. "We are a team. If we remain inseparable, we will be indestructible." His golden eyes changed, his right eye changed to a milky white.

I leaned across the table. "If anything is pertinent, I will inform you. If Zander is close enough to sypher, I will tell him too." I sipped my water. "I will not come between you and your teammate. You can stay blissfully woven and dutiful to each other, then return to your home land in time for your war."

"You can come with us," he posed, causally he and Zander stared back. It was no longer peculiar detecting both their energies mingling in one being.

"We've had this discussion," I groaned. "In honor of the girl I am avenging, I intend to follow her dying wishes. I have a few statements to tell the Emperor at the Opal Lake, wherever that is after I disembowel Stegin."

"The Opal Lake is the birthplace of the Eternals in our world, where their Maker dropped them into a well of clay and freshwater with primal power to mold in their hands. No lies can be spoken nor agendas concealed in the presence of raw, untapped energy. None of the Eleven enjoy trekking there, it reminds them of how far they have fallen from their initial reach of grace. Getting Maruc to take you to Opal Lake without Athromancia will be impossible, unless maybe you have the Overlord of the Veil on your side to vouch for your intentions." The white eye glossed over. His gold one shone brighter.

"No offense, but fuck your Overlord and all the Lords and Ladies, Kings and Queens, and the remaining Eternals in our world. They all are entirely useless in this ordeal. Damn, cowards. I'd be embarrassed to be seen with any of them, let alone have one 'vouch for me'." His foxy face was grinning. Beaming. "If Keenan and I survive, that will be enough. If I am dead, Zander eavesdropped on all that was said, he can run his mouth and have his daddy vouch for him at the scenic fucking lake." The elemental's ears reddened, Zander was booted out of his woven's sight by a roar of laughter. I refrained from joining in his boisterousness so as to not be heard fraternizing without having told Brock my whereabouts. A languid grin crept on my face witnessing his outburst. His laugh continued, shaking the table as his knees repeatedly knocked it around.

He wiped a tear falling from his amber eyes. "I would give almost anything to see his family's reaction to your mouth. It outshines your foolhardy decisions and will undoubtedly divert the attention of the advisors."

"Another reason why I'm not going with you two to play the misfit third wheel and the fool in the court's pompous company," I already felt outcast enough and I was in my home province of Numaal. Cities were not for me. Dresses and small talk were not for me.

He calmed down, the smile stayed. The silence of his room was nice.

"There is no court. We are an invested public, none of us are pompous. Opinionated, but not pompous," he clarified. "You were wrong about Fen, he has never second guessed breaking your chains and escorting you to safety." The first time I met Fen, I made a request of him. He burnt Anna's body. No questions. My heart lifted, knowing he didn't hold anything against me for that or linking myself to his woven. My existence forced him to share his eternal brother. His molten eyes gleamed, they didn't lift from me until I acknowledged him.

"Nikki, savor the weeks ahead. And now that I know you will miss me when I am gone, I will be sure to make them unforgettable for you."

"I expected nothing less," he calmed himself and finished several bites of food. "Nikki, huh?" he gave an exaggerated cringe as he said it.

"Mhmm," I hummed while navigating a dumpling into my mouth with food sticks. Nikki looked disgusted at my failed attempt, I resorted to using my fingers. "Is it your choice of clothes, silk suits and top hats?"

"Is it a problem?" He teased me, throwing a napkin across the table.

My cheeks warmed. "I'm seeking clarification on how much of an act the count's extravagance is."

"And if this amount of luxury is what I am accustomed to in my daily life, would that be a hindrance for our comradery?"

I drank water. "No."

"You are not a good actress; disgust and judgment are evident. I pray that wherever you went as a debted woman you did not get the opportunity to talk excessively or at all."

I scoffed, "You are an ass. I'm sure I did just fine."

"Where did you go?"

"Don't change the subject."

He eased back, reclining in his chair. "My preferences and lifestyle are more aligned with the coalminer, keeping to myself, careful with conversations and making use of my strengths. I also own several silk shirts, bejeweled slacks and iron toe boots. Do I wear them daily? No, maybe once or twice a year. But I own them. A full closet of them." He let a moment pass. "Do you like wearing silks?"

"Wouldn't know."

"Would you wear them daily if you had a closet full of silk gowns?"

"I cannot fight in gowns. They are a hindrance. Not that I wore many dresses, but of the three I have, no. Not even if they were silk." I rolled my eyes. "This conversation is going downhill quickly."

"I disagree." He reached in the cupboard. Out came two stemless wine glasses and a freshly uncorked pink wine. "If you had a closet of silk tunics, fit for riding, fighting and flirting, would you wear them more than twice a week?"

The bastard was smiling as he poured his glass and brought it to his lips. He knew the answer. "Fuck you and yes, I would."

His lips smacked after he swallowed the sip. I sampled the wine. It was enjoyably dry. "Where did you go and disguised as who?"

"Mildred Mcgaffer went to Bjorn's Luncheon." I could not say it with a straight face. I was proud of that name and character design two days ago. Now, the thought of the entire encounter made me blush with discomfort.

"They let an unushered, unknown consort into Bjorn's Luncheon during the largest political gathering of the year?" I bobbed my head. "Your performance sounds noteworthy," he complimented in his profound state of confusion.

"My tits were out." He chuckled politely. "That and I went to meet with Landfell's most beloved and beautiful courtesan, who caters to all the elites, holds their secrets and has knowledge of the tunnels under the estate. I want in those tunnels."

Nikki set his glass down and stared pensively at it. "If this woman is purchased by high-society she is not going to give Mildred answers, she has no freedom nor reason to. Not with the threats of rebel groups *and* deteriorating numbers of Numaalian guards that coincide with the growing number of wraiths. She will be slain if any information is linked back to her." He leaned over his glass, but met my gaze. I broke it. "I'm telling you this because I know you care deeply about others and the guilt that you try hard to suppress will rise again if she meets the consequences."

"When I left, we had agreed upon the terms. We shook on it." I remembered the trace of hope in her gaze as it followed me out the door. Freedom from the sex slave industry, to exist without conditions and expectations and perpetual walking on eggshells. She wanted it. I wanted to give it to her. Not for access to the underground, but because it was a decent thing to do.

"Reiterate the terms for me, please," he beckoned.

"The fewer people involved, the better. A boujee Count Hilderbrand poking his nose around where it needn't be might get it smashed in."

His jaw slacked in aggravation. I ignored his rising frustration as well as one could ignore a blazing fire under your skin. "A name then."

"Promise not to get involved? No Nicholo. No Nikki. No Fen. And if your husband finds out, he stays out of it too until she is comfortable."

"Are you planning on telling this girl everything? She owes you nothing and if you can win her over, then so can somebody else with a sweeter offer. She is accustomed to being bought and auctioned to the highest bidders."

Both my hands grasped the table. I trembled. "Nikki, she has been inside that manor hundreds of times. She knows the staff, passages, locked doors. The only people who have ever loved me were taken in there two years ago. If they are still here, I need to find them. Zander found nothing yet and I promised a grieving father a reunion with his wife, child and a baby. An infant still at the breast Nikki. Don't make me into the enemy." He reached into his pocket and tossed a silk handkerchief across the table. "Do I have sauce on my face?"

"No. Tears." He poured himself another glass and leaned onto the armrest. I wiped my nose in my shirt and spared ruining his garments. I blinked vigorously until all the tears were out of my eyes.

"It's my cycle," I muttered wishfully.

His sigh rumbled the noiseless room. "If it gets dangerous, you tell me. If you threaten my or Zander's identity, I will end it. I'll stay out of your way unless I am forced into it." I agreed. "What is her name?"

"Yolanda d'Loure."

His hands combed through his short, but shaggy blonde locks. It took a long minute to click, but I knew the moment he placed the name for his chair tipped forward when he went reaching for his wine glass. "She is Sage's sister and your current alias."

"A d'Loure family trinket." I pulled out the dual sun necklace from my shirt. "Sage gave this to me, hoping I could sway her sister's ear—if not for my cause, then for a moment of her precious time, only to inform her that Sage was alive and on her way to a new province. To give her sister peace of mind. I may have managed to accomplish both. Remains to be seen." I took a mouthful of wine.

And another when he did not say anything.

He stared at me. Overtly scouring my plain features, wet cheeks and bland choice in clothing. "Nikki, what are you looking at?"

"I am looking at you. What I am looking for is malice or deceit. Ill wishes for certain political parties or a council member's demise. I have not found them."

"Oh, that's good." I said, feeling my lower backache start up. I rounded my spine in my chair to clutch my abdomen. "Why were you looking for them?"

He rattled his head a bit more, still saying nothing. I kicked him under the table. "Ouch! What was that for?" He stood up and massaged his shin. A knot formed under his pant leg.

I stood up too. My cramps were signaling—very strongly—it was time to go lie down and get comfortable for my night watch. "I'm not malicious, but I am short fused. Why would you even think I have a stupid political agenda?"

"Because of your emotionally charged choices and sympathetic nature could be what others deem brilliant, borderlining on perfectly manipulative strategies, which in reality are just dumb luck," Nikki said hoarsely. "You are a contender in a game you didn't know you could play."

"It's a game I didn't know existed. I'm not getting involved in political strategizing, now or ever," I muffled. "I do need to lay down." I carried my dishes to the sink, scrubbing the residual sauce of the porcelain. I took Nikki's from his hand and washed his along with the two wine glasses. They were set aside to dry as Nikki boxed up the remaining food in the ice compartment. First, he tossed me a spare key to his apartment. Then, he tossed me a pair of woolen socks as we walked to his door. My toes wiggled in the warmth. All the candles went out when he turned his back. He intended on seeing the night of my cycle through till completion. "There is no convincing you to stay here?"

"Not when you have yet to tell me about the slumbering monster under your floor boards." He walked close to my back, his eyes examining air vents and tapestries as we walked down a level and barricaded ourselves in my room. I pushed him against a wall, out of sight from Brock who appeared once I called out at the closet, his features were well rested.

I gave a small energetic hop to prove my pep had returned. "Reporting for duty," I mocked the gestures of the guards. He snorted.

"Glad to see you are feeling chipper and your flesh hasn't been scalded off with those heating packs." He pointed to the counter behind me.

"I'd be content bathing in a pool of lava, if it meant alleviating my cramps." I saw his boots readied by the door. A brace and cloak too. "Where are you off to this evening?"

"East Street. It loops around the university."

I adjusted my stance. "Tomorrow night we will ask the count to watch. I have errands that will probably tip over into two or more consecutive nights, if you think both of you can handle things while I'm gone."

Nikki's gaze melted the back of my neck after learning I had more meddling to do. I swatted my arm around the other side of the door, hoping to hit him. I didn't make any contact. Brock said, "We got the spores. Plenty of them since we haven't had to use them in days. I wonder what will happen when your scent is gone."

"Migouri." I said.

"*Migouri.*" It said back with reverent affection. Nikki's fingers wrapped around my wrist. A hot bracelet. It tightened and felt more of a shackle.

"We will find out," I said, keeping my own nerves in check. "Also! Can I borrow some clothes while you are out? I don't have any black tunics."

"Help yourself," he said, pointing behind him. "Do I want to know what you are up to?"

"It will be a pleasant surprise. Hopefully," I wiggled my fingers goodnight. Both sides clicked shut, I locked my brass chain lock in case Brock ventured over to find the count lounging in my room eating whipped cream with me.

I didn't have to make eye contact with the elemental to know he was concerned. I ignored him and went to find a pad of paper and two lead pencils. I pressed them into Nikki's chest and left him scribbling his questions while I retrieved the bowl of cream and two pillows. It was cold on the floor. I arranged three wood logs and tossed dried pine needles in the pit to assist it in catching flame. Nikki's long arms came from behind me and pulled the bark out of my grip. He leaned forward to dig his fingers into the soot. Smoke rose. Ambers ignited. I watched the fire slowly come alive as my guest washed his hands in the sink and gripped the iron tea kettle. I heard it simmer and boil in his grip.

Must be nice to be magical. I dusted off the dirt from my embarrassingly human hands.

Curled into a comfortable position, I began to read Nikki's scribbles. It was sloppier than Zander's but legible. He wanted to know just about everything. I started jotting a summary of the wraith's first encounter with my blood, the responsive tapping, Brock's blood and the singular spoken word.

Nikki sat beside me, upright against the stool of a chair. Two tea cups between us. *You should not permit it to speak. You should not speak words in a language no one understands. It could be a summoning, a spell, a hex or binding. Don't repeat it.*

Do you know Adious? The scholar that rode from the fort here with us.

I know of him. He was a scribe, quieter than me.

I found that difficult to believe. The man was verbose and long-winded. *Did Cultee tell him about our gift? Would he know about this language?*

He was well-rounded, there is a chance he knows the dialect. He paused, tapped his pencil and continued on. *Brock is scouting for him by the university?* I nodded.

He won't approach him. We need confirmation of Adious's involvement from Cultee first. He expressed his approval with a tilt of his head. While he wrote on the paper I stirred the frothy bowl, licking the back of the spoon. I smacked my lips.

Knock. He wanted to see my party trick with the spawn.

Three times I knocked. Three taps came back. I switched up rhythms and beats, it followed me perfectly. His hand covered mine when he had enough. *What does it mean?*

You had silver blood emptied into you, maybe it responds to the descendent magic in you. I'm going to try my blood of silver and dreams once Brock leaves. I circled the above words 'descendent magic' and drew a question mark. *In the unlikely event Anna's blood didn't get filtered out fully, you may still house part of her bloodline, inherited genetics of the family of whom she descended from. She could be from Aditi or Morial lineage, their bloodlines are extensive.* I felt my eyes get wide. *When blessed or immortals use their blood for temporary healing, it is out of the body within three days. Typically. Anna gave you the last of her life, not just a mouthful.*

Her blood sustained me for weeks and healed my wound. I touched my right shoulder. The rusted spear butchered my bones and ligaments, no remnants of the injury remained. *She is with me.* I wrote, debating if I needed to elaborate. *The priestess didn't sense her blood, nor anything amiss with mine. The duke killed us both.* My heart raced. I laid the pen down and rested my head. Keenan would know more about this old blessed blood situation and if he is as ancient as dirt, he may speak it. Although, when I told him what Anna had asked me to tell the Emperor about the *vulborg*, he was baffled and couldn't figure out what it meant without more context. The word meant nothing to him. It was as significant as *migouri* to me now.

I ate my feelings. One spoonful at a time.

Nikki spent his time waiting for Brock to leave for the city by examining my balcony composition, the fit of the windows, the quality of air in the vents, and snooping in each cupboard until he was convinced nothing would surprise him. His neck whipped around impossibly fast when the door adjacent to mine shut into place with a breeze. My lights were dimmed and curtains pulled tautly over them.

"No need to get up, unless you want to move to the bed," he said, eyeing me while opening the closet.

"I was not planning on leaving the floor, it is warmer here. I'll keep my distance so I don't interfere with your scents," I said watching intently. His astute gaze left me to focus on the cutting knife, whose blade dug into his palm. He squeezed ample drops onto the box. Nothing stirred. He wiped his mess across the floor and mesh peepholes. Still nothing.

"Wake. Up." Fennick's tone with lethal. I swallowed another bite of sweet cream. He slammed his heel into the iron sides and dangling locks of its prison. It growled bitterly at the commotion. Stopping when the abuse did.

He knocked without reply. His upper lip was curled as if it was flashing canines that were not there. Not in this form anyways.

"You might be overthinking this," I frowned, finding the bowl on my lap entirely empty. "The wraith might be reactive to me because I am a woman and sacred bleeds are sacred for a reason. They control beings." Nikki took my dish and dropped it in the sink. "See what I mean, my cycle forced your hand in spoiling me and cleaning up my mess. I am magic!" I tossed my hands in the air. "Thank you, by the way."

"You're welcome. And no, nothing about my being here with you is forced by your bleed." He sat in the rocking chair.

"It's enforced by your woven." My lips pursed.

He glared. "He doesn't even know you're on your monthly. He is trapped in an archery tournament alongside members of Duke Hammish's immediate family and landowners from Raj with the priestess overseeing from the ceiling globe. Snooping on her conversations and nuances will benefit his position, allowing him to align himself with those who she and her prince favor. The more parties, billiards and board rooms he attends the better odds we have of discovering what the bloody hell is happening here."

"They will tell him about the wraiths or even the plan to kill the Eternals?"

He licked his lips. Recentering his patience for yet another one of my questions. "The seemingly irrelevant side discussions are those most impactful maneuvers if both parties are aware of the subject at hand. For example, imports of emeralds may refer to the incoming shipment of slaves. The quality of emeralds, their physical condition. The price of the gems correlates to the expense it would take to obtain that specific slave. Chatting about the weather can be an entire dialogue about the health of a person or the internal dynamics or a family to a high lord's court. Which ring one taps while passing by, which horse they ride to visit another's home, who they choose to pin their hair or paint their face are all intentional."

Better Oyoko's grandson than me. "Sounds awful."

"Zander hates it, but he is good at it. With his abilities to sway motives, smell attraction and hear across stone walls, he has an awareness that makes him the best candidate for Numaal's bureaucratic banquets."

Nikki stared passed me, onto the fire. His hands folded across his stomach. "Do you enjoy aristocratic affairs?"

"What I enjoy the most is lounging out in the Burrows, avoiding winter altogether. When I'm feeling up to it, I find contentment in good outcomes, honest leaders and effective policies. But there is no comparing the processes between the three realms. Inherited patriarchal power of a family line, trirulers elected by unseen Divine and an Overlord governed by his own people are as contrasting as the lands on which we live. They are all very different dances, with different tempos and vastly different audiences to appease. I would not want to be caught with my dance shoes on here during the End of the Eternal's Age." My faint smirk was hidden in a pillow. He enjoyed the art of 'the dance' as he called it. I was willing to bet he was decent at it.

"Suppose I should be flattered, you thought I was smart enough to figure all that out. Mildrid Mcgaffy, the mastermind manipulator," I mocked. He started rocking in the chair, the soft squeaks fell rhythmically. I couldn't even walk in the streets outside these walls for five minutes without being overwhelmed, it was a debatably stupid struggle for a grown woman.

Tomorrow night would be easier. I would travel as a shadow, fight as freely and fiercely as I wanted, and not panic about performing as anybody else other than who or what I was.

Chapter Nineteen

I was a transitory shadow flitting about the city.

A few alterations to Brock's tunic and a flexible pair of pants had me feeling at home in my body for I could leap, spring and sprint from rooftop to rooftop and along back-alleys unseen. My breasts were bound down tight. My hair was pinned flat under a deep hood. My face was hidden by a black mask. My green eyes stark against the onyx eyeshadow I smeared across my nasal bridge, undereyes and brow.

I held onto a gutter and swung to the ground. The cold air burned my lungs, I relished the anonymity and liberation that hiding among thousands brought me. Hundreds of thousands.

I held my breath as I approached the massive warehouse. The Pit smelt exactly how I imagined corralled roughens, thugs and prisoners to smell. I was grateful for my mask. In I went, with nothing but a local steel dagger on my hip and an empty sack over my shoulder.

The coliseum was packed.

Above me were rows of bleachers and sectioned off glass rooms where spectators were granted privacy. No red priestess among them. The arena below was made of cement, stone and sand. The passageways to the underground had vertical iron bars and cranks along several portions of the hall to separate the fighters.

The bidding booth was boisterous. Coins, checks and paper pastels were being thrown at financial keepers, while another person was hastily jotting down amounts, account numbers and names of their masters.

To my right, the crowds dispersed. There was more room to roam and breathe. Three unofficial looking security details monitored the threshold to the arena below, their tunics were stained with old blood and the crossbows on their arms were cranked back with tension. Lovely. "Boy, where are you going?"

I stepped closer to the tallest one. He had teeth missing. "I was going downstairs to fight."

The man who leaned against the wooden pillar laughed. His partner didn't. "Who's your master?"

"Myself. I need to earn money." I lowered my inflections and rounded out my articulations to sound more masculine. I did not lower my confidence when I sprinkled the banter with some truths. "It is an urgent matter. I'm new to the city and I have a lady in my life who needs assistance."

"What's in the bag?" The quiet one spoke up. The tattoo on his neck moved as his throat bobbed. The design of a skull.

I shimmied it off my shoulder and tossed it in his hands. "Nothing yet. I expect earnings." He inspected it thoroughly. He seemed disappointed at its bare contents. My sack was tossed on the floor.

"The novice fight pool hasn't started. Won't be until the morning. Are you any good?"

I swiped the bag off the ground, biting back a filthy comment. "Yes. How do I register for the fight pool?"

A gruff fellow spoke to me as if I a dumb, damn fool. He was annoyed. "Pay the fee, write your name and hope for the best."

"Shit," I mumbled. "I haven't made money yet, how am I to pay?"

He spit on the floor and kicked dust over it. "Beats me. You should have thought of that before your scrawny ass showed up here. All you need is one silver."

"Can one of you spare me a silver and when I win, I'll pay you three. One for good faith, one for the inconvenience and another for your well-placed trust?" I posed, looking each of them in the eye. Two spat on the ground, the third left his position on the pillar and walked towards me, sizing me up. I squared my chest and locked eyes with him. They fell to his skull tattoo again.

"I know an entire army that will kill anyone so long as they will be paid in cash, yet not the guts to go in there solo. You will kill for money?" He finally asked, his appearance was slightly tidier than his comrades. Slightly. I noted a recent cut on his forearms starting to scab over.

"I don't murder bystanders off the streets. I'm not a heartless mercenary. I was told those who fight in here are criminals serving their sentence or volunteers, like myself, who made an informed choice. Innocent blood is priceless. I will not spill that."

He fingered the arch of his bow. "How much are you looking to make?

"Seven hundred thousand and forty-three hundred in coin exchange."

"In one night?" The men behind him snickered.

I gave a cocky shrug. "Two at most."

"The novice gladiators don't drag in an audience. Petty coinage is gambled and petty coinage is earned. You will spend years scrapping in there to come close to that amount, if you aren't killed off. What are you trying to buy your lady love, a mansion on a lake?"

I stretched and kept my body limber. "On a lake, no. I can't swim. But I can fight. Some things, sir, are worth fighting for."

"Come with me," he grumbled, picking his teeth with his tongue. I crossed my arms over my flattened chest. "I'm going to see how well you fight and get you a sponsor for the big leagues."

His lackey called after him. "You aren't seriously considering this runt, Warden? He'll break at the sight of the swords, let alone wield one."

I was successfully underestimated.

I went with him, the warden, to a side room with a multitude of wooden chests, envelopes and bank notes. I examined the oak barrels on the wall and noticed a fist with a letter opened plummeting at my freshly recovered flank. I was careful not to show any Ilanthian footwork and went straight to a Montuse tuck and roll. I rose behind him and hit a pressure point to the right of his spine, the eighth vertebra down next to the scapula. His right arm went limp. The letter opener dropped. I casually collected it and put it to his neck. He still had not formed words for what I had just done. I spoke for him. "You will regain sensation and movement within a quarter hour. Did I earn a sponsor?"

He seated himself on the desk behind him. His brown trousers absorbed a puddle of spilt ink. "We don't need your whole life story, but they will need a name for the books. What do I call you?"

I tossed the small letter opener from hand to hand. "Keenan," I decided with a grin, imagining my teacher's face if he ever discovered I used his name in the Pits of Landsfell. "What do I call you?"

He seemed surprised. Pleasantly so. "Rhett," he said. "Give me five minutes."

"Excuse me," I called after him. I cleared my throat to keep my tenor low. "I'll pay you fourth silver, if you can ensure those whom I will be fighting have committed crimes deserving of death. It will make things easier."

He kept walking, his arm lifeless at his side. "Emotions have no place in the arena."

My mouth dried as I sat on a stool next to the mail desk. Watching people's comings and goings, it was too loud to focus on one conversation, so I listened to the ticking clock above my head. When Rhett reentered the nook he had the ability to make a fist. "You were gone seven minutes," I stated, the clicking of the clock synced up with my heartbeat.

His cruel gaze silenced my frivolous commentary. "You got two sponsors. They agreed to give you eighty percent of the earnings with the caveat they decide your opponents. Their purses are deep and they are willing to empty them if you eliminate the pets of their radical adversaries. I will safely gather, count and store your winnings between battles." He pointed to the grey sack around me. "You are free to leave at any point in the night, save mid-fight, and take the earnings with you seeing as you are doing two people, likely many more, a service."

"Killing people is a service?"

"Welcome to the city, Keenan. Killing is a service, skill and occupation for many. What say you to the arrangement?"

My eyes shone above the mask and under the hood. "When do we start?"

"Soon. We go to the weaponry first; you can exchange armor and weapons as you see fit between encounters. There is a privy and bread below in case the nerves in your stomach get rattled."

I stood next to him and pushed in the stool. "There is no meet and greet with these mysterious sponsors?" I asked.

"No," he was firm, skeptical of the question.

"Thank the sun and moon for that. I hate formalities." He relaxed and motioned that I stick close to his heel. His partners laughed at us as he escorted me downstairs saying I will be made into somebody's meal. I rolled my eyes. "I wish they would bet against me and go broke," I mutter to the warden's back.

He cared not about their jives or my remarks.

Down we went again. The air was cooler and moist despite the dozens of fighters and their trainers situated throughout the hallways. "Why do some prisoners wear wrist cuffs, some ankle chains and others nothing?" I asked quietly when we were in private.

"That is decided by their masters, typically it has to do with the gravity of their sins and how unpredictable their behaviors are. Some, like you, are wearing none. A master unto themselves, that does not mean they are sinless." I swallowed, knowing all too well that some crimes were so deep, only inflicting damage on one's heart.

We arrived at a rack of armaments. I took out two sharpened daggers and held them in each hand. "I'll forgo armor," I stated.

"Bread? Water?" He pointed to the desk. I was a woodlander with no antidotes on me.

"I will defer. Thank you for the offer."

His face looked torn between concern and pity. "What are you planning to do when you leave? You will have a target on your head from Colby Debt Maker, if you are moderately successful. You cannot exit the way you came in and I do not recommend the sewers, too predictable. Too occupied."

"I took the rooftops here, but am open to suggestions?"

"Do not go home right away. Nor to your lady. Hide on the rooftops until light has come. Half the men tracking you have a warrant on them and will not risk being seen in daylight. Get a spare change in clothes. Do not come back. Not soon anyways."

He brought me up to the nearest hole, insisting I stay a step behind him, out of the artificial lighting, out of a crossbow's aim. We watched the two figures fight in the arena. A female with a sword, whip and bronze breastplate had been gutted by a man in a full suite of iron.

Heavy, but effective.

The crowd applauded when the match concluded. Her body brusquely dragged off the sand before a crew came out to tidy up the entrails on the sides. "What happened to their bodies?"

"Given to their families if they are free or discarded per their master. There is a mass grave they are carted off too." The wraiths should never find such a place. What a haunting thought. The stone above us rumbled with chairs and feet. "The audience is exchanging. Those who have verified bids are given glass globes and better seating. The rest of the city's scum are cramming into any aisle they can find trying to get a view of the Pit."

"Who am I facing first?" I said quietly and the ceiling above us stormed on.

"His master renamed him Gourger due to his skill with a knife. The name on his criminal record is, Japall Witner."

"What were his crimes?"

The man with the skull tattoo swallowed his annoyance with me. Disbelieving his own sentiments as he stated for my comfort, "His neighbors noticed a smell coming from his home. When they went over to investigate, they found the bodies of four boys decomposing under in his bedroom. None had flesh or organs remaining. They also found a rather large assortment of blades from what I remember hearing." My hands gripped the hilts harder. "He can throw and thrust with both hands equally lethal. His arms are fast, his legs slow."

I nodded, taking notes. I stood calmly while Rhett's fingers drummed soundlessly on the cement wall.

Across the field, behind a metal gate like mine, a figure appeared. On his chest were leather straps, holding several knives of varying curvatures. "Looks like someone already got ahold of his face," I commented to Rhett when I realized his complexion was nothing but groves and sewn skin, no eyebrows and only one ear.

"Even prisons have crimes they cannot tolerate. Criminals taking restorative justice in their own hands." He kicked the gate in front of us. "Get ready, Keenan. There will be no introduction for you besides a name." I tugged my hood down and tightened the leather straps around my gloves and wrist. There was a corroded clank as the gate opened. I walked onto the field mirroring the steps of Japall in a counterclockwise circle, the stands were buzzing, making my ears itch. I discounted them and kept my eyes on my prey. I sprinted towards him. Two blades whizzed past my ear. I jumped behind and used the wall of the stands to launch myself upward, on my descent, I dodged another attack by twisting myself into a backflip.

If I stood up, we would have been nose to nose. That would not do.

Staying low, I kicked out his right knee and as he crumpled, I grabbed a knife fastened to him and used that to slice his carotid. He flopped like a fish without air, grasping at his bleeding neck with both hands.

I rose slowly.

I waited for the guilt to rise. It didn't.

When he stopped thrashing, I walked back to Rhett. The stands behind me were more confused than anything watching the cleaners take his body. Money was brought to my chaperone who dropped a fist full of coins, *gold coins*, and pastels into my bag. He muttered something to the man delivering my earnings. Minutes later, he returned with a case of paper files. He set it down and filtered through it with his dirty hands. He tossed a file at me.

"Romerous Filtch," I stated the name atop the file. "Sentenced to life in prison for stealing resin from the black market. Resin used for the murders of seventeen people including three farmers, two women and eleven children on southern homesteads in attempts to claim land and cattle." I looked up from the paper with sickness seeping in my chest. "How did you obtain these?"

"I believe you requested them. I saw how effective the distaste coursing through you was. It impacted you for the better I'd say."

"Men here just bring them for you to access?"

"There are not many perks to being the Pit's Warden. Take what blessings you can kid," he said, shuffling more papers. "Whenever you are ready, I'll give the signal."

I was ready.

My blades were at my sides when I went to greet Romerous. I strangled him with his own whip. The crowds became more boisterous when I walked off the field.

"A little more showmanship and less execution style will help."

"Help what? I do not intend to come back here, I do not need to make a name for myself."

He gave me another file. "If the crowds are unhappy and threaten security, the games end. The river of money streaming to you is cut off."

"I don't relish standing alone among carnage. I promised nothing about making a spectacle of myself." I opened the folder. 'The Impaler', a spear wielding man charged with treason, was my next pursuit.

Money coins and paper were placed in my bag. Rhett observed the crowd from his peephole, scrounging his face as he did. "Just try not to kill them so fast. That will appease the appetites."

Keenan would cringe if he saw me strutting around the arena, playing with my food before I ate it. I took out 'The Impaler's' Achilles heel on both sides and spent long minutes watching him crawl around the Pit getting jeered at all the while I demonstrated my acrobats. When it was obvious who the winner was, I looked to the crowd for guidance. They all were grinning at the prolonged suffering.

Chanting for me to end him. I did. A blade clean through his heart.

Rhett sounded enthused. "The flips and twirls seem to engage them."

"Bring a circus to town next time." I stretched my arm above my head.

The crowds above us were louder during the transition. Rhett held up the water. I deferred again. I was hardly breathless. He noticed, said nothing and handed me a folder. Paula Helk. Shuttled hundreds of children in the underground slave trade. Including two of her own. Ages three and five.

"Poison ended arrows and a mouth to distract you." I touched my hood, over my right ear and found my antidote missing.

"How does she fair in close combat?" I asked.

"I've not observed too many who achieved close proximity."

A change in approaches was needed. I went to the rack and took a small bow off the wall and a satchel of arrows. Rhett listed the water cracked goblets and I tore at the table cloth wrapping it around the arrowheads and soaking them in lantern oil. "Have you a flint starter?" He coyly gave me a tobacco lighter from his breast pocket. I stared. "Can you show me how it works?"

"The heel of your thumb clicks this wheel here, sparks flint and the propane catches." He spoke a foreign language. I imitated his actions until I got a small flame. "You must be *very* new to Landsfell."

"No backstory. I'm just trying to do the right thing, I wish it wasn't always so fucking hard." I fumbled with the propane stick and grabbed the dagger off the side table. "I'm ready." I said.

The gate groaned open, Paula wasted not one full second in launching her double crossbow across the arena. Two sharp sticks hit the ground at my feet and skidded across the sand. I had to move fast, she already cranked back her lever and set two more. I ran up onto a rock to evaluate her and the surroundings. There was no sufficient place to hide, not for long. I notched the arrow in plain sight of her. She shot at my head, I dodged. Narrowly. The arrow implanted itself into a black banner behind me. A banner? I found the filthy black fabric strung in waves around the arena. "Paula. You are a shit mother!" I shouted while retrieving Rhett's lighter from my back pocket. She shot another round. I succumbed to the crowd and gave them an exquisite series of handless roundoffs and flips until I was clear on the other side of the field. Paula was fast, she already created distance.

"I'm sure your own dead mother would be aghast to know her own boy is a murder. Perhaps, you ended her yourself?" She rocked her hips backwards, her opened shirt appealing to men behind her. I took my chance and pressed my thumb onto the wheel on the lighter. The mechanism was rusting.

I tried again while she laughed. My spine sweat. I spent a long few moments avoiding death while turning the propane lighter. My thumb burned. Finally!

I reached behind and set the entire satchel ablaze. One by one I shot around the arena until the crowds hollered and Paula was forced to back away from the walls because of the flames licking the sides.

I set my bow down and smiled as she navigated around me in the middle. Close enough that her bow, however mechanized, would be of little use. I had seconds, a full sixty at best before the audience began to put out the rowdy fires. I had to make use of the time I had bought myself.

I threw a dagger. It implanted in her left shoulder. Her aim would be off if she tried anything.

I sprinted at her and kicked her in the throat just as she raised her weapon. The scream she let loose was distorted and awful on the ears.

She was on the ground beneath me. Scrambling for air. My knee crushing firm on her neck. I lowered myself to her ear. "My mother would be proud of her daughter." Her cheeks rose into her forever resting face. I had the decency to close her blank, glossy eyes before yanking my blade from her body and hustling back to my iron cave. Rhett took my dagger from my hands and wiped the visible red off onto a towel that hung on his hip. It was warmed under my hood. I exhaled at my keeper, "How many more?" I didn't bother to keep the emotions from my tone.

He pointed to the table where at least seven, eight or nine files lay. I pressed my back against the cool stone wall. "Maybe less if the sponsors opt to pin you against the duke's or Crosby's favorites." Thankfully, I knew Zander was busy tonight and not dropping by the arena to face me. I'd happily face the filth Crosby sent at me.

"I do not meddle in politics. I am here for the exact sum of money with the addition of four silvers for your confidence. Then I will vanish." I stared at him with his rough tattoos, scars and thick brows. "You're worried. Should I be too?"

He spit. "What you faced were the preliminaries, you can take your money and run. Leave the city and get your woman a nice cabin on the plains."

I couldn't help but snort. "Desolation and death are inevitable. I know this and soon everyone will too. I'd rather face them now on my terms." I grabbed the files and read about my next opponent.

I stared at two names. "Lovely. Twins!"

"With maces. Take notice of their thin file. They are volunteers. You beat them, you take their earnings *and* what the sponsors give. That will put you close to three hundred thousand and some odd change." He was still staring at me in a manner I'd expect a wise mentor would before calling me out on how wrong he believed I'd be. He didn't know about the wraiths. If he did he would have that army he knew paid and fighting them. "They are fond of young boys, keep your wits about you and keep your shroud close."

The competitions of the night lasted well into the morning. Rhett sent me off as soon as I had decapitated a knight named Benson in the Pit. He wrapped the bag of money around my torso so tight I winced. There was no time for stairs to the streets, he hoisted me up and out a basement cellar window with instructions to run, change and hide.

I nearly froze on the roof top of a jeweler, burning time until midday had passed and it was safe to climb down the building's trestles with my heavy bag of money flattened to my chest. I paid a drunk girl in a bar a few coppers for her pink, rosy blouse and washed the black off my face in the washroom. My hair was down when I left the tavern, flirting shamelessly with men who offered to escort me to the exit safely. I let them. I tried not to cave into my nerves and sprint to the Arborist, but walk briskly.

Brock and Nikki were having potato hash *in my room* when I unlocked the door to *my* apartment. "You two have three minutes to get out." I shut the door behind me.

"Or what?" Brock asked. I walked over and smelt his breath of sour wine. He was drunk. I flicked his nose then walked to Nikki and swatted him on the back of the head for appearing just as intoxicated.

His sharp fox features were prominent when he smirked. "Night watch was quiet. We were bored waiting for you. You've been gone a full damn day."

"Two minutes!" I shouted from my bedroom. I shut and locked the door behind me. I stripped my blouse off me, revealing blood on my skin and bra. My weighty bag of money I slid under the bed. I needed a bath and the blood hidden in the black fabric needed to soak out if this outfit was ever going to be salvaged.

They were chummy and talking in the dining room. I swiped lounge wear off my bed and opened the door to walk across the hall to the bathroom. I tossed my clothes into the sink with a bar of soap and ran the faucet.

I yelped at the cold water. Coraline hadn't warmed the pipes. I made due. I was a frigid tremoring mess when I emerged with long wet hair soaking the woolen tunic and drapey beige pants.

The count and cripple were submerged in a game of chess, overlooking me in my own chambers as I walked to the kitchenette to boil water for hot tea. Even the screaming tea kettle didn't break their redundant conversation about bishops versus knights as an offensive strategy. I seeped valerian root with lemon balm and wrapped my boney white fingers around the warm clay mug. I shuttered with delight as I began to thaw. My cheeks and ears burned as they regained blood flow.

"Sit," Brock offered with a grandiose wave in the air. He was already pouring me what seemed like a sticky, sweet glass of southern ambrosia.

"I'll pass," I yawned. "I'm going to bundle up in bed." The steam from my cup wafted in my face. I took a deep inhale and found my cherry red nose began to run. I sniffled. A penance for hiding out eight hours on a rooftop in winter.

Nikki spun in his chair. "Do you have the undying urge to tell us where you've been?" His mouth was thin and scrunched to the side, chewing his cheek, he waited for an answer.

"Nope. Do you have the undying urge to leave my apartment so I can sleep without two drunk men clamoring outside my door?"

Brock sighed. "Can we finish the game first?"

"Yeah." I shuffled across the room towards my room. I had pastels to count and coins to divvy up. I waved a pathetic goodbye and left them to their drinking and chess board. I emptied the sack onto my mattress to avoid the harsh clinking and clanking of metal on hard floors.

First, I sorted the coins by material. Coppers, silvers and golds. The paper pastels were in increments of fifty and one hundred and five hundreds. I knew a single gold piece held the same weight as several papers, only I didn't know how much.

My male comrades stumbled out. It was eerily quiet above me.

I couldn't shake the feeling Nikki was up to something mischievous. No sooner did the thought pass was a tipsy count hanging upside down at my window with his hair disheveled and his silks scattered. "Someone is going to see you," I muttered, knowing he could hear me.

"Then you better let me in," he smiled, eyeing the snow falling down around him.

I stood on the bed, gave a smug smirk and shut the curtains over the glass. "Leave before I call Coraline and inform her the count is a peeping pervert."

"I am no such thing!" he hissed. Dramatically wounded.

"I could have been naked."

"You're always cold, you are in layers of blankets." I ignored him. "I saw the money. I smelt the blood on you when you came in. I won't ask, but I want to."

"Are all dreamers so intrusively annoying or just the two I have been forced to interact with?"

He confessed, "All of us."

I sat down on the bed and hugged a pillow. "Yet, another reason for me to avoid going there." I heard him readjust outside, preparing to hoist himself back up to his floor. "How many pastels are exchanged for a single gold coin?"

"One thousand for a gold. One hundred and fifty for a silver."

"Thanks," I yawned again. "I'll need your help, eventually. Assuming that Count Hilderbrandd has a bank account and can write a check for a specific amount."

"His accounts are prolific and he has several, including an open, accessible account in Landsfell."

"Would he be willing to purchase a whore her freedom? I would pay him fully for her cost and extra for his trouble."

"Absolutely." His firm words calmed me. I stopped forcing my eyes open and laid atop my earnings.

Chapter Twenty

The following day, the wraith didn't make a sound, unless prompted by my whispers or knocking. It was an oddly peaceful morning where there was normalcy in cleaning up after the men's mess and relaxing alone with coffee and a nice serving of wheat germ and left-over red velvet cake. Candles were lit with Rhett's rusted lighter and I read poems, even giving a weak attempt to read Malick's governance guide, but found it dull giving the lively state of my heart. Yolanda would see her freedom soon. Or so that was my hope.

I crept upstairs. Nikki wasn't in his apartment. I checked under all the heaps of blankets in the largest owner's room. Nothing. I left a satchel of rose tea on his pillows so he'd known I'd been by.

I recounted my earnings. There were over one million pastels, most of which would be used to free Yolanda, the rest may give her passage to the north to be with her family in Sanctum. I merrily thought about the possibilities for her. And myself. It would be so lovely to have a female counterpart to all this testosterone perpetually invading my space. Even if it was only for the next few days until the gala, even if she only walked by my side a few hours in the tunnels or shared a meal, it would be refreshing.

Anna's blood sang in me. It flurried around my chest and sent my heart fluttering as if she was happy for me current train of thought. She was happy at the notion I'd make a new friend, after I killed my last female friend and sent another to Sanctum. Was I so pathetic I needed a dead Ilanthian celebrating my slacking social victories, even ones that hadn't come to pass? I buried myself in short stories the day's newspaper had to offer.

The door opened and closed delicately. "Did you know there are no female authors in this paper?" I asked Nikki who lifted a cushioned chair from around the fireplace and carried it over to the table, across from me. I still hadn't dropped the newspaper. "My guess is they are ghost writers or have male aliases." I folded the black and white parchment to give a smile to the sharply dressed man in purple sequins and blanket velvets. He kept his top hat on and adjusted the flat ironed collar of his button up.

"My next engagement starts promptly at four in the evening. You have my full attention until then," he stated, beckoning a fresh cup and hot water for his tea, the fresh rose hips tea bag I had left in his room. I filled his cup with water, he heated it in his grip. Once he seemed content, I heaved the weighty bag off the floor.

"Seven hundred thousand and forty-three hundred in pastels. As of four days ago that was the price of her debt. If it has fluctuated, I can accommodate the cost up to one million. She is a courtesan at Madam Maramancien, most have made an appointment to get into the front gates without being spotted by security." I tugged hair behind my ear. "I don't know how it works if you are purchasing her debt outright."

His opened palm reached across the table. "It's done privately with the Madam. I'll be needing that necklace," he spoke softly. I touched my neckline protectively. "How else is she to know the heroine of her story?"

"I'm not anyone's heroine," I corrected sharply. "As you said, I am a reckless fool with dumb luck."

He finished his tea and pensively watched me read the remainder of the paper. "Shall I have my sentries deliver her here?"

"Here is fine. I'll prepare the bed for her as I am sure she is revolted with the notion of sharing it with anybody. I have some clothes in the dresser that may fit and money to get her needs met. There are portions of each meal I can't eat anyways, that she can have too." His tongue ran over his straight teeth as he let out an exasperated sigh. "I will not be asking her to escort me under the estate until she is well and comfortable in her body and in my presence before traveling alone with me into forbidding sectors."

"You have a key to my chambers should you need a proper night's sleep off the floor. I'll keep fruits and pastas in my pantry," he said, with no notion of annoyance at my choices. "I'll take a third of your money to the bank with me now. I can't cash out all of it without knowing which lord or lady is suddenly bankrupt, stolen from or where a large sum of money went missing from last night."

I glared at him. "How many times do I have to tell you, I am no thief! I earned this lot, fairly!"

"Sure." Ugh. He stung my nerves. I walked to the kitchen and refilled my water and drank it facing the frosted window. If I was to calm down, I'd have to ignore him. "Is that why you froze your ass off hiding out for hours before returning here without being followed?"

"I was not about to risk leading wanted criminals to the threshold of this establishment. Ever think they would rob or murder me for my income? No, because for some reason you have it out to assume the worst of me. It is getting old. Especially, now that you can talk," I grumbled. My arms crossed my chest.

"I didn't know you cared so deeply about my opinion."

"Stop flattering yourself, count. I'm fed up with the principles of this entire world, not just your fleeting insecurities." I leaned on the countertop, sipping the chilled water until it emptied. "How much do I owe you for your trouble?"

"Don't insult me," he said, strumming his fingers on the table's edge. "Let's hope she keeps your secrets, Sage d'Loure."

I lifted the paper between our gazes. "I'm meeting Cultee and Zander tomorrow morning, did you need me to relay anything?"

"I am inspecting why Landsfell's outer walls are lacking. I believe I stumbled upon something monumental, tomorrow is too soon to release it without having you witness what I have. You need to relay the message to the captain in your own words. After all I am a gaudy southern count who doesn't involve myself with soldiers and shadows." I felt an actor's exuberance in his tone. "When you aren't in the tunnels, hopefully, I can steal you away for an evening or two. You know, once your black attire is cleaned and dried from the fresh blood soaking it."

"It's already clean," I warned, following up closely with. "And thanks for facilitating the money to get where it needs to go, I don't know much about money or proper purchases."

He rose from his seat twirling an empty cup in one hand and a new oak cane in the other. "It's not a worthy skillset, not nearly as useful as saving lives or performing surgeries. Don't fret about becoming apt with it, not now anyways. You've people in your life to ease that nonsense of a burden, just keep doing what you are doing."

The paper dropped. "Was that a compliment?"

"An encouragement," he said plainly, but the gold flecks in his eyes swirled like melted caramels. "Don't get discouraged by the hustle of the city or warped by the violence of its inner workings. From one woodland creature to another, there is more joy found in simplicity."

"I don't fit in anywhere nor do I have a place to return. I should at least *try* to understand the world around me." I kept the rest of my morbid remarks to myself, although he seemed to know what mortal comments I kept leashed. "If it goes well with Madam, when will she be here?"

"If she doesn't run off with her new freedom, dinner time would be my guess. I'll let Coraline know to bring my serving to your room, so she doesn't think you are without means." My exposed ears reddened. He took several stacks of paper and coins out of the bag and slid them into his plush purple pocket before he left.

Brock had a difficult time sobering up next door, I'm fairly certain he failed to keep down his breakfast. Any tea that I offered him may smell too potent or taste too bitter for his hyper-stimulated pallet. I ignored him the best one could, diving into books and articles about newly appointed knights and guards. I traced my finger tip across my lips. I had slain a knight. I didn't feel one ounce of remorse. I knew what they were capable of, I'd seen their perverseness and disregard for life with my own eyes. Rhett did not hand me a file on that man. I ran out to meet him head on in the Pit, his red cape and his black shield with the sigil of the Resig family crest, all the burning rage I needed to finish my night. I disemboweled him by striking under his plate of armor, one of the many benefits of being an agile five foot five inches against a six something walking iron man.

The evening I had spent stripping linens and replacing them with fresh fitted sheets. I wiped the counters clean and set my makeshift bed in a basket by the fireplace. Every half hour my nose would press against the frosted window, my eyes scouring the masses for a fine lady and her escort. What I wasn't expecting was a lady free of makeup, donning taupe worn pants and matching sweater to pound so vigorously on my door. Knocking on it as brashly as a burly man stumbling out of a tavern. "Cut my hair," she said as a greeting, void of sultry femininity.

She stormed in, inelegant and crass, everything her prior image she buried. Her big brown eyes had been crying, I saw as I shut the door behind her. Yolanda found a pair of shears in the drawer and plopped herself down in front of the table.

"How much?" I asked, watching the light waves tumbled out of the tie that held it up. Her hands sunk into her scalp.

"All of it," she said.

There were tears again. Not ones of regret.

I grabbed the scissors and cut sections out at a time, the floor I had swept was dusted in long locks of hair. When it was about the length of a man's cut, she asked for it to be trimmed shorter. I leveled out her hair and snipped deeper until it was less than an inch long and stood on its own. Her fingers inspected it, she didn't bother to look in a mirror. "I had not realized how heavy that headdress began to weigh, not until I took it off." She was looking at me, now. "I just now realized that I never asked your name. To whom do I thank for striking a bargain with me?"

"I go by Ivy Woodlander and shall go by Ivy until the woman who named me such is avenged. My parents named me Wisteria," I spoke softly. "Sage to the ears here."

"I don't want to know your secrets, I've held too many for too long. But, I want to understand you. Whatever you say I shall not repeat, I do owe you that much out of respect. I'll take you into the tunnels and give you the codes for the access points. Whatever you are looking for, I hope you find it."

I couldn't help myself, so I jumped into my questions. "Have you seen a young boy on the estate? He would be about four or five years old. That is my brother Cobar." Her lips pursed in thought. My fast heart ached as my mouth went on. "There is a woman, with a babe at her breast, Moriah and Rory. They were also taken from our home by capital knights and a priestess. Have you heard whispers of their whereabouts?"

"The prison cells are empty. Years ago there was an escape of magical sorts, felons have been relocated. I do not know where. The Duchess may. I did not visit her side of the manor often; the west is left for you to explore. I will get you there. It is your responsibility to get out."

I nodded. "I am not leaving until I find my family and kill the duke. If I die, stick with my company and they will find you passage out to be with your sister and grandmother if that is what you wish. I've also made water passage arrangements south of the Deadlands if you have the desire to sail out of Numaal and leave the war of the wraiths behind you. Brock, also called Ryholite Stout, is next door and Count Nicholo Hilderbrandd is above us, they frequent here. But, will not know that you have arrived and I want you to feel comfortable and not intruded on by strangers." I pointed in the direction of my company's living arrangements then left when I heard the chimes for dinner. I carried in two trays and shut the door behind me.

Yolanda dove into the bread. "I hate this waistline. They haven't fed me bread in years," her mouth was full as she spoke. Her eyelids fluttered.

"That good, huh?"

"Unbelievable." She dropped her sourdough bread and pointed to my basket. "Is that pumpernickel?" I nodded and pushed it closer to her, she had two fistfuls before I had one.

Between our two appetites, we would be needing a lot more food.

She paused her chewing to guzzle water. "What's a wraith?" I explained the limbs and jaws of a restless and its vicious nature. "These venomous evils are running around the country turning crafters into one of them?"

"Yes. Duke Stegin has more wraiths than citizens in his territory, or is about to once they arrive to Landsfell."

"They are coming here?" I wished I could lead with another topic, not one that caused her to spill her soup in fear.

"Eventually," I said, dapping up her mess spilling across the table. "Cultee Monte is trying to get his brother to listen, to call his province, the visiting provinces and the representative of the royal family to stand and fight before it is too late. Our homeland needs reinforcements. It needs action and someone to fucking tell the truth about what is happening. Stegin knows about the wraiths, they all do, but no one has bothered to stop it. Soon the public will know too." Whether by an attack on the city or by the delightful little gift under the floorboards, they will know.

"When the public finds out, they will be mad. They will demand something be done. That is why the dukes have not spoken about it. They do not want to get removed from their position by a coup, the rebellion or their own people. I bet the rebels already have been tipped off, they may be a hodgepodge group of fighters, seamstresses, whores and criminals, but they would run this ship with a better moral compass than the Montes."

I tapped my fork. "There is a rebellion?"

"It has been in the works for years. A bloke named Bastion is leading it. Four years ago he almost succeeded in dismantling the Monte's; several of the family members got away from the name. I reckon they ran far before either the rebels or their own family tortured them for knowledge. They will be trying something at the gala, that is for certain. I heard a large order of weapons arrived and the cargo was dispersed in minutes to various locations around the city. There are more reasons than wandering wraiths to kill the duke. They won't stop. They want the prince and the king taken out."

"A fallen province is the first step to a fallen family dynasty, a fallen nation and a dying humankind."

"I will not be going north. I will help Bastion once the gala has passed. Seeing as your agenda aligns with his. I'll stick with you until there is an opening to get into his operation."

"Good," my chest warmed. "Have you met this mysterious prince or his father?"

357

"I've walked by their conclaves. There are always a dozen or so in masks, I assume a Resig blood is behind one of them," she said, eying me carefully. "What type of woman is my sister?"

I thought of a resilient Sage behind curtain six and kindhearted Sage helping me in the kitchen. "She is also a fighter. I think she would have joined Bastion if given the option."

Yolandas face seems rounder with no contorting of makeup and the nearly shaved head. "She was always the meeker of us. I knew staying in Madam's company would have broken her, so I took her debt and fucked my way around the nation as good as any conniving highborn bitch. And much prettier too. I never saw little Sage the type to join a rebellion."

"She has more reason than most to hate the Monte line, Captain Cultee she sees fondly, but the duke's bastard son is as vile as they come." Yolanda's face went red, she spewed vulgarities that rivaled my own foul mouth. "I hate to say her miscarriage was a blessing, but it was. Once we had her back on her feet the women in Fort Fell helped us poison Gimlian with several doses of an effective concoction. He is impotent and unable to sire."

"If I see him, I will kill him," she hissed, her neck flushing under her anger.

"You can fight?" I asked.

"No. He doesn't deserve the death of a skilled fighter, he will get me. A retired beauty with an axe of a butcher." I should not have smiled, but I did. We were two livid wildfires feeding off each other.

"Sage is kind and considerate. She wears her emotions for all to see and will help a stranger, even if it means putting herself in harm's way. She has bouncy brown hair that shines glossy on the ends and a delicate manner of maneuvering around the kitchen even with bulking guards roaming about and children hiding under her skirts." I thought of Lorelei holding my blade and Raina pulling two ducks out of the oven to hand over to Zander, wearing matching oven mitts. All of it seemed ages ago. "She is also wicked smart. She drew me a map of the entire city, with details so I wouldn't get lost. Sage spoke with such color it was easy to notice how much she misses the kind parts of the city. Especially a music hall with a pianoforte hidden behind the curtains."

"The old amphitheater. We'd sneak in and watch show after show from the roof. Anything to avoid paying for a ticket," she said. "Those are some of my fondest shared memories as well." She stacked up the empty plates and bowls, and I carried them to the sink.

"Tonight, you ought to rest. There may be old clients out looking for you."

"They will not find the glamorous girl they are searching for, nor will I be found above ground. A night of repose is appreciated, but this time tomorrow we will be walking into a laundromat, that is the closest entrance to the tunnels. Also, the least dangerous and best smelling as luck would have it." She stood. "May I shower?"

"Yes," I motioned down the hall. "Clean clothes are on your bed. You may awake and find me gone. I will be back after breakfast, is there anything you need me to bring back?"

"Tall boots. Size eight. You will need a pair too."

I agreed then spent the night listening to her cry in the shower and later into her pillow.

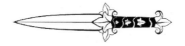

Borders and Binds was the name of the print ship. A quaint name for a large industrial building that consumed an entire block, and sent smoke stacks high into the cloudy morning. Brick and Mortar would have been a more appropriate choice in name given its tattered composition of cement and cinder blocks. I walked around the parameters before I spotted a lone bench. I set down my two shopping bags and closed my eyes. *Zander.* I said softly in my head and in doing so casted my sypher web in every direction.

He found it. *Wisteria.* He swam around our bound and nestled close to the door to my head. A puppy needing affection and overwhelming its master upon arrival. *You are in better spirits.*

I have much to tell you and Cultee! I replied and crossed my legs under a cumbersome skirt. *Nikki burnt down the Wastelands, he got the caravan far enough north into another territory, but there are thousands of wraiths. Also, my blood quieted the wraith and I found Sage's sister. She wants to join some rebellion, but agreed to stay and help me in the meantime.* I opened the door fully to his connection and we merged. Down the slow street meandered a tall hooded male, well over six and a half feet. Zander moved my bags from the bench and sat beside me, his left hand wrapped around mine. I did not pull away, but spun my small fingers around the width of his rough palm. It felt nice. His grin was enough to pull the next question from my mouth. "You found them!" I exclaimed.

"Shh," he rumbled. *I may have found the boy. There is a room within a room in the west tower, it is lined with silver salts. My ears cannot hear beyond that boundary nor can my nose scent who lives there. I saw the launderer washing clothes fit for a child, no maternal or infant clothes or whispers among the duchess's staff. I've tried using Oyoko's power to seep into the room's crevasses, but that salt deters me. The duke has magical items. This terrifies me. Tell Fen to keep his half silver-blooded ass away from the central city. Tell him it is an order.* His fingers roamed up my petite wrist. *Your blood quieted that monster?*

I inhaled the cold air into my lungs and in a cloud exhaled it. *I started my monthly some days back, now it only responds to me. It seems to venerate me, and calls out Migouri. Brock and Nikki both tried bateing it with their bloods, violence and words. They got nothing. I don't know what to expect when my monthly stops.*

Zander tilted his chin to the sidewalk behind me. Cultee strolled in. "The priestess is here with the prince himself. He, and his replicas, have held private conclaves with the dukes of each province," the captain wasted no time in exploding with details, not bothering to sit or greet us.

"Asher said they each left the room with gloves on. That seemed to be the only thing strange about that meeting. Drift, if you see anything amiss with scars, tattoos or trembles—investigate."

Drift's body faced me, yet his words were for the man passing by. "A lot of the buzz I collected is about reinforcing security for the gala, the inner guards and knights are confident Bastion will try something big. The queen's favorite knight was slayed in the Pits. It was obviously both a threat and warning." He moved his free hand around my face pulling strands behind my ear.

I gritted my teeth. "Stop."

"I can't. I missed you," Zander said openly in front of the captain. I smacked his hand away and suppressed the thought of wanting to feel his gentle calloused caress on my cheeks again. My cheeks reddened.

"Ew, Drift." I looked to the captain who slowly continued to walk. "There are passageways under the estate and the city. I found a way in and plan to use them for harboring safety or the element of surprise. I'll have them mapped out and memorized within a few days. Also, the closet is quiet. It reacts to my bleeding cycle. Does Adious know of the wraith we brought? It is speaking a language, nothing we or Count Hilderbrandd know."

"He speculates. I'm not one to trust a man who exclusively believes written logs and proven scientific theories. But if you think understanding *it* will help. I can write him a letter, asking him to tutor you and Rhyolite, then you can interrogate him if you want. Be safe in those tunnels, they are also graves from what I remember of my childhood." He kept walking. "Times are getting desperate. How is tracking the priestess?"

"Social, seductive. Still not as shrewd as she thinks she is. I heard a chat about magical silver salts. Does that mean anything to you? It surrounds a room in the manor. A fine powder," Zander spoke into the tail of the wind.

"Pleadian, perhaps? It's an inherited family heirloom. A tradition my forefather's use to ward off sickness. More silly superstitions. What magic had you heard it wields?"

"Wards against silvers and Eternals."

He gave a scrunched look of confusion over his right shoulder as he waved off passing strangers. "I have access. I'll investigate. Same time. One week. At the bar adjacent to the Inn. Bring the new crew."

Tunnels?

I told you I was getting into that gala. I squeezed his hand. *Do you think my red blood can walk across the salt and get Cobar?"*

You can't cross back with him.

Sweep the line.

The stone is engraved with it. May not be possible.

I sighed. *Then I'll visit.*

He will get tortured to talk. The high lords and ladies are not above playful punishment towards their staff either. Too many innocents will get roped in. Suspicions will be raised. He will be moved.

I felt a warm tear spring loose from my eye. I wiped it on my shoulder. *Yolanda said after the breakout two years ago prisoners haven't been held in the basement dungeons.*

Yolanda d'Loure? The aristocrat's favorite concubine is Sage's sister? Shit. Woah, I did not see that coming. He sounded surprised. *How did you get* her *to help our cause?*

I told you, she supports the rebellion. She has her reasons.

That woman is a courtesan, she can never betray those who've previously bought her–

I stared at him. *She is free now. Living with me. You wouldn't recognize her, she asked me to shave her head last night. I did. She doesn't wear her headdress any more.* I kicked the tall boots in the bag. Size eight. *We start exploring tonight.*

You will reach out immediately if things go wrong. He tapped his temples.

Nothing will go wrong.

He leaned down and buried his lips on the top of my head. *If they do. Call for me.* He planted a kiss there and nuzzled his nose. My traitorous body sunk into his kiss.

You would show up even if it was unwanted. Just like the affection you are giving me now. I tried moving away but his elbow had nestled around my shoulder.

Two Monte shadows are across the street. I don't want them thinking you are of importance to myself or the captain. When I lean in to kiss you, slap me. Storm off. I'll make sure your way home is easy from here. The hand that was laced with mine broke free and reached under my chin to pull my lips upward. My lips parted for him as I steadied my breath. *You are blushing. I'm devastated to leave you like this when you want me to kiss you so badly.*

My eyes widened as he got a rise from me. *Go fuck a fruit basket!* I sprawled out my hand on the side of his face. *Twack.* He did a great job pretending to feel my hit. I was standing and huffing with anger that I did not have to fake. Paper bags in toe, I dashed away from Zander.

One of the spies is Gimly's runt. Avoid any man with an oval pocket watch on a gold chain.

When I calmed down, I replied. *Okay.*

Tell Fen about the pleadian salt. As much as I want him to accompany you in the tunnels, he cannot be led into unsuspecting traps. Every possible plan will go out the window if he is captured or suspected to be of blessed blood.

Because you will turn this nation upside down to see him unharmed and free. Very romantic. Why can't you just use Oyokos's power to implode in the royal palace or the hoard of wraiths at the very least?

We need answers first or it may keep happening generations from now. We need a final fix, not an easy solution.

I turned the corner onto third street and was met with ribbon dancing in a flurry of red. It was dizzying. *It is okay to be scared of your power. I know when not to push, I just want to avoid mass casualties.* I spotted the Arborist in the distance and began stepping towards it, avoiding stepping on feet and bumping into the hundreds of people crammed between here and my destination. My stomach went sour at all the noise and cement building and walkways. Where was nature?

I wield the power of the God of Death. No matter what choices I make, there will always be fresh graves.

And Death has always been a dear close friend of mine. It is no wonder we are woven together. I entered the double doors to the inn, waving at the florist who wheeled in fresh roses. Red and winter white. Their perfume was lovely and soft, like their petals.

I was truly upset to leave you, not just because you and Fen passively calm my hunger. I missed listening to your banter and watching you run around with all your bottled-up passion. I enjoy learning what mischief you have gotten into and what obscene manner you've chosen to get yourself out of it.

I walked up the stairs, pulling the hem of the skirt up. *You are just a bored immortal who found a little toy for entertainment deep in the dungeons.*

I am anything but bored, you have no idea what I would give for a few months of sleep and leisure. You are not a toy, Wisteria Woodlander, prodigy child of the healing arts, raised by blessed and vibrant, leader to the lost. I kept walking up the stairwell and slid into Nikki's room. It was dark. Quiet. A respite from the ruckus of the streets and festival activities. Without lights I felt my way to his bedroom and dropped to the mattresses on the floor for he removed the bedframes to board over windows. I swept my hands in front of me as I shifted around digging through heaps of silks and cottons. Heat intensified.

I am with Nikki. Anything else you need me to relay? I asked Zander.

Slowly, I pulled back a cotton sheet. The firm back of a man was beneath. *Nothing he doesn't already know. Don't get yourself killed.*

Same to you, old man. Humor hummed as he departed.

"Nikki?" I uttered softly into the dark room. The tangle of arms and blanket spun around in response. Golden eyes lit up like bright lamps. They blinked at me, sluggishly orienting him to who the intruder was. They didn't dim as the seconds stretched on. For some reason, I felt the need to ask, "Is it okay if I talk?" as if I was disrupting a rare and sacred moment of solitude for the elemental, who if I forgot his odd sleeping preferences and glowing eyes, seemed no different than a red blood.

He made a groggy noise of approval. I readjusted on his mattress and told him all the brief conversation topics mentioned, putting emphasis on Zander's 'order' he was not to go near where the pleadian was being held or the city center with some priestess powers at large. Nikki stretched and placed a pillow over his head, one eye vaguely visible like a flickering candle. "He said it was an order?"

"Yes."

He didn't look thrilled at the use of his elemental bond to obey. "You are smiling. You are excited to unite with your brother." My hand flew over the lower portion of my face. I was smiling.

"Yes," I said. I missed what was left of my family. The lights under the pillow went out. I scooted off the bed and found my way back to the hallway.

Yolanda was asleep. The two trays of breakfast were untouched. I started to pick at one over a coffee and finished it well before the company joined me. In her high waisted trousers, cropped vest and short hair she could have been mistaken as a wave riding merchant crafter in the south. Were it not for her feminine figure, she could have passed herself off as a seasoned lord of sailing and bartering. "Please, tell me there is sweet bread and extra waffles for breakfast. I'll have fried potato pancakes, banana bread and any hearty substance you offer me." She scarfed down the omelet and raided the cupboard above the stove for crackers and cheese. We were gluttons for the entirety of the morning.

When it was time to slip on our high leather black boots, we behaved more seriously, until Yolanda started shoving rolls of bread into the pockets of my winter tunic for travel snacks. A few hours was far too long to go without food, she reasoned with me. My concluding cycle agreed with her.

The steaming humidity from the laundromat funneled out in puffy clouds causing icicles to congregate on the gutters above. I wafted it as we walked by. Fresh soapy linen. Nothing like the sun dried, pine filled scent that my clothes were heavy with growing up. Clothes in the city were washed in loud scrubbing tubs and heated to dry, the steam riding wrinkles as they hung. Rows and rows of fabric hung, lines filled up all the way to the rafters. It was easy to get disoriented in here, let alone find the closet of broken washboards that guarded a set of descending steps. Yolanda pulled a lantern off the wall and lit it. She pointed down a musty tunnel. "East," she informed, walking hurriedly. "We will explore a quarter of the labyrinth, a few turns and one access point that opens just under the statue of Lord Duggen in Stegin's library. The lock pads are rusty. I want you to practice the code so you don't get frustrated when it comes time to use it and I'm not here."

"Logical," I commented, stopping behind her steps.

"From here to Sir Duggen, all you need to remember is a little phrase. 'Row along a little river'. Right. Left. Left. Right. When you enter through the cemetery, there is a children's tune I sing to carry my feet. But we won't worry about that until we must. I avoid the catacombs. My clients never appreciated when I arrived smelling of death and dust. Although, it beats traveling in the sewage line."

I was grateful for the mildew and dampness. "From here to the statue, how long is the walk."

"Three miles. We only need to be cautious on the last turn, there are preparations being made for the gala. Storage and swords are often kept below for events," she said, swatting a cobweb from the ceiling and jumping back.

"Your sister mentioned as much. The wine your parents bottle is stored in bulk to keep the parties flowing." Her delicate neck and milky skin flexed. "Have you thought about visiting them?"

She nodded. "Those looking for me will stalk my family. Maybe hurt them, to bring me back into the light. They want their secrets buried with me Ivy. If they get into their enemy's hands, their livelihood crumbles."

"Make sense," I said, scrutinizing the pale moss growing between rocks. I placed a sample of it in my breast pocket to examine later.

She spun around to face me, standing just an inch taller. "Seriously?" Her breath was hot with the edge of anger.

"Seriously, what?" I said. My hand instantly found the hilt of the Ilanthian dagger in my shirt. I was not fond of her chipper attitude one minute and rage the next.

Her cheeks puffed up. "I hate these vile nobles! I want nothing more than to exploit their dirty lies and secrets, and you won't even ask!"

"You said you didn't want me to."

She grunted. "I know what I said!" Yolanda gritted her teeth and walked faster. Being down here was prompting a change in her beliefs, I kept my hand close to the dagger. We arrived at a split and made our first right.

"Honestly, I wouldn't know what to ask. I'm far removed from politics and popular opinions."

"Tell me more of your addenda and I can air the dirty laundry of the key players!" She laughed at her own pun.

It was too dark, too unfamiliar, too foreboding in the tunnels. "Not here," I cautioned. My voice decimals lower than hers. She gathered my uneasiness and mindfully held the lamp further out in front of us to extend the reach of our vision. Zander would have names of those in the court he did not have intel on yet. Over the next mile or two I casted a scattered sypher net.

Left.

Left.

"Ivy, the light goes out now. Mouths shut, ears open. Spies, assassins, knights, high born, families, staff alike all pass through this next corridor. It's hard to distinguish foe from faithful down here." Yolanda laced her arm through mine and blew out the handheld lantern. My heart thudded in my chest at the onslaught of darkness. Yolanda, reading my nerves, coiled tighter to me. She placed my right hand on the wet wall next to me, for grounding.

"Give me a minute," I gasped, leaning on the wall with a heavy shoulder. An unexpected incubus arrived in my head. *Why are you fretful?*

Becoming acquainted with the pitch dark. I held the arm in mine tighter. *We are under the estate now. Walking blindly towards an access point.*

Do you have a weapon on you?

Yes.

I pressed off the wall allowing my guide to lead me onward.

Courtesans are professional actresses and actors, yearning to please their audience. Don't be so quick to trust.

Says the man who spent centuries immersed in the act of lying, as he is currently. I just had this conversation with the fox about his characters as a fire wielder, a mute and an extravagant count. I don't know who or what to believe. I will navigate all of you strangers as I see fit.

There was the faintest sound of water dripping to my left. "Foyer fountain, the clay has been cracked for years," she said.

I know Fennick. I know myself. Yolanda, I know by reputation alone.

Shhh! I quieted his stressful chatter. *You are not helping. Tell me names of those you are suspicious of. Yolanda hates everybody in this city apparently. She says that she wants them exposed, or at least their secrets. She may prove to be a great asset if you can give her the benefit of doubt and not be a controlling psycho for once in your life.*

Where does this access point open?

Sir Duggin statue in the library.

My left arm went heavy and hot. *I saw your face once today. That was plenty.*

I changed my shirt. I think you ought to see it. And I get to meet your new, dangerous friend. She also needs to know the proximity of your allies to her enemies.

Be civil.

No fangs. That is all I can promise.

I kicked him out of my mental world, but held onto our line in my hand. The warmth was a lovely counter to the wet floor below me and the cold air around me. We stopped twice, hearing the grumbles of men loading crates in the distance, their light not efficient enough to reach us inching down an adjacent tunnel. We reached a small inlet, my hands were guided above my head. I fumbled with a large metal keypad. "Feel for the numerals. Five-one-five is the combination."

I scrolled through various shapes. My arms and patience grew heavy. The rust on the lock chipped onto my hair, my frustration grew. "Can't I just get a hammer and break it?"

"No. There is ink in it. It will stain your skin and mark you to be fetched and feasted upon by shadows." She shoved bread into her mouth. And another. My stomach grumbled. I bite off a piece and went back to work deciphering the rusted padlock.

I whispered ecstatically. "I got it."

We slid the overhead door and crawled upward. The room was shallow and narrow. There was some light that seeped into the nook from the library on the other side of the wall. A silhouette walked across it. Yolanda flattened her back against the stone and crept backwards. *Zander Veil Halfmoon di Lucient, do not play games. She has been traumatized by the evil in the place enough. As have I.*

"Woodlander?"

Feminine hands and fingernails pull at my skin drawing me away from the voice on the other side of the stone. I turned to her and calmly said in her ear. "I trust him as I trusted you to lead me alone in the dark into my enemy's home. His name is Drift. He came with us from Fort Fell, your grandmother took good care of us." Yolanda was shaking. I let her go. She eased herself halfway in the downwell, ready to leave at a moment's notice. "This is not a trap. We are safe," I reiterated.

It fell on deaf ears.

"Is there room?" He said, running his hand over the wall searching for a groove. A block eased, he squeezed inside the stone room no larger than a closet. In squeezed a two hundred and sixty pound giant.

He stepped on my toe. I punched his gut. "Ouch, you oaf! You didn't wait for a reply. There is no room for your oversized ego in here."

The wall sealed behind us. "Well, I'm here now. I have five minutes before I am obligated to attend some elaborate feast and be forced to use all eleven of the tiny spoons and forks which I bend every damn time. Waste of my bloody time is what it is. Hammish and Colette are gone from the evening and Satoritu Koi is fidgeting with the wrist of that gloved hand, whatever ceremony they did—it was painful. They are up to something that makes me nervous and I am trapped here with Gimly and his father."

"Then leave. You are stealing up all the oxygen in this place," I muttered.

"You are mistaken. My gallant nature has stolen your breath away," he flirted.

I gave him a firm elbow in the ribs. "Your nature is going to force my hand and ensure you never take a breath again. Now, can you shut up so I can introduce you to Sage's sister?"

He straightened and turned his gaze down to where Yolanda was a foot into an escape. "The guards call me Drift, it is a pleasure to meet you Yolanda d'Loure. I have had the pleasure of spending two years with your sister and grandmother," he said, lowering his tone and torso so as to show reverence. "I'm sure you are just as lovely, brave and surreptitious as they were. Raina stole me more hams and beef loins than I care to admit."

"Hi," she said, taken aback either by his size or his words. "I have seen you before. You were at High Tea on the terrace not but a week ago. The blind bloke who wants the king's blessing to be taken into Kathra's inner circle and knighted.'"

"Do you think they bought into my performance?" He asked seriously now. My focus shifted between them in the dark, ready to intervene.

"I did. But seeing how much Gimly openly despised you, I am willing to bet he tarnished your glow to the high council, painted you to be untrustworthy of their conclave and inner circle."

He hinged at his waist, leveling out the intimidation. "Knowing Stegin as you do, which would benefit his standing with the capital more—a snake of a bastard son, conniving and bitter or a warrior horselord, new to the east, easily impressed and adaptable?"

Yolanda wet her lips. "A snake in a pit of snakes will not raise the alarm. The hooves of a horse will do more damage than the venom they are immune to. Gimly is seen as ambitious. You, as a risk. I'd bet no more than a third will vote you in unless you commit a grand act, likely a crime or public prostration, that secures several members in the council to your name."

"You are honest. Okay, I like her." Was all he said before rising and smacking his head on the stone overhand. "Do you have any tips for approaching Duke Koi?"

She swallowed. "Gin and lemon tonics. His wife died in childbirth thirteen years ago. She only drank gin tonics. Now, that is all he sips. He can't even look at his twins without pain. He brought them with him to the festival in hopes to marry them off to be rid of the constant reminder of his wife's death."

"Depressing," Zander said. I somehow thought it was tragically romantic.

"You think conversing with him is depressing, try fucking him," she laughed. I stifled a snort. "To release the wall from this side, step on the corner tile. You are too heavy and it will break, there is already a crack. Ivy, will have to do it," she stated, more comfortable than before.

"I'll happily get him out." I jumped at the chance to rid him. His arms gently wrapped around me, lifting me to the corner. I dug my heel into the stone, and a level released the side wall. I squeezed his forearms in a farewell. My left palm rose to pat his chest. The satin was a strange texture on him. "Enjoy the gin."

"Enjoy the sewer rats," he remarked. Horrendous shivers prickled up my back and down my arms at the thought. Before he squeezed back into the light, he turned behind him. "Wonderful meeting you. I will be around. As for pestering Wisteria as to how she knew, I would be here—that is a moot beseech. I pride myself on surprising her with my mysterious charm."

He left, taking the lighting with him.

"He is obnoxious, but he grows on you."

"That I see," she said, taking my hand and helping me drop under the sliding door. I wasn't sure which segment of my statement she referred to. It was too late to ask, we were back to our hushed creeping along the walls revering the route we came. Soon after the sound of the dripping fountain passed, we lit the lamp. "You lead us back," she insisted. I obliged; my stress vanquished as the flame grew stronger.

The washing tubs were still hard at work, clanking away as we stepped out of the closet of washboards. Back in the apartment, we set our boots next to the locked closet. "Welcome home," Brock hollered through the wall.

"Thanks, buddy," I said, hanging up my layers on the pegs outside the fireplace.

"I would like to meet the rest of your *friends*," she stated confidently, staring at the locked closet between Brock and us. "Just not tonight. I'm tired." Yolanda showered and took her dinner to the room along with a book she borrowed from Coraline. One of my childhood stories. I found some vegetables among the beef cuts to nibble on. I filled the rest of my stomach up with a fizzing apple ale. On the back of a newspaper, sketched the paths I walked today and slid my artistry under the carpet. I would add to it in the days ahead. I smiled a content smile.

Chapter Twenty-One

Nikki had me meet him the night after Yolanda and I trudged through the boggy cemetery to the food cellars in the center of the manor. The entire cemetery was overfilled and in need of purification. We arranged to meet at the burning dumpster, which was more appealing than the rotting mausoleums. I wore all black, as requested by the elemental.

Hooded, masked and armed he didn't see me approach.

As a panther stalked their prey, I stalked him with grace.

I leapt down from the roof top and tied him into a firm choke hold. He was quick to throw my back against a wall. My muscles straightened to protect my spine. I pressed my thumb into the side of his neck, deep into the tension behind the sternal clavicular muscles until it found the weakest spot. His arm gave out as did his lungs. And when his grip faltered, I flipped him over and held a blade to his neck. My knee between his legs kept him stationary on the bricks behind him. "Hi," I exhaled into his chest as it rose steadily beneath me. Under my mask was a prideful grin.

"Hello," he smirked. Still too calm. I narrowed my eyes at his suspicious behavior. There was a sharp jabbing in my left flank. I looked down to see his griffin blade ready to strike.

I offered, "A draw."

He made a scoffing sound. "Not even close. I would be merrily dancing through the beyond and you would be soulless. I won."

My blade was back under my shirt. Nikki came off the wall, but stayed in the shadow of the tarp tents above which collected snow from falling onto the simmering heaps of garbage. "There are monsters beyond the

Veil, I do not want to go there. Completely dead sounds more peaceful," I said, falling in step next to him.

Unable to deny my declaration, he ignored it. "We are going to stay watchful at the iron gates. Stay tight to my side. Keep up."

He moved moderately and swiftly along the abandoned alleyways of the dumping ground. Once we stumbled across more active life we took to the roofs. Stopping every three blocks or so for him to evaluate my fatigue.

His lack of faith in my agility drove me bonkers. "I am the apprentice to an immortal combatant. I will not exhaust after a few hours of playing leapfrog with you, he made sure of that when he stretched our lessons on for days and weeks with little to no rest. I'd be vomiting and still have to swing a sword chasing him through the forest." My mouth twisted. "When I say it out loud it sounds rather barbaric and cruel given I was only fourteen trying to keep up with them."

"Anna trained with you too, or were your mom and dad practiced with the sword?" He enquired while we waited for crowds on the streets below to disperse into the taverns, shops and eateries. I let the silence stretch on. His weight shifted against the chimney. The throngs of people under us multiplied, we'd be waiting until sun down. He pressed on, "Have you spoken to anyone about her?"

"I can't. It would have disclosed too much. My acts of love would be termed acts of treason." We would be on the roof of the paint shop until after the first wave of dinner guests were seated and the bar maidens bustled. I nestled next to Nikki, he wasn't upset when I pulled his black fleece cape over my shoulders to absorb his warmth. Glorious warmth. "Fauna knew there was a woman I loved. And her name." Now, Fauna was dead because I killed her.

Damn, my love was cursed. I was cursed.

My gloved fingers wedged under my arms to retain heat and flexibility; my knees tucked under my chin as I scooted the heels of my boot to my bum.

"Punishment for treason is death. Seeing as you are already guilty of one account, I don't see harm in committing another heinous crime and conversing with yet another elusive Ilanthian." His shoulder next to mine dropped and he leaned over. "I am a marvelous listener. I don't partake in gossip."

I waited for Anna's guidance, what I found was my own intuition. "Death for withholding knowledge of free walking Ilanthians? That decree is ridiculous." I clicked my lips. "Outright stupid. The king is fragile and scared, that mandate makes him look more pathetic than Zander trying to squeeze into a normal sized shirt." Nikki chuckled.

"Wait till you see him get dressed when he has horns and wings. A battle he has yet to win."

I shook my head at the thought. "I don't plan on seeing him undressed. I'll reserve that delightful vision for you." He gave a toothy grin that made his features appear more feline.

The sun was setting and the snow around us piled up slightly, enough to begin hiding our tracks. "What attracted you to Anna?"

I was swallowed by memories and pointed west. I couldn't believe I was doing this. Talking about her. "See that shade of red, just behind Anuli's temple steeple? The red that swirls with deep purples and glimmering oranges?" He nodded following my gaze. "Imagine hair as magnificent as that. Her hair was vibrant and wild. It danced like flames and was just as intriguing. I was twelve when I saw her for the first time. She stepped off the white boat onto the birch dock, a family of three behind her. She called them cousins." Eyes were on the back of my neck. Nikki stopped me from tightening my hood, from receding into the fabric. He was trying to pull me out of my own discomfort emotionally and physically.

"You are safe with me," he said, moving the mask entirely off my face. He did the same, forcing our eyes to meet and air to mingle. My tongue went dry and stuck to the roof of my mouth as I evaluated his words. "Keep talking, Wisteria."

I did. "My parents tried to stop me, calling after me as I ran barefoot from the apothecary, through the gambling merchants and straight to her. I was so startled when I shook her hand. She was warm, they all were. I associated silver bloods to be cold, as if literal chilled metal ran through their veins." I smiled up at the man next to me. "I was wrong. You are all hot blooded. Watching Anna lose her temper at Keenan was akin to unleashing a hurricane. She puts my belligerent mouth to shame. My mother and Elousie, Pine's mom, never let me stay for their arguments. I was removed and brought to different houses. Anna would find her way back to my bed, whatever floor or cot I was sleeping on, within the hours it took her to calm down.

"She was all I knew. My only friend since our commune separated from the other crafters in order to keep them safe after the birth of Rory. My family left everything behind to keep Ilanthians safe. Anna was my world. As I grew up, our relationship evolved. It was as easy as breathing." The sun went down entirely. The red in the sky vanished. The night was colder and darker. "In retrospect, those arguments were important. I should have paid closer attention, but she had me enchanted. Disillusioned." I shook my head roughly between my hands. "I can't for the life of me recall what they were about. Keenan won't speak of it. He won't tarnish her memory for me, but I know there is something out of place, maybe Keenan wanted to leave and she did not? Or the other way around? They all failed when they didn't prepare me for the state of the real world or even educate me on the existence of an entire third realm. They ensured I can save a life, but twice as fast take one. They molded me into two opposite sides of a coin and left me directionless." My head pounded. I rubbed my temples and hopped to my feet. When did a question about my attraction to Anna develop into monologue or anger?

I was not logical. Far from it. "I apologize," I sniffed the cold air to clear my head.

A sad, lamenting purr reverberated up the back of my neck. The empathetic vocals of a woodland fox.

I pivoted around to find a silver head of hair nuzzling against my neck and shoulder. Moving side to side, he buried his nose in my collar bones, as a skulk of familiar foxes often did for comfort. I rested my chin atop his head. Warmth broke through me, slowing the tears that fell. "The further I step away from the Deadlands, the more concerns I have about the people I love." It was a terrifying notion to even consider that maybe they weren't from the Lands of the Gods at all. His nose repetitively nudged the side of my neck and ear, until my chin was up.

Nikki covered his face and hair with layers of dark gray fabrics. "That's better." I felt better, although; nothing about my situation changed. He blinked his golden eyes at me then pointed them down to the street. Hundreds bustled about, far less than thousands. "Let's go." I didn't want to miss the opportunity to dodge suspicious glances, moreover, I didn't want to stand wallowing on a rooftop. He gave me a bent crowbar and kept one in his hands. He jumped onto a dead electric pole and flew down it like a zipline. I got a running start and savored the speed the momentum gave me. A short-lived adrenaline rush that ended in a tuck and roll to avoid a metal flower bed. Nikki no longer lagged for me. He sprinted off before I oriented myself. His array of darkness merged seamlessly with the falling snow, loud chatter and dim street lamps.

My cheeks were wind whipped from the chase when I slowed.

A cart of barreled saffron and spices was stationed to my left. I hid behind it watching the workings of the iron gates which oversaw the import and export exchange. A yip echoed from the hay storage. When the path was clear I back peddled into the stone cylinder. Another sharp bark. This time from above. A rope dropped.

"You insult me," I said.

I kicked off the wooden gate and onto the stone wall, from there I launched myself at a steep angle and gripped the rim of the second story platform. I hoisted myself up on the floorboards and plopped down in a hay bale as Nikki examined our view of the rampart wall from a square window.

The moon had hardly passed its dark phase by two nights. This time next month I will be on a ship sailing towards Ilanthia, over halfway there. I had money now. I could very well buy a formal gown and slip into the gala. One fit to my frame. One of silk. The duke would never see me coming to kill him. Nikki signaled my focus. "This is the scheduled night for the duke's scouts to come back. Two of his trained scouts leave on alternating days. The last ones to come back were greeted at the gate, marked as arrived but never arrived in the barracks."

"Stegin sends precautionary scouts?" I asked baffled. That fact alone countered what picture I had painted in my head given what reports

Cultee and Zander relayed. Suppose someone had to inform him of us woodlanders sheltering silvers all those years ago, I assumed he was making use of Misotaka's priestess lineage. Nikki affirmed my question, with a quick hum. "We are here to discover where they have gone?"

"Yes. Now, get on this ledge with me. Start scouring for suspicious behaviors and red capes altering patrol routes." It was colder on the stone ledge, I scowled at him as a snowy wind whipped in my direction coating my lashes in white. I sniffed my nose and put my chin down under my collars. I watched the same handfuls of men on the wall pass back and forth. Another four men approached the iron gate, their Numaalian shields and reds proudly displayed. Two went up the steps to relieve those on duty and the pair on the ground did the same. I elbowed Nikki. He elbowed back. We were watching the same scene. The groups of men that flanked the right and left of the gate also switched out, it was the normal time to exchange sentries and rangers on the wall.

The new men walked the same routes. A path was worn in the snow from their redundancy. The two on top withdrew arrows from their satchel. "Scouts requesting to enter!" a man hollered from the wall. My heart bobbed in my chest.

The gates were unchained, the hefty iron locks were separated and hauled away. Two mounted men in filthy shades of maroon trotted in and were led to the small assessment stable by the ground guards. They were brought down from their horses by the barn hands and walked to the strategy room adjacent to it.

"We need to get closer," I said. "They are clearly distraught!" A bare finger pressed onto my lips to silence me. Nikki pointed to his ears.

The scouts thanked those in the stall and the women who brought them a warm bowl of food. They and a patrol guard went behind closed doors. "They found evidence of wraiths. He referred to them as crawlers and described what we know to be a bait trap. Darkness is coming," Nikki flexed his bent knees. He was going to jump from the cylinder. I barred his chest.

"I'm coming too," I reminded.

He was tightening his hood when speaking. "I need you to watch the wall, cargo carts and mark any incongruences. I already prepared a hiding spot in the alley to drop my ears. Besides, you will be warmer up here."

"Fine."

"Don't go back without me." He jumped. Landing more feline like than fox. The night absorbed him, his long silent strides, turns and jumps not indenting the snow with expected one-two patterns, no he was far too clever for that. I shivered up on my perch, consciously keeping my focus on any person who had interactions with the scouts, lip reading whatever I could gather. The farm hands were mostly talking to the mounts they cared for, not each other. The rangers on the rampart, walked their normal route, but their eyes were combing the city's internal workings. Poor form for watchmen.

The iron gates had yet to be sealed. I wasn't the only one to notice the gaping metal doors. A crowd of passing brokers and traders made comments about the security of their goods. To which a Numaalian guard ensured, "A late wagon of exports is leaving shortly, their gate will be closed promptly. If you have concerns you can bring it up with High Lord Corrigan, who demanded all rewards from his gambles be shipped off immediately to prevent thieving. I don't make the rules, my brothers." The trader grumbled off without further debate. I marked that particular sentry's small gold stud earring and that he wore his standard sword on his right hip. The rest of him was indistinguishable. Cropped brown hair of an on duty soldier, average build and matched me in years.

The squeaky wheels of a cart rounded the corner, led with one horseman too elderly to swing the sword benched next to him. Too feeble to survive a few days of winter alone. He had no intentions on a long journey to another territory.

There was one final export that departed through the iron gates. Its contents were not a High Lord's winnings, but two lost lives.

The scouts.

Nikki remained below, investigating the scheming and betrayal within the Numaalian guards. I choked down disbelief for the guards that were now on duty blended seamlessly in with the others. They were comrades, calling one another by names and carrying on with their duties with no mention of their depravities. I was shocked that Nikki hadn't intervened yet. By intervene I meant kill or interrogate. I would have done a combination of both if I had been down there, but I am sure he thought of that too, yet another reason he insisted I remained in the overlook.

Hours passed with nothing strange to note. I remained awake and alert until what had to have been around four in the morning, when the next exchange of guards took place, the rangers merrily hustled down from their high post as fresh faces took their spot. Heat moved in. "What did you learn?"

"The stationed guards killed them, they don't want the word getting out. I have their names and bunk numbers in the barracks," he said, handing me a warm cup of vegetable broth. Savory and salty, it went down fast.

"I've pulled off dressing as a man before. I can make it into the barracks if Count Hilderbrandd can't stain his silks," I offered. Sleep sand was in my eyes. I wiped it out.

"The count has money if bribes need to be made. Luckily, I won't have to risk exposure because Asher is available," he said, slipping the empty cup from my grip. "I am not cruel enough to send you into a grotesque grotto of filthy men who have been deprived of females for however many months and years their contract is signed. One whiff of your skin and several heathens will descend upon you."

I rolled my eyes. "I'd kill them all, but unfortunately, I need them alive to fight the wraiths."

"We need to spar. I need to see your physical assets and fragilities," he stated, seriously after scoffing at my eye roll. "At least practice, so your skills don't slack."

I had plenty of recent practice. A great variety of opponents and styles of fighting, I faced and killed them with ease. Efficiently executed them, as Rhett said. Nikki did not need to know that bit of information. Nobody did. "Yeah, I will happily punch you. Now, if you want."

"This is not to be taken lightly," he scolded.

"Is that what you believe I am doing? Taking the expiration of humanity lightly? Taking the death of my family, friends and home as casual news over a cup of morning tea?"

His hands rose, palms open. "Your heat is rising. And so is your voice." He removed his mask and lowered his tone. "My words came out erroneous. I know how serious you are about protecting what you have left and helping others avoid a similar fate. What I was referring to was your concerning lack of ability to prioritize yourself."

"I have adequate amounts of self-preservation," I leaned back against a beam.

Nikki crossed his arms and leaned in. "Not enough."

I pushed his shoulder away. "You are suffocating. Would fighting pacify your need to be right?"

"I don't need to be right," he grumbled. "But I am."

I dusted off my hindquarters and walked over to the straw scattered floor boards. "Best of three? Or first to draw blood?"

"No weapons. First to get compromised," Nikki said, tossing his coat into a hay bale. Such a shame to see the lovely fabric fray with the coarse stalks of straw scratching its inner lining. "Needless to mention the need to stay quiet and out of sight."

"Well, shit. There goes my early morning plans to scamper and scream down the street about an army of crawlers at the iron gate," I rolled up my sleeves and tossed my leather gloves next to his attire. "I'll give you the rare opportunity to strike first because I was raised to respect your elders."

Smiling, he ran at me. His feet were fast, a competent Ilanthian, making his patterned two step approach recognizable. Nikki's crouched stance and fist jabs, however, made him more unpredictable.

Calculatedly, I fought defensive. Dodging him for the first minutes to better observe the manner in which he moved, looking for my window to strike. I stepped backwards, he followed. "I could just let you tucker yourself out throwing lame punches. It is past your bedtime."

"Foxes are nocturnal. I have a few more hours to humiliate you before my ancient bones turn to powder." I tripped his next step, he hopped over my toes and swung an elbow in my face. I dropped to the floor. The heel of a steel boot stomped from above. I shot up via arched back roll and kicked him in the back of his knees. He made hitting the floor look elegant and turned that momentum into his next series of advancements. I leapt up the next level of rafters. I walked out of his reach, balancing on rotten beams and deconstructed floors.

I made an exaggerated yawn, not at all hiding the humor in my eyes. He ran up the walls and met me on the crossing beams. They wavered with the added weight.

The bend in the wet, rotting wood was a sure sign it was failing. I eyed the beams carefully beneath my steps.

When Nikki got close, I jumped to another rafter. He enjoyed making me uncomfortable and persisted to spring himself next to me and come down hard on the planks beneath us. They groaned with frailty. This fucker was going to take us both out.

He ran at me again, this time I chose to mirror his footwork. He looked taken aback when he saw my perfected steps. We sped up, keeping rhythm to a sword dance without a sword. He gave a nod of approval. I said, "If I were to be honest, I would tell you, your left foot lags when it comes out of a standard high strike. And when you block," I ran at him in a traditional chest punch he would recognize. "You block too high." I moved his forearm that barred his chest, his two remaining hearts, downward where it would more effectively save his life.

"Keenan's apprentice has keen eyes. How about she demonstrates offensive maneuvers."

"Gladly. I will even let you choose your method of defeat. Ilanthian or Montuse?"

He cared not. He was already rushing along the creaking beam. My reflexes leapt over him into a front flip. Montuse it would be.

He pivoted and chased me down from the ceiling where I swung on the copper wires that fell loose from the slate roof. I slid my ankle into a nest of string and wires and fought him upside down, while secured. My short lived moment of boasting was threatened when his fist came too close to my cheek. We both knew my confidence just about cost me a shiner and another week's worth of salve on my face. I twisted down and reoriented myself upright.

We fought fist to fist and feet to shoulders until the Landsfell's clock tower chimed and the temples in the area awoke and sang their own morning hymns. I rubbed my wrists, the leather fastenings I had wrapped around them for protection felt tight with all the swelling underneath. He spat out a mouthful of blood. I had gotten him good in the jaw after I paralyzed his lower half with a lucky strike of my thumbs. His teeth cut the inside of his lower lip. Actually, it had split open. But he healed in a matter of minutes. I would need to ice my arms overnight. "Another draw?" I offered, binding up my gloves and tightening my mask and hood.

"Afraid so," he said, wiping the remnants of blood off his chin. "You've my blessing to continue exploring those tunnels."

"I never needed your blessing." I rushed by him and jumped to the first floor, taking shelter behind stacked troughs in a musty corner.

He joined me later. "Thank you for indulging in my request." I eyed him. What a weird comment for the stalker. The woven of my woven.

"Just be grateful I didn't have my sword or a reason to fight with my usual zest," I said, walking out towards the opening. "Tell Asher hello for me."

"I'll have to get to him through the sewers behind the barracks. I'll reek so bad I doubt anyone will approach me for a conversation." The disdain in his voice was palpable.

"Careful. The sewers are occupied," I reiterated Rhett's warning.

"By who? Who told you that?"

I shrugged, stepping into the dim morning light, snow landed on my freckles. "A man who knows the sully mysteries and sleaze of the city. Doubt they are mere rumors given what little I do know of him." Nikki would be making a concerned or disgruntled face if I turned around. So, I walked forward to place fresh imprints on the ground.

After rest and a meal, Brock came over with his chess board. Yolanda eyed his handcrafted metal crutch and missing limb from behind the kitchen counter. "What happened to your leg?" She asked without a hint of misfortune.

Brock leaned over the table and gave a grievous shake of his head at the newcomer. "On my way down from the northern dunes I stumbled across a sleeping fire drake who gnawed it off with his rows of razor teeth." I set up the chess game and let Brock have his fun. Yolanda could use a little of his friendly humor. "I pulled my belt off from my very strapping physique at that time and used it as a tourniquet. With my own hands and blade, I sawed the bone and sewed the flesh with the threads of my shirt. I crawled home in time for dinner. If you think my loss is tragic, you'd pity the drake I slain using the laces of my boots!"

Yolanda threw an apple core at his head. She looked at me. "This is Brock?"

"Yes," I confirmed. "He goes by Rhyolite in the city. Rhyolite, meet Yolanda."

Yolanda sat at the table between us and examined his dangling pant leg. "Does it hurt?" She continued to inquire.

"Not often. A certain woman among us managed an admirable amputation." Heads turned to me. I busied myself arranging pieces.

"She even spent many nights finding pain relief for me even if it meant foraging in dangerous parts of the Southlands."

"That is where you are from? Where those wraiths are?" She asked bluntly, crossing her arms over her endowment. She had two layers of beige sweaters and homely high waisted pants.

"Yes. I was an ironside crafter of the Southlands. Most of this province is overrun with wraiths, they seem unstoppable." I eyed the silent closet behind him and continued to keep to myself. Brock kindly didn't imply the city's probable fate.

A swat on my arm. I looked to my aggressor. "And you cut off his leg?"

"Not all of his story was complete fabrication. They have rows and rows of sharp teeth and a jaw that unhinges to fit a human body in it. He was poisoned. He would have been dead and resurrected into one of them had I not." I seated myself.

"And here I thought imperious lords, haughty ladies and dreadful dukes were the worst things to happen to our nation," Yolanda spun the chess board, she would play black. Brock white.

"What would be worse is learning all those nasty people you mentioned planned and plotted the wraiths in their own nation, among their own kind and are intentionally allowing the massacre," I grumbled. "Among themselves they know and do not speak of it, Drift and Gimly openly conversed about the wraiths to an entire room of the duke's council members the first day of their arrival. They asked him to lessen the gruesome details and refrain from bringing it up in front of the royal court if they could."

Yolanda sipped her water. "I can name everyone in Stegin's council. I can tell you the size of their cocks, their food allergies and what greed haunts their hearts. I could have made each one of those bastards sing me a song. Many I did. Not one made mention of what you described as wraiths or even insinuated to the plague of dying crafters and guards."

"Gimly Monte told me it was a distraction technique the Emperor is using, so the capital would be defenseless when the west came to launch an attack. The peoples of Numaal are not worth protecting, we cost Kathra too much money and resources. Katha is building their walls higher, while ours get burnt down," I swallowed. "He said a lot of bullshit that day. But, I did believe him when he told me Numaal was preparing to kill the last God and Goddess. To cut the head off the snake."

Yolanda moved her knight in front of her line of pawns. "This group of idiots is going to get the rest of us killed. They want to kill our fucking Creators? Bastion has been right all these years. We need a radical shift, not just in Landsfell, but in all the provinces. Sever the major vessels from feeding power to Kathra and stage a coup for the bedridden king."

Brock was smiling as he made room on the board to get his bishop out. "It seems the stars have placed two enraged and spirited women in my path to ensure I will never be uninspired." Yolanda took his rook. He took her knight. She scowled. "How does one go about finding this Bastion?"

"You don't. He finds you."

"Not helpful," Brock said, his foot began to tap out a folk tune when his concentration deepened.

"He tried to rope me into his workings for years. I couldn't accept as a courtesan, what good would I be dead when all he needed from me is my secrets? I wanted to, badly. Word got around that several high borns were purposefully sending messengers on behalf of Bastion to meet them at warehouses. Bastion never sent them. It was a trap. Whoever showed up they killed. And their families. It was an effective way to scare people away from joining the rebellion. I could not tell you what he looks like or much else about him other than his name and mission," she said foolishly. "I'd still follow that stranger than let the current state of affairs persist a day longer."

"And that was before you knew about the hordes of wraiths? Damn, Yolanda, just think of how differently people will think once they realize they have been duped. Once they see a wraith at their fancy gala," Brock stretched his arms overhead.

Yolanda blinked twice. Her emotions were hard to recognize. "What are you arranging?"

"We brought one with us. Captain Cultee's extravagant gift to his brother."

Yolanda wasn't thrilled about the monster in the locked iron box next to us. Who would be? To prove it was even alive I had to demonstrate the peculiar knocking that it copied. "Maybe your captain can connect with Bastion. His reach is greater than any of ours. He was never the ruthless type to abuse his resources."

Brock posed, "Maybe he is Bastion."

"Farfetched, not impossible. He once told me he was on the side that fought for all life," I said.

Yolanda moved her queen backwards to protect her king from Brock's advancing rooks. "The enemy of my enemy is a friend. I agree to meet with the captain. Isn't there a count invited along too?"

"Count Nicholo Hilderbrandd, have you heard of him?"

She hovered her fingers above the checkered squares. "The merchant from the isles?" I nodded. "He is new to the stage, I haven't met him nor did he come into the city often for me to have seen him in the brothels and bedrooms. I heard rumors about his engaging personality and that he was very agreeable on the eyes." I chuckled, wondering if he would be the type to blush at vain complements or dismiss them and carry the conversation onward to something pertinent. "He keeps his circle tight, to be known enough for mid-level invitations and yet not be associated with the backlash of aristocratic affairs. He is clever."

As clever as a fox.

"If you say so," I added, bringing water to a boil. I bought several bags of pasta from Nikki's room along with butter and salt. I stirred and strained it while they set up for another match. Yolanda sulked, after her loss. Leaving Brock to fill the room with his candid humor until she caved into his bad jokes and corrected him on his grammar and how illogical his stories were.

"You need to step up your chess game dearest, you let an unlearnt and illiterate cripple beat you. And if you lead with the same four moves, it will happen again." Yolanda's creases in her forehead softened as she heeded his honest and playful tone. She was bitter about taking direction, but she did. I tossed the salted noodles in a serving bowl. Adious hadn't shown up to tutor us or for us to evaluate him. Brock was disappointed, that much I knew. He didn't always want to refer to himself as the illiterate cripple. But for the sake of a smile and to deviate crossfires, he belittled himself.

Yolanda must have seen something in him that unstiffened her animosity. "Teach me chess and I'll teach you to read."

"Dare I say we just agreed on something? Yes," he jumped at the offer.

Knuckles firmly rapped on the door, the count made his presence known.

In flooded an array of blues and teals, stark against his black vest and slacks. He hung up his top hat next to the fireplace. His cane he set on the chair. He continued to remove his elegant layers until he was in dress slacks and a cotton undershirt. Hints of tattoos crept out of his sleeves by his wrists. "Asher was tickled when you asked about him." He grinned and walked to the kitchen. Nikki stopped in his tracks seeing the bowl of pasta I made. "You were not about to serve that without a sauce or a side, were you?"

My tongue ran over my teeth. "Butter is a sauce. Besides, we already ate a fluffy meal prepared by Coraline. This is just... supplemental."

Nikki looked at Yolanda and lowered himself into a partial bow. "Yolanda d'Loure, I am Nicholo Hilderbrandd, thanks for keeping Sage preoccupied and out of trouble. She owes you an apology for attempting to feed you sloppy, tasteless food. Good thing, I arrived. It likely would have killed you." I smacked him with the flat end of a wooden spatula. "Careful, I rather enjoyed that." He gave a wink that felt more like a warning. My lips pursed.

"Rhyolite, back me up. Butter is a sauce and salt is plenty of seasoning."

Brock said with a wince, "You eat bitter barks, mosses and raw nuts with shells still on them."

"You eat the carcass of dead animals," I shot back.

"Moss. Wet, *fuzzy* moss. Off rocks and sandy river beds," he detailed again with his hands. "It's gritty and gross."

"I know what I eat and I don't have to take a life to sustain mine, you carnivore!"

"The amount of butter you used is not a large enough quantity to qualify as a sauce. Let the man enrich what you prepared." I stepped over and gave Brock a solid swat with the spoon. Firm enough not to be called enjoyable.

My eyes pleaded with Yolanda. She shook her head. Was no one going to support me? "I would have eaten it because I love warm pasta and a free meal. Salt is not a seasoning." I stiffened. "And you better think twice before hitting me with that stick or I will find a fork and retaliate."

Brock ran his hands through his hair, not a man who enjoyed conflict. Nikki rearranged the kitchen. "I moved the knives away from both of you." The knife rack was placed on top of the cabinets, out of our reach. He rummaged in the small ice box until he was satisfied with basil, pine nuts and lemon. By the looks of it, he decided on a pesto. I moved around his busy hands chopping herbs on the slate block to bring him a stone mortar and pestle. I took a small portion of plain salted noodles and ate it by the fire, the rest of the room continued on with pleasantries, which shortly transitioned into a debate of the best chess strategies.

Civil banter filled the room, as did fresh citrus and basil aromas. If I shut my eyes, it almost felt like home, at my parents' cottage in the rich greens of Ferngrove. A community night of sharing food, board games and one too many drinks. I shut them. I wanted to keep them that way. To instill this fleeting, non-momentous moment as a memory. The first memory in years that wasn't remotely off putting or bound to wake me up in terror.

The count sat at the table, offering his perspective on the game of chess—tactfully avoiding Yolanda's curious gaze and probing questions about Septar, a week's journey away at the mercy of the wind and sea.

"I don't buy into your story count. I have reservations about all members of this eclectic team of renegades," she looked at me curled up on the chair. "I feel safe enough, but when the muddy waters clear we shall see what is lurking beneath."

"You are not shackled to us. You are free," I said. "I have spare change to send you off or secure a rental room while you search the city for your rebel leader."

Brock puffed his cheeks. "She says the same shit to me all the time. I keep having to remind her that I want to be wherever she is going. Mostly, to see who is at the receiving end of her resentment. I feel we are close to meeting the culprit who damaged her beyond repair."

I said nothing as the heat rose to my cheeks. People saw me as broken. Maybe, I was. "Rhyolite, you are vexatious."

"You are my only living friend. I expect to be as much," he stated proudly. "Now, stop being your isolated sad self and get over here and pretend to derive pleasure from being social."

"I do enjoy being social," I replied on the short walk to the table. Nikki kicked out a seat across from him to sit in. I plopped down.

"Not in the two years I've known you."

I spun the fork in my hand as if it were a dagger. "I've never been in a city and I find that existing here is over stimulating. It tires me." I gritted at him. "And you never got to see me socialize because by the time I pulled your half dead, fat ass out of the ravine my entire family and love of my life had already been murdered, along with most of the crafters. Who the fucking hell could I hold a conversation with? The restless? Almost everyone we met is dead. Forming new relationships just to watch them end in another unmarked mass grave is stupid." Yolanda and Nikki stared at me. Yolanda horrified, Nikki intrigued. "No offense you two seem... *fine*."

"They seem *fine?* How are they not to take offense to that?" Brock bit back a laugh to keep his voice serious and steady.

Yolanda spoke next, cutting off whatever remark Nikki was going to sling at me. "I am far more than *fine*."

"Yes, you are competing with Sage here to be the most hostile woman in the city. *Fine* does not adequately describe either of you," Brock grumbled sarcastically.

Yolanda flicked his pawns off the chess board. One by one. "If you were forced to do the things I have endured, you'd be rather spiteful too. You've no foundation to judge so harshly on our first meeting." Brock calmly scooped the pieces off the floor and compiled them on his lap.

"You should never have had to tolerate anything that you didn't want, I am sorry about the manner you paid your family's debt. Your worth is immeasurable. I just met you and I already know that much," Brock continued his reserved demeanor until Yolanda concluded he was authentically not a threat.

Count tossed the noodles with the bold green sauce and divided up servings for the table. My arms crossed over my ribs. "Don't waste food, stubborn squirrel," Nikki carped, gracefully holding a fork in his dominant hand. A napkin was already folded on his lap. Dignified, compared to I, who sat with my legs folded beneath me, my small body drowning in a too big cotton chemise, probably hemmed for a man. Such stinging words from an unsuspecting culprit.

"Go dig a hole," I whispered behind my water glass.

My company ate their food while I pushed mine around in the bowl, purely out of spite. Yolanda, looked over Brock to the closet. "Your cycle ended yesterday. Why is it tongue-tied?"

"I cannot fathom a guess," I resolved.

Brock spoke, "I will not complain. Beats living on edge every second and drugging it with resin and spores every other hour. I was getting unwell."

Yolanda refilled the pitcher of water and brought it back to the table. "I don't know much about them, but is it feasible that the human soul is alive inside and they recognize you? If not you, your intent?"

I had watched life and light drain from Fauna's eyes. Her personality rotted away over hours. She was dead. Wholly and irreversibly dead. I could not accept that the Goddesses and Gods fated her, or any of the people I killed, to exist by my side as torment. Punishment for my sins. "Your speculations are as good as mine." No food would settle in my stomach after my imagination manufactured such gruesome notions. Brock reached across the table and happily polished off my late-night snack.

Count replied to Yolanda next. "For years in the Southlands, I have watched bizarre happenings. Even going as far as interrogating them and watching the transition process. Wraiths have no remnant of a soul, not ones we are accustomed to. Now, it is transparently clear that these evils are adapting to the light and studying the best way to dismantle whatever force brave enough to confront them. Landsfell's walls will not hold against the sea of claws and jaws that are coming in waves that will block out the sun. That is why I joined these new friends, to isolate and annihilate this pestilence."

Yolanda must have found the count's statements honest enough, so she went back to restaging the chess board. "Is this your way of apologizing for ruining the previous game?" Brock said.

"I didn't hear you apologize for calling me hostile," she shot back, her pink lips pouting.

"Nor will you. Because you are," he said calmly. Yolanda left the table to bury herself in the room. I chose to do dishes. "That could have gone worse."

My thoughts mirrored Brocks. Nikki brought the remainder of the bowls to the sink. "You need more linens to sleep on. I will carry them down." He pointed to the sheets crammed into the wicker basket. "That is pitiful, you're getting bruises on your hips from tossing around at night." My scrubbing stopped. How had he known about the aches forming on my hindquarters and sides?

"There is no rush," I said, drying my hands on a towel. He avoided my inquisitive gaze by fastening up his layers of clothes by the door. He was going out tonight, I deduced watching him adjust his hat and spin his elegant cloak around his elbow, draping it just so.

"I'll deposit them in a moment. I have bidding wars to attend to with the black market and will not be back until tomorrow morning. I intend to purchase weapons. Now, all we need are people to wield them. Cultee may have people for hire to help with that end of the dilemma." Brock and I waved him off after he dropped a white down blanket and two more pillows on the wooden armchair. "You have a visitor," he said cautiously, lingering at the door to my room.

I peeked at the man, gold chain and oval pocket watch clipped to his lapel. Gimly's shadow. "Perhaps he is here for someone else. We've not met, nor have I introduced myself to many in the city."

"I know you, woodlander," he said my surname as if it were his best kept secret. "My lord beckons you. He is upset. I failed to retrieve you sooner, his tricky uncle switched your lodging arrangements."

"Gimly is not a lord. He is a bastard son, unable to make a name for himself."

The man's face stiffened with a grimace. "Count, you may leave, my business does not concern you. Girl, come with me and I won't kill your friend over there. I believe that was the threat made to you before you left Fort Fell, was it not?" He pointed his sword's tip at Brock. Brock's teeth clenched down.

"I'll go if you promise to bring me back before sunrise and never step foot into this inn again." Nikki hadn't budged. He fixed his stiff eyes on the man. Our recent table conversation played in my mind, there was no need to make new friends, I had a difficult time keeping alive the ones I did have.

The man inched towards the opening. Nikki blocked his foot progressing with an abrupt sweep of his cane. "And if the sun rises before you are home?" He dug inquiringly.

I turned to him and said, "Then it will be the last sunrise you will see before I gouge your eyes out of their sockets and feed them to you."

He and Nikki stared at each other, as two bobcats would before striking the other's neck. "Make yourself reasonable. Face and hair covered," he commanded of me, forgoing any courtesy of acknowledging me when he spoke. When I readied my boots, scarf and layers of tunics he gave a triumphant grin to the count. "Your friends and belongings are safe as long as your medicinal efforts are adequate. Where we are going you will find decent supplies."

A cocky grin moved across my face. I went to Brock and embraced him, softly whispering into his neck. "Stay and keep Yolanda at peace." The squeeze on my shoulder was all the confirmation I needed to soothe that aspect of my mind.

Nikki accompanied the shadow and I to the foot of the staircase, his steps synced up with mine stopping when I was hauled atop a horse, a stranger holding the reins in front of me. Trotting swiftly down the horse lane of the roads granted me a rare perspective to observe the districts I had not ventured down, all were crowded and loud, but also unique in their architecture. The music district was by far my favorite, with band stands and wooden performing platforms arranged every few blocks allowing those meandering up and down the street to drink and dance liberally. So many smiles and laughs, a refreshing sight.

The music faded as we encroached upon a sprawling garden dusted in frost and a few inches of snow. Those tending to the evergreen shrubberies were shoveling snow from the footpaths and sprinkling salt behind their heels. The rod iron gates opened allowing me a full vision of Duke Stegin's manor. It gleamed against the dark and cold backdrop, the massive patios and porches were lit and being prepared for the main event in a week's time. I gave a wave behind me. To where Nikki had been keeping stride unseen, not able to enter the central region or risk the penalty of pleadian salt.

The mount was steered to the right, towards smaller homes. Yet, they had magnificently groomed gardens, on the outskirts of the fenced estate.

Zander felt me right away. He flocked to my presence.

I fully opened my mental doors and yanked Zander's connection. There was no reply, but I sent messages regardless. *Gimly's men fetched me from my room. I'm being brought to heal on the northern estates. In a guest's home by the looks.*

Onward we rode, slowing when flashing lights lured us in. A signal that led us to abruptly dismount and strip the belongings off the free horse. The door opened as we stood on the unlit patio. Gimly.

The man gave me a familiar grotesque grin, eyeing me in a manner that felt criminal. "Petro," he addressed the shadow behind me. "We will signal when we've finished." The door shut behind me. A hand wrapped around my wrist, pulling me through the dark home. I tripped when my feet met the threshold of stairs. My stomach tightened at the dark, the small space, the human shackle around my wrist. His father's dungeons fresh in my mind.

My woven, dispersed my simmering fears with a single phrase. *I am with you.* I felt assured. *Whose house did you enter?*

Remains to be learnt. It is dark and smells like a tavern. There are moans. A man is injured.

Are you armed?

With wits. The lights came on. Intuition was right. It was a small stone wine cellar and on the cot in front of me, the door behind us was shut to block out light and the sounds of discomfort. The olive skinned man with thin eyes and straight hair released the jade buttons on his shirt's cuff, he pulled the red fabric back to reveal an ash gray arm. "A wraith bite," I said, shaking Gimly off my arm. "If I cut the stem of your infection off, your life will be spared." *I believe I am with a high lord or a duke. His hand and arm sustained injuries. A wraith bite.*

"He wasn't bitten, but it's their venom, yes," Gimly grunted from the corner where he opened a massive cabinet of medicines. "You will not cut his arm off. You were brought here to find a manner in which to slow the venom until he has adjusted to it."

I froze. *The high courts are intentionally injecting wraith venom into their own.* "You should not be experimenting with such things. No good can come from it." The injured man tossed a jade hair clip on the bed beneath him.

"We don't need reprimanding from an outsider. You are way over your head, I suggest doing what you were brought here to do, the only thing you are capable of," Gimly pulled a rubber band out and wrapped it around his left arm as a tourniquet. "Poppy milk stopped working days ago."

The man trembled when I flipped over his black palm. His skin was oozing and shedding at the creases. I turned to Gimly. "Can I see what is available to me? Have you needles and syringes?" He moved aside and let me take a full inventory.

The man on the cot cried out, "Cut it off! Let's try again next year on my right side."

"No," Gimly hissed. "If your mind was stronger, we wouldn't be in this situation and you would have adapted like the rest. This is a sign from Anuli." I relayed the conversation to Zander before I got to work. *This isn't an experiment, it sounds as if others have adapted.*

What gifts does blending the blood give them?

Gimly silenced my inquiries. Does Duke Satoritu have an affinity towards jade?

Yes. He started to wear his wedding band around a chain on his neck.

I took as many vials into my hands that fit and came back for a hollow needle. I knelt by the patient. "Do you have any suggestions as to what slows it?" I asked the room.

"Not bayroot or calliope blossom," he said and offered me his purpling arm. I used the backs of my fingers to feel for an accurate temperature on his forehead. It was too sweaty so I felt on his neck. He was cool to touch, and more importantly, I found his necklace and wedding band looped on. *It is Satoritu,* I syphered. "Gimly, what have you tried?"

"Knocking him out until the process is over. Even in his sleep, his mental state is as frail as his heart. Resins, poppy, rotcore."

"Rotcore? That is for equine and cattle use!"

He shrugged. "We were desperate to induce sleep. Nothing we had worked. If he cannot relax and let it infiltrate, then slow it until he stops desiring to join his wife in the Veil."

I couldn't stop myself. "Is that what you did? Allow it to infiltrate you and turn you into a poor specimen of a human?"

"Watch yourself," he warned.

I let it go. For now. "Ginseng proliferates. I'll reconstitute a powder and inject it directly into your arteries. It won't feel good, but if it saves a limb and life, it is worth a try."

Gimly chuckled, "There is that altruistic crafter mentality. Always a sheep in the herd, never the shepherd."

I laughed back. "Oh, certainly we stick together. A pack of wolves more so than a herd of sheep."

"Don't romanticize your lifestyle, it will hurt more when it's extinct." I lowered my fabrics to hide my eyes, they were glaring. "What solution do you want to mix the ginseng with, alcohol or distilled water?"

"Water," I said shortly. "If this fails, find me slippery elm and burdock root. Give the man some alcohol it will vasodilate him and expedite the process. Gin, sounds good. I will drink a glass too," I tossed over my shoulder. "With a twist or two of lemon."

Gimly begrudgingly compiled, the northern duke went still. "There is nothing wrong with forming an alliance with death, or evening wishing it upon yourself as much as others. But if you can do good in this world and combat darkness, life may yet be worth living." I rolled the dried stems and leaves of the ginseng between stone and rock, repeating the process until it was a fine powder. The duke took a long swig of his drink and set it on his knee. He was jittery, I was unsure if it was nerves or withdrawals. As I mixed the water in the injector I hummed a folk tune, eventually I placed my palm on his bouncing knee. "You'll need to be still, sir. Tell me something that you find calming, whether it is a breeze, a voice, a song, a scent. I am here to do you no harm." I untied the tourniquet; it was doing far more damage than good.

I waited for him, the steel needle not yet in my grip. "In the north we have a variety of desert flowers. Ocuya is a pink blossom that never fades a shade dimmer than the sun. It grows on the highest point of the cactus which stands many feet tall. The dunes are decorated in waves of pink florals." The broken blood vessels in his cheeks burst a little more when he smiled. I moved slowly. "It casts a divine perfume over the lands."

"What does it smell like?"

"Less potent than dogwood, sweeter than lilacs. Perfectly balanced." He flexed his fingers and the tip of the needle broke his skin. I wouldn't advance it until I heard him speak again. "My wife embodied ocuya's beauty, toughness and refinement."

"What was her name?"

"Yuki," he spoke with an exhale. While his mind wandered I moved the needle up a particular ugly, dying artery. I injected the first dose. He winced when I pulled out to refill. I asked Gimly to put pressure on the puncture site. He threw a gauze square at me. His conduct remained shitty.

"How did she die?" I inquired. I found another vessel in his arm that would suffice.

"During childbirth, we were not expecting two babies. Kiko and Kaotin have grown into magnificent young adults although I offered no inspiration or emotional availability." He stopped his narrative and groaned as I placed two servings of the liquified herb into his wrist. He swore. I massaged the areas I tried affecting.

"Nature works slower than the toxins of evil spawn. I don't have a foreseeable timeline to see improvement. I'll continue on with burdock." I had watched Gimly prepare my drink, ensuring there was no sleight of hand or a tipping of a vile into the clear liquid. Straight gin. He'd no lemons. I choked it down with what I hoped was a stone set face. My chest burned, my throat salivated to protect my stomach lining. I prepared the next concoction, my gaze dissecting the hands and wrist of the man who handed me the jar of dried tangles of root. Nothing was out of place, hardly a scar. Not a man brave enough to earn one, a snake slithering his way into knighthood. *I don't think Gimly has been initiated into this ritual he seems to know a good bit about.*

There are either too many risks or he is not important enough, Zander replied. *Can you get Satoritu to talk?*

I have a creepy Monte perched on my shoulder. I am working on getting the duke drunk, it doesn't look promising since rotcore and resin didn't touch him. I hate gin by the way. My stomach gurgled. I pushed the glass further away from my nose, its potency sickening. I shivered.

Knowing Gimly is stripped of his functioning manhood is the only reason I have not broken down those doors and swiftly ended this night.

What happened to stealth and meticulous details? Ascertaining alliances in the court?

I have worked out every gruesome detail of Gimly's slow, torturous drawn-out death. The court can go to hell too. I'll save Stegin for you.

My goodness. Zander was losing it.

Before you and I slaughter the nobles and their bratty offspring, you should know Nikki and I watched two of Stegin's scouts get murdered when they returned with news at the iron gate. Their bodies were carted off. Asher is digging around the barracks for clues. Stegin is horrid and gullible, but he is being kept blind.

My arm shook with the strong emotions flooding through it. Emotions that I did not own. *Bloody hell.* I twiddled my fingers as I scanned the shelves to lessen the shakes.

You sound on edge. You feel *on edge.*

He was pacing on the other end. *Do I?*

Yes. I'll work information out of them if I can. Before either of us guts them too soon.

Not soon enough.

Agreed.

He stroked my mental walls. *Does it excite you?*

Knowing their deaths are near? Getting resolutions? Finding my little brother?

Zander's breath twirled up my arm and wrapped around my ribs like a cold plunge into ice water. *Does my being on edge, my restlessness, my desperation* excite *you?*

I dumped out four tablespoons of the root onto the slate cutting board. "I'll need a knife to dice before I pulverize." I set my open palm. *Excite? Hardly.*

I thought we were past the lying.

If you are so damn all-knowing, why bother asking?

Ice penetrated further, his grip around me tightening. Not painful, he would never hurt me in such a manner. It was a jolt, the electricity built between us sucking out the oxygen in the closed, underground cellar I was trapped in. *I want to hear you say it. Say you want me, need me, out loud.*

Gimly pressed the wooden grip of a knife into my hand. My face was red. I beckoned my annoyance with Zander to flood over and into my interactions with Gimlian Monte. Purposefully, I didn't break his eye contact as I peeled back the skin of the root and chopped the plants with precision. No Ilanthian spins, but fast and intentional.

I was a wolf dammit. Not a prey to be stalked by a fox. Not a prey to feed an incubus. Not a prey to be abused by the sinners of Numaal. I broke away from Zander's intense grip to focus on the matters at hand.

I shook him loose, it felt as if icicles went falling to the floor. He growled and sulked away. My arm was in control again.

Keenan would be livid. Hollering at me to 'remain a sheep'. I swore as I finalized an agreement with myself to drop the knife. To drop the bloody knife and all my dignity.

I did. The room quieted as did my head.

I meekly picked it off the floor, Gimly stepped on my hand, the blade pinching into stone and skin beneath his weight. "I'll need those." I referred to my fingers. My voice trembled as he pivoted his boot atop my bruising knuckles. The blade had not pierced my flesh. When he lifted the sole of his foot, I took to inspecting the damage. I swore and I popped my ring finger back into alignment in a fast motion before I chickened out.

That was it. Achy skin and another ugly bruise on my dominant hand.

"Don't bite off more than you can chew." He readied another syringe and distilled water on the side table, while I flexed my grip. Keenan would have me running miles for that dumb stunt. I pushed him and all the tangle of nonsense that surrounded him out of my heart and zoned in on the shrinking flecks of herbs that were ready to be ground with a palm stone. I poured my chaotic thoughts and *excitement* into that batch, my shoulders were taut and burning when I decided the powder was fine enough to enter the vascular system.

"Sir?" I looked up at the duke. His right hand shielded his gray arm, he let me move it. No perceptible developments, no worsening. "Tell me what good you are going to bring into this world, once I save your life." I mixed the browning water and drew it up in the metal piston that fit into my small grip.

"My daughter and son, I will reach out to them. They have no reason to reciprocate the communication," he said softly.

I cleaned my next site. "To stem, to flower, to fruit, the roots need solid ground. Dry soil is better than no soil. That is my experience anyways." The needle tip dove into his forearm, below the crease in his elbow.

"I am out of touch with goodness. This world and the garden I carelessly planted them into, their roots will absorb... from everywhere. Who is to say if what they drink nurtures or necrotizes them?" He wiggled his hideous blistering fingers.

I kept judgment off my face. Any scowl would do the opposite of churning goodness in his dry soul or permit him a space to speak up. "People bloom where they are planted, but they blossom when they meet the sun, the rain and the chatter with the busy bees that pollinate them. This world is vast. I believe there are more forces than goodness and evil, just as I believe there are forces far larger than the Eternals." He gave a panicked scream as my medicine infiltrated his veins and arteries. Sharp, short breathing was what he was reduced to. "Start with soil. Pray for rain." I wiped away the blood with the cloth and finished the vial.

I kneaded his tendons atop the skin that had not yet cracked. He screamed in my ear the entirety of it. "Fight to stay here. Dig trenches to lead water to them. Irrigate frequently. Send help, they need not know who it is from." My hands, one tender, rested on my lap.

His sharp eyes rounded with sorrow. "You have given up on me?"

I shook my head. "No, sir. The opposite. I have faith in you to strengthen your inner beliefs into something you can stand behind. To firm up your resolve and fight this," I looked at his venom-soaked limb. "There is good out there."

Gimly had enough sap for the night, a gruff hand pulled me up to my feet from under my armpit. I straightened before I stumbled into him. My skin griped at the proximity. Gutting him now and torturing Duke Koi for information was a compelling intrusive thought I pulled myself from acting out.

I was a hazard to myself. It became increasingly difficult to convince not to swipe the knife, after Zander expressed how little regard he had for the entire high council. "Upstairs. Wash your filthy hands and wait for Petro to collect you." He turned to Satoritu. "Keep collected." He locked the cabinet and removed glassware and tools, anything he could use to harm himself. The lights went off.

The urge to say final words of encouragement bubbled out. "You will see ucoya again, sir. And dance among their fragrance. Just another example of the beauty in this world worth protecting," I said into the dark. I yelped as my enforcer yanked me up the wooden planks of stairs. My shins scraped beneath my pants.

When I washed my hands, I made sure it was done thoroughly, scrubbing every speck of blood and toxins off my body. I'd burn this shirt and the pair of gloves tonight. *Koi is in the cellar. I did what I could.*

Gimly?

Next to me. He flickered the lights twice to signal for his henchmen. *Alive,* I emphasized before he asked.

For now.

The dark around me felt haunted with the soft cries singing up from the floor below. The place felt haunted. I willed haste to Petro. Gimly arranged the table top counter, resting against the lip of the granite. "What keeps a nosey crafter woman busy in the city?" He asked, not bothering to hide his cocky tone of insinuation.

He knew about the print factory. "I found a few bars, watched a lantern festival and met with your friend, Drift."

"Friend?" He sneered. "We both know there is no friendship between us, just as I know there is no friendship between the two of you. Do you sleep in all your male friends' beds? I heard Brock has his own room. Do you frequent his sheets?"

"I don't fuck my friends," I stated clearly. "I do punch them when they step over the line, I will never hesitate to put a man in their place if they make me uncomfortable." He didn't see the bead of sweat fall down my brow.

"What is the place of a man in your world? Beneath you?"

A clopping of hooves outside. Freedom was near. "Equals, if they aren't an ass." I walked across the dark room to where I knew the front door to be.

Cold metal traced my jaw, my body stiffened.

A blade was at my throat. "If you move or so much as cry I will kill you and give the order for Brock to be fed to the night." Arms wrapped around me, tugged the fabric off my back.

I left my body so it didn't give him a murderous response. I was a shell.

Foul breath coiled at my neck. "I have a message for your *friend.*" His mouth leeched onto my shoulder, the sucking and biting not as enjoyable or playful as my childhood remembered hickeys to be. He was not Anna. No one would measure up to a girl's first love. I winced silently feeling my skin smart and burn where he latched on.

A knock at the door. Gimly moved again. I choked out, "I am sure it will be well received." The knife at my neck pushed me forward. The door opened and I was shoved into Petro's side. I jumped onto the horse when his arms freed me. Once a safe distance from the guest house I called backward. "Gimlian Monte, you have not seen true demons. But you will meet them soon, not even your soul will be left behind when *we* are done with you."

We left him at Satoritu's doorstep, the spooking cries of the duke chasing me off as we rode off the estate.

Chapter Twenty-Two

I had been gone for hours, Brock met me at the door acting as if I had been kidnapped an entire week.

I tossed my gloves into the cold fire pit and slumped over to the table where the letters of the alphabet had been written on parchment. Brock had neatly traced over them. "Yolanda is sleeping. She took a butcher's knife into the room when she went." I drank water and untied my boots. "I am ready when you are." He tapped the cap of the pen eagerly waiting for me to talk.

I told him everything except for the hickey and syphering. He was as dumbfounded as I. Posing all the same questions that raced through my mind, neither of us were able to match the array of puzzle pieces dumped in our possession. Frustration was not a strong enough emotion. Our whole existence was becoming a maddening maze to navigate.

Nikki had made my bed on the floor with a duvet above and below my body for the comfort of my slender bones. My head sunk into a long plush pillow. A lump knocked into my occipital. I reached the case. Ilanthian arnica salve and a written note. *'For your hand.'*

I stopped investing so much energy into how these dreamers came to know what they did and accepted it as I wanted to do with sleep.

Brock slept in the hallway between Yolanda and I. By morning no indication of his sleeping arrangement was left behind. Offending Yolanda wasn't something we cared to do. The three of us talked about the details of what we did understand all while sipping coffee. I spent the rest of the cold day sipping hot whiskey to tolerate the boisterous educational method Yolanda enforced. When she sounded each letter out, Brock would make a face and laugh. Despite their quarries, when Brock did pronounce the letters, he did so with moderate fluency.

With another night of poor quality sleep, none of us were vivacious when we left the inn to cross the street. Count Nicholo and Drift appeared to have spent the entirety of the night and all morning at Bron's Bar and were approaching inebriation when Brock, Yolanda and I walked in. Cultee was alone at the high table finishing up a rolled morning tobacco with his meal. We took an open table just behind Cultee and ordered apple juice. Yolanda called the waitress back to place two side orders of pancakes. And marmalades. And potato hash.

Captain was the first to join us with a casual turn on his bar stool. "Quite the appetite," he said to Yolanda, puffing his cigarette to the nub.

"Well, I am quite the hungry woman. I crave a variety of things that are not ladylike. Rebellions and bread were frowned upon," she retorted cooly to him while her eyes continued to comb through the menu.

"No one here is frowning. We are just as hungry for the same meal if I am reading this correctly."

"Nowadays, I am not picky. As long as it is food and prepared fast. There are other customers that need to eat and have proficient cooks in the kitchen and farmers in the fields, don't you say?" Politics were as indirect as Nikki said they were.

He dipped his chin in agreement. "They are hiring." Cultee pointed to the loud friends in the corner who were drunk and racking wilted jokes to anybody that would pass by. He walked up and plucked them each up by their collar and pulled them to our table, with all eyes on the three of them. "Your jokes are shit. Sit here and sober up so the rest of the city doesn't have to be subjected to your nonsense. I don't even care for your names, just shut up so those who came here to think are permitted to do so." The bartender behind Cultee thanked him and brought the two men lemonade and bread.

I snickered at the pair of dreamers resting shoulder to shoulder, both red in the face and puffy eyed.

When the apple juice arrived I wasted no time in conveying to the table my accord with Duke Koi and since the count wasn't in shape for a reserved tone of speaking, I told Cultee about the scouts. "I will hire mercenaries, pay them half now, half later and pray to the Eternals they keep good on their words. This city needs protecting even if we staff it with criminals and outcasts."

"Are we putting citizens in the tunnels or your militia?" I posed.

"Militia. If the enemy finds a way in and the citizens don't have a way out, they are sitting ducks. It will be a bloodbath. I'll post most around the wall and a hundred or so around the terrace of the gala."

Count Nicholo hiccupped. "I secured three hundred fire lancets. I will give them to you, I am sure it will help sway the greedy to remain loyal seeing as most of them have never fired off a fire hose before. I don't know a man who wouldn't want to try blast one of those things," he grinned when Brock agreed.

"Secured where?"

Nikki hiccuped and wavered in his chair. "In the garbage piles for next month's burning. Green fire-resistant crates, covered in soot and shit. I placed them next to the sewer line for easy distribution." Brock pushed a full canteen of water towards Nicholo. "Also, the restless are coming. We need to light the pyres, make ready the city."

Captain countered, "That will lure them in."

"They. Are. Coming." He managed to stay calm in his tipsy state. "I will volunteer to light them if it means lighting a fire under the asses of these pretentious knights and guards. Lighting them will take off the element of surprise for the city. We don't have much working in our favor, let us at least not be blindsided and have the option to die with dignity."

Zander grumbled, "Speaking of pretentious knights, a spot opened up in the Resig's entourage after the Queen's Knight, Karmic, died in the Pit. I'm going after it."

Cultee's sunken eyes shut as he lowered his chin in agreement with Zander's plan. My gut fluttered to my throat hearing Karmic's name. He was such an easy kill, one thrust under the scales of armor. That was that. Nothing thrilling about him stood out enough to be a royal favorite. Maybe, had I not killed him off so quickly I would have seen something worthwhile. I let my thoughts wind down before I showed something that resembled interest in the previous conversation on my downturned face.

Yolanda poured more syrup on her pancakes, I snuck my spoon under the cascading fluid to sample it. I went back for seconds. Drift spoke so low, it was almost incoherent to the table. "There are wraiths disguised as dukes and landholders. What fires are we lighting inside to reveal them?"

"The gift," Brock said.

He was countered by Drift's harsh words. "Will enlightenment dawn on a confused but living city, or will the battle of Landsfell be a story written before the gala guests lace up their shoes to attend?"

A heavy pause.

Zander's general lack of optimism and zest was felt by the table. Captain wasn't having any of it. "I'll ensure my unruly legion is ready in three days' time, armed with lancets, astute in the peripherals until called to battle. Count and Rhyolite, you will light the beacons and draw the defenders to stand guard. Drift, if they try to collect you for the venom ritual, let them."

"You want him injected?" I grunted.

"I want him to play along. That is why I agreed for him to try and obtain knighthood. We all know he will tear that conclave room apart before that poison shit touches his body." I hummed approvingly, Zander winked at me in my moment of concern for him. I ignored it. "Pleadian is negated by red blood. To break the salt circle, smudge your lifeforce across the parameters. Collette hinted that the prince himself is here among us." I swallowed. A prince with no name, no face, no worthy agenda. "The dukes will not be at the head tables during the ceremony. Three masked replicas will be seated at the four tables and the true dukes will move about the crowds for the night. I have not heard about the royal's diversion technique for the evening or if they plan to formulate one at all."

"Can't we just ask the prince at the gala about the wraiths, the Deadlands, the scouts?" I sighed, not bothering to hide how uninvolved I felt.

"We?" Cultee asked.

"I didn't memorize the tunnels for nothing. I am going dancing too," I stated.

"Dancing? What are you trying to retrieve from inside the manor?" My face warmed at his frank question. I avoided eye contact with the dreamers so as to not rope them into my panic. I lifted my green eyes and studied Cultee up on his bar stool looking more a tired general of war than a stately duke. "We are running out of time, if you decide to trust me, you have to do it soon." Zander's foot found mine under the table. Nothing intimate just our toes touched, just as Nikki's shoulder leaned into Zander. Passive absorption from his wovens.

Zander's twenty-one days were coming up quickly. "My family's death isn't a light conversation to be held at a bar. Find me at your convenience this week, I can make you tea." I opened my arms to the table. "You all are welcome for tea." *Your twenty-one days end the night after tomorrow, Zander. If this place is going down, I need an opportunity to get in and out with Cobar.*

Brock snorted, "Finally! It better be worth the wait or I will be disappointed." I elbowed him. "Now, let's finalize the plans for the coup at the gala."

I can provide a distraction while you search. I am good at that.

Yes, you are loud.

From beneath his dark stubble, his lips turned up. I thought about them on mine as they had been in the kitchen of Fort Fell, curious to how different the kiss would be if he was the one to initiate it. If I hadn't so resolutely shut him down, the stirring inquisitive woman in my core would have likely had her answers met. *How am I to focus when there is a stunning woman staring at me from across the table? All too willingly I will lick that syrup off your chin.* In my mental weakness, Zander slithered in and left me frazzled. Syrup would go well with his cool spiced taste.

I blinked, started at mt own thoughts. It took effort to listen to the plan unfold.

If it went off without a hitch, hundreds of thousands would still die, but we should have answers to prevent the spread of the infestation and a decent man giving orders to the Numaalian guards on the frontlines of the southern country. One who had fought side by side with them and would do so again. Delivering a wraith, paying men for hire, lighting the towers and convincing others to do the right thing.

That last item would be the hardest.

I felt better leaving than when I arrived at the bar. My truths would be known, shortly. What happened after that, didn't necessarily matter if I got Cobar to Keenan, Cultee was sworn in and Duke Stegin was in a grave.

I swirled my tea. What a lie I had told myself.

It *all* mattered. All these lives mattered, but saving them all in their blitheful unknowingness and unpreparedness was a daunting notion. A high mountain and heavy burden if I decided to take them on.

Nights were sleepless enough with the eighteen I killed visiting me often. I decided to stroll down the music district that had caught my attention since I first saw it on Petro's horse. Bodies tumbled into each other, laughter collided, children ran around skirts and buried themselves in powdery delights. I gave two coppers for a sugary pastry. I purchased another and boxed it in my side satchel. Yolanda would certainly enjoy the layers of flakey breads.

I tucked my sweater into the top of my pants and saw my feet moving to the cadence of the night. My boots made me a clumsy dancer. I stepped on two dance partner's toes prior to dismissing myself back to the sidewalks and less available to the participants; were I barefoot, I imagined myself swirling and frolicking like a summer breeze coming to thaw out this dark heart of winter. I was even more graceful with an Ilanthian sword.

The entire span of the street I walked up and down twice, when a seat on a swinging bench presented itself, I took it. The snow that fell was the beautiful type. Bright white against the blue sky, delicate and drifting down slowly as to be admired in all its intricacies. My arms strongly felt the bite of the chilly air when the winds changed. Prickly and alive. Refusing to turn in for the night, I tucked them stiffly under my arms.

Where are you?

I followed a delicate clump of snow with my eyes, watching it until it melted before I replied. *On a bench in the music district.*

Get somewhere with four walls and no audience. If anything happens, place your hands to the ground.

The prickliness turned electrical. *My arms are throbbing. What are you doing? What are you feeling?* I called back apprehensively. His emotional uneasiness before gave my body physical tremors. What the actual fuck was happening to my body?

Finding you.

Waiting for my arms to burn off or for lightning to shoot from them were not options. *Where Carnival Street intersects Fifth.* I stood, pretending to shop around a gem and jewelers, while scouring for four walls. *Broom closet or stable supplies?*

Which has a lock?

I strode further into the alley, shaking out the sharp pain in my hands. *Broom closet. More room too.* I sent, succumbing to crouching on my knees, pretending to tighten my boot as countless passed by with the intentions of buying goods and dancing on the main street behind me.

Good. Fen will find his way to us shortly.

Care to explain?

The ways of the Weaver are not something I am versed in. I just know when she is about to make herself known.

All he had to do was hint at the Weaver for strands of light to start pouring from my palms, pulling me in two separate directions. My limbs quaked, the Weaver threatened to tear them from my body.

Panic and a wild *need* were also pulling me. My body stiffened at the onslaught of feeling a desperate *thirst* for *something*. My mind muddied like a pond on a violently rainy day.

The strands of gold and blues were tightening as Zander came into sight. A breathless tangle of hair and shades of red as he leapt to my side, linking his hand with mine. The light between my hand and his throat disappeared with the contact, while my right hand sent a thin streamer across the city. Beckoning my *second* woven.

"On the ground, Wisteria," he reinforced. I had to step on my hand to ensure it wouldn't shoot back upwards.

How did you know this would happen?

You are not my first woven, I anticipated this to happen again at some point. The voltage in my chest told me it was soon. He merrily greeted a passing group of women, who flirted back with him behind wide laced fans. When they passed, he took to jiggling the lock behind him. Our thread appeared in the space between us. These pestering lights were determined to corrode me. Sweat clung to my sweater. I was itching to get out of it as much as I wanted to shed my skin of this relentless current screaming out in waves of magical storms.

Can everyone see it?

Yes. We are lucky you were sightseeing in the most chaotic and colorful sector. Regardless, we are not taking risks. Get in. He picked the lock.

"I can't move." I was repulsed with how helpless my voice sounded. Who was this woman hijacking me? A figure jumped down from a roof and landed next to me, fancy boots and all. The threads grew thicker, brighter with Nikki inches away. "Don't touch me."

Ah, yes. The woman hijacking me was the omnipotent Weaver of worlds.

"Up and in," Nikki said, his body shielding the alley from the cord of light attaching us. He didn't grab my hand.

"Did you want me to carry you?" Zander offered. He and the elemental entered the shed, clearing off a place to sit on the storage shelves. Them moving away was a magnet yanking me forward. Or a puppet and their marionette master.

The second notion was disgusting.

The day he carried me like a damsel would be the day I died. I moved slowly. Zander rubbed his face watching me. "I thought not."

I didn't crawl on all fours, nor did I roll. It was an ugly combination of the two in which my knees got sullied and my elbows stung as I clopped around.

The door shut behind me. There was no need for light, when the threads provided so much. The light was blinding, add my sweat glistening skin to reflect off and I shone like a beacon. Pressing my back against the corner and my palms into the ground, I willed the force to stop. It didn't, but I would gleefully accept a few minutes of relief just to wrap my head around the intensity of it all. Who cared if I had *two wovens*, I subconsciously accepted that fact weeks ago when learning about my first.

"Two lights. Two threads. Two wovens. Got it." But those two threads also have threads. My mouth was dry, my question came out as a pant. "Who belongs to who?"

The boys eased themselves into a seated position on the shelf, the gold and violet threads adjusted and stilled as they stopped moving. Zander and Nikki had pressed their foreheads together for a long intimate greeting, their arms stayed intertwined as they adjusted to their new close space. Happily resting their hands on each other's knees. Nikki spoke, "We have to interact with it to discern the role it wants us to have in each other's lives."

"Is that not what we've been doing these last weeks? Interacting?" I was yelling.

"We have, but we haven't explored everything. There is no pressure to—from us at least. In fact, I will advise against impulsive exploration and you'll do well to approach one strand at a time unless the Weaver is on a schedule." Nikki said factually, ignoring Zander who shifted his weight and almost collapsed the shelf that they perched on.

My chin clamped down. "I'm not fucking either of you."

Zander sighed and began to twirl his thumbs. "What a great suggestion. It can expedite the process of discovering which bond the three of us are entangled in." Nikki barked, aggressive enough to pull a sincere apology from Zander. "Sorry, I'm not helping the situation, I am aware. It is hard to let this unfold when I have feelings for you Wisteria. I know you are my *corlimor*. What humans would call a soul mate, true love, a forever bride." He left out the part where he was starving and infatuated with peaches.

My head shook. He was insane. And I told him as much. "No, you are not. You are insane."

"I am," he said, all calm and sweetly. How could he say such a ridiculous thing with a straight face?

My parents were soul mates, Zander and I were *not*. I had Anna. "Your feelings are not real. They are imposed." My legs found a vertical beam to kick against, helping me maintain the few feet of space. Goddess, it was hot in here. My neck and face were strained and cherry red.

My left arm shook with his anger that threatened to shatter my ulnar and radial bones. "Do not speak to me of what is real." Zander hissed. "This entire half of the world is unaware of a dreamer realm. A very *real* place. I am a very *real* person who has lived long enough to decipher my own emotions. *Real* emotions. You've felt them through our connection, don't tell me otherwise."

All the things I wanted to say died on the tip of my tongue. Yes, what he said was true. I felt them, his emotions. Perhaps I shared some of them, but I was too scared and too engrossed with my Anna to act on them. I plan to be dead by the time I recover from Anna's hold on my heart. "Will you be upset with me if I don't engage with you now? Or ever?"

"Upset that you are able to keep firm boundaries? Questioning what you don't understand? Never." I grinned. A weak, distressed grin. "You know you will be safe and honored if you choose to reciprocate, otherwise, you wouldn't have pulled me into a tent and fed me."

Also, correct. The bond that enforced what I had done had been alright. "What other types of woven bonds are there?"

Nikki leaned onto his knees, his arms flexed as he strung his fingers together. Zander's hand casually rested on his back. "All woven threads are rare, you need to recognize that. Many who have been stitched try to be private about them due to intimacy, misinterpretation, complicating marriages, or even loving an enemy. But eventually, they all emerge. And all are accepted. Welcomed. This is a blessing." As he spoke, he raised his arms up, our gold thread moved with it. I felt my hand being lured out. I tucked it away under my body weight.

I gritted at the liars, "This does not feel like a blessing."

"Zander and I are brothers, underneath that relationship, I am his to command. A loyalty bond is an easy way to think of it. This is the most common thread people speak of when they talk about an elemental finding their woven. There is also a twin bond, which splits one soul among two born infants. They are a match of equality. A protector bond, which is as it sounds. Amity bond, for plenty of sex and admiration."

I raised my brow. "Zander has unfounded infatuation."

"It is not unfounded. You are not ready to hear me confess my *real* feelings so I will be patient. Patient-*ish*. Even if it takes me another two torturous years," he whispered with a sharpness. My heart shuddered.

"I am not a salvageable lover. So, just stop," I directed. "Nikki, continue. Please."

Bless him, he did.

"The last one I'm aware of is the *corlimor* bond." My eyes darted between their chests, where each spouted a thread directly into me. "All bonds of devotion, love, admiration, lust, protection, and equality merged into one. The vibrant call them soulmates. The water wolves call them mates. Those lucky enough to find their *corlimor* call them a life partner, undeniable. A thread that ties two hearts together until it makes a glorious tapestry." He saw my eyes watching them both nervously. "To our knowledge, no elemental or otherwise has ever had two *corlimor*."

To that I stated nervously. "I doubt any of them had three hearts and donated one to an established woven. Who both then formed another second bond."

"Likely, no." His answer was curt enough to know they had already attempted to research and understand all the possible outcomes. I rubbed my sweat drenched brow on my shoulder.

My mouth was parched, but I had to risk knowing. So I asked, "What do you think I am to you Nikki? What is our bond?" The more I wondered, the less sense it all made. How the fuck did I, a woman who only slept with women and loathes investing in relationships, end up forced together with two wovens? Male wovens!

"One thread at a time, Wisteria or you will get overwhelmed," Nikki cooed.

"I already am overwhelmed!"

"Exactly. You are not ready for me. Consider me your protector woven until you choose to cross that line. You need protection from yourself these days. Until then, I will comfort, listen, guide and rest in close proximity." His voice was dark. A vortex of caution and excitement dragging me into oblivion. I followed the pull, it was a sweet darkness. The pain in my body stopped me from jumping into the vortex.

"This is going to kill me," I announced as they nonchalantly sat gazing at me.

"Also, no," Nikki said. "You are fighting against an unforeseen force to keep your composure. It is difficult."

"Why aren't you two being boiled alive?" I shot back with a short fuse.

The reply came in unison, too steady and strong to be anything other than their bond showing through. "Because we aren't fighting it."

Know-it-alls.

Nikki added, "And we aren't wearing a thick hideous sweater."

He was ignored. "When will she stop this torment?" I grumbled.

"We fought it for weeks," Nikki said. "It wasn't pretty either." I snickered at the thought of the two adolescents fighting their red web of fate in such a public manner. Sitting on my hands, however silly, was necessary, I told myself. "If you combust and go unconscious, I will be hauling you back. I can regulate your body temperature that way. Or you can choose to stop fighting her."

Zander found humor in that option. "Surrender is not in her vocabulary. Wisteria will choose the more arduous selection."

"I *choose* none of this. Prick."

The incubus clicked his teeth with a haughty grin. "Which of us did you say was edgy? Can you refresh my memory?" Zander gave a bright smile through strands of long hair that parted as a curtain would.

I flipped him the bird.

Nikki kicked his feet on the floor boards, gingerly making scuffing sounds. This was going to be a long night. Day. *Week*? I groaned seeing my feet begin to shift to where Nikki's were. My bones winced as I tugged them back and thrusted them against the wooden beam.

The loud music and laughter outside made time pass slower. My counterparts' unhurried, unperturbed breathing was starting to piss me off. They didn't even notice me struggling or breathing three times as fast as I should be, for they were staring at the lights from their chest and stroking it with their eyes.

Every minute, I clawed myself backwards. Gravity was no longer as I understood it. I didn't hold me to earth, but onto these dreamers.

My dirty hands wiped my forehead continuously. Salt streamed down my neck, there had to have been a puddle under me. "Either of you have water on hand?"

Across the closet, a shake of a full waterskin splashed. I licked my lips. "Come over and get it." My mouth gaped. It was Nikki who antagonized me.

"For fuck's sake, now you too? I can't mentally afford to be stuck with two jerks for the next few years. One is plenty."

"You like me," Zander replied before Nikki.

I growled, "That doesn't make you less of a provoking jerk."

"Told you, you like me." His joy danced down our bond, blue waves dotted with yellow rolled down the line. It was entrancing but the intensity was killing me.

I felt like sobbing. "This is Hell. I am sure of it."

My feet were moving on their own again. I hauled them back, my strength noticeably diminished. Nikki hadn't moved. His arm was still extended with the waterskin. His facial features remained pensive. I stared at that waterskin for what felt like hours, ignoring the electricity in the air and magnetism drawing all of us together. Too thirsty to think, I moved attention to Nikki's gold eyes. They shone as a transitioning yellow maple would catch the sun in autumn. "If I sit on that shelf, it will break."

A quirky smile flashed on the fox's face. "Compromise. We will meet you in the middle. We will come to the floor if you agree to that arrangement." The beam of light from my left hand shifted as Zander prepared himself to stand. Our bond tightened with the expectations.

I was quick to pull my hand out of the air and tuck it under the opposite elbow. My heart racing with every jerky movement. The males steadied themselves.

I shook my head. No. Not yet. "What will happen?" I didn't bother elaborating on the question. If they were destined to be my friends, they should have intuition of some magic shit. I felt my sanity slipping away.

Nikki straightened his violet dress shirt and his stiffened cuffs on his sleeves. His beautiful silk cape was disgruntled and in disarray beneath him. But the waterskin was the affection of my eye, reminding me how badly my throat burned. "We can sit side by side on the ground. You can get a drink of water and your muscles can relax. Neither of us will protest if you explore. We can converse, sleep, fight each other until the Weaver takes the threads from sight. The bond isn't painful when you stop fighting it."

I had a lot to say about the repulsive idea of wanting to explore either of them. Zander's cracked grin told me he felt my thoughts travel down the violet line.

A bead of sweat dripped into my eye. My world blurred more. I pressed my forehead into my sleeve, my sweater was heavy. It held all the moisture that was once within my body. I rubbed my lips together, they stuck. I stacked my feet beneath me, my ankles and knees failed to align. I could not stand and I would not ask for bloody help.

Asking for water was enough.

I hit the floor with my fists. The threads of purples and golds and whites trembled.

Zander's low vibrating voice splashed onto my back like a fast-incoming tide flooding ashore. All of what I was feeling—or was about to feel— seemed unavoidable. "All you have to do is nod." His statement was both loaded and unburdening. Tempting and terrifying.

Nodding would be diving into the complexities of unknown threads of fate and simultaneously giving into the Weaver, finding momentary freedom from this struggle.

Eye contact with them felt sheepish.

I kept my head down and hid the delicious reprieve that came a quarter of a second after I nodded.

Chapter Twenty-Three

Crouched on either side, my two wovens placed one firm grip on each of my shoulders. Their touch was the oasis my body needed after the Weaver dragged me through the desert. I was certainly crying from relief.

My own hands clenched in fists under my forehead as I rocked back and forth on all fours, calming my frenzied nervous system. I shook at their touch, which felt like heaven. The darkness helped my headache. The threads vanished when we touched, reemerging the moment we separated. "Do you want that sweater off?" Zander asked softly. "Fen can facilitate better without it."

"Can't," I grumbled, once I was sure I would not vomit if I opened my mouth. "You will overreact. But I will drink water." I lifted my head, a waterskin brushed my lips and waited for my mouth. The liter was guzzled in one go. I nodded my appreciation and used the shelf to pull my torso upright, into a kneeling position. Unsure of what to do with my balmy hands, I placed them on the floor and lowered me into a seated position, irritated by how exhausted this short rendezvous had made me.

Nikki's palm rested at the base of my skull, pulling heat and tension out with his massaging. The air between us was humming loudly. "Where do you want us?" he wondered out loud. I felt for him in the dark and made contact with his silky shoulder. I traced the decadent texture until I found his bare skin, just under the bob of his throat. His flesh was nicer than the silk. I spun my fingertips around his collar as a means of forcing myself to stop caressing him.

"This is ridiculous," I whimpered. No use in apologizing, they expected just foolish behavior from me.

My fingers were already reverting back to stroking silk and skin, they found a chain around his neck on which an acorn was strung. Nikki said nothing nor did he stop my purposeless fondling of his own sweat coated skin. I retraced his throat unwillingly. The bob dipped as he swallowed.

"The fact you think I will overreact if you take off the bulky, wet sweater is ridiculous. Do you think so little of my control and pursuit of you?" Zander said, the air around the three of us hummed louder, morphing into the buzz of static. It made my teeth chatter.

"Shush!" I snapped, swatted at him in the dark. My own voice was too loud for my skull to handle. "Gimly marked my neck to piss you off," I snapped as I touched Nikki's neck brazenly, my fingers inches up to his smooth jawline wanting more of whatever *this* was. My left hand shook as Zander's emotions surged through it. Anger. He growled. The thickness of the rumble and the whistle at the end alerted me that his canines were protruding.

Nikki let a breath go by before asking, as patiently as the first time, "Where do you want us?"

"Sitting?" I suggested.

Nikki shook his head at my words. "How confident. I will not move until you direct me." I could have wept at his attempt to make me feel somewhat less powerless and pitiful. It worked.

"Sit."

I decided that seated would be the most comfortable for all parties involved, especially if this was a lengthy arrangement. They both kicked their legs out from under them. Mentally, I sorted out the image of the three of us. My heart pattered, while my soul sang with a growing sense of... wholeness.

I pushed Nikki's chest until he was no longer able to scoot backward. "Nikki with your back against the wall. I will go here," I said, putting myself between his open knees. My back eased onto his chest and his legs came up around me. I found Zander's forearm and tugged him towards us. He was too vast for my arms to wrap all the way around him. "Zander. You go on my lap, where you can be coddled."

No rebuttal. He laid himself onto the floor, my lap his pillow. Just out of inquisitiveness I ran my fingers over his sternum too. My hand implanted itself over the scars above his heart. It was weighed down by invisible lead, unable to lift it. I left it there and nestled against the warm, firm body behind me, realizing at that moment neither of the pair had their hands on me. Our contact was plenty and initiated solely by me. There was comfort, power, in that.

I inhaled the hot, dense air. "The current in here feels like it is going to spark an explosion." I stared around the dusty broom closet. Clinging just around our bodies was a white outline. "I can see it."

"It is an aura. It should ease when the threads disperse. It might crack sooner with your feistiness and imposed sweater sauna." Zander said. "It's also a clear sign of the physicality of our bonds. Did your body light up when you let Gimly put his mouth on you?" I dug my nails into his skin.

"I didn't *let* him."

Zander wiggled to look up at me from my lap, his beautiful hair scattered across the filthy floorboards. His eyes were both blue and beaming. "No? Then why is he not dead?"

"He dangles Brock's life in front of me for compliance. He is my friend, the one I choose and he means a lot to me," I swallowed. My nails stopped digging into his chest. "Yolanda and Sage want him dead too; they have better reasons than a little hickey."

There was a clicking of his fangs. "When I mark you, it won't be by force, it won't be little and it will be damn more than a hickey."

"I am not a piece of meat to be bitten or a toy to be claimed," I grunted, tossing my head back onto Nikki's shoulder. He lowered his head to rub his chin along my hairline and temple. He sniffed my scalp and ignored my argument with his friend. "Have you ever bitten Nikki?"

"Frequently."

I felt my face skew with confusion.

Nikki spoke in my ear, his warm words settling on my spine. "I often ask him. When I am in the Overlord's Keep among Atticus and his seven sons coming and going, I flaunt my bite as a warning, not a mark of pride or lust. It protects my scent from being picked up by others. He marks me without taking from me these days." Zander made a guttural noise. "Which yes, in our early bonding decades in the name of pursuing sexual exploration and the extent of our thread, I let him give and take from me and I him. Our love is one of brotherhood and purest well wishes for another, not romantic. The physicality was lacking."

Zander crossed his arms across his abdomen. "A short weekend that was. I don't enjoy bland figs, but I ate them."

"Figs are fabulous. Far better than being suffocated by sweaty bat wings," he retorted into my ear.

A giggle escaped. "I presumed you've both sampled a wide variety of fruits." Our aura glowed a little brighter. I grew more than a little warmer. "Speaking of indulging in fruits, this seems a timely opportunity to inform you I have only ever had one type." Nikki's mouth curved into a smile that I felt on my skin. Zander looked dumbly at me, seeking clarification. "I only sleep with women."

Zander pointed his finger closer to me. "Correction. You have only slept with women."

I didn't have the energy to bicker with him. Shutting my eyes, I ignored the finger in my face and submerged my senses in the drone sound that was both inside my inner ear and around the shed. It rang louder than three thousand bells and gongs. My palms pressed over my ears, squeezing my head in between. My hairline was wet with sweat. The intensifying aura was responsible, for I was no longer fighting the Weaver and the two figures next to me were clouds of heat. "Let's just snap the aura," I said through gritted teeth.

"It will peak on its own," Nikki educated. "It won't be longer than a day. If you faint, do I have your blessing to ensure your organs don't get cooked?"

"What does it entail?"

"My hand on your core. From your center I can absorb heat and hatred. My hands do not roam and will be lifted after you are normothermic."

I asked, "Where does my heat go?"

"Into me. My blood lineage of Dradion and Drommal disperse it and exchange it into power. It is harmless to me and if I don't pull all your heat out and turn you into a frozen corpse, then it is beneficial to you at this time, Wisteria."

I lifted up my shirt, just to the bottom of my ribs. "Do it," I directed firmly as I knew he would request. My flat navel flexed with my short, shallow breathing. My skin was slick with sweat. "Now. I refuse to faint in the broom closet and more so loathe the thought of you two carrying me like I was a lush in a tavern."

In the crook of my neck a dark voice scattered my thoughts. "Good girl." Nikki didn't give me time to digest the savageness in his words before his hand pressed on my stomach, just above my belly button. It was sweltering under his touch the coolness came, like little rivers flowing through my body, seeking and destroying pools of lava.

He pulled the heat out from my toes in my boots and from the roots of my hair in a cooling gust that felt akin to a spring breeze running through my veins. When I shivered, the wind slowed. The wetness of the sweater felt like being wrapped in a damp towel in the dead of winter. Which was the reality. With our aura as bright as it was, I watched his hand retreat all the way back to his side, I also saw goosebumps form on my wrist and felt them zoom up my arms. "We will repeat this process later if nothing changes. Tell me to take off your sweater," the dominant and dark voice continued.

I elbowed him in his ribs. Nobody, myself included, would be stripping in this broom closet. Nikki leaned back against the wall, immobile save for the rise and fall of his chest.

Zander was rolling around on my lap, an oversized puppy dog, trying his best to make himself comfortable. "Was I your first kiss with a man?" Two sets of canines were visible in his grin, his uppers and lowers were showing in his slacked mouth. More wolfish than puppy.

"Can't either of you hold a normal conversation? One that doesn't involve the removal of my sweater or what fruits I had?"

Zander rubbed his nose on my leg just above my knee. His hands stretched out on the floor around us. "I love knowing I was the first man to have had that little tongue ring flickering about in my mouth. When I initiate the second kiss as an active participant, I promise to have you gasping from my mouth as if I was all the air your body will ever need."

"Is anyone listening to me?" I shouted, straining my neck. "Tell me *literally* anything else!"

"Was I the first man to see you naked when I helped you dry off the night I found you on the roof?"

I bent my knee and knocked him in the face. "No, you were not," I gritted out while raising the heel of my other foot to kick him. He caught it and wrestled it under his arm. He pouted at my answer, the firm flex of his jaw line caught the aura's light which was brighter.

"Was it Brock? I promise I won't kill whoever it was." He didn't sound harmless. Not at all.

I shook my head, repulsed at his suggestion. "It was the fox. When we went to the pond and hot spring on horseback."

Zander softened. Turning to peaceful putty in my lap. "Good."

"Good?" Could they hear themselves? "Do you two share all your partners?"

"No. Not ever. We honored each other's privacy and intimate affairs. Until, a particular woodlander linked us together more deeply." Zander confirmed looking behind me onto his brother with honest eyes. Something in the pit of my stomach unknotted.

Nikki spoke cooly now, "Incubi don't share. Historically, never. Elementals either keep to ourselves or share pleasure among many, but never our woven. Our tastes in partners have been radically different." He let a particularly strong wave of electricity pass over us and zing across the room.

"Tell me about your past relationships," I said to the room. Anything to get Zander distracted from his fascination with my lack of experience with a man.

Nikki shrugged. "The most *serious* relationship I had, if you could call it that, was with my cousin's friend who lives in Akelis. That lasted all of seven years. I prefer a playful approach to relations, being woven to Zander does come with unconventional understandings. For example, going to war against an undead-dead enemy or spontaneously living in Numaal for years may be seen as a turn off. A lot of our adventures have a high risk of fatality."

"Higher the risk, the higher the reward," I said.

"I'll agree with that."

Zander chuckled. "Don't forget Imuik. You were madly in love with her for six weeks. You convinced yourself to live by the river bed and in a house of sticks to be closer to her. You slept in mud and your own filth."

"Shut up. I was spelled," Nikki hissed. His tone was unamused.

"A water nymph used a love potion on him and traded ten years off her life to get a fae to glamour her more appealingly to attract Fen's fancy. He would have married a mud dweller and sired her hatchlings had Wyatt not found an antidote." Zander's face was lit up with sheer joy. "Best six weeks of my life, by the way."

"Fuck you, dude." Nikki's head rolled side to side. "That potion is ten times stronger than any sway you can pull. It hit my hearts not just my head."

"I only swayed you one time," Zander defended. "When you didn't obey the order to retreat from bloodshed. I wasn't about to abuse your loyalty bond so I summoned a little sway to encourage you to move your fluffy tails to safety. If I had more time and the Draugr weren't on my ass, I would have properly begged you, oh mighty elemental."

I wiggled my legs. "Since you enjoy the sound of your own voice, Zander, tell me the full story of how your ex led darling Nikki into a labyrinth to be slain and how you ended up with such a woman in the first place. Wherever you want to start, I will let you."

The energy soaking our connection was surprisingly unrestricted and tranquil. He gave a big exhale and shifted onto his back. His eyes cleared as they found mine. "She was a family friend. Generations back, her parents and grandparents worked closely with my father and Malick, they were fae and helped in magic regards. When I met her, I didn't feel like an outsider to Veona. She showed me the ropes of the Veil and how to use my charm and sway in the Overlord's house and even in the White Tower.

"It wasn't until Malick gave me his blood did she start aggressively insisting I approach the Empress and Emperor to be the third party in their trilogy. The Veil was plenty for me. I refused her manipulation for thirty years. She believed Fennick was holding back my potential and tying me to the dreamer realm with his elemental nature thriving there under the Eternal Elm. Her family and a society of renegade fae, who supported fae magic ruling the Veil, set to have Fennick killed thinking that would convince me to take the third throne. She would be at the trilogy's side, a fae with influence and power.

"When I found Fen drowning in a water nymph's ice hole. I killed her. I unleashed Oyoko's power and turned her traitorous heart and body into dust. My magic wiped out all life cutting through the center of Veona. I am happy she is dead, but grieved the ninety-four citizens who I sent beyond in my careless fit of fury. Where my magic struck, remains black. Unworkable land, a forever reminder to myself and the people of Veona that Zander, the Lord of Darkness, has power but poor control. The scar of Veona." My air stalled in my lungs. "My father saw to her parents and the renegades' execution after much interrogation and stopped what we hoped was the first and only caravan of fae to send communication and weapons to Numaal's king at that time, Jeorge. All while I saw to repent for my sins by promising the families of those I murdered to make their home a safer place. I will do it. Even if that means painfully locking Oyoko's magic away day after day within myself and turning Numaal inside out to find the source of the lost souls. For them, I have to."

His determination was admirable. One would even say stubborn. It was no wonder the Weaver saw us fit to spend our days butting heads and keeping each other on our toes. "You will find the wraith's origins. You will stop the influx of lost souls. You will protect your home." I had the utmost confidence in what I told him. "You will also stop throwing yourself into a self-induced purgatory. Martyrdom is not the way to earn their forgiveness nor work on forgiving yourself for a mistake."

"My *mistake* costs many their lives and livelihood," he said, brushing his chin and cheek along the fabric of my pants.

"Your mistake uprooted an unfriendly society of fae renegades in cahoots with heart-eating royals. You probably saved millions from a patriarchy of mixing pretentious fae and Goddess killing kings."

His sigh was unenthusiastic. "You still believe that humans ate Anuli's heart?"

"I am not ruling it out," I stood by my mentioning. "I'll have to ask Cultee when I tell him about Cobar."

"What day are you planning on breaking into the manor?"

"The day after next. The same evening that I sit down with Brock, Yolanda and the captain. Hopefully, I can introduce them to my little brother and they can see we aren't so different. Not really." I swallowed. The air was harsh on my throat. I eyed the emptied waterskin.

Nikki spoke, "Count Nicholo will be in attendance."

"Obviously."

"And if you are unsuccessful in retrieving Cobar? Whether he is not there, you get caught or he can't cross the pleadian—what will you do then?"

I craned my neck to view his face. I gave him a firm scowl. "Where is your optimism?"

"Buried in the same place as your common sense." He raised his brows comically.

"He will be there. Alive and well. My blood will break the salt circle. We will make it out safely and onto the boat, with whoever wants to come along, before the war of the wraiths descend on this city." I gave a warning glare.

He returned it with a challenging smirk. "Don't you want to find out where his mother and sister went? Don't you want to stick around and see what becomes of Duke Satoritu and the infected others?" My heart raced with each word he said. "Stay and help Yolanda find Bastion? Stay and watch Zander get knighted or successfully get Cultee sworn in as Duke? Stay and fight for the six hundred thousand humans who will perish? You are one hell of a fighter, you don't think you could defend a city block with ease?" My hand flew over his mouth.

I was weak. I was selfish. He knew it. Zander knew it. I felt tears form and roll down my reddening cheeks.

"I... I..." I fished for words. "My heart cannot hold more right now. It will fail me, if I fail them all."

Nikki watched a tear fall onto his silk shirt, which I had wrecked with my sweat stains already. What was another drop of moisture? "I have one more heart to give."

Quickly, I turned away and buried my face behind my fingers. The tears I shed were tenfold of what they were seconds ago. "Who says shit like that?" My voice was raised.

"Your woven. Your friend," Nikki said casually as if he agreed to bring me a cube of sugar for my tea. "Calm down. You are going to overwork yourself and we have no more water or proper ventilation in here." Gods, I didn't even know what I was feeling anymore or for what reason I kept crying. Maybe fainting and riding the rest of this night out unconscious was the wiser plan.

"Pst," Zander called me. "Hey, little flower?" I nudged him with my knee to show I heard him. "Shall I sing for you?" That sounded glorious. I nodded rapidly. My face remained covered.

The language of the Eternals rolled off his tongue, his teeth shortened permitting the clear cut tone to pour out and over me. I basked in it like a flower in a ray of sun. Soaking in each trill and valley of his magnificent voice. I knew not what he said, but I knew in my heart it was a serenade. A song just for me. A song specifically for this moment. His singing distracted my ears from the relentless loud aura which now lit up the entire closet. "More?" I asked, sensing my tears had slowed.

"After Fen has cooled you off a bit, I will oblige. You can't enjoy my gifts if you droop into a wilted willow." I shook my head at the attempt of a pun, blinking at our glowing flesh. Nikki was examining his skin too, but not as closely as he was eyeing the door. "What do you hear, Fen?"

My own breath I held, trying to hear what the dreamers did. I heard the blasted aura crackling like a pot of water on boil.

The male behind me spoke, "A young girl from the bead store. She is coming to get the dustpan in the corner and the bucket of coiled silver wire on the shelf."

Zander announced, "I jammed the lock when I closed us in."

"I hear the keys in her grip. We have two minutes to come up with a plan."

Zander lifted himself on his knees, his shirt coming untucked in the process. "I have enough in my stores to sway a mind and cast an obscura."

"You will be flying around the city after that unless you feed and you don't enjoy figs, so you better concoct another plan," Nikki cautioned. I had no magic or knowledge of the threads. I was utterly useless and sat there waiting to be discovered by a girl from a bead shop.

One of us got inspired.

We watched Zander take to his feet and disrobe his torso, aggressively popping off buttons as he stripped. I turned my face to the door. As if I could see something beyond that they didn't already sense coming. What I truly did was deprive my eyes of ogling the deep lines and shapes that plummeted into his black leather pants, just above the shiny horselord belt buckle.

Anna had been softer than me. With curves and shapes that formed against my lean body and outline of my own abdominal muscles. The movement behind me distracted my already disorganized mind. Nikki pardoned himself as he stood to fix the two light bulbs hanging from tin circles. The threads were evident as they moved about busily within the ten-foot parameter.

My arms were heavy as I latched onto one of their legs. It was Zander's.

I flinched away as a light flickered on with sparks. "Hello there," Zander said above me.

"Hi," I replied. My right arm was reaching for Nikki who was standing on the shelf swearing loudly as he fused copper electric wires together. The need to touch them both again catered my thoughts. It was ridiculous. Unacceptable, pining behavior. Yet, the Weaver reduced us all to this state of need. They were handling themselves with much more dignity than I.

Zander turned his attention to our elemental. "Any brighter?" The dangling tin lightbulbs were pathetic, yet they did their intended job and took away the stark white glow of our aura. What intention Zander served shirtless and staring down at me latched on his leg... I had an idea, but I didn't want to acknowledge it. Not yet.

Nikki hopped off the shelf and was across the closet with his ear next to the door before I blinked.

A wide calloused palm lowered into my direct vision. I grabbed it with shaking hands. Zander hoisted me upright. Rejecting his touch on the base of my spine would send me crumpling to the floor. Not wanting another moment of sitting, crawling or clawing at that dirty ground, I leaned on his bare chest. His skin glowed. All his scars illuminated, I found them pretty. "There is only one thing two men and a woman would be doing in a locked shed at night," I spoke onto his skin, his jaw locked when he peered down at me.

"It has to be believable," was his response. I unbound my long hair and tossed it over my shoulders. The heat and sweat clinging everywhere would be playing to our benefit. "We are not having sex tonight," he clarified, kicking off his own boots.

I snorted. Obviously we couldn't. "We can't have sex now or ever. You would break me in half."

Nikki shook with laughter, holding a finger to his lips to silence us as Zander opened his mouth to retort. Outside was a discernible sound of a stubborn lock. I steadied my woozy body and waited as the fumbling continued on for several more seconds.

The girl must have walked away because Zander started talking. "I will not break you, Wisteria."

"I studied math and anatomy. I estimate I am a quarter of your size when you are in dreamer boy form." I pulled away enough to imagine him another foot tall, more muscular and with assumably a well-endowed incubus trait. I just shook my head horrified. "You won't break me in half, you will shred me in six pieces. It is not physically possible."

His fingers pressed into my lower back. "It is very possible. Would you like me to prove it to you?"

Nikki butted in, "She is returning with her uncle. Now would be a great moment to rid yourself of that hideous sweater."

"Says the man in full Count Nicholo costume! Why have you gotten into character?" Zander held me in one hand and undid his belt with the other.

Nikki shrugged casually. "Because you haven't told me to strip."

Gods did I want to punch him. "Do you get off on being dominated or are you just trying to give me a scant feeling of control in this fucked up Weaver tapestry?"

"Both," he stated simply.

I saved myself the embarrassment of demanding him to strip and did it for him. Clenching his silky collar in my grip, I ripped downward. Delicate silver buttons and loops were torn and dropping to the floor like shimmering confetti. I swiped his dagger to cut the tie of his cloak around his neck before shoving it back in his belt loop. His tattoos were a dark and complicated contrast to the aura clinging to his skin. Where Zander's torso mimics a sunburst, his was a web of dark stories. Intricate and detailed.

"You see to the rest," I grunted, turning away as his obliques flex under the slightest movements. His ink stained skin and lean muscles made him look terrifying and wild. He was bare from the beltline up when he stepped into my side view. They waited, even though we were seconds away from being found out. They waited. "My master tattoo can't be seen."

"It won't," Nikki reassured. "I will be behind you. My back to the wall, your back on me. When our audience arrives do I have permission to roam my hands? Nowhere private."

Knowing I was about to dive deeper into an experience of unforeseeable intimacy with my new *male* friends, my voice shook, but I managed to reply. "Yes." Before fear reentered, I added. "Nikki, take off my sweater." He peeled the fabric off and tossed the wet mass onto the floor. It was liberating. A faint moan escaped my lips.

Zander purred hearing my noises. He stood dripping in his godly glory. My body quivered with anticipation as he ogled me with hunger. As if I was a Goddess on a pedestal for worship. *Ready?* Zander called down our open line.

Yes, I said, keeping eye contact with his flaming blue irises. His fingers encircled my waist. He effortlessly lifted me off the ground, allowing me to secure my legs to either side of his hips. Heat rushed instantly to my core and my thighs clamped around him tighter, hoping to hide the obvious. Then he moved one of his hands to grip my ass as the other moved my hair aside so he could view the reddened nip on my neck. His mouth descended over that same sensitive spot between my ear and shoulder, he didn't bite atop Gimly's mark. Instead, he begun to lick up the beads of sweat accumulating on my skin. His tongue spun in circles, long and lazy circles, across my clavicle and when he decided to lean me back to lick me from navel to chin, my sternum nearly split in half with exhilaration. I swore my heart fell out of my chest.

My mouth watered for him as I watched him lust after me so sinfully. So purely. So absolutely.

I was panting and he hadn't even kissed my mouth yet. He gave a smug look of self-satisfaction as he eased my body into the awaiting embrace of Nikki, who firmly held my figure so I would not slip out of either of their holds. Nikki's bare chest on my flesh burst every capillary in my face. "You are safe," he said in my ear.

This time I replied. "I know."

His heat swarmed over me. The hand on my thigh was charged with a force that should have terrified me. Only it didn't. It was burning into my flesh only to intrigue me. There were countless new beads for Zander to slurp up with that skillful mouth of his. I wanted to weep from the need building. Craving him, I pulled his mouth closer.

His lips were salty from their travels around my torso. I relished them as if they were sweet. He pulled my lower lip into his mouth, sucking it until it was red and swollen. Hissing, he released it and dove gently into my mouth and coaxed my tongue out to caress his. There was no need for coaxing. My hands wrapped themselves around his neck and tangled themselves in his hair. I held him to me, forgetting how weak and overwhelmed I was minutes ago.

His taste was cool and spicy. His kiss was unrelenting. Which was a lovely thing because I didn't want him to stop. No. At that moment I would happily be torn into six pieces knowing Nikki would put me back together again.

The hand that was on my ass cheek squeezed in a greedy, corporal manner to which I let out a gasp and moved my thin fingers around his neck, threatening his airway. I tightened my grip on his neck and felt him smile and shift his hips deeper into me. As his hard length rubbed into me, I collided harder with Nikki's sweat slicked chest.

A whisper of a warning came in the form of a lock breaking open.

A cold gust of air burst into the room. Nikki's hands now felt like tongues of flames licking sensually and stroking their way closer to my breasts. The deep ache was fully awakened between my legs. Zander broke our kiss enough so that in my blurry peripheral vision I made out two figures standing in the doorway. "What do you say you leave us three to finish our business and I'll leave you three gold coins on your shelf when we are done here? We all can walk away satisfied tonight, eh?"

The worried uncle set his niece behind him, his apprehensive focus on me. He thought I was in distress. Another squeeze on my ass. I grinned boldly. "When you two are finished ravaging me I doubt I'll be able to do much walking."

The pair in the doorway gaped a little longer, weighing the options. The girl's uncle sent her off after catching a glimpse of our debauchery. He raised a stern finger at her when she didn't run off.

Zander cupped my face in his hand, his steady thumb parted my lips before he merged with them. I struggled to catch my breath, but gravitated to him to happily have the rest of my soul and sanity sucked out. I arched my back when warm fingers scattered across the erogenous zone below my belly button at the same time strong wet lips kissed between my breasts. My wicked mind conjured up wild fantasies of them devouring me and tending to the throbbing between my legs.

There was a high-pitched scream and a faint shatter of glass. My eyes flew open. The artificial lighting had erupted, our cover had been compromised. The figures peering into the closet stood gaping at our glow, which pulsated with life of its own.

Nikki grabbed Zander's forearm, low lit gold flames perceivable around his fingertips. "Don't," Nikki advised with lethal undertones, searing his woven's flesh. I smelt the singe of hair and skin.

"There is no other option," his statement was as heavy as the blanket of darkness he cast over our aura, diminishing it significantly. An obscura. His eyes caught on those of the unlucky two to have intruded tonight. I watched the Lord of Darkness convince them to take what items they came here for and reform their memories of the night as easily as molding clay. When the door closed, a famished crescent horned incubus enfolded me into his arms and continued right where we had left off with the obscura gone and our threads blazing.

Only now, he was determined to consume me.

I was tempted to let him.

Chapter Twenty-Four

When the audience left, Nikki's hands dropped from my body and returned to the wall behind him. Just as he promised. His body stiffened as our show concluded.

Zander, however, made no such promise and spun his tongue desperately around the tip of mine, his fangs nibbling my plumping pink lips. "You both need to slow down, we have to talk *this* through." Behind me was an all too rational voice encroaching on my growing desires. I ignored him and pulled Zander's hair to the side to wrap my hands around his horns. I stroked them under his approval.

"Mmm, yes," he growled into my mouth, opening his eyes wider. My grip around his crescent horns slacked when fatigue burned through my arms and they were forced to fall. The back of my head rested on Nikki's shoulder, while I detached from the kiss to breathe.

I needed the heat taken from me, another liter of water and an orgasm. In no particular order. The room was blinding, I am sure the cracks in the foundation seeped light to the outside. "Will the closet catch fire?" I glanced at Nikki who was red in the face and just as sweaty as I.

Nikki huffed against my neck, his lips skirting across my sweat beaded skin. I fought with my body not to turn and face him. "The count's room is safer. Our aura consists of electricity. I don't know which is responsible for the burnt-out lights, that or your arousal." I wiggled my hips at the mention and Zander stroked my thighs in response. Nikki let out a long exhale. "Now, we worry about fainting, fire and a feeding. Are you intending to serve yourself, Wisteria?" The voice next to my ear was too serious for the moment and I was not capable of processing much other than I was hot and wanting a release.

"I think so," I gasped into Zander's face which hovered right next to Nikki and I with a jaw unhinged, delighting in my reply. His splatters of white more prominent across his brow and eyelashes with the magic illumination. His blue eyes wide with lust, a sinkhole of necessity.

His head shook firmly. "Wisteria, that answer does not give consent nor direction." My eyes began to water from the sweltering heat pressure of deciding. One that my body clearly had made for me.

"I will feed you, if I don't faint first." Knowing Nikki's odd behavior, I grabbed his hand and wrapped it around me, pressing it tight to my belly where it was when he worked his elemental magic for the first time. Our fingers knotted together as I held him in place. The storm of warm and cooling rivers rushed through my extremities as he began to remove the excess heat.

Chills and perspiration tingled over me as Zander unfastened my pants and tore them off.

Dropping the entirety of my weight into our woven's arms, Zander got on his knees. Nikki held me vulnerably *open* and upright for our woven's convenience.

My heart skipped at least five beats watching Zander easily maneuver my bare legs onto his shoulders, licking his lips and eyeing his next meal. The wetness between my legs soaked through my panties, which he snapped when he tore them aside to reveal a dripping and eager pussy. "I am in complete control. I will never hurt you." His words were intense and profound. I believed them. "Fen. After this, we flux. Brace yourself and her."

Zander gave several nips to the inside of my thighs as he gravitated towards my spread rosy petals. Riverets of my pussy juice had already made tiny streams down my legs. He was enchanted by what he saw. A roguish grin emerged when he caught sight of the metal hoop above my clit. "It's pierced," he announced in fond disbelief. "Good, this event will be a first for both of us." His statement beckoned pride. Part of me swelled with satisfaction knowing I was his first *any* sort of experience for being over one hundred and ninety years old.

He slowed his breathing and watched me smile down at him from behind my pubic bone. The copper wires in the ceiling broke and zaps of currents shot across the room. Both dreamers growled protectively. Urgency rang through all of us. There was no time for a drawn-out dinner.

A hand caressed my ass and elevated it slightly to bring my opening level with his mouth. The walls around us shuttered with the vibration of our aura which was suffocating the three of us. We were all slick with sweat. My hair fell across Nikki's chest, wrapping on him like drizzles of chocolate. Zander introduced his tongue to my vulva, diving desperately into the folds and swallowing the honey that flowed from my opening.

My left hand secured itself around the base of his right horn as my clit demanded more pressure and attention. He brought his thumb onto my groin to manipulate the blood flow building in my sensitive nub while his strong tongue entered me, working its way deeper until he found it. The spot inside that made my bones shake and my brain fail me. I rolled my hips against his face and Nikki's body, which remained statuesque and unwavering amidst all the messy pheromones.

My lids fluttered, rolling my head back onto Nikki. "Fuck," I groaned into the closet. Zander sucked the swollen bud on the top of my slit until I swore again from the delicious abuse.

I gyrated until the incubus learnt my rhythm and pace. He worked my body for me knowing exactly where and when I needed to be licked and with what pressure. A fast study. For that I was grateful. I had no more energy to exert, only until to come.

"Oh, God Zander," I whimpered, pressing my shoulders backwards to give Zander more access to my imminent pleasure.

"You are praying to me now?" He smirked wickedly.

"Shut up and make better use of that tongue." He did. Fuck was his mouth utterly magical.

I was walking a thin line, seconds away from falling over the edge. He gave me two more thrust of his tongue and finger that sent me over the cliff. With his horn in my hand and my legs around his head we moved as one. My orgasm set off an explosion of light, which Zander tossed an obscure over after he drank in my sexual energy. He palmed my pussy letting me ride out the rest of my orgasm.

Such a gentleman.

"Now," Nikki grumbled at Zander who stood to embrace the pair of us.

No longer did I have a body. I was nothing more than a conscious gust of wind flying high above Carnival Street of the music district.

When my body reformed, it was on the floor. Our threads were white hot lightning. Zander was still propped up between my legs gleaming in peach juice from his nose to his chin while Nikki lay entangled with me, my unruly right hand never released him and it was still firmly pressed to my naked body inches away from the area Zander had just got done exploring with his mouth. His tattooed torso pressed against mine. His hearts thumping in his stoic chest.

I shook his hand free and rolled away. He gave a sarcastic chortle and whispered, "We are beyond the point of feeling shy, wouldn't you say? But, let's keep you modest, little vixen." He reached for the nearest sheet, a black silk one, and draped it over my shoulders, pleased as I moaned at the decadent texture. Beneath his humor, his lips were cracked, his skin grayed, his legs held a tremor. I was not alone in this torment.

Zander was spry, but weariness rattled the two of us who hadn't just eaten.

I was on my knees glaring at the ceiling of Count Nicholo's bedroom. His windows were blocked and boarded, as if he had been preparing for this moment. "Weaver, enough!" I gasped with a scorched throat.

I had no moisture left to cry. So, I begged and bartered. "I swear on Anna's corpse, and if I survive the weeks ahead," I added as a later thought. "that I will live out my life with these woven to whatever end, in whatever capacity, if you stop the lightshow now. The threads and aura are too much. I see you. I hear you. Please, turn it off!"

Either the Weaver heard me and complied or when I fainted, I smacked my skull because blackness licked my vision when the world went dark.

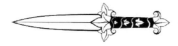

It was cozy on Count Nicholo's bedroom floor among comforters, blankets, sheets and pillows. I stretched my weary limbs in the mounds of softness. The melodious whirl of a fan and the steady respirations of a person nearby were the two subtle sounds my ears gathered. The deafening buzz of the aura was gone. I opened my eyes and adjusted to the darkness. A dim lamp in Nikki's living area remained on, possibly for me to find my way to the bathroom and catch sight of the full pitch of water next to the door.

I crawled to it.

My mouth was so dry from yelling, moaning, crying and kissing, that it was stuck shut. I pried it open and cautiously sipped my first glass of water fearing I may choke. The second, third and forth went down much faster. There were nectarines in a bowl. I peeled and ate two. The sugar rush sharpened my mind, enough to where I cared to investigate the lump of blankets next to me despite already knowing who was under them. Holding the silk fabric under my arms I shimmied across the menagerie of bedspreads and took two layers of pillows off Nikki's head.

There were deep-set circles under his eyes that didn't compliment his usual golden complexion. Sleep was the best method to remedy them, so I left him undisturbed. I buried him with the feathery pillows and left to find the shower. My skin felt as if all the salt in the ocean was stuck on it. The sticky sensation reminded me of cliff jumping with Anna in the peak of summer. When the sun would dry our skin, we would be left salty on the Cliffs of Sound.

A new pair of narrow fitting navy pants, a fresh tunic and white sheer bra lay folded next to towels and floral soaps. A thoughtful deed from one of my wovens. Zander, undoubtedly, had gone back to the duke's manor with one hell of a good excuse for his absence. Hopefully, something more convincing than telling the courts he was 'dining out' for the night.

Cold water fell over me. I tilted my face up at the spout and smiled at the vivid memories of Zander's tongue plunging inside me repeatedly until I came. I washed my body and hair with the orange scented soap before spending many long minutes standing on wet tiles rationalizing the events of the night and working through all the impossibilities. I failed to comprehend the magnitude of the Weaver's might. Just as I failed to comprehend how Zander's use of Oyoko's magic got us from a shed in the city to the bedroom of an apartment unseen.

After I was dressed, I snuck a peek out the bathroom's rectangle window above the sink. It was daylight. Well, past noon. No wonder I was famished.

The kitchen was well stocked. And it was to no surprise that a full salad with legumes and goat cheese sat prepared for me in the fridge when I went scavenging. The note read, *'Help yourself.'* I cleared the bowl and before I left to go back downstairs, I refilled the pitcher of water and scribbled on the back of the card. *'Delicious. Thank you.'*

Yolanda was cleaning up paper and pens when I closed the door behind me. She scrutinized my appearance in her clever head. "Do I want to know?"

"Nope. How is Rhyolite's reading coming along?" I diverted, pouring myself a lukewarm mug of coffee in the kitchenette.

"Good. Wonderful, actually. It is very unproblematic to teach eager learners. He will be reading bulletins in two weeks. Tonight, he is walking me through opening chess strategies. Will you be here?"

I shook my head. "In the tunnels. Unless, Cultee swings by sooner," I said. Her eyes narrowed in a way that made me uncomfortable saying much else. She crossed her arms and followed me to the fireplace, sitting down on a chair adjacent to me. "What?" I said shortly.

"Do you think I am a complete idiot?"

I glanced around the room searching for clues to her outbursts. I found none. "Are you?" I retorted, matching her ferociousness. Still finding no reason for her to raise her voice and suspicions with me.

"You slept with the count," she said flatly, not hiding her offense.

I placed my hand over my chest. "Excuse me?"

"You were gone all evening, night and morning with no warning. I heard the count's shower running and a quarter hour later you show up with wet hair, new clothes and barefoot. You are warm, fed and smell of rich people's foreign gardens. I am no idiot, observing was my secondary job for years."

My stomach fluttered.

I was a poor liar in situations where the evidence was heavily painted against me. So, I went with it. After all, I did sleep with him, just not *with* him. "You asked if you wanted to know. I said no. There is zero reason for you to be sour with me, unless you were worried about me. In which case I am tenderly touched by your sentiments and accept your apology."

Her lips pressed into a thin line and a scowl formed next to her eyes, yet she remained feminine and beautiful. A gift she saw as a curse. When she kept her silence, I set my coffee down and leaned forward. "Sorry, I didn't tell you that I would be gone so long. Truthfully, I didn't expect to be. I bought you a pastry from the music district that was intended to still be warm when I gave it to you."

"Pastry?" She perked up.

"Sugary and flaky, with lemon custard filling. I paid a whole two coppers for it!" My glands salivated at the memory of the desert.

Her mouth crooked to the side. "Two copper coins is a quantity to be excited over?"

"I am a woodlander. I've never held coins until this week, I had no reason to. Any coin seems exciting, especially when I can trade it for fried food with powdery white sugar on it."

"What did you trade with the count to pay for me? If you slept with him for money, I will be livid with you. I may even cut off his dick."

Anger rose in my gut. I was wholeheartedly offended. "He gave me nothing, only use of his time and status to retrieve you with the money I *earned*."

"You've never been to a city, you've never had means or money. Do you expect me to believe that?"

I was as burnt out as the lightbulb in the broom shed. I grabbed my boots by the corner, a coat and my dagger. I ripped down the satchel of remaining pastels I hid under the brim of the chimney vent. "Don't expect me to be back at any particular time."

I did my best not to slam the door when I left or to let Coraline see me angered when I took to the streets. By the time I strutted into the Pit my tears evaporated. The redness on my cheeks was from the wind whipping across the rooftops. I walked past Warden Rhett's scummy looking lackies with their crossbows and tobacco chew. The select coins in my pocket jingled when I came to an abrupt halt at the threshold of Rhett's office door. Or... doorframe as it stood.

The man with the skull tattoo on his throat sat smoking a rolled cigar, its ash piping cherry red as he inhaled. He was reading over parchment papers with hand written notes and burning them in the thick wicked candle. After seven puffs he tapped the loose ash into the glass tray beside him. Now was as good as any to knock. He flourished his hand behind him by way of acknowledging me.

"There is a war coming. Unimaginable beasts will be tearing through these city's walls," I spoke low and articulated each word, stressing my concern. He did look over his shoulder. When he saw my unbound hair, he drew a long drag. "I need you to get me in contact with mercenaries or those who will kill for coin to defend the city." I patted the coins and papers around my torso.

"Lovely lady, I deal with prisoners. They have no future outside of the cell and the Pit. Look elsewhere," his reply forced my hand into my pocket.

I clutched the four silvers and as I placed them one by one in front of him, I said. "One for good faith. One for the inconvenience. Another for your well-placed trust."

Rhett laughed away his brief bewilderment, not bothering to hide wide-eyes behind a thick puff of smoke. "Keenan, are you bribing me with a fourth silver?" He was grinning.

"If my bribe will get you to take two hundred thousand pastels and help protect the innocent, then yes it is a bribe. If you won't help, consider it a thank you for pulling the criminal files of those I fought. It made things easier." I gave a confident tilt of my head.

"I'll take your bribe." My heart almost cracked with relief because my consciousness would be able to rest knowing I tried to help in some way before I left. "When do you need the armed bodies and where?"

"They need to be standing guard within twenty-four hours. I can't tell when the wraiths will come. But they will. We've monsters inside and outside these walls. I'm trying to deal with them both," I swallowed, hearing the resolve in my own voice coming through as confident as I remember Anna speaking when she stepped off the boat. She was not here, even her blood was calm and distant. "Keep most of them around orphanages, temples and sickbays to protect those who can't take up arms. The rest are to be sent to the parameter of the duke's manor. There will be plenty of innocence and ignorance there, hopefully they can discern between the two. If you can occupy a fellow called Gimlian Monte the night of the gala, I'll find a way to get you another silver."

He put out his cigar and swiveled in his chair. "That amount shall secure seventy to your cause. A few may flee at the sight of a deranged nightcrawler and a few short-sentenced inmates may take the money and run, but it is a risk we take." I chewed my cheek.

I released the strap around my neck, my hefty bag swung suspended in the air between us. "We?"

"Others have sought my corrupt and reckless reserves. But they haven't proven themselves in the Pit. Tell me Keenan, how does your lady friend fair? Well, I hope."

"Better than her prior circumstances," I admitted, tossing the bag onto his desk. A variety of coinage spilled out. I was putting faith, money and hope in a stranger. I thought about wishing him good luck in the imminent battle, but that seemed too sentimental or sarcastic. Not knowing what else to add, I backed out of his office. "If you survive, go west."

I wasn't sure why I said what I had, but it felt right. I left out the front door of the big, foul-smelling warehouse and started the long walk to the laundromat.

A lovely silhouette waited for me by the back entrance.

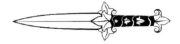

Yolanda held out an ice cream, strawberry flavored, not daring to make eye contact. I took her apology and pulled her inside the tunnels with me by her oversized trench coat. She complained about missing Brock's chess lesson, but I was happy to have convinced her to stay because there was much I did not know about the west wing of the estate. For example, the different servant attires the ladies were expected to wear and how they kept their hair pinned up and under caps.

She waited for me by the entry point to the kitchen stock room while I made a mad dash to steal staff clothes and observe the layout of the duchess's dining chambers. It was small and intimate as Yolanda had said it would be, two stained glass windows portrayed serene wheat fields and the third a bold display of red combined shards arranged in no particular way. The light that shone through it, casting a crimson glow onto her table fit for four, but set for one. I examined the brass locks. Nothing I couldn't pick with practice. I'd need a key, but would settle for the blunt head of a hammer I saw by the store crates.

Mentally, I visualized the hallways and stairwell beyond that door. Cobar was close. Two turns and a winding tower away. I could be there in five minutes.

Zander hadn't reached out since I entered the grounds. Maybe he didn't know what to say to me, no more than I knew what to say to him after... peaches. My stomach fluttered remembering his passionate kiss.

I followed the Weaver's will and called for him. *What excuse did you feed your noble company to cover your absence?* I kept my attention on my palm as I walked back to the store room. I lifted up the floorboards by the fridge and wedged myself down the narrow shoot. There was not even a bite on the hook I cast out to him. No rippling of the water between us. The more I explored our line, the colder it got. A frigid place, where ice clung to my lungs.

There was no door to his soul in sight. *Zander?* My words a pathetic whisper into the abyss when unheard. He must be out in the city or beyond the scope of our syphering.

"Ivy, are you ready to see the duke's dining chambers? If we are lucky, he will be hosting. A great opportunity to eavesdrop."

She steadied me when my feet fumbled on the stone steps in the dark. "Yes," I said, stuffing the brown linen and white cap under my layers to keep the drops of mildew water off them. Our lantern was relit, but I kept a firm hold on her elbow when the passageways narrowed and twisted sharply. She adjusted the blinders on the lantern when the footsteps above us pattered, raising her pointed brows.

"Luck favors us. He is hosting. It's not a dinner or his guests would be seated." She sat down and motioned for me to do the same. Her ears perked up as she called out the voices of those in attendance. "Hammish, Fonzo, Koi..." Oh, good. He survived. My thoughts were short lived for she continued listing more than fifteen people whose names were lost on me, save Gimly, I knew that one. Her brilliance was not lost on me. "Kora, Madonna and Janice do high quality work for Madam Marmacient. I trained them. I was there when they were auctioned. The Montes are hosting a revel in preparation for the gala. Resin and wine are plentiful." She looked ill. "I can still feel the effects of the first time they supplied drugs, we snorted lines of white powders and smoked black shit until I was certain the sky was falling. Nobody makes it out of that room sober or goes to bed alone." She rubbed her temples.

I was going to offer her silence to allow her mind to recover when a booming and boisterous laugh echoed in the room above. Zander was here. Or rather, *there*. In the event.

I brashly shouted out. "Is there a way to see in?"

She didn't reply right away, she chewed on her lower lip. "If you have feelings for the big fellow, I'm going to caution you not to look."

"How can I look in?" It was clear in my tone that I didn't want another argument with her. My ligaments were already trembling with nerves and the familiar emotion of rage.

"You are stupid. Follow me," she further dimmed the lantern.

We took the incline on the right and wedged ourselves deep into a hollow opening yards down. We were between eastern walls. Behind a tapestry worn with holes and just enough space in the rocks to see out. There were just as many men and women wearing headdresses as there were ranked guards and council members in red lounging about on tables and mattresses spread around the room. Smoke fumed everywhere. The lighting was soft, the excessive amounts of candelabras made the atmosphere intimate. I would have liked my first experience with a male to have been somewhere nice and romantic, instead I offered myself in a wretched broom closet. Lame.

A hazy figure of Oyokos paced around the hall, wearing tracks on the carpet. His shadow of a winged body moved unhindered through people and chairs scattered about. It was odd, although I didn't get much time to observe such a mystery because I spotted Zander. My gut twisted. My chest burned as I choked on my gasp finding him directly in the center of the room, straddled by the priestess in red. Neither wore much of anything. Their hips collided. He laughed as her faced flushed deeper.

A face I'd never forget.

Collette was not just any priestess, nor hands down the most beautiful woman in the room with her thick curves and sleek blonde hair—the opposite of whatever I had, but she belonged in the service of the royal family. One look at the jewels around her neck and rings adorning her fingers sent my ice cream spewing onto the floor.

Collette had been with the capital knights into the Southlands. Which meant the men inside barking the orders for the hunt was a male member of the Resig family line. The king or, more likely, the Faceless Prince. My racing heart was nothing compared to my breaking heart. It felt as if Stegin stabbed me. A pain far greater than the rusty end of his spear.

I forced myself into a numb and mute state until Yolanda and I were back onto the bustling streets of drunks, dining and music. Then I buried myself into her shoulder.

It was no coincidence or surprising phenomenon that Count Nicholo exited a tea shop with a goodie bag at the exact moment. A hot hand wrapped around my wrist, pulling my nails away from my chest that I had been clawing at. Skin was under my nails. The pain stabbing through my ribs was raw. Jagged. Merciless. I had to find a way to stop it.

Nikki pinned my arm to my side, forbidding my attempts to rip the disbelief from my chest, by means of tearing my heart out of my body. He did say he had another one for me right? He looked to Yolanda, "What happened?"

"We watched your horselord friend fuck Priestess Collette," she said. "I told her it was a dumb idea to look." As they supported me back to the Arborist, Yolanda told Nikki everything, including how I vomited my strawberry ice cream.

I locked myself in the bathroom to brush my teeth and wash my face. My reflection became unbearable. All it did was remind me that I was not forty pounds thicker with hips and suppleness, or taller to reach his lower lip without standing on my tiptoes, or with a head of silky, blonde hair. I was not a priestess riding Zander under candle light. My chest started to ache again.

When I walked out, Brock poured me a glass of bourbon. I drank it in one go. He poured another. Brock looked at me with gentle eyes. He had sisters and would often tell me stories of when they would come home mourning the stupidity of men or plotting the end of their relationship.

"Men are dumb," I sniffed my running nose.

"We are," he agreed, placing a comforting hand between my shoulder blades. The arteries from my heart to all my extremities spasmed. It felt like I was being stabbed in my lungs. I bent over. "Sit before you fall." A chair swung around and knocked my knees out, I landed on the cushion as Nikki intended.

My head snapped in his direction. "Don't speak. I will not listen to you defend your friend." He raised his hands in surrender and walked to the firepit. I glared at his back with daggers shooting from my eyes knowing he would have done just that. Defend Zander's actions, name and reputation until death. A loyalty woven who couldn't fathom his precious master in the wrong.

I grabbed the second glass of liquor and drank it hoping it would thaw out the ice clenching my sides. Brock raised a concerned brow. "You don't invest in relationships. This is bigger than Drift's foolishness. What is it?"

"How much do you remember about the attacks of the capital knights?" I asked the quiet room.

Brock stabilized his breathing. "All of it." Yolanda observed Brock's acrimony and hurt as his own memories resurfaced.

"Good. Then you can recall the black carriage which housed a man giving the orders and the priestess riding alone relaying the commands to the barbaric knights. Collette is that same priestess statured in human blood and red rubies. The foul man who gave those orders has to be a male of the royal family." My stomach clenched saying it out loud. The fire cackled louder across the room.

"If the Torval Prince is not an ally of his own countrymen, he is likely a supporter of the wraiths. This city is doomed. We need to collect anyone who will listen and leave," Brock's voice struggled to rid the tremor.

Yolanda rose and grabbed the bourbon from the counter. "If you go around telling your stories and suspicions, you will be killed for defamation. If you intend to leave here alive, you keep your mouth shut."

Brock looked up at her with his nose crinkled. "You're not leaving with us?"

Yolanda shrugged. "I haven't decided. But what I do know is that as much as I enjoy your enthusiasm for chess, you will be teaching me how to fight from now on."

Brock agreed. Nikki spoke up. "I will get you a sword fit for your frame. Sage, have you a sword?"

Him referring to me as *Sage* felt itchy on my skin. My body betrayed me and replied. "I will need one. Also, two daggers and a thigh strap."

"Demanding," he sighed. "I guess I am burdened with the cost to pay for the mistakes of my friend. I will get them to you by tomorrow morning if you swear not to use them on him."

The laugh that escaped was full of venom, it rattled my aching chest. Gods, did my heart hurt! "I guess I will have to find my own weapons then. Too bad I just donated the rest of my pastels to our cause."

"Are you ready to let me talk or do you want me to fetch Cultee, so we can all say our piece without your bitterness running rampant?" Nikki's zest bit at me.

I drank more bourbon and welcomed the dizziness that bubbled up to my brain. After midnight the three weeks were up. "Get the captain." I grabbed my third glass and took it to a bench outside where I waited for my shadow to find me in the falling snow.

It didn't take long. He was reliable and consistent, I knew he would come.

Nikki climbed down the side of the apartment complex on a flimsy escape ladder, begrudgingly I made room for him next to me.

"I'll summon Cultee after we chat," he wasn't dressed in his finery, but in various shades of black cotton. I strummed my nails on the empty glass in my grip. "After you went unconscious and the threads faded, Zander and I got to talking. He overheard members of high society talking about an exclusive circle among them. They call themselves the Remnants. He refused to take the venom, but he succeeded in getting recruited by the royal family's most active supporters. Since he was fed, he planned to let Collette collect him, then use his *sway* and *charm* to get answers from her. Last I heard, he thinks they got their hands on something terrible that makes Oyoko's blood curdle in his veins."

I couldn't look at him, even though questions and snarky comments were eagerly waiting to bubble out like an uncorked bottle of champagne. He continued, "I am confident something went wrong, that these Remnants are welding magic or objects of magic. Our sight went out. I can't reach him or see into his world." My gut twisted. "When you were on the estate, did you sypher?"

My head shook. "It was distant and cold. I couldn't find him. It might be that he was too *preoccupied* to notice a little voice in his head."

He cracked his back over the bench and groaned in frustration. "What magic can interfere with the bond of the Weaver?"

"Am I supposed to know the answer to that?" I scoffed, hiding my concern.

Nikki scooted closer, wrapping his arm around my shoulders before I shimmied far enough away from his grasp. I was caught in his warmth. His voice a sharp whisper, "You are the only sustenance that he physically *can* consume, without deathly repercussions. And coincidentally, the only force he *wants* to feed from."

"Save your bullshit. I know what I saw." I was gripping the glass tightly.

"*Corlimors* cannot engage in intimacy with anyone other than their woven or they risk dying, Wisteria," he educated.

I scrunched my nose. "I slept with other women after the dungeons, sometimes several at once. I guess I have no *corlimor* then."

He just batted his pale lashes and said calmly. "You had no knowledge of threads, it wouldn't have tied you to the fate of demise. But, once you see the truth, there is no forgiveness for those who choose differently. No going back or denying them."

So, celibacy was in my future? Lovely. "That sucks," I grumbled, crossing my arms over my chest. "Besides, none of us know what we are to each other, he made assumptions," I stated.

Nikki smacked his lips. "Weaver threads aside, the personal vow he made to never let harm befall you will also send him into the beyond if he carried out any act that would hurt you. Because whether you can admit it out loud or not, you developed feelings for him. And being the fool hearted man he is, he allows you to carry on avenging your past lover in profound blind rage instead of bringing you to see the present moment and stop living in your past. Your heartache and jealousy are proof enough. He did not and will not betray you." His hand released my shoulder. His arm moved away as he stood adjusting the hood over his blond, white hair, which had grown since we've arrived in the city.

My cold ears I tucked deeper into the scarf Raina made me. "I know what I saw, he was uninhibited. No rules or vows applied."

He cracked a devious grin. "One day, you will know real desire and inhibition when you are consumed with no restraint. Then you will look back on this moment and laugh."

I was not amused, not when my mind vividly replayed his hips rolling up under Collette's thick thighs and his flirty eyes ogling her breasts in his face. I outright ignored Nikki's last statement. "When I get Cobar out, I'll see what information I can gather from the west wing."

"Wise. A spellbound grandson of Oyokos, in the wrong hands, is a terrifying weapon to wield. Let's hope they don't realize who they have captive."

He left me with that dreadful thought for several long hours until Cultee arrived.

Chapter Twenty-Five

All but Zander gathered in my small apartment to listen to my confessions.

The more I talked, the more Anna's death felt insignificant... or maybe too coincidental... Brock was the first one to speak to me after hearing about my need to kill Cultee's half-brother and just how equipped I was to do it. Just as I was both a woodland healer and a moderately trained Ilanthian physician. "All this time, you could read?" He said bitterly. I nodded. "I don't give two shits about who you loved, protected or forged the names of. You should have taught me how to write my own name!" He crossed his arms over his chest.

My teeth cut into my lip as I succumbed to a smile. "Sorry. After the hunt for silver bloods, I couldn't risk more people knowing and being hunted for knowledge. And now, we have loads more to worry about than escorting the remaining Ilanthians out of this fallen nation. Like defending a city and seeing Cultee sworn in as duke."

Yolanda rose a bottle of wine. "And finding Bastion to overthrow the Faceless Prince."

Cultee's knuckles ran back and forward across his grey bearded chin and cheek. "And gathering intel about these Remnants." He gave a discouraged human growl. "When my father was in power, the tutors who oversaw my education mentioned something about Anuli's temples housing valises of her compassion, moments of her empathy enshrined to remember her deeds after she departed." Captain tapped the toes of his shoes repeatedly. "I'm inclined to say, the term

Remnants was mentioned then, but under different contexts. I didn't listen to those old buffoons well enough. My sister ought to have."

"Excuse me," I intruded, while he was on the topic of Goddesses. "In your office at Fort Fell, there was a book with historical text and artwork in it. One painting depicted Numaal's royal family eating the heart of Anuli, the crest of the two headed raven embellished in the scene. Is it true? Did your tutors teach about her death?"

He opened his palms. "Aditi painted that." He was reverent. "The reason for her death is a perpetual debate among scholars, it has been for hundreds of years. Her brother Taite was there, but the scribes who questioned him documented his refusal to speak of Anuli's last act of compassion, whether it was a sacrifice or an act of insanity during the great war. Either way, her heart was missing from her chest cavity when the temple staff entered the palace. 'The death of all red and silver bloods became too much for her to handle and her heart shattered' is how my mother described it to me as a young child. The particulars may be too disturbing for young minds."

Yolanda's nose pinched. "Her heart was missing? Why isn't that taught in the elementary years of public education? Scat, I've been in and out of those temples, sleeping with the celibate for years, and have heard nothing of Anuli's death outside of it being one of peace yet so horrendous. Taite drank himself into oblivion and made sure his vessel was entirely removed from earth when he left. Heart ache and suicide do not remove an organ from a splayed open sternum." I touched my still aching heart, wondering if it truly wasn't possible where magic was concerned. My body was tender from Zander's stupidity and from clawing at my chest when we emerged from the tunnels. "I know my way around the temples. I will go pay the Goddesses a visit if I can sober up in time," Yolanda said with resoluteness. She set down the bottle in her hand and gave me her best nod of confidence.

Cultee turned to me, his fixed gaze soft, yet stormy. "Do what you must to see your family to safety, I would not dare to stop either of you. If you stumble across a woman named Calabress, tell her I sent you. Encourage her to leave these lands with your friend Keenan by whatever honesty you feel appropriate." Cultee's knuckles ran back and forward across his grey bearded chin and cheek. "I will investigate the society of Remnants, while you deal with the wraith. It will no longer be an adequate gift, nor as profound of an offering as we need to turn heads. Kill it. Burn it. We will need a better gift for Stegin if the battle doesn't end our scheming sooner. I trust you to think of one before the gala. One that the lords and royals will applaud, something they need. I will collect it here, three hours after midday." I nodded, relieved at his acceptance for all I dumped onto his shoulders.

He turned to Nikki. "Count Nicholo, get in touch with Drift. Inform him of the changes in our plan. You and Brock will light the pyres as you take leave for the southern docks the morning of the gala. If our story makes it to the Land of the Gods, try and get it to the ears of Athromancia and Maruc, so they may intervene or at the very least, be alerted that Numaal is in civil turmoil and its rulers are seeking its demise. I will send word to prepare rested mounts, enough for Yolanda and Calabress to join the company, should they choose." Yolanda fussed with the shredded hems of her pants giving no indication of her choice.

Cultee surveyed the room fondly. "I pray to the Eternals that we are not the sole assembly of good will fighting in the east. I pray that our ragtag endeavors are enough to give truth and peace a chance to permeate these lands once more. I pray that we and our fellow countrymen and women remain safe now and in many years to come. I pray that good will prevail, peace will grow, joy will blossom and love will unite nations." Cultee got onto his knees and prostrated himself on the floor. Count Nicholo followed suit, the rest of us lowered our heads reverently.

The captain left, his prayers his means of a farewell. Brock invited Yolanda over to his living space to practice holding the guard's sword he got from Fort Fell. I was too tired to be of much assistance given the early hour and how much bourbon I drank. Brock showed her how to use her body weight to give the sword momentum. Nikki rubbed his tired eyes and watched me ready my bed on the hard floors. "If you threw up your ice cream, that means you haven't eaten since the salad I prepared. You expended far more energy the night of the threads than you have eaten in over a week. How are you not hungry?"

I rolled on my side. "I didn't say I wasn't. However, I am emotionally exhausted, a little drunk, a lot tired and I need to dream up the most impressive gift for the gala." He prodded the logs in the pit with the iron rod. "Besides, I'll throw up whatever I eat for however long this gnawing pit, that is my indignity of letting a man of Zander's reputation near me, festers in my gut."

"I am impressed by the numerous ways you have concocted to express every emotion aside from the root of what you are feeling." He pulled a chocolate bar from his breast pocket and tossed it at me. "I feel enlightened. Who knew jealousy had so many other names."

I was peeling the tin wrapper off the dark salted chocolate bar. "If you stay longer, I will inform you of all the adjectives I have compiled to call you an ass." The chocolate was delightful. The chunks of almonds were particularly scrumptious. "You have good taste in desserts, that is the sole reason I've decided to keep you."

"Keep me?" he questioned.

I hummed, "Mhmm, keep you alive that is."

His pointed tongue ran over his teeth. "You sleep. I will pack up my valuables. Tomorrow, I will swing by to watch you kill that," he pointed to the closet. "Rhyolite and I have a discussion to be had about strategies—this time not about the chess board, but the thirty pyres to be lit by two men on the run." Brock agreed from across the open doors. His boot tapped my bare feet that were poking out of the white comforter. "Thank you for sharing your story tonight, I can see the relief on your face. It must have been hard to carry all those memories alone and hide your truth." Mist covered my eyes. What was he doing? "Good luck with Cobar tomorrow night. I hope to meet him before we all become travel buddies dashing through the Deadlands."

Knowing he could hear me, I whispered a soft good night before the door shut and locked behind him.

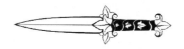

455

The count brought lunch with him when he arrived back at my apartment eight hours later. He also presented Yolanda with her first sword to which he gifted her a sheath with sage leaves imprinted on the leather. Wrapping the belt and steel around her waist, she sniffed back emotions and gave him a gruff response from across the room, "Thank you."

The count had crafted a new brace for Brock's stump, one that did not pinch with rust as he moved. He strapped the leather belts around his thigh and adjusted the bend on the metal rods. There was no boot at the bottom of this make, just a metal stamp. Brock seemed to manage better than he did with the one I made for him, and he could do so without the use of a crutch or cane. Nikki tapped my shoulder. I looked up from my barley soup. Hot liquid dripped down to my chin when I saw the gifts he brought for me.

Sure, the slender sword, daggers and leg straps were fine, but my heart nearly burst when I saw the small winter boots, jacket and warm garments fit for a child. "We can't deliver the child to his dad as a snowball, that wouldn't be considerate enough to earn us a seat on his ship."

I held up the sweet mittens meant for little hands and the cobalt blue ear protection. Cobar was my age, twenty-two, but he would be seen as a boy still early in his single digit years. "It's perfect. He will need them, winter was never a season he enjoyed, the mud puddles had frozen over," I said, lost in a fond moment in time.

"Good to hear. Now, make use of the weapons and kill that wraith so I can finish mapping out our escape from the city," he wiggled his brow and began to move the tiny table and empty chair away from the closet, taking with it my bowl of soup. I scowled and tossed my spoon down to pick up the sword he brought. It wasn't Ilanthian steel, but it rang with quality forging.

"Do something fun!" Brock jested as a rowdy adolescent would have. I indulged him, revolving the sword around my wrist and blindly twirling a dagger between the fingers of my non-dominant hand. That would have to suffice until I had room for a sword dance. Brock handed over the key Drift had given him weeks ago. I opened the vent into the box. Knocking three times as I approached. *Knock, knock, knock.*

I tilted my head tilted. "Maybe I don't need to sedate it first."

"Maybe it will just lay there paralyzed and silent and let you decapitate it because it got addicted to the scent of your period?" Brock grunted sarcastically. "Now is not the time for experimenting, Sage." Yolanda looked over at Brock at the use of my fabricated name, the leather sheath still in her grip.

"Alright, toss me some bathroom towels." I tried to make the process quick and as clean as possible. Count stood behind me with used shower towels, his sword drawn and pointed down at the iron box exposed by the upturned floorboards. Blue capped spores floated into the vents; I heard its muscles stiffen. *Migouri*, it exhaled one last time before its vocal cords froze.

I sent in another teaspoon of spores to be safe.

My dagger lay clenched between my teeth, while my hands busied nervously opening the three separate locks Pine and Zander decided to place. I was ready. I pulled the towels down and had a dagger in my right fist before I pried opened the box that seemed more of a coffin given the circumstance. Brock and Nikki carried it the rest of the way out.

Yolanda disappeared from my peripheral vision. Its shackled limbs did nothing to hinder the foulness of its stench or convince the sane mind it was harmless. Its elongated body parts appeared snapped and discombobulated as if Zander had broken each one of them intentionally before stuffing it into the coffin. I was certain he did.

Its empty wide beady eyes found mine. They did not show any emotion. No fear. No hint of a smile or panic. No remembrance of me or lost humanity. There was no need for me to hesitate. I slit its throat. It gurgled and oozed onto the towel I wrapped around the neck. Then I kept at it, sawing until I severed the spinal corn and tendons holding its head to its body. There was a heartbeat behind me. Fennick's family heirloom beckoned me. I took it from the hip of his owner, stabbed the body's chest, wiped it clean and returned it to the count. For once there was no comment of my thieving, but approval in his eyes as I strode past him to wash my hands. Yolanda, under Nikki and Brock's watchful eyes, crept closer to observe the body.

"Count, if I cut it into pieces, can you move them to the trash incinerator?"

"There is no need to further soil your hands. I have plenty of crates upstairs for packing up my room, I can get this corpse off your hands after lunch once you help carry the box upstairs," the count informed me, then went back to reassuring Yolanda who was horrified at the notion it was once a human body. A child. A mother. A grandfather. Somebody's someone.

I scrubbed my hands twice to remove all the foul-smelling black blood from them, lost in the notion of how romantic even a mundane life would be if I was somebody's someone until I was grey and aged with sunshine lines in my face. I gathered up the last of my soup and finished it. "How can you possibly eat after guillotining a head?"

My shoulder rose to my ears. "I am hungry and a bit of a sadist," I offered.

"Ew," she said with a heavy note of disgust. She gawked at the figure in the box until the smell became too strong and she demanded the lid be closed and secured. She didn't touch her afternoon tea as the boys in the room spread a rough outline of a city map on the table and began to circle where the oil buckets and wooden stock piles of each tower were.

Brock chewed on his soft pencil, his teeth marks making little grooves as he studied landmarks and street names. "Wouldn't it be faster to light them from *outside* the city? Where we wouldn't have to hide or be stopped every few minutes?"

"So much easier and faster. And a lot less of a risk because there are no patrolling sentinels on the outside of the city. But we are only two bodies, if we both start in the north and separate around the parameter it would take hours to see you again on the south side to start our trek down."

"What if you were three bodies?" Yolanda swallowed.

Brock looked happy, yet disturbed. "Are you offering to come with us?"

"Yes. I can ride next to Brock. I can light the pyres that require climbing, he can light the ones that require an arrow. Even if we each only light a few, the guards on the wall will follow suit and light theirs."

Count spun his pencil around his knuckles. "They are trained to warn the city, to call soldiers to their defensive positions, but we do not know who among them is corrupt. We will not leave this city until they are all burning bright with copious amounts of oil that they cannot be extinguished." The table agreed. "Yolanda, how are you on horseback?"

"Fair. I've attended hunting games," she said. Count Nicholo flipped over the paper and began sketching his own, proportionally accurate, layout of Landsfell including the stables and six gateways in and out of the city. "What about *Sage*, the kid and the horselord? Won't they be available to help too?"

"I was unsuccessful in getting a hold of my friend. I'll try again today, but as of now let's assume he will be taken off guard by the change in plans and that Cultee will inform him amid the chaos of the gala where we have gone. I don't see him leaving until Cultee is standing in control of the city, until the royal family gives the order to protect Landsfell with their knights side by side with the guards. He can fight and figure things out later, once he is in his correct state of mind." Nikki's eyes shifted to me, I didn't meet them but I felt them burning through my skin. Per usual.

His attention on me prompted me to speak. I swore I smelt my flesh singed under his gaze. "Yolanda, I told you I can't leave until I have killed the duke. I am not an oath breaker." My eyes shot across the room. The gold in his eyes greeted me. "There are too many variables involved for me at this time to plot. I am getting Cobar tonight. If I don't get him tonight, I will not be going south. I stay in the city until I find where they have taken my family. Keenan will sail you all to safety if you tell him I sent you, I don't need to be there for him to care for you. I promise that much."

A pencil was thrown at my head. "Real mature, Rhyolite." I threw it back at him, he swatted it away. It scattered across the floor.

"I go where you go. Do what you need to do and meet us at the port or I will not board that ship. I will turn into a wraith and hunt your stupid ass

459

down for years," Brock said. I was glad to know the secrets I kept from him changed nothing of our friendship, he was a true friend. Nikki was smiling at the ironside's grit and stubbornness, I supposed it reminded him of his loyalty to Zander. Such fools.

"I will catch up with you. I have two legs and you have one, it shouldn't be that difficult." Two more pencils were chucked at me.

I swore in my typical manner.

"I was being serious," he said, shaking his head. The count was glued to Brock's earnest pledge.

I stood up and swung my arms around his neck, placing a big smacking kiss on his cheek. "So was I. I will find you, my friend."

He grabbed my forearms, locking me to the back of his wooden chair. "You better because if I find you first, I will be a royal pain in your ass."

"You already are," I reminded.

"This is nothing," he warned.

I believed him.

Chapter Twenty-Six

After Yolanda and I facilitated moving the wraith's coffin upstairs, I left with a canteen of water and my west wing's servant attire folded into my satchel. Yolanda had braided my hair and pinned it up under the white cap before I left. On each of my legs a dagger was fastened, I began to feel more of myself again with each stride I took down the long passageways. I was armed and my purpose rekindled. All I had to do now was ignore the urge to cut out Zander from my life and disband our syphering. It was as comfortable as swallowing thumb tacks, but I managed to do the opposite.

I cast out my nets in each direction and called for him around each corner I took. It was strange to feel absolutely nothing on the other side of the thread, not even a tug of acknowledgement. Twice, I thought I perceived the door rattling on his end, but it remained locked. I remained isolated. I pressed my hands against the wet stone walls of the tunnels and screamed louder for him until his name became my only thought. The rattling was silenced.

I would never tell Nikki to his face, but he was right. Something was absolutely amiss.

To add to the frustration, staff occupied the Duchess's kitchen. Two females prepped and cleaned for an afternoon snack, their feet hustling on the stones above my head. I took this time to strip my pants and tunic and wear the unsightly, shapeless brown dress. At least it was loose enough to hide the daggers on my legs. I did what I could to preserve the white house slippers from the damp grim beneath me.

Crouching on the top step under the entrance, I pressed my ear to the floor above. Between the clacks of tea pots and clamor of iron pans I listened.

"...her chambermaid overheard."

"If he was on his deathbed, why would his sole son be here? He should be in the capital getting sworn in as the next king of Numaal."

"Miranda has no reason to lie. Collette said he would be dead any day now, if he isn't already. The healers have given up and he refuses to send for the physicians of Akelis, after they pulled all their kind out of his land."

"Maybe Miranda did not lie, she only misheard. They speak in riddles."

"Her dad owns land in Tranwellton, she isn't an idiot."

"Her dad sold her into slavery to afford the house in Tranwellton, she was raised by idiots. Selfish idiots."

The dish water ran. I heard nothing above the pipes and faucet. When it stopped, their conversation was over. Their soft steps padded into the dining area where a timid speaking Duchess Kacey dismissed the two girls. While she ate, I went back to rifling through concepts for a suitable gift. When I came up empty, I shouted for Zander until his door rattled. Then I shouted more.

He never opened it.

But I refused to believe that he was not trying. He always tried too hard. He was trapped inside.

Just as I was trapped under the damn cellar door until the duchess saw herself out with the two spears at the entrance. After it was quiet, I waited longer, ensuring no one returned to claim forgotten items or fuss with the perishables.

I emerged from the tunnels as Mildred. Where there once was a rust headdress, now were rows of braids and a simple cap. My gaze was kept low and humble, I counted my steps just as I counted all the exits, halls and windows around me. A gaggle of cleaning maids strode by, I paused in a groove and increased the pace of my strides as I turned down the opposite direction they flocked. There were countless rooms I wished I could have stopped and admired, the painting gally was one of them. The library was the other.

Up the stairs I dashed, feeling lucky that I had not bumped into trouble. A benefit of hosting a winter gala for the nation, more workload and more staff to see it done. The door to the music chamber was left open and just as Zander described it, a smaller square room was built amid the raised ceiling, next to the pianoforte, and surrounded in a thin rope of silver, coarse salt. Pleadian.

There was a single door and window facing a great stained glass window, in which the western setting sun lit up dimly. I walked across the line and opened the door. That solved the mystery of Anna's silver blood being filtered fully from my system. I was a red blood through and through.

My head and heart did all they could to hold onto her essence.

It was a simple room made cozy with picture books, a children's art corner and a colorful bedding. Were it not for the locks on the door, the bloodied fingernail scratches under the window and the eerie solitude, it would have been a homely retreat spot. To visit. Not to be locked in.

He wasn't here. His mattress gave a little as I sat down to mourn, my right hand stroking over the groves his little fingers dug into the stone wall over the years he has been here. My head throbbed behind my eyes and my sinuses burned. Regret. Regret was punishing me for not coming sooner. I choked down the vomit rising in my throat and grabbed the nearest paper and crayon. I drew a lilac and purple and green bands of wisteria climbing around the page. Where my tears hit the paper, it became translucent.

Sissy is here.

I left the note under his blanket for him to find. And walked out of the gilded cage, wondering when he would be back tonight. If it was worth me hiding close by and risking both our lives. I circled around the music room, looking for a desk, a box, a window or vent to hide in and wait the night out. "Hello, there." I heard the voice before I caught sight of a woman dressed as I, she was a little taller and perhaps ten years older than I.

Shuffling, shyly towards her I noted her high cheekbones and a strong face I couldn't place. "Hello. I was just passing by, tempted to dabble my inexperienced fingers on the pianoforte," I made a snorting sound and hid my blush by dropping the top of my head.

"And that wishful thinking alone has brought tears to your eyes?" Her white slippers moved closer. I felt for my face. There were tears. I let them fall and dug around in my head for a believable lie.

"My mother played. I haven't seen her since my father sold me to the slavers passing through Tranwellton." I looked up at her. "It seems silly missing such an abstract thing such as the sound of her fingers practicing scales."

She continued closing the distance between us. "You are a fresh face. When were you purchased from Tranwellton?"

"Two months ago. Landsfell is as lovely as I dreamt it would be," I gave a goofy grin, my sweaty palms wiping against the front of my fabric.

"The slaver route from Transwellton was closed over a year ago. If you are going to lie, do better research. What business have you with the boy?"

My hands sagged to my sides, my fingers caressing the blades under the gown. "None." I lied again.

"I have brought him his meals everyday since he has been here. Those nosey enough to poke their heads where they do not belong, get them removed." Good. He was being fed. "It is a moot point in asking your name, just to hear you lie again. If you came to sneak a peek at the silver, you are too late. He has gone to his exams for the day and by the time he returns it will be well after your shift has ended and he will be too tired to talk. If you came to kill the silver, I will strike you down before you get an opportunity to pose a threat to a child." Her jaw flexed in her ferocity. She stationed herself well between the obvious exit and me.

Gods, I didn't have time for games. The entire persona of Mildred went out the window. Ivy was here now. And she wanted answers. "And what if I came to free Cobar?"

Her nose flared at the mention of his name. "Then I would ask—why would I let you take him from one prison to another, where there is no guarantee of food or warmth?" Her brown hair was falling loose from her cap.

"I am sure his father will give him far more food and warmth than this cold place of secrets and solitude. Where are his mother and the young babe?" I slowly backed away, making towards the piano.

She followed. "Who are you?"

"Someone who loves him." The piano stood between the two of us now, my hands rested atop the lid. "Where are Moriah and Rory?

"Why would I tell a stranger? Are you planning on robbing them of their blood too?" My gut twisted. I leaned onto the instrument to maintain composure.

"What do these *exams* entail?"

She looked surprised, as if I was a true idiot. "They experiment on him. Not much lately. As of recent months, they have stopped the invasive procedures and have just been collecting his blood. They told me it cures wraith bites, but I don't believe it. Not for one second."

I was crying again. Ugly weeping, was more accurate. "What do *you* believe they do with it?" I risked knowing.

"Drink it. Inject it," she tossed a hanky across the smooth black surface of the string instrument. My thumb traced the initials C.M. "I may be old fashioned in my beliefs, but how we treat all life matters." I gaped at her, at Cultee's younger sister. Calabress.

The minute that passed was unnervingly long. I observed her strong chin and curve of her brows, recalling the same dark brown eyes on the captain's face. I sniffed my tears and spoke, "I agree. So, does your brother. He told me something similar when we rode out from Fort Fell into the dangerous Southlands to rescue the rest of us crafters." I held up the hanky, addressing the C.M. "You're Calabress Monte, are you not?"

"Cult mentioned me?" She looked shocked.

"Several times. Yesterday, when I told him I was going to free Cobar, he asked me if I ran into a girl named Calabress, to convince you to leave here by whatever means necessary." I shook my head abruptly. "I didn't expect it to be so easy to bump into you." She shushed me and scolded my loud mouth, which echoed in the vaulted room. "This place will be swarming with demons this time tomorrow. You can leave with me. With me and Cobar."

"Who are you?" she pressed again.

"An angry crafter who loved the wrong race, who watched capital knights rape and murder her own family, and steal away the rest. Where are Moriah and Rory?"

"They were moved to Kathra last autumn." My blood went still. She eyed the hallway and lowered her voice to a whisper. "Myself and his chambermaid are the only familiar faces Cobar sees. The only ones who are willing to heat up his food before he eats it. To sing him songs before the moon ascends. To sew close the holes in his sweaters. He doesn't talk to us. He doesn't trust us. I doubt Cobar will ever trust a Numaalian, what makes you think he will go with you if given the opportunity?"

"We grew up together. He is my perpetual baby brother," I announced, holding back a river of grief in my throat. "I promised his dad I would reunite our family."

"That was stupid," she muttered.

"I knew it would be difficult."

She rolled her eyes. "It's a suicide mission. How many times do you think I have tried to cart the kid off?"

A noisy herd of women were walking down the hall, we both sprinted out of view behind Cobar's prison. "Then help me," my whisper was jagged and desperate.

She pressed her finger to her lips and motioned I keep my back against the wall. We waited for the steps to pass along. "What is my brother up to?"

"We are getting him sworn in as duke. I am going to kill the current one." I lifted up the hem of my dress and flaunted my blades. "After I get Cobar to safety."

"He *loathes* high society," she expressed her doubt.

I grumbled, "Who doesn't? He and his comrades have arrived at the conclusion he is better equipped to defend innocents against the wraiths because he has been fighting them for years. No one else has. No one else raises a brow or sword at the mass graves in the south. He can do it. He may not like it. But, he can." I peeked my head around the corner of the prison. A billowing dress was seen rounding the other side. I grabbed Calabress' wrist and tugged her along still prattling, "I would follow him and I am notoriously skeptical of people sporting red. That must count for something." She shushed in my ear. I sealed my lips.

The pattering paused. "The council already suspects my brother is up to something, but believes he is the same understated man he was when he left Landsfell a decade ago. If I go missing, they will lock him away or worse."

"So, you won't come with me?"

"If my brother is going to run this city, I will stay here and help him."

"Wraiths are coming. Thousands of undead monstrosities."

Calabress pursed her mouth. "If my brother is here, I am here." She would not leave.

I gave a deep sigh from the shaking parts of my lungs. "And if my brother is here, I will tear down each wall and rip out the entrails of whoever stands in my way."

A stranger's voice piped up. A blade was now in my grip again. The voice shouted, "Calabress? I know you are here. Duchess Kacey is looking for you."

"Fucking shit," she swore. Cultee was correct about her mouth. "We can't be discovered talking. It's death for us and whatever hope you have for your brother and mine. Carson is a snitch."

I grabbed her wrist and spun her back to me, my blade at her throat. She screamed reflexively. "Play along," I said sharply in her ear. She nodded against the steel on her neck.

I called back, "Oh, she is here, Carson darling. But, she is rather busy at the moment." A female staff member came into view, her face white with terror. She stopped dead in her tracks. "Calabress has done a mighty good job at keeping her mouth shut so far, your duke would be proud of her devotion."

To my surprise the maid didn't wet herself or run. "The boy won't be returning tonight. Not after I tell them about you." She panted and began a slow creep backward.

"I am not here for the silver blooded child." I danced the blade deeper into Calabress' flesh as the lie escaped my dry lips. She squirmed against me. "Not even for your cowardice of a duke. I want to know what evil magic this society of Remnants weld and why. I want to know who is shooting down Stegin's scouts and preventing them from warning the nation of the imminent onslaught."

She shook her head, beads of sweat shone on her upper lip. "I know nothing about either of those." Her hands were up, her eyes pleaded with mine. She was telling the truth. "Let her go and I won't scream."

"I am not as fond as your duke in killing the people of his own province. My intent is not to kill Calabress, nor you for that matter." My green eyes glinted in her direction. I felt a cocky smile on my face. "Tell me, what weaknesses you've noticed in Priestess Collette."

The young girl named Carson scrunched her face, frantically trying to give me an answer. "Or what?" she asked bravely. Her gull sparked my own.

"Or you lose the ten second head start I was planning on giving you before I chased you down like the mouse you are. I supposed with your loose lips for gossip, that makes you a rat really." My grin broadened.

"Other than pining after her owner and her fascination with the new gemstone walking stick, there is none."

My blade moved aside, I pushed Calabress towards Carson. I shouted, "One. Two. Three. Four." By then the pair figured out what I was up to and sprinted out the door. I hollered after them. "Five. Six!" I shouted at their back down the long hallway. I bolted towards the dining hall. "Seven!"

Security would be chasing me by the time I hit ten. I moved quickly.

I fumbled with the stone slab next to the pantry, slithering myself into the crawl space of the tunnels and locking the padlock above my head before I left. I didn't bother to change right away, I sat in the dark, finalizing my gift for those blood drinking demons and convincing myself that Calabress would comfort Cobar wherever he was taken tonight.

My costume I dumped in the dirty hamper bin and ran behind the hanging cloth lines to shimmy my pants on and readjust my blades. When I busted down the door to the apartment and entered alone, neither Brock or Yolanda said anything. The pity on Yolanda's face was enough to make me ill. "I'm going back in tomorrow," I stated, kicking off my boots by the door.

Brock's voice was tender, but he reminded firmly, "The gala is tomorrow. The tunnels will be full, the hallways protected. The battle will ensure no one goes in or out of the city. Not easily anyways. Getting close enough to kill the duke is one thing, leaving with the kid is another. How can you accomplish both?"

"Underestimating me now too, Brock?" I said, chalking up a chummy smile.

"Never. Call me curious." Wise man.

"I will be escorted through the front doors, armed by knights and delivered to my enemy." I moved my gaze from Brock's baffled look to Yolanda's sinister smile. "Yolanda, I require your help yet again."

"You're the gift," she said, smirking. She leaned onto her elbows. "Now, let's wrap you up as the most alluring present."

Chapter Twenty-Seven

Yolanda insisted I slept in the bed while she ran errands. I was glad I did; it gave me privacy to mourn the seasons of Cobar's painful existence and torture myself with guilt for not intervening sooner. Every time I closed my eyes, I saw his tiny claw marks under the window or envisioned him being ripped away from his mother and sister, who were no doubt being *experimented* on. Keenan would be driven violently mad if he knew any of this. Reuniting them was the remedy.

I sipped my morning coffee while sitting on a stool locked in the bathroom. Yolanda was hard at work. She had been since sunrise. We all had a busy night and an early start to our big day. The boys were waiting for her to finish making me into a masterpiece, as she referred to it, so they could pack up and start lighting the pyres before the city finished breakfast.

"Almost, done," she said, dipping another crystal into a pot of glue and carefully pressing it onto my face. The winter gala was a masquerade and my mask consisted of countless diamond-like shards glued around my cheekbones and eyes, which she had painted skillfully with shimmery makeup. I was given instructions not to rub my eyelashes no matter how much my face itched and not to eat oily foods because it would smudge the red lip stain. I was already uncomfortable under the layers of mascaras and glitz.

While she directed me into a red thong and translucent skirt, I placed all my woodlander jewelry on. My ears, nose, lip, tongue, breasts, and navel were all decorated with traditional vials. I added my own poisons to the ensemble. The polished ring on my finger shone brightly with the minuscule glass bead I placed in its prongs.

Yolanda placed a few more opals down my sternum, another sheer red bit of fabric was tied around my chest. She stepped back with prideful eyes. I looked into the mirror, not recognizing myself in the slightest. Not until I moved the mass of beautifully curled hair laced with lilacs and glanced at the tattoos on my spine, did I remember. "Don't cry. It will ruin all my efforts."

"You're a genius," I said, watching my plump red lips move in my reflection. I *was* delicious to look at. Sultry, confident, and luxurious. I strapped two daggers to my thighs, my excitement for the evening ahead returned slowly.

I felt and looked like a feminine Goddess reincarnated to raise hell.

Yolanda spun me in a circle and did a final exam. "You are an easy canvas to work with, Ivy Woodlander."

There was an impatient fist on the door. I ignored it and took Sage d'Loure's sister into my arms. "Wisteria. My parents named me Wisteria, Anna called me Ivy. After I fulfill my promise to her, I hope angry Ivy can find peace and I may blossom back into wild Wisteria."

"I look forward to meeting her," she hugged back. "Now, let's go before these idiots break down the door."

Brock yelled, "We are not idiots! This whole plan is damned and doomed if we wait any long for the two of you to ..." He stopped talking when the door swung open. He looked at me and looked away quickly. "Did you forget to get dressed this morning?" He hollered. He was limping towards the exit with his bags already strapped across him. Yolanda dressed for winter, grabbed her travel bag and the sword Count Nicholo gifted her. Count took a long white hooded cloak off the wall and gestured I step into it. His eyes pupils widened with each step I took towards the outstretched garment. They were coals simmering with a wicked heat lurking behind them. I fussed with my tongue ring, tapping it against my teeth. The fabric hit my shoulders.

"Silk!" I exclaimed merrily. I tied a knot at my neck and twirled in my bare feet. "This is a lovely farewell gift."

A firm arm halted my merriment. "Not farewell. I will leave a trail for you to find us in the woods. We will wait at the docks for a half day. If you are not there, go west with Drift."

I gave him a soldier's salute. Brock grumbled, "Cover up and hug me." I complied. He patted my back lightly, as if he was scared to break me. "Remember, I will make your life a living hell if you don't come back for me." He left abruptly. Yolanda winked and went down the stairs with Brock.

Nikki pulled me aside, away from the door. He placed his fingers under my chin and brought my gaze up to meet his. The darkness was slow to dissipate, but the gold did return. "Living life without a woven is an arduous burden. Most kill themselves shortly after losing one. The threads are strong, as you now know, and none of us are immune to them. If one of us dies, the other two will live with unspeakable pain." He pulled up his sweaters to reveal a scar tattered chest. "Paralyzing, perpetual pain, that makes the Weaver's short stint in the broom closet seem like a cakewalk." He dropped his shirts.

"Why are you telling me all this?" I asked.

He straightened his stance. "You need to understand how profound this moment is. I am trusting you with not only the life of my brother, but mine. Bring him back to us, I can't live long if he remains lost or if you are dead. I demand you both in my life and alive."

I blinked. My long eyelashes brushing the mask of gems. "Are you sentimental or just outrageously selfish?"

"Shut it," he followed up quickly.

"I'll be safe. You do the same," I insisted. Then it was quiet. I calmly set my right-hand square onto his chest. His hands swiftly enveloped mine and held me to him. A sign of relief escaped his lips. I closed my eyes and felt the two hearts pounding away, beating as one beneath my palm. His pulse was faster than mine. "I'll get him back." His eyes were still closed, his grip around my wrist still tight.

"I know," he stated factually.

"I mean, if there is one way to lure a spell-bound reclusive incubus out it's with one of two things, jealousy or peaches." His eyes finally opened and were filled with light. Relief dawned.

My hand stayed pinned to him until he was standing in the hallway, saddle bags and weaponry untouched at his feet. "Yolanda will think I am fucking you again for money if you don't get down there. I mean, do I look like a complete whore?" I snorted, sarcastically and pointed to my ass cheeks hanging out. He was shaking his head, biting back what was bound to be an enraging comment. A comment that never left his lips. He pulled away, my hand slowly felt the effects of gravity and dropped to my sides.

I stood alone, locked in the room with the sword in my hand. I kept the window open, listening for outbursts in the nearest districts. It didn't take long for the distant rumblings of pandemonium to pervade avenues and streets as people were seen fleeing establishments and festivities to run home. I counted six pyres from my window that had burst into flame and sent smoke wafting into the snowy winds. By the time Cultee came to collect me, the guards below had managed to get their armor on and find their swords.

When he entered and saw the gift I prepared for him, he rubbed his temples. "There is no other way. I need another chance to get Cobar and slay Stegin. Drift needs a slap in the face, he doesn't know the plan yet, and the royals need a healer. I am the master of my craft, the best Numaal has ever had. I heard rumors, the king is dying, if not dead already. If the prince wants him alive, he will see value in me. I can barter just about anything for the life of a king." Cultee waved his hand in the air, pretending to listen.

"I know I will not be changing your mind, so get a blanket and follow me into the carriage. We will be in there for a few hours, waiting to see if the gala commences amid the battle preparation. My brother is foolish enough to continue the party even with half in attendance. Boots, too!" He called. I gathered up my long white silk train and popped up my hood which was deep set and hung low over my mask. My red lips peeked out.

The blinds were drawn in the carriage. He finally admitted, "It's a brilliant plan. I only wish I didn't care so much about your outcome."

"At least, our comrades succeeded this morning. All the pyres are lit, people are moving to safety and will hopefully remain cautious for the night ahead. That's a good omen," I tried conveying any sense of optimism, despite feeling like I wanted to hide away in a haystack and wade out the battle. "Another fantastic omen of success is that I met Calabress."

Now, his attention peeked. "Did she agree to leave?"

"No," I stated. "Where her brother is, she will be. She is staying in the palace, helping you however she can from the inside now and when you take control of it." I crossed my arms and frowned across the carriage. "After all I told you about my transgressions and secrets, you didn't think to tell me that Calabress was your sister?"

"It didn't seem relevant. You figured it out well enough, and would have helped either way without knowing she was my little sister," he said.

I took this time to take in his cut and combed hair, which grayed about the tips of his ears. He oiled his trimmed beard with a musky cologne and had his family crest polished and fastened to his breast pocket. He wore nothing extravagant, his scars and calluses all the adornments he needed, all the medals of honor the world needed to see.

"Tell me what I am walking into."

He did. He spoke about the commencement speech, tables of imitators, the event agenda, the gift giving, the banquet food service, the dances and the offering acceptance.

Outside the carriage, midday passed into early evening. The pyres stayed lit, but there was no ringing of gongs to send the men from the barracks to the outer wall. At least, they had their armor on and swords sharpened. Cultee pointed out that most had started to sober up after weeks of celebrating the deep of winter's arrival. Sober sword swinging and spear throwing were preferred to the alternative.

The jostle of the carriage's wheel sent me sliding across the leather seat on the silk robe. I steadied myself against the frosted window, my fingers imprinted themselves on the cloudy surface. I flexed them when my bones felt frigid, burying them into the plaid woolen blankets across my lap, my steel sword on top.

"Stay a step behind me. We are the fifth gift to be presented. Shall I introduce you?"

I shook my head, my lustrous curls framing my face. "No. I am done hiding."

"You'll have to captivate their focus to earn their ear. If not them, the crowd. They will do what they must to appease those who've risked showing up. Entertainment and extravagance, before disemboweling and demanding," he said, watching his reflection on the smooth surface of my blade.

"Where will Drift be?"

"Behind the table of three Stegin Monte decoys in gold stag masks. There is where I will be standing once I have unleashed you to the crowd."

The ring around my finger spun in circles. "The royals?"

"On a balcony, flanked by knights. Collette will have her scrying board with her. Silvers will be spotted if they enter the city's vicinity," he stated as a caution, to which I acknowledged by dipping my chin.

A loud knock on the roof of the cart disrupted our conversation. The air in my lungs froze. "Oy, they are here. Moving in with the setting sun." Asher. It was Asher.

"Asher!" I called, knocking my knuckles where I heard the initial knocks from.

"Miss Ivy? What are you doing here?" He whispered back.

Cultee grunted. "No time you two. Get the horn and blow it through the street until all the eyes on the ramparts see what is lurking in the shadows. Don't stop. Do you hear me, guard of Numaal?"

"Yes, sir," his voice was clear. The trials of this season had transformed Asher into a man. I was willing to bet his freckles didn't disappear under a scarlet blush when he said his departing words. "Bring them to their knees, Ivy Woodlander."

I intended to.

Our carriages were pulled along, another gruesome ten minutes of waiting built up a strum of tension in my chest waiting to hear Asher's horn blasting down the center of Landsfell. "The speech has concluded. Liquor is flowing and the gifts are being unwrapped with eager hands. We are next to be escorted in."

I shoved the blankets off my lap and took off the boots, not only did they not match my scant white and red clothing, but they were not authentic to the woodlander ways. I pulled my hood low over my dazzling eyes, portions of the fabric provided warmth and modesty when I stepped out of the carriage. Eight men in red encircled us. "Captain," several referred to him respectfully, crossing their spears over their chest.

"Men of the realm, my kin. Stand vigilant. You heard the horn, tonight will be long," Cultee replied and followed them forward. My long billowing train rippled behind me, the men were shrewd enough not to step on it. What a debauchery that would be. A sin that would not permit them entry to peace beyond the Veil.

Up the black stone steps we strode, my stark cape and bare toes beckoned the eyes of onlookers before we even crossed the threshold of the great ballroom.

The harp's sophisticated melodies and the polite chatter of socialites reached my ears. It was hard to keep my head down. My blood thrummed wildly as I tucked the sword under my left arm, snug to my body. I strained my eyes, frantically looking in my peripheral vision to obtain details of my surroundings. The servers were plentiful. Offering food, champagne, wine and tobacco generously to the crowd. Chains rattled. A crisp snap of a whip settled the qualm.

It wasn't Cobar kept in chains, I exhaled gratefully, but a massive wolf the size of a bull thrashing against the man who tugged at her collar. Her ribs were protruding, its maw was marred. Perhaps, a previous gift.

Cultee's worn boots halted. My feet mimicked the movement, the chilly granite a reassurance beneath my bones. "Captain Cultee Monte of Fort Fell," he was received by a voice that did not belong to Stegin. "I am as much pleased as I am encouraged by your appearance tonight."

My chaperone straightened. "I am here, as a man of Numaal. With me, a woman of Numaal." He stepped aside and flourished an arm open.

Show time.

Chapter Twenty-Eight

I strut past him with my chin up enough so the room could witness my self-assuredness and painted lips peeking out from the shimmery pureness of the hood. I must have gotten too close for the nearest table's comfort for a set of sword bearers blockaded my advancement. I smiled and pulled my hood back. They surveyed my features with unconcealed satisfaction. One congratulated Cultee on what a specimen he decided to share with the courts.

I gave a flirtatious wink and explored the scene.

The stag masks were meticulously well-designed, all three with different sizes and shapes of horns encompassing their heads, all with shades of blonde peeking out. Zander was not at the southern province's assigned seating. Neither was Gimly for that matter. The tables were clothed in red toppers and winter red roses, thorns uncut and unruly. The five gold trimmed chandeliers hung low enough to touch, where the average man would have to walk around them. Innumerous candles dripped wax from each intricate prong, lighting up the murals of clouds painted on the ceiling.

Time was of the essence, I reminded myself as I stared at the two men in front of me. "Gentleman," I greeted coyly, ensuring they got a good look at the contents dangling from my ears and the hoops on my face. I moved my robe enough for them to view the daggers strapped to my thighs. "Thank you for volunteering!" I said loud enough for the nearest tables to overhear.

"You may have them, if you remove that insulting *white* cloak," the middle man spoke up. The loathe for Akelis' White Tower and those who ruled it was palpable.

I licked my lower lip. "Impatient, aren't we?" Raising my brow, I *very* slowly untied the strings at my neck, allowing the fabric to ripple off my body. My lack of garments was to their liking. The sword under my arm lowered to hook the white fabric off the floor and slung it over to their laps. It floated elegantly and settled across them.

Stegin's table gave a laugh and a dismissive wave to his guards, who sheathed their steel and followed me as I positioned them perniciously where I needed them. The room buzzed with intrigue. Weightless on my feet I swiped two corked bottles of bubbles and placed both in one guard's grip, the other I instructed to move a spare table under the chandelier in the center. He complied and returned to his post.

My back to the prince's balcony and the high lord seating, I set the sword on the table, to better collect my hair and move it to the side. The full length of my crafter tattoo stared at them.

The grumbles were slow initially. But they amplified.

"I am Ivy Woodlander. Daughter of Alister and Lily Woodlander. The last master of my craft. The prodigy child of the south who can heal better than her ancestors and who can operate as well as any Ilanthian physician. As of recent years, the skills I have been perfecting conflicts with my woodland nature to mend. But, since the Southlands are no more, I don't have an issue with demonstrating a few tricks of survival I learned over the last years of fighting wraiths alongside my country men and captain." I acknowledged Cultee who did not move from his spot in the center of the floor.

With all eyes on me, it felt like the arena of the Pit. 'Showmanship.' Warden Rhett would have said.

I took the daggers from my straps, spinning them in my hands as I strolled around the room engaging the audience with my cocky grin, permitting them to eye my backside. Plenty of sticky gazes clung on the lowest portion of my tattoo, the lilacs and sprays of ivy on my all too visible ass cheeks. From across the hall I let the two daggers loose, there were hollers as the unexpected guests who startled.

The two champagne bottles were uncorked with the tips on my blades, that were nestled in the wall behind the wide-eye guard. Numbly, he stared at the liquid flowing over his hands. Even when I plucked the bottles out of his grasp and took two deep swallows from each, all he managed to do was blink. I adjusted his collar for him and laughed.

Applause broke out politely from the three impostor dukes in gold lion masks then spread to the other spectator tables. I rewarded the felines and stags by refilling their goblets with the remainder of the bubbly, leaping into a series of flips and handsprings once they overflowed. I sprawled myself across the table as they sipped their wines. My eyes moved upwards.

I flashed by Cultee and jumped onto the table beneath the chandelier. I walked on my hands and looped my legs around the hanging metal prongs, hoisting myself up onto the large candelabrum using the strength of my legs. Sword clenched between my teeth, I lifted myself upwards towards the ceiling.

To better view who resided on that balcony. To better barter with my enemy.

My legs steadied me as I counted the sentries surrounding the parameters, one hundred men in red was not nearly enough to guard the five thousand that occupied the enormous estate. We would need all the aid this scummy city could muster. I wonder how many wraiths that powerful jaw of the wolf could ripe through, if it didn't rip through me first?

I had climbed high enough now to enter the direct line of sight of the Faceless Prince in his black raven mask. The red priestess on his lap was hastily scrying with sand on the side table. Checking my blood no doubt. Two bulking figures stood adjacent to the prince.

Zander was one.

The knight who violated and slaughtered my family was the other.

Keeping my shit together was vital, I hastily tried to collect my scattering thoughts which left me faster than I could comprehend them.

I called to the room, "Even among the crafters, whose only means to spread national news was through word of mouth and windrider ships, we knew of King Resig's deteriorating health. Collette was bragging yesterday of his death, pity your knights murdered and raped your nation's own men and women, my family included, or we may have come to his aid sooner. I may have offered my aid."

The gossip of the crowd grew. I fed them, "It's true. Collette was there, barking the orders of a man in a black carriage. If she won't vouch for it, hundreds will. Hundreds that are alive and well who roam with truth and anger. Evil hasn't killed all of us off. Nor, will it." The prince, unreadable behind a mask of a beaked black raven, sat immobile and seemingly unperturbed. "Thankfully, the capital knights forgot to kidnap several well-loved and kind hearted Ilanthians on their hunt, permitted by the nation's dukes. They were befriended. We were taught how to read, fight and given the secrets of the society of Remnants," I lied. Collette's beautiful face fell beneath her feathery red mask. "The missing guards and growing number of restless, venomous monsters is coincidentally suspicious? It doesn't take a university student to decipher simple facts." Below me, people were shifting uncomfortably. Many opted to leave.

Many had already run out. When they swung open the doors to leave, they were greeted with the horns of battle, the cries of children, the calls of soldiers lifting up arms.

The prince pulled Collette closer, whispering in her ear. She rose in her fitting red gown, and walked to the balcony's edge. "What is it that you want dear? A confession? Bloodshed?" She was all but screaming above the uncertainty below.

The noise in the room escalated. Confused lords merely looked up, waiting for direct orders from their prince.

"This nation's secrets have already been spilt. More will be revealed in time, and in a much more dramatic manner I can assure you." I spun my sword in a way that even those unstudied in combat knew it was Ilanthian. "As for bloodshed, that is inevitable. The wraiths you failed to stop are coming. Coming fast. They will be here before dinner settles in your stomachs."

"There is much you don't know. Stop your nonsense before Havnoc stops your heart," she eyed the knight in sharp layers of black armor. His horns were straight and sharp on either side of his helmet.

"*Havnoc*," I repeated. "I now have the name of my mother's rapist. An ugly name for an ugly brute." He laughed low as I glared. When his tongue flicked out in a suggestive manner, I hissed and bite the air. A threat to bite it off and shove it up his—Collette's staff slammed into the granite beneath her.

"What do you want, Woodlander?"

"Since the prince's silence is confirmation enough for his own people to hear his betrayal, I will give him one last opportunity to redeem himself." The prince's mask dipped, showing engagement with my proposal. "Despite the lack of honorable leadership in Numaal, I think we can influence tonight's outcome. Make Cultee Monte the duke of the southern province, allow him to command *all guards* present *and* the capital knights you have brought with you. He has fought evil. I have fought at his side."

"And in return?" The priestess posed.

I let out a mirthful laugh of hysteria. "As if saving his life, reputation and Numaal isn't enough? You ask what I will give in return?" I leapt over to the balcony, quickly finding my way to Zander's side. Tugging his arm, I brought him close enough to plant a kiss on his cheek. His hands tucked behind his back as Havnoc's were.

Staring at his stoic face, I wasn't ready for the influx of syphering. *Bone shards. The Remnant's carry bone. Collette's staff. Break. Break it!* Our bond was tight on either end. Unable to open his door, he shook it violently. *Get me out! Break it!* The sheer panic of a descendant of a mighty God was painful. He couldn't hear any thought I sent him. Another kiss on the cheek will have to suffice. "Good to see you again, Drift."

My eyes found the glossy wood and golden staff in the priestess's left hand. The balcony was high enough that if I jumped, I would break my legs, it should break the fancy walking stick. I hopped onto the banister and walked one foot in front of the other, sensually prowled, was a more accurate term. Whatever I had to do to lure my woven out of his shackles. "Landsfell is under attack. We will not survive if we do not fight unified and tactically. Legalize Cultee Monte as duke and give him full command of the militia here tonight. Now!" I was nose to nose with Collette, her outlined lips grimaced.

The prince got up from his chair. "Friends of my beloved city of Landsfell and those from beyond, I, Prince of Numaal, Son of King Resig, hereby declare Cultee Monte the current, indisputable duke of the southern province." His voice was neither weak nor strong, youthful or old. But what it was, was absolute. I watched his demeanor, it was not that of a son grieving his father's death or someone who particularly was surprised that he was confronted and exposed. "All enlisted guards are his to command. The Knights of the Crimson Cohort will stay under Duke Cultee's command and will not return until the city is set right."

In an instant, Captain Cultee took control of the room below. The staff were called upon to escort the attendees deeper into the manor for safety, while those with any skill in combat were pulled forward, destined for a sword and shield within the minutes that would follow. The prince stepped backward. Two whistles and his bulky bodyguards took to his side. "Woodlander, come," his words hit me strongly.

My blood pounded in my ears. "Come," the raven face demanded again. My lips tasted coppery and dry. Anna's memory resurfaced violently.

I blinked and the raven cocked its head with piqued interest. "Ivy Woodlander, you *will* come." The Weaver tolerated none of that. She shocked my chest and I yelped, losing my balance.

"Can't," I said, gasping from the electric shock. "I have a battle to fight, family to avenge." I turned to Havnoc. "I will fucking kill you. Just not tonight. I want you to lie awake at night wondering when I will castrate that tiny cock of yours and cram it down your throat, which I will slit shortly after." I spit on his breastplate.

The prince whispered in Collette's ear. The opportunist I was grabbed her staff and let go of the balcony.

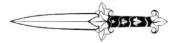

My aloof limbs scarcely accomplished a distance that would have been easy if I were in a proper state of mind. The sword fell from my hand while I held tightly to the linked chain chandelier. I loosened my grip, the flesh on my palm torn open, but I descended a safe distance to jump to the floor. I vaulted in the air, hurling the staff down with as much momentum as I had.

Like a cat, I landed on my feet. Around me lay the shattered fragments of Collette's stick. Among the wood and gold, rested a long black brittle bone. A femur. "Don't touch it," Zander shouted midleap from the balcony. Somehow the floor beneath him did not splinter with the impact of his weight. Unphased, he hurriedly put on leather gloves and wrapped the femur in layers of leather skins. He knotted it to his waist. We both eyed it with distaste.

Together, we turned up at the balcony. It was empty.

His hand found mine. My fingers wrapped tightly around his. The tremble in his hand was enough to rattle my empathy. *Wisteria.* Down our bond stormed a breathtaking display of colors, he doused me in all his presence. Yellows of joy and gratefulness. Blues, like his eyes, of contentment and steadfast. Red of anger and release. Brown of disgust.

Grey of fear and dread. White of his commitment. The gold sun swam around gleefully in Zander's cage, he let me stroke it. Only once, before grey swept me away and set me a safe distance away from Oyoko's power. His lips kissed the smooth skin on the inside of my wrist.

Little flower. I was scared. For the first time in decades, I was scared. If they knew who I was, this world would be demolished. He pivoted to face me, his left hand stuck in my hair, around the stem of a lilac. His blue and white gleamed of relief. And when Fennick blinked gold, I felt his body relax. *I knew you would come, but part of me was scared you wouldn't see it through after what you stumbled upon in the pre-festivities. None of that was real.* My skin crawled, hearing him speak about it. Repulsion hit me and I pried my hand away from him. He held tighter. There was no strawberry ice cream to vomit, but I had plenty of bile. I pulled away. He held tighter. *Stop. I was spellbound by the bitch with her wand, but she was not immune to my magic, nor was the company. I set up a scene to play in everyone's minds, once they entered the room. You and Yolanda saw what I needed the world to see.*

I didn't reply right away, there was much disarray sprinting about that it was easy to get distracted. He called my name again, his grip slacking in worry. *When I looked into the room, I thought I saw the great shadow of Oyoko's wearing holes in the carpet pacing. That was you. The* real *you, albeit, you were immaterial.*

His cool breath swept across my bare torso when he exhaled. *You saw me.*

You had wings, your form was of mist and moonlight. You moved through furniture. Zander's head came down to rest on my shoulder, his hand slid around my waist. My skin turned into pinpoints at his touch. It was that moment he seemed to remember I was mostly naked. And that we weren't alone. His attention caught on my erect nipples shining through the sheer fabric. I collected my sword off the ground while he unbuttoned his dress shirt at a superhuman rate.

"Put it on," he growled, using his body to shield me from the golden masked aristocrats. "They are plotting. They are as shocked as everyone else that the prince agreed to your terms and left. Their sentiments of abandonment may work for us as a whole." The hem of his red garment hung above my knees. I lifted the ends to tie them tailed in a knot around my waist. Not liking my legs exposed, he reached to undo the knot, I hit his hand with the hilt of the sword.

"I can't fight in a pillow case." Pinching his bearded scowl between my bleeding fingers, I forced him to look at me. *I am going to get Cobar before they take him to Kathra. I'll head to the southport next, Nikki, Brock and Yolanda lit the pyres and left this morning.* "Stay with Cultee. See him equipped for success, this city must stand." *Then fly until you find me.*

I will always find you, Wisteria. I released his chin only to wrap my arm around his neck. Our lips pressed together softly as we shared our last mingling breaths. *I will search until there is no notion of time, until the world stops turning and the stars stop burning. I chose you* before *the Weaver even intervened. You gave me your name and I vowed my life to you before she ever tied us together for a lifetime. Even without the Weaver binding us, I would have chosen you and you would have been stuck with me pursuing you.*

I know. I said, after his statements sunk in.

We separated before we entered a deeper lip lock. We drew our swords, and ran in opposite directions. His eyes stayed on me until I rounded the corner.

Chapter Twenty-Nine

The layout of the tunnels, I memorized.

The format of the estate however… Well, I figured the west wing would be west. I sprinted out of the great hall chasing the setting sun. Forty seconds into my endeavors I slammed directly into the back of a noble. He was so busy shouting a name he didn't notice me wedging myself around him pulling cotton fuzz out of my mouth. Backtracking, I ran down the staff hallway, which was hopefully not in use.

It was. They all were. Frustration exploded. I swore.

Hundreds of people shook with fear and confusion blocked yet another route. Fancy folks were piling in behind me, I weighed my chances of success by climbing the outside of the brick residence and roof hopping to the west wing. Capital knights would surely steal away Cobar, those who made use of his blood here would be presumed dead or taken with him. My heart was in my throat when I fought my way back into the great hall with elbow jabs and pushing. Rhett popped out from behind a banister, calling for his men. They were off to dismantle the royal escorts and mounts by the sound of it. I hoped they succeeded.

I passed unnoticed.

Cultee and Zander had cleared much of the disorder before exiting with their newly acquired men. The main doors would remain a jar until the inner city had been compromised. In the corner, the prowling wolf snapped at the passing guards armed with steel, her ten-foot chain latched onto the thick bars of a heater unit.

I made a dash towards the she-wolf. Arms up, hands open I strode into her radius. "I won't hurt you," I said, after the hairs on her spine stood on end. Beneath her grey fur rested an iron collar. I took out one of the pins holding my flowers in place and held it out for her to observe. Her unnerving eyes did not blink. They were hardened with abuse. They were also cognizant.

"I can try to pick that lock." I pointed to her neck. Her teeth bared at my moving hand. I tucked it back to my side. The ground was cold on my bare, knobbed knees. I set my sword down and let her sniff me. "I have seen wolf packs bounding up the Cliffs of Sound, but I've never seen one as big and beautiful as you. Nor have I seen one so alone. You must miss your family." She made a gruff, short exhale through her muzzle. "I miss mine too," I offered.

The wolf broke eye contact, she padded closer, her neck within reach. My motions were slow and deliberate. Startling her would cost me a limb. The head of my hair pin jabbed around aimlessly until I found the press lever. It slipped the lever twice. "Cheap, bloody, damn piece of crap hair pin!" I yelled, feeling my bleeding hand tenderize with each passing second. The wolf's tail lowered as I brought myself directly in front of her. "Almost...Got it!" The iron collar clunked between her paws, she took one look at it on the ground and pummeled through the lines of people. I think I smiled. I worked the rest of the chain off the heater and tossed it by the steps.

My fingers reached for my sword when a distinctly familiar wave of jasmine hit me.

My blood awakened with unexpected delight. "*Stegin*." I mirthfully stated his name. "I had been praying Oyokos would deliver you to me." I spun on my knees and jumped upright. Stegin kept his sword held at the ready. His blonde pony slicked back behind a gemstone encrusted dragonfly mask. "And to repay the God for honoring my request, I will send you to meet him."

He loosened the cuff around his neck, his veins bulging. He flexed his wrist and spun his heavy longsword with both of his. "You've demoted me from my title and given my lands, home and wealth to your homely Captain of Fort Fell." I advanced. He backstepped into a more spacious location of the great hall.

It was impossible to stifle the laugh that erupted. "I've done much more than that and after I kill you, I will erase your name from the world. I will ask Maruc to banish your existence and wipe clean any trace of you and your bastard son."

Spit foamed at the corner of his mouth. His chest was red and heaving with anger. "Such hate? For not sending aid to a cause damned from the very beginning? For not recognizing my scouts being plucked off one by one when half my troop went missing the years prior?"

We moved in a circle, two swings of a blade apart. "Do I not look familiar?" I gave a childish one, two skips, blindly whirling my sword behind me. "No? Perhaps you can recall the girl who you stabbed with a rusty spear in your dungeon who later escaped after you murdered the love of her life. I've returned to take your life and make a spectacle of your poor choices. Do you have anything you want to say before I humiliate you further?" His lips trembled at my arrogance.

He gripped his ten fingers around the sword and lifted it to strike. "It is a futile fight, one I yielded to a decade ago. You cannot win, but you can join the conquest. I'm not a Remnant, but I facilitated their expansion by my own free will. My choice allowed Cultee to ride south with his life, permit his sister food and shelter and give my son an opportunity to prove himself as a man."

His words constricted my throat. "I'd rather die standing, than be a spineless worm." *Enough talking!* I had to remind myself. *Cobar!*

"The Dark King will come for you!"

I smiled. "I know the Lord of Darkness, he is my friend, my woven," I whispered. The truth in my words fueled my fight. "He has already laid his claim to me."

I struck first. Second. Third. Nothing powerful or fancy, just gauging his ability and response time. He managed to block my blows, but was not a contestant for anything fun. I frowned coming to the realization his death would be boring compared to all the ways I envisioned him stuck to the wall with his rusty spear head.

He tripped on the wolf's chain while avoiding my single-handed swipes. Inspiration dawn.

Stegin Monte's death would be quick, but it would also be unforgettable. The vial from my belly button, I removed and uncorked. The spotted spores infiltrated his body, muscle by muscle he froze. There was a loud clamor when his weapon and body hit the floor.

The great hall stared, and wisely, did not interfere as I ripped off his mask. They did not meddle as I encircled his neck with the iron collar. Did not plead with me as I dragged his limp body to the chandelier and fastened the end of the chain to its base. I cracked my neck and prepared for the completion of my vow to Anna. "You permitted the royal family, their priestess and knights to hunt aimable, innocent silver *and* red bloods living peacefully *together* on your lands. They slaughtered the crafters and fed us to the night walkers to *become* a soulless army." I raised my voice to engage with the crowd of the royal family's supporters. "They stole an Ilanthian mother who taught me to heal and read, an infant who I watched be birthed into this world—*our world*—and a child who I could not have loved more than if he came from my own mother's womb. You experimented on them! You cut into their bodies! You and your secret society are drinking their blood! Children!" I shouted loudly.

I recomposed myself and looked around the room. The wolf was perched on a buffet table, gorging on anything edible. The staff dared not move. The party guests looked ill. If they were scared of me and the truths I spilt, they were not equipped to survive outside these walls. Nonetheless, they were deserving to live in whatever compound and in whatever manner they saw fit.

Stegin's breathing was wet, his eyes went wide when I stood before him with my sword point pressed into his right shoulder. "You robbed Anna and I of our time together, of our last goodbyes. You robbed me of happiness and answers. There will be no final words for you." At that, I thrust my sword where he had stuck me two years ago. His eyes misted. No noise came.

When I released the latch that held the candelabra low, some sounds escaped. The sound of a broken neck and collapsing airway.

The former duke's body thrashed as it swung many meters above. The blue sky and white fluffy clouds painted behind him was a far too serene backdrop for his shit-stained pants and bloody vomit. His excrements spattered around the pristine stone floor. He was dead in seconds.

When I heard the agonizing wallows of my least favorite bastard, I found the nearest window and ran west, rooftop to rooftop.

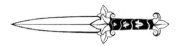

The stained glass windows of Duchess Kacey's dining room were lit up from within. With no latch to weasel inside, I had to break it. The loose bricks from the rooftop were slammed into the image of the grain field time and time again until I hit the weakest corner just right. The sound of breaking glass was muted by a gust of snowy wind blowing down from the north.

I entered, landing on slivers of glass. Bloody footprints followed me as I ran to the music chamber, toward Cobar's prison.

Gimlian Monte had arrived first. His foul grin wide as he pressed a knife to a child's throat. The child didn't fight against the grip or bother open his eyes, he calmly stood, accepting death. "I grew up here. I know this house better than most." He snickered seriously. "You killed my family, now I will kill yours. Poetic, isn't it?"

One move from me and Cobar would be dead. So, I didn't move. "What do you want in exchange for his life?" I asked.

His hazel eyes opened and he put a face to the voice. "Sissy!" Cobar exclaimed. Well, he whimpered.

"Sissy is here for you. Your dad is waiting for us," I responded. Hope rekindled in his eyes.

Gimly nestled the blade deeper. The tender brunette winced. "Drop your weapons, Ivy. Then we can negotiate for the boy. We can fight over who gets the biggest piece of his corpse." Two daggers and a sword were on the floor before he finished his statement. I kicked them over to him, my arms remained above my head, hands open.

A third party entered. Gimly and I boarded our defensive stand to incorporate Priestess Collette. "The boy isn't yours to negotiate with Gimlian," she said, caressing a black whip. "Release the boy and stand behind me. You are coming to the capital."

He didn't move, he countered her with questions. "She strung my father up from the ceiling and embarrassed the entire patriarchy. You want me to just give her what she came for?" He was breathing so hard, sweat was on his upper lip. "Are you allowing her and the boy to leave *alive*?"

"Alive, but not well. Yes." Her voice was monotone and unamused. Collette unfurled the length of the whip at her side. There were three metal tails on the end. My bare back was already cringing. "The girl will earn the boy's release by being flogged. After that, we will make another deal." She finally showed emotion by curling up her lips. "I assume you also want to see Moriah and Rory delivered to safety, right woodlander?"

Cobar was limp in Gimly's arms, shaking with relief. I dipped my chin in her direction. She ordered Gimly to drop the boy and strip my garb. Cobar was on his knees staring at me. For him, I showed no fear. For him, I gave a lively twirl as Zander's shirt was pulled from me. "Cobar, my sweet brother. Can you go to the pianoforte and practice the keys for me? Don't stop until I come to you, okay?" He was sprinting across the room towards the instrument. His tiny, fumbling fingers struck the black and white key.

The loathsome cockroach Gimly was, he unbound all my clothes and traced his fingers up my body. "Piece of shit," I muttered. He smacked my legs. "Don't pretend you are interested, your dick is limp and your seed is dead."

He smacked my face. "You?"

I spit out blood. "Obviously, you pervert. Now, I made you impotent and the last of your filthy line." He raised his hand to strike me again. That is when I made the decision to flip my ring around.

I caught his wrist and dislodged his elbow to bring him to his knees. I twisted a little more and he was screaming, flat on his belly. He wouldn't notice the little cut my ring made with all the unpleasant sensations I inflicted. I stepped over him and braced myself on the nearest wall. "Are we doing this Collette or are you going to stand there admiring me with raging jealousy?"

The first whip took away my ability to breathe.

The second, my body's ability to stand upright.

Music of childhood melodies echoed as I convulsed on the floor. Spatters of my blood hit the wall and began to pool under me by the fifth strike.

I heard joy in the Priestess's voice. "Your back is unrecognizable. Your master mark is shredded."

"Play louder, Cobar," I managed to say. Screams threatened to tear through me as the bones on my spine shuddered with blinding pain. They spasmed with the next blow, I vomited on the floor.

My nose, throat and eyes burning as I heaved in agony.

Cobar was worth it. All life is worth fighting for. At this moment, I wasn't fighting with weapons or words, I was fighting to stay alive.

"On your feet," she said. I was disoriented. My hands could not find the wall in front of me. "On. Your. Feet!"

She lashed again. I shrieked and felt myself breaking.

The piano continued despite the door opening and closing for the second time. I spit bile out of my mouth and turned to see who was unfortunate enough to stumble upon this mess. A black raven mask walked past me. The prince snatched the leather stick and whip from his priestess and brought his open gloved palm to meet the side of her face. "I see I made a grievous mistake in trusting you to deliver the proposal. Your reformatory education starts when we get back to Kathra. Keep that whip on hand and I'll demonstrate how to wield it during your lessons as it strikes your back until you've reeled in your independence."

"Yes, my grace. Sorry, my grace," Collette trembled.

"Havnoc, enter!" the prince called. The knight entered. I tried my damnedest to compose myself in the knight's presence.

"Here, my liege," he grumbled, laughing at my attempt to appear threatening.

"Find me a salve and fresh towels for our woodlander friend. I will need my crest already heated," he said. My stomach churned again. The knight left to fulfill his master's wishes. "Ivy, was it?" I involuntarily trembled so badly I couldn't gesture a reply. "I take responsibility for how this unfolded, this was not how I envisioned she would have delivered my proposal. How distasteful! Cobar is yours to take, no one will stop you. This was meant to be a gesture of good faith so when she offered, on my behalf, the lives of Rory and Moriah for your hand in marriage, it would have been better received."

I rested on my knees, gaping at him.

He placed a finger to my lips. I wanted to bite it off.

"Don't reply yet. If you deny me now, I have no reasons left to convince myself to let you and the boy escape tonight. You have one year and one day to come to the capital to claim your friends and your title, as Queen Wisteria Torval of Numaal." I blinked dumbly, settling onto my hindquarter fighting the urge to cry as the smallest breeze from the fans met the fresh fileted muscles of my back.

In walked Havnoc. Gimly grinned at what he held in his possession, a white hot brander in his hands, a circle with two ravens. One glance at his ugly face and I knew it was meant for me. My chest rose and fell fast. My body couldn't take more abuse. "Shh, shhh," the Faceless Prince cooed, brushing my curls away from my back. Blood soaked the ends. I recoiled from his touch. "Collette was to mark you in a manner that set you aside from other women so when you came to Kathra and requested me, I could spot you. Slaves have scarred backs, you are not a slave, oh no. You are the lucky lady to wear my personal emblem seared on their flesh."

"No," I choked, finally finding words. "No!"

"You will wear this with pride one day, my darling."

"Cobar, louder!" His fists clunked around the keys, holding no tune.

There was no running, no crawling, the molten iron met my shoulder. It seared and sizzled when it contacted wet blood. My flesh blackened and blistered on contact. When it lifted, the pain persisted. I slunk across the floor, biting back a mangled scream that refused to escape in the presence of my enemy. I reached my sword.

A foot stepped on my hand. "Now, now love. We are not done yet. I have medicine and clothes for you." Wet towels dabbed my wounds, thick layers of petroleum salve coated my back. I was lifted upright and given feminine pants, Zander's shirt and the coat off of the prince's back. "Put it on. I want to see how you look in proper golds and crimsons." I did. Only to end this encounter soon. "Yes, yes. I have chosen well." He adjusted my bloody hair and rubbed my lifeforce together between his fingertips. "One year and one day, woodlander."

Collette, Gimly and Havnoc flanked him as he departed.

The door shut.

Chapter Thirty

Cobar was in my arms. I knelt to inhale the earthy scent of his hair and wipe his tears and snot on the despicable coat. It was him. He was in my arms. Alive.

I had done it.

"Sissy!" he screamed and buried himself deeper into my chest.

"Cobar, let's get out." He refused to let go, I did not blame him. Nor would I protest how painful his touch felt. Were it anyone else I would have thrown them off me, for my flesh—what was left of it—burned. If I was going to carry him, I would need liquid anesthesia and something to make me dumb enough to see this through.

On our way out of the Duchess's kitchenette, I drank a half canister of amber liquid and stole two full pocket canteens of potent port wine. There was a pair of homely white shoes on the shelf. I stole those. "Around my neck," I instructed Cobar on where to hold me. The least ruined locations. Thin arms swung behind my knot of hair.

There would be people in the tunnels, it was unavoidable. But with the rooftops inaccessible with Cobar and the hallways packed to the brim, I took the risk.

Flickering lights shone eerily down passage ways. The confusing shouts from above and from those using the tunnels echoed. Cobar buried into my neck. He repeated his name and mine, as if he had forgotten both in the years of his lamenting. I took another deep swing of the port. I gagged it down with particulates of my blood before shoving back into the coat pocket and gripping my sword in my dominant hand.

The cemetery's egress would be the one least used. "Hold your breath. We will be out soon," I said, hurrying along with a limp. The filth of the dead mucked up the puny servant slippers I wore. The sypher rope tightened.

Location? Status? Zander was more overbearing than a commander on the field.

Cobar and I made it to the graveyard, we've a mile or more until we reach the stables by the Iron Gate. Stegin is dead. Gimly left with the royal's entourage. We emerged from a tombstone. I set my sights on the men, and women, in commoners attire wielding fire lancets, aimed outside the stone and wicker walls.

Pinks and blue swarmed over me. *You must be relieved and elated, Wisteria.*

The journey is not done yet, my friend. Physically, I was falling apart. Mentally, my wellbeing shattered the moment that Prince Torval of Numaal branded me as his. Neither of these things I would tell him. *Is the way to the stables clear?*

There are no wraiths meandering, but plenty of citizens. Within a quarter hour they will crash upon us like waves upon the rocks. The guards on the wall can already hear the breathing of restless. Hurry.

I am trying. I'm carrying my brother. I said as an excuse for my sluggish pace. I started off in the direction of the gate. We would not make it out of the city before the battle started. *Where are you?*

Boiling cauldrons of oil and hoisting them up to the ramparts.

I waited a long moment before I asked. *Do you have enough of Oyoko's magic to dissolve us and reappear in the stables?*

You don't think you can make it.

I know we won't make it.

Zander appeared, ragged and handsome in his sleeveless undershirt. There must have been blood on my face. *Was the price of the boy's freedom bleeding you out?* Gritty, rough grey colors rubbed on our connection.

Stables. I redirected him. *We can talk about what happened later. Once I am on a ship and you have saved this city.* Smokey tendrils inked from his body. *Don't growl, you will scare my brother.*

He stuck his tongue out at me. I mimicked his gesture. *Is that the fucking prince's overcoat?*

I resorted to shouting. "Later!"

"It is, isn't it? He did this to you? I hate this," he grumbled and took my hand. I pressed it to my lips. *I wish I had enough magic to flux you right to Fennick.*

He knelt and brought himself eyelevel with Cobar. "Hello, brave boy. I am Zander, I'm Wisteria's friend. Can I touch your shoulder and help you get into the stables?"

Cobar looked at me with round eyes. "Sissy?"

"He is harmless," I replied to my brother. Zander's nose wrinkled.

Cobar gave his blessing and the three of us dissolved into the night.

I landed on my ass in a hay bail. Screams were everywhere. Zander tossed me a proper pair of boots and led over a readied mount. "Don't stop for anything. I'm sure Fen brought all your necessities." He got me to my feet, I waved off kisses. Cobar hadn't known me to be with anyone else besides Anna.

That conversation would not be held here.

"I am pretty sure I see Asher up there boiling himself like a lobster. You better go," I said flippantly. Zander walked out of the stables, dodging a fire lancet that some fool had set off. It blasted the building across the street, immediately bursting up into fifteen-foot flames. My mount struggled to keep composure. She pulled backwards on the reins and cornered herself.

I tried to coax her out, there was no strength in me to lead her confidently. The screaming from the civilians made her nerves worse. If the wooden roof hadn't caught fire, I might have thought my method of bribery successful. She bucked the walls and broke away. Her hooves collapsed the beams above. I held Cobar tight. He held back. I choked on pain as his legs wrapped around my waist.

Sharp pains gripped my spine so violently, there was no convincing my legs to move. A fine suited man lifted us up and out of the falling piles of timber, getting struck across his torso in the process. His shirt caught flames, illuminating his memorable face and jade jewelry. Dismayed, I screamed.

Satoritu Koi laughed as he fought off the embers, rolling on the ground. "Consider this my act of goodness, woodlander."

He grimaced a grin, until his face went white and he cowered back to the city center.

A nip pierced my left elbow, the arm that held Cobar's weight. The she-wolf padded beside me, her features more human than wildling. She was a dreamer being. "There are others like you in my company. We are going to board a ship and sail to Ilanthia. You are welcome to join us."

Her reply was the lowering of her massive body. "Are you fast?"

She snarled, taking my question as an insult. I finished one of the canteens and tossed it into the smoldering flames. I sat Cobar behind her shoulder blades and I behind him. She was the size of a small mare. We sat comfortably with our legs on either side of her body. Her muscles rippled beneath us as she rose and prowled to the street. "Iron gates. We run south for a week. We will be sprinting straight through a hoard of things trying to kill us." I let out a laugh. "But, that isn't a new concept to either of us. We will be fine," I said to hide my edgy nerves.

Horns blew.

Time in Landsfell suspended. Everyone sucked in a long breath of air, including me. It wasn't until I heard the booming voice commanding the ramparts, did I remember they stood a fighting chance.

Death was on our side for once.

Orders had been given to seal the gates and barricade.

Sensing the urgency, the wolf moved quickly around the buildings. Her steps were dizzying and agile. Cobar's fingers disappeared into the thick grey fur on her neck to keep a hold. I did the same after she leaped up a full flight of stairs in one bounce and nearly sent me on my ass. The view from the top of the ramparts did just that.

The horizon teemed with the undead. The murky, ominous storm of restless had finally arrived to unleash hell and tear through the last lives of the south. They flocked to the fire. Sprinting on their gangly legs, screeching with their elongated jaws of steel. In the backdrop, the stomachs of many churned in seeing their enemy descend without fear, without fatigue, without a spark of consciousness.

They funneled towards the gate. It was well armed with arrows, fire and hot oil. They were smart, they would learn this strategy would get them nowhere. But, before they wised up we would need to escape to the left. There was a narrow gap between them.

My thighs clamped down when I saw the wolf's intentions.

A few yards away Cultee stood with flaming arrows. He fired them at will alongside his men. "My Captain, my duke!" I made myself known above the chaos. "It has been an honor. Protect our backs!" He lit two more arrowheads and lowered his head as a farewell.

I braced Cobar under my chin. My grip tight around the wolf's neck as she leapt from the wall. Considering the height we dropped from it was a graceful landing. Not poised enough for my wounds. My back split open and the raw meat of my ribs and neck grated against the fabric. I exhaled a deep sob and urged us onward.

Calling her fast would have been an insult. She was swift; effortless in her pouncing between unaware wraiths who were too riled up with the light, warmth and fresh blood beyond the rampart. Within minutes we left the hoard of several thousand strong a league behind. After an hour, the noise of battle cries, horns and steel turned to silence. My eyes watered from the cold air her speed created when she sent it whipping at my face. Cobar buried his nose in her neck for warmth. I drank sticky, sweet wine to distract from the stinging tenderness of the blood on my shirt drying and getting ripped off, drying and getting ripped off, each time weight was shifted from front paws to back paws.

Soon, my watery eyes became real tears. The cold weather contrasted my burn so vividly, it was as if I was getting branded again. And again. There was no reprieve for my flesh. The pain and the tears persisted. I buried my blanches and put my forehead on Cobar's back, letting his presence absorb my silent weeping. Yolanda's gemstones she had glued flaked off in the pattern my tears flowed.

"My friends left a trail," I managed, catching her sniffing the air with flaring nostrils. She had already picked up on their scent, her wolfly grin told me we were close. "You can rest." She shook her ears, but the pace notably slowed, her breathing more of a pant. We stopped once to relieve ourselves. The second time we stopped was an hour before the sun broke and it was to unite with the other half of our company.

Brock had a large fire lancet aimed in our direction. His jittery finger stayed on the trigger until we entered their clearing. Nikki lowered his bow, his keen eyes spotted the matting in my hair. I gave him a wary look, I was not in a mood to answer too many questions. The wolf laid down in a fresh mound of snow. She was built for this climate.

I nudged Cobar awake and slid him off the wolf's back in unison with me. Neither of our legs worked, we tumbled into a kneeling position. "Cobar, I would like to introduce you to my friends." He buried his cold hands into my sleeve. I pointed to the rose cheeked amputee. "That is Brock. He is an underhill. He traded with the same merchants as Eliousie's husband each summer and he lost his leg fighting the bad things that kept you up at night. He is one of the good guys, okay?" I felt his chin bob. Brock smiled wide, charming the kid. Nothing in his eyes saw him as an oddity or a rare treasure. I exhaled a breath I didn't know I held.

Nikki hid his weapons and took off his hat. "That is Nick. He has traveled to many of the same places as your dad and he is full of fanciful stories." Nikki wiggled his fingers in our direction, Cobar peeked his chin off my elbow.

Yolanda pulled a saddle bag off the ground and slowly walked over with it. "I am Yolanda d'Loure. I keep these fools in line. You ought to know by now how much mischief your sister gets herself into." Yolanda knelt in the snow with us. She untied the bag and held up small sized winter clothes.

Cobar took a breath. "Sissy and mischief go together better than butter on toast." Yolanda laughed; I concealed a joyful tear by reaching into the bag for articles of clothes. What a relief part of his innocence had been spared!

"Right you are. Would you like to get dressed before or after breakfast?" She asked the youth kindly.

"Before," he said, biting his dried lips. He flinched when she too quickly pulled out a sweater and fleece bottom.

"I'll go get you some apples and rye bread, while you get snuggled warm," Yolanda excused herself having watched Cobar bury himself in the crook of my arm. Nikki was watching, he saw everything. So, I hid my grimace when Cobar hugged my oozing welts.

The wolf behind me rested, her eyes were shut. "She is not a threat. She is one of us," I pointed to the large canine. "Without each other neither of us would have made it out of Landsfell alive." Brock admired her from a distance. Yolanda continued her cautious stance. "Can you bring over my warm garb too? This top coat is from the prince, I don't know if it is laced with bone shards to manipulate me. The remnants of *something*." The last of the beverages I finished off, it warmed my chest. I tossed the canister in the snow and worked on finding the zipper piece under gold tassels. Such fruity, frivolous fashions. Nikki had a cobalt blue wool and sheepskin long coat in his hands waiting for me. I pointed on the ground, an acceptable distance from Cobar and I where he could drop it without posing a threat, or getting a good look at the layers of fabric I bled through.

I told the collective about the state in which I left the city under siege and the events of the night. The Remnants, the femur in Collette's staff, Captain's promotion to duke and the prince's agreement to donate a section of his knights to Landsfell's cause.

"Did you handle Stegin?" Brock asked, delicately avoiding grotesque wording or talk of Anna. He adjusted the first of three saddles.

I pulled Cobar's trousers up to his navel and tied the string taut. He wiggled his fingers into mittens and allowed me to cover his head and reddened ears with the flaps of a fur rabbit hat. I placed a large wet kiss on his nose. His food was ready, but he stayed wrapped to my side. He held my leg while I shimmied out of the prince's coat. "I wouldn't be here if I didn't."

There was no resisting the draw of the icy snowflakes piled behind me. I laid my back flat onto the surface. Trembling with pain and delight as the cool, dampness permeated the oversized red shirt, soaking and softening the scabs that extended the entire length of my back. The burn on my right shoulder blade swelled and blistered as minutes passed on. I wondered if Nikki sensed my burnt skin with his elemental magic.

Yolanda sliced the apple and two pieces of rye. She spread a blanket on the ground and patted for Cobar to join her for a snowy winter sunrise picnic. "Wisteria?" She tossed a floppy waterskin at my head. I twisted it open and drank liberally.

"That is my name now, yes," I said contently after I swallowed. Cobar took the apples off the blanket. He settled his bum onto my feet and ate them there.

"It seems like there is more to the evening you have yet to disclose," Yolanda probed, offering to butter my brother's bread.

"Much. Best discussed after my favorite tiny silver blooded boy sleeps," I nudged him with my toes.

Cobar said with a mouth stuffed with bread, "I'm not tiny anymore, I'm twenty-one now, Sissy."

"My apologies, Sir Cobar Woodlander. Should I offer you a nice strong brewed coffee for lunch instead of cranberry juice? Or maybe tell your dad you are too mature for enjoying muddy puddles in spring?"

He giggled. That sound melted my heart. "Are you crying again?"

"Me? Never!" I exclaimed.

He gave a charming smirk that showed both of his dimples, a trait he inherited from Moriah. "She missed me so much she hasn't stopped crying," he educated Yolanda.

"I cried because you played the piano so damn awful it hurt my ears," I retorted.

"That is your fault. You told me to play *loudly* because you didn't want me to turn around and watch them. Or listen," he crumpled up his face into an adorable scowl.

I pinched his cheeks. He had grown a little. Easily he could pass as a six, maybe a petite, thin seven-year-old. "Did my conniving trickery work?" I prayed it had.

"Yes," he confessed. "I want to know why they made you cry. Was it because of me?"

I pushed myself up right and wrapped my arms around him. "No, Cobar. I wept for the broken state of our world." My lips pressed into his cheek. I made sure he felt my lips upturn. "Now, I rejoice, knowing the fragments of it will be re-forged, melded and made invincible." He shuttered and sank into me. Frank, bright blood dripped behind me. I gulped down my worries.

Nikki understood on some level. He was quick to relocate the disposed jacket over the area of white snow behind me that was now stained with blood, protecting the remainder of the child's naivety. My head intentionally turned away from my woven's all too stern gaze. My cuts were nothing for him to fret over. "Your canteen has run dry," Brock noted. "Do you need herbs to take away your hunger pains?" He tiptoed around my condition. I denied the slice of apple Cobar held up to my lips.

"Yes. Poppy is preferable. Even resin. No willow," I instructed. Willow would bleed me out. He rummaged in his side satchel. "How much time do we have left to rest? My new comrade needs respite." The wolf quickly blew air from her nostrils, not a sneeze, but a dismissal of my statement. "Or not." Her front paw inched closer. The boy on my lap petted her leg. She retracted her long claws and let him near.

Brock tossed a tin container.

I pried it ajar slowly so as to not spill the liquid contents. I didn't ask where he got it. I was just so happy that he had it. I licked the lid and slid the tin into my breast pocket. "These lands are abandoned. We've agreed the entire hoard set its sights on Landsfell, but we will not be taking unnecessary risks or loitering. We set out as soon as we finished saddling up and eating." The effects took a minute to calm my overawed system. But when relief came in delirious deliciousness, I was able to fully expand my lungs without spasms and turn my neck not caring about the pulling blisters. I felt audacious enough to run the rest of the way across the Deadlands. Maybe I would ask the water wolf and the fire fox to a race?

Everyone mounted their horses, the wolf lowered herself for us to straddle her. Cobar gave her an affectionate rub behind the ear as he settled his grip in her thick winter coat. "I am fine," I insisted, when Yolanda questioned my stamina. And as the day passed with little respite, I proved myself wrong. Despite the mushroom antibiotic doses that I snuck in my mouth with food, water and little physical exertion, a fever built. I was a damn fool.

We slept for two hours in the last hours of daylight and were on the move again when night came. Nikki thought he heard something in our wake that sounded unfriendly. None of us questioned him.

The quantity of our sleep was scant. The quality of my sleep was poor. Cobar didn't leave me. Not to pee, not to eat and not to sleep. There was no way for me to change clothes, clean my injuries while hiding them from my brother. Nikki couldn't get me alone. It drove him mad and strung his tension higher. His jaw flexed everytime he eyed me.

The following afternoon, I helped him roll his sheepskin bedroll. We let Cobar do most of the work, he spun himself up like a cinnamon bun. I took the opportunity to place my hand on Nikki's shoulder. He removed his glove and reached across his chest to touch his skin to mine. His fingers intertwined immediately. I squeezed them back.

"No need to thank me for saving your star-crossed loyalty lover boy. It was merely a coincidence," I lied cockily. I gave a gingerly squeeze to his deltoid. He didn't cheer up. I rolled my eyes. "Always so grumpy when you fret and fuss about nothing."

He sucked his teeth. "Nothing, eh?"

I sipped more poppy milk and leaned over to sort out the laughing cinnamon bun. Warm wetness trickled down my ribs, blood streamed into the fabric of my waist line. It was sticky. It was Gods awful. How fortunate, I was drugged beyond caring. "A little more than nothing. Let the fever rise, it will flush my system." Cobar tumbled back into my arms. I knew Nikki smelt the fresh blood. The muscles in Nikki's neck and jaw feathered. He was paler than usual.

At night, we moved conservatively. We carried no lanterns or torches; the ripening moon was all we needed. The snowy downfall ensured our vigilance, but also provided a peaceful trek. It was rare when one of us would interject our voices into the soundless Deadlands of ash and snow. Even the wolf padded reverently across the frosted fallen forests. On the third night, my fever peaked and the poppy milk was the only thing I could keep down. Cobar's next words made me feel delusional. "Sissy, I know Anna is dead." He sounded so sure.

The boy had been through unimaginable torments that lasted days, weeks, months on end. He was not the same child who planted coriander and cabbage with me in the springtime and would run into the arms of any friendly red blood. No, he had been changed in ways I didn't know. I couldn't stomach the details of the Remnant's playtime with him, but Anna's blood assured me, he could handle the truth of her passing. "She is." Brock and Nikki exchanged looks and dropped back to offer support should we need them.

A whimper escaped him. "She loved you so much. Only death could take her away from you. That is how I know she must be dead."

I slumped onto Cobar's shoulders, an embrace, but also a resting pose for my failing body. "She loved you too. Insanely so, or she wouldn't have chosen you to sail across the world with her on a ship. She wouldn't have taught you how to explode crockpots with soda and vinegar or paint with acrylics on peoples nightstands whilst they sleep." A weak snuff. "It's perfectly alright to miss her. I miss her everyday."

"I already forgot the sound of Rory's babbles and the smell of mom's perfume. I can't remember the vespers of Akelis' temples or the taste of oakmoss in Ferngrove. What if I start to forget Anna too?"

I swallowed the wariness coating my throat. I had shared these exact thoughts too many times to tally. I'd be damned if I permitted them to fester in his untainted heart. "Then I will remind you of her flaming hair, short temper and unconditional love whenever you ask it of me. Just as I will tell you that your mother wore rose oil on the ends of her hair and across her wrists. For the record, Rory doesn't babble, she screams and wakes up the entire house if she isn't content with her swaddle."

Cobar pulled my arm and wrist around his waist, demanding a hug, craving comfort. "Your arms are all sweaty. Sissy, you can change your shirt and eat my portion of bread if your tummy has a virus. Bread helps. You haven't been lively, you're too sleepy. That's no fun."

I pushed aside a fictional realm where we were all at peace and well and said, "It's not a tummy bug, brother. When I was fighting in the duke's manor, I got a few good size scrapes on my back. Can you sit with Yolanda while Brock and Nikki wash out the germs?"

"I am a woodlander, I can help heal too," he defended his status. "They broke my bones to watch them fuse together and drank my blood until I lost the light of the God Orion in my eyes. I can manage the scrape on your back."

Nikki trotted over to the dreamer wolf, who hardly cast a glance. "Cobar, we need to chat, man to man, male to male." Cobar looked up at him bouncing in the saddle at our side. "We all need to make it to your father's ship. We all need to maintain the ability to protect each other and your sister is the best fighter here and is downplaying her injury because she loves you and wants to keep you in her arms as long as you want to be there. Wraiths are out here. I can feel them following our scent from the north." Our scent? *My* scent? "We need her to defend herself, you and us or your father will be missing you eternally. Please, let me assess the severity of the wound and fix what I can."

Cobar gritted down. "Fine. But, if I can help, you will call me. I know how to stitch and slather." The count agreed.

Yolanda rode next to Nikki. "Nicholo, they are coming?" We were still two days off the shore. She didn't bother to hide her worry.

"Yes. I can feel it in the air and smell their evil encroaching. The wolf senses it too or she would be nudging us awake and setting the pace ten miles more each day." I lazily rubbed the wolf's ribs.

"Wisteria will need to hold her ground, letting her infection fester, is not an option if you are considering shaving time off our arrival," my woven said with plenty of feist.

He lowered his voice, "Wolf sistren, lead us to a stream."

Chapter Thirty-One

Yolanda set up the picnic spread with dry cheeses, raisins and jerky that Cobar and I avoided. Brock brought back fresh water in the drinking canteens and placed them next to the pile of wet linens. I knelt frozen facing my brother while Nikki layered the soaking towels over Zander's single layered dress shirt to soften the scabs enough to pull the fabric off. Yolanda worked on plucking the glue and gemstones off my neck and face and flicking them aside. "Now would be an appropriate time to sip poppy," Nikki said. Brock wrapped another wet towel around my head and neck, roughly massaging the dried, matted blood off me.

Before I intoxicated myself, I winked at Cobar. "Honestly, if you want to sleep it would be far more entertaining than watching these blokes try and do a woodlander's job."

Pouting, he crossed his arms. "I'm not watching. Brock stuck me way over here. I can't see much of anything behind the bags and bushes."

"You are ten feet away. You can see plenty," Brock retorted dryly. Yolanda paused her work to go and sit by our youngest travel partner. Five or six drops of milky essence pooled in my mouth. When my head rushed, I signaled for them to start.

Brock was in my ear, "Focus on even inhales and exhales." He knotted my hair atop my head in a messy bun, the style my mother wore around the house on hot summer nights.

When I felt hands moving around my waist breaking away the hold the bloodied cloth had on my flesh, all breathwork went out the window. I decided to put my attention on keeping my face immobile and brow wrinkle free. Anything to keep Cobar's mind at ease.

The metal tails of the whip made rows of overlapping slashes in every direction, when they got to the exposed bone on my spine. I shouted for Brock. "Brock! Towel over my face!"

"Don't pull away from him," he said, wringing out a fresh handkerchief and covering my forehead to my chin. Behind the cold cloth, hot tears flowed.

"Nikki, finish this before I change my mind!" I erupted. The hands on my body moved faster and rougher. I bit down on the fabric dangling in front of my face. Shivering more now from the liters of frigid stream water they doused me with, then the fever racking my body. I gagged when they ripped open a wound that spanned from the top of my left shoulder down to my right buttock.

Anxiety set in and I lost feeling in my limbs.

Poppy wouldn't help now as much as it would after the procedure "Brock?" I called for my faithful friend between pants. "I need you." He dropped his supplies and moved around until he was nose to nose with me. He opened his arms allowing me to lean into him and bury my silent screams, his hands on my flexed elbows kept the shaking to a minimum, allowing Nikki to work as carefully and detailed as he could. The shirt was free from my skin, now they needed it off.

"Lift your arms, Wisteria. Brock will guide them out of the sleeves, I will see to applying pressure where I see fit," Nikki stated assuredly.

I protested in raspy yelps when the two of them attempted to move my right arm above my head. Any extensive motions threaten to rip the blisters and tight skin of the burn. Brock was in my ears reassuring me, even as I pushed him away with fists and words, he found a way to get that damn shirt off my neck.

Brock pried my sweaty fingers off of his cloak to detangle me and place a blanket over across my chest. The stunned silence was enough to prompt a reply from me. "Don't say anything. Just... just... fix what you can." I curled into myself. My head fell onto Brock's lap. Poppy milk dripped into my mouth.

They whispered as my mind lifted to the dreary clouds 'There is no skin left to sow.' 'The prince branded her.' 'She won't talk, not with the kid here.' 'What salve regrows flesh and muscle?' Count Nicholo pulled out llanthian arnica and smeared the entire jar on my back. He and Brock tore wide strips off blankets and made them into wraps to lock the moisture in to encourage regranulation and keep foreign invaders out. They drained a pocket of infection and cut off the necrotic skin that surrounded the raven emblem and irrigated my right scapula vigorously with water from the stream.

When it was time to rise, a warm hand snuck under the blanket and pressed on my navel. The searing pain from the burn and aches of the infection were pulled out with elemental magic. He soothed the chills by gifting me a normal body temperature. Then he was gone, burying the towels and tunic, before I thanked him. Ridding the evidence of *migouri* passing through this particular clearing.

"Are you too high to ride?" Brock asked after I crawled over to Cobar and stole a cheese chunk from his hand. I rested on my forearms and plucked raisins from the bowl as if I were a bird. I was an earth squirrel, I smiled to myself.

"Probably."

Cobar, pleased with my improved mood, brushed my hair from my face and picked up where Yolanda left off in picking the glitters from my cheek, nasal bridge and brow. "You are well now, Sissy." He squished my face. I kissed his nose.

Yolanda interrupted, by cleaning up the food baskets and clicking her tongue at me to move. "The wolf is restless. We move. Cobar, you can pick who to ride with."

He chose Nikki, which put me behind Brock and Yolanda with the luggage. The wolf scouted ahead and our three mounts galloped behind her as night swallowed the charred woods. Our speed fluctuated in intervals. When I wasn't dozing off, I was admiring the unbelievable swiftness of the wolf, bobbing and weaving through the darkness. Sporadically, Brock would wake me to adjust my slacking grip. As the night progressed, the wariness left my bones. When we stopped for an early morning slumber, I managed to sleep.

Sure, I woke up wrenching in pain. That was easily remedied with poppy and a hug from Cobar.

The winds changed. Even to my human senses, I felt they were different. Darker, more malicious.

They carried the howls of the restless alongside the flurries of snow. This would be our last stop until the docks. We divided up food and water portions and discussed the plan for the final leg of the journey. We all carried flint stones and erok wood in case we needed light as an aid or distraction.

The troop took care of its needs and broke down the camp. Cobar decided to ride with Brock and pester him with ten thousand questions about living without his foot. Yolanda and I did a dreadful job at withholding our amusement when he imitated Brock's limp. Brock pulled the kid into the saddle and gave him the reins.

That left me with Nikki.

I anchored myself to him. My arms snug around his waist, pressing my chilly chin between his shoulder blades and relishing the inferno he was. He kept his torso straight and eyes keenly sweeping across the path ahead, but he did offer me two words before he spurred the horses hinder. "Start talking."

I did.

I told him everything in detail, up to the point when the wolf leapt off the ramparts with us on her back, including the manner I strung up the duke as I would a fancy decoration, Collette's scourging and the prince's bargain. "Zander and Duke Cultee were running that shitshow when we left. Good riddance," I saluted the sky.

When he didn't reply to my epic tale of magnificence, I squeezed his torso. He sounded lost in thought when he did speak, "I think you leaving the city, saved it. Even if a third of that horde decided to track down your scent, that would exponentially raise the city's chance of survival."

"Good thing Collette painted the walls with my blood then."

He clicked his teeth at me. "Bad news is you still are bleeding and I'd estimate minimum of fifteen hundred demon spawn are racing towards us as we speak. Whatever the wraiths sense in you, the prince did too or he wouldn't have proposed a future with you then send you off into a city under siege."

My body shuddered at the notion of waking up every morning next to the mask of the raven or, more likely, in a prison cell with my body controlled by the black bones of the Remnant. "Where was Anuli buried?"

"The bone fragments are not hers. Gods and Goddesses don't leave behind bodies when they die. The stars reclaim them after eleven cycles of the moon and we are left with their memories which we devote to shrines and temples to preserve," he derailed my train of thought and ushered it back to the present. "Wraiths are as fast as that water wolf you dragged along, and they don't fatigue or stop for comforts like we do. Let's pray the ocean crashes upon us before they do."

"I'm a better fighter than swimmer. I reckon you are too," I stated, stretching my chin to his shoulder. He was hidden beneath scarfs and a hood, his amber eyes fell to me once before reverting back to the outstretched rock and rotting wood.

"I swim fine," he said curtly. "I just don't particularly enjoy my senses being doused out."

"You can't see people's heat when they are in water, can you?" I took the lack of reply as my answer. "That explains why you panicked when you found me swimming in the hot spring."

"You vanished abruptly. And no, I don't panic," I heard him say after I moved my chin.

"Must be nice." I checked the poppy stash, it was halfway used up. I gave myself an allotted two drops on alternating hours, cutting off my intake entirely when the wolf made an aggressive snarl, when she sprinted back to us her muzzle was dripping in black. Taking a page from Nikki, I chose not to panic and instead took the bow from the saddle and tied the arrow satchel around my waist.

Brock locked Cobar behind his iron grasp and reared his horse. "Last one to the ship earns privy duty!" he barked and galloped off due south. Three horses and a wolf were locked in a dead sprint, the haunting clicks and wallows were progressively getting louder. The foliage shook and snapped as we darted through it. The wraiths nipping at our tails.

The pristine snow was no longer. Footprints imprinted the hillside. I knew where we were. "This was Ferngrove. The dock is six miles southeast." The structures we passed in a blur were hardly recognizable as homes or grain storage. But, they were. My grandfather and mother had built them up by hand over years. I spent many years upkeeping it.

It was impossible not to envision my home and garden commune, farming on the hillside. Creatures swarmed over the land like beetles devouring crops in late autumn. Several encroached too close to Brock and Cobar. I sent arrows through their skulls. Momentum forced Yolanda to keep her head down and bum out of the saddle, she and the wolf led the pack of us in the mad dash. Nikki and I jostled. "Hold me," he demanded.

"I thought your preference was for me to dictate you," I quipped, releasing another arrow. This one I sent at the legs of the wraith running in stride with us. Its trip and tumble lead to a cascade of tripping wraiths. I lowered my weapon triumphantly.

Nikki griped, "Wisteria! Now!"

My arms locked around him, our bodies moved as one in the saddle. "If I didn't know better, I'd say you sound a wee bit panicked."

He ignored my comment. "Start calling for your friend! Make noise. Alert him."

"Keenan! Incoming!" I bellowed into the night. "Prepare the ship! Keenan!"

Cobar joined in with a heart plucking, "Papa! Papa! I'm here! Papa!"

We hollered until we heard it. The horn of Athromancia's Bloodsworn legionnaire reverberating over the descent from the valley.

The rocky waters of the ocean came into view. The moon illuminated everything with its reflection on the surface. Salvation was in sight.

Keenan was on the water, readying a merchant ship crewed by waveriders.

Chapter Thirty-Two

"Papa!" Cobar wept, seeing his father alive within a mile's reach. Keenan had a sword in each hand and charged towards us off the docks, metal gleaming on either side of him. The men manning the boat released the sail and tied down the jib, long paddle ores were on each side, the wide spoons dipped in the water while awaiting departure.

The wind blew against us as we flew down the mountain on sets of hooves. Icicles accumulated on my lashes despite a fire elemental taking the brunt of the wind's whipping fists. Brock called ahead, "The horses have to be set loose."

Nikki agreed. He had reverently left the reins to rest on the horse's sweat drenched neck under the mane of coarse tawny hair. He prayed to Dradion and Drommal, asking them to lead him to a safe land of sweet grass and protect him from darkness. I hadn't known my calculated count of a woven was so tender. It did make sense, being as he himself was a woodland creature. Perhaps, there was instinctually empathic for animals. "You will need help dismounting, we will slow but, cannot stop completely. Our mounts got us this far, they deserve a shot at freedom."

"What do you propose?"

"After my feet leave the stirrups, wrap your legs around me—arms around my neck. I'll try to make it nimble, no promises I won't roll. Brace your back." He had already grabbed things of value and strapped them to his person. "Then run like hell."

Keenan was close now. Gods did I miss him.

There was a fierceness in his gaze that I hadn't seen before as he spun his dual blades and widened his stance. Like he meant to kill. This was not the man I saw in training or in warding off a few wraiths at a time. He was taking what may very well be his last stand and it was difficult to remove my eyes away from his intensity. Fast and with the practice of an immortal, he prepared himself for the onslaught. We didn't slow until we passed him and the dock was within the distance of a short sprint.

Nikki's legs rose and mine encircled him, my arms so tight around his neck I obscured his throat, he remained unflinching. It took all but a second for him to adjust to the weight of me and find a new equilibrium, within a blink we were jumping off the horse's back. He landed on all fours like a cat, his body hard against me. My jaw ached from the impact hitting his firm muscles. He slid me off his back to catch Yolanda who leapt at him.

Yolanda and I ran.

My weaponry bounced at my hip and the bow string around my torso severed my wounds open as the wooden dock thudded beneath our boots. The same birch one I ran barefoot on years ago to welcome Anna. The merchants dropped the plank bridge for us to cross. Yolanda went first. The wolf was already aboard and greeted her with a sniff. I dared to look back.

Nikki was under Brock's weak side urging him on and Cobar clung to his father with all his might. Neither of the pairs were making fast enough progress. I pulled the arrows back and let loose. One by one, two by twos, the wraiths fell. My arrows didn't slow the mass of them, but it prevented them from gaining. Keenan and Cobar got to the planks of the dock first. "Board!" He hollered, rushing by me with his son in his arms. I stayed planted launching arrows at will until my friend's clumpy metal footing hit the flat planks. "Now, Ivy! I will not lose you too, damn it!"

Yolanda was dragging me up the incline to the main deck by my elbow, muttering all sorts of filthy nonsense as she did all while I landed a satisfying arrow through the esophagus of a wraith five feet away from chewing my woven's legs off. "You really enjoy living life on the edge, don't you?" she said, making room for our final company's arrival. Brock leaned onto the main mast to catch his breath, gaping horrified at the quantity of restless that had come for us. Over two thousand swarmed the hillside.

It was an appalling sight. The night made them appear infinite.

"Enjoy it? No. I thrive off it," I replied, watching the waveriders pull the bridge from our boat to the land aboard. Someone among them gave the command to shove off the dock and row. They did.

Or rather, they *tried.*

Our enemies were incapable of fear. They piled themselves onto the shore and into the waters, creating inlets where there were none. The ores of our ship weren't yet taken up by the time they figured out how to drown themselves in a sacrificial manner allowing their own kind to consume us.

If we didn't move fast enough, they would latch onto the boat.

Cedar and tobacco centered me. Keenan, garbed in his usual brown leathers and fitting boots, wept with his arms extended to me. The lines in his tired face flattened with joy where there once was hopelessness, when I rushed into his embrace. His hands gripped either side of my face and I accepted a kiss on the brow. "Daughter of mine, I am forever in your debt and yours to command," he cried. I cried. My heart was still beating too fast with adrenaline to relish this moment for what it was. A fucking miracle.

A silver moonlit blur moved by us. Nikki grabbed the fire lancet Brock had brought with him and centered it on the bow of the boat. He looked back at Keenan, Cobar and I. His face was unreadable.

He crept closer, observing the familial interaction and finally muttered a phrase or perhaps a name that was of no importance to me. "*Ikke nin Kynigan?*" my woven said with the inflection of a question.

Keenan blinked at Nikki. Nikki's knuckles were white. "Ay?" my guardian replied, setting myself and his son at an arm's length away.

I had never seen Nikki's jaw so clenched. "I don't see the one who you serve."

Keenan replied with calamity. "Not here."

Nikki's silver hair fell over his line of sight, he was beautifully built of magic and man. With pursed lips, he choked out, "Does she know?"

Keenan shook his head *'no'* then Nikki's knuckles smashed into his face. The crunch of a fractured nose was my queue to intervene.

I moved in and twisted Nikki into a headlock. He didn't fight me. His arms eased as he went limp. "Whatever shit you two have to settle, you will do it in the afterlife if we don't get away from the shore." He tapped out of the choke hold. I was the first to stand and make it to the fire lancet. Nikki was stunned for a half second on the floor. Wraiths had arrived and were knocking dents into the hull of the boat.

"Anyone standing, sit your asses down and row!" I yelled at the crew after watching the wide mouth of a wraith chomp a hole through the dock. They could demolish our ship. Easily.

Half the ores and benches were still vacant, Keenan was pacifying his son and I'm fairly certain I overheard Nikki tell Brock, Yolanda and the crew he was half Ilanthian and apologize for not saying something sooner in case they were taken in for treason. I took metal arrow tips and sent them whizzing onto the shore. I had to stop the wraiths from crawling into the water if we were to have a snowball's chance in hell to make it to open water.

I stomped down the aisle. "If you have energy to talk, then you have energy to heave an ore!" I shouted, my friends separated and found seats among the crafters eyeing me with surprise. There were about forty of them all together, who fell into a rhythm of grunts and counting with each pull of the paddles. The boat rocked with strained effort. "You do not stop rowing until the sounds of their foul mouths are softer than the wind, until their memory is a distant nightmare! Row for your lives and for the lives of those you promised to remember!" Cobar clung onto Keenan as he moved to the further portion of the boat to steer the rudder.

The haunting shrieks of the night were now louder than my own thoughts. There were so many of them surrounding us! *Don't panic,* I exhaled to myself watching them leap in the waters off the dock.

I held up a spare bow that was hooked to the stern. "If you consider yourself a decent aim, follow me!" A man my father's age tied off the last knot on the starboard side volunteered his skills.

I called for the wolf at the stern to follow me to the bow. Her maw was still open and panting with exhaustion from the mad dash that lasted days. "No amount of gratitude is enough to thank you for saving Cobar and I. I don't have any right to ask you what I am about too, but for the sake of your own life and the lives of those on this ship, I need you to use your element." Her icy eyes were a window into her depleted soul. There was bitterness, hatred and confusion stewing behind them. "When you feel the boat break free, muster a current. Get us out of here. Please," I added, plenty desperate. Her eyelids drooped over her eyes as she sprawled herself out on the deck. Her breathing slowed. Energy conservation.

The archer had brought down a fair amount of spawn snapping their jaws at us, I grabbed an oil lamp and lit the ends of both satchels. We steadied ourselves, for the boat felt like a bucking horse as it tried to unstuck itself. "There!" I pointed to the few dozen wraiths who linked themselves into a chain from the dock and latched onto the hull beneath us. We aimed our arrows down their throats. We killed time and time. They were fast to rearrange themselves and grab hold again.

The darkness grew shrewder as more and more took notice of the wicked brilliance. More chains of limbs and claws were forming, this time they intended to anchor onto the portside, we'd never leave. Not unless someone brought down the docks to buy us time and severed the chain from the shore. "We are damned," the man adjacent to me gasped.

There was no need to look behind.

The image of my new friends and familiar acquaintances, all from different walks of life and races, worked as one to see themselves off to a better and brighter future. I had given a father and son back their relationship, I helped Landsfell by getting them an honest duke, I had held my vow to Anna mostly fulfilled and trusted my wovens to deliver her message to the Emperor. Those on that ship collectively had enough of Numaal's dirty secret and influence elsewhere to make a difference.

And I, a tired, bled out human girl, I would stand my ground on the soil drenched in my ancestral blood, if it made their tomorrow better.

Poppy milk slipped down my throat. Too much, my mother would have said. Not enough, was my initial thought. Then it hit me. The high. The aloofness that took the pain from my body and worries from my mind.

I was far from invincible, but for the sake of my friends and family, I pretended I was. "Wolf, do not turn back. Do not let any of them turn this ship around," I uttered below.

The fire lancet I readjusted until the aim was on the post of the docks locking it upright. I didn't give myself time to imagine how pissed Brock and Keenan would be. I'm sure Nikki and Zander would be just dandy, they survived this long without the likes of me, they would get on just fine without a mortal girl holding them back.

I set off the explosion.

The impact was so bright and loud, no one saw me leap off the bow and launch myself onto the backs of the wraiths.

I swung down hard and fast. I severed two heads, several arms, and what might have been a leg.

The chain broke.

The boat rocked forwards, tasting its first bite at freedom. The water wolf saw to the rest realizing the leash was loosened. Unnatural currents swept the ship forward, and with manpower assisting her, they were gliding over the dark wide ocean. They were twenty, fifty, one hundred feet away and cruising straight out, while I choked on icy water and vermin blood.

My boots weighed me down, I kicked them off. They sank to the bottom while my body fought against a shared fate. I gagged as slimy skinned slithering things touched my clumsy legs. In the water I was as uncoordinated as a baby foul learning to walk, the cold robbed me of what control I had over my lean limbs. I kicked and scooped my way along the shoreline where death awaited me with beady eyes.

I'd much rather stay quaking in the lapping water, eventually my lungs would freeze, and a sleepy death would come for me. That was a much more peaceful exit from earth. Atop the waves I floated, I glanced at my numb right hand to ensure steel was in its grasp. I managed that much. The injuries on my back were kissed by salt and ice, cleansing and cooling. If I exited now, frostbite would have my toes and fingers before morning, that is if I lasted that long. The ship vanished out of my vision. I swore I heard Keenan screaming at me from a full league away, something about being brash and over confident.

I smiled with chattering teeth.

My enemies were packed together. A dense shield that no matter how many times I slashed and struck with my blade, it would never break. Arrows were a decent option... If I had thousands... A forest fire would be grand... if I had magic or oil. What did I have? A sword and two threads from the Weaver.

The battle of Landsfell should have ended and its new council should be mending what had been broken. I hope he had enough magic left after fighting to take to the skies.

Zander! I tugged on our line, pulling compulsively until it tightened. He didn't answer, he wasn't near enough yet to sypher. But he felt me. *I left the boat. I am going to swim for a cavern.* I spotted the rock formation that sat over the underwater entrance to a cozy cave Anna and I discovered and camped out in. I prayed we left comforts in there.

Between the temperature of the ocean and the condition of my body, not much air could be held in my lungs. I rolled onto my stomach and dove beneath the choppy surface. Treading water was hard enough in the warm seasons. Productive swimming in the winter when the waters shocked my inner ears and skin prickled until it burned, felt impossible. Unable to make progress on my own, I let the currents drag me along. *By swim I meant, splashing desperately as I try not to die.* I humored the half human listening in.

Our connection was getting more colorful. He couldn't have been too far off.

Unfortunately, any distance greater than an arm's length away was too far.

The floor of the ocean was as dark as peering up into a starless night. Someone called my name. I heard it as clearly as my own thoughts. I kicked away from the pitch black tendrils beckoning me downward, I threw a left hook for good measure. No, the darkness wasn't solid or supernatural. But it was everywhere. The bottom of a sand bank. The bubbles left my mouth and streamed upward to the surface. I reached out as if I could grab onto one hoping it would float me up to where I could breathe. They slipped through my fingers. My muscles immobilized, they no longer obeyed me.

Suspended in a state between life and death, I watched as the surface tension of the water shattered with the impact of two enormous wings and a solid body diving downward.

Death had sent his grandson to save me.

Chapter Thirty-Three

It was cold. So unbearably cold.

And when my fingers and toes began to thaw, I remember wishing they had been cut off because my nerves burned so deeply that my bones were forever etched with that ache. Zander put a leather glove in my mouth for me to bite down on, for if I screamed any more they would flood into our hidden cove. His large hand softly held the back of my head onto his bare chest, his other fumbled with the lantern left on the floor.

It sparked on, illuminating the hollow limestone sanctuary and the form of the man holding me. "I want to see," I whisper with chattering teeth. My hands on his hard, rippling stomach pushed my face away from him enough to notice his entire statue had bulked significantly, he was kneeling with his wings drying splayed on either side of him. Wings that had tears and fresh blood trickling out of the stretchy white and black leathery webbing. I reached around him and with my painful fingertips caressed the bones and muscles of his wings that held their powerful structure.

I used my reserves up. I ran half the way here. Took two days. The wraiths slashed my wings. I turned my chin up. His fangs gleamed behind his parted lips. *Don't worry. I'll mend.* I curled a finger. He understood and lowered his head down so I could examine his horns. The moon crescents were wrapped in his messy hair. I sorted them out and placed my lips over the chip missing from his horn, holding him into my chest for an extended minute. Questioning if I was alive.

He was smiling when he lifted his head. Gods, he was so much taller than me and he was only on his knees! If he stood up, well...he couldn't, not in this confined space. Hell, not in any house in Numaal.

Take off the wet clothes, there is a trundle of blankets we are going to wrap you in.

I paused and sat backwards onto my bum. *I have something to tell you and you are not going to lose your shit, okay?*

He took a pile of blankets and sat them next to us. His face already contorted with distaste. *You really seem to think I can't handle myself. This is the second time you've tried to hide from me. I will make no promises.*

Zander. I didn't jump off that damn ship to save everyone, only to have you bring down this cavern and bury me under rocks.

He leaned forward, my face between his warm hands. His mouth in my ear. "I *will* never *hurt* you." I shivered and rubbed my cheek against his unshaven beard. *You are a bigger danger to yourself than I will ever be.*

And don't you forget it. I went deep into our bond, ignoring the many layers of Zander Veil Halfmoon de Lucient and walked right up to the imprisoned magic, radiating behind bars. He allowed me to caress the sun twice before distracting me by attempting to remove my frost coated tunic.

He gave an impatient sigh. *I saw you hovelling across the cemetery with Cobar in your arms, smeared in your own blood. I know you have injuries.*

Wait! I found his wrist and held him at bay.

I told him about the branding and the prince's proposal. He said nothing and began to remove my garments with delicate urgency. He spun me around and wrapped my legs in a blanket, gave me another to hold onto as he untied the wraps, one by one. *The salt water was probably the best thing for them.* I referred to my lashes after minutes passed without him saying anything. The emblemed cauterized the open vessels by my shoulder and Nikki had tended to the blistering infection not two days ago. Other than pain management and rest, I needed water and food.

You won't accept the deal.

I don't want to, no.

He washed and rinsed the bandages in the ocean water and laid them out to dry. *You probably didn't want to jump off the boat and leave your family and woven behind either, but you did.*

Maybe I won't be alive in a year to follow through with anything.

Wings wrapped around us, blocking out most of the dim light. The sheer strength and size of the peeked bat wings compelled my hand to touch them again. I avoided the sores and gaping holes. Zander's hands were on the non-injured parts of my hips, his thumbs toying with the thin strap of the thong. *You will be alive. We will conjure another plan to free them.* He kissed my temple. *I swear.*

His right hand begun inching around my waist. Gentle fingers skimmed from my pubic bone, swirling across my bare breasts and ending on the point of my chin. He tipped my head back. I was gazing up at his handsome face painted as a speckled stallion, his new dreamer features cast unfamiliar shapes on the stone walls and ceilings. *Just a kiss.* My mouth was already open when he lowered his full lips into my mine. I reached up and grabbed a fistful of horns and hair, securing his mouth on mine. It was a lovely distraction from the searing pain of the cold and the spasms on my fileted back.

If we were going to be stuck in here for heaven knew how long, then we should make the most of it. *I want more than just a kiss. I want it all, even if you break me into six pieces. I'm not afraid of you,* I declared. His wings flew behind us, almost as if he attempted to take flight. Growling, he sucked the tip of my tongue, his teeth caught on the piercing. I really did want him. I wasn't embarrassed of my growing physical needs, outright curiosity or afraid of the sexual penetration. I sent him calming colors via our bond and allowed the resoluteness of my decision, my choice, my wants to sit firmly and unshakeable at his door.

I opened my eyes when he separated our mouths.

You have no idea how long I've been waiting to hear you say that. I could have done without the whole 'breaking you into pieces' part. He added some space between us. His needs began to shake our thread, yet he said, *I want us to be loud and tumble playfully. Here we must be stifled and neither of us can lay on our backs.*

I thought you wanted to be the first man I ever slept with?

His nose flared. *Not as much as I want you to be the last woman I will ever sleep with.* He was an incubus. He couldn't have been serious. *Only you. I swear it if you will have me.*

"You are mine." I surprised myself when I agreed easily. He was mine, mine alone to share in intimacy.

I pivoted to face him and rose from my knees to even out the height difference. Standing, I was inches above him, placing his gaze across from my breasts which were as exposed as the rest of me because I dropped the blankets by my feet. The blue halo around his eyes shone almost crystalline white. *Worry not about our backs, I am creative. I just hope you are moderately limber,* I smirked.

Wild Wisteria, I expect nothing less. I moved closer until the round swells of my breast basked in his uneven exhales. He didn't pull away when I re-engaged in our kiss, quite the opposite. His hands found places to hold my cold body while I lost count of how many different strokes of kissing he had after I felt him spelling out his name, his *very long* name, in my mouth and against the strained muscles of my neck.

With each passing moment of yielding into our desires, *carefully* yielding, our bodies struggled to keep things from escalating too quickly or moving the wrong way and damaging his wings or my spine any further. *Are we doing this?* I asked before I shoved him into a better angle to straddle him. His reply left my heart racing. His reply was guiding my hand just below that tarnished gold horselord belt buckle. His erection ardently pressed into my hand, almost tearing the thin fabric between us. He was hung like a fucking stallion.

As I unclasped his belt to yank his trousers down, he took the liberty of spreading my legs and inserting his middle finger inside me. Moving it in and out until my juices flowed over his knuckles, pooling in his palm. *Fuck. You are ready for me.* I paused taking off his clothes to enjoy the firm pressure he applied just below my pubic bone. He tried two fingers in my pussy in a rolling motion, my body tensed, and he reverted back to one finger. I bit back a moan. *You are so tight.*

That is problematic? I couldn't help the slight nervous energy I felt trickling down our connection.

Only if I don't last long enough to please you. He got rid of the rest of his pants and shirt. I moved his face towards the light and stepped back to imprint this moment of Zander Veil Halfmoon di Lucient kneeling naked, eager to please me. Not just any girl, his woven. He looked beyond me, into my soul. He looked past the smeared makeup and half bejeweled gems on my face, the royal crest burned onto me and my temporarily fragile state and looked at me as if I was on a pedestal being worshiped in the finest temple in Akelis. *I want you. I will always only want you.*

I said nothing.

He grinned. A dangerous seductive grin. *I don't need to tell you because you already know how devoted I am to you, to us. But I will never stop saying it.* Our connection had a life of its own. It tied us closer and closer, until it forced me to nod.

His eyes roamed rampantly, devouring each imperfection and freckle on me. I returned the favor and let go of the consequences of wanting him by admiring the way his hair was always a kinky mess from his braids and how it managed to perfectly fall in front of his devilish grin and dimple to amplify his white teeth. I watched as each breath he took flexed his abs and how his cock twitched when he noticed me staring at it. It was difficult not to be intimated when its length rose above his belly button.

I placed my left hand over his heart. *Can you manage to sit?* A second later he laid a blanket behind him and lowered himself, leaning back on his arms slightly so I could straddle him. My knees and thighs nestled on either side of him, his wings curved around to tickle my forearms.

I won't move until you are situated. If you can't take it all, then stop so I can work you. Zander leaned on his elbows, his neck a warming pink color from all the excitement of breaking his two years of celibacy. I wrapped first one hand, then the other, around his cock. It was thick. Way girthier than his fingers teasing me. I twisted as I stroked the velvet wrapped steel, enjoying the frequent throbs in my curious hands. Moving my ocean tousled hair to the side I lowered my mouth down to the part I found most intriguing. *Wisteria, what are ...* I cut his bemusement off by licking his shaft from the base to the tip, already leaking salty cum. I sucked off the little pearl bead that accumulated on his tip. "Wisteria, fucking Goddess, Woodlander..."

You've tasted me. It is only fair. His size filled my mouth to where if I tried to take even a third of him in, I would choke. I used my hands to milk him and used my tongue to spin around the tip as I hallowed my cheeks. When I looked up his eyes were shut and his head hung limp. His fangs practically pierced the skin of his lower lip as if he was restraining a mighty roar all the while our sypher bond exploded with descriptive commentary of how many times he has imagined my smart mouth gagging on his dick and how if I didn't stop what I was doing, the fun was going to end before it got interesting.

I rolled my eyes and removed my mouth. He stared at me, shaking his head. *Roll your eyes at me again, little flower and see what happens.* His dick was glossy with my spit, I moved my hips up and rocked my soft, open vulva on him.

What are you going to do, Zander? I leaned forward and put more pressure on my clit by gyrating it on the hard head of his penis.

Things that you haven't attempted or even fantasized about, but that will make you question your sanity time and time again. He watched my bouncing breasts and the way I curled onto his broad chest repositioning myself to get closer to what I wanted.

When my desire moved deeper, I needed Zander to release my ache.

Stopping my desperate hips, I held his erection upright and eased the tip inside. Just the tip at first, and Hell, I gasped at the sheer girth. True to his word, Zander was motionless, save his lusty eyes blinking as he watched me take him for the first time. Slowly, I moved up and down, each time sliding a bit more into me. Halfway, I clawed his chest when my eyes started to water. The burn of the stretching was causing my breath to hitch.

I felt full. I couldn't fathom being stuffed more. But the ache deep inside me, demanding that I try.

Beneath me, Zander appeared as gorgeously sculpted and as statuesque as a historic marble sculpture, and just as hard. *I'm not stopping.* I told him after I collected myself from the feeling of disbelief that had yet to completely pass. I burned with the stretching of him inside me, balanced on the edge of a knife between needing more pleasure and stopping to allow the discomfort to pass.

I see that. Fucking stubborn. I dropped lower on his shaft. I slid up to the top and did it again, this time with a little sway of my hips. His wings shuddered.

He wasn't all the way in, but I doubt he would ever be, when I got reasonably comfortable working myself with his cock. I reached back and grabbed my ankles. This angle did wonders for my pleasure. Moans escaped when I found the spot I had been searching for.

I rolled and bounced until I reached a point where I did not want to wait any more. I *could not* wait any longer. *Fuck me, Zander.* Hands traced their way to where my hips met my inner thighs. His thumbs parted the slender folds of my pink lips watching in ecstasy as they swallowed him. The ring on the hood of my clit was begging for attention.

He was disciplined and considerate when he began to fuck me. Slight hip lifts and light grips pulled me down onto this cock so I didn't tear. I sunk into him when his pace picked up and his cock rubbed against the glorious spot I discovered. *You're doing alright? Not splitting into six pieces?*

I released my ankles and found the magic inside was still stirring, the fire was still being stoked. My hands groped him, started at that tantalizing 'v' I had spent weeks trying not to ogle. Then his abs, his scars, the cords of strength moving under his skin. It was all so masculine. Godly and masculine.

You are moaning again. He sounded both cautionary and immensely pleased with himself and he lay there letting me use him.

I took him by the horns and locked eyes with him. "Then shut me up." His mouth took to me as if I were all the sustenance he would ever have. A few more sounds and sighs escaped as he explored my uncharted territory. *More pleasure than pain.* I reassured the beast beneath me, inside me, surrounding me.

Pleasure, lots of it was seconds away from escaping with his slow pumping of his hips. He pivoted his cock and rolled until he brought me closer.

Zander tasted it in the air, on my saliva, on my skin and down our thread. His hand wove into my hairline to bring my face next to his and held our lips near, he was ready to eat and stifle my orgasm. After his next thrust, my knees locked down and he did just that.

I sputtered, trying to keep quiet as he kept thrusting and elongating my orgasm. "Holy…. fuck you, Zan..der… Just fuck!" I panted.

A starved Zander let my cum drip onto him and used it to his advantage. His hips worked harder and faster. His hands anchored me onto him so he could fully fuck me. He lifted me up and down as if I was weightless. Slamming down onto his cock again and again.

Gentleness was replaced by desperation and I was there for it. I assured down our line.

I bounced, wanting to see his face flushed with more longing. His wings trembled and when he was about to come, his fingers hastily made their way back to my clit. He spun me in circles until I split open for the second time.

My nails dug into his flesh, right over his heart, and we came together.

His face a silent scream of release and around us violet swirls and black whorls of magic filled the caves. They floated around like a flurry of downy baby bird feathers and when I reached for them, they disintegrated in my hands. I looked back down at Zander whose skin glowed a dark hue of indigo and whose horns were aglow, a stark shade of white. Truly crescent moons holding all the starlight in the sky.

I felt utterly human. Simple. Lackluster. Mortal.

Don't. Zander advised sensing my drop in energy.

Don't what? I played. *Roll my eyes at you? I think I will. Everyday.*

He pouted and kissed innumerous times along my scalp, inhaling deeply as he did. *I will happily reprimand you. Everyday.*

I folded onto his chest, him and his warm cum still inside me. He placed blankets over our legs and crossed his brow, ciphering out how to keep the rest of me warm as my droplets of sweat chilled on my skin. *I will wrap your back. Then bury you in dry blankets next to me. I am not as warm as Fen, but I am above freezing.* I nodded and pointed down to our intimate bits.

I'm stuck. He laughed. I was sore too, I noticed when the afterglow dimmed slightly. When he realized my legs were too shaky and that I was serious, he laughed harder. I punched him in the gut. To silence himself he kissed me. Damn that charming grin. *I'm too proud to ask for help.* Is what I sent him as a means to do just that... ask for help.

Yes, my little flower. Hold tight. His magically mending wings clicked down his spine as he maneuvered from sitting to kneeling to standing all with me in his arms and with all of him inside of me. He separated us, paying special care to how he set me down. I held onto his waist when my knees gave, the rest of him towered above me, far out of reach. I reached down between my legs feeling his come slide down my thighs. There were traces of blood.

I squeezed my legs together and felt my intimate parts slightly swollen. *I'll have to pay special apologies to your tender pussy tomorrow. Only my tongue. I'll be gentle.* He promised.

I look forward to it.

Zander, not fond of his horns scraping the limestone deposits above, grabbed the cotton wraps and went to his knees to spin them around me. Then I was spun in one sheet and two blankets and laid to rest on top of Zander's chest as he reclined. His fingertips gently tracing the features of my face, my ears, anything within reach. I watched his swirly, artful magic essence blow about the cave.

Do you think they've given up their search? I sent the dazed horselord.

No. They are still out there. Some are scattering to the Cliffs of Sound. Few have splashed into the ocean. Most are waiting. Thousands.

I sighed. *I'm hungry.* And in need of poppy milk. *Can you see if Anna left anything in that chest?*

His arm reached across the pile of our drying clothes and dug around in the chest. *Empty. Sorry, I can flux the both of us after this form heals. It won't be this week though.*

I nodded against his chest. *Fluxing?*

I call it fluxing. I don't know if there is a proper name for magically disintegrating, traveling and recomposing. But that's what I termed it, since I am the only one I know capable of doing it. I felt his calloused finger brush my lips, instinctually, I puckered them to kiss him. His warm and fuzzy reaction felt like our bond was dipped in the nostalgia of a childhood memory full of giddy joy. I shut my eyes so I didn't roll them. I was already feeling sore, it was too soon to be reprimanded. *You came here with Anna?*

I shut my heavy eyelids. *Yes. We stumbled upon it when the tide was low and when we needed an escape, we'd hide out here. Never more than two nights or the commune would think we ran into the restless or ran off to elope.* I yawned. *I feel less spiteful now that Stegin is dead. But, I know this is only temporary. I seemed to have stumbled across another door to open while trying to close the other one. And anger finds a way to slither in. The same anger awakens each time we fail to find answers to our growing lists of questions.*

Zander made a lower hum that rumbled in his chest. *I saw your work swaying from the ceiling. You are a much more imaginative fighter then even those in the dreamer realm.* I accepted his compliment. *That was one hell of a way to close that door.*

I am glad there are things in this world that still surprise you.

I have much to learn, Wisteria. I will be forever learning when I am with you, just as you will be educated in all the magnificent ways there is for a halfbred incubus to make you come.

Looking forward to being a diligent student. I propped my head up on my chin. *However, it was a bad idea on the Weaver's part to link two immortals to a mortal who values revenge more than her own life. I'll be decrepit and dusty in the blink of an eye. Then you and your husband will have to bury me and live out the rest of your days grumpy and bored.*

The Weaver doesn't make mistakes.

True. She might have the foresight to see we will all be dead in the near future. He pinched my nose. I smack him away, grimacing at the painful movement. *If you want an optimistic spin on the tragedy, how about we die together and are protected from suffering broken threads.*

He let a few breaths cycle. *I am elated to know you would suffer without me.*

I pinched his side. *What you heard was that you are insufferable.*

He ignored me. *Wait until I tell Fen how devastated you would be without us.*

You meant delighted, right?

He looked at me long and hard. *You promised the Weaver that if you survived, you would live out your days—to whatever end, in whatever capacity—with your two Woven. It's a good time to inform you of the gravity of the threads you mock.* I readied myself. Some small part of me felt as if I was being disciplined or sitting in a reading lesson with Moriah critiquing me over my shoulder.

Wisteria, you couldn't tolerate the threads pulling us near in the shed without going crazy or unconscious. When one of us dies, imagine that feeling, but magnified with each passing day, years, decades. That intensity will drag you across the world as you look for its end. When you discover it has no end, that you have no partner, no tie, no completion, that you have and will continue to follow a tortuous path that will not conclude, not ever, until you have nowhere else to look for peace and completion but in death. You are just empty, desperate and missing parts of your soul and are so tired of never feeling whole, so you will tell yourself anything and you will do anything to get it to stop. You decide your only choice is to go beyond into the Veil claiming the Weaver brought you there.

So, you do. You end your existence hoping that you are either reunited with your woven on the other side or that darkness brings all of it to a finite end so you can rest in solitude, unsearching. My breath quaked as it exhaled. *That is what it will be like to lose a woven. Too many times and in far too many situations, have I feared the break of my bond. You saved Fennick's life by endangering yours tonight, I can't repay you for that. If I didn't show up before you drowned, Fennick and I would have already joined you beyond. That I can promise.*

I blinked, sifting through the heaviness of his words. I felt selfish for my short lifeline, not having to wander the world broken. *The beyond isn't ready for us, yet. We need to sharpen our swords first before we slaughter that army of shadow building up outside of Veona.* He squeezed my shoulders.

I think that the Weaver knew how special you are and knew how much you needed to teach Fen and I, and blessed us all in ways we can't yet fathom. If our thread lasts as long as your lifetime, it will be the most wonderful fifty years. There was no sadness in his tone. No sadness in the manner he looked at me.

I'll be old and brittle.

And wise, beautiful, blunt, fierce, happy and never lonely.

He was too far out of my reach to kiss and my arms were tied to my side. So, I settled for placing a kiss over his heart. *Corlimors* felt too otherworldly, too complex and entailed too much. *I could use another friend. One that knows their way over Thalren and the fastest way to the Emperor and Empress's front door.*

It just so happens I do. His charming dimple appeared as he thought of the adventure ahead. His black hair clung to him in shades that were so dark it was impossible to fathom their depth. I ran my fingertips over his hard nipples and firm side body, relishing the way he moved beneath me. Such power in a dense form, such strength rippling under my touch. It was intoxicating. I pressed my lip onto his scars, his magic spurred and sputtered around the room at the simplest of touches.

He gave a carnal growl and tightened his hands laced in my hair. A pleasant pull on my scalp had me lost in the sweet memories of fondling and fucking we made moments ago. The memories that make my cheeks burn and pussy weep. Zander sniffed the air around us, pleased with himself.

One jab in his stomach and he continued detailing the journey ahead of us all while I smoothed over the massive, jagged scar on his heart with my lower lip. It was warmest directed over his left rib cage, where Nikki's heart beat for them both. *The scenic route is the quickest.* He was chipper and spoke with fondness. *On foot and in flight, we will go past the griffin nests in Howling Hills, through my mother's town of Waning Star and into my father's city of Veona. In the Veil, we will walk through the portal that links Akelis to Veona. You will be pounding on the White Tower demanding an audience in three weeks. Keenan's ship should have arrived by then.*

First, we rest. Then, I'll scavenge like a squirrel to find you food and we can fly far enough away from the wreckage of this shore.

Fly? My eyes widened.

Don't tell me that my little flower is afraid of heights?

A tight grimace locked on my face. *This little flower has roots. Not wings.*

I will be careful not to damage them when I uplift you and place you into safer, softer soil.

Don't drop me. My petals would get ruined, I added warily.

The strong fingers in my hair clenched and with a fistful of brunette strands Zander pulled my chin off his torso and lifted my mouth to his. *I would never drop my most precious cargo.* His kisses were slow and languid. It felt like drinking from a fountain of caramel and chocolate and just as sweet. Maybe he didn't have to dig up berries and winter greens. Maybe I could survive off his tongue alone. *I will never allow anyone to harm you. And those that have already committed that crime will die one thousand deaths before I permit them to enter their destination of torment beyond.* I supposed I also enjoyed his violence. Yes, it excited me. That was the most romantic promise I had ever heard, one that instigated my lips to crush onto his with need and fervor. His length was already stiff granite beneath my body, yet he pulled back and left me grieving the loss of his tongue. I pouted. *Definitely a succubus.*

I didn't wait for him to draw me back in, I leapt as soon as the opportunity presented itself, nestling my thighs on either side of his cock. Even beneath the blankets the tip of him rocking against my core ignited a fire that demanded to be fed. His name was already falling off my lips and echoing around us like a prayer being answered.

Ocean blue embers took the place of his eyes. He raised his white and black brow and surrendered to my long strokes. Then we had ourselves a decadent feast, telling ourselves that sometime after a drawn out breakfast buffet we'd leave the cavern and fly west. As soon as we could keep our mouths off each other we'd be on our way.

If only it were so simple to keep my hands off my woven.

The threads of fate have been stitched onto their souls.
The adventure continues in

The Lies of the Eternals

Book Two of the Realm Weaver Trilogy

ABOUT THE AUTHOR

B.B. ASPEN

Bethany has been immersed in fantasy realms since childhood and ensures her three daughters grow up running barefooted and talking to backyard fairies. When she isn't writing or dreaming about far off fictional worlds she is traveling the one she lives on, gathering magic, lore and inspiration from the many beautiful countries she has crossed off her bucket list. She plans to retire on a cruise ship then live in the woods practicing earth magic under the moon with a community of self-loving women who want to change the world. And have a garden. A big one. With Crystals, coffee cups and books on every surface.

Bethany rocks many roles in this realm including a full time registered nurse, mother of three wildlings, indie author and happy wife of the man who holds down their chaotic home and lets her live out the adventures inside her head.

@B.B.Aspen_Author

Stay wild.

B.B. Aspen

Scan below to stay up to date on B.B. Aspen's magic.

Including book release dates, new fantasy series, leave reviews, follow her indie author journey & add her to your TBR piles with ease.

Made in the USA
Columbia, SC
04 September 2024

4571095e-451b-41be-84f7-46a8f6dd5ed1R01